From My People

Other Works by Daryl Cumber Dance

Honey, Hush! An Anthology of African American Women's Humor

Shuckin' and Jivin': Folklore from Contemporary Black Americans

Folklore from Contemporary Jamaicans

Fifty Caribbean Writers: A Bio-Bibliographical and Critical Sourcebook

Long Gone: The Mecklenburg Six and the Theme of Escape in Black Folklore

New World Adams: Conversations with Contemporary West Indian Writers

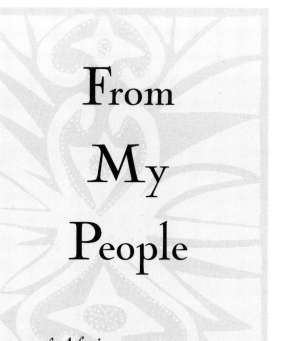

From My People

400 Years of African American Folklore

Edited by Daryl Cumber Dance

W. W. Norton & Company

New York London

Copyright © 2002 by Daryl Cumber Dance

Since this page cannot legibly accommodate all the copyright notices, pages
721–31 constitute an extension of the copyright page.

The text of this book is composed in Cochin
with the display set in FC-Nicholas Cochin
Composition by Allentown Digital Services Division of R R Donnelley & Sons
Manufacturing by Haddon Craftsmen, Inc.
Book design by Chris Welch
Production manager: Julia Druskin

Library of Congress Cataloging-in-Publication Data

Dance, Daryl Cumber.
From my people: 400 years of African American folklore / Daryl Cumber Dance.
p. cm.
Includes bibliographical references and index.
ISBN 0-393-04798-9
1. African Americans — Folklore.   2. Tales — United States.   3. Legends —
United States.   I. Title.
GR111.A47 .D36 2002
398.2'089'96073 — dc21   2001044843

W. W. Norton & Company, Inc., 500 Fifth Avenue, New York, N.Y. 10110
www.wwnorton.com

W. W. Norton & Company Ltd., Castle House,
75/76 Wells Street, London W1T 3QT

1 2 3 4 5 6 7 8 9 0

Dedicated to my son Allen Cumber Dance,
a bright, handsome, generous, and supportive individual
who would make any mother proud, but an inveterate Trickster,
who almost always makes me worry a little but laugh a lot

*For my people everywhere singing their slave songs
repeatedly: their dirges and their ditties and their blues and
jubilees, praying their prayers nightly to an unknown god,
bending their knees humbly to an unseen power.*
—Margaret Walker, "For My People"

Contents

Chapter 2 * Folk Music * 70

Spirituals and Other Freedom Songs

*B*lues

*B*allads and *O*ther *F*olk *S*ongs

Chapter 4 * Folk Arts and Crafts * 209

Carvings and Sculptures

Pottery

Dolls and Other Toys

Musical Instruments

Everyday Objects

Graffiti

Chapter 5 * Sermons and Other Speeches * 250

Chapter 6 * Family Folklore and Personal Memorates * 356

Chapter 7 * Soul Food * 422

Chapter 8 ✱ Proverbs and Other Memorable Sayings ✱ 454

Chapter 9 * Folk Rhymes, Work Songs, and Shouts * 474

Chapter 10 * Riddles and Other Verbal Tests
and Contests * 538

Chapter 11 * Superstitions and Other Folk Beliefs * 553

Chapter 12 * The Rumor Mill * 616

Chapter 13 * Techlore * 647

Color illustrations follow page 208.

Color Illustrations

Acknowledgments

I have been supported and assisted in numerous ways by myriads of folk as I prepared this book. I regret the impossibility of individually naming each of them as I express my gratitude to a few notable mainstays.

First of all, I want to thank my editor, Amy Cherry, who conceived the idea for this collection and offered me the opportunity to prepare it.

The work on this anthology was begun while I was in residence at the Center for Advanced Study in the Behavioral Sciences in Stanford, California (1998–99). Though this anthology was not my major research project at the Center, perusing folklore collections offered a relaxing change from my daily writing there. At the end of the grant year, I found myself quite far advanced on this anthology. For support at the Center, I am grateful to the Andrew W. Mellon Foundation.

Special acknowledgment must be offered to Sw. Anand Prahlad, a former student and now a noted scholar of African American proverbs, and Trudier Harris, renowned folklorist and literary critic, both of whom consulted with me throughout the preparation of this

anthology, offering ideas, materials, and helpful reviews and cri-
tiques. If I had effectively incorporated all of their suggestions, this
would be a more impressive achievement; because of their help it is
immensely better than it otherwise would have been.

I am indebted to Regenia Perry, not only for her superb scholarship on Black folk art but also for her generous support of this project through allowing me to reproduce works from her impressive
collection (hers is among the largest of the folk art collections dedicated exclusively to African American work). She helped me make
selections, provided the prints, and offered some interesting commentary about the works and the artists. My visits with her were de-
lightfully entertaining, and I came away not only with prints from her
collection but also with copies of her books and articles.

I also wish to acknowledge William and Ann Oppenhimer for
opening their home and their remarkable collection of folk art to me,
for their information and advice about the art, and for their gen-
erosity in allowing me to photograph pieces for this collection.

I am grateful to Barbara Gray and Jacquelyn Thomas for sharing
their wonderful collections of Black dolls with me.

I thank Benjamin C. Ross, church historian of the Sixth Mount
Zion Baptist Church in Richmond, Virginia, for the informative tour
of the archives at his church and for the materials on the Reverend
John Jasper that he provided.

I am indebted to Alfonzo Mathis for taking pictures of the Virginia
State University Marching Band and of a step show, and for pro-
viding me information about significant aspects of both performances.

I wish to thank the many storytellers who have shared their tales,
anecdotes, and proverbs with me through the years and whose stories still continue to echo in my head, though I don't always remember who told me what — Marie Hunter, Delores Robinson, Calvine
Battle, Beatrice Buck, Charles Calender, Eugene Mundle, Hopson
Lipscomb, and numerous others.

A very special note of appreciation is due my mother, the late
Veronica Bell Cumber, whose tales, recipes, and proverbs enrich this
collection. Her inspiration, encouragement, and love of Black folklore has influenced this and all of my prior work in countless ways.

I want to thank my extensive E-mail circle of friends whose messages regularly provide me a delightful reprieve from the work and

problems of daily life. They forwarded me many of the selections in the chapters on Techlore and Rumors. Among them are Judy Anderson, Connie Edwards, Daryl Lynn Dance, Carlyse Ford, Laverne Spurlock, Clara (Mikki) Hoggard, Tadelech Dance, and Elaine Crocker.

I gratefully acknowledge all of the great cooks who improvised and passed soul food recipes along for generations. For sharing those recipes from their families with me I thank Ethel Morgan Smith, Joanne V. Gabbin, Francis Smith Foster, Carol F. Boone, Wendolyn Wallace Johnson, Esther Vassar, Quincy Moore, Nikki Giovanni, Dorothy Montague, Martha Gilbert, Rozeal Diamond, and deceased friends Oswald Diamond and Ruth Richardson.

Many individuals at libraries, museums, and other similar institutions deserve individual thanks, but lest I overlook some, I shall offer a general acknowledgment to the staffs of the libraries at Stanford University, the University of Richmond, Virginia Commonwealth University, the University of Virginia and the Virginia State Library; and the staffs of the Virginia Historical Society, the Folk Art Center (Williamsburg), the Mariners' Museum (Newport News, Virginia), the Hampton University Museum, and the Black History Museum of Richmond, Virginia.

I am grateful to my graduate assistant, Rob Mawyer, for his able assistance during the final preparations of this manuscript. I am also grateful to Julia Pastore for her work with permissions for this volume, and to Lucinda Bartley and Nancy Palmquist, who helped with the editing.

I thank Wendy Levy and Kathy Zacher of the English Department, University of Richmond, for clerical support.

A number of other individuals provided material, leads, addresses, and a variety of other help. Thank you Beatrice Buck, Robert C. Vaughan, Elizabeth Thompson, Carolyn Adams, Eva Brinkley, David Hoggard, Elizabeth Dade, Al Rozier, Kathy Albers, Michael Williams, Richmond Police Officer Debbie Allen, LaFonda Davis, Annie Brooks, Margaret Crews, Ebony Chivon Rector, Roland L. Freeman, Gwendolyn Nixon, James S. Ghaphery, Juanita Boylan, Susan Roach, Sybil Kein, and Clinton A. Strane.

I also thank my children, Warren, Taddy, Allen, Robin, Daryl Lynn, Yoseph, and Veronica, for their loving encouragement and support.

Introduction

Folklore is the boiled-down juice of human living. It does not belong to any special time, place, nor people. No country is so primitive that it has no lore, and no country has yet become so civilized that no folklore is being made within its boundaries.
—Zora Neale Hurston,
"Go Gator and Muddy the Water"

There is probably no body of materials as rich and informative, as interesting and entertaining, as tragic and painful, as humorous and healing, as honest and imaginative, as provocative and disturbing, as broad and diverse, as universal and distinctive, as African American folklore. Those truly interested in African American life and culture need to begin their quest for knowledge here. Acclaiming the power and wonder of Negro folklore, novelist Ralph Ellison has written in *Going to the Territory:*

> But what we've achieved in folklore has seldom been achieved in the novel, the short story, or poetry. In the folklore we tell what Negro experience really is. We back away from the chaos of experience and from ourselves, and we depict the humor as well as the horror of our living. We project Negro life in a metaphysical perspective and we have seen it with a complexity of vision that seldom gets into our writing.

Folklore is an important source for the study of any racial or cultural group because it provides so much that is missing from traditional scholarly sources. We are coming to realize that the facts of historical studies and the data of sociological treatises, while indispensable in the quest for an overall view of the history and culture of a people, do not completely achieve that goal of revealing to us the *full* picture. Historical and sociological studies often fail to offer a human, individual perspective; and despite their claims to objectivity, they are limited by the biases of individual scholars. A volume of history is after all but one person's interpretation of the sources at his or her command. The choice of sources, the limitation of sources, the possibilities of varied interpretations, the personal leanings of the scholar, time constraints, and a number of other variables all undoubtedly color the history that he or she produces.

While folklore is an important source for the study of any group, it is critical and indispensable as a source in our consideration of the African American experience. This fact is best illustrated in a well-known and widely disseminated folktale, the version of which I borrow here from John Oliver Killens's *Black Man's Burden:*

> A little boy had read numerous stories in his children's books about various life and death struggles between a man and a lion. But no matter how ferociously the lion fought, each time the man emerged victorious. This puzzled the boy, so he asked his father, "Why is it, Daddy, that in all these stories the man always beats the lion, when everybody knows that the lion is the toughest cat in all the jungle?"
>
> The father answered, "Son, those stories will always end that way until the lion learns how to write."

Certainly the "history" of African Americans in this country has been written for hundreds of years with few or (all too often) no contributions from the subjects themselves. It was a history largely written from the perspective of Whites, most of them racists who felt compelled to use their studies to defend their system of slavery and segregation. It was written from the perspective of those who operated and profited from a system of slavery and who had never experienced Black culture, Black life, Black conditions. Traditionally what has been presented as the history of African Americans is a history of lies, distortions, and misinterpretations. It is a history that maligns Blacks as everything from happy and contented slaves and clowns to barbaric and monstrous beasts. It is a history that insists that Blacks are a people without a history, culture, distinctiveness, or meaningful traditions. It is, as the folk so aptly put it, not history but "*his* story." And "his story" denies in the most demeaning manner African American culture and history. As James Baldwin reminds us in *No Name in the Street,* "the key to a tale is to be found in who tells it."

The Negro who is pictured in these "histories" is unrecognizable to most of the folk that one of John Langston Gwaltney's informants referred to as "just drylongso[1] Black people"—for the simple reason, as another of his informants astutely observed, that things "mean one thing to us and something else to white people." And if we want to know what things mean to many drylongso Black people, our best source is unquestionably the African American folk tradition.

John Little, a runaway slave, noted, " 'Tisn't he who has stood and looked on, that can tell you what slavery is—'tis he who has endured" (cited in Norman R. Yetman, ed., *Life Under the "Peculiar Institution"*). Although not too many John Littles left written accounts, a surprising number orally passed on their experiences through their children and their children's children so that it is indeed possible, even to this day, to hear the voices of those who "endured." The interpretation of those voices is a matter of some serious import to those interested in America's history.

It is also important to note that traditionally history has been concerned with rulers, wars, powerful forces, and grand adventures, events far removed from the folk whose voices are heard in the oral traditions. Mr. Dooley, in Finley Peter Dunne's *Observations by Mr. Dooley* humorously, but forcefully, reinforces this point:

> "I know histhry isn't true, Hinnessy, . . . because it ain't like what I see ivry day in Halstead Sthreet. If any wan comes along with a histhry iv Greece or Rome that'll show me th' people fightin', gettin' dhrunk, makin' love, gettin' married, owin' th' grocery man an' ebin' without hard-coal, I'll believe they was a Greece or

[1]*Drylongso* is an African American folk expression meaning ordinary or regular.

Rome, but not before. Historyans is like doctors. They are always lookin' fr symptoms. Those iv them that writes about their own times examines th' tongue and feels th' pulse an' makes a wrong dygnosis. Th' other kind iv history is a post-mortem examination. It tells ye what a counthry died iv. But I'd like to know what it lived iv."

Similar details of the lives and loves and hopes and fears—what ordinary African Americans "lived iv"—are the stuff of the folk tradition. This is indeed a necessary component in the study of American culture, for one of the lessons that must be learned from history is that it is not merely the rulers and the intelligentsia and the wealthy and the Whites who influence history and whose lives are of significance to us. The so-called powerless folk are actors in the drama as well and likewise contribute to the events that transpire in a nation's life. A lowly female slave creeping away from her master's bed, a common male slave plotting revolt, an ordinary mother slave singing a spiritual, and a conjure doctor concocting a potion to cast a spell on his master were all reflecting the past, responding to the present, and influencing the future. Their experiences are as necessary in truly understanding American history (Black and White) as those of any prominent figure. We must realize then that the facts of historical studies, the data of sociological treatises, the imaginative accounts of literary works—while indispensable in the quest for an overall view of the history and culture of a people—do not completely achieve that goal of revealing to us the full picture.

The folk tradition, for numerous reasons, may present a much more honest, objective, and direct reflection of a people than can be found in what those in the academy usually designate history, or sociology, or literature. First of all, folklore is a group creation that by its very being—its conception, transmission, and survival—reveals a great deal about the realities of the life of that group—about their experiences and reactions to those experiences. I am not proposing, of course, that all folktales be viewed as literal history: not all of them are true accounts of events—though many indeed have their origins in actual incidents from everyday life. The important point is that even when they deal with fictional events, those tales, when carefully analyzed, reveal the true soul of the people who created them. It is in the folklore of a people that we find out most about their values and concerns, their innermost thoughts and desires. Folklore indeed tells us what people "lived iv." The revelations therein are often greater than even the creators of the tales themselves realize. A tale's growth and continued existence is contingent upon its acceptance by a larger group. The modifications it undergoes will reflect the soul of the group within which it circulates, so that when a tale can properly be called a folktale—when it has a currency among a certain group, when it exists in variant forms—we should be aware that it is thereby an item of some significance in understanding something about that group. As Frantz Fanon notes in *Black Skin, White Masks*, "When a story flourishes in the heart of a folklore it is because in one way or another it expresses an aspect of the 'spirit of the group.' " In the Black community, an item of folklore will not be admitted or even listened to if it does not reveal the unique characteristics of African American materials that some may call soul, others spirit, still others style. Castigation awaits the speaker whose material is not consistent with the group's specifications and values.

While folktales are among the largest group of oral folk items, while they represent the most easily accessible genre in the oral folk tradition, and while they have a peculiar significance because of the way they can project and comment upon a complete situation, this anthology aptly demonstrates that those interested in the full range of African American folklore will find wealth aplenty in numerous other forms, oral and otherwise—notably songs, styling out, sermons and speeches, family legends and memorates, soul food, proverbs and other memorable sayings, rhymes, worksongs, shouts, riddles, verbal tests, contests, folk art and crafts, graffiti, superstitions, rumors, and techlore. My goal in this collection is to acquaint readers with the broad range of folk expressions, from the creations of enslaved Africans to contemporary forms.

My efforts to include contemporary materials have reinforced the need for new definitions of folklore in a twenty-first-century world. Those whose earlier definitions of folklore limited it to "popular antiquities" or "archaic" beliefs and customs that circulate only in the oral tradition certainly never envisioned such things as photocopiers and computers. Many of them would have looked for folklore only in isolated societies, far removed from the modern workplaces and subways of cities such as New York City, Los Angeles, or Chicago, where new forms, such as photocopied sheets, E-mailed rumors, urban legends, rap, breakdancing, and subway graffiti, are constantly being spawned daily. Obviously earlier proscriptions that folklore only circulates in variant forms must be modified to take into account new media of circulation, such as photocopied sheets, E-mails, and Web sites, not to mention CDs, television programs, and nightclub comic shows. The degree to which such "standardization" or "formalization" of materials removes them from the realm of folklore is an issue that will continue to be debated for many years.

A close study of a number of these modern forms, such as I attempt in individual chapters in this book, will in fact reveal that there is much more of the traditional in these "new" expressions than many of their practitioners realize. Rap, stomping, graffiti, and many popular new dances are simply slightly modernized variants of long-standing traditional practices. The photocopied sheets, E-mails, jokes, tales on Web sites, and comic revues continue to retain traditional motifs, form, structure, and tones.

This anthology also includes a number of selections by creative writers, pieces that are folkloristic literature rather than actual folklore collected in the field. I have included such works when these authors seem to be transcribing folk events that they have witnessed rather than imaginatively creating those events. Certain pieces presented in the creative work of writers such as Paul Laurence Dunbar, Zora Neale Hurston, James Weldon Johnson, Langston Hughes, and others (all of whom were close students of Black folk culture) are arguably more authentic than many of those provided by folklore collectors. When I was collecting folklore in the 1970s for my book *Shuckin' and Jivin': Folklore from Contemporary Black Americans*, several of my informants had not heard of Dunbar but recited verses from him that they had learned from family and friends. His work, growing out of the folk tradition, was easily accepted back into the folk culture. I also include here a number of sermons from trained theologians who continue to use elements from the folk tradition that they learned long before they attended college and divinity schools. Several recent studies of the Black folk sermon, such as those by Dolan Hubbart and Gerald L. Davis, likewise include such works in their analyses. I recognize that there may be some debate about the distinction between folklore and literature, between the folk sermon and the learned oration, but I include a limited number of carefully selected items here because of the strong folk influence upon them; in each instance I also provide some commentary to highlight their sources. On the other hand, I have been careful to exclude folk imitations, or works by those who consciously mimic folk art. Rather, I have attempted to include a few clear and natural evolutions or evocations of folk expressions.

As you peruse these chapters, you will discover that the classifications I have attempted do not achieve distinct and clear-cut differentiations. The fluidity of folk forms is remarkable. All of these forms are related and interrelated. Quilting includes socializing with its tale-telling and feasting; sermons are not mere oral discourse but a kind of styling out; talking can be just as much a work of art as a painting; songs are narratives, and narratives incorporate songs; graffiti and toasts often reflect the same goals. The lines of demarcation are never clear between family legends and folktales, rhymes and songs, rumors and urban legends. Numerous items included in one chapter could conceivably be situated elsewhere in the book.

As in any effort at a folklore anthology, I am limited in my ability to convey the full context of the folk event, during which the folklore arose. Your appreciation of oral items transcribed here would be enriched if you could hear, see, and feel the dynamic presence and voice and drama of a mesmerizing performer. Your appreciation would be enlarged were you privy to the explanatory commentaries of the tellers and the responses of the audience during the actual performance. Your appreciation would be increased had you experienced or witnessed the precipitating events that motivated the folk expression. Your appreciation would be enhanced were you able to observe other activities in conjunction with the oral expressions: tonal variations, meaningful gestures that occur during a recitation, games played during the singing of a particular song, dances accompanying a song. I have taken many paths (some of them a bit roundabout) to attempt to provide you with as great a sense of the folk piece as the limitations of my format here allow. I provide the texts of many forms — tales, songs, proverbs, rhymes, and so on — but you must use your imagination to conceive of their delivery. The rhythms, the tones, the modulations, the gestures cannot be incorporated into the pages of a book. Occasionally, I have provided some contexts for selected pieces to help you to better envision the whole event.

In some instances, I am not even able to provide the text of a folk practice that is not easily reproduced on the page, such as the ring shout. In such situations, I can offer only summary-descriptions provided by viewers—and in a few situations a photograph.

As I compiled this anthology, I wrestled with the overall issue of the source of the texts of African American folklore. Some of the most beautiful performances of Black people are provided by observers who could see nothing but barbarism and ignorance when they looked at Negroes. Where the only other option was to drop such items completely, I have included a number of these pieces, trusting that readers will look through and beyond these sources' narrow views and hopefully appreciate the subject despite the limitations in presentation. I faced other problems too: the material may not be fully representative; it may have been dangerously expurgated or edited by an outsider; it may reflect the prejudices of the folk collector more than the views of the teller; and it may even have been censored by the teller himself. Elsie Clews Parsons, for example, reported in *Folk-Lore of the Sea Islands, South Carolina* that obscene tales were absent in Carolina; yet she acknowledged that her informants wouldn't tell her toasts and men's tales, and she included several riddles with an obscene suggestiveness that she obviously did not recognize. She also observed that another collector of Black folklore, A. M. H. Christensen, "told me that, faithful recorder as she was, on this point she had been selective: the stories she found 'vulgar' she had not taken." Howard Odum and Guy Johnson likewise omitted a great deal of material because of its perceived obscenity. Even Langston Hughes, given the times and publishing exigencies, cleaned up the toasts to the point that his versions would have limited usefulness to a student of the form. I, myself, have done some limited expurgations of the toasts and a few other items in this anthology because I did not want young people to be denied access to this rich heritage because of concerns about profanity.

Furthermore, in order to make the selections more readable, I have also regularized spelling in a few instances in which transcribers of the material used exaggerated dialect and misspellings, as was popular in treating Black speech until well into the twentieth century.

I have done this with great caution, seeking not to standardize the speech so much as to prevent its nuances and rhythms from being lost amid an unreadable, mutilated, buffoonish, minstrel-type gibberish. In other words, in carefully selected cases, I have made very minor changes to try to restore passages to a recognizable African American vernacular expression. For example, I have sometimes changed *wur* to *were*, *consequens* to *consequence*, *I'z* to *I's*, *uv* to *of*, *nuthin'* to *nothin'*, *doan't* to *don't*, *gin'ral avrig* to *general average*, *tur'ble trub'le* to *terrible trouble*, *sed* to *said*, *furloserfers* to *philosophers*, *nu* to *new*, *sezee* to *says he*, *wen* to *when*, etc.

My goal throughout my career and in this anthology has been to collect, transcribe, preserve, and respect the integrity of the folk text. As I have worked in the field over the last thirty years, I have been keenly aware that my informants, the depositories of the knowledge of the past, have entrusted their histories and stories to me in the faith that I will respect, protect, and preserve them. That trust is an obligation that has motivated me here and elsewhere to strive for the most honest and representative texts.

Finally, in judging collections of folk texts, I have had to consider the possibility that informants will eliminate certain materials or modify them before sharing them with some folklorists. I remember the first time I collected the popular parrot tale about a maid stealing hot biscuits from her mistress, "Hot Biscuits Burn Yo' Ass" (Chapter 1): the teller carefully expurgated the narrative, and the audience of older ladies did not respond at all to the story, which they all knew. Finally one lady spoke up, and said, "Aw, Sadie, you know that ain't the way that ends," and she proceeded to provide the usual obscene punch line. The original teller's attempt to explain her variation cannot be heard on my tape because of the loud outburst of the audience, both in response to the proper punch line and to the original teller's unsatisfactory and clearly unacceptable attempt to change the tale. I experienced other similar incidents where tellers obviously responded to me as a collector: some males, for example, would not tell me certain tales. In other instances the group was restrained by a member of the audience. My problems, however, were infinitesimal when compared with those faced by some White collectors. The selectivity oftentimes practiced by Black folk approached by White collectors was noted by Zora Neale Hurston:

Folklore is not as easy to collect as it sounds. The best source is where there are the least outside influences and these people, being usually under-privileged, are the shyest. They are most reluctant at times to reveal that which the soul lives by. And the Negro, in spite of his open-faced laughter, his seeming acquiescence, is particularly evasive. You see we are a polite people and we do not say to our questioner, "Get out of here!" We smile and tell him or her something that satisfies the white person because knowing so little about us, he doesn't know what he is missing. The Indian resists curiosity by a stony silence. The Negro offers a featherbed of resistance. That is, we let the probe enter, but it never comes out. It gets smothered under a lot of laughter and pleasantries. The theory behind our tactics: "The white man is always trying to know into somebody else's business. All right, I'll set something outside the door of my mind for him to play with and handle. He can read my writing but he sho' can't read my mind. I'll put this play toy in his hand, and he will seize it and go away. Then I'll say my say and sing my song!" (*Mules and Men*)

Such different reactions are clearly illustrated in studies of the WPA collections of narratives from former enslaved African Americans: The South Carolina WPA collectors were all Whites, and the accounts indicate that those who were enslaved were well fed, well clothed, and generally well treated by kindly masters. A completely different image of slave life emerges from the tales Black scholars at Fisk, Hampton, and Southern University collected. The narratives Blacks collected also contain many more details about "sensitive" subjects, such as life in the slave quarters, miscegenation, and Black anger, hatred, and resistance. We can conclude that these variations may have had something to do with, among other things, choices the tellers made based upon the race of the collectors as well as the choices the interviewers made about what they recorded, whom they recorded, and the questions they asked.

I have brought these and other considerations to the choices of selections I include in this anthology. I have considered the quality of the collectors and the collections from which I have reproduced material. I have chosen, where possible, material taken directly from the folk. Despite the fact that in many instances I would have preferred to provide a more objective, open, and inclusive version of some items, I have made every effort to present the most representative, accurate, and interesting account available. In instances where I have used literary sources, I have attempted to choose selections from writers who were most appreciative of, sensitive toward, and faithful to the actual folk sources. However, at times I found it necessary to include descriptions by academic observers writing for an audience far removed from the folk community and utilizing terms that their subjects would never understand as descriptive of their actions. Their didactic, verbose, pompous, and theoretical presentation is often so alien to their subject matter that it threatens to obscure rather than illuminate. Yet in some instances theirs are the only descriptions available of particular gestures, actions, dances, and music. But when I have had to select a source undesirable for one reason or another, I have chosen the least compromising one. In every case I have considered the quality of the text as well and made every attempt to provide the version that would likely merit the approval of a demanding folk audience.

There is, unfortunately, some truth to the folk expression, "You've got to go there to know there," but my goal in this anthology is to take you there in every way that the printed word and the reproduced picture can possibly do.

As you read this collection, you will note many of the distinctive qualities of the folklore from the African American community. At the same time that you appreciate its uniqueness, it is also important to note that remarkably similar items of folklore circulate in other countries and a variety of racial and ethnic groups. The same motifs, the same character types, and indeed the same tales have frequently been collected from one part of the globe to the other. Certainly nothing reinforces the kinship of humanity across oceans and time more than folklore. Thus at the same time their tales, language, style, songs, and proverbs tell us about the African Americans' experience in America, they reveal a great deal about Blacks as a part of a universal family.

May you be enlightened, inspired, and entertained as you enjoy four hundred years of folklore from my people.

From
My
People

Chapter 1

Folktales

A story, a story.
Another story is coming.
Stop talking and listen.
Let it go, let it come.

—African Griot's Preamble as cited in Endesha Ida Mae
Holland, *From the Mississippi Delta*

S tripped of family and friends, every possible belonging, even language, name, and religion, the kidnapped Africans did manage to smuggle a few revered comrades aboard the slave ships that transported them to America: Brer Rabbit and Brer Anancy, whom Guyanese author A. J. Seymour called "the unregistered passenger[s] of the Middle Passage."[1] These and the other familiar animals of African folklore remained in the minds and memories of enslaved Africans and undoubtedly provided a source of strength to help them cope with their conditions in the American South (where Brer Rabbit disembarked) and the Caribbean (where Brer Anancy chose to stay). Aboard the slave ships and on the plantations, Brer Rabbit and Brer Anancy had little trouble evading their enemies, for they were little and wiry, fleet and crafty, smart and treacherous. They could hide in remote corners and briar patches, and it was hard to ever get one's hands on them, and harder still to keep them in one's grasp. And if nothing else prevailed, they could talk their way out of anything. The newly captured Africans per-

[1]Interview with Daryl Cumber Dance, February 13, 1979.

*

haps began to appreciate their animal friends even more in the American South and the Caribbean, where they recognized their skills and attributes as crucial to their own survival in a slave society, in which they too were always in conflict with more powerful creatures who seemed determined not only to rule over everything, to hoard everything, and to make all the rules, but also to ensnare and ultimately to devour them. Here more than ever they enjoyed the victories of Brer Rabbit and Brer Anancy over the predatory Wolf and Bear. Here, more than ever, the antics of Brer Rabbit and Brer Anancy were relished and even emulated at times. For just as the revered weaker animals managed to defeat their larger enemies and to secure the best food, the prized possessions, the desired privileges, and even the choice ladies, the enslaved people sought ways to win precisely those same prizes—prizes inexorably denied them in antebellum society. And Brer Rabbit and Brer Anancy became their models for the indirection, trickery, masking, and verbal dexterity that the enslaved men and women would have to bring into play to survive with some sense of dignity. It is no surprise then that the Brer Rabbit and Brer Anancy tales were among the most popular in the slave communities. Brer Rabbit and Brer Anancy were no models of virtue—they were greedy and deceitful, and often immoral and vindictive, even vicious at times. But given the nature of their conditions and the savagery of their enemies (to which, of course, the slaves related), their behavior was understood, applauded, and emulated in the slave community. While Brer Anancy tales were occasionally collected in the United States, it is Brer Rabbit that is the main subject of these tales. The Brer Rabbit tales here are frequently the same ones found throughout the Caribbean with Brer Anancy as the protagonist.

Because the Brer Rabbit tales were fables that at least on their surface did not appear subversive, they could be safely related, even in the presence of Whites; in fact, Negro slaves sometimes regaled their White charges with these yarns. However, another related cycle of tales, the Slave John anecdotes—which focused explicitly upon the very issues the animal fables camouflaged in symbolism—had to remain underground, carefully concealed among the slaves. In these tales, John (also sometimes Tom, Jack, Sam, Efan, or Rastus) is always trying to outwit Ole Massa. Rarely does John achieve the kind of physical victory over his master that Brer Rabbit achieves over Fox or Bear (whom Brer Rabbit sometimes kills). Often John simply tries to humiliate Ole Massa, avoid some work, steal some food, or win some privilege denied him. Naturally these exploits often land him in a strait out of which he must talk his way. Much of the humor in these tales involves John's lying, scheming, and cajoling as he attempts to escape discovery or punishment.

Another popular body of tales during slavery and afterward is the etiological tales, those explaining how things came to be as they are. The paradox of slavery and its aftermath required some explanation of the situation of the Negro: Why was he a slave in a society founded upon the tenets of freedom and equality? Why was he so poor and deprived in a wealthy society? Why was he so powerless in a strong nation? Why was he Black in a White world? These tales purport to be myths explaining the role of God in creating the racial situation that exists in America. As I have argued in great detail in *Shuckin' and Jivin'*, these tales do not reflect the Black man's acceptance of his own inferiority, as many have contended;[2] rather they are satirical commentaries on White society. In all of the tales, which on the surface seem to make fun of the Black man's color, hair, poverty, and laziness, we see the Black personae operating in an absurd situation growing out of White hypocrisy, White values, White prejudices, and White economic institutions, which conspire to punish the Black subject, no matter what he does. These tales are not really myths, but parodies of myths. Indeed they are jokes, and the butts of the jokes are only ostensibly Blacks—the real target is the racist American system.

While most of the etiological tales in the African American repertoire deal with racism, a number explain how animals got their physical features, and a few deal with other issues, such as sexism.

Another body of folktales deals with the exploits of the ba-a-d man—*ba-a-d* is, of course, in the Black community a term of commendation rather than condemnation. It is another instance of African Americans' reversal of the values of the larger community, of changing the joke and slipping the yoke, as Ralph Ellison would say.

[2]See Fred O. Weldon, "Negro Folktales"; and John Lomax, "Self-Pity in Negro Folk-Songs."

The enslaved people knew that the White slaveowners hated and feared the "ba-a-d nigger" because he violated their laws and moral codes; the enslaved folks themselves admired the "ba-a-d nigger" and relished his exploits for exactly the same reasons. Obviously Brer Rabbit and Slave John are early examples of ba-a-d men, but others growing out of slavery, like High John de Conquerer, and those evolving later, like Stagolee, gave new meaning to ba-a-dness. As I have written in *Shuckin' and Jivin'*:

> The Bad Nigger of folklore is tough and violent. He kills without blinking an eye. He courts death constantly and doesn't fear dying, probably because he is willing to do battle with the Devil as well as with his human enemies (and he frequently defeats even the Devil). He values fine clothes and flashy cars. He asserts his manhood through his physical destruction of men and through his sexual victimization of women.

(A number of accounts of this figure may also be found in the toasts in chapter 9.)

A close relative of the ba-a-d man in Black folklore is the Preacher, who likewise is a lecherous woman-chaser and booze-drinker, a stylish dresser, a driver of big cars, a lover of eloquent language, and an all-around rascal. But because he is a hypocrite posing as a pious leader of his people (unlike the ba-a-d man, who loudly trumpets his iniquity), the Preacher is usually treated with disdain in the folklore, while the ba-a-d man is applauded. Many of these tales focus on other principals in the church, including the deacons and the old sisters. Although much of the humor directed toward the Black church in this body of folklore lampoons the institution, it does not reflect a negative bias towards the church in the Black community. The Black church has been the most influential institution in the Black community from slavery to the present. It has been the source and support of most Black education and Black political movements. Its ministers have been the revered leaders in the community and the nation. Yet Black folks, like their counterparts in other times and in other groups, have derived and inspired laughter by lampooning their religious leaders, particularly by revealing the moral defects of those who present themselves as exemplars. And many of the tales in this body are told by devout Christians, deacons, ministers, and the wives of ministers, a fact clearly reinforced by my own fieldwork.

Ghost tales are another body of folklore popular in the African American community. Those tales that reflect a belief in ghosts are included in chapter 11. Here I include, rather, the scare tales, those in which individuals are frightened by events that are not supernatural in origin.

A final group represented here includes the ethnic tales. Despite the fact that African Americans themselves have been victimized by the racial stereotyping of the larger society, they have embraced some of the common stereotypes of other ethnic groups in their own folklore. At various periods, often reflecting historical interactions with specific groups, tales abound about the greedy Jew, the stupid Irishman, the numskull Pole, the impoverished Puerto Rican, the wetback Mexican, the Chinese laundryman, and the Vietnamese storekeeper.

De Ways of de Wimmens

· *From James R. Aswell,* God Bless the Devil ·

Most folks say de *six* day was Satdy, 'cause on de *seventh* day didn't de Lawd rest an look his creation over? Now hit *may* been Satdy dat he done de *work* of makin man an woman, but from all de signs, he must *thought up* de first man an woman on ol unlucky *Friday.*

Satdy *aw* Friday, de Lawd *made* em. Den he made a nice garden an a fine house wid a cool dogtrot faw dem to set in when de sun git hot. "Adam an Eve," he say, "here hit is. Git yo stuff together an move in."

"Thank you kindly, Lawd," say Eve.

"Wait a minute, Lawd," say Adam. "How we gwine pay de rent? You ain't create no money yet, is you?"

De Lawd say, "Don't worry yo haid bout dat, Adam. Hit's a free gift faw you an de little woman."

So de man and woman move in an start to red up de house to make hit comfortable to live in. And den de trouble begun.

"Adam," say de woman, "you git de stove put up while I hangs de curtains."

"Whyn't you put up de stove," say Adam, "an me hang de curtains? You's strong as me. De Lawd ain't make neither one of us stronger dan de other. Howcome you always shovin off de heavy stuff on me?"

" 'Cause dey's man's work and dey's woman's work, Adam," say Eve. "Hit don't look right faw me to do dat heavy stuff."

"Don't look right to who?" say Adam. "Who gwine see hit? You know dey ain't no neighbors yet."

Eve stomp de flo. She say, "Jes cause hit ain't no neighbors yet ain't no reason faw us actin trashy behind dey backs, is hit?"

"Ain't dat jes like a woman!" say Adam. Den he set down and fold his arms. "I ain't gwine put up no stove!" he say. "An dat *dat*, woman!"

Next thing he know ol Eve lollop him in de talk-box wid her fist an he fall over backward like a calf hit by lightnin. Den he scramble up an was all over her like a wildcat. Dey bang an scuffle round dere to de house look like a cyclone wind been playin in hit. Neither one could whup, cause de Lawd had laid de same equal strenth on dem both.

After while dey's both too wore out to scrap. Eve flop on de baid and start kickin her feets an bawlin. "Why you treat me so mean, Adam?" she holler. "Wouldn't treat a no-count ol hound like you does po me!"

Adam spit out a tooth an try to open de black eye she give him. He say, "If I had a hound dat bang into me like you does, I'd kill him."

But Eve start bawlin so loud, wid de tears jes sopping up de bed-close, dat Adam sneak out of de house. Feelin mighty mean an low, he set round awhile out behind de smokehouse studyin whut better he do. Den he go find de Lawd.

De Lawd say, "Well, Adam? Anything bout de house won't work? Hit's de first one I ever made an hit might have some faults."

Adam shake his head. "De house is prime, Lawd. De *house* couldn't be no better dan hit is."

"Whut den, Adam?" say de Lawd.

"To tell de truth," say Adam, "hit's dat Eve woman. Lawd, you made us wid de equal strenth an dat's de trouble. I can't git de best of her nohow at all."

De Lawd frown den. "Adam!" he say. "Is you tryin to criticize de Lawd? Course you's of de equal strenth. Dat de fair way to make a man an woman so dey both pull in de harness even."

Adam tremble an shake but he so upset an miserble he jes has to keep on. He say, "But Lawd, hit reely ain't equal tween de two of us."

Lawd say, "Be keerful dere, Adam! You is *des*putin de Lawd smack to de face!"

"Lawd," say Adam, "like you says, we *is* equal in de strenth. But dat woman done found nother way to fight. She start howlin an blubberin to hit make me feel like I's a lowdown scamp. I can't stand dat sound, Lawd. If hit go on like dat, I knows ol Eve gwine always git her way an make me do all de dirty jobs."

"Howcome she learn dat trick?" say de Lawd, lookin like he thinkin hard. "Ain't seed no little ol red man wid hawns an a pitch-fawk hangin round de place, is you, Adam?"

"Naw, Lawd. Thought I heard Eve talkin wid somebody down in de apple orchard dis mawnin, but she say hit jes de wind blowin. Naw, I ain't seed no red man wid hawns. Who would dat be, anyhow, Lawd?"

"Never you mind, Adam," say de Lawd. *"Hmmmmmmmm!"*

"Well," say Adam, "dis woman trouble got me down. I sho be much oblige if you makes me stronger dan Eve. Den I can tell her to do a thing an slap her to she do. She do whut she told if she know she gwine git whupped."

"So be hit!" say de Lawd. "Look at yoself, Adam!"

Well Adam look at his arms. Where befo dey was smooth an round, now de muscle bump up like prize yams. Look like hit was two big cawn pones under de skin of his chest an dat chest hit was like a barrel. His belly hit was like a washboard an his laigs was so awful big an downright lumpy dey scared him.

"Thank you kindly, good Lawd!" say Adam. "Watch de woman mind me now!" So dat Adam high-tail hit home an bust in de back do.

Eve settin down rockin in de rocker. Eve lookin mean. Didn't say a mumblin word when Adam come struttin in. Jes look at him, jes retch down in de woodbox faw a big stick of kindlin.

"Drap dat stick, woman!" say Adam.

"Say who?" say de woman. "Who dat talkin big round here?"

Wid dat, she jump on him an try to hammer his haid down wid de stick.

Adam jes laugh an grab de stick an heave hit out de window. Den he give her a lazy little slap dat sail her clean cross de room. *"Dat* who sayin hit, sugar!" he say.

"My feets must slip aw somethin," say Eve. "An you de one gwine pay faw hit out of yo hide, Adam!"

So de woman come up clawin an kickin an Adam pick her up an whop her down.

"Feets slip agin, didn't dey?" say Adam.

"Hit must be I couldn't see good where you is in dis dark room," say Eve. She riz up an feather into him agin.

So Adam he pick her up an thow her on de baid. Fo she know whut, he start laying hit on wid de flat of his hand cross de big end of ol Eve. Smack her wid one hand, hold her down wid tother.

Fo long Eve bust out bawlin. She say, "Please quit dat whackin me, Adam honey! Aw please, honey!"

"Is I de boss round here?" say Adam.

"Yas, honey," she say. "You is de haid man boss."

"Aw right," he tell her. "I *is* de boss. De Lawd done give me de mo power of us two. From now on out an *den* some, you mind me, woman! Whut I jes give you ain't nothin but a little hum. *Next* time I turn de whole song loose on you."

He give Eve a shove an say, "Fry me some catfish, woman."

"Yas, Adam honey," she say.

But ol Eve was mad enough to bust. She wait till Adam catchin little nap. Den she flounce down to de orchard where dey's a big ol apple tree wid a cave tween de roots. She look round till she sho ain't nobody see her, den she stick her haid in de cave an holler.

Now, hit *may* been de wind blowin an hit *may* been a bird, but hit sho sound like somebody in dat cave talkin wid Eve. Eve she sound like she *com*plainin dat she got a crooked deal an den hit sound like she sayin, "Yas — Yas — Yas. You means on which wall? De east wall? Oh! Aw right."

Anyhow, Eve come back to de house all smilin to herself like she know somethin. She powerful sweet to Adam de rest of de day.

So next mawnin Eve go an find de Lawd.

Lawd say, "You agin, Eve? Whut can I do faw you?"

Eve smile an drap a pretty curtsy. "Could you do me a little ol favor, Lawd?" say Eve.

"Name hit, Eve," say de Lawd.

"See dem two little ol rusty keys hangin on dat nail on de east wall?" Eve say. "If you ain't usin em, I wish I had dem little ol keys."

"I *declare!*" say de Lawd. "I done fawgot dey's hangin dere. But,

Eve, dey don't fit nothin. Found em in some junk an think maybe I find de locks dey fit some day. Dey been hangin on dat nail ten million years an I ain't found de locks yet. If you want em, take em. Ain't doin me no good."

So Eve take de two keys an thank de Lawd an trot on home. Dere was two dos dere widout no keys an Eve find dat de two rusty ones fit.

"Aaah!" she say. "Here's de locks de Lawd couldn't find. *Now*, Mister Adam, we *see* who de boss!" Den she lock de two dos an hide de keys.

Fo long Adam come in out of de garden. "Gimme some food, woman!" he say.

"Can't, Adam," say Eve. "De kitchen do's locked."

"I fix dat!" say Adam. So he try to bust de kitchen do down. But de Lawd built dat do an Adam can't even scratch hit.

Eve say, "Well, Adam honey, if you go out in de woods an cut some wood faw de fire, I maybe can git de kitchen do open. Maybe I can put one dem cunjur tricks on hit. Now, run long, honey, an git de wood."

"Wood choppin is yo work," say Adam, "since I got de most strenth. But I do hit dis once an see can you open de do."

So he git de wood an when he come back, Eve has de do open. An from den on out Eve kept de key to de kitchen an made Adam haul in de wood.

Well, after supper Adam say, "Come on, honey, les you an me hit de froghair."

"Can't," say Eve. "De baidroom do is locked."

"*Dad*blame!" say Adam. "Reckon you can trick dat do too, Eve?"

"Might can," say Eve. "Honey, you jes git a piece of tin an patch dat little hole in de roof an while you's doin hit, maybe I can git de baidroom do open."

So Adam patched de roof an Eve she unlock de baidroom do. From den on she kept *dat* key an used hit to suit herself.

So dat de reason, de very reason, why de mens *thinks* dey is de boss and de wimmens *knows* dey is boss, cause dey got dem two little ol keys to use in dat slippery sly wimmen's way. Yas, fawever mo an den some!

An if you don't know *dat* already, you ain't no married man.

Why the Black Man's Hair Is Nappy

· *From Daryl Cumber Dance*, Shuckin' and Jivin' ·

I collected this tale in Richmond, Virginia.

All right now, we going to our races; we going to find out where the Black people got their hair from, and how they got it. When it was time for the Lord to give hair, He called all three of these men, and this is what he said. Well, first he called the white man to come on and get his hair. All right, the white man he went right on up there and got his hair. So the Lord called the Jew man to get his hair. So the Jew man went up there and got his hair, and said, "Thank you, Lord."

So when it got down to the Black man, the Lord called him. And do you know what the Black man said? Black man said, "Lord, ball it up and throw it to me." And it's been balled up ever since.

Why the Whites Have Everything

· *From Daryl Cumber Dance*, Shuckin' and Jivin' ·

I collected this tale in Richmond, Virginia.

God was making the worl' and He called de people, you know, de white people to get a bag and de colored people to get a bag. De colored people went to get the little light bag and the white people get the big, heavy bag; and the heavy bag [there] was money in it, and the light bag ain't have nothin' in it. And they say dat's why us ain't got nothin' today; white people got it all.

Upon This Rock

· *From Daryl Cumber Dance*, Shuckin' and Jivin' ·

I collected this folktale in Richmond, Virginia.

On the side of a mountain once, the Lord summoned three people to help Him with a project, one being a Black man, one being an Italian, and the other Jewish. And the Lord said, "I am simply looking for people to follow simple directions." And He said, "I simply want the three of you to go out and bring me back a stone, or as much stone as you'd like." And so the Black man, thinking that it was a timed thing, rushed right back with a pebble. The Italian took a couple of hours, and finally he came back with a wheelbarrow piled with crushed stone. And they waited until midnight. Finally they heard a rumbling. And the Jew was shoving a mountain. So the Lord in His patience blessed the stones and said, "These stones I will now turn into bread." Well, the Black man had a biscuit. The Italian had a wheelbarrow *filled* with loaves of bread. And the Jew had a *bakery,* of course.

So the next day, the Lord said, "Same gentlemen, same assignment. Go out and fetch stones." Well, the Black man was *extremely* happy for a second chance. So sometime later that evening, the Italian was the first one back, with his same wheelbarrow filled with stones. And the Jew took very long to come, but here he is with his mountain. And they waited until midnight. The Black man didn't show . . . Two A.M. . . . Three A.M. . . . Four A.M. . . . Well, just about dawn they heard a rumbling sound. And a whole avalanche of mountains and boulders—just everything—was being hurled at the Lord. And finally the Lord said, "Upon *these* rocks I'll build my church."

And the Black man said, "I be *damned* if you will. You gon' make *bread* today!"

Why the Rabbit Has a Short Tail

· *From Richard M. Dorson,* American Negro Folktales ·

Dorson collected this tale from Sarah Hall.

Once upon a time Brother Rabbit had a long bushy tail. And every time he'd see Brother Fox he'd shake it at him and wave his tail in the Fox's face. Brother Fox studied and studied how to get even with the Rabbit. Well, he went to fishing and he had good luck. As he was coming home from fishing, the Rabbit run out and says, "Brother Fox, how did you catch all these fish?" (The Rabbit loves fish.) Brother Fox said to himself, "Now's my time to get even with the Rabbit." Out loud he said, "Any cold night, all you got to do is to go down to the creek and hang your tail in the water, and let it hang there from sundown to sunup the next morning, and you'll have more fish than you can pull out."

He meant that his tail would freeze in the ice. "All right," said Brother Rabbit, "I believe that I'll go fishing tonight." So he took with him a blanket, and his pole, and bait, and sit on a log with his tail in the water in the middle of the creek, all night long. It growed so cold, he began to shiver, and shiver, and he shiver. All night he set there and shuck and shiver. But he's thinking about the fish he's going to have in the morning. Late that morning the sun begin to rise, so the Rabbit tried to pull his fish. But his tail was froze too tight in the ice. He pulled and he pulled, but his tail stuck fast. The Rabbit begin to be afraid that the Man would come along and see him. So he thought he would call for help. "Help! Help! Help!"

Brother Owl heard Brother Rabbit. He says, "I wonder where Brother Rabbit's at. I heered him holler for help." So he flew over the creek, and there he seen Brother Rabbit sitting on a log. And he flew down to help Brother Rabbit. He caught a holt of his right ear and begin to pull. It grewed longer and longer. The Rabbit said, "Why don't you catch my left ear?" He caught hold of his left ear, and he began to pull. He pulled and pulled, but it grew longer. The Rabbit says, "Brother Owl, don't you see what you did! You pulled and pulled my ears until my best friend won't know me. Why don't you catch my tail?"

So the Owl grabbed a holt of his tail, and begin to pull. He pulled and pulled, and off went the Rabbit's tail. So the Rabbit been having long ears and short tail ever since from that day to this.

I stepped on some tin and it bent,
And I skated on away from there.

How the Black Man Lost His Wings

This popular tale was reproduced from memory and probably influenced by the many versions I collected as well as those I heard growing up.

God told Saint Peter that he thought he would give wings to every-body in heaven. The Black man was so happy to hear it that he couldn't wait for them to give 'im his. He decided he would just go get them himself. So he sneaked in the room where God had the wings and grabbed the first two he saw. He was so excited, he didn't even notice that he picked up two left wings. He put 'em on and started to fly. He was flying all one-sided, bumping all up into walls, knocking things off tables, almost hitting the angels and other peoples in heaven.

Saint Peter heard all the commotion and he come rushing out, say, "Hey, what you doing with those wings? Who gave you those wings?"

The Black man say, "I got 'em myself."

Saint Peter say, "What! What you say? You went in God's storeroom and took those wings without permission!" He say, "Gimme those wings. Just gimme those wings." And Saint Peter took the Black man's wings from him and put 'im out of heaven.

Black man just laughed and say, "Hey, hey, you may have took my wings and put me out of heaven, but, hey, hey, I had a flying good time while I had 'em."

The False Message: Take My Place
· *From Elsie Clews Parsons,* Folk-Lore of the Sea Islands, South Carolina ·

Once there was a man. He only had daughter. So he had a garden with cabbage and turnip. So every day he will go to work and leave the girl to mind the house. A rabbit come up there one day, and say, "Little girl, your father say you must turn me in the garden." The girl turn him in. He eat much as he want to eat. "All right, little girl, turn me out now." The girl turn him out. That night her father come from work, and the girl asked her father about it. The man say, "No, I ain't tell Ber Rabbit anything. When he come back to-morrow, you turn him in, and let him stay until I come." So next day the rabbit come, the girl turn him in. And most time for the girl father to come. "All right, little girl, turn me out now." The girl say, "I ain't got time now." The rabbit wait a while longer. "All right, little girl, turn me out now." The girl say, "I'm washing the grits to put in the pot now."

So her father come. "Ber Rabbit, what you doing in my garden?"

Ber Rabbit say, "That little girl turn me in here." The man catch Ber Rabbit and put him in a sack and hang him up in the tree, and gone in the woods to get a load er switch. A wolf came along in the time. So the wolf said to Rabbit, "What is the matter?" The rabbit say, "O man! I'm going to heaven. You want to go?" The wolf say, "Yes." Told the wolf to open the sack and come in. "And let me go out and tie you up in here." The rabbit tie the wolf in the sack and gone. The man come, say, "What you doing in here?" The wolf say, "Ber Rabbit put me in here." The man say, "All right, when I done with you, when you see a sack again, you will run from it." So he beat the hide off the wolf.

> *And I went around the ben'.*
> *There was a crooked six pen'.*
> *There was my story end.*

The Goldstone

· *Adapted from Louise-Clarke Pyrnelle, "Diddie, Dumps, and Tot"*
in Plantation Child-Life ·

Aunt Edy was the principal laundress, and a great favorite she was with the little girls. She was never too busy to do up a doll's frock or apron, and was always glad when she could amuse and entertain them. One evening Dumps and Tot stole off from Mammy, and ran as fast as they could clip it to the laundry, with a whole armful of their dollies' clothes, to get Aunt Edy to let them "iron des er little," as Tot said.

"Lemme see what yer got," said Aunt Edy; and they spread out on the table garments of worsted and silk and muslin and lace and tarlatan and calico and homespun, just whatever their little hands had been able to gather up.

"Lord, chil'en, if yer washes deze fine clothes yer'll ruin 'em," said Aunt Edy, examining the bundles laid out; "de suds'll take all de color out'n 'em; s'posin' yer jes press 'em out on de little stool ober dar wid er nice cole iron."

"Yes, that's the very thing," said Dumps; and Aunt Edy folded some towels, and laid them on the little stools, and gave each of the children a cold iron. And, kneeling down, so as to get at their work conveniently, the little girls were soon busy smoothing and pressing the things they had brought.

"Aunt Edy," said Dumps, presently, "could'n yer tell us 'bout Po' Nancy Jane O?"

"Dar now!" exclaimed Aunt Edy. "Dem chil'en never is tired er hearin' dat tale; pears like dey like it mo' an' mo' eb'y time dey hears it"; and she laughed slyly, for she was the only one on the plantation who knew about "Po' Nancy Jane O," and she was pleased because it was such a favorite story with the children.

"Once'pon er time," she began, "dar was er bird name' Nancy Jane O, an' she was guv' up ter be de swif'es'-fly'n thing dar was in de air. Well, at dat time de king of all de fishes an' birds, an' all de little beasts, like snakes an' frogs an' worms an' tarrypins an' bugs, an' all sich ez dat, he were er mole dat year! An' he was blin' in bof his eyes, jes same like any udder mole; an', somehow, he had heard some way dat dar was er little bit er stone name' de gol'-stone, way off fum dar, in er muddy crick, an' if he could git dat stone, an' hol' it in his mouf, he could see same ez anybody.

"Den he begun ter study how was he fur ter git dat stone.

"He studied an' he studied, an' 'peared like de mo' he studied de mo' he couldn' fix no way fur ter git it. He knowed he was blin', an' he knowed he travel so slow dat he 'lowed 'twould be years pon top er years befo' he'd git ter de crick, an' so he made up in his mind dat he'd let somebody git it fur 'im. Den, bein' ez he was king, an' could grant any kind er wish, he sent all roun' thu de country eb'ywhar, an' 'lowed dat any bird or fish, or any kind er little beast dat would fetch 'im dat stone, he'd grant 'em de deares' wish er dey hearts.

"Well, man, in er few days de whole earth was er movin'; eb'ything dar was in de lan' was er gwine.

"Some was er hoppin' an' some was er crawlin' an' some was er flyin', jes 'cord'n to dey natur'; de birds dey 'lowed ter git dar fus', on 'count er fly'n so fas'; but den de little stone was in de water, an' dey'd had to wait till de crick run down, so 'twas jes 'bout broad ez 'twas long.

"Well, while dey was all er gwine, an' de birds was in de lead, one day dey heard sump'n gwine f-l-u-shsh- f-l-u-shsh- an' sump'n streaked by like lightnin', and dey look way ahead, dey did, an' dey seed Nancy Jane O. Den dey hearts 'gun ter sink, an' dey give right up, cause dey knowed she'd outfly eb'ything on de road. An' by'mby de crow, what was always er cunnin' bird, says, 'I tell yer what we'll do; we'll all give er feast,' says he, 'an' git Nancy Jane O ter come, an' den we'll all club togedder an' tie her,' says he.

"Dat took dey fancy, an' dey sent de lark on erhead fur ter catch up wid Nancy Jane O, an' ter ax her ter de feast. Well, man, de lark he nearly kill hisself er flyin'. He flew an' he flew an' he flew, but peared like de faster he went de furder erhead was Nancy Jane O.

"But Nancy Jane O, bein' so fur er start of all de rest, an' not er dreamin' 'bout no kind er devilment, she 'lowed she'd stop an' take er nap, an' so de lark he come up wid 'er, while she was er settin' on er sweet-gum limb, wid 'er head under 'er wing. Den de lark spoke up, an', says he, 'Sis Nancy Jane O,' says he, 'we birds is gwinter give er big feast, cause we'll be sure to win de race any how, an' bein' ez we've flew so long an' so fur, why we're gwine ter stop an' rest er spell, an' give er feast. An' Brer Crow he 'lowed 'twouldn' be no feas' atall lessen you could be dar; so dey sent me on ter tell yer to hol' up tell dey come: dey's done got seeds an' bugs an' worms, an' Brer Crow he's gwine ter furnish de corn.'

"Nancy Jane O she 'lowed ter herself she could soon git erhead of 'em agin, so she 'greed ter wait; an' by'mby hear dey come er flyin'. An' de nex' day dey give de feast; an' while Nancy Jane O was eatin' an' er stuffin' herse'f wid worms an' seeds, an' one thing er nudder, de blue jay he slip up behin' her, an' tied 'er fast ter er little bush. An' dey all laugh an' flopped dey wings; an' says dey, 'Good-bye ter yer, Sis Nancy Jane O. I hope yer'll enjoy yerse'f,' says dey; an' den dey rise up an' stretched out dey wings, an' away dey flewed.

"When Po' Nancy Jane O seed de trick what dey played her, she couldn' hardly stan' still, she was so mad; an' she pulled an' she jerked an' she stretched ter git aloose, but de string was so strong, an' de bush was so firm, she was jes er wastin' her strengt'. An' den she sat down, an' she 'gun ter cry ter herse'f, an' ter sing,

Please on-tie, please on-tie Po' Nancy Jane O!
Please on-tie, please on-tie Po' Nancy Jane O!

"An' after er while here come de ole bullfrog Pigunawaya. He says ter hisse'f, says he, 'What's dat I hear?' Den he listen, an' he hear sump'n gwine,

Please on-tie, please on-tie Po' Nancy Jane O!

an' he went whar he heard de soun', an' dar was de po' bird layin' down all tied ter de bush.

" 'Umph!' says Pigunawaya, says he, 'Ain't dis Nancy Jane O, de swiftest-flyin' bird dey is?' says he; 'what ail 'long yer, chile? what yer cryin' bout?' An' after Nancy Jane O she up an' told 'im, den de frog says:

" 'Now look a here; I was er gwine myse'f ter see if'n I could'n git dat gol'-stone; hit's true I don't stan' much showin' long o' birds, but den if'n eber I gits dar, why I can jes jump right in an' fotch up de stone while de birds is er waitin' for de crick ter run down. An' now, s'posin' I was ter ontie yer, Nancy Jane O, could yer take me on yer back an' carry me ter de crick? an' den we'd hab de sho' thing on de gol'-stone, cause soon's eber we git dar, I'll git it, an' we'll carry it both together ter de king, an' den we'll both git de deares' wish of our hearts. Now what yer say? speak yer mind. If'n yer able an' willin' ter tote me from here ter de crick, I'll ontie yer; ifn yer ain't, den fare yer well, cause I mus' be er gitten' erlong.'

"Well, Nancy Jane O, she studied an' studied in her mind, an' by'mby she says, 'Brer Frog,' says she, 'I b'lieve I'll try yer; ontie me,' says she, 'an' git on, an' I'll take yer ter de crick.' Den de frog he climb on her back an' ontied her, an' she flopped her wings an' started off. Hit was mighty hard flyin' wid dat big frog on her back; but Nancy Jane O was er flyer, man, yer heard me! an' she jes lit right out, an' she flew an' she flew, an' after er while she got in sight er de birds, an' dey looked, an' dey see her comin', an' den dey 'gun ter holler,

Who on-tied, who on-tied Po' Nancy Jane O?

"An' de frog he holler back,

Pig-un-a-wa-ya, Pig-un-a-wa-ya, hooo-hooo!

"Den, gentlemen, yer oughten seed dat race; dem birds dey done dey level best, but Nancy Jane O, spite er all dey could do, she gained on 'em, an ole Pigunawaya he sot up dar, an' he kep' er urgin' an' er urgin' Nancy Jane O.

" 'Dat's you!' says he; 'git erhead!' says he. 'Now we're gwine it!' says he; an' presently Nancy Jane O shot erhead clean befo' all de rest; an' when de birds dey seed dat de race was lost, den dey all 'gun ter holler,

> *Who on-tied, who on-tied Po' Nancy Jane O?*

"An' de frog, he turnt roun', he did, an' he wave his hand roun' his head, an' he holler back,

> *Pig-un-a-wa-ya, Pig-un-a-wa-ya, hooo-hooo!*

"After Nancy Jane O got erhead er de birds, den de hardest flyin' was through wid; so she jes went 'long, an' went 'long, kind er easy like, tell she got ter de stone; an' she lit on er' simmon-bush close ter de crick, an' Pigunawaya he slipt off, he did, an' he heist up his feet, an' he give er jump, kerchug he went down inter de water; an' by'mby here he come wid de stone in his mouf. Den he mount on Nancy Jane O, he did; an', man, she was so proud, she an' de frog bof, tell dey flew all roun' and roun' an' roun', an' Nancy Jane O, she 'gun ter sing,

> *Who on-tied, who on-tied Po' Nancy Jane O?*

An' de frog he answer back,

> *Pig-un-a-wa-ya, Pig-un-a-wa-ya, hooo-hooo!*

"An' while dey was er singing' and enjoyin' of deyselves, here come de birds; an' de frog he felt so big, cause he'd got de stone, 'til he stood up on Nancy Jane O's back, he did, an he took 'n' shook de stone at de birds, an' he holler at 'em

> *O Pig-un-a-wa-ya, Pig-un-a-wa-ya, hooo-hooo!*

"An' jes ez he said dat, he felt hisself slippin', an' dat made him clutch on ter Po' Nancy Jane O, an' down dey bof' went together ker-splash, right inter de crick.

"De frog he fell slap on ter er big rock, an' bust his head all ter pieces; an' Po' Nancy Jane O sunk down in de water an' got drownded; an' dat's de end."

"Did the king get the stone, Aunt Edy?" asked Dumps.

"Why no, chile; don't yer know de mole he's blind 'til yet? If'n he could er got dat stone, he could er seen out'n his eyes befo' now. But I ain't got no time ter fool 'long er you chil'en. I mus' git marster's shirts done, I mus'."

And Aunt Edy turned to her ironing-table, as if she didn't care for company; and Dumps and Tot, seeing that she was tired of them, went back to the house, Tot singing,

> *Who on-tied, who on-tied Po' Nanty Dane O?*

and Dumps answering back,

> *Pig-un-a-wa-ya, Pig-un-a-wa-ya, hooo-hooo!*

Mr. Rabbit and Mr. Frog Make Mr. Fox and Mr. Bear Their Riding Horses

· *From Richard M. Dorson*, American Negro Folktales ·

Dorson collected this tale from John Courtney.

Mr. Rabbit and Mr. Frog were courting two girls, and Mr. Bear and Mr. Fox were liking them too. Mr. Fox and Mr. Bear they had the best going, the girls cared most for them. So Brother Rabbit went down to Brother Frog's house, and built up a scheme to play on Brother Bear and Brother Fox. So they set a night that they were going to the girls' house, an off night from what Brother Bear and Brother Fox were courting. And so they went on a Friday night, and they told the girls, "Brother Fox and Brother Bear's our riding-horses. You're crazy about them boys but there ain't nothing to them."

So the girls says, "Oh no, I can't believe that."

So Brother Rabbit told them, says, "I'll prove it if you'll be my girl friend." And Brother Frog said he would too. So they set a night that they was going to prove it, in the following week. So that evening Brother Fox and Brother Bear come over to Brother Rabbit's house.

Brother Rabbit say, "You just the man I want to see." So Brother Rabbit say, "We ought to go to some extra girls' house tonight, we need some more girls." So they finally made it up and begin to get ready. They carried them a saddle apiece, Brother Rabbit and Brother Frog, and hid them by Brother Bear's girl friend's house. So they went on that night down to this extra girl's house. So they stayed there till nine o'clock. Brother Bear and Brother Fox they had to stay by their girl friend's house. So they all got ready and started out. Brother Rabbit took sick. Brother Rabbit was so sick, Brother Bear 'cided to try to tote him. So Brother Frog he had a bellyache. So that made him sick too.

So Brother Fox said, "Well we'll just tote them two guys up here and we'll stop over."

Brother Bear told them, says, "Crawl up on my back, Brother Rabbit, I'll tote ya." And Brother Fox told Brother Frog to crawl up. Both of them was so sick, he could get up there but he couldn't stay up there.

Brother Rabbit told him, says, "I just can't stay on your back. I gotta get something to hold to." Brother Rabbit told him, "I know what, I see the very thing I can hold to." [*Excited*] Brother Frog say the same thing. So Brother Rabbit say, "Here's some saddles here, here's the very thing we can hold on to." So they put the saddles on, and Brother Rabbit and him climbed up in the saddle. Both of 'em was so sick they couldn't hardly stay in the saddle.

And when they got to the girls' house, Brother Bear say, "Now you've got to get down, Brother Rabbit, at the steps. This is far as I can carry you."

So Brother Rabbit told him, says, "You take me to the top steps, we can make it." He had done put him a pair of spurs on he and Brother Frog. So when they got up to the top step, Brother Rabbit popped them spurs to Brother Bear. Brother Bear ran right on in his girl friend's door. Brother Rabbit said, "I told you Brother Bear was my riding horse."

Brother Frog said, "I told you Brother Fox was my riding horse."

Bobtail Beat the Devil

· *From Daryl Cumber Dance,* Shuckin' and Jivin' ·

I collected this folktale in Richmond, Virginia.

They had a saying: they say that "You beat Bobtail and *Bobtail* beat the Devil." So the way it come about, say the Devil and the Rabbit (we call him Bobtail, you know) got to talkin'. Say the Rabbit said to the Devil, say, "I tell ya what let's do, Mr. Devil." Say, "Let's go in croppin' together this year. We gon' plant corn." He say, "You have all the bottom; I'll have all the tops."

The Devil say, "All right."

So when it come to gather the crops, the Rabbit had the feed and the corn, and the Devil didn't have nothin' but roots, you know. So the Devil was put out 'bout it. He say, "Aw, that ain't no fair. I — I'll crop you again next year, but I'm gon' have all the tops you had."

He say, "Naw, I'll tell ya whatcha do. Let's raise sweet potatoes next year. I'll have all the bottoms; you have all the tops."

He say, "Awright."

So when they went to gather in all the crops, the Devil had the vines and the Rabbit had all the sweet potatoes. So he beat the Devil each time. That's why they say, "Bobtail beat the Devil."

Making Butter

· *From Elsie Clews Parsons,* Folk-Lore of the Sea Islands, South Carolina ·

Once upon a time Ber Rabbit and Ber Wolf made a plan together, and promise not to break it. "Let us go out into the woods and catch any cow that we can catch, and milk it, and set the milk!" And after the milk has been set and turn to hard milk or clabber, then they would churn it together. They had wanted a kagful of butter to put up. So after they had churned the milk and the butter came, they put the butter up into the kag and buried it into a woods. And both of them promised faithfully not to walk the road that led by the side which the butter was buried. Ber Rabbit is a very schemy man. He told that he would not go that road, don't care what happen, through the woods. So one day Brother Wolf was standing in his door, looking out, studying what he was going to find to eat that day, when to his eyes he saw Ber Rabbit just a-coming down the road in full speed. "Heh, there, Ber Rabbit!" said Ber Wolf, "where are you going in that road?"—"O Ber Wolf!" said Ber Rabbit, "my sister had a pretty girl-child, the finest child you have ever seen."—"What is the child's name?" said Ber Wolf. "Her name is Just-Begin. You must excuse me for coming this side, but my sister said that I must be sure and come." And he went into the wood and scrape off the top of the earth off the kag, and started into the butter. He took a good deal of it, to last a week or two. And he did this over and over again, until Ber Wolf said, "Well, Ber Rabbit, let us go and see how the butter is getting on!" Ber Wolf's wife told him, "See here! that brother of yours who is Ber Rabbit is just eating all of that butter, because his sister she cannot have children so fast." And so Ber Wolf and Ber Rabbit went to the woods and started to dig. They dug and dug until they came to the kag. And when they sounded the kag, it sounds as if it is empty. Ber Wolf did not say anything, but took the top off. And while he was taking it off, Ber Rabbit got a pain in his stomach and beg for excuse to go. And Ber Wolf said, "No, not now." And he said, "I must go. Do let me go!" So he went; and while he was away, Ber Wolf open the kag, and the kag was empty. And Ber Wolf tried to catch him; but all Ber Rabbit said was, "Your sister is a fool! Your mother and father are fools, your whole family are fools, and you are the biggest fool! Ha, ha!"

Some Are Going, and Some Are Coming

· *From Daryl Cumber Dance,* Shuckin' and Jivin' ·

I collected this folktale in Charles City, Virginia.

The Rabbit was coming along, and he looked down in this old deep well (you know how the wells used to be), and he looked down in this well, and he saw what he thought was a piece of cheese down there, but it was only a reflection of the moon. And he said, "Well, I'll git down here and git this piece of cheese." It was two buckets, you know, it was two buckets; you know how people used to have one bucket goes down and the other one goes up. So he got in this bucket at the top, and he say, "I'll go down and get it." So he went on down in this bucket. Then when he got down to the bottom and reached for the cheese, it was only a reflection of the moon. And he didn't have any way to get *up,* and he say, "I'm down here now in this *water,* nothin' but this moon reflection 'n' . . ."

And after a while the Fox came by. He looked up there and the Fox was at the top of the well. And the Fox say, "Brer Rabbit, what ya doin' down there?"

He say, "I'm down here eatin' *cheese.* I'm down here eatin' this cheese. Can't ya see this big cheese down here?"

"Yeah, I see it."

"Come on down, Brer Fox, 'n' get a piece, ya know. Come on down. It's nice."

So the Fox got in the other bucket and he was coming on down. And when they got about half—you know, when they got about, you know, even Stephen, you know, when the Fox was going down and the Rabbit was coming up, he say, "Brother Fox, I tell ya, that's the way it is in life. Some are going and some coming." And *he* got on up, you know. Some going and some coming.

The Tar Baby

· *From Daryl Cumber Dance,* Shuckin' and Jivin' ·

I collected this folktale in Richmond, Virginia.

The animals were tryin' to *catch* Brer Rabbit; and Brer Rabbit would go down to the spring to get water. They thought that would be a good way to catch him. And so they made a Tar Baby and set it up at the spring 'cause Brer Rabbit was very inquisitive. And Brer Rabbit went down to drink, and he saw this Tar Baby; and he said, "Uh, who're you?" And he didn't say nothing, so then Brer Rabbit said, "You better tell me who you are!" And so the Tar Baby didn't say anything. So then Brer Rabbit went up there and say, "Well, I'll *slap* ya!" And the Tar Baby didn't say anything, so he slapped the Tar

Baby, and his hand stuck, but the Tar Baby still didn't say anything. So then he say, "I'll kick ya!" And he kicked 'im and his foot stuck. So then he said, "Well, I got another foot; I'll kick ya with that!" And he kicked 'im and *that* foot stuck. And then he said, "Well, I got another hand—I'll slap ya." And so he slapped 'im with the other hand, and *that* stuck. He said, "Now you think you smart, but I got a head—I'll butt ya!" So he butt 'im and *that* stuck. So when the animals came to catch him he was all stuck on the Tar Baby, and he say, "Oh-oh, oh! Turn me loose, turn me loose!"

They say, "We gotcha! We gotcha!"

He say, "Well, I tell you what you do. You throw me in the *briar* patch, because I don't like briar patches. You just throw me in the briar patch and you'll have me—then you kin keep me *forever.*"

So then they took him and throwed him in the briar patch, and he say, "O-o-oh!" when he got in the briar patch. "O-O-OH! This is where I was *born* and *raised*—right in the briar patch!"

Then he ran on down through the briars.

Buh Squirrel an' Buh Fox

· *Adapted from Charles C. Jones*, Negro Myths ·

Buh Squirrel was very busy gathering hickry nuts on de groun to put away to feed himself an his family in the wintertime. Buh Fox been er watching him, an befo Buh Squirrel see him, he slip up and grabbed him. Buh Squirrel was scared and tremble all over, an he begged Buh Fox for let him go. Buh Fox tell him say he been trying to catch him a long time, but he hab such sharp eyes, an keen ears, an spry legs, he manage to dodge him; an now when he got him at last, he mean for kill him an eat him. When Buh Squirrel find out dat Buh Fox ain't going to pity him an turn him loose, but dat he fixin for kill him an eat him, Buh Squirrel say to Buh Fox: "Ain't you know that nobody ought to eat vittles before they say grace over 'em?" Buh Fox him mek answer: "Dat so"; an wid dat he put Buh Squirrel in front o' him, an he fall on his knee, an he cover his eye wid his hand, an he turn for say grace.

While Buh Fox do dis, Buh Squirrel manage for slip 'way; an when Buh Fox open his eye, he see Buh Squirrel done run up de tree where him couldn't tetch him.

Buh Fox fine he couldn't help himself, an he call after Buh Squirrel an he say: "Never mind, Boy, you done git away now, but de nex time me clap dis hand on top of you, me gwine eat you fust and say grace afterward."

The best plan for a man is to make sure of his vittle befo he say thanks for 'em.

How Brer Wolf Caught Brer Rabbit
· *From Donald J. Waters,* Strange Ways and Sweet Dreams ·

One night Brer Rabbit went to Brer Wolf cabbage patch to steal cabbage. Brer Wolf been missin' his cabbage long time, so he tuck an' set a trap that swung up high in de air. So when Brer Rabbit got his bag of cabbage and started home he got caught in de trap. By an' by, Brer Possum, he come by, an' Brer Rabbit he begin to sing, "Swing high, I see up in Heaven, Swing high, I see up in Heaven."

Brer Possum say, "What you doin' there Brer Rabbit?"

"Lor, man, I can see way up in Heaven. Don't you want to see? Pull down dat stick and you can see too."

Brer Possum pull down de stick and up de trap went. Brer Possum begun to sing, "Swing high, I don't see no Heaven. Swing high, I don't see no Heaven."

By an' by, Brer Wolf came to de patch an' when he seed Brer Possum, he say, "I catch you, you been eatin' my cabbage."

When Brer Possum went to 'splain, Brer Rabbit broke out, "Mash his mouf, Brer Wolf, he givin' you imp'dence." Blip! Brer Wolf hit him in de mouf. "Look at him Brer Wolf, he makin' faces at you, hit him agin." After Brer Wolf got through with Brer Possum, an' took him down, Brer Rabbit he gone home wid de cabbage. Den Brer Wolf 'lowed dat he was gwine to get even wid Brer Rabbit, an' Brer Possum and Brer Fox 'low dat dey'll jine wid him, so de gave a supper an' 'vites Brer Rabbit an' say dat he gwine to kill him. Brer

Rabbit grab up he banjo an' say, "Do, Brer Wolf let me play one more tune befo' I die." Den he begin to play, "I have a fing fang, fing fang, finger. I have a fing fang, fing fang finger, — Boo." "I can't half play 'lessen I have some cake an' wine."

Den Brer Fox give him some cake an' wine. Den he sang "Re-o-be Rabbit, Brack-eye Rabbit, Re-o-be Rabbit, O."

All dat time he was gettin' to de do'. By an' by he 'lowed dat he want a little air, dat he can't half play widout mo' air; all de folks was carried away over de music, 'cause Brer Rabbit was the best singer gwine, so dey move from befo' de do'. Den Brer Rabbit say, "Let's all dance," so, dey all dance round de room, an' when Brer Rabbit got to de do' he jump out. Brer Wolf say, "Catch him! Catch him!"

Brer Rabbit hollowed, "Why didn't you catch me when you had me?" Den he jes took out for home.

Straighten Up and Fly Right

· *From Richard M. Dorson,* American Negro Folktales ·

Dorson collected this tale from John Blackamore.

Do you know where the title of the song "Straighten Up and Fly Right" comes from — the song by Nat King Cole?

One day the Buzzard was sailing around the sky looking for food. He hadn't found none, when he spied a Rabbit looking for a cool place to rest, in the midday sun. So he decided he'd try to get him. So he lights down beside the Rabbit, and spoke to him. Asked him how was he doing. Rabbit says he's pretty hot. Buzzard tells him it's cooler up where he came from, and suggested the Rabbit go for a ride. The Rabbit didn't know what to think about that: "It's closer to the sun and should be hotter up there." But since Buzzard looked so rested and cool, finally he accepts. He gets on the Buzzard's back, and they sail around up in the sky. When he thought the Rabbit felt all cool and comfortable, Buzzard assures him they are going to make a landing. Down he roars, about a hundred feet straight down in a power dive, and then zooms back up. And the Rabbit falls off. So he had the Rabbit for lunch.

Next day when he's looking for food, he sees a Squirrel. So he comes down and lights beside the Squirrel, asks him how did he feel. Squirrel told him he's pretty hot. Buzzard says, "It's cool where I come from. Why don't you take a ride with me?" Since the Squirrel had been accustomed to the trees being cooler up high, he accepted; he figured it would be cooler the higher up he got. So they went sailing way on up. And the Buzzard gave him time to cool off. By the way, a small Monkey was in the top of the tree, watching the Buzzard play his trick on the Squirrel. When the Buzzard gets the Squirrel cooled off, he takes another power dive, and goes right back up, so the Squirrel falls off his back. And he eats the Squirrel for dinner.

Next day the Monkey watches the Buzzard. When he sees him coming, he gits out where the Buzzard can see him, and pretends to be hot. Buzzard lights down beside him, says "Good day," and asks him how he feels. So the Monkey tells him the sun is burning him up, and he wishes he knew where there was a cool place. Buzzard tells him it's cool where he came from, and asks him to take a ride with him. The Monkey accepts. So they sails around. When he figured the Monkey had got all cooled off, the Buzzard started to make another power dive. But the Monkey wraps his tail around the Buzzard's neck. "Let go, you're choking me." "Then straighten up and fly right. You won't have no Monkey for dinner today."

> The buzzard took the monkey for a ride in the air.
> The monkey thought that everything was on the square.
> The buzzard tried to throw the monkey off his back.
> The monkey grabbed his neck and said,
> "Now listen Jack,
> "Straighten up and fly right."

De Two Fren an' de Bear

· *Adapted from Charles C. Jones*, Negro Myths ·

Two fren, dem went on a journey together. Dem haffer go through one thick swamp where full er bear an' other varmints. Dem promise for stand for one another, an' to help one another out if de varmint attack dem. They didn't get halfway through de swamp when one big black Bear jump outer de bush and make fur dem. Instead of one o' dem stand for help fight him, he left his friend and climbed one tree. De other friend had heard it said that Bears wouldn't eat dead people, so him lay down on de ground, and hold his breath, and shut his eye, and make out say him dead. De Bear come up to him, and smell him, and turn him over, and try for see if he was breathing. When he saw he wasn't breathing, he gone off a little way an' he watch him. Den he turned back an' smell him again, an' notice him close. At length he make up his mind say de man was dead for true; an' with dat he left him for good an' gone back in de wood. All dis time de other friend was squinched up in de tree watching what been gwine on. He was so scared he wouldn't do nuthin' for help his friend or try for run de Bear off.

When he find de Bear gone for sure, he holler to him friend say: "What de Bear been tell you? Him an' you seem like you have close conversation." Then his friend make answer: "He been tell me never for trust nobody where call hisself friend, and where gwine run like a coward soon as trouble come."

De Eagle an' His Chillun

· *Adapted from Charles C. Jones,* Negro Myths ·

De eagle, him is a wise bird. He make his nest on one tall pine tree close to de ribber, or de sea, where nothin' kin git at him. He satisfied wid two chillun. He take good care of 'em. Every hour he fetch 'em snakes an' fish, an' he guards 'em from wind an' rain an' fowl hawks, an' make 'em grow fast. When dem wings are covered wid feathers an' are strong enough for dem to fly, what Buh Eagle do? He won't leave dem chillun in de nest for get lazy an' live on deir father and deir mother, but he take dem on his wing, an' he sail over de sea, an' he tell the chillun: "De time come for you for make you own livin'. Me feed you long enough. Now you have to look out for youself." Wid dat, he fly from under dem, an' the young birds, when dem find out deir mother ain't gwine carry 'em no furder, an' dat dem have to shift for demself, dem try deir wing an' sail off in de element to hunt vittles.

People ought to take notice of Buh Eagle an' do just as him do. When you chillun git big enough for work, make 'em work. Don't let 'em sit about de house doing nothing, an' expecting deir father an' mother for find vittles and clothes for 'em. If you does, you chillun gwine make you shame, an' dey will turn out trifling. Dey will keep you dead poor, too.

Do same like Buh Eagle. Mind you children well when dem little; an' soon as dem big enough for work, make 'em work.

Buh Lion an' Buh Goat

· *Adapted from Charles C. Jones*, Negro Myths ·

Buh Lion been a hunting, an' he spy Buh Goat lying on top er big rock, workin' his mout an chewin'. He creep up for ketch um. When he git close to um he notice um good. Buh Goat keep on chewin'. Buh Lion try for fine out what Buh Goat was eatin'. He ain't see nothing but de naked rock where he lay down on. Buh Lion was 'stonished. Buh goat keep on chewin' and chewin' and chewin'. Buh Lion cant make de ting out, an he come close, an he say: "Hay! Buh Goat, what you eatin'?" Buh Goat was scared when Buh Lion rise up befo um, but he keep a bold heart and he answer: "Me chew dis rock, an if you dont leave, when me finish, me guine eat you." Dis bold threat save Buh Goat. Bold man git outer difficulty while a cowardly man lose his life.

De Dyin' Bull-Frog

· *Adapted from Charles C. Jones*, Negro Myths ·

One time Old Bull-Frog been very sick and expectin' for to die. All his friends in de pond collect round him and his fambly, for nurse um an' take dem las' look at um. Dat Old Frog been hab a young wife and heap er lil' chillun. He was very trouble in his heart 'bout who gwine mind his fambly after he gone. When his voice begin to fail um, an' just befo' he died, he say: "Me friends, who gwine take me wife when de breath leave dis yer body?" His friends all holler out at de top er dem voice: "Me me! Me me! Me me!" Den he inquire: "Who er you gwine mind me lil' chillun?" For some time he ain't heard no answer; and den de answer come back to him one by one from all over de pond, in a deep voice: "Not me. Not me. Not me!"

Heap er people willin' for notice a pretty young widow, when dem no want bother long another man's chillun.

The Elephant and the Whale
· *From Alcee Fortier,* Louisiana Folk-Tales ·

One day Compair Lapin [Rabbit] and Compair Bouki [Hyena] were going on a journey together. Compair Lapin often took Bouki with him to make fun of him, and to hear all the news which Bouki knew. When they reached the seashore, they saw something which was very strange, and which astonished them so much that they stopped to watch and listen. It was an elephant and a whale which were conversing together.

"You see," said Bouki, "they are the two largest beasts in the world, and the strongest of all animals."

"Hush up," said Lapin, "let us go nearer and listen. I want to hear what they are saying."

The elephant said to the whale: "Commère Baleine, as you are the largest and strongest in the sea, and I am the largest and strongest on land, we must rule over all beasts; and all those who will revolt against us we shall kill them, you hear, commère."

"Yes, compair; keep the land and I shall keep the sea."

"You hear," said Bouki, "let us go, because it will be bad for us if they hear that we are listening to their conversation."

"Oh! I don't care," said Lapin; "I am more cunning than they; you will see how I am going to fix them."

"No," said Bouki, "I am afraid, I must go."

"Well, go, if you are so good for nothing and cowardly; go quickly, I am tired of you; you are too foolish."

Compair Lapin went to get a very long and strong rope, then he got his drum and hid it in the grass. He took one end of the rope, and went to the elephant: "Mister, you who are so good and so strong. I wish you would render me a service; you would relieve me of a great trouble and prevent me from losing my money."

The elephant was glad to hear such a fine compliment, and he said: "Compair, I shall do for you everything you want. I am always ready to help my friends."

"Well," said Lapin, "I have a cow which is stuck in the mud on the coast; you know that I am not strong enough to pull her out; I come for you to help me. Take this rope in your trunk. I shall tie it to the cow, and when you hear me beat the drum, pull hard on the rope. I tell you that because the cow is stuck deep in the mud."

"That is all right," said the elephant. "I guarantee you I shall pull the cow out, or the rope will break."

Compair Lapin took the other end of the rope and ran towards the sea. He paid a pretty compliment to the whale, and asked her to render him the same service about the cow, which was stuck in a bayou in the woods. Compair Lapin's mouth was so honeyed that no one could refuse him anything. The whale took hold of the rope and said: "When I shall hear the drum beat I shall pull."

"Yes," said Lapin, "begin pulling gently, and then more and more."

"You need not be afraid," said the whale; "I shall pull out the cow, even if the Devil were holding her."

"That is good," said Lapin; "we are going to laugh." And he beat his drum.

The elephant began to pull so hard that the rope was like a bar of iron. The whale, on her side, was pulling and pulling, and yet she was coming nearer to the land, as she was not so well situated to pull as the elephant. When she saw that she was mounting on land, she beat her tail furiously and plunged headlong into the sea. The shock was so great that the elephant was dragged to the sea. "What, said he, what is the matter? that cow must be wonderfully strong to drag me so. Let me kneel with my front feet in the mud." Then he twisted the rope round his trunk in such a manner that he pulled the whale again to the shore. He was very much astonished to see his friend the whale. "What is the matter," said he. "I thought it was Compair Lapin's cow I was pulling."

"Lapin told me the same thing. I believe he is making fun of us."

"He must pay for that," said the elephant. "I forbid him to eat a blade of grass on land because he laughed at us."

"And I will not allow him to drink a drop of water in the sea. We must watch for him, and the first one that sees him must not miss him."

Compair Lapin said to Bouki: "It is growing hot for us; it is time to leave."

"You see," said Bouki, "you are always bringing us into trouble."

"Oh! hush up, I am not through with them yet; you will see how I shall fix them."

They went on their way and after a while they separated. When Compair Lapin arrived in the wood, he found a little dead deer. The dogs had bitten him so that the hair had fallen off his skin in many places. Lapin took off the deer's skin and put it on his back. He looked exactly like a wounded deer. He passed limping by the elephant, who said to him: "Poor little deer, how sick you look."

"Oh! yes, I am suffering very much; you see it is Compair Lapin who poisoned me and put his curse on me, because I wanted to prevent him from eating grass, as you had ordered me. Take care, Mr. Elephant, Compair Lapin has made a bargain with the Devil; he will be hard on you, if you don't take care."

The elephant was very much frightened. He said, "Little deer, you will tell Compair Lapin that I am his best friend; let him eat as much grass as he wants and present my compliments to him."

The deer met a little later the whale in the sea. "But poor little deer, why are you limping so; you seem to be very sick."

"Oh! yes, it is Compair Lapin who did that. Take care, Commère Baleine." The whale also was frightened, and said: "I want to have nothing to do with the Devil; please tell Compair Lapin to drink as much water as he wants."

The deer went on his way, and when he met Compair Bouki he took off the deer's skin and said: "You see that I am more cunning than all of them, and that I can make fun of them all the time. Where I shall pass another will be caught."

"You are right indeed," said Compair Bouki.

Polly Tells on the Slaves

· *From Richard M. Dorson,* American Negro Folktales ·

There is a large cycle of polly parrot tales; several others are included in Dorson,
and I collected a number when I was compiling *Shuckin' and Jivin'*.

Back in slavery days Old Marster and his wife would go to town to shop. And the slaves'd take the time to have a big party—there was so much food it wouldn't be missed. They would cook cakes and pies and potatoes and kill chickens and bring out their fiddle and dance. But no matter how they pledged themselves to secrecy, Old Marster would know all about it when he came back. And then one day one of the maids who worked in the house heard the poll parrot reviewing all the things they had done at the last party.

"Pass the 'tater pie."

"Gimme another piece a chicken."

"This is good cake."

"Are you going to dance now, are you going to dance now?" [*Croaky*]

"Swing your partner."

(They go off—they lose interest in the conversation.)

So they knew how the Marster knowed about them—Polly had told them. They had gradually stopped the parties, and Marster thought soon it would stop altogether. Next time Marster went to town they draped a black cloth over his head and put him under the washpot. When Marster came back he asked Polly what she'd seen.

"Polly don't know. Poor Polly been in hell all day." (Darkness is her idea of hell.)

Hot Biscuits Burn Yo' Ass

· *From Daryl Cumber Dance,* Shuckin' and Jivin' ·

I collected this folktale in Richmond, Virginia.

This was a maid, and she went to work for these people. So this lady had to go away to do some shopping or something. So this maid had to cook while she was gone. They had a Polly Parrot, and he was hanging up there, and this little girl, she didn't know he would talk. So she had to cook dinner, and so she went on and cooked biscuits and other foods to go along with it.

So then when the lady came in, she had dinner all ready. She wanted the lady to go right on to the table and eat, but the lady, she went somewhere and sit down. The Parrot had seen this maid put these hot biscuits (when she saw her coming, she grabbed some out of the pan and put over there for her[self], you know, under the cushion in the chair). So this here Parrot told his mistress, "Hot biscuit burn [yo' ass]! Hot biscuit burn [yo' ass]!"

Lookin' for Three Fools

· *From Jack and Olivia Solomon,* Ghosts and Goosebumps ·

That gal, Tildy Moore, had done had her cap sot fer John Spencer fer nearbout a year. She had been drappin' hints an' sideise looks all along, but John was young an' skittish an' didn't ketch on fast. Howsomever, one bright May day in church, when he finely seen her kinda cuttin' her eye tward him, he reared back an' tuck notice.

After church, when ever'body was bunchin' around askin' the reverend to dinner an' braggin' to each other 'bout their crops an' just generally bein' sociable, John he sashayed over to where Tildy was prancin' around her maw an' a passel of other women-folks.

"Might I have the pleasure of seein' you home, Miss Tildy?" he sat her, tippin' his hat as clever as you please.

"Why, John," Tildy sorty giggled, "you'll have to ast Maw; but I wouldn't mind."

Ole Miz Moore was hard put to keep a straight face, she was that pleased, but she put on her solidest look an' said, "Well, I reckon you can walk home with John but don't you all dast meander an' dally on the way fur I'll be a needin' you to help about dinner."

Well, the two on 'em they strolled down the road to her house — 'tw'nt more'n two mile — an' John he pulled up a cheer on the piazzer clost to whur old man Moore was a-settin' an' they talked about this an' that while the wimmen was a-scarin' up dinner.

Whilst she was a-settin' the table the old lady seen the syrup pitcher was near bout dry, so she said, "Tildy, you run to the smokehouse an' fetch some mo'lasses."

Tildy tuck the pitcher and went out tuh the smokehouse, and she stayed, an' she stayed, an' she stayed.

'Twa'nt so very long 'till her maw got right oneasy and so she called and she called but Tildy didn't answer. So her maw throwed a cloth over the table to keep the flies offen the vittles and she tuck 'n went to the smokehouse to see what the matter was.

Well, there sot Tildy by the syrup kag with her knees drawed up an' her chin on her hands, and the syrup just a-runnin out over the edge of the pitcher and makin' a puddle on the dirt.

"Well, my goodness, Tildy, whatever in the world's got possission of ye?" she yelled at the gal.

Tildy lifted up her head and looked at her maw with sorty bland, starin' eyes, "Why Maw, I'm jest a-thinkin' and a-thinkin' about whatever shall we name our fu'st child when me an John git mar'ied."

"Well, now, Tildy, I declare that is to be thought about," the old lady said, an' she sot down in the puddle of syrup beside Tildy an' put her hands on her knees an' her chin on her hands and started a-helpin' her think.

Now they is hardly a patienter man to be found that that old man Moore are sometimes, but mealtimes when he was hungry was not one of them times. Him an' John got to talkin' less and less and he commenced fidgetin' worser and worser. Finely he couldn't stand it no longer so he tuck his feet off the bannister and went stompin' into the kitchen a-walkin' his mad walk. There was the table all kivered up, but no wife and no Tildy.

He yelled out, "Maw, whur ye at?" When he didn't git no anser he was mad enough to chaw up sawdust an' spit out scantlin's. Then he looked out the back door an' seen the smokehouse door open an' got awful oneasy, thinkin' maybe they had both went out an' got snake bit.

He tore out down them back steps and went abustin' out to that smokehouse like the devil beatin' tanbark and poked his head in the door. His eyes near bugged out. There sot Tildy and her maw with their hands on their knees an' their chins on their hands, a-thinkin', an' the syrup was apourin' out and amakin' a reg'lar lake.

"Old woman, what on earth air ye a-doin'?" he hollered.

Old Miz Moore raised them blank eyes ov hern an' told him, "We air just a-tryin' to think up a name fer the fu'st child when John and Tildy get mar'ied," she said.

That tuck the old man up short. He said, "Well, now that is somp'n to be thought about," he said and down he sot in the syrup an' begun a-helpin' 'em think.

Well, John like to wore out that rawhide cheer bottom a-fidgitin'. He didn't know should he go home or should he stay. Finely he sot jest as still as he could an' strained his ear a-listenin' for them people. He didn't hear nothin'. Well, it got to where he jes' couldn't hold himself in no longer. He had to know what the matter was, manners or no manners. So he up an' went to see if he could find 'em. He even hollered for the ole man a time or two, but it bein' Sunday he wouldn't holler too loud. Finely he seen the smokehouse door open an' he went a'sailin' out there as hard as he could tear an' looked inside.

There was the whole kit an bilin' of the Moores, a-settin' half-leg deep in syrup with their hands on their knees an' their chins on their hands lookin' into space.

John, he scratched his head an' kicked his foot an' said, "Excuse me, y'all, but did you git bad news?"

The old man didn't so much as raise his head, an' he told him, "We're a-thinkin' up a name for the fust chile when you an Tildy git mah'ied!"

Well that fair tuck John's breath away for a minute an' then he said, "Well, I never! If that don't beat anything I ever see. I bet I kin go on up thisyere road as fur's it goes an' I won't never find three more as big fools as y'all. If I do, I'll come right back an' marry the gal!" He didn't say no more, but he stuck his hat on his head an' went off down the road. It was a powerful thin-settled country up around there an' he had to walk a right smart piece before he come to another house. This was an old house an' the boards on the kiver had this here green moss-stuff a-growin' out thick all over 'em. Well, right out in the front yard he seen a man a'tryin' to drive a old skinny cow up the ladder that was a leanin' up against the house.

John stopped dead an' for a spell he just gaped at the man. Finely he made so bold as to ast him, "Mister, I'm a stranger in these here parts but I shore would like to know what you're tryin' to do?"

The man, he worked his chaw of tabacco over to one side of his mouth an' spit at a horsefly an' near'bout hit it, an' then he said, "Why, I'm a tryin' to git this here consarned creetur to go up thar 'n eat that there moss offen them shingles but, dang her contrary hide, looks like she'd ruther starve plum to death than to climb that there ladder."

John ast him, "Well then, why don't you scrape the dad-burn stuff off and let her eat it down here? Looks like if them rafters ain't strong enough to hold up her weight. She shore will ruin the top o' your house!"

The ol' man, he reached down an' got that cow by the tail, but afore he twisted her, he turned around to John an' he says, "Well, son, I been a-pasturin' my stock since your grandpa wa'n't no bigger than a groundpuppy an' I reckon I can still pasture my cow with-outen no advice from any of you soft-headed Spencers."

An' with that he twisted that critter's tail so hard that she run up nine rungs of the ladder an' stood there swayin'. Now John thought he might step up an' fetch the ol' man a slap an' then he thought he mightn't, for he was a-lookin' for fools an' not fights. So he went on with his hands in his pockets a-cussin' an' a-hawkin' an' a-spittin', lowin' he'd done found one fool.

Along late in the evenin' he come to the next house. It was after night an' the moon was a-shinin' when he seen it. An' he seen somp'm else which surprised him a heap. A woman was a-tearin' round an' round the house a-pushin' a wheelba'r, an' ever' time she made the third trip around she'd shove the wheelba'r up inside the house an' dump it. Then she'd skeedaddle back out and run around agin, an' there wa'n't anything in that ba'rr. Well, John he watched and he watched an' he figgured an' he figgured an' he couldn't make it out. Finely he busted out as polite as he knew how, "Please, ma'am, mought I ast what you're a-doin'?"

She was a little woman an' swift. "Son, I ain't got no time to an-swer no foolish questions. Here I've been a-scourin' floors all after-noon an' tain't but three hours 'til moonset with me still havin' to haul in enough moonshine to dry the parlor floor."

An' she kept right on a-goin'.

John didn't have nothin' a-tall to say to that. He just scratched his head as he went on off and said to hisse'f, "Well, that shore makes two."

He was so wore out and hungry he didn't go but jus' a few mile fu'ther on till he laid down under a tree with his coat fer a piller an' slep' till big daylight. Then he got up an' went on.

Jest about sun'up he come around a bend in the road an' there sot a house. They wa'nt nobody stirrin' an' no smoke comin' outen the chimbly but it looked like somebody must stay there so he went to the door an' knocked. He didn't git no answer so he knocked again. 'Bout that time he heard a funny bumpin' noise to'rd the back side of the house, an' bein' brash an' young, he went around to see what that noise mought be.

Well, they was a man under a peach tree in the back yard an' he didn't have on a thing but his shirt and drawers. His pants was a-hangin' on a limb of the peach tree an' that air man would jump up as high as he could an' kick at the top of the breeches with both feet an' fall back an' bump hisself on the ground. That was what was makin' the bumpin' noise. He'd git right back up an' dust off where he had bumped hisself and jump 'n kick at the breeches again.

John was too weak tuh talk loud but he spoke up as stout as he could an' said, "Mister, mought a pore stranger ast ye what ye're a-doin'?"

"I'm a-tryin' to put my britches on, smart aleck, what does hit look like I'm a-doin'?"

That made John sorter mad so he said, "Well, why in the dickens don't ye take 'em down from there, then, and step into 'em one foot at the time?"

The man turned around and looked at John like he could go plum through him, and then he reared up his head and said, "Boy, this here is how my paw and his paw afore him put on their britches, and what was good enough fer them is shore-Gawd good enough fer me!" Then he give a pertic'ler hard jump and got one foot in the breeches and fell kerbip, a-sprawlin'. "Most made hit that time," he said. But ol' John Spencer never heard him for he was half way back to Tildy's house by that time, 'cause he had sure enough found him three bigger fools than Tildy and her maw and paw.

Uncle Monday

· *From Zora Neale Hurston,* Go Gator and Muddy the Water ·

Uncle Monday was the name he told the people, so that is all anybody knew to call him. The talk about him is mixed up with both Eatonville and Maitland. Eatonville for a number of reasons, and Maitland because that is where the lake is.

They say that when Uncle Monday is not a man, he is the big alligator that lives in Lake Belle. That when he goes back to join the waters there is bellowing and turmoil among the gators all night long in the lake. The brutes are acknowledging his mastery and paying homage. He has ruled and been king since the days of the haughty Osceola. Uncle Monday was a great African medicine man that got captured and sold into slavery but soon made his escape from a rice plantation in Georgia or South Carolina and made his way down into the Indian country which is now Florida. He made medicine among them with the escaped slaves and fought as fiercely as the best against the white man's arms. But by reason of one disaster or another, the Indian-Negro forces were pushed south and south and south. The war party with which Uncle Monday was fighting made its last stand around Fort Maitland. For the dark-skins that day there was nothing but dying and fleeing. But not for Uncle Monday. He assembled all that was left of the forces on the shore of Lake Belle. They had been driven from the shore of Lake Maitland. What is now Lake Belle was deep in a forest. Uncle Monday announced to the remains of the army that in Africa he had belonged to the crocodile clan. He had been advised that all was lost, so far as their resistance to the white man's arms was concerned. He would go to join his brothers and wait. Someday he would come again and walk these shores in peace. So before them all he made a great ceremony, drummed and danced to the rhythm beat out by blacks, danced until his face grew longer and very terrible, till his arms and legs began to change, until his skin grew thicker and scaly and his voice came like thunder. And from the lake came alligator voices to answer his own. A thousand gators swept up to the banks of the lake and made a lane between the ranks and he glided majestically into the water between the rank and file of thundering gators and they disappeared after him. That was the way he left the land, and they tell many stories of how he came back.

Anyhow, when he lived in a tiny hovel on the shore of Blue Sink, Old Judy Bronson felt pangs of professional jealousy. She kept saying with more and more passion that the awe and worship showered on Uncle Monday was going to waste. She said that he was not even as good a hoodoo doctor as she was, and what was more, work that he might do, she could not only undo it, she could and would "throw it back on him." That statement insinuates a great deal of power indeed. Nobody ever heard Uncle Monday say one word about it one way or another, except to comment when he was told about it one night for the hundredth time, "The foolishness of tongues is higher than mountains." He made no move to "prove and fend" about Old Judy's slander at all.

But one late afternoon, Judy told her half-grown grandson to fix her a pole so that she could go fishing. This was startling to all of her family, for she had given up going fishing years ago and said repeatedly that she could not be bothered sitting on fishing ponds and having the red bugs and the mosquitoes eating her old carcass up. So they were surprised but not pleased when she ordered somebody to dig her some bait and rig up a pole for her to go fishing all by herself around sundown. Neither did they like the idea of her going to Blue Sink Lake, which is deep and bottomless only a few steps from shore almost everywhere around it. They tried to stop her, but she cut them off short with, "I just got to go, so hush up jawing and do like I told you." So the old woman went against herself down to Blue Sink to fish that sundown.

She said nothing but [baited] her hook and she soon wanted to go especially since before she could get her hook baited and get it into the water, it was nearly dark. She didn't like to walk through the brush anyway after it got too dark to see where she was going, but somehow she could not get the consent of her mind to get up and run like she wanted to. Look like she felt the dark slipping up on her and grabbing hold of her like a varmint.

When the dark was finally there for good, she got so scared that she lost use of herself about the legs. Then she heard a wind start up the hill a little way off and come rushing down upon her and the lake and in the twinkling of an eye she found herself falling into the lake. And she was so afraid! She had always been afraid of water and darkness even when they were separate things. And the two together were more terrible than she could find words to tell afterwards. And both of these elements held her in their claws. She was in the lake, terrible Blue Sink, and she could not get out. She was afraid to struggle for fear that she would slip off into the deeps. Or some foul varmint might be attracted to her struggles and get her. But she could not stay there either, so she began to try to get to her feet and found out that she had no power at all in her limbs. It was all that she could do to support herself on her hands to keep her head above water. Finally she found the power to scream for help. Maybe somebody in the far-off village might hear her cry. But the moment that the squall left her lips, something huge hovered over her and the water and told her, "Hush! Your tongue, your bragging, lying tongue, has brought you here and here you will stay until I decide for you to leave." Judy could make out nothing of form and outline in the darkness, but she swore that it was the voice of Uncle Monday. Then a brilliant beam of light fell clear across the lake like a flaming sword, and she saw Uncle Monday walking across the lake from the opposite side to where she was and in the luminosity on either side of the reddish ray, the light ray that pointed dead at her from the opposite side of the lake like a monster spear made out of light, swam a horde of alligators like an army behind their leader. Uncle Monday was dressed in strange clothes and he walked proudly like a king down that shimmering band of light to where she laid there in the edge of the lake and about to drown and die of terror. "When you quit putting your ignorance and your weakness against me, you can get out of the water. I put you here and here you will stay until you bow down and acknowledge." Old Judy say she fought against it in her mind because she hated the man or whatever he was for stealing away her living and her prestige in the community. But fear rode her down. "I am going, but I shall leave a messenger and a guard. When you bow down somebody will find you, but not until." Then the light on the lake began to fade until it was gone and the man and his swimming escort was gone. There was a slight disturbance in the water and a huge alligator glided up beside her and stationed himself motionless along beside her so close that she could not help touching him when she breathed. Then her will gave away, and she was willing to bow down and acknowledge that she was weak and nothing beside Uncle Monday. She could not have done even a hundredth part of what she had seen and felt tonight. So inside she began to beg for mercy. Then she said it out loud, and almost at once she saw a flambeau moving down the hill towards the water and she heard her grandson calling her and telling the rest that she just had to be around there some place because he knew she had come to this lake. So she made a sound and they found her.

Her folks kept telling Judy that she had had a stroke and fallen in the lake and imagined all the rest of it. But to the day of her death she maintained that it all really happened. So she never fooled with hoodoo work anymore, and she never made any more slighting remarks about Uncle Monday again. She gave up the doctor's medicine and sent for him to put her on her feet again, and she did walk around a little while before she died.

Sweet-the-Monkey

· *From Ann Banks*, First-Person America ·

Ralph Ellison collected this WPA narrative from Leo Gurley in New York
in 1939.

I hope to God to kill me if this ain't the truth. All you got to do is go down to Florence, South Carolina, and ask most anybody you meet and they'll tell you it's the truth.

Florence is one of those hard towns on colored folks. You have to stay out of the white folks' way. All but Sweet. That the fellow I'm fixing to tell you about. His name was Sweet-the-Monkey. I done forgot his real name, I cain't remember it. But that was what everybody called him. He wasn't no big guy. He was just bad. My mother and grandmother used to say he was wicked. He was bad alright. He was one sucker who didn't give a damn bout the crackers. Fact is, they got so they stayed out of *his* way. I cain't never remember hear tell of any them crackers bothering *that* guy. He used to give em trouble all over the place and all they could do about it was to give the rest of us hell.

It was this way: Sweet could make hisself invisible. You don't believe it? Well here's how he done it. Sweet-the-monkey cut open a black cat and took out its heart. Climbed up a tree backwards and cursed God. After that he could do anything. The white folks would wake up in the morning and find their stuff gone. He cleaned out the stores. He cleaned out the houses. Hell, he even cleaned out the damn bank! He was the boldest black sonofabitch ever been down that way. And couldn't nobody do nothing to him. Because they couldn't never see im when he done it. He didn't need the money. Fact is, most of the time he broke into places he wouldn't take nothing. Lotsa times he just did it to show em he could. Hell, he had everybody in that lil old town scaird as hell, black folks and white folks.

The white folks started trying to catch Sweet. Well, they didn't have no luck. They'd catch im standing in front of the eating joints and put the handcuffs on im and take im down to the jail. You know what that sucker would do? The police would come up and say, "Come on, Sweet," and he'd say, "You all want me?" and they'd put the handcuffs on im and start leading im away. He'd go with em a little piece. Sho, just like he was going. Then all of a sudden he would turn hisself invisible and disappear. The police wouldn't have nothing but the handcuffs. They couldn't do a thing with that Sweet-the-Monkey. Just before I come up this way they was all trying to trap im. They didn't have much luck. Once they found a place he'd looted with footprints leading away from it and they decided to try and trap im. This was bout sunup and they followed his footprints all that day. They followed them till sundown when he came partly visible. It was red and the sun was shining on the trees and they waited till they saw his shadow. That was the last of Sweet-the-Monkey. They never did find his body, and right after that I come up here. That was bout five years ago. My brother was down there last year and they said they think Sweet done come back. But they cain't be sho because he won't let hisself be seen.

The Coon in the Box

· *From Richard M. Dorson,* American Negro Folktales ·

Dorson collected this tale from John Blackamore.

Once upon a time there was a Boss had a servant on his farm, kind of a handyman. Every night this handyman, Jack, would go down to the Boss's house and listen while he ate supper, so he'd know what Boss was going to do the next day. One night when Old Boss was eating supper he told his wife he was going to plow the west forty acres the following day. After Jack heard that he goes home to bed; next morning he gets up earlier than usual, and gets the tractor out and hooks up the plow. When Old Boss came out Jack was all ready to go. So he said, "Well Jack, we're going to plow the west forty acres today." He said, "Yes, Boss, I know, I got the rig all set up." Well, Old Boss didn't think much about it. He gets on his horse and goes in there and shows Jack how he wants him to plow it up.

So the next night when Boss sits down to eat his supper Jack goes on down to his favorite spot where he could hear everything. He heard his Old Boss tell his wife that he was going to round up all the livestock for shipping. Next day Jack gets up early, and gets the Boss's horse ready that he always rides when he rounds up the livestock. When Boss comes out later, he starts to tell Jack what he's got on the program. Jack cuts him off and says, "Yes, Boss, I know, we're going to round up the livestock this morning. I got your horse all saddled and ready to go." So Boss says, "Jack, what puzzles me is, every morning when I get up you tell me what I'm going to do before I tell you." And he wants to know what's happening, how did Jack know what he's gonna do. Jack says, "Well I don't know, I just knows." So Boss says, "Well, something funny going on." Jack says "Maybe so, but I know."

So they goes on to round up the livestock, and at the end of the day Boss sits down at the supper table again. And Jack takes the same position at the window, so he can hear everything that's talked about. Boss tells his wife about he's going to clean out the stable the next day, to use the waste to fertilize the fields. So the next morning Jack was out in the stables cleaning 'em out, before Old Boss was up.

Boss eats breakfast and he goes on out to the barn, sees Jack busy working. So he asks Jack, "How did you know I wanted the stables cleaned out today?" Jack says, "That's all right, I knowed you wanted to get it cleaned out so I went and got it started so I could hurry up and get the job done." So Boss says, "Yes, that's right, but what puzzles me is how a nigger like you can figure out what I'm going to do every day before I tell you." He says, "Well that's all right Boss, I know everything." So Old Boss shook his head and walks on up. So that night he was still puzzled at suppertime. Jack was still at the window. He listened to what his Boss was talking about. Old Boss told his wife, "Well this handyman we got around here, he's the smartest one I ever seen. Every morning I go out to tell him what to do he's already done it or he's telling me what we are going to do. And I don't know what to do about it."

So he was going up to the council next night, where the landlords have their meeting every Wednesday night to discuss their crops and problems. When Old Boss comes out of the house to go to the meeting, Jack had his rig all ready. Old Boss says, "Well thank you, Jack." And Jack says, "I hope you have a good time at the meeting, Boss." So Old Boss went on down to the meeting and he was telling the other landlords about this smart nigger he had down at his place. All the other councilmens laughed at him. But it didn't tickle Old Boss. He says, "You guys think I'm joking, but that's the truth." So one smart aleck he jumped up and said, "There ain't no nigger that smart." Everybody laughs again. So Old Boss got peeved. He says, "Well, all you crackers think it's so damn funny; I'll bet money on my nigger, 'cause he knows everything." Everybody begins to get quiet then, except this smart aleck. He says, "Well Jim, since you think so much of your nigger, I got $100,000 to say that I can outsmart your nigger." Old Boss called the bet. He said, "Now any of you other crackers in here think that's so funny and want to bet, I'll cover you too." So everybody kicks in with $100,000 apiece. When the total was counted up the bet run over a million dollars. So this Carver — that was the smart aleck — he says, "Well, you can expect us down tomorrow about two o'clock, and we'll have something your nigger can't tell us about."

Old Boss went home. Old Jack was still up waiting, so he could find what's going to happen tomorrow. Old Boss went into his bedroom, and he sat down side of the bed and he commenced to telling his wife what he was doing. And he said he was going to give a big barbecue the next day, so he needed to have food and drinks ready for the crowd when they come on down. Then he went on to bed.

Next morning old Jack was still sleeping when Old Boss got up. He was making himself scarce. He knowed they had some kind of a trick for him; he didn't want Old Boss to think he was so smart any more. So Old Boss rapped on the door, said, "Jack, get up, it's day." He says, "Coming, Boss." Old Boss walks on off and went on back in the house. And Jack was so used to Old Boss getting up and he being ready for him ahead of time, he begins to prepare for the party, without the Boss even telling him. When Old Boss come out, he says, "That's right, Jack, that's right. We're going to have a big party this afternoon, and I got a lot of money bet on you." Jack wanted to know then what for he had his money bet. So Old Boss said, "Well you know—you're trying to kid me that you don't know."

When the crowd had all of them gathered around they called Jack. Jack came around slowly. Old Boss said, "Come on up, Jack, come on up, don't be bashful." So Mr. Carter, the smart aleck, he says, "Well darky, they tell me you're pretty smart around here." So Jack says, "Aw, I wouldn't say that." Old Boss says, "Oh he's just trying to be modest." Then Old Boss said to Jack, "Didn't you tell me the other day that you know everything?" So Jack stretches his head and says, "Yes, that's right," rather slowly, scared to call the Boss a liar. So Mr. Carter says, "All right, let's get down to business, we got a lot of money bet on this. And I want you to tell us what it is, 'cause if you don't, I'm going to have your head tomorrow." Then Carter he called Jim over to tell him what the surprise was, before Jack would tell them. Carter told Jim it was a box in a box in a box in that box, and in the small box was a coon. And why they had him in so many boxes was so that Jack couldn't hear the coon scratch.

And then Jack started scratching his head and trying to tell them what was in the box, although he didn't really know. So Carter asked him again, "Well Jack, what do you say is in the box?" Jack started repeating what Carter had said. He says, "In the box, in the box, in the box." And he decided that he didn't know in his mind what, so he just scratched his head and said, "You got the old coon at last." (He was using that as an expression.)

So Old Boss grabbed him and shook his hand and said "Thanks, Jack, thanks, that's just what it is, a coon in them boxes."

The Mojo

· *From Richard M. Dorson,* American Negro Folktales ·

Dorson collected this tale from Abraham Taylor.

There was always the time when the white man been ahead of the colored man. In slavery times John had done got to a place where the Marster whipped him all the time. Someone told him, "Get you a mojo, it'll get you out of that whipping, won't nobody whip you then."

John went down to the corner of the Boss-man's farm, where the mojo-man stayed, and asked him what he had. The mojo-man said, "I got a pretty good one and a very good one and a damn good one." The colored fellow asked him, "What can the pretty good one do?" "I'll tell you what it can do. It can turn you to a rabbit, and it can turn you to a quail, and after that it can turn you to a snake." So John said he'd take it.

Next morning John sleeps late. About nine o'clock the white man comes after him, calls him: "John, come on, get up there and go to work. Plow the taters and milk the cow and then you can go back home—it's Sunday morning." John says to him, "Get on out from my door, don't say nothing to me. Ain't gonna do nothing." Boss-man says, "Don't you know who this is? It's your Boss." "Yes, I know—I'm not working for you any more." "All right, John, just wait till I go home; I'm coming back and whip you."

White man went back and got his pistol, and told his wife, "John is sassy, he won't do nothing I tell him, I'm gonna whip him." He goes back to John, and calls, "John, get up there." John yells out, "Go on away from that door and quit worrying me. I told you once, I ain't going to work."

Well, then the white man he falls against the door and broke it open. And John said to his mojo, "Skip-skip-skip-skip." He turned to a rabbit, and run slap out the door by Old Marster. And he's a running son of a gun, that rabbit was. Boss-man says to his mojo, "I'll turn to a greyhound." You know that greyhound got running so fast his paws were just reaching the grass under the rabbit's feet.

Then John thinks, "I got to get away from here." He turns to a quail. And he begins sailing fast through the air—he really thought he was going. But the Boss-man says, "I will turn to a chicken hawk." That chicken hawk sails through the sky like a bullet, and catches right up to that quail.

Then John says, "Well, I'm going to turn to a snake." He hit the ground and begin to crawl; that old snake was natchally getting on his way. Boss-man says, "I'll turn to a stick and I'll beat your ass."

How?

· *From Daryl Cumber Dance,* Shuckin' and Jivin' ·

I collected this folktale in Charles City, Virginia.

It was said that this large plantation owner had many slaves, and for one reason or another the Devil appeared to him one day and said that he was going to take the man's slave whose name was John.

And the plantation owner said, "Why John?"

He said, "Well, it's just John's time."

He said, "Please don't take *John.*"

And the Devil said, "Well, what's so special about *John?*"

He said, "Well, John is my record keeper." Says, "I don't keep any records. I keep no books whatsoever. John has a memory that's *fantastic,* and he just doesn't forget *anything.* I can ask him about my crops and what I made last year, and all I have to do is tell him and I call him back and ask him what I made and how many bushels of corn and what have you, and John has the answer [snap of the finger] just like that."

So say the Devil said, "That's unbelievable. Are you sure about that?"

He said, "I'm positive."

So the Devil said, "Well, will you call John up here? I want to talk to John—I want to test him out now. If he doesn't prove you're right, I'm going to have to take John."

So the Master called John up, and he said, "Now, Mr. Devil, you can ask him anything you want."

So the Devil said to John, say, "*John, do you like eggs?*"

And John said, "Yes, sir," and immediately the Devil disappeared.

Well, it was two years to the [day] and John was in the corn field plowing the corn, laying beside the corn, and it was a hot day. John had stopped the mule and sat under a tree. He had his old straw hat just fanning himself, you know. The Devil pops out of the ground, and he says one word to John; he says, "*How?*"

John says, "Scrambled."

Uncle Jim Speaks His Mind

· *From J. Mason Brewer,* Worser Days and Better Times ·

A white preacher was preaching to a group of slaves one night, and he was talking about the gates of gold that the white folks would walk through, and the streets of silver and gold that they would walk on. He stopped and said, "Now you darkies need not worry, for God has some mighty good asphalt streets and some cement streets for you all to walk on." When he finished preaching about where the white folks would walk, he called on Uncle Jim, a very old slave, to lead the congregation in prayer. So Old Jim got down on his knees and said in a feeble voice, "Lord, I heared de preacher talking about where de white folks would walk, and us poor slaves would walk, but Lord, I done come up like de bulrushes wid my head bowed down, like de rushes covered wid de morning dew. Lawd, I knows dat I's your child and when I get to heaven I's gonna walk any damn where I please."

Pompey

· From Margaret Young Jackson, "An Investigation of Biographies and
Autobiographies of American Slaves Published between 1840 and 1860" ·

The following tale presented as a conversation between master and slave was
recorded from a slave, Peter Randolph.

Pompey, how do I look?

O, massa, mighty.

What do you mean "mighty," Pompey?

Why, massa, you look noble.

What do you mean by "noble"?

Why, sar, you just look like one *lion.*

Why, Pompey, where have you ever seen a lion?

I see one down in yonder field the other day, massa.

Pompey, you foolish fellow, that was a *jackass.*

Was it, massa? Well, you look just like him.

Thirteen Years

· *From E. C. L. Adams,* Tales of the Congaree ·

Tad: Is you hear 'bout dat nigger dey turn loose yesterday?

Voice: No, we ain' hear nothin' 'bout him. We hear dey turn a nigger
loose. How come dey turn him loose?

Tad: He were innocent.

Scip: Wuh dat got to do wid it?

Tad: De ooman wuh scuse him say dat.

Scip: How long he serve 'fore she say dat?

Tad: De judge guin him thirty years an' he ain' serve but thirteen on
'em.

Scip: He ain' serve but thirteen on 'em. I wonder how come dat.

Tad: De ooman say he ain' guilty.

Voice: Wuh is he been scuse on?

Tad: He been scuse er rape an' have two trial 'fore dey convict him,
but dey was in doubt, so de judge guin him de benefit er de doubt
an' guin him thirty years. Dey say dat kep' 'em from lynchin' him.

De real reason dey say was: dis nigger have land wuh he rent to dese white folks an' he want he land back for he ownt nuse, an' de white folks dey wants de land, so dey charge him wid rape, an' he loss he farm an' he spend thirteen long years in prison. Dey say he ain' have no friend an' he would write letter to de diff'ent governor an' plead wid 'em an' say:

"Please, Governor, help me. I am innocent."

An' de governor wouldn't pay no 'tention to him, an' he labor for thirteen long an' weary years—thirteen long years out er dis short time 'lowed a man in dis world.

Voice: Is he pray?

Tad: You know dat nigger pray, but good as prayer is, dere is times when it ain' no good—when you got to suffer for de sins er you' forefathers. Well, dat was dat nigger.

Reverend Hickman: You is wrong, brother. God is answer dat nigger' prayer. He jes leff him dere awhile to try he faith, an' 'sides dat, I reckon he done some wrong er some kind.

Voice: You ain' explain how dey 'cide dis nigger is innocent after he wear stripe an' chain for thirteen year.

Tad: Well, it were a white ooman wha' send him dere, an' she were mighty sick an' she knowed ef she ain' hurry up an' do sump'n, she were guh bu's' hell wide open. She know she done a innocent man wrong an' she time was comin'. She know when God Almighty hand you over to de devil, it ain' make no diff'ence wuh you' color—black or white or yallow, high or low—dat ole man don't fool wid you, dat one thing he don't do. You kin lay anything to de devil but dat—he don't never neglect he duty. When God hand a sinner over to de devil, He done satisfy in He mind dey ain' no 'count—dey ain' worth savin'—an' de devil don't waste no time puttin' de fire to 'em.

Well, dat ole ooman find out she guh leff dis world, an' she guine wey dey will burn a cracker wuss dan a cracker would burn a nigger in dis world. An' she say as she feel dat death is approachin', she would like to tell de trute for one time in she life, an' she own up dat dis nigger ain' never done nothin' to her an' she wants to acknowledge her wrong an' be saved.

Scip: De way I see it, she tryin' to save she self. She ain' care nothin' 'bout de nigger.

Voice: It looks dat er way.

Reverend Hickman: My brother, you mustn't have evil thought. Maybe she is repent in de name er de Lord an' is been thinkin' 'bout de nigger.

Scip: She must er been thinkin' 'bout de nigger.

Tad: Yes, she sho' was thinkin' 'bout de nigger.

Scip: I reckon she jes natu'ally couldn't been thinkin' 'bout bein' saved ef she had er leff dat nigger out her thought.

Voice: Le's we pray for she.

Reverend Hickman: It ain' guh do no harm.

Scip: Is you reckon it will do good?

Reverend Hickman: Prayer never is hurt nobody.

Scip: I reckon de Lord will see it all an' use He judgment.

Reverend Hickman: He ain' guh hold it 'gainst we.

Voice: I reckon it best we pray. It might help we sometime.

Reverend Hickman: Have faith.

Scip: Dat's 'bout all we got.

Reverend Hickman: Dat nigger had faith an' is free.

Scip: Him an' faith had a hard time for thirteen years.

Reverend Hickman: Well, de judge guin him thirty, an' faith tooken dat down.

Scip: It look to me like faith on de part er dat nigger ain' had nothin' to do wid it.

Tad: He are free. Dey all on 'em kin say dat.

Scip: He free. How 'bout de ooman?

Reverend Hickman: I stick to wuh I say in de first place: have faith. De ooman have faith an' she still is free.

Tad: You reckon faith kep' her free?

Reverend Hickman: Faith—I always preaches faith.

Scip: Faith in what? Thirteen years er faith. Faith in law; faith in God; faith in de everlastin' punishment dat would come to dis ooman, ef dis man had er served he full time. Faith in de court; faith in de liar dat testify; faith in dis sneakin' hag dat is tryin' to escape hell fire. Don't tell me 'bout no faith.

Reverend Hickman: Repent an' you will be saved.

Voice: Amen!

Tad: I b'lieve in repentance.

Reverend Hickman: My brother.

Scip: Repent.

Reverend Hickman: Repentance is de easiest way.

Tad: Dat's wha' I say.

Voice: Wuh is you all say?

Scip: All you all niggers has too much to say.

Reverend Hickman: Luh 'em say wuh dey has a mind to say.

Scip: I ain' kin stop 'em.

Tad: We talkin' to we.

Scip: Is you all forgit how to laugh? Laugh an' I jine you.

Why the Guardian Angel Let the Brazos Bottom Negroes Sleep

· *From J. Mason Brewer,* The Word on the Brazos ·

When a Brazos Bottom Nigguh git mad he mad sho' 'nuff. He don' know much else, but he know how to fight, an' he know who to fight too—he fight his own color. Anytime a Texas Nigguh git bad de peoples say, "Dat Nigguh mus' be from de Brazos Bottoms," 'caze dey hab de record for bein' de baddes' Nigguhs in de whole state.

Jes' de same, mos' all of 'em goes to heabun when dey dies. Dey done heerd Gawd's voice lack de prophet 'Lijuh an' paid heed on to hit. When Guv'nuh E. J. Davis (what dey call de Nigguh Guv'nuh 'caze he de fuss guv'nuh attuh dey 'clare de Nineteenth of June), die an' go to heabun, de Guardian Angel tuck 'im 'roun' an' showed 'im de peoples he used to rule ovuh when he was de Nineteenth of June Guv'nuh of Texas. Evuhwhar he'd go, he'd see a putty bright spot along de heabunly lane, an' de Guardian Angel'd say: "Dem's yo' white folks; dese heah's yo' Meskins; dere's yo' Germans." Dey was all wide awake an' quiet lack, wasn't keepin' no noise, jes' settin' 'roun' in de sunshine lookin' at de putty flowers an' a smilin' at one anothuh. De Guv'nuh powful happy to see his ole frien's 'joyin' dey-se'f an' he ain't payin' much heed to whar he's haidin'; so he almos' stumble ovuh a dark spot in de lane 'fo' he seed hit.

"What's dis?" he say to de Guardian Angel.

"Shh! be quiet!" say de Angel. "We gonna haf to tiptoe by heah; dem's dem Brazos Bottom Nigguhs of your'n. Don' wake dem up, 'caze dey raises hell evuhwhar dey goes!"

You May Fall In Yourself

· *From Daryl Cumber Dance,* Shuckin' and Jivin' ·

I collected this tale in Richmond, Virginia.

It's sad but this is a slavery-time story, too. Seems like after the slave was abolished, his ex-master left 'im a lil' piece o' ground where his lil' cabin used to stay on. Nobody paid it any mind, but it so happened that a railroad company wanted to run a track through there and the land got valuable. And those poor people—they wanted it, wanted to get 'im out of it. They couldn't *take* it away from 'im 'cause it was given to 'im by this owner where died. So they did everything they could to aggravate 'im and worry 'im to make 'im—just make 'im jump up and leave 'cause they wanted the property. So this man— this white fellow—had a son. They both of the same type.

And that day the old man [ex-slave] had just cooked 'im a 'possum, had it in the stove baking while he was sleep. And this poor white fellow came in and looked around to see what he could steal there, to agitate, and he saw the old man sleep. He smelled the 'possum, and he opened the oven door, looked in at it, all browned up. His first idea was to grab it and carry it off and eat it. And he happened to look up on the shelf and saw this rat poisoning. He say, "Oh, I know what I'll do. I'll git him—I'll git his land." So he took that rat poisoning and put it *all* over that 'possum, and left it back in the stove. He say, "Now, if he eat that, I'll get the land."

Well, now he had a son who was just on his type. The son didn't know the daddy had been in there. So, he come around, snooping around to see what he could do to this old fellow. And he smelled this 'possum, looked in the stove, there it was. So he carried it off and ate it . . .

And the next day the daddy had a funeral for his only son. And he put the poison down for the ole slave fellow and his son ate it and killed him.

You dig a ditch for your fellow man, you may fall in yourself.

I'll Go as Far as Memphis

This is one of my mother's favorite tales. A version appears in *Shuckin' and Jivin'*.

This Black man had lived in Mississippi all his life, but times had gotten so bad there with Jim Crow and lynching and all that he decided that he would go North like a lot of his people. So he went North and he was doing *fine*. I mean he had gotten to the top. Then one of his friends called him and begged him to come back to Mississippi and help his folks because times were so hard. So he thought and thought. Finally he said, "I'm going to have to talk to the Lord about it."

So his friend called him again, and said, "Well, what did the Lord say?"

He said, "I told the Lord that my friends in Mississippi needed my help and I asked Him if He would please go back South with me."

"So what did God say?" his friend inquired.

He said, "The Lord told me, 'I'll go as far as Memphis.' "

Shall We Gather at the River

Reproduced from memory. I have collected several versions of this tale.

This preacher was preaching one Sunday about the need for abstinence. He say, "For my part, you can take all the whiskey in the world and throw it in the river."

The old Deacon, sittin' in the front pew, say, "A-A-A-men!"

The minister say, "For my part, you can take all the wine in the world and throw it in the river!"

The old Deacon clapped his hand, say, "A-A-A-men, preach it, Pastor, A-A-A-men!"

Ole minister was getting carried away. He say, "I say, ha, I say, HA-A-A, you can take all the alcohol in the world, HA-A-A, and *throw* it in the river!"

The Deacon jump up, say, "A-A-A-men, preach it, Pastor, A-A-A-men!"

When the minister ended his sermon and sat down, the ole deacon jumped up, say, "Let us sing page 314, 'Shall We Gather at the River.' "

Gone to Meddlin'

This tale is reproduced from memory. I have collected many versions.

This minister was in the pulpit preaching, preach-ing-g-g! He say, "We must quit this running around and follow the teachings of God."

Old Sister say, "A-men, preach it, Pastor!"

The minister say, "We must quit this backbiting and love each other."

Another Old Sister say, "Tell the truth, Pastor! A-men!"

The minister say, "We have to stop all this drinking alcohol and live sober lives."

Both sisters say, "A-men, you preaching the word today, Pastor! A-a-a-men!"

The minister say, "And another thing, we must quit all this snuff dipping—"

The Old Sister cut 'im off, say, "Now you done quit preachin' and gone to meddlin'."

Can't Get In

This tale is reproduced from memory. I have collected many versions through the years.

This Negro went to a White church one Sunday. The minister's text was "Come all ye that labor and are heavy laden." The minister cried out, "Come! Come all! The Gospel is free to all alike. God calls everybody to his kingdom. In God's house everyone is welcome!"

The Negro was so surprised at this warm welcome that he jumped up and went up front to join. The preacher say real quiet to 'im, "Go in my study and I'll talk with you after the service." So the ushers showed the Negro to the study.

After church services, the minister came in the study and say, "Now look, we don't want to rush this matter. I think you better take a week and reflect on this. Seek the Lord's guidance. See if he directs you to join *this* church."

The next week the Negro came back and met with the minister

and said that yes, he was certain. God had led him to join this church. But the White minister was adamant. He said, "I don't believe you have really consulted God. Take another week and be sure God has spoken to you."

The minister was surprised, but relieved, that the Negro didn't come back. One day several weeks later he met him on the street and he said, "I guess God told you that ours was not the church for you."

"As a matter of fact," the Negro said, "when I talked to God about joining your church, God told me, 'It might take you a long time. *I* been trying for twenty-five years to get into that church, and I haven't made it yet.'"

The One-Legged Grave Robber

· *From Richard M. Dorson,* American Negro Folktales ·

Dorson collected this tale from Mary Richardson.

Old Mistress died, and when they carried her to the cemetery they put a watch on her, and a gold ring on her finger. And too they put some money in there to pay her fare across Jerdan's River. Well, there was a one-legg'd man lived with the white people and worked in the yard, he wanted the jewelry, but he couldn't get down there on his one leg. And there was a two-legg'd man stayed on the place who wanted it too, but he was afraid to go alone to the cemetery. So he said to the one-legg'd man: "Come on go with me. I'll wheelbarrow you down there tonight, and we'll dig her up and get that jewelry offa her. You don't have to do nothing but just sit in the wheelbarrow; I'll do the digging." So the other says, "All right."

Come night, the two-legg'd man wheelbarrowed him down back of the field, where his old mistress was buried. So he said, "You just sit there; I'll dig the dirt offa her, get down to the coffin, and I'll open it." He taken the dirt off the top of the coffin, and got down to where the box was nailed on top. So he said: "Phew, I'm about here, about got to her. I just believe I'll rest some now, and then we'll lift her out again, and set her up, and take the jewelry off her." So he sits down on the coffin. But they hadn't driv all the nails down right good, and when he aimed to get up, his pants caught a nail. The one-legg'd man standing up on the top said. "What's the matter, John, is she got you?" John didn't say nothing. He tried to get up again, and the nail caught again and pulled tight. So the one-legg'd man repeats, "Is she got you?" John said, "I don't know whether she got me or no, but when I get loose I ain't got time to fool with that wheelbarrow."

So the one-legg'd man says, "Well, I'll go on." And he gets outa the wheelbarrow and starts to the house on his hands and one foot, and he beat the two-legg'd man to the house.

They ran off so fast, they left the cemetery open, and left the wheelbarrow down at Old Miss's grave. So the two-legg'd man crept down there next morning to get it—the wheelbarrow would have betrayed them. And they never got the gold or jewelry off her. But the one-legg'd man beat the two-legg'd man to the house.

Big Fraid and Lil' Fraid

This tale is reproduced from memory.

This lil' boy was always goin' out by hisself at night. Walking all through the woods. Anywhere he wanted to go. All by hisself. So this man said to him one night, "Boy, ain't you afraid to be walking all out here in the woods at night by yourself?"

"A Fraid?" he say. "What's a Fraid? I ain't never seen a Fraid."

The man say, "You keep hanging out in dese woods by yourself at night, you gon' see a Fraid, and he gon scare you too."

So this man decided he was gon' teach this lil boy a lesson—give him a good scare the next night he catch him out in the woods by hisself.

So he looked out his window one night and saw the boy wandering on out in the woods again. He say, "I'm gon' teach him a lesson tonight."

So the man grabbed a sheet and threw it over his head and started on through the woods to cut the lil' boy off. The man didn't notice that his pet monkey, as always, was imitating what he saw his master do. Soon as the man ran out the door, the monkey grabbed a pillowcase, threw it over his head and started on out to the woods behind the man.

The lil' boy was strolling along, singing and skipping, and the man jumped out at him, yelling "Boo! Boo!" thinking he was gon' scare the boy. But just at that time, the monkey jumped on the man and near bout scared him to death. The man *lit* out, screaming and yelling, monkey right behind him covered with that pillowcase.

The lil' boy yelled, "Run, run, Big Fraid, or Lil' Fraid'll catch ya!"

"Run, run, Big Fraid or Lil' Fraid'll catch ya!"

The Irishman and the Moon

· *From Donald J. Waters*, Strange Ways and Sweet Dreams ·

Once upon a time there were ten Irishmen who were always on the lookout for something to eat. One bright moonlight night they took a walk by the side of a river, and the greediest one of all espied the reflection of the moon in the water and he thought it was cheese. So he said to his companions, "Faith, boys, there's green cheese! Let's get it." The others answered, "Sure an' we will, if you kin find some way for us to reach it." No sooner said than done. He made a leap into the air and caught hold of the bough of a tree which stood near by, and bade the rest of them make a long line by swinging one on to the other's feet until the man at the end could reach what they thought was cheese. The weight was more than the first man could stand, so he thought he would lighten up by letting go his hold long enough to rest his hands, being perfectly ignorant of what would happen if he did so. Of course they all fell pell-mell into the river and stirred up the water so much that when they did manage to crawl out they could not see the reflection of the moon. Then they all declared that the last fellow had stolen the cheese and gone. To see whether they were all there, after everyone denied taking the cheese, they thought that they should be counted, so the very cleverest one of all stood the rest in a row and began to count. Instead of counting from one to ten and including himself either as first or last, he only said, "Me myself, one, two, three, etc.," and the consequence was that he only counted nine. He repeated this for sometime, and getting tired of it and calling it a slow way to find out the thief, they all got little twigs, and forming themselves in a row, each one stuck a hole in the ground with his twig. After this was done, they took turns to count the holes and at last really saw that all ten were still there. As to where the cheese went they never could tell, and they lamented for weeks afterward over the lost piece of green cheese.

The Irishman and the Watermelon

· *From Donald J. Waters,* Strange Ways and Sweet Dreams ·

Two Irishmen were walking along one day and they came across a wagonload of watermelons. Neither one had ever seen a watermelon before, and they inquired of some Negroes who were working nearby, what they were and what they were good for. The Negroes answered their questions very politely, and then as it was their dinner hour, sat down in the shade to eat. The Irishmen concluded to buy a melon and see how they liked it. They went a little distance and cut the melon, but taking pity on the poor Negroes, decided to share it with them. "Faith!" they said, "Guts is good enough for Naygurs." So they cut the heart out of the melon and gave it away, and ate the rind themselves.

John and the Twelve Jews

· *From Richard M. Dorson,* American Negro Folktales ·

Dorson collected this tale from John Courtney.

Once upon a time there was twelve Jews and they had a porter boy. His name was John. John had been traveling all over the United States with those Jews, and everywhere they go you know, where they get off y'know, they tip John you know. And John would have something to help support hisself in the place y'know while he was there. So they went to Chicago y'know. They came from New York to Chicago. They give John, oh, a big pocket of money. John had a big time y'know. And they all got ready to go y'know, he'd go get all of 'em their grips y'know, and he'd put 'em, load 'em all on the train y'know. And then John he'd be standing there when they'd get on y'know. And when the last one get on, why John he get right on up behind the boss, y'know. And he say, "Okay John, you all loaded and ready to go?"

So John traveled with them y'know for quite a bit of time, like he'd been with 'em for years. So they left Chicago for Los Angeles, California. And so John loaded their things. So when they got to Los Angeles, the train pulled up, the porter put the box down. John got off y'know, and John took all their grips off y'know and set 'em down, taken 'em off. John got all their grips sorted out y'know before they came out. Okay. The first big boss came out y'know, he came right down y'know, his coat fastened, picks his two grips y'know, and never looked back. John looked at him y'know. Okay. Here comes the other, the second one. He come down, he picks up his two grips y'know, never looked back, steps right on.

John said, "Well, maybe the other one's got the money." So here come the third one down. He picks up his grips, step down, and never looked back. So John still thought about it y'know, getting worried about the money. And so here come the fourth one. The fourth one picked up his grips, and he never looked back. Fifth one came down and picked up his grips: he never looked back. John ain't got nothing. So here come the sixth man. The sixth man come down, he picks up his grips, never looked back. So John begin to frown, "That's half of 'em y'know." So John looked all around y'know at the porter and the porter looked at him y'know. And so John looked, "Here come the seventh one down." And he done the same thing, the seventh. He picked up his grips. The eighth one, he picked up his, and he ain't looked back. John just kept frowning. So the ninth one he picked up his ones. He never looked back. The tenth one did the same. The eleventh man he was a big, heavy-sot, great big feller. He wagged down, he got his grips y'know, and he looked back at John. John he never said a word. John all frowned up. "That's the eleventh man y'know." John said, "Well maybe Old Boss is got the last one." Old Boss is long, tall. He come down y'know, he's *tall*. He picks up his grips. John looks at him. So he picks up his grips and set 'em over there on the side, y'know, and he turned around to John. Run his hand in his pocket, got his billfold out y'know.

John says, "Cap'n," says, "let me tell you something." Says, "Y'know they just telling a damn lie on you-all." Say, "I . . . I . . . I thought that like hell y'know, for a long time. I'se been thinking it like hell." Said, "But I'm going to tell you," said, "they sure told a damn lie. They say you-all killed Christ. But you didn't kill him."

He said, "What's the matter, John?"

He said, "You-all just worried hell out of him."

The Irishman at the Dance

· *From Richard M. Dorson,* American Negro Folktales ·

Dorson collected this tale from Silas Altheimer.

A slave from the Old States (Carolina and Virginia) told me this when I was a child, when the railroads first began to build, sixty years ago.

There were building a road through Virginia and the Carolinas, and the contractor had many slaves and some white men, Irishmen. And there was one Irishman, Pat, had recently come from Ireland, and never seen a colored man. A dance was given in the area, and the white men were invited to the dance. They had to go through a bottom and across a creek to reach the seat of the dance. And of course when they arrived Pat went in and took his seat, and stood very still in one place, and the other boys began to talk to the many beautiful girls at the dance, and choosing their partners.

There was a big black man sitting in the corner, with red eyes, and he was tuning his fiddle. And after a while when the dancers were ready, they were all assembled on the floor. The fiddler began to play and the dancers began to move around the room, promenading we'd call it. Pat sat there and all at once he jumped up, he couldn't stand it any longer, and so he ran out. He got lost, and he tramped around the whole night in the mud, and fell in the lagoon. So he pulled himself out, and next morning, just before day, when the train was heating up to go out, Pat coursed in, all muddy and wet, about seven o'clock. So the boys began to laugh and tease him about leaving the dance. "Well Pat, how did you enjoy the dance?" They didn't know what had become of him.

When they asked him, Pat gave his conception of the dance. He said, "When I got there, there were many beautiful girls there. And the boys began to enjoy theirselves, chatting with the young ladies. But the Devil was sitting in one corner, and he had a little red babe in his arms. And he pulled its ears, and it was all I could do to sit there. And finally he picked up a stick and whaled the baby across the back, and of all the racket I ever heard, there it was. And the people were flying around, hunting the door. And no one could find it but me."

How Hoodoo Lost His Hand

· *From Richard M. Dorson,* American Negro Folktales ·

As folklorist Sw. Anand Prahlad has observed, this is one of the few tales collected that substantiates Zora Neale Hurston's contention that African Americans regarded Moses as a conjurer.

The Israelites was captured and carried down in bondage under Egypt. And Moses was born there. And they was killing all males, to keep the Hebrew children from multiplying so fast. And when Moses was born his mother kept him hid three months. Then when she could keep him hid no longer, she made a basket of bulrushes and slime. And so she carried him down and put him in the river, where Pharaoh's daughters went down to bathe. When they seen him he was a fine Egyptian boy. Then the daughter carried him to the King, Pharaoh, and begged her daddy to let her keep him and 'dopt him. So he agreed. "Go out and find you a nurse, an Israelite woman, for they'd know how to take care of this baby." So she goes out and hires an Israelite woman, who was his mother.

So he waxed and grewed fast, and learned all the Egyptian words and languages. So Pharaoh made him a ruler then, when he seed how smart he was. So one day he walks out and he sees a Hebrew and a Egyptian fighting. So he killed this Egyptian, looked all around and seed nobody, and buried him in the sand. A couple of days after he went out and he seed two Hebrews fighting. He said, "Why do you all strive against one another, and you'se brothers?" One said, "You want to kill one of us like you did that Egyptian the other day?"

So Moses got scared and run away into Middin. He stayed there forty years and married this Ethiopian woman (which is a colored woman). One day he was out minding his father-in-law's sheep, and the Lord spoke unto Moses and said, "Pull off your shoes, for you is on holy ground. I want you to go back and deliver my children from Egypt." He said, "Moses, what is that you got in your hand?" Moses said, "It's a staff." He said, "Cast it on the ground." And it turned to a snake. And Moses fleed from it. The Lord said, "Go back and pick it up." So Moses picked it up, and it turned back to a staff. The Lord said, "Go back and wrought all these miracles in Egypt and deliver my children from bondage."

So Moses goes on back. He goes in to Pharaoh and told him what the Lord had told him to do. Pharaoh said, "Who is he?" "I can show you what He got power to do." And he cast his rod on the floor, and it turned into a serpent. Pharaoh said, "That ain't nothing. I got a magikin can do that." So he brought his magikins and soothsayers in, and they cast their rods on the floor. So theirs turned to snakes. And they crawled up to Moses' snake, and Moses' snake swallowed up their snake. And that's where hoodoo lost his hand, because theirs was the evil power and his was the good. They lost their rods, and he had his and theirs too.

Mary Bell

· *From Elsie Clews Parsons,* Folk-Lore of the Sea Islands,
South Carolina ·

Once upon a time there was a man had one daughter. Every man come to marry her, she said, "No." So a man came, all over was gold. And she married him. He had a horse name Sixty-Miles, for every time he jump it was sixty miles. So they went. The more he goes, his gold was dropping. Mary Bell wanted to know why his gold was dropping. He said, "That is all right." They reached home soon. He gave her a big bunch of key and take her around to all the room in the house. "You can open all the room except one room; for if you open it, I will kill you." She start to wonder why her husband didn't want her to open it. So one day she open it. It was great surprise. She saw heads of woman hanging up. She also saw a cast of blood. Her key dropped in the blood, and she couldn't get it off. So she began to mourn. The Devil daughter told her not to cry. She took three needles and gave it to her. "He is coming; but when you first drop one, there will be a large forest, and so on." She went and get Sixty-Miles, and she went. Now the Devil came from the wood. He had a rooster. He told his master, "Massa, massa, your pretty girl gone home this morning 'fore day. Massa, massa, your pretty girl gone home this morning 'fore day." The Devil look about the house for his wife, he didn't see her. So he went to get Sixty-Miles, and he couldn't find it. So he get Fifty-Miles. Start after her. He spy her far down the road. He said, "Mary Bell, O Mary Bell! what harm I done you?"

> *"You done me no harm, but you done me good. Bang-a-lang!*
> *Hero, don't let your foot touch, bang-a-lang!*
> *Hero, don't let your foot touch!"*

The Devil catch at her. She drop a needle, and it became a large forest. He said, "Mary Bell, O Mary Bell! how shall I get through?"—"Well," said she, "go back home, get your axe, and cut it out." And he did. He saw her again, and catch at her. She drop another needle, and a large brick wall stood in the way. He said, "Mary Bell, how shall I get through?"—"Go get your shovel and axe, and dig and pick your way." He done just the same way. And he get through all right. He spy her again. He said, "Mary Bell, what harm I done you?"

> *"You done me no harm, but you done me good. Bang-a-lang!*
> *Hero, don't let your foot touch."*

He catch at her. She step into her father's house. The Devil get so mad, he carry half of the man's house.

> *I step on a t'in', the t'in' bend.*
> *My story is end.*

The Clever Companions

· *From Elsie Clews Parsons,* Folk-Lore of the Sea Islands,
South Carolina ·

Sev'al mans have gone to see de king daughter. An' de meracle the king put befo' dem no one could do it. So Jack say he would go an' see if he could marry de king daughter. So de king tol' Jack dat he mus' go an' pitch his tent one hund'ed miles from him, an' come back nex' mornin'. An' he tell him what meracle he want him to do. So Jack goin'. He meet one man dat standin' up lookin'. An' Jack ax him what was his name. He say his name Seer-All. De nex' man he meet, he had a long ear. Jack ax him what was his name. He say his name is Hear-All. He ax him if he want a job. Tell him, "Yes." Tol' him, "Jump in!" De nex' man he seen, he seen a man brushin' de dus' off his feet. He ax him what was his name. He say his name was Run-Well. He ax him if he want a job. Tell him, "Yes." Tol' him, "Jump in!" De nex' man he meet, he met a man jumpin' up an' down. He say his name was Hard-Bottom. He ax him if he want a job. Tell him, "Yes." Tol' him, "Jump in!" So dey pitch deir tent one hun'ed miles from de king dat night. Nex' mornin' Jack went to de king. Say dat a flock of ducks are comin' over de house, an' one particular duck he mus' shoot. An' ven de flock of duck come over, Seer-All pick up de gun an' pint at de duck. An' the ol' lady come down, an' say, "Don't shoot! It's me." So de king tol' Jack he mus' go two hund'ed miles dat night an' pitch his tent, an' come to-morrow mornin', an' he will tell him what meracle he will want him to do. Nex' mornin' Jack gone to de king. De king had an orange-tree in de garden, an' he tol' Jack one particular orange he mus' shoot. An' Seer-All pick up the gun an' pint at the right orange. An' the ol' lady come down, an' say, "Don't shoot! It's me." So the king tol' Jack that he mus' go one t'ousan' miles an' pitch his tent, an' come to-morrow mornin', an' he will tell him what meracle he will want him to do. An' Jack went. An' nex' mornin' Jack come. So de king tol' Jack it was a bull in de pen, an' he mus' go an' tie dat bull. An' de bull were ravin'. Jack jumped up, an' come down between de bull-horns, an' began to tie him. An' de ol' lady come down, an' began to sing,

"Don't tie um, my son! it is me." So de king tol' Jack dat he mus' go two t'ousan' mile an' pitch his tent, an' come to-morrow mornin', an' he will tell him what meracle he will want him to do. Nex' mornin' Jack gone to de king. An' de king tol' Jack dat his wife was very sick, an' he mus' go an' get some healin'-water, an' he mus' go t'ree t'ousan' miles, an' he mus' make it back in five minutes. So Run-Well start off. An' de ol' lady tu'n a witch, an' stop Run-Well in de road, an' began to look his head until he didn' had but two minutes more. An' Seer-All look up, an' seen de ol' lady lookin' Run-Well head. An' Seer-All pick up de gun an' p'int at de ol' lady. An' Run-Well gone an' git de healin'-water, an' made it back in five minutes. Den Jack married de king daughter. An' Jack moder been put up on a steeple, an' had one grain of rice to eat, 'til Jack married de king daughter. An' she was so glad Jack married de king daughter, 'tel she fell down an' break her neck.

The Laziest Man

· *From Jack and Olivia Solomon,* Ghosts and Goosebumps ·

Nick Weldon was an awfully lazy man. He would not work at anything. All he did was eat and lie back with his feet cocked in the air, while he looked until he fell asleep. His parents fed him till he was a man grown but they finally worked themselves to death and left Nick to shinny for himself. The neighbors, as is the custom of good neighbors, brought over a lot of good things to eat after his mother died and he ate them all. After that he was hungry.

Everybody in the community knew he was too lazy to live but they were sorry for him and finally got into the habit of sending a child around once in a while with a plate of victuals for him to eat. Several families kept this up for a month or two and in this way Nick kept alive. But he was getting lanky on the uncertain food, and still he made no effort to do a thing for himself. Finally, the good neighbors got tired of being put upon in such a manner and got together to talk the matter over.

It was a hopeless case, they decided, and Nick must be disposed of once and for all. They could not continue to waste the time and supplies to care for him, and so he must die. Of course they could just refuse to send him any more food and he would soon die of starvation. But that, they felt sure, was too cruel a death for even Nick. So they decided to haul him out to the boneyard and knock him in the head.

Early the next morning two of them took a cart and drove over to get Nick. When they told him why they were there he offered no protest so they lifted him into the cart and started down the road.

It was a long drive to the boneyard and after they had gone a long way they were stopped by a man who wanted to know where they were going. He had not heard of Nick, so they told him the whole story.

"Why," he offered generously when he had heard the tale, "I can spare a bushel of corn. I'll give him that and he can live a while longer. It is a bad thing to kill a man and I don't want to see it done."

At that Nick slowly turned his head in the cart so he could see the man. "Is it shelled?" he asked in a whiny drawl.

The charitable man answered, "Why, no, but the four of us can shell it in just a little while."

"Ne'mind," whined Nick, "jes' drive on to the boneyard, boys!"

The Lazy Man

· *From Elsie Clews Parsons,* Folk-Lore of the Sea Islands,
South Carolina ·

'Bout a man who was goin' to be married. He was so po', he had to go 'roun' to de citizen an' ask help. Dey all assis' him in clothin' an' in weddin'. Done all dey could for him. Promise den if he live, he ketch up again an' he give all return. Dey give him enough so he could live a while widout goin' to work. Dey get so hard on him, dey 'peal back to his wife. Said, "Oh, I remember my promise!" She ask him, "What was your promise?" Said, "I promise all of my people that help me when I was goin' to get married, I live quite a while on dat. Times gettin' hard for me. I got to go to work. I believe dat is my trouble."—"I believe it is," she says. "Now, dis is de en' of de week. I have to go to work Monday. Wake me up on Monday mornin'." She did. When she call upon him, said, "I kyan' work Monday, Monday is Sunday broder. Wake me Tuesday mornin'." Tuesday mornin', when she call upon him, he said, "Kyan't work Tuesday, Tuesday is Monday broder. Wake me Wednesday mornin'." She call upon him Wednesday mornin'. "Kyan't work Wednesday, Wednesday is de middle of de week," he says. Says, "Well, de week goin' fast. De rations goin' fas'. Wake me Thursday mornin'." She call upon him. "Kyan't work Thursday, Thursday is day o' fas'."—"Two more days. Got to work, cause de neighbors is tired of us. Have somet'in' to eat Sunday." Said, "Kyan't work Friday, Friday is hangman day. Everybody go see a man hang. Call me Saturday mornin'." She call upon him Saturday mornin'. "Kyan't work Saturday, Saturday is jus' de same as Sunday. Wake me up Monday. Have somet'in' to eat nex' week." Kep' on wid dat. Nex' week met a man wid some money. While he roamin' out, get him to talk. He killed de man, took away his money. Nex' Friday he was hang. Everybody wen' to see *him* hang.

Chapter 2

Folk Music[1]

All music is folk music. I ain't never heard no horse sing.
—Louis Armstrong

N o aspect of American culture is more familiar and popular worldwide than African American folk music. From
the moment Europeans observed Blacks singing in Africa
and its diaspora, they responded with amazement and fascination, al-
beit often with disdain and contempt for aspects of these sounds that
they found unfamiliar and discordant. Soon after the end of the Civil
War, European heads of states as well as their subjects en masse enthusiastically embraced the Fisk Jubilee Singers and their spirituals.
In the twentieth century, blues and jazz found a home in Paris and
have continued to be popular all over the world. By the end of the
twentieth century, hip-hop culture and rap music were the rage in
Japan and numerous other Asian and European countries where
American rap stars are embraced and new rappers are spawned.

One of the earliest and most beautiful, poignant, and enduring
forms of African American folk music is the spiritual, what W. E. B.
Du Bois called the "Sorrow Songs": "They that walked in darkness
sang songs in the olden days—Sorrow Songs—for they were weary

[1]Certain forms of Black music that are sometimes recited or shouted, such as
work songs, street cries, ring shouts, and field shouts, are included in chapter 9.

at heart" (*Souls of Black Folk*). Though they are sad songs that express the difficult situation the slaves endured ("Nobody Knows de Trouble I See"); they are also optimistic, signifying the singer's confidence that he would win freedom ("Soon I Will Be Free"). The enslaved singers saw themselves as the chosen people ("We Are the People of God"), and they were assured that they would get to heaven ("I'm Bound for the Promised Land") and that certain other folks would not ("Everbody Talkin' 'bout Heaven Ain't Going There"). They delighted in a Jesus who is more an Old Testament warrior than a New Testament man of humility ("Ride on King Jesus"; "The Man I Serve Is a Man of War"). Their spirituals are aggressive songs of a people determined to be free ("Before I'd Be a Slave I'd Be Buried in My Grave"), and in which escape is a common theme. Of course, like so much of African American folklore, the essence of the spirituals is masked—in this case, in the cloak of religion. When they implored, "Go down, Moses, way down in Egypt land / Tell Ole Pharaoh to let my people go," and entreated, "Swing low, sweet chariot, comin' for to carry me home," they were singing more about freedom from slavery and escape to the North than of the Bible and heaven.[2]

Despite the fact that the spirituals were often denigrated by Whites and aspiring Blacks, they did not disappear with slavery. Their beautiful melodies remind us not only of the sufferings of enslaved African Americans, but they also continue to provide support and sustenance to Blacks and all oppressed people seeking freedom and equality. If any single buttress sustained Martin Luther King Jr. through his struggle for Civil Rights, it was the spiritual. In the King movement, as in slavery, the spiritual voiced the plight, communicated the message, comforted the sufferers, uplifted the marchers, and celebrated the victories. No wonder then that his most memorable speech, "I Have a Dream," culminates in the anticipation of "that day when all of God's children, Black men and White men, Jews and Gentiles, Protestants and Catholics, will be able to join hands and sing in the words of the old Negro spiritual, 'Free at last! Free at last! Thank God Almighty, we are free at last.' "

Rivaling the spiritual in international acclaim is certainly the blues,

---

[2]This is not to argue that there were not some truly religious elements in the spiritual or that they served merely and exclusively as masks.

which Langston Hughes called those "sad funny songs—too sad to be funny and too funny to be sad." In *Shadow and Act* Ralph Ellison offers one of the most succinct definitions of the blues: "The blues is an impulse to keep the painful details and episodes of a brutal experience alive in one's aching consciousness, to finger its jagged grain, and to transcend it, not by the consolation of philosophy but by squeezing from it a near-tragic, near-comic lyricism. As a form, the blues is an autobiographical chronicle of personal catastrophe expressed lyrically." Both definitions recognize that while the blues is about bad times, the blues is not merely a sad song. The blues is its own reward; it provides its own antidote; it offers its own relief; it is its own celebration that the blues singer can survive and give voice to his or her pain. The blues enables transcendence. One old bluesman is quoted as saying, "the blues regenerates a man" (Sterling A. Brown, "Been Acquainted with the Blues So Long"). And the old blues line declares:

> *Yes, I'm blue, but I won't be blue always,*
> *Because the sun is going to shine in my back door someday.*

Rap music, today's most widespread and popular form of folk music in the Black community and beyond, grew out of the Bronx as a part of the popular hip-hop culture[3] of the 1970s. No form is so new and at the same time so traditional. To listen to contemporary rap is to hear the braggadocio of the great African epic poem, *Sundiata;* the rhyming couplets and the sexually explicit, inflammatory, provocative, and misogynistic brags of the toast; the formulaic lines of earlier "rappers" of the likes of H. Rap Brown; the masked language of the slave trickster; the autobiographical narrative of the blues; the utilization of the human voice as an instrument of the scat singers; the commentary on social and political and economic problems of the day of the street-corner orators; the incorporation of music of the Black sermon; the projection of the image of the ba-a-d nigger in conflict with the police of "Stagolee"; the crude ver-

---

[3]Hip-hop culture is usually considered to include break dancing, graffiti, deejays, and rap music. Thus hip-hop embraces visual art, dancing, instrumental music, singing, rhyming, and "talking that talk" (as the deejay does).

bal attacks upon one's enemies of the dozens; the signifying of the Signifying Monkey;[4] and the rhythms and drum beats of—well, of all Black music. How applicable to contemporary rappers is the description of the Griot in the introduction to the *Sundiata:* "He . . . is a master of circumlocution, he speaks in archaic formulas, or else he turns facts into amusing legends for the public, which legends have, however, a secret sense which the vulgar little suspects." And how similar are both of these to the American deejay, the Jamaican toaster (a deejay reciting smart jingles), the Jamaican dub poet, the Trinidadian Calypsonian, the West Indian Rapso poet, and the Trinidadian Pan poet.[5] Indeed the only things new about contemporary rap are its use of modern technology for a new manipulation of sound and practices that require new terms to describe them, such as "scratching" and "sampling" and "dubbing"; and its performers' names. Note, however, that performers' choice of ba-a-d names like Public Enemy, Grandmaster Flash, Fresh Prince, NWA (Niggas with Attitudes), BWP (Bitches with Problems), LL Cool J, is traditional; consider The Great McDaddy, High John de Conqueror, Duke Ellington, Lady Day, Count Basie, Nat King Cole, Prince,[6] and the legendary Ba-a-d Niggers and Wild/Sassy Women. Even the rappers' contemporary attire—such constantly changing items as designer tennis shoes, leather jackets, gold chains, baggy pants, NASCAR fashions[7]—have a number of parallels in outré costuming

[4]Signifying, the subject of Henry Louis Gates Jr.'s *The Signifying Monkey,* is not simply defined. It usually includes loud-talking, berating, harassing, or putting down someone. The signifier is always a person of great eloquence and wit and he makes subtle use of irony and indirection so that his victim may not fully comprehend the attack being made upon him or her.

[5]For a brief introduction to the West Indian forms mentioned here, see Stewart Brown et al., *Voice Print.*

[6]It is also true that a certain amount of signifying was going on when Blacks chose names that are titles, since this assured that Whites who addressed them would unwittingly accord them the respect of a title, since they almost certainly were going to call them by their first name.

[7]Though rappers and their fans are not racing enthusiasts, NASCAR's colorful race-theme pants and logo-dotted jackets, hats, and T-shirts have become popular with them: "It's about style, they say—not sport" (CNN's Stacey Wilkins, "Nascar Drives Rapper Fashions," April 11, 2000).

worn by entertainers through the years (see chapter 3, "The Style of Soul").

A number of other twentieth-century musical forms, such as gospel, bebop, jazz, and zydeco,[8] have continued to enjoy great popularity in the United States and beyond. Though they, like the earlier forms that spawned them, had their genesis in the Black community, their creators were more likely to perform them in the recording studios and Northern nightclubs and urban churches than in the plantation cabins where slaves intoned the spirituals, or on the street corners and barbershops and Southern prisons where the Leadbellys sang traditional blues, or the honky-tonks where the Bessie Smiths and the Ma Raineys belted out their songs. Furthermore, contemporary forms are more quickly adopted by the White community. Indeed, American audiences today are very likely to be more familiar with White jazz performers than Black. Thus finding traditional versions of more recent music, even those that have origins in the Black folk community, is problematic.

Whatever the form, however, certain general characteristics can be noted about Black music. It almost always takes the form of call and response between a singer and an audience. Thus, recorded music will never take the place of the live performance where folks flock to hear their favorite blues singer, where singer and audience become one, where the singer sings her blues and the audience talks back to her—as described by Sterling Brown in his poem "Ma Rainey" in *Southern Road:*

> *When Ma Rainey*
> *Comes to town,*
> *Folks from anyplace*
> *Miles aroun',*
> *From Cape Girardeau,*
> *Poplar Bluff,*

[8]Zydeco, which dates to the first quarter of the twentieth century, is a variant of Cajun music, one inspired by blues, rhythm and blues, and the rhythms of Haitian migrant workers. Zydeco was made popular by Clifton Chenier, who was dubbed "The King of Zydeco." Lorenzo Thomas defines zydeco as "the dance music of African-American creoles in southwestern Louisiana" ("From Gumbo to Grammys").

Flocks in to hear
Ma do her stuff;
Comes flivverin' in,
Or ridin' mules,
Or packed in trains,
Picknickin' fools. . . .
That's what it's like
Fo' miles on down
To New Orleans delta
An' Mobile town,
When Ma hits
Anywheres aroun'.

. . . . . .

O Ma Rainey,
Sing yo' song;
Now you's back
Whah you belong.
Git way inside us,
Keep us strong. . . .
O Ma Rainey,
Li'l an' low;
Sing us 'bout de hard luck
Roun' our do'
Sing us 'bout de lonesome road
We mus' go. . . .
I talked to a fellow, an' the fellow say,
"She jes' catch hold of us, somekindaway.
She sang Backwater Blues one day . . .

. . . .

An' den de folks dey natchally bowed dey heads an' cried,
Bowed dey heavy heads, shet dey moufs up tight an' cried,
An Ma lef' de stage, an' followed some de folks outside.
Dere wasn't much more de fellow say:
She jes' gits hold of us dataway.

Black music is also improvisational. Whether in church, on a chain gang, or in a blues club, the leader (or someone else) can offer a word, a phrase, an idea, a retort, a sound, and it may be taken up to create a new verse in that song. Adding new verses to the same tune can sometimes go on indefinitely.

Traditionally songs in the Black community use the Black idiom—to varying degrees, of course. "Ain't" is generally preferred to "aren't"; word endings are frequently dropped; and words are run into each other—instead of "one of these days," the singer will almost invariably sing "onenadesedays" or use Brown's "somekind-away" for "some kind of way." *D*s frequently substitute for *t*s. Such uses of the Negro idiom are, of course, frowned upon by many African Americans, and my friends and I, like most American Blacks, often reminisce about teachers and choir directors who made us enunciate carefully, never dropping our *t*s and always sounding the endings of our words. But as soon as we finished singing "Lift-t ev-e-ry voice-e and sing-g-g till earth and hea-ven ring-g-g," we went around the corner intoning, "You ain't nothin' but a houn' dog . . ."

Black music does not rely merely on words. As Sterling Brown has noted, "Ma Rainey didn't have to sing a word, she would just moan and groan, and the audience would groan with her" *(SAGALA)*. The groan, the hum, the nonsense syllables, the yell, and the scatting are just as important as words in conveying a message and an emotion.

Nor does African American music rely merely on formal instruments. While talented musicians can make pianos moan, drums talk, and saxophones wail, they can also make music with spoons, pans, and a variety of improvised instruments. And then the body can always be called into play to provide a beat—foot stomping and tapping, hand clapping, body slapping, and varied uses of the mouth can suffice when there are no drums or pans or extraneous sources around.

Finally, in communal settings, there is an element of competition in music. Instrumentalists will vie with one another in offering improvisations on a theme; choir singers will compete in offering their versions of the same song; the instrumentalist will try to duplicate the sound of the human voice and the singer will respond by reproducing the sound of the instrument.

The following description (quoted in Eileen Southern, *The Music of Black Americans*) of a performance of patting juba[9] from around

---

[9]Patting juba refers to the slapping of the hands, legs, and body to produce a rhythm. It stems from an element of the slave dance referred to as juba.

1850 illustrates some of the continuing characteristics of this traditional music, whose form has changed so little that it might be mistaken for a contemporary rap performance:

> The young, brown-skinned woman stood in the middle of the group, patting out a beat on the ground with her feet, at the same time beating out a rhythm on her chest and legs with her hands. People crowded closer, caught by the quiet, distinct, funky sound. Suddenly she began to rhyme, fast and furiously. As people listened, swayed and swung to the beat, she shot poetic insults at friends nearby, to their chagrin and the crowd's delight. She rhymed about her experience, things that both she and her audience had seen and experienced. She kept that same funky rhythm as the dancing crowd went crazy with loud screams and shouts.

* S P I R I T U A L S   A N D   O T H E R   F R E E D O M   S O N G S *

Every Time I Feel the Spirit

· *Traditional* ·

Every time I feel the Spirit moving in my heart,
  I will pray.
Every time I feel the Spirit moving in my heart,
  I will pray.
Up on the mountain my Lord spoke,
Out of his mouth came fire and smoke.
Every time I feel the Spirit moving in my heart,
  I will pray.

Many Thousand Gone
· *Traditional* ·

No more auction block for me,
No more, no more.
No more auction block for me,
Many thousand gone.

2. No more peck o' corn for me
3. No more driver's lash for me
4. No more pint o' salt for me
5. No more hundred lash for me
6. No more mistress' call for me

I'm Gon' Live So God Can Use Me
· *Traditional* ·

I'm gon' live so God can use me,
Anywhere, Lord, anytime.
I'm gon' live so God can use me,
Anywhere, Lord, anytime.
2. I'm gon' work so God can use me
3. I'm gon' pray so God can use me
4. You ought to live so God can use you

Swing Low, Sweet Chariot
· *Traditional* ·

Swing low, sweet chariot
Comin' for to carry me home.
Swing low, sweet chariot,
Comin' for to carry me home.

I looked over Jordan, and what did I see?
Comin' for to carry me home.
A band of angels comin' after me,
Comin' for to carry me home.

Swing low, sweet chariot
Comin' for to carry me home.
Swing low, sweet chariot,
Comin' for to carry me home.

If you get there before I do,
Comin' for to carry me home.
Tell all my friends I'm comin' too,
Comin' for to carry me home.

Swing low, sweet chariot
Comin' for to carry me home.
Swing low, sweet chariot,
Comin' for to carry me home.

Go Down, Moses

· *Traditional* ·

Go down, Moses,
Way down in Egypt land,
Tell ole Pharaoh,
Let my people go.

When Israel was in Egypt's land
Let my people go,
Oppressed so hard they could not stand,
Let my people go.

Go down, Moses,
Way down in Egypt land,
Tell ole Pharaoh,
Let my people go.

"Thus said the Lord," bold Moses said,
"'Let my people go.
If not, I'll smite your firstborn dead,
Let my people go.' "

Go down, Moses,
Way down in Egypt land,
Tell ole Pharaoh,
Let my people go.

No more shall they in bondage toil,
Let my people go;
To lead the children of Israel through,
Let my people go.

Go down, Moses,
Way down in Egypt land,
Tell ole Pharaoh,
Let my people go.

Oh, Mary, Don't You Weep
· *Traditional* ·

Oh, Mary, doncha weep, doncha moan,
Oh, Mary, doncha weep, doncha moan,
Pharoah's army got drownded,
Oh, Mary, doncha weep.

Steal Away
· *Traditional* ·

Steal away,
Steal away,
Steal away to Jesus.

Steal away, steal away home.
I ain't got long to stay here.

My Lord, he calls me,
He calls me by the thunder;
The trumpet sounds within-a my soul,
I ain't got long to stay here.

Steal away,
Steal away,
Steal away to Jesus.
Steal away, steal away home.
I ain't got long to stay here.

Oh, Freedom

· *Traditional* ·

Oh, freedom,
Oh, freedom,
Oh, freedom over me,
And before I'd be a slave,
I'd be buried in my grave
And go home to my Lord
And be free.

No more moanin',
No more moanin',
No more moanin' over me,
And before I'd be a slave,
I'd be buried in my grave
And go home to my Lord
And be free.

3. No more weepin'
4. There'll be prayin'
5. There'll be shoutin'

Nobody Knows de Trouble I See

· *Traditional* ·

Nobody knows de trouble I see,
Nobody knows but Jesus.
Nobody knows de trouble I see,
Glory, hallelujah.

Sometimes I'm up, sometimes I'm down,
Oh, yes, Lord.
Sometimes I'm almost to the ground,
Oh, yes, Lord.

Nobody knows de trouble I see,
Nobody knows but Jesus.
Nobody knows de trouble I see,
Glory, hallelujah.

What make ole Satan hate me so?
Oh, yes, Lord.
Because he got me once and he let me go.
Oh, yes, Lord.

Nobody knows de trouble I see,
Nobody knows but Jesus.
Nobody knows de trouble I see,
Glory, hallelujah!

No Man Can Hinder Me

· *Traditional* ·

Walk in, kind Savior,
No man can hinder me.
Walk in, sweet Jesus,
No man can hinder me.

Oh, no man can hinder me.
Oh, no man, no man, no man can hinder me.
O no man, no man, no man can hinder me.

See what wonder Jesus done,
No man can hinder me.
See what wonder Jesus done,
No man can hinder me.

Oh, no man can hinder me.
Oh, no man, no man, no man can hinder me.
O no man, no man, no man can hinder me.

3. Jesus make de dumb to speak
4. Jesus made de cripple walk
5. Jesus give de blind his sight
6. Jesus do most anything
7. Rise, poor Lazarus from de tomb

I Been 'Buked and I Been Scorned

· *Traditional* ·

I been 'buked and I been scorned,
I been 'buked and I been scorned,
Chillun, I been 'buked and I been scorned,
I'se had a hard time, sure's you born.

You can talk about me as much as you please,
You can talk about me as much as you please,
Chillun, talk about me much as you please,
Gon' talk 'bout you when I get on my knees.

Sometimes I Feel like a Motherless Child
· *Traditional* ·

Sometimes I feel like a motherless child,
Sometimes I feel like a motherless child,
A long way from home.

Oh, I wonder where my mother's gone,
I wonder where my mother's gone,
I wonder where my mother's gone,
A long way from home.

Rock-a My Soul
· *Traditional* ·

Rock-a my soul in the bosom of Abraham,
Rock-a my soul in the bosom of Abraham,
Rock-a my soul in the bosom of Abraham,
Rock-a my soul in the bosom of Abraham,
Oh, rock-a my soul!

Uncloudy Day
· *Traditional* ·

Oh, they tell me of a home far beyond the skies,
Oh, they tell me of a home far away.
Oh, they tell me of a home where no storm clouds rise,
Oh, they tell me of an uncloudy day.

Oh, they tell me of a home where my friends have gone,
Oh, they tell me of that land far away;

Where the tree of life's in eternal bloom
And sheds its fragrance through the uncloudy day.

John Brown's Body
· *Traditional* ·

Thomas Wentworth Higginson in *Army Life in a Black Regiment* and numerous other contemporary observers note that "John Brown's Body" was a favorite of Negro soldiers during the Civil War. Though some scholars have suggested that the song originally referred to a Sergeant John Brown, those who adopted it generally regarded it as a paean to the abolitionist John Brown who was hanged for his armed takeover of the arsenal at Harper's Ferry. I include variants to the song in parentheses.

John Brown's body lies a-mouldering in the grave (clay),
John Brown's body lies a-mouldering in the grave (clay),
John Brown's body lies a-mouldering in the grave (clay),
But his soul goes marching on. (His truth is marching on.)

Glory, glory, hallelujah,
Glory, glory, hallelujah,
Glory, glory, hallelujah,
His soul goes marching on.

2. John Brown died that the slave might be free
3. He captured Harper's Ferry with his nineteen men so true
4. He's gone to be a soldier in the Army of the Lord

A verse cited by Eileen Southern (*The Music of Black Americans: A History*) as one circulating during the war years follows:

We are done with hoeing cotton, we are done with hoeing corn,
We are colored Yankee soldiers, as sure as you are born;
When Massa hears us shouting, he will think 'tis Gabriel's horn,
As we go marching on.

My Army Cross Over

· *From Thomas Wentworth Higginson,* Army Life in a
Black Regiment ·

Higginson said he could get no satisfactory explanation of "mighty Myo," though
one soldier thought it meant the river of death. Higginson speculates it may come
from the African word *Maya,* which means death in the Cameroon dialect. He
describes this song as a "grandly jubilant" marching or rowing song.

My army cross over,
My army cross over,
O, Pharaoh's army drownded!
My army cross over.

We 'll cross de mighty river,
   My army cross over;
We 'll cross de river Jordan,
   My army cross over;
We 'll cross de danger water,
   My army cross over;
We 'll cross de mighty Myo,
   My army cross over. (*Thrice.*)
O, Pharaoh's army drownded!
   My army cross over.

One More Valiant Soldier

· *From Thomas Wentworth Higginson,* Army Life in a
Black Regiment ·

Higginson speculates that his soldiers may have substituted *soldier* for what he
expects might have been *soul* in the original of the song that follows. He noted that
this was a very "ringing song" that was sung when the soldiers were marching or
rowing.

One more valiant soldier here,
One more valiant soldier here,

One more valiant soldier here,
  To help me bear de cross.
O hail, Mary, hail!
  Hail, Mary, hail!
Hail, Mary, hail!
  To help me bear de cross.

Ride In, Kind Saviour

· *From Thomas Wentworth Higginson,* Army Life in a Black Regiment ·

Higginson notes that sometimes "hinder me" was changed to "hinder *we.*"

Ride in, kind Saviour!
  No man can hinder me.
O, Jesus is a mighty man!
  No man, &c.
We're marching through Virginny fields.
  No man, &c.
O, Satan is a busy man,
  No man, &c.
And he has his sword and shield,
  No man, &c.
O, old Secesh done come and gone!
  No man can hinder me.

We'll Soon Be Free

· *From Thomas Wentworth Higginson,* Army Life in a Black Regiment ·

Higginson points out that Negroes had been jailed in Georgetown, South Carolina, at the outbreak of the Civil War for singing the following song, which took on additional meaning for Black soldiers.

We'll soon be free,
We'll soon be free,

We'll soon be free,
    When de Lord will call us home.
My brudder, how long,
My brudder, how long,
My brudder, how long,
    'Fore we done sufferin' here?
It won't be long (*Thrice.*)
    'Fore de Lord will call us home.
We'll walk de miry road (*Thrice.*)
    Where pleasure never dies.
We'll walk de golden street (*Thrice.*)
    Where pleasure never dies.
My brudder, how long (*Thrice.*)
    'Fore we done sufferin' here?

We'll soon be free (*Thrice.*)
    When Jesus sets me free.
We'll fight for liberty (*Thrice.*)
    When de Lord will call us home.

When Dat Ar Ole Chariot Comes

· *From Sarah Bradford*, Harriet, the Moses of Her People ·

This is a song that Tubman would sing to alert slaves to an upcoming escape.

When dat ar ole chariot comes,
I'm gwine to lebe you,
I'm boun' for de promised land,
Frien's, I'm gwine to lebe you.

I'm sorry, frien's, to lebe you,
Farewell! oh, farewell!
But I'll meet you in de mornin',
Farewell! oh, farewell!

Lay This Body Down

· *First version of this old slave song taken from W. E. B. Du Bois,* The
Souls of Black Folk; *second version from Thomas Wentworth Higginson,*
Army Life in a Black Regiment ·

I walk through the churchyard
    To lay this body down;
I know moon-rise, I know star-rise;
I walk in the moonlight, I walk in the starlight;
I'll lie in the grave and stretch out my arms,
I'll go to judgment in the evening of the day,
And my soul and thy soul shall meet that day,
    When I lay this body down.

I know moon-rise, I know star-rise;
    Lay dis body down.
I walk in de moonlight, I walk in de starlight,
    To lay dis body down.
I'll walk in de graveyard, I'll walk through de graveyard,
    To lay dis body down.
I'll lie in de grave and stretch out my arms;
    Lay dis body down.
I go to de Judgment in de evening ob de day
    When I lay dis body down;
And my soul and your soul will meet in de day
    When I lay dis body down.

Ain't Gon' Study War No More

· *Traditional* ·

I'm gonna lay down my sword and shield,
Down by the riverside, down by the riverside, down by the
    riverside,

Gonna lay down my sword and shield,
Down by the riverside.
Ain't gon' study war no more.

Ain't gon' study war no more,
Ain't gon' study war no more.
Ain't gon' study-e-e war no more.

Gonna put on my long white robe.
Down by the riverside, down by the riverside, down by the
     riverside,
Gonna put on my long white robe,
Down by the riverside.
Ain't gon' study war no more.

Ain't gon' study war no more,
Ain't gon' study war no more,
Ain't gon' study-e-e war no more.

I Heard from Heaven Today

· *From William Francis Allen et al.,* Slave Songs of the
United States ·

I have changed "yearde" to "heard."

Hurry on, my weary soul,
And I heard from heaven today.
Hurry on, my weary soul,
And I heard from heaven today.

My sin is forgiven and my soul set free,
And I heard from heaven today.
My sin is forgiven and my soul set free,
And I heard from heaven today.

My name is called and I must go,
And I heard from heaven today.

My name is called and I must go,
And I heard from heaven today.

Soon I Will Be Done wid de Troubles o' the World

· *Traditional* ·

Soon I will be done wid de troubles o' the world,
Troubles o' the world, troubles o' the world,
Soon I will be done wid de troubles o' the world,
Going home to live wid God.

No more weepin' and a-wailin',
No more weepin' and a-wailin',
No more weepin' and a-wailin',
Going home to live wid God.

Soon I will be done wid de troubles o' the world,
Troubles o' the world, troubles o' the world,
Soon I will be done wid de troubles o' the world,
Going home to live wid God.

2. I want to meet my mother
3. I want to meet my Jesus

I Want to Go Home

· *From William Francis Allen et al.,* Slave Songs of the United States ·

I want to go home.
Dere's no rain to wet you,
O, yes, I want to go home,
Want to go home.

[Repeat, substituting each of the following for the second line.]

2. Dere's no sun to burn you

3. Dere's no hard trials

4. Dere's no whips a-crackin'

5. Dere's no stormy weather

6. Dere's no tribulation

7. No more slavery in de kingdom[10]

8. No evil-doers in de kingdom

9. All is gladness in de kingdom

Wade in de Water

· *Traditional* ·

Wade in de water,
Wade in de water,
Wade in de water, children,
God's gonna trouble de water.

See that band all dressed in white,
God's gonna trouble de water.
The leader looks like an Israelite
God's gonna trouble de water.

Wade in de water,
Wade in de water,
Wade in de water, children,
God's gonna trouble de water.

See that band all dressed in red,
God's gonna trouble de water.
It looks like the band that Moses led,
God's gonna trouble de water.

[10] A note in Allen indicates that this verse was added after the Emancipation Proclamation, an assertion that I question because it is impossible for collectors to determine when something was added and because it was so common for the enslaved people to sing of better conditions in heaven or elsewhere.

Ole Time Religion

· *Traditional* ·

Gimme me that ole time religion,
Gimme that ole time religion,
Gimme that ole time religion,
It's good enough for me.

Gimme me that ole time religion,
Gimme that ole time religion,
Gimme that ole time religion,
It's good enough for me.

It was good for my ole mother,
It was good for my ole mother,
It was good for my ole mother,
And it's good enough for me.

Gimme me that ole time religion,
Gimme that ole time religion,
Gimme that ole time religion,
It's good enough for me.

It brought me out of bondage,
It brought me out of bondage,
Yes, it brought me out of bondage,
And it's good enough for me.

Gimme me that ole time religion,
Gimme that ole time religion,
Gimme that ole time religion,
It's good enough for me.

It was good for the Hebrew children,
It was good for the Hebrew children,
It was good for the Hebrew children,
And it's good enough for me.

Gimme me that ole time religion,
Gimme that ole time religion,
Gimme that ole time religion,
It's good enough for me.

Somebody's Knocking at Your Door
· *Traditional* ·

Somebody's knocking, somebody's knocking,
Somebody's knocking at your door.
Oh-O, sinner, why don't you answer?
Somebody's knocking at your door.

Sounds like Jesus, sounds like Jesus,
Sounds like Jesus at your door.
Oh-O, sinner, why don't you answer?
Somebody's knocking at your door.

No Hiding Place
· *Traditional* ·

There's no hiding place down there, down there,
There's no hiding place down there.

Oh, I went to the rock to hide my face;
The rock cried out, "No hiding place,
There's no hiding place down here."

Oh, the sinner man, he gambled and fell;
He wanted to go to heaven, but he went to hell.
There's no hiding place down there, down there,
There's no hiding place down there.

Heaven, Heaven

· *Traditional* ·

I got shoes,
You got shoes,
All o' God's children got shoes.
When I get to heaven
Gonna put on my shoes,
Gonna walk all over God's Heaven,
Heaven, heaven,
Everybody talkin' 'bout heaven ain't going there,
I'm gonna walk all over God's Heaven.

I got a harp,
You got a harp,
All o' God's children got a harp.
When I get to heaven
Gonna play on my harp,
Gonna play all over God's Heaven,
Heaven, heaven,
Everybody talkin' 'bout heaven ain't going there,
I'm gonna play all over God's Heaven.

I got a robe,
You got a robe,
All o' God's children got a robe.
When I get to heaven
Gonna put on my robe,
Gonna walk all over God's Heaven,
Heaven, heaven,
Everybody talkin' 'bout heaven ain't going there,
I'm gonna walk all over God's Heaven.

I got a wings,
You got a wings,
All o' God's children got wings.

When I get to heaven
Gonna put on my wings,
Gonna fly all over God's Heaven,
Heaven, heaven,
Everybody talkin' 'bout heaven ain't going there,
I'm gonna fly all over God's Heaven.

O Canaan

· *From Frederick Douglass,* Life and Times of Frederick Douglass ·

Douglass writes, "A keen observer might have detected in our repeated singing of
[these lines] something more than a hope of reaching heaven. We meant to reach
the *North,* and the North was our Canaan. [The lines] had a double meaning. On
the lips of some it meant the expectation of a speedy summons to a world of
spirits, but on the lips of our company [fellow slaves planning escape] it simply
meant a speedy pilgrimage to a free state and deliverance from all the evils and
dangers of slavery."

O Canaan, sweet Canaan,
I am bound for the land of Canaan.

I thought I heard them say
There were lions in the way;
I don't expect to stay
 Much longer here.
Run to Jesus, shun the danger,
I don't expect to stay
 Much longer here.

Michael, Row de Boat A-Shore

· *From William Francis Allen et al.,* Slave Songs of the
United States ·

I have changed a few spellings for clarity and omitted a few lines.

Michael row de boat a-shore
Hal-le-lu-jah!

Michael row de boat a-shore
Hal-le-lu-jah!

2. I wonder where my mudder dere
3. I see my mudder on de rock gwine home
4. O you mind your boastin' talk
5. Boastin' talk will sink your soul
6. Jordan stream is wide and deep
7. Jesus stand on de other side

Were You There?

· *Traditional* ·

Were you there when they crucified my Lord?
Were you there?
Were you there when they crucified my Lord?
Were you there?
Oh, oh, sometimes it causes me to tremble, tremble, tremble.
Were you there when they crucified my Lord?

2. Were you there when they nailed him to the cross?
3. Were you there when they pierced him in the side?
4. Were you there when the sun refused to shine?

Done wid Driber's Dribin'

· *Traditional* ·

Done wid driber's dribin',
Done wid driber's dribin',
Done wid driber's dribin',
Roll, Jordan, roll.

Done wid massa's hollerin',
Done wid massa's hollerin',

Done wid massa's hollerin',
Roll, Jordan, roll.

Done wid missus' scoldin',
Done wid missus' scoldin',
Done wid missus' scoldin',
Roll, Jordan, roll.

Dry Bones

· *Traditional* ·

Dem bones, dem bones, dem *dry* bones,
Dem bones, dem bones, dem *dry* bones,
Dem bones, dem bones, dem *dry* bones,
Oh, hear de word of de Lord.

Ezekiel connected dem *dry* bones,
Ezekiel connected dem *dry* bones,
Ezekiel connected dem *dry* bones,
Oh, hear de word of de Lord.

Toe bone connected to de foot bone,
Foot bone connected to de ankle bone,
Ankle bone connected to de leg bone,
Leg bone connected to de knee bone,
Knee bone connected to de thigh bone,
Thigh bone connected to de hip bone,
Hip bone connected to de back bone,
Back bone connected to de shoulder bone,
Shoulder bone connected to de neck bone,
Neck bone connected to de head bone,
Oh, hear de word of de Lord.

Dem bones, dem bones, dem *dry* bones,
Dem bones, dem bones, dem *dry* bones,

Dem bones, dem bones, dem ∂ry bones,
Oh, hear de word of de Lord.

Dem bones gonna walk all around,
Dem bones gonna walk all around,
Dem bones gonna walk all around,
Oh, hear de word of de Lord.

Dem bones, dem bones, dem ∂ry bones,
Dem bones, dem bones, dem ∂ry bones,
Dem bones, dem bones, dem ∂ry bones,
Oh, hear de word of de Lord.

Song of the Coffle Gang

· *From William Wells Brown,* The Anti-Slavery Harp: A Collection
of Songs ·

Brown notes that this song "is said to be sung by Slaves, as they are chained in
gangs, when parting from friends for the far-off South."

See these poor souls from Africa,
Transported to America:
We are stolen and sold to Georgia, will you go along with me?
We are stolen and sold to Georgia, go sound the jubilee.
See wives and husbands sold apart,
The children's screams!—it breaks my heart;
There's a better day a coming, will you go along with me?
There's a better day a coming, go sound the jubilee.
O, gracious Lord! when shall it be,
That we poor souls shall all be free?
Lord, break them Slavery powers—will you go along with me?
Lord, break them Slavery powers, go sound the jubilee.
Dear Lord! dear Lord! when Slavery'll cease,
Then we poor souls can have our peace;
There's a better day a coming, will you go along with me?
There's a better day a coming, go sound the jubilee.

A Song for Freedom

· From *William Wells Brown*, The Anti-Slavery Harp: A Collection
of Songs ·

Brown notes that this song is sung to the tune of "Dandy Jim."

Come all ye bondmen far and near,
Let's put a song in massa's ear,
It is a song for our poor race,
Who're whipped and trampled with disgrace.

My old massa tells me O
This is a land of freedom O;
Let's look about and see if 'tis so,
Just as massa tells me O.

He tells us of that glorious one,
I think his name was Washington,
How he did fight for liberty,
To save a threepence tax on tea.

My old massa, &c.

And then he tells us that there was
A Constitution with this clause,
That all men equal were created,
How often have we heard it stated.

My old massa, &c.

But now we look about and see,
That we poor blacks are not so free;
We're whipped and thrashed about like fools,
And have no chance at common schools.

Still, my old massa, &c.

They take our wives, insult and mock,
And sell our children on the block,
Then choke us if we say a word,
And say that "niggers" shan't be heard.

My old massa, &c.

Our preachers, too, with whip and cord,
Command obedience in the Lord;
They say they learn it from the book,
But for ourselves we dare not look.

Still, my old massa tells me O,
This is a *Christian* country O, &c.

There is a country far away,
Friend Hopper says 'tis Canada,
And if we reach Victoria's shore,
He says that we are slaves no more.

Now hasten all bondmen, let us go,
And leave this *Christian* country O;
Haste to the land of the British Queen,
Where whips for negroes are not seen.

Now if we go, we must take the night —
We're sure to die if we come in sight,
The bloodhounds will be on our track,
And woe to us if they fetch us back.

Now haste all bondmen, let us go,
And leave this *Christian* country O;
God help us to Victoria's shore,
Where we are free and slaves no more.

Get on the Bus

· *From the* Richmond Times Dispatch, *Sunday, August 6, 2000* ·

On July 16, 1944, Irene Morgan refused to give up her seat on a Greyhound bus to a White couple. When she had boarded the bus in Gloucester County, Virginia, she sat four rows from the back in the area then designated for colored people, but as more Whites boarded, the driver told her that she had to move further back. She refused, and the sheriff was called; when the sheriff attempted to force her out of the seat, she resisted, kicking him three times. When a nightstick-wielding deputy threatened to beat her, she said she would fight back. Found guilty of resisting arrest and of failing to move to the back of the bus, she appealed the latter to the Supreme Court. When the court found the Virginia law flawed in that it impeded interstate transportation, civil rights advocates staged a version of the Freedom Rides, singing the following song as they moved through the state on an interstate bus.

Get on the bus,
Sit anyplace,
'Cause Irene Morgan
Won her case.

I'll Overcome Some Day
We Shall Overcome

The lyrics to "I'll Overcome Some Day" were published in Charles Albert Tindley's 1923 *New Songs of Paradise,* but the song was very likely circulated in the folk tradition long before then. The 1989 videotape of the song, "We Shall Overcome," begins with Blacks in an isolated church in John's Island, South Carolina, singing "I Will Overcome." One member of the group declares that it was a "part of the slavery song . . . the old people always sang it." On that same videotape blues singer Taj Mahal recalls that his mother used to sing "I Will Overcome." The song was adopted by protesting workers in Charleston, South Carolina, in 1945; a variant, "We Shall Overcome," became the anthem of the Civil Rights movement in the 1960s. Since that time it has been adopted by people all over the world. As Harry Belafonte proclaims in "I Shall Overcome," "It is probably the most powerful song in the world today. It belongs to everyone."

It is not possible to reproduce all of the verses to "We Shall Overcome." Eileen Southern, professor emerita of music at Harvard University, declares that at varied demonstrations Civil Rights activists made up *hundreds* of verses to this simple melody (*The Music of Black Americans*). Many participants in that movement will recount the exact moment and situation that gave birth to specific new verses. In the videotape one participant gives a moving account of her introduction of "We are not afraid" one night when she was a part of a group of Civil Rights workers who were being held by Whites who had raided the Highlander Center in Tennessee. She declares that raising their voices in song, declaring "We are not afraid," emboldened the Civil Rights workers on that occasion.

Numerous others around the world have declared the indescribable power of the song. I can personally attest to the authenticity of the testimony of one leader of the Southern Christian Leadership Conference who commented, "You really have to experience it to understand the kind of power it has for us. When you get through singing it, you could walk over a bed of hot coals, and you wouldn't even feel it!"

The lyrics to "We Shall Overcome" are from the song as I have heard it sung on countless occasions.

I'll Overcome Some Day

"Ye Shall overcome if ye faint not."

This world is one great battlefield
With forces all arrayed;
If in my heart I do not yield,
I'll overcome some day.

I'll overcome some day,
I'll overcome some day.
If in my heart I do not yield,
I'll overcome some day.

[Additional verses:]
Lord make me strong some day
I'll be like Him some day

We Shall Overcome

We shall overcome,
We shall overcome,
We shall overcome some day.
Oh, deep in my heart, I do believe
We shall overcome some day.

[Additional verses:]
We shall all be free
We are not afraid
We'll walk hand in hand
We shall live in peace
The Lord will help us through

We's Free

· *From* The Negro in Virginia, *compiled by Workers of the Writers'*
Program of the Work Projects Administration in the state of Virginia ·

Collected from Fannie Berry.

Niggers shoutin' an' clappin' hands an' singin'! Chillun runnin'
all over de place beatin' tins an' yellin'. Ev'ybody happy. Sho'
did some celebratin'. Run to de kitchen an' shout in de
winder:

> Mammy don't you cook no mo'
> You's free! You's free!

Run to de henhouse an' shout:

> Rooster, don't you crow no mo'
> You's free! You's free!
> Ol' hen, don't you lay no mo' eggs,
> You's free! You's free!

Go to de pigpen an' tell de pig:

> Ol' pig, don't you grunt no mo'
> You's free! You's free!

Tell de cows:

> Ol' cow, don't you give no mo' milk,
> You's free! You's free!

An' some smart alec boys sneaked up under Miss Sara Ann's winder an' shouted:

> Ain't got to slave no mo'
> We's free! We's free!

∗ B L U E S ∗

Many of the following blues lyrics exist in many variant forms, and most have been recorded by several artists.

Po' Boy 'Long Way from Home

· *From Howard W. Odum, "Folk-Song and Folk-Poetry as Found in the Secular Songs of the Southern Negroes"* ·

Though Odum does not use the word "blues" in describing this and the next song, "Look'd Down de Road," both of which he includes in his 1911 essay, they are clearly blues songs, incorporating many of the lines that would continue to be repeated in the blues for the remainder of the twentieth century. Odum notes that each of the lines is repeated three times.

I'm po' boy 'long way from home,
Oh, I'm po' boy 'long way from home.

I wish a 'scushion train would run,
Carry me back where I cum frum.

Come here, babe, an' sit on yo' papa's knee.

You brought me here an' let 'em throw me down.

I ain't got a frien' in dis town.

I'm out in de wide worl' alone.

If you mistreat me, you sho' will see it again.

My mother daid an' my father gone astray,
You never miss yo' mother till she done gone away.

Come 'way to Georgia, babe, to git in a home.

No need, O babe! try to throw me down,
A po' little boy jus' come to town.

I wish that ole engeneer wus dead,
Brought me 'way from my home.

Central gi' me long-distance phone,
Talk to my babe all night long.

If I die in State of Alabam',
Send my papa great long telegram.

[In the same way the following "one-verse" songs are added:]

Shake hands an' tell yo' babe good-by.

Bad luck in de family sho' God fell on me.
Have you got lucky, babe, an' then got broke?
I'm goin' 'way, comin' back some day.
Good ole boy, jus' ain't treated right.

I'm Tennessee raise, Georgia bohn.
I'm Georgia bohn, Alabama rais'.
"If I die in Arkansa',
Oh, if I die in Arkansa',
If I die in Arkansa',
Des ship my body to my mother-in-law.

"If my mother refuse me, ship it to my pa.

"If my papa refuse me, ship it to my girl.

"If my girl refuse me, shove me into de sea,
Where de fishes an' de whales make a fuss over me."

[And then, after this wonderful rhyme and sentiment, the singer
    merges into plaintive appeal, and sings further, —]

"Pore ole boy, long ways from home,
Out in dis wide worl' alone."

Look'd Down de Road

· *From Howard W. Odum, "Folk-Song and Folk-Poetry as Found in the
Secular Songs of the Southern Negroes"* ·

Odum observes that each line is repeated twice.

Look'd down de road jes' far as I could see,
Well, the band did play "Nearer, my God, to Thee."

I got the blues, but too damn mean to cry.

Now when you git a dollar, you got a frien'
Will stick to you through thick an' thin.

I didn't come here fer to steal nobody's find.
I didn't jes' come here to serve my time.

I ask jailer, "Captain, how can I sleep?"
All 'round my bedside Police S. creeps.

The jailer said, "Let me tell you what's best:
Go 'way back in yo' dark cell an' take yo' rest."

If my kind man quit me, my main man throw me down;
I goin' run to de river, jump overboard 'n' drown.

Frisco Rag-Time

· *From Howard W. Odum, "Folk-Song and Folk-Poetry as Found in the
Secular Songs of the Southern Negroes"* ·

Got up in the mornin', couldn't keep from cryin',
Thinkin' 'bout that brown-skin man o' mine.

Yonder comes that lovin' man o' mine,
Comin' to pay his baby's fine.

Well, I begged the jedge to low' my baby's fine.
Said de jedge done fine her, clerk done wrote it down.

Couldn't pay dat fine, so taken her to de jail.

So she laid in jail back to de wall,
Dis brown-skin man cause of it all.

No need babe tryin' to throw me down,
Cause I'm po' boy jus' come to town.

But if you don't want me, please don't dog me 'round,
Give me this money, sho' will leave this town.

Ain't no use tryin' to send me 'roun',
I got plenty money to pay my fine.

W. C. HANDY

The Hesitating Blues

Hello Central, what's the matter with this line?
I want to talk to that High Brown of mine,
Tell me how long will I have to wait?
Please give me 2 9 8,
Why do you hesitate?
What you say, can't talk to my Brown!
A storm last night blowed the wires all down;
Tell me how long will I have to wait?
Oh, won't you tell me now —
Why do you hesitate?

Procrastination is the thief of time,
So all the wise owls say, "One stitch in time may save nine."
Tomorrow's not today, and if you put off,
Somebody's bound to lose.
I'd be his, he'd be mine,
And I'd be feeling gay,
Left alone to grieve and pine,
My best friend's gone away.
He's gone and left me the Hesitating Blues.

Sunday night my beau proposed to me;
Said he'd be happy if his wife I'd be,
Said he, "How long will I have to wait?
Come be my wife my Kate,
Why do you hesitate?"
I declined him just for a stall,
He left that night on the Cannon Ball;
Honey, how long will I have to wait?
Will he come back now — Or will he hesitate?

Procrastination is the thief of time,
So all the wise owls say, "One stitch in time may save nine,"
Tomorrow's not today, and if you put off,

Somebody's bound to lose.
I'd be his, he'd be mine,
And I'd be feeling gay,
Left alone to grieve and pine,
My best friend's gone away,
He's gone and left me the Hesitating Blues.

W. C. HANDY

Joe Turner's Blues

You'll never miss the water till your well runs dry,
Till your well runs dry.
You'll never miss Joe Turner till he says "Goodbye."
Sweet Babe, I'm goin' to leave you, and the time ain't long,
No the time ain't long.
If you don't believe I'm leavin', count the days I'm gone.

You will be sorry, be sorry from your heart, uhm, uhm,
Sorry to your heart, uhm, uhm,
Someday when you and I must part.
And every time you hear a whistle blow,
You'll hate the day you lost your Joe.

I bought a bull-dog for to watch you while you sleep,
Guard you while you sleep.
Spent all my money, now you call Joe Turner "Cheap."
You never 'preciate the little things I do,
Not one thing I do.
And that's the very reason why I'm leavin' you.

You will be sorry, be sorry from your heart, uhm, uhm,
Sorry to your heart, uhm, uhm,
Someday when you and I must part.
And every time you hear a whistle blow,
You'll hate the day you lost your Joe.
Sometimes I feel like nothin',

Somethin' throwed away, somethin' throwed away.
And then I get my guitar, play the blues all day.
Now if your heart beat like mine, it's not made of steel,
No tain't made of steel,
And when you learn I left you this is how you'll feel.

You will feel sorry, be sorry from your heart, uhm, uhm,
Sorry to your heart, uhm, uhm,
Someday when you and I must part.
And every time you hear a whistle blow,
You'll hate the day you lost your Joe.

W. C. HANDY
The St. Louis Blues

Published by Pace & Handy Music Company in Memphis in 1914, "St. Louis Blues" became the first million-selling blues song and the first song to have a short film made of it (starring Bessie Smith). Versions of "St. Louis Blues" were recorded by Esther Bigeou in 1921, Katherine Henderson in 1928, Bessie Smith in 1925 and 1929, Jim Jackson in 1930, Cab Calloway in 1930, and Lena Horne in 1941.

I hate to see de evenin' sun go down,
I hate to see de evenin' sun go down,
'Cause my baby, he done left this town.

Feelin' tomorrow lak ah feel today,
Feel tomorrow lak ah feel today,
I'll pack my trunk, make ma gitaway.

St. Louis woman, wid her diamond ring,
St. Louis woman, wid her diamond ring,
Pulls dat man roun' by her apron strings.

'Twant for powder and for store-bought hair,
If it weren't for powder and for store-bought hair,
De man I love would not gone nowhere.

Got de St. Louis blues, jes blue as I can be,
Dat man got a heart lak a rock cast in the sea —
Or else he wouldn't gone so far from me.

Been to de Gypsy to get ma fortune tole,
To de Gypsy done got ma fortune tole,
'Cause I'm wild bout ma Jelly Roll.

Gypsy done told me "don't you wear no black."
Yes, she done told me, "don't you wear no black.
Go to St. Louis, you can win him back."
. . . .
I loves dat man lak a schoolboy loves his pie,
Lak a Kentucky Col'nel loves his mint an rye,
I'll love ma baby til de day ah die.

PERRY BRADFORD
The Lonesome Blues

During Perry "Mule" Bradford's youth, his family lived for a while next to the
Fulton Street Jail in Atlanta, where he heard the Black inmates singing the blues.
This experience obviously was the source of his life's work as a writer, performer,
and producer of the blues. David A. Jasen credits Bradford with opening the
recording field to blues singers when he persuaded a record company to record
the first blues record — Mamie Smith singing his "Crazy Blues" in 1920 (*Beale
Street and Other Classic Blues*).

I'm just as lonesome as I can be —
Thinking of the one that don't care for me —
he keeps me worried thinking all the time
'Cause he told me to my face —
had another one to take my place.
Tell me pretty daddy
Why do you treat me so?
I'm going to the furniture store to buy a rocking chair,
If the blues overtake me, going rock away from here.
Tell me how long, Babe, do I have to wait,

'Cause I want you back—I don't want to hesitate.
I am lonesome and I'm worried, yes down deep in my heart—
'Cause I know, I know the best of friends must part.
Listen to my plea,
Honey come back to me.

I woke up this morning, morning, morning downhearted and
    blue
Didn't have no one, no one, no one to tell my troubles to.
I went to the fortune teller, and then she said to me,
Dear girl, you surely have got them lo[n]esome blues.

W. C. HANDY

Beale Street

I've seen the lights of gay Broadway,
Old Market Street down by the Frisco Bay,
I've strolled the Prado,
I've gambled on the Bourse.
The seven wonders of the world I've seen,
And many are the places I have been.
Take my advice folks and see Beale Street first.

You'll see pretty Browns in beautiful gowns,
You'll see tailor-mades and hand-me-downs,
You'll meet honest men and pickpockets skilled,
You'll find that business never closes till somebody gets killed.

I'd rather be here than anyplace I know,
I'd rather be here than anyplace I know,
It's goin' to take the Sergeant for to make me go,
Goin' to the river, maybe, by-and-by,
Goin' to the river, and there's a reason why.
Because the river's wet and Beale Street's done gone dry.

You'll see hog-nose restaurants and chitlin' Cafés,
You'll see jugs that tell of bygone days
And places, once places, now just a sham,
You'll see golden balls enough to pave the New Jerusalem.

I'd rather be here than anyplace I know,
I'd rather be here than anyplace I know,
It's goin' to take the Sergeant for to make me go,
Goin' to the river, maybe, by-and-by,
Goin' to the river, and there's a reason why.
Because the river's wet and Beale Street's done gone dry.

You'll see men who rank with the first in the nation
Who come to Beale for inspiration.
Politicians call you a dub
Unless you've been initiated in the Rickriters Club.

I'd rather be here than anyplace I know,
I'd rather be here than anyplace I know,
It's goin' to take the Sergeant for to make me go,
Goin' to the river, maybe, by-and-by,
Goin' to the river, and there's a reason why.
Because the river's wet and Beale Street's done gone dry.

If Beale Street could talk,
If Beale Street could talk,
Married men would have to take their beds and walk,
Except one or two, who never drank booze
And the blind man on the corner who sings the Beale Street
    Blues.

I'd rather be here than anyplace I know,
I'd rather be here than anyplace I know,
It's goin' to take the Sergeant for to make me go,
Goin' to the river, maybe, by-and-by,
Goin' to the river, and there's a reason why.
Because the river's wet and Beale Street's done gone dry.

CHRIS SMITH AND W. C. HANDY

Long Gone

Clearly motivated by the old work song (see "Long Gone" in chapter 9), Chris Smith wrote the lyrics to the following blues song; W. C. Handy composed the music.

Did you ever hear the story of Long John Dean?
A bold, bank robber from Bowling Green,
Was sent to the jailhouse yesterday,
Late last night he made his getaway.

He's Long Gone from Kentucky, Long Gone.
Ain't he lucky?
Long Gone and what I mean,
He's Long Gone from Bowling Green.

Long John stood on the railroad tie
Waiting for a freight train to come by,
Freight train came just puffin' and flyin',
Ought a seen Long John grabbin' that blind.

He's Long Gone from Kentucky, Long Gone.
Ain't he lucky?
Long Gone and what I mean,
He's Long Gone from Bowling Green.

RICHARD M. JONES

Trouble in Mind

This song has been recorded by countless artists.

Trouble in mind.
I'm blue, but I won't be blue always,
'Cause the sun's gonna shine round my back door someday,
    some day.

I'm gonna lay my head on some lonesome railroad line,
jus' let the two nineteen come on and pacify my mind.

I'm all alone, don't ask me why, and the lights are burnin' low.
Yes I have never seen so much trouble in my life before.
My good girl she has gone, and there's no more talkin' now,
but, Oh, no Lord! You can't keep a good man down.

I'm all alone, don't ask me why, and the lights are burnin' low.
Yes I have never seen so much trouble in my life before.
My good girl she has gone, and there's no more talkin' now,
but, Oh, no Lord! You can't keep a good man down.

W. C. HANDY

Careless Love

If I were a little bird
I'd fly from tree to tree;
I'd build my nest way up in the air
Where the bad boys could not bother me.

Love, oh love, oh careless love,
Love, oh love, oh careless love,
You've broke the heart of a many poor girl
But you'll never break this heart of mine.

When I wore my apron low,
When I wore my apron low,
When I wore my apron low,
He always passed right by my door.

Now I wear my apron high,
Now I wear my apron high,
Now I wear my apron high,
And he never, never passes by.

BESSIE SMITH
Backwater Blues

Bessie Smith and other blues musicians wrote songs commemorating the famous
Mississippi flood of 1927. The catastrophe caused more than a thousand deaths
and left 100,000 people homeless, many of them impoverished Blacks, at a time
when no federal emergency relief aid for flood victims was forthcoming.

When it rains five days and the skies turn dark as night
When it rains five days and the skies turn dark as night
Then trouble's takin' place in the lowlands at night

I woke up this mornin', can't even get out of my door
I woke up this mornin', can't even get out of my door
There's been enough trouble to make a poor girl wonder where
  she want to go

Then they rowed a little boat about five miles 'cross the pond
Then they rowed a little boat about five miles 'cross the pond
I packed all my clothes, throwed them in and they rowed me
  along

When it thunders and lightnin' and when the wind begins to
  blow
When it thunders and lightnin' and when the wind begins to
  blow
There's thousands of people ain't got no place to go

Then I went and stood upon some high old lonesome hill
Then I went and stood upon some high old lonesome hill
Then looked down on the house where I used to live

Backwater blues done call me to pack my things and go
Backwater blues done call me to pack my things and go
'Cause my house fell down and I can't live there no more

Mmm, I can't move no more
Mmm, I can't move no more
There ain't no place for a poor old girl to go

BESSIE SMITH AND CLARENCE WILLIAMS

Jail-House Blues

· *From* Bessie Smith 1923: The Chronological Classics, *recorded in
1923 by Columbia Records* ·

Thirty days in jail with my back turned to the wall,
Thirty days in jail with my back turned to the wall,
Look here Mr. Jail-keeper, put another gal in my stall.
I don't mind being in jail, but I got to stay there so long, so long,
I don't mind being in jail, but I got to stay there so long, so long,
When every friend I had is done shook hands and gone.
You better stop your man from tickling me under my chin,
You better stop your man from tickling me under my chin,
Because if he keeps on tickling I'm sure going to take him on in.
Good morning blues, blues how do you do,
Good morning blues, blues how do you do,
Say I just come here to have a few words with you.

JIMMIE COX

Nobody Knows You When You're Down and Out

Performed by Bessie Smith.

I once lived the life of a millionaire,
Spending my money, I didn't care,
Always taking my friends out for a good time,
Buying champagne, gin, and wine.
But just as soon as my dough got low,

I couldn't find a friend, no place I'd go,
If I ever get my hands on a dollar again,
I'm gonna squeeze it and squeeze it till the eagle grins.

Refrain:
Nobody knows you when you're down and out,
In your pocket not one penny
And your friends you haven't any.
And soon as you get on your feet again,
Ev'rybody is your long lost friend.
It's mighty strange, without a doubt,
But nobody wants you when you're down and out,
Nobody wants you when you're down and out.

IDA COX

Wild Women Don't Have the Blues

I hear these women raving about their monkey-man,
About their trifling husbands and their no-good friends.
These poor women sit around all day and moan
Wondering why their wandering papa don't come home.
Now when you got a man don't never be on the square,
Because if you do he'll have a woman everywhere.
I never was known to treat no one man right,
I keep them working hard both day and night.

I've got a disposition and a way of my own,
When my man starts to kicking I let him find a new home,
I get full of good liquor, walk the street all night,
Go home and put my man out if he don't act right.
Wild women don't worry,
Wild women don't have the blues.

You never get nothing by being an angel child,
You'd better change your way an' get real wild.

I wanta' tell you something, I wouldn't tell you no lie,
Wild women are the only kind that ever get by.
Wild women don't worry,
Wild women don't have the blues.

MA RAINEY

Last Minute Blues

Recorded in Chicago, December 1923.

Minutes seem like hours; hours seem like days,
It seems like my daddy won't stop his evil ways.
Seem like every minute is going to be my last,
If I can't tell my future, I will tell my past.
The brook runs into the river, river runs into the sea,
If I don't run into daddy, somebody'll have to bury me.
If anybody asks you, who wrote this lonesome song,
Tell them you don't know the writer, but Ma Rainey put it on.

CHARLES COW COW DAVENPORT

I Ain't No Ice Man

Recorded in New York on May 8, 1938.

I ain't no iceman, I ain't no iceman's son,
But I can keep you cool until the iceman comes.
I ain't no wood chopper, I ain't no wood chopper's son,
But babe I can chop your kindling until the wood chopper
    comes.
Baby I ain't no stove man, I ain't no stove man's son,
But I can keep you heated up babe until the stove man comes.
Baby I ain't no butcher, and I ain't no butcher's son,
But I can furnish you plenty of meat baby until the butcher
    comes.

I ain't no milkman, I ain't no milkman's son,
But I can furnish you plenty of cream baby until that milkman
 comes.

Miscellaneous Blues Lines

Following are some traditional blues lines that appear in variant forms in
many songs.

I ain't good lookin',
Got no great long hair,
But I got ways, Baby,
That can take me anywhere.

•

I'm a big fat mama,
the meat shaking on my bones,
I'm a big fat mama,
the meat shaking on my bones,
Everytime I shimmy, shimmy,
a skinny gal lose her home.

•

You abuse me and mistreat me,
Dog me around and beat me.

•

When a woman gets the blues,
She tucks her head and cries.
But when a man gets the blues,
He catches a freight and rides.

•

I never miss my water till my well run dry
And I never miss sweet [name of woman] until she said good-
    bye.

    •

One of these mornings, and it won't be long,
You gonna look for me, baby, and I'll be gone.

    •

I'm gonna pack my suitcase, get on down the line.

    •

I woke up this morning, my sweet woman had gone.
I stood by that bed, and I hung my head and moaned.

    •

I woke up this mornin' just 'bout the break of day,
Found that my friend done took my gal away.

    •

I woke up this morning, blues all round my bed.
I woke up this morning, blues all round my bed.
I felt just like
Somebody in the family was dead.

    •

Woke up this mornin', blues all round my head.
Woke up this mornin', blues all round my head.
Had a dream that I was dead.

    •

Now she ain't good looking, and she don't dress fine,
But the way that woman love me, make me lose my mind.

.

I got the blues,
But I'm too damn mean to cry.

.

If you see my milk cow,
Tell her to hurry home,
'Cause I ain't had no good loving
Since she been gone.

.

It must be jelly 'cause jam don't shake like that.

PORTER GRANGER AND EVERETT ROBBINS
'Tain't Nobody's Business If I Do

Many artists, including Bessie Smith, performed this favorite, popular song.

There ain't nothin' I can do,
Or nothin' I can say,
That folks don't criticize me,
But I'm going to do just as I want to, anyway,
And don't care if they all despise me.

If I should take a notion
To jump into the ocean,
'Tain't nobody's business if I do, do, do, do.

If I go to church on Sunday,
Then just shimmy down on Monday,
'Tain't nobody's business if I do, if I do.

If my friend ain't got no money,
And I say, "Take all mine, honey,"
'Tain't nobody's business if I do, do, do, do.

If I give him my last nickel,
And it leaves me in a pickle,
'Tain't nobody's business if I do, if I do.

Say, I would rather my man would hit me,
Than jump right up and quit me,
'Tain't nobody's business if I do, do, do, do.

I swear I won't call no copper,
If I'm beat up by my papa,
'Tain't nobody's business if I do, if I do.

The New York Glide

Writer unknown. Recorded by Ethel Waters.

Everybody's going crazy
About the different dances of the day;
Everybody in this whole entire world
Is trying to learn the dance and sway;
Here's one dance you ought to learn,
It's something simply grand;
Now folks, it is so simple
Anyone can understand.
And if you'll take a chance,
I'll show you how to do this dance:

Just grab your partner
'Round the waist,
Hook her lightly
In her place,
Just lay back and do the shimaree,

Buzz up to your baby like a bumblebee.
Then lay back and do that eagle rock;
Please, professor, don't you ever stop,
Swing your partner, then you slide;
That's the New York Glide!

You can all have your tickle toe,
I mean, that's a dance you can do,
But if you should once see this dance,
I know that you would be amused;
Anywhere you hear this tune,
It sneaks up on your mind;
And if you love good music,
Why, you're going to keep in time;
And when you hear that band,
You'll say this dance is simply grand!

Just grab your partner
'Round the waist,
Pull her lightly
In her place;
Just lay back and do the shimaree;
Buzz up to your baby like a bumblebee.
Then lay back and do that eagle rock;
Please professor, don't you ever stop;
Swing your partner, then you slide;
That's the New York Glide!

SAM THEARD AND FLEECIE MOORE
Let the Good Times Roll
This version recorded by B. B. King.

Hey everybody, let's have some fun,
You only live for once and when you're dead you're done.
So let the good times roll, let the good times roll,
And live a long long.

I don't care if you are young or old no no, get together and let
    the good times roll.

Don't stand there moaning, talking trash,
If you wanna have some fun, you'd better go out and spend
    some cash,
And let the good time roll,
Let the good time roll.
I don't care if you young or old, get together and let the good
    times roll.

Don't stand there moaning, talking trash,
If you wanna have some fun, you'd better go out and spend
    some cash;
And let the good time roll,
Let the good time roll.
I don't care if you young or old, get together and let the good
    times roll.

Hey mister landlord, lock up all the doors,
When the police comes around, tell them Johnny's coming
    down.
Let the good times roll,
Let the good times roll,
And Lord I don't care if you young or old,
That's good enough to let the good times roll.

Hey everybody!
Tell everybody!
That B.B. and Bobby's in town.
I got a dollar and a quarter,
And I'm just raring to clown.
Don't let nobody play me cheap,
I got fifty cents to know that I'm gonna keep,
Let the good times roll.
I don't care if you young or old,
Let's get together and let the good times roll.

Jimmy Crack Corn

· *Traditional* ·

When I was young I use to wait
On Master and give him his plate,
And pass the bottle when he got dry,
And brush away the blue tail fly.

Chorus:
Jimmy crack corn and I don't care,
Jimmy crack corn and I don't care,
Jimmy crack corn and I don't care,
My master's gone away.

When he ride in the afternoon,
I follow him with a hickory broom;
The pony being rather shy
When bitten by a blue tail fly.

One day he ride around the farm,
The flies so numerous they did swarm;
One chanced to bite him on the thigh —
The devil take the blue tail fly.

The pony run, he jump, he pitch;
He tumble Master in the ditch.
He died and the jury wondered why —
The verdict was the blue tail fly.

They laid him under a simmon tree;
His epitaph is there to see:
"Beneath this stone I'm forced to lie,
A victim of the blue tail fly."

Old Master's gone, now let him rest,
They say all things are for the best;
I'll never forget, till the day I die,
Old Master and that blue tail fly.

Charleston Gals

· *From William Francis Allen et al.,* Slave Songs of the
United States ·

As I walked down the new-cut road,
I met the tap and then the toad;
The toad commenced to whistle and sing,
And the possum cut the pigeon-wing.

Along come an old man riding by:
Old man, if you don't mind, your horse will die;
If he dies I'll tan his skin,
And if he lives I'll ride him again.

Hi ho, for Charleston gals!
Charleston gals are the gals for me.

As I went a-walking down the street,
Up steps Charleston gals to take a walk with me.
I kep' a walking and they kep' a talking,
I danced with a gal with a hole in her stocking.

Hi ho, for Charleston gals!
Charleston gals are the gals for me.

Marry Me

· *From Howard W. Odum, "Folk-Song and Folk-Poetry as Found in the
Secular Songs of the Southern Negroes"* ·

This song, which reflects some of the courtship verses popular in early Negro
lyrics, also suggests the early popularity of strolling (see chapter 3, "The Style of
Soul").

Yes, there's going to be a ball,
    At the negro hall;
        Ain't you goin'?
Lizzie will be there,
    Yes, with all her airs;
        Don't you want to see the strolling?

Ha, ha, Miss Lizzie, don't you want to marry me—marry me?
I will be as good to you as anybody—anybod-e-e,
    If you'll only marry me.

Yes, I goin' to the negro hall,
    Have a good time, that's all,
        For they tell me Miss Lizzie will be there;
An' you bet yo' life,
    I goin' win her for my wife,
        An' take her home to-night.

Well, Miss Lizzie could not consent,
    She didn't know what he meant,
        By askin' her to marry him;
Well, Miss Lizzie couldn't consent,
    She didn't know what he meant,
        By askin' her to marry him.

So he got down on his knees,
    "O Miss Lizzie, if you please,
        Say that you will marry me;
An' I'll give you every cent,

> If I git you to consent,
>   If you'll only marry me."

Frankie and Johnnie

· *Traditional* ·

Frankie was a good woman,
That everybody knows.
She paid a hundred dollars
For Albert's one suit of clothes.
He was her man, but he done her wrong.

Frankie and Johnnie were lovers,
Lordy, how they could love,
Swore to be true to each other,
True as the stars up above.
He was her man, but he done her wrong.

Frankie went down to the barroom,
To buy her a bucket of beer.
She says, "Oh, Mister Bartender,
Has my Johnnie been here?
He was my man, but he done me wrong."

Well the bartender he told Frankie,
"I don't want to tell you no lie,
Johnnie was here 'bout a half-hour ago
With that gal named Nellie Bly,
He was your man, but he done you wrong."

Frankie went looking for Johnnie
And she found him with Nellie Bly.
She shot him through the heart,
And stood there watching him die.
He was her man, but he done her wrong.

Frankie said to the sheriff,
"What's going to happen to me?"
The sheriff said to Frankie,
"It's murder in the first degree.
He was your man, but he done you wrong."

Last time I heard of Frankie,
She was sittin' in her cell.
She say, "Johnnie was untrue to me,
That's why I sent him to hell.
He was my man, but he done me wrong."

The Lynchers

· *From E. C. L. Adams,* Tales of the Congaree ·

What did de lynchers say?
Bertha bleated like a goat
When dey shot her down.
What did Bertha say?
I ain't done no wrong at all,
Just tried to 'fend my little home;
I can only weep and moan,
White folks got my body,
   Oh, Lord! Have mercy on my soul,
   Have mercy, have mercy on my soul.

What did de big boss say?
He say I is hog tie
And unable to do my duty.
What did de Lowmans say?
I ain't done no wrong at all,
Just tried to 'fend my little home;
I can only weep and moan,
White folks got my body,
   Dear Lord! Have mercy on my soul,
   Have mercy, have mercy on my soul.

What did de government do?
Dey say dere was no evidence,
And dey feared de murder crew.
What did Demon say?
I ain't done no wrong at all,
Just tried to 'fend my little home;
I can only weep and moan,
White folks got my body,
> *Oh, Lord! Have mercy on my soul,*
> *Have mercy, have mercy on my soul.*

What did old man Lowman do?
For liquor dey did claim to find,
Dey [give] him two years on de gang.
What did de poor nigger say?
I ain't done no wrong at all,
Just tried to 'fend my little home;
I can only weep and moan,
White folks got my body,
> *Oh, Lord! Have mercy on my soul,*
> *Have mercy, have mercy on my soul.*

What did de lynchers do?
Put a bullet in my mother,
Kilt a babe unborn.
What did de Lowmans say?
I ain't done no wrong at all,
Just tried to 'fend my poorly home;
I can only weep and moan,
White folks got my body,
> *Oh, Lord! Have mercy on my soul,*
> *Have mercy, have mercy on my soul.*

What did de murderers do?
Open up de jail door;
Dragged de helpless from dere cell.
What did de weeping woman say?
I ain't done no wrong at all,

Just tried to 'fend my little home;
I can only weep and moan,
White folks got my body,
   Oh, Lord! Have mercy on my soul,
   Have mercy, have mercy on my soul.

What did de noble heroes do?
Dey butchered helpless niggers,
['Cause] dey had a mind for murder.
What did de screaming woman say?
I ain't done no wrong at all,
Just tried to 'fend my little home;
I can only weep and moan,
White folks got my body,
   Oh, Lord! Have mercy on my soul,
   Have mercy, have mercy on my soul.

What did de lynchers do?
Dey shot a helpless woman
In de back begging mercy.
What did de weeping woman say?
I ain't done no wrong at all.
Just tried to 'fend my little home;
I can only weep and moan,
White folks got my body,
   Oh, Lord! Have mercy on my soul,
   Have mercy, have mercy on my soul.

What did de lynchers say?
We shot a bunch of niggers,
And we'll kill some white folks, too.
What did de bruised and weeping woman say?
I ain't done no wrong at all,
Just tried to 'fend my little home;
I can only weep and moan,
White folks got my body,
   Oh, Lord! Have mercy on my soul,
   Have mercy, have mercy on my soul.

* Z Y D E C O A N D
B A L L A D S F R O M
L O U I S I A N A C R E O L E S
O F C O L O R *

SYBIL KEIN

Zydeco Calinda

· *From the album* Creole Ballads & Zydeco ·

According to poet, folklorist, and composer Sybil Kein, "Zydeco Calinda" is perhaps the oldest of the Zydeco songs. Kein's comments to me in a letter provide important information about this song. She wrote:

Calinda was a slave dance which was noted by the Dominican missionaries who first witnessed it in the West Indies. . . . However, this dance was soon banned in the colonies as it was considered very lewd. Curiously there is written evidence that the nuns in the Caribbean did this dance on Christmas in their convents. The extant verse is verse number one. I wrote the second verse.

1. Allons dansé, Calinda,
   Allons dansé Calinda
   Pendant ta mère est pas là
   pour fais faché yé vieille femmes.
   C'est pas tout monde qui connais
   Dansé, dansé de longtemps.
   Pendant ta mère est pas la, Allons dansé, Calinda!
   Ét Toi!

2. Allons dansé Calinda,
   Allons dansé Calinda.
   Si to fais sa, Calinda
   To fais bontemps, Calinda.
   Allons dansé Calinda,
   Allons dansé, Calinda.
   Si to fais sa, Calinda,
   To fais bon temps, Calinda!

1. Come dance the Calinda
   while your mother is not home
   to make the old women angry.
   It is not everyone who knows
   how to dance the old dances.
   While your mother is not home,
   come dance the Calinda. And you!

2. Come dance the Calinda,
   come dance the Calinda.
   If you do that,
   you will have a good time.
   (repeat)

SYBIL KEIN

Salé Dame

· *From the album* Creole Ballads & Zydeco ·

Sybil Kein first heard this song from her great aunt Julia Boudreaux more than forty years ago. She notes that her "Aunt Tee" (Ms. Boudreaux) drank bourbon. Kein's version here is based on the folk song which exists in several versions.

Chorus:
Salé, Salé Dame, Salé Dame Bonjour.
Salé, Salé Dame, Salé Dame Bonjour.
Salé, Salé Dame, Salé Dame Bonjour.
Salé Salé Dame, Salé Dame Bonjour.

Verse:
Denise cuit filé gumbo;
Mo l'aimé filé gumbo
Denise l'aimé bois bon duvin,
Mo l'aimé mo bourbon

(repeat Chorus)

[Translation:]

Chorus:
Salty Woman, Salty Woman, Salty Woman, good day.
Salty Woman, Salty Woman, Salty Woman, good day.
Salty Woman, Salty Woman, Salty Woman, good day.
Salty Woman, Salty Woman, Salty Woman, good day.

Verse:
Denise, she cooks file gumbo,
Me, I like file gumbo.
Denise, she drinks her cherry wine.
Me, I like my bourbon.

(repeat Chorus)

SYBIL KEIN

Éh, La Bas

· *From the album* Creole Ballads and Zydeco ·

"Éh, La Bas" is a greeting, comparable to hello or aloha. According to Sybil Kein this is *the* most popular of the Creole songs in New Orleans. In her letter to me, Kein provided other interesting information about the song:

My mother remembered hearing this song on Carnival day when she was a teenager. It was sung by men dressed as women who played small guitars (c. 1922). They would try to outdo each other by making up the most and sometimes the most risqué verses, all in the manner of the calypso men of the West Indies. They made them up in Creole as they sang them. Mardi Gras for Creoles was celebrated on Claiborne Avenue between St. Bernard Avenue and Canal Street. It was a beautiful, tree-lined street where families had picnics and small groups of musicians entertained. The arrangement of this tune is mine as is the last verse about going to Bourbon Street (a street in the French Quarter where there are night clubs which cater to bar top dancing and the like).

The last verse about going to Bourbon Street is Kein's addition to the folk song.

Éh, La Bas, Éh, La Bas, Éh, La Bas, chèr;
comment sa va?
Éh, La Bas, Éh, La Bas, Éh, La Bas, chèrie;
comment sa va?

1. Mo donné li so café.
   Mo donné li so dusucre.
   Et tout quichose mo donné li,
   li té tres satisfé.

2. Mo chèr cousin, so cher quizine;
   mo l'aimé so laquizine.
   Mo mangé bien, mo bois duvin,
   et sa pas couté-moin narien.

3. Mo allez dans la halle
   pour cherché coubion.
   Le coubion, li té pas bon,
   et sa donne-moi ledérangement.

4. Mo allez à la rue Bourbon
   pour cherché pour yé beau garçons.
   Yé beau garcons pas gain l'argent
   mais yé donne moin plen bon temps.

   [Translation:]

   Hello over there, dear
   (repeat)

1. I gave him his coffee,
   I gave him his sugar.
   I gave him everything
   and he's very satisfied.

2. My dear cousin, I love her dear kitchen.
   I eat well, I drink wine
   and that does not costs me anything!

3. I went to the market
   to buy some fish.
   The fish was not good
   and it gave me diarrhea.

4. I went on Bourbon Street
   To look for some young men.
   They had no money
   but they showed me a good time.

SYBIL KEIN

Maw-maw's Creole Lullaby

· *From the album* Creole Ballads & Zydeco ·

This lullaby is one that Sybil Kein's mother sang to her and her twelve siblings.
Kein notes in a letter to me, "I would stand with my feet on the side of the rocker
she sat in while she rocked the newest baby to sleep. This is where I heard the
song for many years. I added verse two because I could often see the moon from
the window in my mother's room."

1. Fais dodo, mo l'aime mo ti chère,
   Fais dodo, dodo sans douleur.
   Fais dodo, mo l'aime mo ti chère,
   Fais dodo, dodo sans douleur.
   (repeat)

   Maw-Maw gain gateaux,
   Paw-Paw gain bonbons
   Yé donne sa à toi,
   si bébé dodo.

2. Fais dodo, la lune dans le ciel-la
   Fais dodo, li brille pour toi.
   Fais dodo, la lune dans le ciel-la.
   Fais dodo, dodo jist pour moi.

Maw-Maw gain gateaux.
Paw-Paw gain bonbons.
Yé donne sa à toi,
si bébé dodo.

Fais dodo, mo l'aime mo ti chère.
Fais dodo, dodo sans douleur.
Fais dodo, mo l'aime mo ti chère.
Fais dodo, dodo sans douleur.

[Translation:]

1. Go to sleep, I love my little dear one.
   Go to sleep, sleep without grief.
   Go to sleep, I love my little dear one.
   Go to sleep, sleep without grief.

2. Go to sleep. The moon's in the sky there.
   Go to sleep, it shines for you.
   Go to sleep, the moon's in the sky there.
   Go to sleep, it shines for you.

   Mama has some cake
   Papa has candy.
   They give that to you
   if baby goes to sleep.

   Go to sleep, I love my little dear one.
   Go to sleep, sleep without grief.
   Go to sleep. I love my little dear one.
   Go to sleep, sleep without grief.

❋ R A P ❋

The often bitter, obscene, and misogynistic lyrics of contemporary rap have created much controversy in American society: the media and community groups have attacked raps; rap groups have been hauled into court;[11] recording companies have pulled their music from the shelves; and presidential candidate Bill Clinton assailed Sister Souljar during his campaign.[12] The more that society attempts to repress and protest and argue with the lyrics, however, the more publicity they give to the songs and the rappers—often increasing their popularity.

As offensive as much rap is (and the so-called gangster rap often overshadows the clean rap and the Christian rap, the rap designed to save and teach), the rappers are usually speaking to issues of concern to the young Black audiences who embrace them (but audiences far removed from the problems of the urban ghettos that they usually address have also become enthusiastic fans). Their raps are their weapons, and they have proven to be very powerful ones.

Because permissions for reprinting raps are generally so expensive, only one of the selections that I intended to use is reproduced here. Rap selections, however, are listed in "Audio-Visual Resources" and can easily be obtained on cassettes and CDs.

[11]The most publicized case was the trial of 2 Live Crew on obscenity charges, where noted critic Henry Louis Gates Jr. defended them on the grounds that rap is a traditional form of Black folklore.

[12]Clinton attacked Sister Souljar for allegedly declaring, "If black people kill black people, every day, why not have a week and kill white people?" Immediately Sister Souljar was in demand on TV talk shows and the college lecture circuit.

DE LA SOUL

Ghetto Thang

· *From the album* 3 Feet High and Rising ·

Poj is Posdnuos (b. Kelvin Mercer) and *Dove* is Trugoy the Dove
(b. David Jolicoeur).

Poj:

(Mary had a little lamb)
That's a fib, she had two twins though
And one crib
Now she's only fourteen, what a start
But this defect is ground common in these parts
Now life in this world can be such a bitch
And dreams are often torn and shattered and hard to stitch
Negative's the attitude that runs the show
When the stage is the G-H-E-T-T-O

Dove:

Which is the one to blame when bullets blow
Either Peter, Jane, or John or Joe
But Joe can't shoot a gun, he's always drunk
And Peter's pimping Jane, and John's a punk
Infested are the halls, also the brains
Daddy's broken down from ghetto pains
Mommy's flying high, the truth is shown
The kids are all alone
'Cause it's just the ghetto thang
IT'S JUST THE GHETTO THANG (WORD)

Poj:

Who ranks the baddest brother, the ones who rule
This title is sought by the coolest fool
Define coolest fool? Easy, the one who needs
Attention in the largest span and loves to lead
Always found at the jams, but never dance

Just provoke violence due to one glance
The future plays no matter, just the present flow
When the greeting place is the G-H-E-T-T-O

Dove:
Lies are pointed strong into your skull
Deep within your brain against the wall
To hide or just erase the glowing note
Of how to use the ghetto as a scapegoat
Truth from Trugoy's mouth is here to scar
Those who blame the G for all bizarre
So open up your vents and record well
For this is where we stand, for the true tell
Ghetto gained a ghetto name from ghetto ways
Now there could be some ghetto gangs and ghetto play
If ghetto thang can have its way in ghetto rage
Then there must be some ghetto love and ghetto change
Though confident they keep it kept, we know for fact
They lie like ghettos form, 'cause people lack
To see that they must all get out the ghetto hold
The truth they never told
'Cause it's just the ghetto thang
IT'S JUST THE GHETTO THANG (WORD)

Pos:
Do people really wish when they blow
Out the cake candles, and if so
Is it for the sunken truth which could arise
From out the characters in which the ghetto hides
Roses in the ring supply their shown relief
Granted it's planted by their shown belief
Kill and feed off your own brother man
Has quickly been adopted as the master plan
Posses of our people has yet to provoke
Freedom or death to them, it's just a joke
What causes this defect, I don't know

Maybe it's the G-H-E-T-T-O

IT'S JUST THE GHETTO THANG (WORD)

Standing in the rain is nothing felt
When problems hold more value, but never dealt with
Buildings crumbling to the ground
Impact noise is solid sound
But who's the one to say this life is wrong
When ghetto life is chosen strong
We seem to be misled about our dreams
But dreams ain't what it seems
When it's just the ghetto thang

IT'S JUST THE GHETTO THANG (WORD)

Chapter 3

The Style of Soul

God created black people, and black people created style.
—George C. Wolfe, *The Colored Museum*

While the distinctive style of soul is evident in every aspect of the African American's folk expression from juba to jive[1] and from proverbs to prayers, and while we shall view it in every chapter in this book, it is important in any study of Black folk culture to carve out some small space that focuses on what is generally called in the folk community *style, stylin'*, or *stylin' out*, a certain distinctive manner of walking, dressing, talking, dancing, being. Style is, unfortunately, the most difficult aspect of culture to document in recorded words or even pictures, though it is clearly evident in any firsthand observation of particular individuals in the community. Style is also the area of Black life that has most often been reduced to caricature and stereotype since it often teeters on the edge of exaggerated display. The most common adjective that the outside community has used to describe Black style has been "ludicrous," and its efforts to interpret and picture it in newspaper cartoons, minstrel shows, vaudeville performances, stage dramas, and

---

[1] I borrow here an expression that serves as the title of Clarence Major's *Juba to Jive: A Dictionary of African-American Slang.*

TV situation comedies have ranged from the patronizing or sympathetic to the vicious and malevolent. No matter what the motive, efforts at presenting African American style almost always denigrate it.

Despite the larger community's historical demeaning of African American style (as indeed it has all too often demeaned every other area of Black culture), the fact is that it has evinced an ongoing fascination with that style. From the beginning, Whites' descriptions of enslaved people reflect an obsession with their dress, their speech, their laughter, their demeanor, and their rhythm. Whites have demonstrated the same measure of disdain and fascination toward everything from the way enslaved people patted juba during slavery to the way frat brothers stomp in step shows; from the way they strut down the road with a load on their heads to the way women handle their babies; from the way players sported zoot suits to the way rappers flaunt huge gold chains; from the way chicks roll their eyes to the way cool cats speak. Often these observations of Black style are followed by efforts in the larger community to imitate it, a practice that in the 1990s gave us the blended term "wiggers"—White youths who attempted to act like "niggers." Among the de rigueur items for these young White males were the caps turned backward on their heads and the baggy pants, both popularized by inner-city Black youngsters. Indeed as early as 1927, H. L. Mencken declared, "No dance invented by white men has been danced at any genuinely high-toned shindig in America since the far-off days of the Wilson Administration; the debutantes and their mothers now revolve their hips to coon steps and coon steps only" (Mel Watkins quotes Mencken in an undated *American Mercury* article in his book *On the Real Side*). And many are the White comedians, jazz musicians, rock-and-roll stars, and rappers who have written of their close observation of their Black mentors and their conscious efforts to imitate them.

Though there are African Americans who reject, ridicule, and disassociate themselves from those traits manifesting Black style, many others proudly acclaim it as an affirmation of their racial identity, one that distinguishes them as "hip," "cool," "groovy," "down," "with it," "in the know"—or whatever the current slang is that denotes a person with style. Ralph Ellison noted in *Shadow and Act* that as he and his friends in Oklahoma observed "the eloquence of some Negro preacher, the strength and grace of some local athlete, the ruthlessness of some businessman-physician, the elegance in dress and manners of some headwaiter or hotel doorman," they were developing their own "Negro American style." He continued, "We recognized and were proud of our group's own style wherever we discerned it — in jazzmen and prizefighters, ballplayers and tap dancers; in gesture, inflection, intonation, timbre and phrasing. . . . [We] recognized within it an affirmation of life beyond all question of our difficulties as Negroes." In *Steppin' on the Blues,* Jacqui Malone confirms the "great significance [African American performing artists attach] to personal style and dress" and goes on to point out elements of the distinctive style of many of the great performers. Many would argue that without style, one does not have Soul.[2]

A significant aspect of style, especially for young Black males, is in their stance. At varied times, certain postures are cool. These postures may be defined by the way one puts his hand in his pockets, in his belt, by his sides, behind his back; by the position of his legs and feet; by the tilt of his head and shoulders.

One of the first observable aspects of style in the Black community is the way the individuals move. Black motion is ideally a kind of dance; and human bodies, like the inanimate objects to which Robert Farris Thompson refers in a different context in *African Art in Motion,* "are made more impressively themselves by motion." A youthful and graceful body is a thing of beauty, made even more so when it is in motion. In African American communities, people are judged by the way they (literally) walk that walk. The most notable aspect of this style is what, among men, has various been called by such terms as *bop, slide, bebop, dip,* and *shooting the agate.*[3] With head and hands held in a certain position, the man struts out in a cool, jivey motion designed to distinguish him from the squares, and "individualist enough to distinguish him from other 'cool' folks as well."[4] The

[2]Clarence Major defines soul as "the essence of blackness." Jimmie Lee declares, "It's not soulful to try and spell out exactly what soul is" (*Soul Food Cookbook*).

[3]Jelly Roll Morton describes shooting the agate in the selection from *Mister Jelly Roll.*

[4]The quoted phrase is a critical addition suggested by Trudier Harris (letter to Dance, August 25, 2000).

walk must, of necessity, change periodically, lest the "hicks" copy it, but certain basic characteristic of its style convey its lineage. Among women "the walk" is characterized by the subject's graceful balance—head held high, long neck straight, shoulders back, hips swinging—moving with the grace of one who can and does/did walk three miles over rough terrain without spilling a drop of a full container of water balanced on her head. Hers is the carriage of one who, in the words of Maya Angelou, walks "like [she's] got oil wells / Pumping in [her] living room" ("Still I Rise"). In her popular "Phenomenal Woman," Angelou's speaker explains why she, who does not fit the model of the beautiful woman, is so attractive to men that they swarm around her and fall down on their knees before her: the secret, among other things, is in "the grace of my style"—the way she flashes her teeth, swings her waist, curls her lips, arches her back, clicks her heels, and strides. Angelou's is the portrait of a woman with that ineffable something called style.

Another expression of style is found in marching, stepping, and dancing. These activities of African Americans have also attracted the attention of outside observers, who have again noted, ridiculed, and copied everything from the Cakewalk and Turkey Trot through the Charleston, Black Bottom, and Lindy Hop, to the moonwalk. Always outsiders have been amazed at Black rhythm and polyrhythm. In varied tones, voyeurs express amazement at how dancers can coordinate movements of the hands, hips, shoulders, arms, knees, and feet. They are awed at the spectacular feats the dancers and their partners can accomplish with their bodies. Most bewildering, of course, are the constant variations Black dancers add to their routines, thus frustrating onlookers determined to copy their intricate steps. Indeed, Langston Hughes asserted, "house-rent parties began to flourish [during the Harlem Renaissance]—and not always to raise the rent either. But, as often as not, to have a get-together of one's own, where you could do the black-bottom with no stranger behind you trying to do it, too" (*Big Sea*).

In dance, as in other folk expressions, Black people sometimes mask and ridicule. As Jacqui Malone points out, there has been a long history of Black "derision dancing," beginning with the cakewalk, which was a conscious parody the Negroes did of the masters' minuet.

Whatever the dance in the Black community, an important element is style, grace, and flair. This is no doubt an influence from Africa, where, Robert Farris Thompson tells us, the goal is to add something to one's dance or walking "to show [one's] beauty, to attract the attention of those around" the dancer *(African Art in Motion)*. One of his informants compared good dancing to the "smart motion of the leopard in the forest or to the iridescent vibration of the feathers of the Pin-Tailed Whydah, when shaking his plumage during the mating season to display his feathers to full effect." Natural grace and flair are certainly elements that continue to be prized in dancing among African Americans.

Most Black children grow up observing and learning to dance. I have often seen tiny children get out in the aisle or up on the stage during musical performances to join in dances. It is not unusual for them to joyously clap their hands, tap their feet, swing their shoulders, and move their heads to the rhythms of music even before they can walk. Children's play incorporates dances of many sorts, and the influence of dance can be seen in several popular games, such as jumping double-dutch.

Group dances have long been popular in Black communities. Groups of dancers always flock to the floor at Black socials for the Soul Train or varied other line dances or to join a group doing coordinated routines, such as the Mashed Potato, the Funky Chicken, the Birdland, the Macarena, the Madison, the Electric Slide, the New Electric Slide, or the Booty Call.

A combination of marching and dancing has also marked several Black folk forms, among the earliest of which was the funeral march. This seems to have been common during slavery, but has disappeared in most places, except in New Orleans, where it still occasionally takes place. Despite the band's sad tone as the family and friends march to the grave, it strikes up a lively melody on the return. These marches bear some similarities to the street marches and parades seen in celebrations, such as the Negro Election parades of eighteenth-century New England,[5] which William D. Piersen sug-

---

[5] Jane deForest Shelton discusses these in detail in "The New England Negro." She dates the marches to at least 1756, when the enslaved (and later free) Negroes of Connecticut elected their own governor and lieutenant governor and held a "grand" parade, dinner, and dance afterward in Derby.

gests may be the genesis of America's contemporary inaugural and other political parades ("African-American Festive Style"). Other popular parades of note in Black communities include the Jonkonnu (John Canoe, John Kooner, John Kuner) parades in eighteenth- and nineteenth-century North Carolina; the antebellum Pinkster parades in New York; the parades sponsored by Marcus Garvey and his Universal Negro Improvement Association in Harlem in the 1920s; Chicago's 1912 State Street Carnival; varied cities' Juneteenth[6] or Emancipation or Liberation parades; Brooklyn's annual Labor Day "Mas" Parade;[7] FAMU's (Florida A&M University) performance in Miami's Orange Blossom Classic Football Game Parade and halftime show;[8] and New Orleans's annual Mardi Gras, in which Blacks often parody the White Carnival societies and burlesque famous local Whites. Elsewhere in the Diaspora several celebrations similar to Mardi Gras are held: Carnival in Trinidad and Brazil, and Festival in Jamaica. In most of these parades costuming is a major part of the style. With Garvey, military attire was de rigueur; and, of course, in Mardi Gras there are some of the most elaborate outfits imaginable. In all of the parades, large groups of people often fall into synchronized, intricate steps as they march through the streets—stepping, twisting, swaying, sliding, kicking, rotating their pelvises, twirling their bodies, throwing batons, changing directions, weaving in and out, achieving interesting and signifying formations. Ralph Ellison's Invisible Man uses a street parade to drum up support for the Brotherhood, organizing a "People's Hot Foot Squad" to "[drill] fancy formations" and a group of majorettes who "pranced and twirled and just plain girled." These forms may be found in military groups in the United States armed forces from the Revolutionary War and the Civil War, where Black military bands became famous, until the present day. Black sergeants have often

---

[6]In June 1865, the enslaved people of Texas learned—two and one-half years later than most Americans—that they had been freed. Juneteenth is a combining of June and nineteenth, the day the news was announced by Union General Gordon Granger. It was officially declared a state holiday in 1980.

[7]This celebrates Trinidad's independence and includes masking.

[8]Every Black college, of course, has its homecoming and other football parades.

led their troops in foot-stomping syncopation performed while singing lyrics, both the steps and the songs growing directly out of Black tradition. These kinds of performances have become most familiar to a larger public through the half-time shows of Black college bands at major league football games.

It should be noted that the bands are not the only ones dancing during parades. African Americans are often not merely observers but participants in the show. The practice of a group of people dancing behind the bands is so popular in New Orleans that it is called the Second Line.

Closely related to the marching bands and the stomping military units are the fraternity and sorority step shows or stomp shows, now so popular on both Black and White college campuses, in which the African American Greeks develop lyrics and intricate steps to attack their competitors and to sing the praises of their own groups. These are closely related to the fraternity and sorority lines, which were popular when I was in college in the 1950s. We dressed alike and went out on the campus in a synchronized line, singing, marching, and stepping. Now much the same performance is given on a stage and called a step show.

Also related is the *stroll*, a practice of simply walking down the street styling and showing off one's fashions. In August 1927 the *New York Times* reported the practice of Blacks with "enviable physique[s]" who "strutt[ed] the streets of the 'Black Belt' . . . in the latest and newest creations of the tailor's and dressmaker's art." An interesting illustration of strolling is found annually at the popular CIAA basketball tournament,[9] during which an unidentified dandy, dubbed Mr. CIAA, strolls through the bleachers throughout the game dressed in an expensive and stylish suit with identically colored shirt, tie, hat, socks, shoes, and umbrella. He changes four or five times during the game, and when he reappears wearing a new color (including yellow, purple, powder blue, and white — always in attire

[9]The Central Intercollegiate Athletic Association's annual championship between historically Black Southern colleges is one of the big events of the year for these schools. To accommodate the large crowds that travel from all over the nation to attend, the tournament is always held in big city coliseums rather than on any of the college campuses, and Southern cities vie for the privilege of hosting the games.

matching the color of one of the member schools of the CIAA Conference), the announcers often make note of his entrance and the audience gasps and applauds. Though he has become an icon at the games, having been on the scene for more than fifteen years,[10] his appearance is not without controversy—some of the macho men consider him much too effeminate. (See the color photo section for pictures of Mr. CIAA.)

Another expression of the distinctive African American style can be seen in gestures and kinesics. Men, in particular, tend to develop varying styles of handshakes, slaps, "giving skin," and other greetings. The raised fist is another powerful, often male, icon. Black women are noted for a number of gestures: eye-rolling, eyebrow-arching, head-bobbing, neck-swiveling, hip-swinging, finger-pointing, and several other gesticulations that form a dynamic vocabulary of their own. All of this is a part of their sassiness, a term used to denote a mixture of impudence, sauciness, wit, self-assurance, determination, and style.

Another element of African Americans' style is their hair. Certainly no more elaborate and striking hair styles can be created by any ethnic group than Africans, whose hair texture allows many forms of cutting, shaving, braiding, cornrowing, weaving, twisting, coiling, locking,[11] knotting, and bushing not possible with straight hair. Historically African cultures have developed distinctive hair styles and decorations, including the use of combs, shells, beads, colored buttons, yarn, and strips of rags. African women have also perfected an unending array of wraps with gorgeous cloths. Despite the numerous striking and distinctive Black hairstyles, many African and Diaspora Black women often reveal a marked preference for straight hair. They have devised a number of processes to straighten

---

[10]CIAA aficionado Al Rozier told me that in the past, several people would stroll through the stands in stylish outfits, but when Mr. CIAA came on the scene and upstaged all the others with his fashions, it became a one-man show. Though no one I talked with knew his name, he was identified in a newspaper article as Abraham "Ham" Mitchell.

[11]Dreadlocks have become popular since the assent of the Rastafarians in Jamaica in the second half of the twentieth century. Though the origins of the movement go back at least to the thirties, it did not receive much attention until the sixties and seventies.

their curly or kinky hair and a number of ways in which to style it. The first Black female millionaire,[12] Madame C. J. Walker, made her fortune by developing hair straighteners, and the beauty salon remains among the most profitable businesses in Black communities from Africa and Europe to America and the Caribbean. With the weave today, some might argue that tossing her long (often blond) hair (a practice of White women so long satirized in the Black community) is now a part of the Black woman's styling out. It also used to be quite fashionable for Black men to straighten or process their hair (a procedure that Malcolm X describes in painful detail in *The Autobiography of Malcolm X*), although it is no longer a common practice.

A major aspect of the style of soul is clothing. Given the pitiable, drab, and coarse clothing (if any) allotted to the enslaved people, it is amazing how often descriptions of slave runaways and of slaves in church and at parties indicate quite elegant clothing of the finest fabrics and the most elaborate accoutrements, such as gold lace, silver buckles, silk hats, kid gloves, and the like. It was not unusual, as Shane and Graham White indicate in *Stylin'*, for slaves to be more stylishly dressed than their owners on certain occasions. While it is clear from accounts of both Whites and Blacks that often these fashionable outfits resulted from hand-me-downs from owners or of actual thefts (or "borrowings") of their masters' clothes, it also appears that at least a few Blacks found varied ways through their craftiness, industry, and talents to secure or make some fine clothing of their own—clothing that inspired some awe from observers. One of the most popular of the slave tales describes Slave John's delight when his master left home, whereupon he dressed up in the White man's finest clothes, got out his best wine, had the table set with his finest silver, and grandly hosted a party for all the slaves (see "Abe and Dinah" in *Shuckin' and Jivin'*).

From the time that Elizabeth Keckley served as dressmaker for First Lady Mary Todd Lincoln, a number of Black designers have influenced fashion, though they often have not received the media at-

---

[12]In a recent book, *On Her Own Ground: The Life and Times of Madam C. J. Walker,* A'Lelia Bundles, Madam Walker's great-great-granddaughter, says that Walker was never a millionaire per se—but history generally accords her this honor, and by today's standards her wealth far exceeded a million dollars.

tention enjoyed by their successful White counterparts. Black designers are as likely to find their motivation in African and African American fashion that developed in the folk context as in New York and Paris fashion houses. Afro-inspired designs are notable too for their beautiful color combinations, frequently making use of red, green, black, and gold, which symbolize African unity. Generally it is suggested that red represents the blood shed, green represents the African lands, black represents the color of African people, and gold represents the riches stolen from Africa.

It is perhaps important to acknowledge that African Americans have always both imitated and parodied White fashions. Tuxedos, top hats, derbies, French berets, military uniforms, nylon stockings, pointed toe shoes, bonnets, hot pants, straight flowing hair, and scores of other popular European and White American styles from the seventeenth century to the present day have been eagerly copied and shown off or caricatured by Negroes.

Fashionably dressed African Americans attract favorable attention within their communities. Frances Smith Foster asserts that Elizabeth Keckley's "manner was so dignified and her attire so grand that many worshipers [at the Fifteenth Avenue Presbyterian Church in Washington, D.C.] arrived early in order to witness the arrival of the woman they knew as 'Madame Keckley' " (*Written by Herself*). And slave narrator Gustavus Vassa notes how much more attention he received from women when he dressed in the "Georgia superfine blue clothes" he purchased upon receiving his freedom.

Each era, of course, has its own faddish styles, and time does not permit a full discussion. Many periods have much in common as might be seen by a closer look at the zoot-suit culture of the 1930s and the hip-hop cultures of the past three decades. In every period Black men and women who are styling out manifest a preference for hats and other headwear. Men have adorned themselves variously in large wide-brimmed hats, derbies, the big knitted "tea-cozy" caps made popular by the Rastafarians, and athletic caps turned backward. It is interesting to note that one of the items in the John Jasper museum is a wide-brimmed hat, characteristic of the stylishness of the popular slave minister (see selections from Jasper in chapters 3 and 5). In addition to their elaborate headwraps, Black women undoubtedly design the most unique hats of any group.

Often the larger culture is so disturbed about some Black styles that it attempts to prohibit or restrict them. During slavery, for instance, many Whites castigated Blacks who dressed "above their condition" and some laws were even passed outlawing such dress attire for Blacks. In *Stylin'*, Shane and Graham White point to a 1735 South Carolina edict forbidding slaves to wear their owners' cast-off clothes, and William Wiggins cites a law in Massachusetts prohibiting "men and women of meane condition" from wearing "the garb of gentlemen." Shane and Graham White also identify a 1942 regulation that made zoot suits illegal; and a few localities have attempted to outlaw pants that fall down below the hips and reveal underwear (a style popular during the waning years of the twentieth century).

Everything from the way African Americans tell their tales, through the manner in which they move, to the choice of their outfits reflects the style of soul. The striking style of a number of its Black citizens has forever changed the nature of American life: the moment John Jasper stepped into the pulpit, American preaching would never be the same; the moment Sojourner Truth strode onto the stage, a new drama enlivened political debate; the moment Marcus Garvey marched out into New York streets, parades took on a new fervor; the moment Josephine Baker brought the house down in *La Revue nègre* in Paris, the Jazz Age took on new meaning; the moment Jackie Robinson walked onto the Brooklyn Dodgers field, American professional sports would never be the same;[13] the moment Muhammad Ali declared himself the greatest, boxing acquired a new and unaccustomed panache; the moment Martin Luther King proclaimed his dream, a new level of rhetoric was born; and the moment FloJo[14] sprinted to Olympic victory with her haute couture

[13]Much might be noted about distinctive aspects of the Black basketball and football players as well—their style of play, showmanship, celebratory dances, and the like. Something of an exaggeration of this style has kept the Harlem Globetrotters a popular phenomenon for years. For one commentary on this frequently noted aspect of Black sports, see Jeff Greenfield, "The Black and White Truth about Basketball," in which he calls the distinction between Black and White players "a question of style": . . . " 'White' ball . . . is the basketball of patience and method. 'Black' ball is the basketball of electric self-expression."

And let's not even mention Dennis Rodman!

[14]Florence Griffith Joyner was generally referred to by the media as FloJo.

tights, long, glittering nails, and flowing hair, a new glamour astounded the world of racing. According to Ralph Ellison (in his discussion of what America would be like without Blacks), African American style is what gives this nation its "color." He goes on to declare, "Without the presence of Negro American style, our [American] jokes, our tall tales, even our sports would be lacking in the sudden turns, the shocks, the swift changes of pace (all jazz shaped) that serve to remind us that the world is ever unexplored, and that while a complete mastery of life is mere illusion, the real secret of the game is to make life swing" (*Going to the Territory*).

Many of the selections here are accounts by White viewers because they were the most frequent or only early recorders of Black life and characters. Despite the denigrating tone of a number of them, they convey (if we can read beyond the racist stereotyping) some sense of the style of soul among early African Americans.

HARRIET BEECHER STOWE
Looking Down on Her
· *From Dorothy Sterling,* We Are Your Sisters ·

Though Sojourner Truth, as described in the following account by noted novelist Harriet Beecher Stowe, is not dressed in the finest of fabrics, some element of style is to be noted in her turban. But the real element of style obvious here is Truth's charisma, sassiness, and a seeming conceit in her carriage that evidently disconcerts the famous White woman accustomed to perceiving Blacks as inferior people.

I do not recollect ever to have been conversant with any one who had more of that silent and subtle power which we call personal presence than this woman. Her tall form is still vivid to my mind. She was dressed in some stout, grayish stuff, neat and clean, though dusty from travel. On her head she wore a bright Madras handkerchief, arranged as a turban. She seemed perfectly self possessed and at her ease; in fact there was almost an unconscious superiority, not unmixed with a solemn twinkle of humor, in the odd composed manner in which she looked down on me.

SOLOMON NORTHUP

The Poetry of Motion

· *From* Twelve Years a Slave ·

Here Northup recalls his pleasure in playing the violin and the popularity it
afforded him as an entertainer at White and Black gatherings, the most
memorable of which were the Christmas dances. The sarcastic swipe at White
slave owners also reveals Northup's pride in Black style.

The Christmas dance! Oh, ye pleasure-seeking sons and daughters of idleness, who move with measured step, listless and snail-like,
through the slow winding cotillion, if ye wish to look upon the
celebrity, if not the "poetry of motion"—upon genuine happiness,
rampant and unrestrained—go down to Louisiana and see the slaves
dancing in the starlight of a Christmas night.

WILLIAM WELLS BROWN

Corn-Shucking and Christmas Festivities

· *From* My Southern Home: or, The South and Its People ·

The pleasures enjoyed by the slaves in the few entertainments allotted them is
recalled by William Wells Brown in his accounts of the annual corn-shucking and
Christmas celebrations on the plantation in St. Louis.

An old-fashioned corn-shucking took place once a year, on "Poplar
Farm," which afforded pleasant amusement for the out-door negroes
for miles around. On these occasions, the servants, on all plantations, were allowed to attend by mere invitation of the blacks where
the corn was to be shucked.

As the grain was brought in from the field, it was left in a pile near
the corn-cribs. The night appointed, and invitations sent out, slaves
from plantations five or six miles away, would assemble and join on
the road, and in large bodies march along, singing their melodious
plantation songs.

To hear three or four of these gangs coming from different directions, their leaders giving out the words, and the whole company

joining in the chorus, would indeed surpass anything ever produced by "Haverly's Ministrels," and many of their jokes and witticisms were never equalled by Sam Lucas or Billy Kersands.

A supper was always supplied by the planter on whose farm the shucking was to take place. Often when approaching the place, the singers would speculate on what they were going to have for supper. The following song was frequently sung:

All dem puty gals will be dar,
    Shuck dat corn before you eat.
Dey will fix it fer us rare,
    Shuck dat corn before you eat.
I know dat supper will be big,
    Shuck dat corn before you eat.
I think I smell a fine roast pig,
    Shuck dat corn before you eat.
A supper is provided, so dey said,
    Shuck dat corn before you eat.
I hope dey'll have some nice wheat bread,
    Shuck dat corn before you eat.
I hope dey'll have some coffee dar,
    Shuck dat corn before you eat.
I hope dey'll have some whisky dar,
    Shuck dat corn before you eat.
I think I'll fill my pockets full,
    Shuck dat corn before you eat.
Stuff dat coon an' bake him down,
    Shuck dat corn before you eat.
I speck some niggers dar from town,
    Shuck dat corn before you eat.
Please cook dat turkey nice an' brown.
    Shuck dat corn before you eat.
By de side of dat turkey I'll be foun',
    Shuck dat corn before you eat.
I smell de supper, dat I do,
    Shuck dat corn before you eat.
On de table will be a stew,
    Shuck dat corn before you eat.

Burning pine knots, held by some of the boys, usually furnished light for the occasion. Two hours is generally sufficient time to finish up a large shucking; where five hundred bushels of corn is thrown into the cribs as the shuck is taken off. The work is made comparatively light by the singing, which never ceases till they go to the supper table. Something like the following is sung during the evening:

De possum meat am good to eat,
    Carve him to de heart;
You'll always find him good and sweet,
    Carve him to de heart;
My dog did bark, and I went to see,
    Carve him to de heart;
And dar was a possum up dat tree,
    Carve him to de heart.

Chorus. —Carve dat possum, carve dat possum children,
    Carve dat possum, carve him to de heart;
    Oh, carve dat possum, carve dat possum children,
    Carve dat possum, carve him to de heart.

I reached up for to pull him in,
    Carve him to de heart;
De possum he began to grin,
    Carve him to de heart;
I carried him home and dressed him off,
    Carve him to de heart;
I hung him dat night in de frost,
    Carve him to de heart.

Chorus. —Carve dat possum [etc.]

De way to cook de possum sound,
    Carve him to de heart;
Fust par-bile him, den bake him brown,
    Carve him to de heart;
Lay sweet potatoes in de pan,
    Carve him to de heart;

De sweetest eatin' in de lan',
    Carve him to de heart.

Chorus. — Carve dat possum [etc.]

Should a poor supper be furnished, on such an occasion, you would hear remarks from all parts of the table:

"Take dat rose pig 'way from dis table."

"What rose pig? you see any rose pig here?"

"Ha, ha, ha! Dis ain't de place to see rose pig."

"Pass up some dat turkey wid clam sauce."

"Don't talk about dat turkey; he was gone afore we come."

"Dis is de las' time I shucks corn at dis farm."

"Dis is a cheap farm, cheap owner, an' a cheap supper."

"He's talkin' it, ain't he?"

"Dis is de tuffest meat dat I is been called upon to eat fer many a day; you's got to have teeth sharp as a saw to eat dis meat."

"Spose you ain't got no teef, den what you gwine to do?"

"Why, ef you ain't got no teef you muss *gum it*!"

"Ha, ha, ha!" from the whole company, was heard.

On leaving the corn-shucking farm, each gang of men, headed by their leader, would sing during the entire journey home. Some few, however, having their dogs with them, would start on the trail of a coon, possum, or some other game, which might keep them out till nearly morning.

To the Christmas holidays, the slaves were greatly indebted for winter recreation; for long custom had given to them the whole week from Christmas day to the coming in of the New Year.

On "Poplar Farm," the hands drew their share of clothing on Christmas day for the year. The clothing for both men and women was made up by women kept for general sewing and housework. One pair of pants, and two shirts, made the entire stock for a male field hand.

The women's garments were manufactured from the same goods that the men received. Many of the men worked at night for themselves, making splint and corn brooms, baskets, shuck mats, and axe-handles, which they would sell in the city during Christmas week. Each slave was furnished with a pass, something like the following:

Please let my boy, Jim, pass anywhere in this county, until Jan. 1, 1834,
and oblige   Respectfully,

JOHN GAINES, M.D.
"Poplar Farm," St. Louis County, Mo.

With the above precious document in his pocket, a load of baskets, brooms, mats, and axe-handles on his back, a bag hanging across his shoulders, with a jug in each end — one for the whiskey, and the other for the molasses — the slaves trudged off to town at night, singing:

> Hurra, for good ole massa,
>   He give me de pass to go to de city.
> Hurra, for good ole missis,
>   She bile de pot, and giv me de licker.
>   Hurra, I'm goin to de city.
>
> When de sun rise in de mornin',
>   Jes' above de yaller corn,
> You'll fin' dis nigger has take warnin',
>   An's gone when de driver blows his horn.
>
> Hurra, for good ole massa,
>   He giv me de pass to go to de city.
> Hurra for good ole missis,
>   She bile de pot, and give me de licker.
>   Hurra, I'm goin to de city.

PAUL LAURENCE DUNBAR

The Party

· *From* Lyrics of Lowly Life ·

Born to parents who were former slaves, the poet Dunbar grew up absorbing accounts of slave life from them and became one of the most prolific recorders of the nineteenth-century American folk experience. This poem is a valuable source for multiple aspects of the culture of enslaved African Americans, including celebrations, food, dance, speech, dress, courtship, and religious beliefs.

Dey had a gread big pahty down to Tom's de othah night;
Was I dah? You bet! I nevah in my life see sich a sight;

All de folks f'om fou' plantations was invited, an' dey come,

Dey come troopin' thick ez chillun when dey hyeahs a fife an'
   drum.

Evahbody dressed deir fines'—Heish yo' mouf an' git away,

Ain't seen no sich fancy dressin' sence las' quah'tly meetin' day;

Gals all dressed in silks an' satins, not a wrinkle ner a crease,

Eyes a-battin', teeth a-shinin', haih breshed back ez slick ez
   grease;

Sku'ts all tucked an' puffed an' ruffled, evah blessed seam an'
   stitch;

Ef you'd seen 'em wif deir mistus, couldn't swahed to which was
   which.

Men all dressed up in Prince Alberts, swaller-tails 'u'd tek yo'
   bref!

I cain't tell you nothin' 'bout it, y' ought to seen it fu' yo'se'f.

Who was dah? Now who you askin'? How you 'spect I gwine to
   know?

You mus' think I stood an' counted evahbody at de do'.

Ole man Babah's house-boy Isaac, brung dat gal, Malindy Jane,

Huh a-hangin' to his elbow, him a-struttin' wif a cane;

My, but Hahvey Jones was jealous! seemed to stick him lak a
   tho'n;

But he laughed with Viney Cahteh, tryin' ha'd to not let on,

But a pusson would 'a' noticed f'om de d'rection of his look,

Dat he was watchin' ev'ry step dat Ike an' Lindy took.

Ike he foun' a cheer an' asked huh: "Won't you set down?" wif a
   smile,

An' she answe'd up a-bowin', "Oh, I reckon 't ain't wuth while."

Dat was jes' fu' style, I reckon, 'cause she sot down jes' de same,

An' she stayed dah 'twell he fetched huh fu' to jine some so't o'
   game;

Den I hyeahd huh sayin' propah, ez she riz to go away,

"Oh, you raly mus' excuse me, fu' I hardly keers to play."

But I seen huh in a minute wif de othahs on de flo',

An' dah wasn't any one o' dem a-playin' any mo';

Comin' down de flo' a-bowin' an' a-swayin' an' a-swingin',

Puttin' on huh high-toned mannahs all de time dat she was
   singin':

"Oh, swing Johnny up an' down, swing him all aroun',

Swing Johnny up an' down, swing him all aroun',

Oh, swing Johnny up an' down, swing him all aroun',

Fa' you well, my dahlin'."

Had to laff at ole man Johnson, he's a caution now, you bet—

Hittin' clost onto a hunderd, but he's spry an' nimble yet;

He 'lowed how a-so't o' gigglin', "I ain't ole, I'll let you see,

D'ain't no use in gittin' feeble, now you youngstahs jes' watch
me,"

An' he grabbed ole Aunt Marier—weighs th'ee hunderd mo' er
less,

An' he spun huh 'roun' de cabin swingin' Johnny lak de res'.

Evahbody laffed an' hollahed: "Go it! Swing huh, Uncle Jim!"

An' he swung huh too, I reckon, lak a youngstah, who but him.

Dat was bettah 'n young Scott Thomas, tryin' to be so awful
smaht.

You know when dey gits to singin' an' dey comes to dat ere
paht:

"In some lady's new brick house,

In some lady's gyahden.

Ef you don't let me out, I will jump out,

So fa' you well, my dahlin'."

Den dey's got a circle 'roun' you, an' you's got to break de line;

Well, dat dahky was so anxious, lak to bust hisse'f a-tryin';

Kep' on blund'rin' 'roun' an' foolin' 'twell he giv' one gread big
jump,

Broke de line, an' lit head-fo'most in de fiahplace right plump;

Hit 'ad fiah in it, mind you; well, I thought my soul I'd bust,

Tried my best to keep f'om laffin', but hit seemed like die I must!

Y' ought to seen dat man a-scramblin' f'om de ashes an' de
grime.

Did it bu'n him! Sich a question, why he didn't give it time;

Th'ow'd dem ashes and dem cindahs evah which-a-way I guess,

An' you nevah did, I reckon, clap yo' eyes on sich a mess;

Fu' he sholy made a picter an' a funny one to boot,

Wif his clothes all full o' ashes an' his face all full o' soot.

Well, hit laked to stopped de pahty, an' I reckon lak ez not

Dat it would ef Tom's wife, Mandy, hadn't happened on de spot,

To invite us out to suppah—well, we scrambled to de table,
An' I'd lak to tell you 'bout it—what we had—but I ain't able,
Mention jes' a few things, dough I know I hadn't orter,
Fu' I know 't will staht a hank'rin' an' yo' mouf'll 'mence to
    worter.
We had wheat bread white ez cotton an' a egg pone jes like gol',
Hog jole, bilin' hot an' steamin' roasted shoat an' ham sliced
    cold—
Look out! What's de mattah wif you? Don't be fallin' on de flo';
Ef it's go'n' to 'fect you dat way, I won't tell you nothin' mo'.
Dah now—well, we had hot chittlin's—now you's tryin' ag'in to
    fall,
Cain't you stan' to hyeah about it? S'pose you'd been an' seed it
    all;
Seed dem gread big sweet pertaters, layin' by de possum's side,
Seed dat coon in all his gravy, reckon den you'd up and died!
Mandy 'lowed "you all mus' 'scuse me, d' wa'n't much upon my
    she'ves,
But I's done my bes' to suit you, so set down an' he'p yo'se'ves."
Tom, he 'lowed: "I don't b'lieve in 'pologisin' an' perfessin',
Let 'em tek it lak dev ketch it. Eldah Thompson, ask de
    blessin'."
Wish you'd seed dat colo'ed preachah clean his th'oat an' bow
    his head;
One eye shet, an' one eye open—dis is evah wud he said:
"Lawd, look down in tendah mussy on sich generous hea'ts ez
    dese;
Make us truly thankful, amen. Pass dat possum, ef you please!"
Well, we eat and drunk ouah po'tion, 'twell dah wasn't nothin'
    lef,
An' we felt jes' like new sausage, we was mos' nigh stuffed to
    def!
Tom, he knowed how we'd be feelin', so he had de fiddlah
    'roun',
An' he made us cleah de cabin fu' to dance dat suppah down.
Jim, de fiddlah, chuned his fiddle, put some rosum on his bow,
Set a pine box on de table, mounted it an' let huh go!
He's a fiddlah, now I tell you, an' he made dat fiddle ring,

'Twell de ol'est an' de lamest had to give deir feet a fling.

Jigs, cotillions, reels an' break-downs, cordrills an' a waltz er two;

Bless yo' soul, dat music winged 'em an' dem people lak to flew.

Cripple Joe, de ole rheumatic, danced dat flo' f'om side to middle,

Th'owed away his crutch an' hopped it, what's rheumatics 'ginst a fiddle?

Eldah Thompson got so tickled dat he lak to los' his grace,

Had to tek bofe feet an' hol' dem so's to keep 'em in deir place.

An' de Christuns an' de sinnahs got so mixed up on dat flo',

Dat I don't see how dey'd pahted ef de trump had chanced to blow.

Well, we danced dat way an' capahed in de mos' redic'lous way,

'Twell de roostahs in de bahnyard cleahed deir th'oats an' crowed fu' day.

Y' ought to been dah, fu' I tell you evahthing was rich an' prime,

An' dey ain't no use in talkin', we jes had one scrumptious time!

No Other Preacher Could Walk like Him

· *From William E. Hatcher,* John Jasper: The Unmatched Negro Philosopher and Preacher ·

This account from an old woman in the Reverend John Jasper's church follows her description of his sermons, his devotion to his church, his love of children, and his friendliness. I might add that Jasper was a very tall and striking man. I have regularized the heavy dialect of this piece.

Brer Jasper had a walk mighty remarkable. When he went in de streets he was so stately and grave like that he walk different from all de people. Folks would run out of all de stores or out on deir porches, or turn back to look when Jasper come 'long. Oh, it made us proud to look at him. No other preacher could walk like him. You felt de ground got holy where he went 'long. Some of 'em say it was equal to a revival to see John Jasper moving like a king 'long de street. Often he seemed to be wrapped up in his thoughts and hardly to know where he was. De people feared him so much—wid such a loving kind of fear, that they hardly dared to speak to him.

HERMAN MELVILLE

The Handsome Soldier

· *From* Billy Budd, Sailor ·

This selection from the opening of *Billy Budd* reflects the usual ambivalence about race seen in noted novelist Herman Melville's portraits of Black characters. But despite disparaging terms such as "barbarous" and comparisons to animals, Melville nonetheless suggests the charisma of his subject.

In the time before steamships, or then more frequently than now, a stroller along the docks of any considerable seaport would occasionally have his attention arrested by a group of bronzed mariners, man-of-war's men or merchant sailors in holiday attire, ashore on liberty. In certain instances they would flank, or like a bodyguard quite surround, some superior figure of their own class, moving along with them like Aldebaran[15] among the lesser lights of his constellation. That signal object was the "Handsome Sailor" of the less prosaic time alike of the military and merchant navies. With no perceptible trace of the vainglorious about him, rather with the offhand unaffectedness of natural regality, he seemed to accept the spontaneous homage of his shipmates.

A somewhat remarkable instance recurs to me. In Liverpool, now half a century ago, I saw under the shadow of the great dingy street-wall of Prince's Dock (an obstruction long since removed) a common sailor so intensely black that he must needs have been a native African of the unadulterate blood of Ham[16]—a symmetric figure much above the average height. The two ends of a gay silk handkerchief thrown loose about the neck danced upon the displayed ebony of his chest, in his ears were big hoops of gold, and a Highland bonnet with a tartan band set off his shapely head. It was a hot noon in

---

[15]Taurus, the Bull, where it forms the animal's eye.

[16]I.e., black, from the belief that God's curse in Genesis 9.25 made Ham and his descendants black.

July; and his face, lustrous with perspiration, beamed with barbaric good humor. In jovial sallies right and left, his white teeth flashing into view, he rollicked along, the center of a company of his shipmates. These were made up of such an assortment of tribes and complexions as would have well fitted them to be marched up by Anacharsis Cloots[17] before the bar of the first French Assembly as Representatives of the Human Race. At each spontaneous tribute rendered by the wayfarers to this black pagod of a fellow—the tribute of a pause and stare, and less frequently an exclamation—the motley retinue showed that they took that sort of pride in the evoker of it which the Assyrian priests doubtless showed for their grand sculptured Bull when the faithful prostrated themselves.

FREDERICK LAW OLMSTED

Colored People of Richmond in 1852

· *From* The Cotton Kingdom ·

Olmsted gives us a sample here of the range of dress of the colored people he saw in Richmond on Sunday, December 15, 1852. The fine dress here is not commonplace and throughout this volume he frequently describes the coarse, plain clothing of most of the enslaved people he saw elsewhere.

The greater part of the coloured people, on Sunday, seemed to be dressed in the cast-off fine clothes of the white people, received, I suppose, as presents, or purchased of the Jews, whose shops show that there must be considerable importation of such articles, probably from the North, as there is from England into Ireland.

Many, who had probably come in from the farms near the town, wore clothing of coarse gray "negro-cloth," that appeared as if made by contract, without regard to the size of the particular individual to whom it had been allotted, like penitentiary uniforms. A few had a better suit of coarse blue cloth, expressly made for them evidently, for "Sunday clothes."

Some were dressed with foppish extravagance, and many in the

---

[17]Melville knew of the Prussian-born Baron de Cloots (1755–1794) from Thomas Carlyle's *The French Revolution*, part 2, book 1, chap. 10.

latest style of fashion. In what I suppose to be the fashionable streets, there were many more well-dressed and highly-dressed coloured people than white; and among this dark gentry the finest French cloths, embroidered waistcoats, patent-leather shoes, resplendent brooches, silk hats, kid gloves, and *eau de mille fleurs*, were quite common. Nor was the fairer, or rather the softer sex, at all left in the shade of this splendour. Many of the coloured ladies were dressed not only expensively, but with good taste and effect, after the latest Parisian mode. Some of them were very attractive in appearance, and would have produced a decided sensation in any European drawing-room. Their walk and carriage were more often stylish and graceful. Nearly a fourth part seemed to me to have lost all African peculiarity of feature, and to have acquired, in place of it, a good deal of that voluptuousness of expression which characterizes many of the women of the South of Europe.

There was no indication of their belonging to a subject race, except that they invariably gave the way to the white people they met.

Fashion Plates

· *From Shane and Graham White,* Stylin' ·

This account, from the September 6, 1931, issue of the *New York Times*, reports that Seventh and Lenox were the "two favorite avenues of Harlem where folks go a-strollin'."

Both men and women display the latest creations of the art of the tailor and the dressmaker. There is a type of youthful Negro who affects garments of a daring cut and pattern, with exaggerated built-up shoulders and with wasp-like waists. These garments are frequently of delicate pastel shades. One gets the impression their wearer is all shoulders and is gorgeously upholstered from head to foot. It is said of Harlem that its fashion plates are several jumps ahead of the rest of the world.

Zora Neale Hurston

Hurston, who acclaimed herself "Queen of the Niggerati," was often called the Queen of the Harlem Renaissance and was once introduced by Fannie Hurst as "The Princess Zora." Most often described as flamboyant, she evoked all the contradictory and ambivalent responses that those who style out usually do.

She was tall and tan and stylish, expansive and difficult, playful and brilliant. —*Rosemary L. Bray, "Renaissance for a Pioneer of Black Pride"*

She was flamboyant and yet vulnerable, self-centered and yet kind, a Republican conservative and yet an early black nationalist. —*Robert E. Hemenway,* Zora Neale Hurston: A Literary Biography

Zora had a great deal of flamboyance, a great deal of personal power. Imagine in 1937, to be a black woman in America and talk about loving your indigenous self, be as black as you want to be—and it's beautiful. —*Elizabeth Van Dyke, quoted in Rosemary L. Bray, "Renaissance for a Pioneer of Black Pride"*

Once, dressed for a party in a flowing white dress and a wide-brimmed hat, she found herself sharing an elevator with a would-be Casanova. As they approached the first floor, he made his pass, and Zora responded with a roundhouse right that put him flat on the floor. She stepped out of the elevator, never looking back at the man laid out behind her. —*Robert E. Hemenway,* Zora Neale Hurston: A Literary Biography

Zora Neale Hurston . . . is a perfect book of entertainment herself. —*Langston Hughes,* The Big Sea

I have given myself the pleasure of sunrises blooming out of oceans, and sunsets drenching heaped-up clouds. I have walked in storms with a crown of clouds about my head and the zigzag lightning playing through my fingers. The gods of the upper air have uncovered their faces to my eyes. I have found out that my real home is in the water, that the earth is only my stepmother. My old man, the Sun, sired me out of the sea. —*Hurston on her own life*, Dust Tracks on a Road

The late Zora Hurston first swung into my orbit when she was a new graduate of Barnard College.

She walked into my study one day by telephone appointment, carelessly, a big-boned, good-boned young woman, handsome and light yellow, with no show of desire for the position of secretary for which she was applying. Her dialect was as deep as the deep south, her voice and laughter the kind I used to hear on the levees of St. Louis when I was growing up in that city. As Zora expressed it, we "took a shine" to one another and I engaged her on the spot as my live-in secretary.

What a quaint gesture that proved to be! Her shorthand was short on legibility, her typing hit-or-miss, mostly the latter, her filing, a game of find-the-thimble. Her mind ran ahead of my thoughts and she would interject with an impatient suggestion or clarification of what I wanted to say. If dictation bored her she would interrupt, stretch wide her arms and yawn: "Let's get out the car, I'll drive you up to the Harlem bad-lands or down to the wharves where men go down to the sea in ships."

Her lust for life and food went hand in hand. She nibbled constantly between meals and consumed dinner off the stove and out of the refrigerator before the meal was served. "Sorry I ate all the casaba melon for tonight's dessert, I was hungry for so many years of my life, I get going nowadays and can't stop."

This was before her first book. Up to this time she had mentioned only vaguely her writing intention and ambitions.

One day after reading the manuscript a strange young man had submitted for my opinion, I dictated a letter to him. When Zora gave it to me to sign, she pointed out that she had added a final paragraph of her own, something to this effect: "I, the secretary, have also read your manuscript. I think better of it than Miss Hurst. Atta-Big-Boy!" —*Fannie Hurst, "Zora Hurston: A Personality Sketch"*

LANGSTON HUGHES

Rent Parties

· *From* The Big Sea ·

Here Hughes discusses the evolution of rent parties in Harlem during the Harlem Renaissance of the 1920s.

Then it was that house-rent parties began to flourish—and not always to raise the rent either. But, as often as not, to have a get-together of one's own, where you could do the black-bottom with no stranger behind you trying to do it, too. Non-theatrical, non-intellectual Harlem was an unwilling victim of its own vogue. It didn't like to be stared at by white folks. But perhaps the down-towners never knew this—for the cabaret owners, the entertainers, and the speakeasy proprietors treated them fine—as long as they paid.

The Saturday night rent parties that I attended were often more amusing than any night club, in small apartments where God knows who lived—because the guests seldom did—but where the piano would often be augmented by a guitar, or an odd cornet, or somebody with a pair of drums walking in off the street. And where awful bootleg whiskey and good fried fish or steaming chitterling were sold at very low prices. And the dancing and singing and impromptu entertaining went on until dawn came in at the windows.

These parties, often termed whist parties or dances, were usually announced by brightly colored cards stuck in the grille of apartment house elevators. Some of the cards were highly entertaining in themselves:

We got yellow girls, we've got black and tan
Will you have a good time?—YEAH MAN!

A Social Whist Party

—GIVEN BY—

MARY WINSTON

147 West 145th Street   Apt.5

Saturday Eve., March 19th, 1932

GOOD MUSIC   REFRESHMENTS

HURRAY

COME AND SEE WHAT IS IN STORE FOR YOU AT THE

Tea Cup Party

GIVEN BY MRS. VANDERBILT SMITH

at 409 Edgecombe Avenue

New York City

Apartment 10-A

on Thursday evening, January 23rd, 1930

at 8:30 P.M.

ORIENTAL — GYPSY — SOUTHERN MAMMY — STARLIGHT

and other readers will be present

Music and Talent — —Refreshments Served

Ribbons-Maws and Trotters A Specialty

Fall in line, and watch your step, For there'll be
Lots of Browns with plenty of Pep At

A Social Whist Party

Given by

LUCILLE & MINNIE

149 West 117th Street, N. Y. Gr. floor, W,

SATURDAY EVENING, NOV. 2ND 1929

REFRESHMENTS JUST IT   MUSIC WON'T QUIT

If Sweet Mamma is running wild, and you are looking
for a Do-right child, just come around and
linger awhile at a

SOCIAL WHIST PARTY

GIVEN BY

PINKNEY & EPPS

260 West 129th Street   Apartment 10

SATURDAY EVENING, JUNE 9, 1928

GOOD MUSIC   REFRESHMENTS

Railroad Men's Ball

AT CANDY'S PLACE

FRIDAY, SATURDAY & SUNDAY,

April 29–30, May 1, 1927

Black Wax, says change your mind and say they
do and he will give you a hearing, while MEAT
HOUSE SLIM, laying in the bin
killing all good men.

L. A. VAUGH, *President*

OH BOY   OH JOY

The Eleven Brown Skins

OF THE

Evening Shadow Social Club

ARE GIVING THEIR

Second Annual St. Valentine Dance
Saturday evening, Feb. 18th, 1928
At 129 West 136th Street, New York City

GOOD MUSIC   REFRESHMENTS SERVED

SUBSCRIPTION   25 CENTS

---

*Some wear pajamas, some wear pants, what does it matter
just so you can dance, at*

A Social Whist Party

GIVEN BY

MR. & MRS. BROWN

at 258 W. 115th Street, Apt. 9

SATURDAY EVE., SEPT. 14, 1929

The music is sweet and everything good to eat!

Almost every Saturday night when I was in Harlem I went to a
house-rent party. I wrote lots of poems about house-rent parties, and
ate thereat many a fried fish and pig's foot—with liquid refreshments
on the side. I met ladies' maids and truck drivers, laundry workers
and shoe shine boys, seamstresses and porters. I can still hear their
laughter in my ears, hear the soft slow music, and feel the floor shaking as the dancers danced.

WILLIE MORRIS

Going Negro

· *From* North Toward Home ·

Morris recounts in this selection his ambivalence as a Southern White boy who
accepted and acted out all the prejudices and cruel racist behavior toward Blacks
at the same time that he experienced an "ineluctable attraction of niggertown."
His unquestioning acceptance of Southern racism was so great that when he
discovered that his life had been saved when he was an infant by a Negro doctor
called to his home because no White doctor could be found, his only question was,
"Which door did he come in?" Obviously the maintenance of a Southern tradition
that required that Blacks enter only the back doors of White residences was more
important than the small detail that he had been treated by a man whose act of
mercy required that he be subjected to such ignomiry. The following passage also
serves as a description of Negro style—at least as it appeared to
Southern White boys.

There was a stage, when we were about thirteen, in which we "went
Negro." We tried to broaden our accents to sound like Negroes, as
if there were not enough similarity already. We consciously walked
like young Negroes, mocking their swinging gait, moving our arms
the way they did, cracking our knuckles and whistling between our
teeth. We tried to use some of the same expressions, as closely as possible to the way they said them, like: "Hey, *ma-a-a-n*, whut you *∂o*in'
theah!," the sounds rolled out and clipped sharply at the end for the
hell of it.

My father and I, on Sundays now and then, would go to their
baseball games, sitting way out along the right field line; usually we
were the only white people there. There was no condescension on our
part, though the condescension might come later, if someone asked
us where we had been. I would say, "Oh, we been to see the nigger
game over at Number Two."

"Number Two" was the Negro school, officially called "Yazoo
High Number Two" as opposed to the white high school, which was
"Yazoo High Number One." We would walk up to a Negro our age
and ask, "Say, buddy, where you go to school?" so we could hear the
way he said, "Number *Two*!" Number Two was behind my house a
block or so, a strange eclectic collection of old ramshackle wooden
buildings and bright new concrete ones, sprawled out across four or

five acres. When the new buildings went up, some of the white people would say, "Well, they won't be pretty very *long.*"

Sometimes we would run across a group of Negro boys our age,
walking in a pack through the white section, and there would be
bantering, half-affectionate exchanges: "Hey, Robert, what you *doin'*
theah!" and we would give them the first names of the boys they
didn't know, and they would do the same. We would mill around in
a hopping, jumping mass, talking baseball or football, showing off for
each other, and sounding for all the world, with our accentuated expressions and our way of saying them, like much the same race. Some
days we organized football games in Lintonia Park, first black against
white, then intermingled, strutting out of huddles with our limbs
swinging, shaking our heads rhythmically, until one afternoon the
cops came cruising by in their patrol car and ordered us to break it
up.

On Friday afternoons in the fall, we would go to see "the Black
Panthers" of Number Two play football. They played in the discarded uniforms of our high school, so that our school colors—red,
black, and white—were the same, and they even played the same
towns from up in the delta that our high school played. We sat on the
sidelines next to their cheering section, and sometimes a couple of us
would be asked to carry the first-down chains. The spectators would
shout and jump up and down, and even run onto the field to slap one
of the players on the back when he did something outstanding. When
one of the home team got hurt, ten or twelve people would dash out
from the sidelines to carry him to the bench; I suspected some injuries
might not have been as painful as they looked.

The Panthers had a left-handed quarterback named Kinsey, who
could throw a pass farther than any other high school passer I had
ever seen. He walked by my house every morning on the way to
school, and I would get in step with him, emulating his walk as we
strolled down to Number Two, and talk about last Friday's game or
the next one coming up. We would discuss plays or passing patterns,
and we pondered how they could improve on their "flea-flicker"
which had backfired so disastrously against Belzoni, leading to a
tackle's making an easy interception and all but walking thirty yards
for a touchdown. "Man, he coulda *crawled* for that touchdown,"
Kinsey bemoaned. Once I said, "You got to get another kicker," and

Kinsey replied, "Lord don't *I* know it," because in the previous game the Yazoo punter had kicked from his own twenty-yard-line, a high cantankerous spiral that curved up, down, and landed right in the middle of his own end zone. But this was a freak, because Kinsey and many of his teammates were not only superb athletes, they played with a casual flair and an exuberance that seemed missing in the white games. A long time after this, sitting in the bleachers in Candlestick Park in San Francisco, I saw a batter for the New York Mets hit a home run over the center-field fence; the ball hit a rung on the bleachers, near a group of little boys, and then bounced back over the fence onto the outfield grass. Willie Mays trotted over and gingerly tossed the ball underhanded across the wire fence to the boys, who had been deprived of a free baseball, and that casual gesture was performed with such a fine aristocracy that it suddenly brought back to me all the flamboyant sights and sounds of those Friday afternoons watching Number Two.

ALAN LOMAX

Shooting the Agate

· *From* Mister Jelly Roll ·

Jelly Roll Morton describes the "style" of the guys with whom he used to sing in New Orleans as a young man.

Those boys I used to sing with were really tough babies. They frequented the corners at Jackson and Locust and nobody fooled with *them*. The policemen was known never to cross Claiborne Avenue and these tough guys lived five blocks past Claiborne at Galvez, way back of town!

It was a miracle how those boys lived. They were sweetback men, I suppose you'd call them—always a bunch of women running after them. I remember the Pickett boys—there was Bus, there was Nert, there was Nonny, there was Bob. Nert had a burned hand, which he used to wear a stocking over, and he was seemingly simple to me. All these boys wanted to have some kind of importance. They dressed very well and they were tremendous sports. It was nothing like spending money that even worried their mind. If they didn't have it, somebody else would have it and spend it for them—they didn't care. But they all strived to have at least one Sunday suit, because, without that Sunday suit, you didn't have anything.

It wasn't the kind of Sunday suit you'd wear today. You was considered way out of line if your coat and pants matched. Many a time they would kid me, "Boy you must be from the country. Here you got trousers on the same as your suit."

These guys wouldn't wear anything but a blue coat and some kind of stripe in their trousers and those trousers had to be very, very tight. They'd fit um like a sausage. I'm telling you it was very seldom you could button the top button of a person's trousers those days in New Orleans. They'd leave the top button open and they wore very loud suspenders—of course they really didn't need suspenders, because the trousers was so tight and one suspender was always hanging down. If you wanted to talk to one of those guys, he would find the nearest post, stiffen his arm out and hold himself as far away as possible from that post he's leaning on. That was to keep those fifteen, eighteen dollar trousers of his from losing their press.

You should have seen one of those sports move down the street, his shirt busted open so that you could discern his red flannel undershirt, walking along with a very mosey walk they had adopted from the river, called shooting the agate. When you shoot the agate, your hands is at your sides with your index fingers stuck out and you kind of struts with it. That was considered a big thing with some of the illiterate women—if you could shoot a good agate and had a nice highclass red undershirt with the collar turned up, I'm telling you were liable to get next to that broad. She liked that very much.

Those days, myself, I thought I would die unless I had a hat with the emblem Stetson in it and some Edwin Clapp shoes. But Nert and Nonny and many of them wouldn't wear ready-made shoes. They wore what they called the St. Louis Flats and the Chicago Flats, made with cork soles and without heels and with gambler designs on the toes. Later on, some of them made arrangements to have some kind of electric-light bulbs in the toes of their shoes with a battery in their pockets, so when they would get around some jane that was kind of simple and thought they could make her, as they call making um, why they'd press a button in their pocket and light up the little-bitty bulb in the toe of their shoes and that jane was claimed. It's really the fact.

RALPH ELLISON

Rinehart, Poppa

· *From* Invisible Man ·

In this scene the Invisible Man has attempted to disguise himself by wearing shades and the widest hat he can find, when he is approached by a group of men who mistake him for a popular hustler named Rinehart.

A couple of men approached, eating up the walk with long jaunty strides that caused their heavy silk sports shirts to flounce rhythmically upon their bodies. They too wore dark glasses, their hats were set high upon their heads, the brims turned down. A couple of hipsters, I thought, just as they spoke.

"What you sayin', daddy-o," they said.

"Rinehart, poppa, tell us what you putting down," they said.

Oh, hell, they're probably his friends, I thought, waving and moving on.

"We know what you're doing, Rinehart," one of them called. "Play it cool, ole man, play it cool!"

Honky Tonk Bud

This is merely the introduction to the main character of this toast, who considers himself to be styling out. I recorded this in Richmond in November 1974.

Honky Tonk Bud, the hip cat stud,
Stood diggin' a game of pool.
Though his pockets was saggin',
Bud wasn't braggin',
'Cause he knew he was looking *real* cool.
Now he was choked up tight in his white on white,

And on his head supported a lead
That supposed to been a gold Stetson crown.
It was the first frame of a nine-ball game,
Hip Bud stood digging the play.

JANE DE FOREST SHELTON

The Election Day Festival

· *From "The New England Negro"* ·

Shelton provides a 1766 resignation letter from one of the slave "governors,"
which indicates that the practice of electing a slave governor and lieutenant
governor goes back at least to 1756. These election-day festivities, as the following
account shows, included a "grand" parade followed by a dinner and dance
in Derby.

The people assembled at Derby, Oxford, Waterbury, or Hum-
phreysville, as was ordered, the Governor and his escort in uniforms—anything but uniform—that were hired or borrowed or
improvised for the occasion, according to fancy or ability. Mounted
on such steeds as could be impressed into the service—remnants of
their former selves—they mustered outside the village, and with all
the majesty and glitter of feathers and streaming ribbons and uniforms, with fife and drum, made their way by the main thoroughfares, sometimes stopping to fire a salute before a squire's house, to
the tavern which was to be the centre of festivity. Then the Governor,
dismounting, delivered his speech from the porch, and the troops
"trained." Then the clans gathered with more and more enthusiasm
for the election ball. Families went entire, a babe in arms being no
drawback, as the tavern-keeper set apart a room and provided a
caretaker for them. Sometimes more than a dozen little woolly-heads
would be under surveillance, while the light-hearted mothers shuf-
fled and tripped to the sound of the fiddle. New Haven and Hartford,
as well as intervening towns, were represented. Supper was served
for fifty cents each, and they danced and feasted with a delight the
more sedate white man can hardly appreciate, spinning out the night
and often far into the next day. To their credit it must be recorded
that although they were not strict prohibitionists, their indulgence

was limited. The influence of the Governors was for moderation, which was generally observed.

A newspaper notice of more than fifty years ago strikes the keynote of the great day:

ATTENTION, FREEMEN!

There will be a general election of the colored gentlemen of Connecticut, October first, twelve o'clock, noon. The day will be celebrated in the evening by a dance at Warner's tavern, when it will be shown that there is some power left in muscle, catgut, and rosin.

By order of the Governor,
From Headquarters.

ALICE MORSE EARLE

Pinkster Day

· From "Pinkster Day" ·

Earle asserts that the American celebration of Pinkster Day originated among the Dutch in New York; *Pinkster* derives from the Dutch word for Pentecost. She points out that the celebrations were nowhere more gloriously celebrated than by the Negroes on Capitol Hill in Albany; and notes that in his account of the Negroes' celebration in *Satanstoe,* James Fenimore Cooper says it was held in the area then known as City Hall Park. Following are Earle's reproductions of accounts by "Munsell" and "Dr. Eights" of the Negroes' Pinkster celebrations.

Pinkster was a great day, a gala day, or rather week, for they used to keep it up a week among the darkies. The dances were the original Congo dances as danced in their native Africa. They had a chief—Old King Charley. The old settlers said Charley was a prince in his own country, and was supposed to have been one hundred and twenty-five years old at the time of his death. On these festivals old Charley was dressed in a strange and fantastical costume; he was nearly barelegged, wore a red military coat trimmed profusely with variegated ribbons, and a small black hat with a pompon stuck on one side. The dances and antics of the darkies must have afforded great amusement for the ancient burghers. As a general thing, the music consisted of a sort of drum, or instrument constructed out of a box with sheepskin heads, upon which old Charley did most of the beating, accompanied by singing some queer African air. Charley generally led off the dance, when the Sambos and Phillises, juvenile and antiquated, would put in the double-shuffle heel-and-toe break-down. These festivals seldom failed to attract large crowds from the city as well as from the rural districts.

Dr. Eights, of Albany, wrote still further reminiscences of the day. He said that, strangely enough, though all the booths and sports opened on Monday, white curiosity-seekers were, on that first day, the chief visitors to Pinkster Hill. On Tuesday the blacks all appeared, and the consumption of gingerbread, cider, and applejack began. Adam Blake, a most elegant creature, the body-servant of the old patroon Van Rensselaer, was master of the ceremonies. Charley, the King, was a "Guinea man" from Angola—and I have noted the fact that nearly all African-born negroes who became leaders in this country, or men of marked note in any way, have been Guinea men. He wore, always, portions of the costume of a British General, and had the power of an autocrat—his will was law. Dr. Eights says the Pinkster musical instruments were eel-pots covered with dressed sheepskin, on which the negroes pounded with their bare hands, as do all savage nations on their tom-toms. Their song had an African refrain, "Hi-a-bomba-bomba-bomba." Other authorities state that the dance was called the "Toto Dance," and partook so largely of savage license that at last the white visitors shunned being present during its performance.

THOMAS WENTWORTH HIGGINSON

The Route Step

· *From* Army Life in a Black Regiment ·

Here Higginson describes the marching his colored Civil War troops enjoyed when they felt free to improvise.

Soon we debouched upon the "Shell Road," the wagon-train drew on one side into the fog, and by the time the sun appeared the music ceased, the men took the "route step," and the fun began.

The "route step" is an abandonment of all military strictness, and nothing is required of the men but to keep four abreast, and not lag behind. They are not required to keep step, though, with the rhythmical ear of our soldiers, they almost always instinctively did so; talking and singing are allowed, and of this privilege, at least, they eagerly availed themselves. On this day they were at the top of exhilaration. There was one broad grin from one end of the column to the other; it might soon have been a caravan of elephants instead of camels, for the ivory and the blackness; the chatter and the laughter almost drowned the tramp of feet and the clatter of equipments. At cross-roads and plantation gates the colored people thronged to see us pass; every one found a friend and a greeting. "How you do, aunty?" "Huddy (how d' ye), Budder Benjamin?" "How you find yourself dis mornin', Tittawisa (Sister Louisa)?" Such salutations rang out to everybody, known or unknown. In return, venerable, kerchiefed matrons courtesied laboriously to every one, with an unfailing "Bress de Lord, budder." Grave little boys, blacker than ink, shook hands with our laughing and utterly unmanageable drummers, who greeted them with this sure word of prophecy, "Dem's de drummers for de nex' war!" Pretty mulatto girls ogled and coquetted, and made eyes, as Thackeray would say, at half the young fellows in the battalion. Meantime the singing was brisk along the whole column, and when I sometimes reined up to see them pass, the chant of each company, entering my ear, drove out from the other ear the strain of the preceding. Such an odd mixture of things, military and missionary, as the successive waves of song drifted by! First, "John Brown," of course; then, "What make old Satan for follow me so?" then, "Marching Along"; then, "Hold your light on Canaan's shore"; then, "When this cruel war is over" (a new favorite, sung by a few); yielding presently to a grand burst of the favorite marching song among them all, and one at which every step instinctively quickened, so light and jubilant its rhythm, —

> All true children gwine in de wilderness,
> Gwine in de wilderness, gwine in de wilderness,
> True believers gwine in de wilderness,
> To take away de sins ob de world, —

ending in a "Hoigh!" after each verse, — a sort of Irish yell. For all the songs, but especially for their own wild hymns, they constantly improvised simple verses, with the same odd mingling, — the little facts of to-day's march being interwoven with the depths of theological gloom, and the same jubilant chorus annexed to all; thus, —

> We're gwine to de Ferry,
>> De bell done ringing;
> Gwine to de landing,
>> De bell done ringing;
> Trust, believer,
>> O, de bell done ringing;
> Satan's behind me,
>> De bell done ringing;
> 'T is a misty morning,
>> De bell done ringing;
> O de road am sandy,
>> De bell done ringing;
> Hell been open,
>> De bell done ringing; —

and so on indefinitely.

The little drum-corps kept in advance, a jolly crew, their drums slung on their backs, and the drum-sticks perhaps balanced on their heads. With them went the officers' servant-boys, more uproarious still, always ready to lend their shrill treble to any song. At the head of the whole force there walked, by some self-imposed preeminence, a respectable elderly female, one of the company laundresses, whose vigorous stride we never could quite overtake, and who had an enormous bundle balanced on her head, while she waved in her hand, like a sword, a long-handled tin dipper. Such a picturesque medley of fun, war, and music I believe no white regiment in the service could have shown; and yet there was no straggling, and a single tap of the drum would at any moment bring order out of this seeming chaos. So we marched our seven miles out upon the smooth and shaded road, — beneath jasmine clusters, and great pinecones dropping, and great bunches of mis[t]letoe still in bloom among the branches.

EDWARD WARREN

John Koonering

· *From* A Doctor's Experiences in Three Continents ·

Despite Warren's racist descriptions, his air of superiority, and his exaggerated
dialect, his firsthand account of the John Canoe festival does provide significant
details of the celebration.

One of their customs was playing at what they called "John
Koonering," though this was more of a *fantasia* than a religious
demonstration; that it had, however, some connection with their religion is evident from the fact that they only indulged in it on
Christian festivals, notably on Christmas day. The *leading* character
is the "ragman," whose "get-up" consists in a costume of rags, so
arranged that one end of each hangs loose and dangles; two great ox
horns, attached to the skin of a raccoon, which is drawn over the
head and face, leaving apertures only for the eyes and mouth; sandals
of the skin of some wild "varmint;" several cow or sheep bells or
strings of dried goats' horns hanging about their shoulders, and so
arranged as to jingle at every movement; and a short stick of seasoned
wood, carried in his hands.

The *second* part is taken by the best looking darkey of the place,
who wears no disguise, but is simply arrayed in what they call his
"Sunday-go-to-meeting suit," and carries in his hand a small bowl or
tin cup, while the other parts are appropriated by some half a dozen
fellows, each arrayed fantastically in ribbons, rags, and feathers, and
bearing between them several so-called musical instruments or
"gumba boxes," which consist of wooden frames covered over with
tanned sheepskins. These are usually followed by a motley crowd of
all ages, dressed in their ordinary working clothes, which seemingly
comes as a guard of honor to the performers.

Having thus given you an idea of the *characters* I will describe the
performance as I first saw it at the "Lake." Coming up to the front
door of the "great house," the musicians commenced to beat their
gumba-boxes violently, while characters No. 1 and No. 2 entered
upon a dance of the most extraordinary character—a combination of
bodily contortions, flings, kicks, gyrations, and antics of every imaginable description, seemingly acting as partners, and yet each trying

to excel the other in the variety and grotesqueness of his movements. At the same time No. 2 led off with a song of a strange, monotonous cadence, which seemed extemporized for the occasion, and to run somewhat in this wise:

> My massa am a white man, juba!
> Old missus am a lady, juba!
> De children am de honey-pods, juba! juba!
> Krismas come but once a year, juba!
> Juba! juba! O, ye juba!

> De darkeys lubs de hoe-cake, juba!
> Take de 'quarter' for to buy it, juba!
> Fetch him long, you white folks, juba! juba!
> Krismas come but once a year, juba!
> Juba! juba! O, ye juba!

while the whole crowd joined in the chorus, shouting and clapping their hands in the wildest glee. After singing a verse or two No. 2 moved up to the master, with his hat in one hand and a tin cup in the other, to receive the expected "quarter," and, while making the lowest obeisance, shouted: "May de good Lord bless old massa and missus, and all de young massas, juba!" The "rag man" during this part of the performance continued his dancing, singing at the top of his voice the same refrain, and striking vigorously at the crowd, as first one and then another of its members attempted to tear off his "head gear" and to reveal his identity. And then the expected "quarter" having been jingled for some time in the tin cup, the performers moved on to visit in turn the young gentlemen's colony, the tutor's rooms, the parson's study, the overseer's house, and, finally, the quarters, to wind up with a grand jollification, in which all took part until they broke down and gave it up from sheer exhaustion.

PAUL LAURENCE DUNBAR

The Colored Band

· *From* Lyrics of Love and Laughter ·

In this poem, Dunbar captures the spirit and rhythms of a colored marching band
as well as the responses of the neighborhood to the performance. The people
delight not only in the music but also the steps and the outfits. Here the narrator
applauds the performers' style and soulfulness, which he is convinced cannot be
matched by White bands.

W'en de colo'ed ban' comes ma'chin' down de street,
Don't you people stan' daih starin'; lif' yo' feet!
Ain't dey playin'? Hip, hooray!
Stir yo' stumps an' cleah de way,
Fu' de music dat dey mekin' can't be beat.

Oh, de major man's a-swingin' of his stick,
An' de pickaninnies crowdin' roun' him thick;
In his go'geous uniform,
He's de lightnin' of de sto'm,
An' de little clouds erroun' look mighty slick.

You kin hyeah a fine perfo'mance w'en de white ban's serenade,
An' dey play dey high-toned music mighty sweet,
But hit's Sousa played in ragtime, an' hit's Rastus on Parade,
W'en de colo'ed ban' comes ma'chin' down de street.

W'en de colo'ed ban' comes ma'chin' down de street
You kin hyeah de ladies all erroun' repeat:
"Ain't dey handsome? Ain't dey gran'?
Ain't dey splendid? Goodness, lan'!
W'y dey 's pu'fect f'om dey fo'heads to dey feet!"
An' sich steppin' to de music down de line,
'Tain't de music by itself dat meks it fine,
Hit's de walkin', step by step,
An' de keepin' time wid "Hep,"
Dat it mek a common ditty soun' divine.

Oh, de white ban' play hits music, an' hit's mighty good to
  hyeah,

An' it sometimes leaves a ticklin' in yo' feet;

But de hea't goes into bus'ness fu' to he'p erlong de eah,

W'en de colo'ed ban' goes ma'chin' down de street.

○ The Zulus

· *From Lyle Saxon et al.,* Gumbo Ya-Ya ·

The Zulu Social Aid and Pleasure Club, developed in 1909, is the oldest Black
Mardi Gras marching club in New Orleans. Something of their style is suggested
in the following description from the 1940s, but it seems the observer here is not
fully aware of the fact that the Zulu parody the lavish and racially exclusive
White Carnival societies. Their blackening of their already black faces is a parody
of the Whites' parody of Blacks, reminiscent of Blacks in Blackface in the
minstrels.

The Zulus emerged as a Mardi Gras organization in 1910, marching on foot, a jubilee-singing quartet in front, another quartet in the
rear. Birth had come the year before, when fifty Negroes gathered in
a woodshed. William Story was the first king, wearing a lard-can
crown and carrying a banana-stalk scepter. By 1913 progress had
reached the point where King Peter Williams wore a starched white
suit, an onion stickpin, and carried a loaf of Italian bread as a scepter.
In 1914 King Henry rode in a buggy and from that year they grew in-
creasingly ambitious, boasting three floats in 1940, entitled respec-
tively, "The Pink Elephant," on which rode the king and his escort,
"Hunting the Pink Elephant," and "Capturing the Pink Elephant."

It was in 1922 that the first yacht—the *Royal Barge*—was rented,
and since then the ruler of the darker side of the Carnival has always
ridden in high style down the New Basin Canal.

Gloom was in the air before Johnny Metoyer went to glory. He
had been president and dictator of the organization for twenty-nine
years, but had never chosen to be king until now. And this year he
had announced his intention of being king, and then resigning from
the Zulu Aid and Pleasure Club. This, everyone had agreed, probably meant disbanding. It just wouldn't be the same without ole John.
Even the city officials were worrying. It seemed like the upper class
of Negroes had been working on Johnny, and had at last succeeded.

The Zulus had no use for "stuck-up niggers." Their membership is
derived from the humblest strata, porters, laborers, and a few who live

by their wits. Professional Negroes disapprove of them, claiming they "carry on" too much, and "do not represent any inherent trait of Negro life and character, serving only to make the Negro appear grotesque and ridiculous, since they are neither allegoric nor historical."

When, in November, 1939, word came that Johnny Metoyer was dead, people wouldn't believe it. The night the news came, the Perdido Street barroom was packed. Representatives of the Associated Press, the United Press and the local newspapers rubbed shoulders with Zulus, Baby Dolls and Indians. The atmosphere was deep, dark and blue. Everybody talked at once.

"Ain't it a shame?"

"Poor John! He's gotta have a helluva big funeral."

"Put him up right so his body can stay in peace for a long time to come."

Somebody started playing "When the Saints Come Marching In," written by Louis "Satchmo" Armstrong, Metoyer's bosom friend. Then it is suggested that a telegram be sent to Armstrong. He's tooting his horn at the Cotton Club on Broadway, but it is felt he'll board a plane and fly down for the funeral.

A doubt was voiced that any Christian church would accept the body for last rites. "John was a man of the streets, who ain't never said how he stood on religion." Probably, others said confidently, if there were enough insurance money left, one of the churches could be persuaded to see things differently. Of course, he would be buried in style befitting a Zulu monarch. Members must attend in full regalia, Johnny's body must be carried through headquarters, there must be plenty of music, coconuts on his grave. Maybe Mayor Maestri could be persuaded to proclaim the day a holiday in Zululand.

But Johnny had a sister; Victoria Russell appeared on the scene and put down a heavy and firm foot. All attempts to make the wake colorful were foiled. "Ain't nobody gonna make a clown's house out of my house," said Sister Victoria Russell.

Even the funeral—held on a Sunday afternoon, amid flowers and fanfare and a crowd of six thousand—was filled with disappointments. Louie Armstrong had not been able to make the trip down from New York. Sister Russell banned the coconuts and the Zulu costumes. . . .

Outside [of the church] waited a fourteen-piece brass band and eighteen automobiles. Thousands marched on foot. The band struck up "Flee as a Bird," and the cortège was on its way toward Mount

Olivet Cemetery. Everyone was very solemn, and there was not a smile visible. All Zulus wore black banners draped across their chests and their shoulders.

Then, after the hearse had vanished into the cemetery, the entire aspect of the marchers changed. The band went into "Beer Barrel Polka," and dancing hit the streets. Promenading in Mardi Gras fashion lasted two hours, ending in Metoyer's own place of business, where the last liquor was purchased and consumed. Sister Russell, returning to the scene, then ordered all Zulus out.

Photograph of King Zulu

From Lyle Saxon et al., Gumbo Ya-Ya. *Permission of Pelican Publishing Company, Inc.*

The Black Indians

· *From Lyle Saxon et al.,* Gumbo Ya-Ya ·

Even before the advent of the Zulus, Blacks used to dress up as Indians and run
through the crowds at Carnival. The Black Indians continued to appear in
Carnival though the years, though later they became more organized.

Suddenly, this Mardi Gras afternoon [1940], there appeared on a
street corner a lone figure of an elaborately garbed Indian. He stood
there, a lighted lantern in one hand, the other shading his eyes, as he
peered into the street ahead, first right, then left. This Indian's face
was very black under his war paint, but his costume and feathered
headdress were startlingly colorful. He studied the distance a moment, then turned and swung the lantern. Other Indians appeared,
all attired in costumes at least as magnificent as the first, and in every
conceivable color.

A second Indian joined the first, then a third. These three all carried lanterns like good spy boys must. Then a runner joined them, a
flag boy, a trio of chiefs, a savage-looking medicine man. Beside the
first or head chief was a stout woman, wearing a costume of gold and
scarlet. She was the tribe's queen, and wife of the first chief.

A consultation was held there on the corner. The chiefs got together, passed around a bottle, and argued with the medicine man
until that wild creature, dressed in animal skins and a grass skirt,
wearing a headdress of horns and a huge ring in his nose, jumped up
and down on the pavement with rage. When, at last, it was decided
that since there was no enemy tribe in sight, they might as well have
a war dance, Chief "Happy Peanut," head of this tribe of the Golden
Blades, emitted a bloodcurdling yell that resounded for blocks,
"Oowa-a-awa! Ooa-a-a-awa!"

Tambourines were raised and a steady tattoo of rhythm beat out.
Knees went down and up, heads swayed back and forth, feet shuf-
fled on the pavement, as they circled round and round.

The Queen chanted this song:

The Indians are comin'.
Tu-way-pa-ka-way.
The Indians are comin'.

Tu-way-pa-ka-way.
The Chief is comin'.
Tu-way-pa-ka-way.
The Chief is comin'.
Tu-way-pa-ka-way.

The dances are wild and abandoned. Unlike the songs, there may be detected traces of modernity, trucking and bucking and "messing-around" combined with pseudo-Indian touches, much leaping into the air, accompanied by virile whooping. All this is considerably aided by the whiskey consumed while on the march, and the frequent smoking of marijuana.

The tribes include such names as the Little Red, White and Blues, the Yellow Pocahontas, the Wild Squa-tou-las, the Golden Eagles, the Creole Wild Wests, the Red Frontier Hunters, and the Golden Blades. The last numbers twenty-two members, and is the largest and oldest of those still extant.

The Golden Blades were started twenty-five years ago in a saloon. Ben Clark was the first chief and ruled until two years ago, when a younger man took over. Leon Robinson—Chief "Happy Peanut"—deposed Clark in actual combat, as is the custom, ripping open Clark's arm and gashing his forehead with a knife. That's the way a chief is created, and that is the way his position is lost.

Contrary to the casual observer's belief, these strangest of Mardi Gras maskers are extremely well-organized groups, whose operations are intricate and complicated.

Monthly meetings are held, dues paid and the next year's procedure carefully planned. All members are individually responsible for their costumes. They may make them—most of them do—or have them made to order.

The regalia consists of a large and resplendent crown of feathers, a wig, an apron, a jacket, a shirt, tights, trousers and moccasins. They vie with each other and with other tribes as to richness and elaborateness. Materials used include satins, velvet, silver and gold lamé and various furs. The trimmings are sequins, crystal, colored and pearl beads, sparkling imitation jewels, rhinestones, spangles and gold clips put to extravagant use. Color is used without restraint. (Flame, scarlet and orange are possibly the preferred shades.)

Amazingly intricate designs are often worked out in beads and brilliants against the rich materials. A huge serpent of pearls may writhe on a gold lamé breast, an immense spider of silver beads appears to be crawling on a back of flame satin. Sometimes a chief will choose to appear in pure white. A regal crown of snowy feathers, rising from a base of crystal beads, will adorn his head, and all other parts of his costume will be of white velvet heavily encrusted with rhinestones and crystals. All costumes are worn with the arrogance expressed in such songs as

Oh, the Little Red, White and Blues,
Tu-way-pa-ka-way,
Bravest Indians in the land.
Tu-way-pa-ka-way.
They are on the march today.
Tu-way-pa-ka-way.
If you should get in their way,
Tu-way-pa-ka-way,
Be prepared to die.
Tu-way-pa-ka-way.
Oowa-a-a!
Oowa-a-a!

Ten years ago the various tribes actually fought when they met. Sometimes combatants were seriously injured. When two tribes sighted each other, they would immediately go into battle formation, headed by the first, second and third spy boys of each side. Then the two head chiefs would cast their spears — iron rods — into the ground, the first to do so crying, "Umba?," which was an inquiry if the other were willing to surrender. The second chief replied, "Me no umba!" There was never a surrender, never a retreat. There would follow a series of dances by the two chiefs, each around his spear, with pauses now and then to fling back and forth the exclamations, "Umba?" "Me no umba!" While this continued, sometimes for four or five minutes, the tribes stood expectantly poised, waiting for the inevitable break that would be an invitation for a free-for-all mêlée. Once a police officer was badly injured by an Indian's spear. After that occurrence a law was passed forbidding the tribes of maskers to carry weapons.

Today the tribes are all friendly. The following song is a warning
against the tactics of other days.

Shootin' don't make it, no no no no.
Shootin' don't make it, no no no no.
Shootin' don't make it, no no no no.
If you see your man sittin' in the bush,
Knock him in the head and give him a push,
'Cause shootin' don't make it, no no.
Shootin' don't make it, no no no no.

The Golden Blades marched all day through main thoroughfares
and narrow side streets. At the train tracks and Broadway came the
news the spy boys had sighted the Little Red, White and Blues.

The tribes met on either side of a vacant space of ground, and
with a whoop and loud cries.

"Me, Chief 'Happy Peanut.' My tribe Golden Blades."

The other replied: "Me, Chief 'Battle Brown.' My tribe Little Red,
White and Blues."

Palms still extended, they spoke as one, "Peace."

Then they met, put arms around each other's necks. Together they
proceeded toward the nearest saloon, the two tribes behind them
mingling and talking, the medicine men chanting a weird duet:

Shh-bam-hang the ham.
Follow me, follow me, follow me.
Wha-wha-wha-follow me.
Wha-wha-wha-follow me.
Shh-bam-hang the ham.
Wha-wha-wha-follow me.
Wha-wha-wha-follow me. . . .

At the bar, the chiefs gulped jiggers of whiskey, then small beers
as chasers. Members of both tribes crowded about and imbibed
freely.

ALAN LOMAX
Didn't He Ramble
· *From* Mister Jelly Roll ·

Following is Jelly Roll Morton's brief description of a funeral march.

Of course, as I told you, everybody in the City of New Orleans was always organization minded, which I guess the world knows, and a dead man always belonged to several organizations—secret orders and so forth and so on. So when anybody died, there was always a big band turned out on the day he was supposed to be buried. Never buried at night, always in the day and right in the heart of the city. You could hear the band come up the street taking the gentleman for his last ride, playing different dead marches like *Flee as the Bird to the Mountain.*

In New Orleans very seldom they would bury them in the deep in the mud. They would always bury um in a vault. . . . So they would leave the graveyard . . . the band would get ready to strike up. They'd have a second line behind um, maybe a couple of blocks long with baseball bats, axe handles, knives, and all forms of ammunition to combat some of the foe when they came to the dividing lines. Then the band would get started and you could hear the drums, rolling a deep, slow rhythm. A few bars of that and then the snare drummer would make a hot roll on his drums and the boys in the band would just tear loose, while second line swung down the street, singing . . .

Didn't he ramble?
He rambled.
Rambled all around,
In and out the town.
Didn't he ramble?
He rambled.
He rambled till the butchers cut him down.

That would be the last of the dead man. He's gone and everybody came back home, singing. In New Orleans they believed truly to stick right close to the Scripture. That means *rejoice at the death and cry at the birth. . . .*

A Different Style

· *From Ann Banks,* First-Person America ·

White jazzman Muggsy Spanier reflects on his attraction to and efforts to emulate the style of Black musicians.

At first I started out as a drummer. Those days I used to go down to hear Joe Oliver at the Dreamland Cafe on Thirty-fifth and State. Before that, Joe played at the Pekin Cafe. I was too young to go inside and they didn't start playing till twelve o'clock at night, but I used to stand outside and listen. They used to have matinee dances at the Dreamland and I'd ditch school and go out there. I'd put on my brother's long pants and go there and listen to them and get up early and go to school in the morning. I must have been about thirteen years old at the time and I was still playing drums. But finally I went to my mother and I told her I wanted to play a cornet and she bought me one on time. She paid $125 for it. I'll never forget it. It was a real pretty thing.

When the Dixieland band began to make records I bought all I could get and played them on my victrola and played my cornet with the recording. After that Joe'd let me sit in with his band. That was unheard of in those days up North here, a white person playing with Negroes. There were few white guys they'd let sit in with them, but they let some because some couldn't play that way with any other band. Then I met the fellows from the New Orleans Rhythm Kings and I hung around with them. The Rhythm Kings was the best band put together at the time. Their style affected me. It was a different style; at the time the rage was sweet music and laughing cornets.

I learned how to play from listening to Joe Oliver a lot. Joe would play with that little mute and get some wonderful effects and I decided I'd do that too, which I'm still trying to perfect. When Louie [Armstrong] joined the band he didn't do much because he was the second trumpet man, but I liked to listen to him play those pretty parts against what Joe was doing.

RALPH ELLISON

Learning to Swing

· *From* Shadow and Act ·

Ellison explains how he and his peers were initiated into mixed but related elements of Black jazz and marching.

You see, jazz was so much a part of our total way of life that it got not only into our attempts at playing classical music but into forms of activities usually not associated with it: into marching and into football games, where it has since become a familiar fixture. A lot has been written about the role of jazz in a certain type of Negro funeral marching, but in Oklahoma City it got into military drill. There were many Negro veterans from the Spanish-American War who delighted in teaching the younger boys complicated drill patterns, and on hot summer evenings we spent hours on the Bryant School grounds (now covered with oil wells) learning to execute the commands barked at us by our enthusiastic drillmasters. And as we mastered the patterns, the jazz feeling would come into it and no one was satisfied until we were swinging. These men who taught us had raised a military discipline to the level of a low art form, almost a dance, and its spirit was jazz.

JACQUI MALONE

Stepping: Regeneration through Dance in African American Fraternities and Sororities

· *From* Steppin' on the Blues ·

"Regeneration of Soul" is the homecoming theme at Howard University, where hundreds line the bleachers of Burr Gymnasium at the largest fundraiser of the week-long celebration: the annual homecoming step show. A halftime guest appearance by the Muslim Girl Training and General Civilization Class, Nation of Islam is ending as the drill team of young women marches off the floor. The gymnasium starts to buzz with excitement in anticipation of the show's second half, a battle of Howard's fraternities in stiff competition for the first place trophy.

All eyes are riveted on the gold, black, and silver sphinx painted on a canvas pyramid that stands in one corner of the gymnasium. The Alpha step team announcer begins: "Ladies and gentlemen, good evening. For us as a people of African descent, the turn of the century brought darkness. But all hope was not lost. For in the year 1906, seven bright lights stood upon the Nile to guide us to peace. From that vision, from that dream, in 1907 Beta was made. And the vision is a reality, a reality that started off very small."

Rap music blares from the speakers as ten African American boys (ages six to nine) burst through the front flaps of the pyramid and perform their versions of the latest hip hop steps. The crowd is ecstatic. When the music stops, the ten boys freeze in angulated stances, proudly displaying the Alpha Phi Alpha hand signal. After their exit, the announcer sets the stage for the Alpha step team: "But now, ladies and gentlemen, that small dream is a reality. And now, the brothers from Beta are here to make it happen. To the Howard University Homecoming step show theme, 'Stepping in Sequence,' showtime proudly presents 'Standing Room Only, the Brothers of Alpha Phi Alpha.'"

The "aesthetic of the cool" swings into operation when, one by one, the twelve Alphas emerge from the pyramid. For this year's show they've chosen a Boyz II Men look: black Bermuda shorts, black baseball caps, white long-sleeved dress shirts with ties, black socks, and heavy-soled black shoes.

The men of Alpha Phi Alpha strut, glide, and pimp across the floor as they slap five, coolly acknowledge the crowd, exchange hugs with their brothers, and "profile" their way to center stage. In the words of the vernacular, they are "dead up in the tradition." With heads bowed, feet firmly planted in a wide stance, and arms crossed, each member waits for the first call from the step leader. It is unquestionably *show time*. They are about to perform one of the most exciting dance forms to evolve in the twentieth century: stepping, a complex multilayered dance genre created by black American Greek-letter fraternities and sororities.

Spike Lee's 1988 film *School Daze* provided the first widespread exposure for this ritual dance form, which began on college campuses. Since that time it has been featured on such television shows as "A Different World" and the "Arsenio Hall Show," in music videos, in television commercials, at regional dance conferences, and in a one-hour documentary produced by Jerald Harkness. In January 1993, the Alpha Phi Alpha step team of Howard University performed on the Mall in Washington as part of President Clinton's inaugural celebration. During December 1994, the Alphas were invited by the Soweto Dance Theater to Johannesburg, where they performed, taught stepping, and took classes in South African dance forms.

Stepping features synchronized, precise, sharp, and complex rhythmical body movements combined with singing, chanting, and verbal play. It requires creativity, wit, and a great deal of physical skill and coordination. The emphasis is always on style and originality, and the goal of each team is to command the audience with stylistic elements derived primarily from African-based performance traditions. Even though the choreography is prearranged, competition ensures an element of surprise and helps keep standards high, not an easy feat when the onlookers are aficionados who understand all of the codes of the genre and eagerly look forward to something new and unique at each performance. Their enthusiastic participation is what gives a step show its dynamic quality. "The spirit of stepping," writes dance critic Sally Sommer, "is what I would wish for all dancing."

A step, which usually lasts from one to five minutes, is defined as a complete choreographed sequence or series of movements. It can be verbal, nonverbal, or a combination of the two. Women and men perform on separate teams, and at Howard University fraternities and sororities are judged separately, although they appear in the same shows.

What we call stepping today grew out of song and dance rituals performed by Greek-letter chapters as a way of expressing loyalty toward their organizations. Over a period of approximately fifty years, this constantly changing dance form has evolved and absorbed many cultural influences, including military drilling, black social dances, African American children's games, cheerleading, vocal choreography, martial arts, the precision marching of historically black college bands, South African "gumboot" dancing, music videos, acrobatics, and American tap dancing. Like many other vernacular forms, stepping has the ability to assimilate almost anything in its evolutionary path and still retain its distinctive character.

Because the most characteristic movements and body stances of stepping are based on traditional western and central African dance styles, many practitioners of the form believe that it "came from Africa." But this is a somewhat misleading point of view, especially when one considers how cultural transference takes place. It would be more accurate to view stepping as a uniquely African American dance genre that was created in the United States but is, in the words of Roger Abrahams, "animated by the style, spirit, and social and aesthetic organization of sub-Saharan Africa." . . .

While doing research on cornshucking ceremonies among slaves in North America, Roger Abrahams found substantial evidence to support the view that African Americans preferred to dance on planks rather than the bare ground because they acted as sounding boards for the complex rhythms that were produced. What we see in stepping is a 1990s version of the same practice. Most step teams prefer using hard-soled shoes on wooden surfaces in order to amplify the sound.

Sorority and fraternity members also use canes and sticks as percussive devices. The use of canes, staffs, and sticklike objects has been noted in the dances of many traditional African cultures. Among such nomadic groups as the Mbuti, who have no drums, sticks and other implements are carried for musical purposes and used in conjunction with rhythmic stamping, hand clapping, complex body movements, and vocal techniques. Dancing with sticks is not usually seen in the Kongo area, but in northern Zaire and Sudan, where the martial arts are very popular, the use of sticks is coupled with dancing and chanting. Sticks are used for dancing by the Zulu, in South Africa, and among various cultures in Zambia and Mozambique.

Slaves brought to North America commonly used sticks to beat time on the floor. In African American dance acts of the 1920s through the 1940s, canes were often used to add flare and variety to stage presentations. The Berry Brothers were internationally famous for their acrobatic strut and cane dancing. In a display of perfect rhythmical timing and incredible agility, they could twirl their canes with lightning speed, bounce them off the floor, slide them down their arms, and throw them in the air, while tapping or performing flashy spins and knee drops.

Although Kappa Alpha Psi is reputedly the most skillful at using canes, several of Howard's step teams have adopted this practice. Through the use of canes, sticks, or the hands and feet, large step teams sometimes separate into three or four carefully spaced sections and function like drum choirs, each performing a different rhythm at the same time. Multiple meter is present in the body movements of the individual performers as well. Usually they dance at least two rhythms simultaneously, although at times three rhythms are played, particularly when canes are used. At the 1991 Howard University homecoming step show, the University of Virginia Kappas coordinated sharp head turns with three different rhythms: one with their canes, another with their feet, and a third with their left hands pounding against their chests.

Call and response between the step master or whoever gives the first call and the other members of the team happens on a verbal and nonverbal level. As an introduction for a step that is done blindfolded, the Alphas of Howard moved to the following call-and-response pattern:

Leader: Brothers!
Team: Ice!
Leader: A Phi
   A Phi A
   Uh, get *down!*
Team: Got to get down!
   Got to get down!
Leader: Get *down!*
Team: Got to get down!
   Got to get down!
Leader: Get *down!*
Team: Got to get down!
   Got to get down!
Leader and Team: A Phi A Alpha Brothers
   have *got* to get down! . . . Uh, you know!

There is a continuous call-and-response pattern between spectators and dancers. Audience members spring to their feet with the exuberance and enthusiasm of a football stadium crowd, and during the most virtuosic movements, the steps evoke verbal support and encouragement: "Break it down, y'all!" "Get it, girl!" "All right!" "Work it out!" "Go, Sherri!" "Get down, Chris!" Whistles, yells, barks, and numerous other verbal incantations almost drown out the performers. When teams don't quite meet the mark, a Howard step show audience can be as tough as the Apollo Theater crowds of the thirties and forties. Moving off beat, dropping props, or forgetting choreography can mean instant defeat for any competing team.

The special connection between the step show audiences and performers at Howard grows out of a shared knowledge of language and gesture that constitutes what Gerald Davis calls an *aesthetic community,* "a group of people sharing the knowledge for the development and maintenance of a particular affecting mode or 'craft' and the articulating principles to which the affecting mode must adhere or oppose" in performance. The audience members become both participants and observers, and the entire presentation of each team is designed specifically to elicit as much positive response as possible.

While the audience's reaction depends greatly on the movement skills of the performers, speech—witty speech, chanting, and verbal play—holds a crucial role in the overall presentation. Steppers can trace the traditions of eloquence in speech to sub-Saharan Africa. Ethel M. Albert's study of speech behavior in the traditional kingdom of Burundi is, according to Abrahams, characteristic of writings on African peoples:

> Speech is explicitly recognized as an important instrument of social life; eloquence is one of the central values of the cultural world-view; and the way of life affords frequent opportunity for its exercise. Sensitivity to the variety and complexity of speech behavior is evident in a rich vocabulary for its description and evaluation and in a constant flow of speech about speech. Argument, debate, and negotiation, as well as elaborate literary forms are built into the organization of society as means of gaining one's ends, as social status symbols, and as skills enjoyable within themselves.

When African slaves arrived in North America, they brought with them a "sensitivity to a wide variety of speech activities and a highly systematic sense of appropriateness in regard to content, formality, and diction."

Many observers of slave life have commented on the African American everyday use of proverbs, speeches, and movement nu-

ances. The leaders of such slave festivities as cornshucking ceremonies were selected for their ability to rhyme and improvise in a
witty manner. Cornshucking captains and set callers at dances seized
these opportunities to engage in social commentary: "The notion of
employing song or rhyme for making oral commentary came directly
from the various African cultures from which the slaves were taken."

In keeping with the traditions of their ancestors, the festivities of
slaves were occasions to celebrate through the use of song, dance,
music, and language. This winning combination is maintained at step
shows, where oral commentary and verbal play are central to the
overall success of the event. The rhymes, however, are not improvised, but rehearsed in advance and are delivered more often by a
group than by an individual.

Because stepping is rooted in a traditional African worldview that
values communication that is interactive and interdependent, the language of stepping must be entertaining as well as functional. The forms
of discourse used at Howard step shows grew out of a much larger system of terms or figures of speech that are present in the verbal play of
African American communities throughout the Americas. Among the
most widely used terms in the United States are *woofing, playing* (as in
playing the dozens), *marking, sounding, signifying, shucking, jiving, cracking, rapping,* and *joning.* These "ways of talking" function as floating
terms that to some degree vary in definition depending upon the community in which they are used. Abrahams insists that "many of the
names for these ways of speaking change constantly from time to time
and place to place, but the patterned interactions and the relations between the types of situated speech remain essentially constant."

Although the patterned interactions were present in the step
shows, most of the students did not describe their actions with these
terms. For example, none of the students used the terms *signifying*
("to imply, goad, beg, boast by indirect verbal or gestural means"),
sounding (a verbal dueling strategy that involves direct taunts), or
marking (when a speaker, through direct quotes, reproduces the
words, voice, and mannerisms of the targeted person or group). The
umbrella term used by Howard's stepping community to cover all
three verbal dueling strategies is *cracking.* Geneva Smitherman defines *cracking* as a way of "putting down" someone or showing disre-
spect for them, either in fun or seriously.

Usually fraternities crack on other frats, and sororities limit their cracks to rival female groups. In this practice we see a close link to the songs of allusion/dances of derision of African music and dance styles. By diminishing the status of their opponents through witty verbal surprises, sorority and fraternity members draw cheers from the audience. As Smitherman points out, "excellence and skill in this verbal art helps build yo rep and standing among yo peers." Delivered with just the right amount of rhythmical punch, a successful crack can bring the house down. In the following combination of marking and rapping, the Deltas of Howard parody the trade steps of the AKAs and Zetas:

> *Leader:* What is a Delta?
> *Team:* It is a serious matter . . . (performed in the song and dance
>   style of AKAs)
> *Leader:* That is definitely not a Delta!
>   Sorors, what is a Delta?
> *Team:* Woo-pee-dee, Woo-pee-dee . . . (performed in a Zeta
>   style)
> *Leader:* That is not a Delta!
>   Sorors, *what* is a Delta?
> *Team:* Devastating, captivating, oh so fine
> My soul stepping sisters gonna blow your mind.
> Many are called, but the chosen are few.
> Delta Sigma Theta's gonna rock it for you!

Saluting, a term coined by the fraternities and sororities, is a way of paying tribute to another group. Through a combination of movement, song, and speech, fraternities salute sororities and vice versa. In a seven-minute salute to fraternities at the Howard 1991 homecoming step show, the Delta Sigma Theta twenty-two-member team captured the characteristic stepping styles, calls, and hand signals of the Kappas, Alphas, Sigmas, and Omegas. The step leader began the call as the Deltas prepared to stomp their way into a marching-band-like formation:

> *Leader:* Here's what you've been waiting for—D S T
> *Team:* Here's what you've been waiting for.

We are that mighty, mighty Delta squad!
Here's what you've been waiting for.
We are that mighty, mighty Delta squad!
Here's what you've been waiting for.
We are that mighty, mighty Delta squad!

Positioned in four sections across the gymnasium floor, they took turns performing takeoffs on the stepping style of each fraternity. The longest and last segment of the salute was preserved for the Delta soul mates, Omega Psi Phi:

Leader: I said my D, my D, my D
Team: S T
   My Q, my Q, my Q
   Psi Phi
Leader: I said my Q, my Q, my Q
   Psi Phi
Team: My Q, my Q, my Q
   Psi Phi
   (continue chant until they change formation)
Leader and Team: All of our love and peace and happiness, we
      want to give to Omega.
   All of our love and peace and happiness, we want to give to
      Omega Psi Phi.
   (repeat)
Leader: Sorors!
Team: Yes!
Leader: I said, my sorors!
Team: Yes!
Leader: I said, how do you feel about Omega Psi Phi?
Team: I like to roop, roop
   roop, roopity, roop.

With hard-pumping body language, the Deltas broke into a series of typical Omega-like movements. The stands exploded with barks, cheers, and stomps, leaving no question about who would take home the women's first place trophy.

ALFONZO MATHIS

Step Show at Virginia State University

These step show pictures were taken in the fall of 2000. Figures 1 and 2 show the
Phi Beta Sigma brothers doing their steps. Figure 3 shows the Omega Psi Phi
brothers "gritt'n," a practice also popular with the VSU band. According to
Mathis, "gritt'n" is used to show which individual is the most intense about his
performance, and it is an exaggerated version of what is called "game face" in
sports.

1

2

3

Permission of Alfonzo Mathis.

ALFONZO MATHIS

The Virginia State University Marching Band

These pictures of the Virginia State University Marching Band were taken in the fall of 2000. As Mathis told me, the performance begins as the band enters the field, playing a powerful song to show off its volume—usually a testament to how much brass it has; the band members then march into formations and intricate configurations in a corps-style sequence. Next, the dancers are introduced, and while they perform the band remains stationary. Figure 1 shows the band "gritt'n" (see figure 3 in the previous selection). Figure 2 shows the dance group The Essence of Troy, their name playing on the name of the VSU football team, The Trojans. (In earlier days, as Mathis informed me, majorettes provided the cheesecake, but now times have changed and the feeling is that crowds needed a little more excitement. Now all the HBCUs [Historically Black Colleges and Universities] have a sex-appeal dance troupe. Hampton's dancers are called Ebony Fire, Norfolk State's Hot Ice, and Virginia Union University calls its dancers The Divas.) The next pictures show the band's dance routine, which climaxes the performance. When the drum major signals (3), the flag girls (in the short white skirts), who had remained in the back during the first part of the show, drop their flags and move to the front. They lead the rest of the band in performing a spirited dance routine to the latest popular music hit, either rhythm and blues or hip-hop (figures 4 and 5).

1

2

3

4

5

Permission of Alfonzo Mathis.

The Twist

· Photographs by Daryl Cumber Dance ·

LaFonda Davis of Richmond, Virginia, kindly allowed me to photograph her twist turned up in a bun, which was styled by Wanda Brown. Though LaFonda's own hair is quite long (below the shoulders), she uses hair extensions in her twists because they give her hair extra body and because they help the style to stay longer. Though her twist will last about a month, LaFonda spends about three hours having her hair restyled every two weeks.

Dreadlocks

· Photographs by James Mairs ·

Myshiel Massa, a pre-school teacher in New York, poses in her dreadlocks.

CLINTON A. STRANE, *Mr. CIAA, Strolling at the CIAA*
Figures 1 and 2 were photographed at the 1999 CIAA Basketball Tournament
in Winston-Salem, North Carolina; and figure 3 was photographed at the 2000
tournament in Raleigh, North Carolina. *Permission of Clinton A. Strane.*

MR. IMAGINATION (GREGORY WARMACK), *Self-Portrait and Self-Portrait as an African King*

Mr. Imagination (Gregory Warmack of Chicago, Illinois) fashioned *Self-Portrait* out of a paintbrush, which serves effectively to create the hair. The top of *Self-Portrait as an African King* is made out of a tiny paintbrush, with the body created from foil and the base from bottle tops. *Collection of William and Ann Oppenhimer; photographs by Daryl Cumber Dance. Permission of Gregory Warmack.*

EARNEST WHITE, *New Orleans Jazz Band*

Earnest (Bunky) White of Newport News, Virginia, began painting in the late 1980s. White uses his brushes to capture on canvas familiar events, people, and places in his community. His subjects range from tender, playful memories of his childhood to the anguishing problems of homelessness, crime, and hunger faced by modern society. This picture painted in 1990 or 1991 was motivated by his longtime interest in New Orleans jazz bands and funeral marches, which he had observed a couple of times (telephone conversation, September 3, 2000). *Collection of William and Ann Oppenhimer. Permission of Earnest White.*

NELLIE MAE ROWE, *Pig on Expressway*

Nellie Mae Rowe was born July 4, 1900, in Fayette County, Georgia. From 1930 on, she lived in Vinings, Georgia. As a child she learned from her mother to make quilts and dolls. In 1948, Rowe began decorating her house and yard. The display drew visitors from all over. She made dolls and chewing-gum sculptures. After 1976, she concentrated on making drawings using crayons, colored pencil, and pencil on paper. She died in 1982. *Collection of Judith Alexander. Permission of the Rowe estate.*

JOHNNY W. BANKS, *My Grandfather's Funeral*
Johnny W. Banks was born in San Antonio, Texas. His work is autobiographical,
much of it dealing with scenes from his childhood. He recalled, according to
collector Regenia Perry, that his teachers often scolded him for drawing in class.
He often depicts Juneteenth celebrations, picnics, and religious scenes. *Collection of*
Regenia Perry.

SARAH ALBRITTON, *He Lifted Me*

Sarah Albritton, who was born in Arcadia, Louisiana, in 1936, began working as a cook's assistant at the age of nine. She has spent her life catering, farming, working in the community, and painting. She says that *He Lifted Me* was inspired by guardian angels who encouraged her, such as her friends Susan Roach and Peter Jones. "God saw fit to bring the three of us together. So with you all's encouragement and being the mouthpiece for me, and helping me and encouraging me to paint . . . God has lifted me." Note that Albritton places a folklorist with a microphone and an artist with an easel to the left in the painting. *Photograph by Peter Jones. Narrative as told to and transcribed by Susan Roach. Permission of Sarah Albritton.*

Home Is a Place
I photographed this mural on an abandoned building on Second Street in Richmond, Virginia, on August 1, 2000. *Photograph by Daryl Cumber Dance.*

ANDERSON JOHNSON, *Portable Pulpit*
Anderson Johnson, an itinerant minister, carried this pulpit around with him. William Oppenhimer told me that his wife, Ann, was upset that he was crass enough to offer to buy it from Johnson, but the owner responded positively to his request, and now it is a prized piece in their extensive collection (interview, August 16, 2000). Johnson used egg crates and ice-cube trays in fashioning his pulpit. Rolled, painted paper gives the illusion of candles. Faces are painted on the sides of the creation. *Collection of William and Ann Oppenhimer; photograph by Daryl Cumber Dance. Permission of the Johnson estate.*

ROBERT HOWELL, *Fish*

Robert Howell was born in Powhatan, Virginia, where he still lives on
several acres that he has transformed into a wonderland of large-scale
sculptures. As collector Ann Oppenhimer told me, he transforms an array
of discarded materials, such as roofing tin, tree limbs, carpets, mops, and
broken furniture, into animals and people with "movement, animation,
and life" (interview, October 17, 2000). *Hampton University Museum, Hampton,
Virginia.*

1

Black Dolls

All of the Black dolls shown here are from the impressive collection of Barbara Radcliffe Grey of Richmond, Virginia. Grey started her collection in 1976 when she retired from the Richmond Public School System, perhaps, she has laughingly said, to compensate for "her children" that she missed (interview, July 30, 2000). Then when people told her there simply weren't that many Black dolls around, she was further motivated to continue collecting. She has recently begun to make dolls herself, particularly sock dolls. Museums frequently solicit for display her collection, which now numbers around two hundred. Grey also frequently loans her doll-sized slave quarters, constructed from wood taken from actual slave quarters in Goochland, Virginia. The nineteenth-century sock doll in figure 1 was just returned from the Smithsonian before our interview, while her crib and other related items were still at the Smithsonian. That doll, one of the oldest in her collection, is stuffed with straw and has a real silver clip on her collar; she holds her baby in her arms. Grey's collection includes various types of dolls from slavery

4

to the present; their dresses, suits, hair decorations, undergarments, cribs, chairs, and miscellaneous accoutrements provide a wealth of additional illustrations of Black crafts. The doll pictured in figure 2, c. 1910, has a cloth body and no facial features except button eyes. Figure 3 features a pair of rag dolls that Grey estimates are more than 100 years old. Their eyes are made of buttons and their noses and mouths are embroidered. The pair of broom dolls in figure 4 represent a popular kind of early Black doll; they too feature eyes of buttons and embroidered noses and mouths. Grey also has a number of "Topsy-Turvy" dolls similar to the two in figure 5 arranged so that you can see both the Black and the White dolls. Reportedly these dolls allowed a slave playing with a Black doll to simply turn it over so that the skirt would cover the Black face and the doll would appear to be White. Then when the interlopers left, another flip covered the White face and the child would have a Black doll again. *Collection of Barbara Radcliffe Grey; photographs by Daryl Cumber Dance.*

HARRIET POWERS, *Bible Quilt*

Harriet Powers, a former slave living in Athens, Georgia, had refused to sell her quilt to Jennie Smith when an offer of $10 was made for it in 1886. Unfortunately she was forced by financial exigencies to sell what Roland L. Freeman describes in *Communion of the Spirits: African American Quilters, Preservers, and Their Stories* as "everyone's favorite African-American quilt" to Smith in 1890 for $5. The descriptions of the eleven panels—provided by Powers, elaborated by Jennie Smith, and abbreviated by me—inform that the scenes include (in order) "Adam and Eve in the Garden of Eden, naming the animals," "A continuation of Paradise, but this time Eve has 'conceived and born a son,'" "Satan amidst the seven stars," "Cain 'is killing his brother Abel,'" "Cain goes into the land of Nod to get him a wife," "Jacob's dream when 'he lay on the ground,'" "The Baptism of Christ," "'Has reference to the Crucifixion,'" "Judas Iscariot and the thirty pieces of silver," "The Last Supper," and "the Holy Family." *National Museum of American History, Smithsonian Institution.*

JOSIE ELLA NEWBURN, *Nine-Patch Quilt*
This quilt was created by Josie Ella Newburn of Arkedelphia, Arkansas, who was born around 1902, and given to Cozetta Gray Guinn. Close-ups reveal some of the individual designs, including liberty bell. *Collection of Cozetta Gray Guinn; photograph by Daryl Cumber Dance.*

LOUISA GILL, *Dog Quilt*
This quilt was done by Louisa (pronounced Lou-eye-sa) Gill, Cozetta Gray Guinn's maternal grandmother, whom she called "Aunt Ted." Born in 1874 or 1875 in Bigelow, Arkansas, Gill, who died in 1944, made this quilt around 1940–41. It was first owned by Guinn's aunt in Chicago, passed on to her daughter, then to Guinn's mother, then to Guinn's sister, and finally to Guinn. In a conversation with me on March 9, 1999, Guinn recalled watching her grandmother piece quilts, cut out patterns, and sew the quilts. *Collection of Cozetta Gray Guinn; photograph by Daryl Cumber Dance.*

NORA EZELL, *Martin Luther King Jr. Quilt*
Here the quilter Nora Ezell provides numerous scenes from the life of King, titles of his writings, lines from his speeches, and panels of related events — including Rosa Parks's refusal to give up her bus seat and the passage of the Voting Rights Act. *Robert Cargo Folk Art Gallery. Permission of Nora Ezell.*

YVONNE WELLS, *Two Quilts of the Civil Rights Movement*
Yvonne Wells is a quilter from Alabama who has been drawn to making story
quilts on everything from race matters and religion to baseball. *Yesterday: Civil
Rights in the South* is a history of the Civil Rights movement. *Portrait of a King*
depicts Martin Luther King Jr. surrounded by various events from the 1960s.
Robert Cargo Folk Art Gallery. Permission of Yvonne Wells.

PEARLIE POSEY, *Hens Quilt*
As a child in Yazoo City, Mississippi, Pearlie learned to quilt from her grandmother. Quilting was a very personal and emotional activity for her; her mother died when Pearlie was five years old after spending her last days piecing quilt tops for her young daughter with the understanding that Pearlie's grandmother would turn them into quilts to remind Pearlie of her mother's love. Pearlie also made quilts, such as this 1981 *Hens Quilt*, for her children, explaining, "Then if the Lord take me and leave you . . . I say you'll have some covers"

(Maude Wahlman, *Signs and Symbols*). *Pearlie Posey (1894–1984), Yazoo City, Mississippi, 1981. Cotton and synthetics, 71" x 69". Collection of the Museum of American Folk Art, New York; Gift of Maude and James Wahlman, 1991.52.02.*

SARAH MARY TAYLOR,
Mr. Fletcher Quilt
Sarah Mary Taylor learned to quilt from her mother, Pearlie Posey (see her *Hens Quilt*). For Taylor, quilting is an artistic endeavor: "When I be doing it, be trying to see how pretty I can make it, just how I picture it in my mind" (Maude Wahlman, *Signs and Symbols*). *Sarah Mary Taylor (b. 1916), Yazoo City, Mississippi, 1990. Cotton and cotton blends, 77 ½" x 62". Collection of the Museum of American Folk Art, New York; Gift of Marion Harris and Dr. Jerry Rosenfeld, 1995.10.01.*

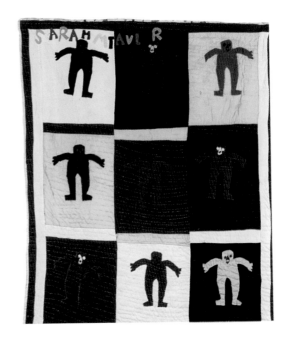

JOHN LANDRY, *Queen's Float*
This miniature Carnival Float was fashioned by New Orleans native John Landry. Landry was always fascinated by the Mardi Gras floats and used to make necklaces and toys out of carnival beads thrown from them when he was a little boy. After he retired, he began to design miniature replicas of the elaborate Mardi Gras floats out of plastic and glass beads (Perry, *What It Is*). *Collection of Regenia Perry.*

Jewelry Box
This jewelry box made from matchsticks was purchased by William and Ann Oppenhimer at a flea market. They were told that it was probably made by a prisoner as a gift to the woman whose name appears on it. *Collection of William and Ann Oppenhimer; photograph by Daryl Cumber Dance.*

Graffiti in Richmond, Virginia
This item displaying the artist's tag was photographed in the Church Hill neighborhood in July 2000. One of the legendary seven hills in Richmond (there really aren't seven), Church Hill is the city's oldest neighborhood. It had become almost completely Black by the mid-twentieth century, but with urban gentrification, Whites are returning to some parts of Church Hill and restoring some of the interesting antebellum homes. *Photograph by Daryl Cumber Dance.*

1

2

Graffiti in Richmond's North Side
In the mainly residential North Side, the sites struck by the graffiti artists are a bit different than in some of the business areas. Several garage doors and even the sides of garages are covered in graffiti as seen in figure 1.
An abandoned building provided the opportunity for a few "artists" to display the tags shown in figure 2. One wonders if the "Mofia" were a poor speller's attempt to spell "Mafia." It's very likely that the "Crip" that I saw written on one street, but not pictured here, was meant to suggest the infamous gang. There is almost no gang activity in Richmond, however, and no indication that the Crips have any organization here. *Photographs by Daryl Cumber Dance.*

Chapter 4

Folk Arts and Crafts

The Spirit woke me up and said, "Carve Wood."
—Folk sculptor Jesse Aaron

*What my mother teaches me are the essential lessons of the
quilt; that people and actions do move in multiple directions
at once.*
—Elsa Barkley Brown, "African-American Women's
Quilting"

A frican American art clearly originated in Africa, where art
is manifested in all aspects of communal life. The art of
Africa, like its music, is both aesthetic and functional, and
it is designed for and used in activities of everyday life, religious ceremonies, and social affairs. African artists were and are carvers in
wood, ivory, and bone; sculptors in stone, clay, bronze, gold, and
iron; and spinners and weavers of textiles. African motifs, subjects,
designs, styles, and materials are evident in much work produced
by Blacks throughout the Americas. Though African forms have
evolved considerably over the years and have blended with European and White American forms, many aspects of the style of contemporary American folk art still reflect a prominent African
influence.

Among the traditional arts and crafts produced by enslaved and
freed Blacks in this country were personal art objects, ceramics, bas-
ketry, earthenware, trays, bowls, grave decorations, woodcarvings,
furniture, musical instruments, toys, fabrics, and quilts. African-
inspired architecture includes, among numerous others, the wrought-
iron balconies in New Orleans, shotgun houses found throughout the

South, a cylindrical quarter for enslaved Africans in Virginia that resembles Tembu houses in South Africa, and carved mantels with an African mask motif in North Carolina.

Much African American folk art depicts religious subjects, such as Biblical events and popular Biblical characters, especially Jesus and angels. Also prevalent subjects in Black folk art are a variety of fish, fowl, and animals—especially the snake, the lizard, the alligator, the pig, and the monkey, several of which have religious symbolism as well. Frequently treated in folk art are political figures: representations of Martin Luther King Jr., John F. Kennedy, and Abraham Lincoln are commonplace. Whether their subject stems from personal, religious, or political sources, Black artists, like musicians and storytellers, use their expressions to celebrate the things they prize and to attack those they despise, often in a signifying manner.

Traditionally, a number of crafts are taught to children and passed on in the family, one of the most common being wood carving, a popular form in Black communities in Africa and the New World. Among the most clear-cut representations of African influences on American wood carving are walking sticks and canes. Here, as in Africa, where canes were traditional badges of power, the canes tend to have very symbolic carvings, the snake being an ever-present icon.[1] Often the handles are carved into heads or faces. One of the most polished illustrations of an early woodcarving is of a preacher carved between 1860 and 1890 (reproduced later in this chapter).

Basket weaving is another traditional craft that continues to be popular in a few areas of the United States and throughout the Caribbean. Roadside stands in the Deep South, especially in South Carolina and Georgia, feature items that have been made by Black artisans for more than three centuries from grass, reeds, leaves, straw, rushes, palm or oak strips. Their works include coiled baskets,

---

[1] The snake is often viewed with reverence in Africa and the Diaspora. The snake, particularly the python, is often associated with gods, especially Damballa. Often what one sees is not to be regarded as a mere snake, but a being incorporating the spirit of a god or an ancestor. Sometimes snakes may also represent evil spirits or witches. African beliefs about snakes also often incorporate Christian beliefs, which view the snake as the tempter. These conflicting interpretations are dramatized in numerous African literary works, most notably Chinua Achebe's *Things Fall Apart.*

pocketbooks, hats, trays, mats, fans, and chairs. A number of items made out of traditional materials and often following traditional designs also incorporate modern trinkets.

Enslaved African Americans also made a variety of musical instruments. Fiddles and banjos were crafted from pine boards and the gut of a slaughtered cow, or from gourds and horsehair. Other instruments commonly made in the Black community included the single-stringed washtub bass, rattles, tambourines, castanets, flutes, gong whistles, and double-stringed cigar boxes. Drums, the most popular of all of the instruments, were often made from barrels with an ox hide stretched across one end. An upturned bucket could, without any modifications, become an effective drum. Music has also been produced using a number of other common items, including bottles, spoons, and sticks.

From slavery until the present, many Black families have fashioned a whole host of toys to keep their children occupied, including dolls, dollhouses, balls, checkers, dominoes, kites, whirligigs, windmills, spinning tops, bows and arrows, slingshots, wagons, wheelbarrows, airplanes, skateboards, seesaws, and tree swings. Though I grew up in a relatively prosperous rural family that provided store-bought toys, I, like virtually every other child in my rural community, had a swing hanging from the large walnut tree in the front yard and a glider on my front porch. Many of my friends had seesaws made by their fathers and uncles. One of the most delightful "toys" in my childhood memories is an elaborate dollhouse made by a neighbor and set in his front yard. Each of the rooms featured ornate furniture that he had also created. I spent hours gazing in the varied windows of this magical miniature house.

From the days of slavery as well, another craft practiced in the Black community was pottery. Often African Americans fashioned small items for their personal use. They made their stoneware vessels of local clay. As Regenia Perry has pointed out, "The facial features of the vessels are frequently tormented; however, some examples are static, smiling and a few are suggestive of a voice raised in song" ("Black American Folk Art"). The eyes and teeth were sometimes made of white clay, offering a contrast to the darker colors with which the pottery was glazed.

Many slave girls grew up learning from their mothers how to spin, weave, and sew. Slave women often carded and spun threads and wove fabrics. They made dyes out of indigo, varied barks, leaves, and herbs. After producing, bleaching, and/or coloring varied fabrics, the slave women sewed and knitted and embroidered garments for their masters and themselves.

Though quilting is not generally considered an African tradition, Sule Greg C. Wilson notes in *African American Quilting*, that it has been found in ancient Egyptian robes and that West Africans use quilted finery for ceremonial occasions. He also points out that the traditional narrow-strip weaving, which is a hallmark of West African textile work, has influenced the preference for patterns that flow in slender strips observed in African American quilting. It is clear that this quilting has been influenced by both African and European traditions. Decorative quilts have long been a viable part of the tradition of women in a number of European groups in this country. Blacks have, however, made of their quilting a unique art form. Their quilts often use African motifs, images, patterns, fabrics, and appliqué techniques. There are some standard patterns, such as the Dresden Plate, Bowtie, Saw Tooth, Double Wedding Ring, Field of Diamonds, the Crazy Quilt, and the Strip Quilt, but most accomplished quilters modify these patterns or create unique designs reflecting their own attitudes and styles. Quilts made in the White community are generally more precise, subdued, and refined and are usually consistent in reproducing traditional patterns. Black quilts are often bolder in color and design, less consistent and precise in following the standard patterns, and often make no pretense at following those patterns. Black quilts are often compared to jazz music in their improvisation and rhythmic composition. During slavery quilts sometimes incorporated secret codes to guide escaping slaves on the Underground Railroad, as suggested in Jacqueline Tobin and Raymond Dobard's *Hidden in Plain View: The Secret Story of Quilts and the Underground Railroad* and in Sule Greg C. Wilson's *African American Quilting*. Many free Black women attended quilting bees, where neighbors gathered in a very social atmosphere to sew, tell tales, and sing. The hostess would serve food and drink.

One final form of folk art requires extended commentary. The oldest form of expression, dating back to prehistoric eras, is graffiti, now regarded by some as a most annoying form of defacement of property against which the full power of the law must be brought; others see it as the latest art form, a big business where "graffiti artists" are paid for their work.

For varied reasons, graffiti has enjoyed a popularity among some inner-city African Americans, partly because traditionally in this country, it is an underground activity, one that provides an opportunity for expression of an idea without identification. Artists struck, leaving their messages usually written with spray-paint cans, in subway trains, on the sides of buses, trucks, and trains, in bathroom stalls, on highway overpasses, on signs and posters, on rocks, in the hallways of schools, on windowpanes, on trees, on the outside walls of buildings, on rooftops, on sidewalks, in the sand—on virtually any surface on which they could work unobserved.

Graffiti, like many forms of folklore, is often an individual statement of identity. Robert Reisner and Lorraine Wechsler speculate in their *Encyclopedia of Graffiti* that graffiti began when "prehistoric man placed his hand on a cave wall and traced the outlines of his fingers with pigment. It was his way of saying 'I exist.'" For contemporary graffiti artists, it continues to provide a way of proclaiming one's nom de plume, displaying one's unique, identifying symbol or tag, asserting one's fame, expressing one's love, declaring one's affiliation, expressing one's philosophy, and attacking one's enemies. Much graffiti focuses on the forbidden, discussing in the most explicit terms lewd and hostile ideas that society constrains individuals from expressing openly. Often graffiti reflects racial and religious prejudices and hatred in the most obscene of terms. Quite a bit of it, especially that found in bathrooms, deals in sexual perversions, often focusing on the genitalia, sexual relations, oral sex, sodomy, or homosexuality. A great deal of it is scatological, focusing on excrement, flatulence, and the like.

In places like Los Angeles, graffiti became the mechanism for young males, especially gang members, to mark territories and assail enemies. Graffiti has also become an international forum for artists who try to outdo one another with more elaborate tags, bigger "masterpieces," and numbers of hits (places where they paint their graffiti). Their artistry became more and more sophisticated. They began to develop three-dimensional letters and pictures. Contemporary graffiti seems to emphasize the artistry (pictures, dimensions, color, visual appeal) as much as the message; much earlier graffiti was all writing and the artist had a message to communicate rather than a creation to share.

Graffiti became a significant part of the hip-hop culture that developed in New York in the 1970s. As graffiti artists began to receive media attention, they began to organize meetings (at places called writers' corners or benches) to make plans, settle disputes, and "bench" (watch and critique art on passing subway trains). United Graffiti Artists was soon formed, and the work of some of the subway artists was collected and exhibited in museums. Magazines developed. Some of these later developments displeased some of the artists, who declared, "Real writers bomb trains: not magazines."[2] Like other forms of the hip-hop culture, the graffiti craze moved elsewhere—to small American towns and to Mexico, Canada, and Europe. European artists were so eager to come and work in New York that the Americans hosted "Pilgrimages to Mecca."[3] Now, of course, beginning with the first one in 1994, numerous Web sites provide a safer medium for graffiti than the ones utilized by the original artists, who sometimes stole their paint and sneaked into the sites that they "bombed." Further, as Susan A. Phillips notes in *Wallbangin': Graffiti and Gangs in L.A.*, some modern practitioners reject the label "graffiti" and prefer that their work be called aerosol or spraycan art.

A glance at the slave potter, the inner-city wallbanger, and everything in between thus reveals the rich body of folk art produced by African Americans. While Black folk arts and crafts, often referred to as material culture, take many forms, it is interesting to note their common deviations from the Western "norms" of beauty, balance, structure, and logic. First of all, Black artists often make use of things that are considered old, ugly, useless, trash. Thus they work with rags, toothpicks, chewing gum, popsicle sticks, matchsticks, soda pop tops, tree stumps, driftwood, paintbrushes, brooms, mud, newspaper, etc., etc.

Black folk art is almost always flat and unbalanced. Figures with big popping eyes, grimacing teeth, and misshapen bodies challenge

[2]"History Part I," www.at149st.com/hpart1html.
[3]"History Part II."

the Western sense of the beautiful. William Ferris has noted, "The preference for ugliness is an aesthetic choice which reverses traditional white concepts of beauty somewhat like the black use of 'bad' to mean 'good' " (quoted in Livingston and Beardsley, *Black Folk Art in America*). It is important to reinforce the fact that Black folk art reflects, like many forms of Black folk expression, a love of improvisation and a desire to surprise, to switch around, and to disallow complacent expectations. It reflects too an African culture that does not share America's traditional standards of beauty.

Regenia Perry sums up some of the major characteristics of African American folk art in *What It Is:*

> The folk artist's orientation is essentially noncommercial, an unself-conscious artist who frequently creates for his own pleasures and the decoration of his home and environment. Folk art disobeys most of the elements and principles of fine art, and is almost invariably flat, colorful, and illogical in space relationships. Much of the subject matter is imaginary, and the works are frequently made of simple or cast-off materials. The very unpretentiousness of folk art is probably its most appealing characteristic. The viewer is able to enjoy its aesthetic appeal without having to participate in elaborate mental exercises. Folk art is childlike without being childish.

Additional folk art appears in the color photo section.

✳ C A R V I N G S   A N D
S C U L P T U R E S ✳

Seated Figure Holding a Bowl

This figure, carved in Fayetteville, New York, between 1836 and 1865, is
sometimes called "Child with Bucket." I prefer the description provided by
Regenia Perry, who notes that similar figures with bowls are common in the
Congo region of Africa and in some Yoruba territories *(What It Is)*.

Abby Aldrich Rockefeller Folk Art Museum,
Williamsburg, Virginia.

MISSIONARY MARY PROCTOR

My Aunt Betsey Told Me

"My Aunt Betsey" was created on a drawer panel using paint and glue.
Missionary Proctor's work is commonly done on doors and drawer panels.

Garde Rail Gallery.

Country Preacher

One of the best known of the slave wood carvings, this figure of a preacher was
carved of pine in Kentucky between 1860 and 1890.

Anonymous, American, 19th century,
Country Preacher, *1860–1890, white*
pine, 29 in. high, Elizabeth R. Vaughan
Fund, 1956.1199. Photograph ©2000,
The Art Institute of Chicago, All Rights
Reserved.

HENRY GUDGELL

Walking Stick

Henry Gudgell, a slave blacksmith, wheelwright,
coppersmith, and silversmith in Livingston County, Missouri,
probably carved this walking stick for John Byran, a friend
of his master who suffered a knee injury during the Civil War.
Regenia Perry speculates that the cane was probably done
between 1865 and 1867 ("Black American Folk Art").

JAMES HAMPTON

The Throne of the Third Heaven of the Nations Millennium General Assembly

James Hampton's renowned sculpture, c. 1950–64, is made of
furniture, lightbulbs, jelly jars, cardboard, and miscellaneous
other discarded items that he covers with aluminum and gold
foils. On tablets adorning the *Throne*, Hampton recorded the
religious visions that inspired this work. After his death in
1964, the *Throne* was discovered in a garage that he rented.
Mike Walsh writes in "The Miracle of St. James Hampton,"
"[Hampton's] central motivation for building the Throne was
as a tribute to his God. He believed, quite literally, in the
Second Coming, and his work on the Throne was in
preparation for that event. He also claimed to have
communed regularly with the Almighty during the Throne's
construction."

*Yale
University
Art Gallery.*

*Smithsonian American Art Museum, Washington, DC/Art
Resource, NY.*

J . B . A N D E R S O N

Male Angel

J. B. Anderson carved this male angel from white oak with a chainsaw.

*Collection of William and Ann Oppenhimer of
Richmond, Virginia; photograph by Daryl Cumber
Dance. Permission of J. B. Anderson.*

STEVEN ASHBY

Large Lady in Beige Outfit

Ashby made this painted wood and mixed media piece in 1970.

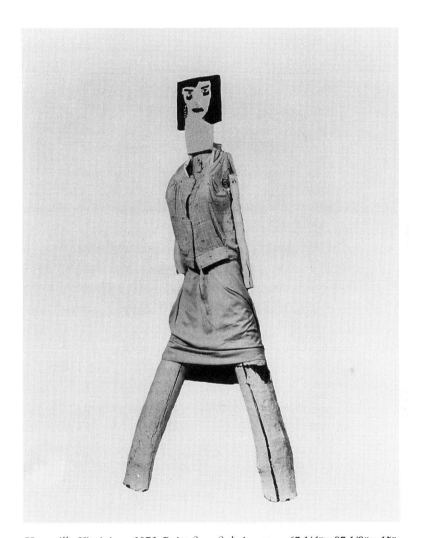

Upperville, Virginia, c. 1970. Painted wood, hair, cotton, 63 1/4″ × 27 1/2″ × 15″ deep. Collection of the Museum of American Folk Art, New York; Gift of Chuck and Jan Rosenak. 1978.17.01.

❋ P O T T E R Y ❋

Afro-Carolinian Face Vessel

This mid-nineteenth-century glazed stoneware face vessel is one of a group of
unique pieces in Georgia and the Carolinas variously dubbed, Regenia Perry
points out, "plantation pottery," "voodoo pots," "grotesque jugs," "slave jugs," and
"monkey jugs." Given the fact that many of these face vessels are too small to have
been used as containers, Perry speculates that there is some link between them
and religious spirits. She further notes the similarity of many of these vessels to
Bakongo figural sculptures of Zaire *(What It Is)*.

National Museum of American History,
Smithsonian Institution.

Dave's Pottery

Some of the largest handmade vessels from the nineteenth century were created and inscribed with rhyming couplets by a South Carolina slave known only as Dave. One plaintively meditates, "I wonder where is all my relations / friendship to all and every nation." A jar, dated June 27, 1840, declares, "Give me silver or either gold / though they are dangerous to the soul" (Allison Germaneso, "I Made This Jar").

Jug, 1836. American: Southern United States. Ceramic. David Drake, Edgefield district, SC, 1800-ca.1. Alkaline-glazed stoneware. 17 1/4″× 13″× 13″ (43.8 × 33 × 33 cm). High Museum of Art, Atlanta, Georgia; Purchased with funds from the Decorative Arts Endowment 1997.193.

* D O L L S   A N D   O T H E R
T O Y S *

RUTH POLK PATTERSON

Toys Fashioned in the Polk Family
· *From* The Seeds of Sally Good'n ·

In addition to counting games, the Polk children were entertained by homemade toys. A special toy that had an African origin was the "bull roarer," which Arthur Polk made for his children. A "bull roarer" is a musical instrument common among African and other non-Western cultures. The West African writer Chinua Achebe mentions the instrument in his works. The bull roarer was made by whittling a thin piece of wood, about six inches long and two or three inches wide, into a special shape with a hole carved in one end. A piece of twine was tied through the hole, and when the string was whirled around rapidly, the piece of wood made a loud, roaring sound. Arthur Polk knew the exact shape and size to carve the bull roarer in order to produce the right sound.

A favorite summer pastime for the young was propelling a "hoop and pad" up and down the lanes between the Bullock and Polk farmsteads. A "hoop and pad" was made by taking an iron band from a worn-out wagon wheel hub and rolling it along the ground with a paddle. The wheel was kept upright by the paddle, which was made from a short strip of wood or a stick to which was attached a tin flap on one end. The tin flap was often made from a flattened snuff box, which was nailed to the stick, curved around to fit the narrow band of iron, and maneuvered in such a way as to steer the rolling wheel along the desired route.

Other homemade toys included the "bean flip," cornstalk horses, corncob dolls, and a variety of whistles. The "bean flip" was a slingshot made from a forked tree branch, with rubber bands made from old inner tubes attached as straps. The ammunition was held in a piece of leather cut from a cast-off shoe and tied to the rubber bands to form a small slingshot. Small rocks were used for ammunition, and the toys were used for target practice or to shoot birds for food.

The making of cornstalk horses was both a skill and an art. The "horses" were soon discarded rather than used to play with, so the main purpose in making them was to see who could make the best horse. Dry cornstalks were stripped of the hard covering, and, using the soft center for the body and head, the horse was put together by thin strips made from the hard outer stalk. The strips of stalk were cut into desired lengths, sharpened on the ends, and used as pins to attach head and body, or used in larger strips for legs, tail, and ears. Careful details of ears, eyes, legs, and tail provided for individual creativity and personal imagination.

Corncob dolls were made by using a cob for the body and making the head from a goldenrod plant that formed, in the middle of the stalk, a large round tumor that turned brown and hard in the fall of the year. The round tumor was broken off with a long stem on one end. The stem was pushed into the soft center of the cob, forming a perfect neck and head. The head was then adorned with cotton for hair and bits of paper for eyes, nose, and mouth. The cob body was then dressed in the fashion that could best be devised by using scraps of cloth, ribbon, and threads. The girls would vie to see who could design the most fabulous fashions for her individual family of dolls. Store-bought dolls were seldom brought home, but when they were they were soon cast aside in deference to the children's own creations.

Common twine provided another source for toys. Forming designs and playing tricks with string made for hours of entertainment for the Polk children. String was used to make a "Jacob's Ladder" and a "cat's cradle," which were intricate designs threaded between the fingers of both hands. String was also used to "cut off" one's fingers; this was done by looping the thread through the fingers, thus cutting them off. "Spinning buttons" were made by threading twine through the holes of buttons, winding it up, and then pulling the elasticized twist of twine back and forth to spin the button with a buzzing sound. It was a real trick to be able to tie a knot in a string without turning loose the ends of the string. Of course, live "kites" were improvised by tying a string to the leg of a captured June bug and setting the green and gold creature free to fly the limits of its hand-clutched tether.

Black Raggedy Ann

Pictured here is an unusual colored version of the popular Raggedy Ann doll.

*Collection of Jacquelyn Thomas of Richmond,
Virginia; photograph by Daryl Cumber Dance.*

Banjo

This banjo was used by an African American family in Smyth County, Virginia, in
the 1800s. It is displayed at the Virginia Historical Society with a rum bottle of
the age and type sometimes presented to slaves at Christmastime.

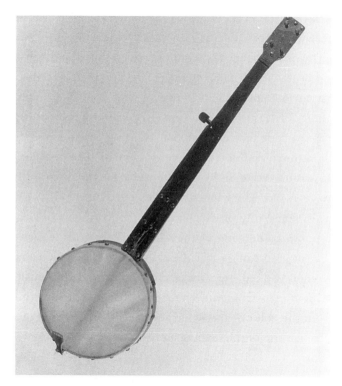

Virginia Historical Society, Richmond, Virginia.

BENJAMIN HENRY BONEVAL LATROBE

New Orleans Musical Instruments

· *From* Impressions Respecting New Orleans (*sketches*) *and*
The Journal of Latrobe ·

Following are Benjamin Henry Boneval Latrobe's description and sketches of
slave instruments that he saw being played in a New Orleans public square in
February 1819.

The music consisted of two drums and a stringed instrument. An old man sat astride of a cylindrical drum, about a foot in diameter, and beat it with incredible quickness with the edge of his hand and fingers. The other drum was an open-staved thing held between the knees and beaten in the same manner. They made an incredible noise. The most curious instrument, however, was a stringed instrument, which no doubt was imported from Africa. On the top of the finger board was the rude figure of a man in a sitting posture, and two pegs behind him to which the strings were fastened. The body was a calabash. It was played upon by a very little old man, apparently eighty or ninety years old. The women squalled out a burden to the playing, at intervals, consisting of two notes, as the negroes working in our cities respond to the song of their leader. Most of the circles contained the same sort of dances. One was larger, in which a ring of a dozen women walked, by way of dancing, round the music in the center. But the instruments were of different construction. One which from the color of the wood seemed new, consisted of a block cut into something of the form of a cricket bat, with a long and deep mortise down the center. This thing made a considerable noise, being beaten lustily on the side by a short stick. In the same orchestra was a square drum, looking like a stool, which made an abominable, loud noise; also a calabash with a round hole in it, the hole studded with brass nails, which was beaten by a woman with two short sticks.

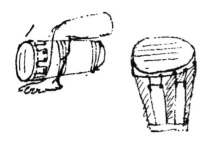

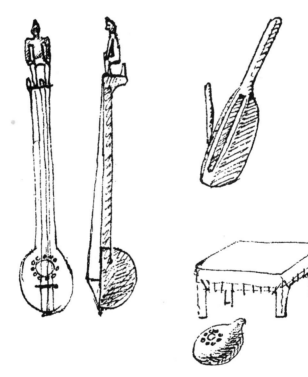

✳ E V E R Y D A Y
O B J E C T S ✳

A B R A H A M   L I N C O L N   C R I S S

Animals

The innovative Abraham Criss fashioned a variety of striking animals that
achieved a remarkable verisimilitude. Criss often made the bodies of his animals
from a special mixture of sawdust and glue that looks eerily realistic. The goat in
figure 1 has the actual legs of a deer. The turtle in Figure 2 has a practical
purpose: Criss designed it as a seat for a child.

1

2

Collection of William and Ann Oppenhimer; photographs by Daryl Cumber Dance.
Permission of Shirley Criss Fields.

Lamp

The shade of this lamp is fashioned out of Popsicle sticks. The base and the two large figures are carved wood, while the small figure is made from Criss's glue-and-sawdust mixture.

Collection of William and Ann Oppenhimer; photograph by Daryl Cumber Dance. Permission of Shirley Criss Fields.

Rocking Chair

This drawing of a rocking chair made by slaves is from the Sam Houston Home.

Pearl Davis, Hickory Rocking Chair, *Photograph ©
2001 Board of Trustees, National Gallery of Art,
Washington.*

Quilting Parties

· *From Ann Banks, First Person America* ·

This 1938 WPA narrative collected from Mayme Reese in New York by Dorothy
West tells us something about the folk practices surrounding the designing,
making, and selling of quilts.

We used to have quilting parties at least twice a year. Say there'd
be three or four ladies who were good friends; one time we would
meet at one house and one time at another. You'd keep on that way
until the quilt was finished. If I was making the quilt, I'd set up the
quilting frame in my house and the other two or three ladies would
come and spend the day quilting. I'd have it all ready for the quilting to start. You'd decide before how you were going to make the
stitches: if you were going to have a curving stitch, you'd sew one
way; if you were going to quilt block fashion, you'd sew that way. I
might have been sewing scraps together for a year until I got the
cover all made. Then when my friends came, there wouldn't be anything to do but start working on the padding. If there were four
ladies, each would take an end.

The ladies would come as early in the morning as they could.
Sometimes you all had breakfast together. If you didn't you had dinner together and a little snack off and on during the day. If it was at
my house and nobody was coming early enough for breakfast, I'd
put something on the sideboard that everybody could reach if they
got hungry before time to sit at the table. Sometimes there'd be sweet
potatoes, some smoked pork, bread, maybe some syrup, and things
like that. Then when you had dinner, there'd be the regular things
everybody had at home. If somebody came way in from the country
or a town eight or nine miles away, they'd have supper and stay all
night.

Depending upon how many quilts you needed a year or just
wanted to make, there'd be that many quilting parties for ladies who
were intimates. If none of my friends were going to make quilts in a
year, then they'd keep coming to my house maybe twice a week until
we got it finished. If you worked right along and didn't stop to talk —
course most of the time we stopped to gossip a little — you could finish a quilt in a day or two. That depended on the pattern, too. If

somebody else was making a quilt, we'd go to their house and ex-change labor till they got their quilt done.

Whenever we had a quilting party, the men folks had to look out for themselves. They ate cold food if they came in hungry in the day and if we finished working soon enough, they'd get their supper on time. If we didn't, they just had to wait. They didn't mind. If they fussed, we'd remind em about keeping warm in the winter.

Sometimes we'd take our quilts out to the country fairgrounds for exhibition in the fall. Each lady picked out her best quilt—the pret-tiest color, the prettiest pattern, and the best stitches—and took it to the fair to try to win the prize. It didn't make any difference if your prettiest quilt had been quilted by three or four other people; you al-ready had the pattern and you'd already put the pieces together, so that much was your own idea. And that counted more than the help you got when you were putting it on the frame. Sometimes a church club would make a quilt and enter it in the name of the church. Even if they put it in the club's name, the club would give the money to the church if they won. Once I won the prize for my own quilt and once I was one of a group that won. The prize was most often five dollars, sometimes ten. One year they couldn't get the money together and they gave the winner some prize preserves, some pieces of fancy-work, and something else that had won first prize in other contests instead of the money. Course you'd rather have the money because everybody could can fruit and do tatting and crocheting and things like that and they could make their own things. But you couldn't act nasty about it. Anyhow, it didn't happen but once as I remember it.

Sometimes rich white women would hear that such and such a per-son had won the prize for pretty quilts and they'd come and ask that person to make them a quilt. Sometimes they'd make it and sometimes they wouldn't. If they did make it, they'd get around five dollars. Sometimes they'd furnish the scraps; most of the time, though, they'd buy pieces of goods and give it to the person who was making the quilt to cut up. They'd get different colors and say what pattern they wanted.

Some of the churches would have quilting parties. Not every church did that, but those that did had quite a few woman members come to quilt. They'd get some little boys to take the quilting frame to the church in the morning and then they'd go in the afternoon. I guess they'd quilt for two, three hours. Most of the time they'd be making the quilt to sell to raise money for the church.

Things like that were nice. Sometimes I wish I could go back to that kind of life for a while, but times have changed so. They won't ever be like that again. But I guess it's just as well. Nowadays, there are other things to occupy people's minds.

Key Basket

This tooled leather key basket is reported to have been made by an inmate at the slave penitentiary in Richmond, c. 1845–50. Note the intricate design of diamonds and hearts. Key baskets were designed to hold the large and cumbersome keys of the period.

Virginia Historical Society, Richmond, Virginia.

"Tramp Art" Bureau

This bureau, from around 1890, descended in the family of Fred Lander of Lynchburg, Virginia, an African American physician, and his wife, Georgia, a schoolteacher. The mirror can be pivoted to access a sewing kit on the back. This interesting piece of decorative furniture is often referred to as "tramp art," the term used (beginning in the 1950s) to identify a form of folk art that was popular from the 1870s to the 1950s. The lore is that tramp art was produced by "tramps" who sold it for food, shelter, and pocket change. Using for the most part cigar boxes and wood from fruit crates, these craftsmen notched, layered, and whittled highly embellished picture frames, elaborate boxes, and furniture such as the bureau pictured on the following page.

Virginia Historical Society, Richmond, Virginia.

Basketmaker and His Tools

Georgia basketmaker Charles Wilson is pictured here with one of his baskets and his tools.

The Georgia Historical Society, Savannah, Georgia.

EDWARD LEE ATKINS

Crafts

Edward Lee Atkins of Charles City County began making varied crafts out of
wood when he retired in 1988. Best known for his Christmas reindeer-head
mailbox ornaments, he also makes wastebaskets, baby rockers, paper-towel
holders, toilet-tissue holders, and laundry hampers. Figures he has crafted adorn
his property, including the boy and girl at play in his yard in the first picture. His
reindeer mailbox ornament, a toilet-tissue holder, and two towel holders are
featured in the second photograph.

Photographs by Daryl Cumber Dance. Permission of Edward Lee Atkins.

Making Mullet Net

Beamon Lee is pictured here making mullet net at St. Simons Island, Georgia, in March 1948.

The Georgia Historical Society, Savannah, Georgia.

Purse Seine

Tidewater, Virginia, fishermen, many of whom were Black, made purse seines, like the ones shown here. These seines were dropped into the sea and tightened like a purse string to catch menhaden.

From the collections of The Mariner's Museum, Newport News, Virginia; photograph by Daryl Cumber Dance.

✳ G R A F F I T I ✳

Hand Signs from the 79 Family Swan
Bloods, 1996

Phillips offers the following explanation for this item: "The first hand signs '7, 9,
F' for 79th Street Family; the second represents the swan itself. [The assorted
numbers to the right] represent streets that constitute the extended territory of
the Swans neighborhood. The composition ends with the common rhyme "CK
[Crip Killas] all day."

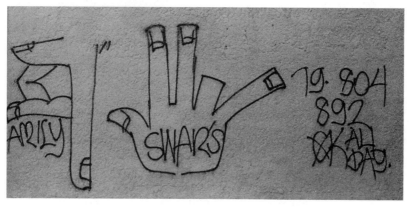

From Susan A. Phillips, Wallbangin': Graffiti and Gangs in L.A. *Permission
of Susan A. Phillips.*

Pirus Rule the Streets of Bompton
[Compton] Fool's

Phillips explains that because Crips avoid using the letter *B*, and Bloods the letter *C*, the offending letter will be scratched out in graffiti. Note that *Bompton* is used here instead of *Compton*.

From Susan A. Phillips, Wallbangin': Graffiti and Gangs in L.A. *Permission of Susan A. Phillips.*

No More Prisons

This item was photographed in Jackson Ward, the oldest Black neighborhood in Richmond, Virginia. Adjoining the city's downtown, Jackson Ward in its heyday was called "The Wall Street of Black America." Including historic Second Street, the neighborhood was home to numerous Black businesses: the first bank owned by a woman or a Negro (Maggie Walker's Consolidated Bank), several real estate companies, hotels, restaurants, retail stores, and theaters, as well as elegant homes. However, the area suffered urban blight following the integration of public facilities.

The blunt "No More Prisons" obviously comments on the expensive investment Virginia (and other parts of the country) has made in prisons, spending much more to incarcerate a largely Black male population than to educate them.

Photograph by Daryl Cumber Dance.

Graffiti on Second Street

I photographed the graffiti in the first picture at a garage on Richmond's historic Second Street, where the mechanic told me that his own truck had been covered with graffiti while parked at his home on the intersecting Clay Street. The second item was on a wall across the street from the garage. Both photos were taken in August 2000.

Photographs by Daryl Cumber Dance.

A Bum Was Here

Readers cannot possibly appreciate the commentator's note, "It smells like a bum was here," unless they experience firsthand the stench of this graffiti-filled area of an underpass on Lombardy Street in Richmond, Virginia. The walls provide some privacy to the area, which I expect—given the number of empty liquor bottles and beer cans and the graffiti—is a hangout for Richmond's homeless. I was shocked that an area that is outside in the air could retain such an overpowering odor of urine and beer. When I finished taking the pictures, I felt stifled, and for the rest of the day I seemed unable to escape the stench and the feeling of suffocation. The other graffiti signs say "Shabazz the Strugglar!" and "Justice Be Allah."

Photographs by Daryl Cumber Dance.

Graffiti at Maggie L. Walker High School

These photographs were taken at the once-popular Richmond high school named for the first female and first Black banker, Maggie L. Walker. Its now-abandoned state is typical of the many Black institutions lost to school integration.

Photographs by Daryl Cumber Dance.

Moving Graffiti

Trailers, trucks, vans, and other vehicles seem to be popular sites for graffiti, as can be seen in the truck trailer photographed in Richmond's Newtown area and the van photographed in Jackson Ward in August 2000.

Photographs by Daryl Cumber Dance.

A Few Items from the *Encyclopedia of Graffiti*

The *Encyclopedia*, compiled by Robert Reisner and Lorraine Wechsler, records graffiti from a variety of sources around the world, not many of them areas that one would expect to find graffiti written by Blacks. For example, none of the many universities where they collected graffiti is a historically Black school. There are a few selections from two major Black communities, however — Harlem and Watts. Though it is not possible to determine the race of the writers, the following selections speak to issues that reflect concerns of the Black community. It is clear that some of the responses are written by others. Most of these were collected during the late 1960s and 1970s period of Black militancy.

Black is beautiful.
> *(written underneath)*

Death is black.
Is death beautiful?
> *— Trailways bus station, Pittsburgh*

Black is whats happening.
> *(written underneath)*

As long as it doesn't happen to me!
> *—Men's room, John Jay College of Criminal Justice, New York City, 1972*

Harlem is Mecca, blood brothers only.
> *—Harlem, New York City, c. 1970*

NAACP stands for Negroes Are Always Colored People.
> *(written underneath)*

No, it stands for Never Antagonize Adam Clayton Powell.
> *— Place not indicated, but I would guess New York*

Soul Nation, Brothers Only.
> *—Harlem, New York City, c. 1970*

Today is a new day for all black people. Today we kick ass.
> *—IND subway, New York City—April 5, 1968, the day after the murder of Martin Luther King Jr.*

Power to all Blacks by any means necessary.

— *Watts, Los Angeles, 1970*

Free Bobby Seale.

(written underneath)

Free the people.

(written underneath)

Free me.

— *Watts, Los Angeles, 1970*

Chapter 5

Sermons and Other Speeches

You read books; God himself talks to me.
–Sojourner Truth, cited in Nell Painter, *Sojourner Truth*

We're down here, Lord, chewin' on dry bones an'
swallerin' bitter pills. We can't do nothin' without You.
–Preacher in Camden County, Georgia, cited in Lydia
Parrish, *Slave Songs*

The oratory of great Black speakers is an internationally recognized aspect of American culture.[1] Based in the black church and dedicated frequently to social reform, its greatest practitioners, whether illiterates like Sojourner Truth or university-trained scholars like Martin Luther King Jr., believed that they were inspired by God. Like Truth, most know the Bible but also feel that God speaks directly to them.

The Black sermon and the rhetorical practices growing out of it are characterized by the use of improvisation, popular formulaic lines, and familiar expressions ("I've been to the mountaintop"); the

[1] In 2000 a panel of 137 academics selected Martin Luther King's "I Have a Dream" as the greatest political speech of the twentieth century. Among the top ten speeches selected, three were by Negroes: King's, Malcolm X's "The Ballot or the Bullet," and Barbara Jordan's keynote address to the Democratic National Convention in 1976. The seven other speeches that placed were by American presidents. The panel submitted their votes on the speeches to Stephen Lucas of the University of Wisconsin–Madison and Martin Medhurst of Texas A&M, who analyzed the ratings and reported on them in *USA Today* (*Jet* 97, January 17, 2000).

insistence upon audience response ("Can I get an amen?"); the use of repetition and parallel structure ("I have a dream that . . . ;" I have a dream that . . ."); the incorporation of metaphors, similes, allegory, alliteration, euphony, parallelism, balance, personification, antitheses, hyperbole, repetition, rhyme—the whole range of poetic techniques; the use of the vernacular;[2] the use of wordplay, wit, and humor; and the focus upon political and sociological issues of relevance to their audience.[3] The orator often hammers away at a catchy phrase that will grab the listeners' attention to the point that they will enthusiastically echo it, as in Jesse Jackson's "Keep hope alive" or "I am *somebody.*" The power of such a single dramatic phrase is nowhere more effectively demonstrated than in an incident involving Sojourner Truth, who is described by Nell Painter as "first and last an itinerant preacher." A single phrase she uttered has echoed through the ages. The story apparently originated with Wendell Phillips, but the account of it comes from Harriet Beecher Stowe: Frederick Douglass had just spoken in a meeting in Faneuil Hall in Boston, declaring that Blacks would never gain justice in America unless they resort to violence: "It must come to blood: they must fight for themselves, and redeem themselves, or it would never be done." Stowe continues:

> [I]n the hush of deep feeling, after Douglas[s] sat down, she [Sojourner Truth] spoke out in her deep, peculiar voice, heard all over the house,—
>
> "Frederick, is God *dead?*"
>
> The effect was perfectly electrical, and thrilled through the whole house, changing as by a flash the whole feeling of the audience. Not another word she said or needed to say; it was enough. ("The Libyan Sibyl")

[2]Even the most educated of Black preachers speak in the language of the people as the congregation demands. Thus one will note variations in the rhetoric of some preachers depending upon their audience.

[3]It is important to note that the Black church has spawned most of the leaders in the fight for freedom, justice, equality, and dignity in America—including, notably, Nat Turner, Sojourner Truth, Frederick Douglass (it is not commonly known that Douglass was a licensed AME Zion Church preacher), Adam Clayton Powell Jr., Martin Luther King Jr., Malcolm X, and Jesse Jackson.

As that story indicates, the Black preacher is a master of timing. His voice achieves a remarkable range of intonations (one can only imagine the many possible variations in pitch and tone and volume with which Truth delivered that electrifying retort).

The Black preacher's sermon is an operatic concerto, building in a rhythmic fashion from the introduction of a theme to a dramatic and emotional crescendo. His voice is used as a dramatic instrument in ways not possible to effectively describe; for one example, the traditional minister uses a *grunt,* sounding something like "Haah!" to fill in gaps, to create rhythm, and to build drama. As the sermon becomes more fervent, the "Haahs! increase in intensity and finally in themselves provoke emotional responses. The Black minister also makes use of the Bible and spirituals, often beginning with a Biblical passage and ending with a popular spiritual, as King ends his "I Have a Dream" speech with "Free at Last." The successful minister makes use not only of his powerful oratory and his captivating singing voice (he often breaks into song), but of all sorts of body movements: he claps his hands, prances, dances, rocks, jumps up and down, and stomps, often waving his hands frenetically. He suddenly freezes, then he dramatically starts again (sometimes with a loud clap of the hands and a sudden shift in the direction in which he was moving); he may leave the pulpit and move through the audience, comforting, cajoling, challenging, inviting, accusing. His hand gestures and facial expressions add impact and often humor to his delivery. The handkerchief to wipe the sweat of his brow is a necessary stage prop.

If indeed, the minister is successful, by the time he reaches his conclusion, people will be fervently responding to him — some parishioners will be happy (possessed by the spirit to the point that they require assistance from the ushers), and others will be converted (sinners who will have found the Lord and are now ready to come forth and join the church).[4]

The minister is not the only speaker in the Black church. The deacon — who assists him in the pulpit, offers prayers, and may even in-

---

[4]I should emphasize that I am speaking here of the traditional Black church and preacher. It is true that many Black churches hold very sedate services in which the minister stands erect at his lectern and provides a scholarly discourse while the audience listens quietly, without ever uttering an amen. In such churches spirituals and gospels are also often taboo.

troduce the minister—is also a speechifyer. He too has heard the word of God and must testify. Many in the congregation are often moved during and immediately after the sermon to offer their own testimonies. All these "speeches" are traditional and follow a set pattern even at the same time that they are personal and spontaneous. Of course, the major goal here is to bring lost souls to God, and that whole process is an interesting ritual as well. Often the unconverted will sit in the front on the mourners' bench, generally sent there by their parents or guardians, who pray for their salvation. Numerous Black authors have written of those long days and nights on the mourners' bench (night services are held for a week during the annual revival) waiting to hear God speak to them, none more movingly than James Baldwin in his autobiographical account of John Grimes wrestling with the Spirit on the dusty floor of the Harlem storefront church in *Go Tell It on the Mountain.* Once God has spoken, once the seeker has crossed over, the convert is called to testify. From the time of their conversion until their Baptism, the proselytes are expected to declare their saved state to anyone who will listen. These conversion-experience speeches are also traditional at the same time that they are individual testimonies.

Even when God and Allah, Christianity and Islam, are never mentioned, the religious fervor and the popular elements of the folk sermon continue to be prominent elements in the oratory growing out of Black communities. Everyone, from street-corner orators speaking about political issues, to defense lawyers appealing to jurors,[5] to the Black Panthers preaching militant responses to oppression, to high school students campaigning for student government positions, finds their messages more successful in Black communities if they make use of some of the elements of the traditional Black sermon.

[5]Johnnie Cochran's closing argument in the well-known O. J. Simpson trial of 1994–95, from its conception in memories of Biblical passages and echoes "of the Little Union Baptist Church" *(Journey to Justice)* through its use of every element of Black oratory just described, can be studied as a textbook example of the power of oratory growing out of the Black church and community. And despite the few non-Black faces on the jury, Cochran was unquestionably addressing them as community: "These are my people. I know their hearts and they know mine. And when the time comes, that's how I'm going to speak to them—heart to heart" (his description of the jury months before the closing argument).

SOJOURNER TRUTH

Ain't I a Woman

· *From Frances Dana Gage, "Sojourner Truth," published in the National Anti-Slavery Standard on May 2, 1863* ·

I have included Sojourner Truth's well-known "Ain't I a Woman" speech that she delivered at a women's rights convention in Akron, Ohio, in 1851, even though in recent years scholars such as Carleton Mabee and Nell Irvin Painter have challenged the accuracy of Truth's feminist comrade Frances Dana Gage's account of that speech (an account published some twelve years after the event), suggesting that the repetition of "Ain't I a Woman" was devised by Gage and not Truth. I might note that such repetitions were consistent with the varied accounts of Truth's speeches, all of which have come down to us only from the accounts of members of the audience who heard them. However, even Painter, after several encounters in her classroom and in conferences, recognized the depth and scope of the Black community's embrace of the Truth who electrified audiences and silenced strong White men as she declared, "Ain't I a Woman," and ends her book, "The symbol we require in our public life still triumphs over scholarship." What a reinforcement of the persistence and value of legends!

As Painter earlier informs, "Black oral culture of the late twentieth century produced a composite Sojourner Truth, comprised of one single, speech act dated 1851—or often, 1852. This Truth faces down a hostile audience, defies doubters as to her sex, rips open her bodice to bare her breast, and shouts, sneering, 'and ain't I a woman?!!' 'Ar'n't' becomes 'ain't' in the interests of authenticity."

I reproduce Gage's account, making minor changes in the dialect to reflect the familiar versions that circulate in the Black community and dropping a few brief passages generally omitted. Gage's descriptions appear in parentheses.

Well, chillen, where dere's so much racket dere must be somthin' out o' kilter. I think dat, twixt the niggers of de South and de women at de Norf, all a-talkin' 'bout rights, de white men will be in a fix pretty soon. But what's all this here talkin' 'bout? Dat man over dar say dat woman needs to be helped into carriages, and lifted over ditches, and to have de best place everywhar. Nobody eber helps me into carriages or over mud-puddles, or gives me any best place; (and, raising herself to her full height, and her voice to a pitch like rolling thunder, she asked) And ain't I a woman? Look at me. Look at my arm. I have plowed and planted and gathered into barns, and no man could head me—and ain't I a woman? I could work as much and eat as much as a man—when I could get it—and bear de lash as well—and ain't I a woman? I have borne thirteen chillen, and seen 'em mos' all sold off into slavery, and when I cried out with a mother's grief, none but Jesus heard—and ain't I a woman? . . . If my cup won't hold but a pint and yourn holds a quart, wouldn't you be mean not to let me have my little measure full? Dat little man in black dar, he say woman can't have as much right as man 'cause Christ wasn't a woman. *Whar did your Christ come from?*

(Rolling thunder could not have stilled that crowd as did those deep wonderful tones, as she stood there with outstretched arms and eye of fire. Raising her voice still louder, she repeated,)

Whar did your Christ come from? From God and a woman. Man had nothing to do with him. . . . If de first woman God ever made was strong enough to turn de world upside down, all dese togeder ought to be able to turn it right side up again.

FREDERICK DOUGLASS

My Slave Experience in Maryland

· *From the* National Anti-Slavery Standard, *May 22, 1845* ·

Following is one of Douglass's earlier speeches, delivered to the American Anti-Slavery Society on May 6, 1845.

I do not know that I can say anything to the point. My habits and early life have done much to unfit me for public speaking, and I fear that your patience has already been wearied by the lengthened re-marks of other speakers, more eloquent than I can possibly be, and better prepared to command the attention of the audience. And I can scarcely hope to get your attention even for a longer period than fifteen minutes.

Before coming to this meeting, I had a sort of desire—I don't know but it was vanity—to stand before a New-York audience in the Tabernacle. But when I came in this morning, and looked at those massive pillars, and saw the vast throng which had assembled, I got a little frightened, and was afraid that I could not speak; but now that the audience is not so large and I have recovered from my fright, I will venture to say a word on Slavery.

I ran away from the South seven years ago—passing through this city in no little hurry, I assure you—and lived about three years in New Bedford, Massachusetts, before I became publicly known to the anti-slavery people. Since then I have been engaged for three years in telling the people what I know of it. I have come to this meeting to throw in my mite, and since no fugitive slave has preceded me, I am encouraged to say a word about the sunny South. I thought, when the eloquent female who addressed this audience a while ago, was speaking of the horrors of Slavery, that many an honest man would doubt the truth of the picture which she drew; and I can unite with the gentleman from Kentucky in saying, that she came far short of describing them.

I can tell you what I have seen with my own eyes, felt on my own person, and know to have occurred in my own neighborhood. I am not from any of those States where the slaves are said to be in their most degraded condition; but from Maryland, where Slavery is said to exist in its mildest form; yet I can stand here and relate atrocities which would make your blood to boil at the statement of them. I lived on the plantation of Col. Lloyd, on the eastern shore of Maryland, and belonged to that gentleman's clerk. He owned, probably, not less than a thousand slaves.

I mention the name of this man, and also of the persons who perpetrated the deeds which I am about to relate, running the risk of being hurled back into interminable bondage—for I am yet a slave;— yet for the sake of the cause—for the sake of humanity, I will mention the names, and glory in running the risk. I have the gratification to know that if I fall by the utterance of truth in this matter, that if I shall be hurled back into bondage to gratify the slaveholder—to be killed by inches—that every drop of blood which I shall shed, every groan which I shall utter, every pain which shall rack my frame, every sob in which I shall indulge, shall be the instrument, under God, of tearing down the bloody pillar of Slavery, and of hastening the day of deliverance for three millions of my brethren in bondage.

I therefore tell the names of these bloody men, not because they are worse than other men would have been in their circumstances. No, they are bloody from necessity. Slavery makes it necessary for the slaveholder to commit all conceivable outrages upon the miserable slave. It is impossible to hold the slaves in bondage without this.

We had on the plantation an overseer, by the name of Austin Gore, a man who was highly respected as an overseer—proud, ambitious, cruel, artful, obdurate. Nearly every slave stood in the utmost dread and horror of that man. His eye flashed confusion amongst them. He never spoke but to command, nor commanded but to be obeyed. He was lavish with the whip, sparing with his word. I have seen that man tie up men by the two hands, and for two hours, at intervals, ply the lash. I have seen women stretched up on the limbs of trees, and their bare backs made bloody with the lash. One slave refused to be whipped by him—I need not tell you that he was a man, though black his features, degraded his condition. He had committed some trifling offence—for they whip for trifling offences—the slave refused to be whipped, and ran—he did not stand to and fight his master as I did once, and might do again—though I hope I shall not have occasion to do so—he ran and stood in a creek, and refused to come out. At length his master told him he would shoot him if he did not come out. Three calls were to be given him. The first, second, and third, were given, at each of which the slave stood his ground. Gore, equally determined and firm, raised his musket, and in an instant poor Derby was no more. He sank beneath the waves, and naught but the crimsoned waters marked the spot. Then a general outcry might be heard amongst us. Mr. Lloyd asked Gore why he had resorted to such a cruel measure. He replied, coolly, that he had done it from necessity; that the slave was setting a dangerous example, and that if he was permitted to be corrected and yet save his life, that the slaves would effectually rise and be freemen, and their masters be slaves. His defence was satisfactory. He remained on the plantation, and his fame went abroad. He still lives in St. Michaels, Talbot county, Maryland, and is now, I presume, as much respected, as though his guilty soul had never been stained with his brother's blood.

I might go on and mention other facts if time would permit. My own wife had a dear cousin who was terribly mangled in her sleep, while nursing the child of a Mrs. Hicks. Finding the girl asleep, Mrs. Hicks beat her to death with a billet of wood, and the woman has never been brought to justice. It is not a crime to kill a negro in Talbot county, Maryland, farther than it is a deprivation of a man's property. I used to know of one who boasted that he had killed two slaves, and with an oath would say, "I'm the only benefactor in the country."

Now, my friends, pardon me for having detained you so long; but let me tell you with regard to the feelings of the slave. The people at the North say—"Why don't you rise? If we were thus treated we would rise and throw off the yoke. We would wade knee deep in blood before we would endure the bondage." You'd rise up! Who are these that are asking for manhood in the slave, and who say that he has it not, because he does not rise? The very men who are ready by the Constitution to bring the strength of the nation to put us down! You, the people of New-York, the people of Massachusetts, of New England, of the whole Northern States, have sworn under God that we shall be slaves or die! And shall we three millions be taunted with a want of the love of freedom, by the very men who stand upon us and say, submit, or be crushed?

We don't ask you to engage in any physical warfare against the slaveholder. We only ask that in Massachusetts, and the several non-slaveholding States which maintain a union with the slaveholder— who stand with your heavy heels on the quivering heart-strings of the slave, that you will stand off. Leave us to take care of our masters. But here you come up to our masters and tell them that they ought to shoot us—to take away our wives and little ones—to sell our mothers into interminable bondage, and sever the tenderest ties. You say to us, if you dare to carry out the principles of our fathers, we'll shoot you down. Others may tamely submit; not I. You may put the chains upon me and fetter me, but I am not a slave, for my master who puts the chains upon me, shall stand in as much dread of me as I do of him. I ask you in the name of my three millions of brethren at the South. We know that we are unable to cope with you in numbers; you are numerically stronger, politically stronger, than we are—but we ask you if you will rend asunder the heart and [crush] the body of the slave? If so, you must do it at your own expense.

While you continue in the Union, you are as bad as the slaveholder. If you have thus wronged the poor black man, by stripping him of his freedom, how are you going to give evidence of your repentance? Undo what you have done. Do you say that the slave ought not to be free? These hands—are they not mine? This body— is it not mine? Again, I am your brother, white as you are. I'm your blood-kin. You don't get rid of me so easily. I mean to hold on to you. And in this land of liberty, I'm a slave. The twenty-six States that blaze forth on your flag, proclaim a compact to return me to bondage if I run away, and keep me in bondage if I submit. Wherever I go, under the aegis of your liberty, there I'm a slave. If I go to Lexington or Bunker Hill, there I'm a slave, chained in perpetual servitude. I may go to your deepest valley, to your highest mountain, I'm still a slave, and the bloodhound may chase me down.

Now I ask you if you are willing to have your country the hunting-ground of the slave. God says thou shalt not oppress: the Constitution says oppress: which will you serve, God or man? The American Anti-Slavery Society says God, and I am thankful for it. In the name of my brethren, to you, Mr. President, and the noble band who cluster around you, to you, who are scouted on every hand by priest, people, politician, Church, and State, to you I bring a thankful heart, and in the name of three millions of slaves, I offer you their gratitude for your faithful advocacy in behalf of the slave.

FREDERICK DOUGLASS

What to the Slave Is the Fourth of July?: An Address Delivered in Rochester, New York, on 5 July 1852

Following is a brief section of Douglass's speech, in which he responds to some of the arguments of the supporters of slavery. The version here was published in a pamphlet by Lee, Mann & Company that same year. (A very different version of the speech appears as *The Meaning of July Fourth to the Slave*, published by the Chicago Chapter of the National Black Caucus of Librarians in 1976.)

For the present, it is enough to affirm the equal manhood of the negro race. Is it not astonishing that, while we are ploughing, planting and reaping, using all kinds of mechanical tools, erecting houses, constructing bridges, building ships, working in metals of brass, iron, copper, silver and gold; that, while we are reading, writing and cyphering, acting as clerks, merchants and secretaries, having among us lawyers, doctors, ministers, poets, authors, editors, orators and teachers; that, while we are engaged in all manner of enterprises common to other men, digging gold in California, capturing the whale in the Pacific, feeding sheep and cattle on the hill-side, living, moving, acting, thinking, planning, living in families as husbands, wives and children, and, above all, confessing and worshipping the

Christian's God, and looking hopefully for life and immortality beyond the grave, we are called upon to prove that we are men!

Would you have me argue that man is entitled to liberty? that he is the rightful owner of his own body? You have already declared it. Must I argue the wrongfulness of slavery? Is that a question for Republicans? Is it to be settled by the rules of logic and argumentation, as a matter beset with great difficulty, involving a doubtful application of the principle of justice, hard to be understood? How should I look to-day, in the presence of Americans, dividing, and subdividing a discourse, to show that men have a natural right to freedom? speaking of it relatively, and positively, negatively, and affirmatively. To do so, would be to make myself ridiculous, and to offer an insult to your understanding. There is not a man beneath the canopy of heaven, that does not know that slavery is wrong *for him.*

What, am I to argue that it is wrong to make men brutes, to rob them of their liberty, to work them without wages, to keep them ignorant of their relations to their fellow men, to beat them with sticks, to flay their flesh with the lash, to load their limbs with irons, to hunt them with dogs, to sell them at auction, to sunder their families, to knock out their teeth, to burn their flesh, to starve them into obedience and submission to their masters? Must I argue that a system thus marked with blood, and stained with pollution, is *wrong?* No! I will not. I have better employments for my time and strength, than such arguments would imply.

What, then, remains to be argued? Is it that slavery is not divine, that God did not establish it; that our doctors of divinity are mistaken? There is blasphemy in the thought. That which is inhuman, cannot be divine! Who can reason on such a proposition? They that can, may; I cannot. The time for such argument is past.

At a time like this, scorching irony, not convincing argument, is needed. O! had I the ability, and could I reach the nation's ear, I would, to-day pour out a fiery stream of biting ridicule, blasting reproach, withering sarcasm, and stern rebuke. For it is not light that is needed, but fire; it is not the gentle shower, but thunder. We need the storm, the whirlwind, and the earthquake. The feeling of the nation must be quickened; the conscience of the nation must be roused; the propriety of the nation must be startled; the hypocrisy of the nation must be exposed; and its crimes against God and man must be proclaimed and denounced.

What, to the American slave, is your 4th of July? I answer: a day that reveals to him, more than all other days in the year, the gross injustice and cruelty to which he is the constant victim. To him, your celebration is a sham; your boasted liberty, an unholy license; your national greatness swelling vanity; your sounds of rejoicing are empty and heartless; your denunciations of tyrants, brass fronted impudence; your shouts of liberty and equality, hollow mockery; your prayers and hymns, your sermons and thanksgivings, with all your religious parade, and solemnity, are, to him mere bombast, fraud, deception, impiety, and hypocrisy—a thin veil to cover up crimes which would disgrace a nation of savages. There is not a nation on the earth guilty of practices, more shocking and bloody, than are the people of these United States, at this very hour.

Go where you may, search where you will, roam through all the monarchies and despotisms of the old world, travel through South America, search out every abuse, and when you have found the last, lay your facts by the side of the everyday practices of this nation, and you will say with me that, for revolting barbarity and shameless hypocrisy, America reigns without a rival.

Prince Lambkin's Oration on the American Flag

· From *Thomas Wentworth Higginson,* Army Life in a Black Regiment ·

Higginson describes a scene in which his colored soldiers celebrate by singing and speaking. On this occasion no less than seven soldiers are encouraged to ascend the pedestal and deliver speeches, all of which he describes as "good, without exception." In his speech Prince Lambkin reminded the audience that he had predicted this war, gave an account of President Lincoln's election, and told how Florida slaves refused to work on the fourth of March because they anticipated that they would be freed on that day. Lambkin then went on to provide the following oration on the flag, causing Higginson to conclude, "there will be small demand in this regiment for harangue from the officers; give the men an empty barrel for a stump, and they will do their own exhortation."

I have regularized the spelling of a few words in Higginson's transcription.

Our mas'rs dey have live under de flag, dey got dere wealth under it, and everything beautiful for dere chillen. Under it dey have grind us up, and put us in dere pocket for money. But de first minute dey think dat ole flag mean freedom for we colored people, dey pull it right down, and run up de rag o' dere own. (Immense applause) But we'll never desert de ole flag, boys, never; we have live under it for *eighteen hundred sixty-two years*, and we'll die for it now.

Sister Lucy

· *Fragment of a sermon from E. C. L. Adams*, Tales of the Congaree ·

I seen our sister in life,
An' she done her duty,
She served her God
An' done her earthly labor
As best she knowed how,
An' listened for the blowin' of the trumpet.
Death had no fears for her,
For the blowin' of the trumpet,
The Master's trumpet,
Was the music that she loved;
The blowin', the blowin' of the trumpet,
The Master's trumpet.

At the mornin' sunrise,
She was on her row,
An' when the sun had set,
Her daily task was done;
An' when the night was come
She knelt in prayer beside her bed
An' listened for the blowin' of the trumpet,
The Master's trumpet,
The music that she loved,
The blowin', the blowin' of the trumpet,
The Master's trumpet.

She had met the world
Wid strength an' grace;
Although her life was trailed by hardship,

Love was in her heart for man
An' in her soul for God.
An' she listened for the blowin' of the trumpet,
The Master's trumpet,
The music that she loved,
The blowin', the blowin' of the trumpet,
The Master's trumpet.

Wid a frosty life behind her,
Wid misery savage
As a hungry hound
Ever wid her,
She never lost her faith in God,
An' she listened for the blowin' of the trumpet,
The Master's trumpet,
The music that she loved,
The blowin', the blowin' of the trumpet,
The Master's trumpet.

Silas

· *Fragment of a sermon from E. C. L. Adams,* Tales of the Congaree ·

De body of Silas
Stiff on de coolin'-board lies.
De battle of life is done;
His soul has passed
To his far-off home —
Passed through de pearly gates.
He passed in de night,
His soul's gone forward,
But his body is left
For de weepers and mourners,
For de singers of songs
And de prayer of prayers.
His soul's gone onward
To de golden throne.

He has no regrets,
His labors was hard
And he passed in de night,
In a heavenly flight,
By a holy light.
He's gone to his home —
His far-off home —
To de golden throne.

Potee's Gal

· *From E. C. L. Adams*, Tales of the Congaree ·

My brothers and sisters, death takes on the shadows of night for the body of Brother Silas. It takes on for those who knew him the colors of darkness, but such is the will of God and such the workings of His mind.

It takes on for those who knew him the colors of darkness, but such is the will of God and such the working of His mind. He never intended for us to fully understand. If He showed us everything, we would think we knew as much as He does. God has put death amongst us to impress us with the importance of living the right sort of life.

Preacher: God has let death drop upon us like a dark and angry cloud.
    Voices in the Congregation:
      Angry cloud. Angry cloud.
    Shrill Voice of Old Woman:
      Dark, dark and angry cloud.
Preacher: Lightning flashes and thunder rolls.
Preacher: And lightning flashes, flashes and strikes. It may be you or me, for thunder is the voice of God and lightning is the flashing of His eye and the thunder bolt He hurls from His heights on high. He does not miss you, my brother or my sister. His aim is always true, and your mortal body is destroyed. Such is the will of God and the cloud that has dulled the world and your senses rolls away, and the soul of the dead is either lifted into the world of eternal

light, or cast into the everlasting shadows of unending night amidst the flames and groans of the sinful and the wicked—cast down, down, down into the night.

Preacher: Brother Silas is dead,
He rests from his labor,
And he sleeps,

Shrill Voice of Sister:
He sleeps, oh, he sleeps.

Preacher: Where the tall pines grow
On the banks of a river.

Another Voice:
On de banks of a river.

Several Voices:
On de banks of a river.

Preacher: His trouble is done,
He has left this world
On the wings of glory.

Voice:
On de wings of glory!

Preacher: Out of life's storm,

Another Voice:
On de wings of glory!

Preacher: Out of life's darkness,

Several Voices:
On de wings of glory!

Preacher: He sails in the light
Of the lamb.
Away from his troubles,
Away from the night,

Congregation:
In the light, in the light of the lamb!

Preacher: He's gone to the kingdom above,
In the raiment of angels,

Voice of Sister:
In the raiment, in the raiment of angels!

Preacher: To the region above;
And he sleeps,

Voices Chanting throughout the Congregation:

He sleeps, oh, he sleeps,
    On de banks of a river.
Preacher: Where the tall pines grow,
    On the banks of a river.
    Congregation:
      Wid de starry crowned angels,
      On de banks of a river.
Preacher: And the flowers are blooming
    In the blood of the lamb.
    Shrill Voice of Sister: (Taken up by congregation chanting and
      swaying:)
      De blood of de lamb!
      In de blood of de lamb!
Preacher: And the birds are singing,
    Where the wind blows soft
    As the breath of an angel;
    And he sleeps,
    Where the tall pines grow
    On the banks of a river.
    Voice:
      An' he sleeps!
    Another Voice:
      Wey de tall pines grow.
Preacher: And his spirit is guarded
    Several Voices:
      On de banks of a river.
Preacher: By a flaming-faced angel,
    Sister:
      Yes, Jesus, a flamin'-faced angel,
      On de banks of a river.
Preacher: Standing on mountains of rest
    And he sleeps where the tall pines grow,
    On the banks of a river,
    Where the wind blows soft
    As the breath of an angel,
    He sleeps where the tall pines grow.
    He sleeps, oh, he sleeps.
    Congregation:
      He sleeps, oh, he sleeps.

Preacher: May God in His mercy and loving kindness look down
with pity on Brother Silas and rest his soul in peace.

*(During the sermon the congregation sways, beat their hands against their
thighs or their knees and move their feet, keeping time with the rhythm of the*
PREACHER'S *sermon.)*

Preacher: The congregation will sing.

(They respond with:)

"Set Down Servant"

I know you tired, set down,
I know you tired, set down,
I know you tired, set down,
Set down and rest a little while.

Refrain:

Oh, set down, servant, set down,
Oh, set down, servant, set down,
Oh, set down, servant, set down,
Set down and rest a little while.

I know you been runnin', set down,
I know you been runnin', set down,
I know you been runnin', set down,
Set down and rest a little while.

Refrain:

Oh, set down, servant, set down,
Oh, set down, servant, set down,
Oh, set down, servant, set down,
Set down and rest a little while.

Know you been cryin', set down,
Know you been cryin', set down,
Know you been cryin', set down,
Set down and rest a little while.

Refrain:

Oh, set down, servant, set down,
Oh, set down, servant, set down,
Oh, set down, servant, set down,
Set down and rest a little while.

Talked wid de death angel, set down,

Talked wid de death angel, set down,

Talked wid de death angel, set down,

Set down and rest a little while.

Refrain:

Oh, set down, servant, set down,

Oh, set down, servant, set down,

Oh, set down, servant, set down,

Set down and rest a little while.

You know your time comin', set down,

You know your time comin', set down,

You know your time comin', set down,

Set down and rest a little while.

Refrain:

Oh, set down, servant, set down,

Oh, set down, servant, set down,

Oh, set down, servant, set down,

Set down and rest a little while.

JOHN JASPER

The Sun Do Move

· *From William E. Hatcher,* John Jasper: The Unmatched Negro
Philosopher and Preacher ·

"The Sun Do Move" is the best known of all the sermons by the legendary
Richmond, Virginia, minister, John Jasper, and the best known of all early folk
sermons. He is reputed to have delivered it 253 times between 1878 and 1901, and
when it was rumored that he would be preaching it for the last time, 2,500 people
packed into Sixth Mount Zion Baptist Church to hear it on March 8, 1891.
Allowed to serve as an itinerant preacher while enslaved, Jasper continued to
work as a minister after emancipation, founding the Sixth Mount Zion Baptist
Church on Brown's Island in Richmond on September 3, 1867. Originally the
congregation worshiped in an abandoned Confederate horse stable. They moved
into the present location at the corner of St. John and Duval Streets in 1869. That
structure was renovated and extended in 1925 and was, in 1996, placed on the
National Register of Historic Places and on the Virginia Historic Landmarks
Register.

Ironically, in 1955, the church was slated for demolition along with more than six
hundred houses in the Black neighborhood. Protests resulted in rescuing the

historic church from destruction, though the community, including the home in which the Reverend John Jasper had lived, did not escape. As can be seen in the picture I took from the church window, the highway goes right around the church, literally cutting it off from much of the remaining community. The church is separated from the highway only by a massive wall that some have called the Walls of Jericho. The impact of urban renewal and expressway construction on this Black community and many others in Richmond and throughout the nation is the subject of numerous memorates and rumors that circulate in African American communities, which are convinced that their neighborhoods are always the ones sacrificed. Sixth Mount Zion Church historian Benjamin C. Ross shared with me the fact that the city wanted to dig up Reverend Jasper's grave, so the church dug him up and reburied him at Woodlawn Cemetery. It is also widely rumored that wood from Reverend Jasper's home—demolished to construct Interstate 95—was used to make a gavel for the mayor of the city. Though Mr. Ross cannot verify that claim, he noted that several Richmond mayors have lifted the gavel and proclaimed that source.

The following text is obviously a reconstruction. Hatcher likely followed the tendency of his time to exaggerate Black dialect, and I have slightly modified his text to make it more readable. It is interesting to note that William Wells Brown was present on another occasion and wrote a detailed account of the famous sermon. He observed that "the more educated class of the colored people . . . did not patronize Jasper. They consider him behind the times, and called him 'old fogy' " (*My Southern Home, or The South and Its People*). Noting the venerable audience attending this sermon and the throngs who couldn't get in, Brown adds, "these people had not come to be instructed, they had really come for a good laugh." Brown's own accounts of passages of the speech are in Standard English, offering an interesting contrast to the heavy dialect of Hatcher's version. For contrast, I present a few lines from Brown's account—singular in that Brown often presents sermons in dialect and in fact uses heavy dialect in his account of the deacon's prayer preceding Brown's sermon in this instance (see "Let My People Go" in this chapter):

If the sun does not move, why did Joshua command it to "stand still"? Was Joshua wrong? If so, I had rather be wrong with Joshua than to be right with the modern philosophers. . . .

The sun rises in the east and sets in the west; do you think any one can make me believe that the earth can run around the world in a single day so as to give the sun a chance to set in the west? . . .

Those who doubt these things that you read in Holy Writ are like the infidel,—won't believe unless you can see the cause.

And now the full sermon as recorded by Hatcher.

'Low me to say dat when I was a young man and a slave, I knowed nuthin' worth talkin' 'bout concernin' books. Dey was sealed mys-

teries to me, but I tell ya I longed to break de seal. I thirsted for de
bread o' learnin'. When I seen books I ached to git into em for I
knowed dat dey had de stuff for me, an' I wanted to taste deir con-
tents, but most of de time dey was barred against me.

By de mercy of de Lord a thing happened. I got a room-feller—he
was a slave, too, an' he had learned to read. In de dead of de night he
give me lessons outen de New York Spellin' Book. It was hard
pullin', I tell ya; harder on him, for he know'd just a little an' it made
him sweat to try to beat somethin' into my hard head. It was wuss
wid me. Up de hill every step, but when I got de light of de lesson
into my noodle I fairly shouted, but I knowed I was not a scholar. De
consequence was I crept 'long mighty tedious, gittin' a crumb here
an' dere until I could read de Bible by skippin' de long words, toler-
able well. Dat was de start of my education—dat is, what little I got.
I make mention of dat young man. De years have fled away since
den, but I ain't forgot my teacher, an' never shall. I thank my Lord
for him, an' I carries his memory in my heart.

'Bout seven months after my gittin' to readin', God converted my
soul, an' I reckon 'bout de first an' main thing dat I begged de Lord to
give me was de power to understand His Word. I ain' braggin', an' I
hates self-praise, but I bound to speak de thankful word. I believes in
my heart dat my prayer to understand de Scripture was heard. Since dat
time I ain't cared 'bout nuthin' 'cept to study an' preach de Word of God.

Not, my brethren, dat I's de fool to think I knows it all. Oh, my
Father, no! Far from it. I don' hardly understand myself, nor half of
de things roun' me, an' dere is millions of things in de Bible too deep
for Jasper, an' some of 'em too deep for everybody. I don't carry de
keys to de Lord's closet, an' He ain' tell me to peep in, an' if I did I'm
so stupid I wouldn't know it when I see it. No, friends, I knows my
place at de feet of my Marster, an' dere I stays.

But I kin read de Bible and git de things whar lay on de top of de
soil. Outen de Bible I knows nothin' extry 'bout de sun. I sees his
courses as he rides up dere so gran' an' mighty in de sky, but dere is
heaps 'bout dat flamin' orb dat is too much for me. I know dat de sun
shines powerfully an' pours down its light in floods, an' yet dat is
nothin' compared wid de light dat flashes in my mind from de pages
of God's book. But you knows all dat. I knows dat de sun burns—oh,
how it did burn in dem July days. I tell ya he cooked de skin on my

back many a day when I was hoein' in de corn fiel'. But you knows all dat, an' yet dat is nothin' dere to [compare] to de divine fire dat burns in der souls of God's chillun. Can't ya feel it, brethren?

But 'bout de courses of de sun, I have got dat. I have done ranged through de whole blessed book an' scored down de las' thing de Bible has to say 'bout de movements of de sun. I got all dat pat an' safe. An' lemme say dat if I don't give it to you straight, if I gits one word crooked or wrong, you just holler out, "Hol' on dere, Jasper, you ain't got dat straight," an' I'll beg pardon. If I don't tell de truf, march up on dese steps here an' tell me I's a liar, an' I'll take it. I fears I do lie sometimes — I'm so sinful, I find it hard to do right; but my God don't lie an' He ain't put no lie in de Book of eternal truf, an' if I give you what de Bible say, den I boun' to tell de truth.

I got to take you all dis afternoon on an excursion to a great battlefield. Most folks like to see fights — some is mighty fond of gittin' into fights, an' some is mighty quick to run down de back alley when dere is a battle goin' on, for de right. Dis time I'll 'scort ya to a scene where you shall witness a curious battle. It took place soon after Israel got in de Promised Land. You member de people of Gideon make friends wid God's people when dey first entered Canaan an' dey was monstrous smart to do it. But, just de same, it got 'em into an awful fuss. De cities roun' 'bout dere flared up at dat, an' dey all joined deir forces and say dey gwine to mop de Gideon people off of de groun', an' dey bunched all deir armies together an' went up for to do it. When dey come up so bold an' brave de Gideonites was scared outen deir senses, an' dey sent word to Joshua dat dey was in trouble an' he must run up dere an' git 'em out. Joshua had de heart of a lion an' he was up dere directly. Dey had an awful fight, sharp an' bitter, but you might know dat General Joshua was not up dere to git whipped. He prayed an' he fought, an' de hours got away too peart for him, an' so he asked de Lord to issue a special order dat de sun hold up awhile an' dat de moon furnish plenty of moonshine down on de lowest part of de fightin' ground. As a fact, Joshua was so drunk wid de battle, so thirsty for de blood of de enemies of de Lord, an' so wild wid de victory dat he tell de sun to stand still 'til he could finish his job. What did de sun do? Did he glare down in fiery wrath an' say, "What you talkin' 'bout my stoppin' for, Joshua; I ain't never started yet. Been here all de time, an' it would smash up everything if I was to start?"

Naw, he ain' say dat. But what de Bible say? Dat's what I asked to know. It say dat it was at de voice of Joshua dat it stopped. I don't say it stopped; ain't for Jasper to say dat, but de Bible, de Book of God, say so. But I say dis; nothin' kin stop until it has first started. So I knows what I'm talkin' 'bout. De sun was travelin' long dere through de sky when de order come. He hitched his red ponies and made quite a call on de land of Gideon. He perch up dere in de skies just as friendly as a neighbor where comes to borrow something, an' he stand up dere an' he look like he enjoyed de way Joshua waxes dem wicked armies. An' de moon, she wait down in de low ground dere, an' pours out her light and look just as calm an' happy as if she was waitin' for her escort. Dey never budged, neither of 'em, long as de Lord's army needed her light to carry on de battle.

I don't read when it was dat Joshua hitch up an' drove on, but I suppose it was when de Lord told him to go. Anybody knows dat de sun didn't stay dere all de time. It stopped for business, an' went on when it got through. Dis is 'bout all dat I has to do wid dis particular case. I done showed ya dat dis part of de Lord's word teaches ya dat de sun stopped, which show dat he was movin' befo' dat, an' dat he went on afterwards. I told ya dat I would prove dis an' I's done it, an' I defies anybody to say dat my point ain't made.

I told ya in de first part of dis discourse dat de Lord God is a man of war. I 'spec by now you begin to see it is so. Don't ya admit it? When de Lord come to see Joshua in de day of his fears an' warfare, an' actually make de sun stop stone still in de heavens, so de fight kin rage on 'til all de foes is slain, you obliged to understand dat de God of peace is also de man of war. He kin use both peace an' war to help de righteous an' to scatter de host of de aliens. A man talked to me las' week 'bout de laws of nature, an' he say dey can't possibly be upset, an' I had to laugh right in his face. As if de laws of anything was greater dan my God who is de lawgiver for everything. My Lord is great; He rules in de heavens, in de earth, an' down under de ground. He is great, an' greatly to be praised. Let all de people bow down an' worship befo' Him!

But let us git along, for dere is quite a big lot mo' comin' on. Let us take next de case of Hezekiah. He was one of dem kings of Judah—a mighty sorry lot I must say dem kings was, for de most part. I inclines to think Hezekiah was 'bout de highest in de general average, an' he was no mighty man hisself. Well, Hezekiah he got sick. I dare say dat a king when he gits his crown an' finery off, an' when he is prostrated wid mortal sickness, he gits 'bout as common lookin' an' grunts an' rolls, an' is 'bout as scary as de rest of us po' mortals. We know dat Hezekiah was in a low state of mind; full of fears, an' in a terrible trouble. De fact is, de Lord strip him of all his glory an' landed him in de dust. He told him dat his hour had come, an' dat he had better square up his affairs, for death was at de door. Den it was dat de king fell low befo' God; he turned his face to de wall; he cry, he moan, he begged de Lord not to take him outen de worl' yet. Oh, how good is our God! De cry of de king moved his heart an' he tell him he gwine to give him another show. Tain't only de kings dat de Lord hears. De cry of de prisoner, de wail of de bondsman, de tears of de dyin' robber, de prayers of de backslider, de sobs of de woman dat was a sinner, mighty apt to touch de heart of de Lord. It look like it's hard for de sinner to git so far off or so far down in de pit dat his cry can't reach de ear of de merciful Savior.

But de Lord do even better dan dis for Hezekiah—He tell him He gwine to give him a sign by which he'd know dat what He said was coming to pass. I ain't acquainted wid dem sundials dat de Lord told Hezekiah 'bout, but anybody dat has got a grain of sense knows dat dey was de clocks of dem ole times an' dey marked de travels of de sun by dem dials. When, therefore, God tol' de king dat He would make de shadow go backward, it must have been just like puttin' de hands of de clock back, but, mark ya, Isaiah expressly say dat de sun returned ten degrees. There you are! Ain't dat de movement of de sun? Bless my soul. Hezekiah's case beat Joshua. Joshua stop de sun, but here de Lord make de sun walk back ten degrees; an' yet dey say dat de sun stand stone still an' never move a peg. It look to me he move roun' mighty brisk an' is ready to go any way dat de Lord orders him to go. I wonder if any of dem philosophers is roun' here dis afternoon. I'd like to take a square look at one of dem an' ax him to explain dis matter. He can't do it, my brethren. He knows a heap 'bout books, maps, figgers an' long distances, but I defy him to take up Hezekiah's case an' 'splain it off. He can't do it. De Word of de Lord is my defense an' bulwark, an' I fears not what men can say nor do; my God gives me de victory.

'Low me, my friends, to put myself square 'bout dis movement of de sun. It ain't no business of mine whether de sun move or stand still, or whether it stop or go back or rise or set. All dat is outta my hands entirely, an' I got nothing to say. I got no the-o-ry on de subject. All I ax is dat we will take what de Lord say 'bout it an' let His will be done 'bout everything. What dat will is I can't know except He whisper into my soul or write it in a book. Here's de Book. Dis is enough for me, and with it to pilot me, I can't git far astray.

But I ain't done wid ya yet. As de song says, dere's more to follow. I invite ya to hear de first verse in de seventh chapter of de book of Revelations. What do John, under de power of de Spirit, say? He say he saw four angels standin' on de four corners of de earth, holdin' de four winds of de earth, an' so forth. 'Low me to ax if de earth is roun', where do it keep its corners? A flat, square thing has corners, but tell me where is de corner of an apple, or a marble, or a cannon ball, or a silver dollar. If dere is any one of dem philosophers where's been takin' so many cracks at my old head 'bout here, he is cordially invited to step forward an' square up dis vexing business. I here tell you dat ya can't square a circle, but it looks like dese great scholars done learn how to circle de square. If dey kin do it, let 'em step to de front an' do de trick. But, my brethren, in my po' judgment, dey can't do it; tain't in 'em to do it. Dey is on de wrong side of de Bible; dat's on de outside of de Bible, an' dere's where de trouble comes in wid 'em. Dey done got out of de breastworks of de truth, an' as long as dey stay dere de light of de Lord will not shine on deir path. I ain't caring so much 'bout de sun, though it's mighty convenient to have it, but my trust is in de Word of de Lord. Long as my feet is flat on de solid rock, no man kin move me. I'se gittin' my orders from de God of my salvation.

The other day a man wid a high collar and side whiskers come to my house. He was one nice Northern gentleman who think a heap of us colored people in de South. They are lovely folks and I honours 'em very much. He seem from de start kind of strict an' cross wid me, and after while, he broke out furious and fretting, an' he say: "Allow me Mister Jasper to give you some plain advice. Dis nonsense 'bout de sun movin' where you are gettin' is disgracin' your race all over de country, an' as a friend of your people, I come to say it's got to stop." Ha! Ha! Ha! Mars' Sam Hargrove never hardly smash me dat way. It was equal to one of dem ole overseers way back yonder. I tell him dat if he'll show me I'se wrong, I give it all up.

My! My! Ha! Ha! He sail in on me an' such a storm about science, new discoveries, an' de Lord only knows what all, I never heard befo', an' den he tell me my race is against me an' po ole Jasper must shut up his fool mouth.

When he got through—it look like he never would—I tell him John Jasper ain't set up to be no scholar, an' don't know de philosophies, an' ain' tryin' to hurt his people, but is working day an' night to lif 'em up, but his foot is on de rock of eternal truth. Dere he stand and dere he is goin' to stand til Gabriel sounds de judgment note. So I say to de gentleman who scolded me up so dat I heard him make his remarks, but I ain' heard where he get his Scripture from, an, dat 'tween him an' de word of de Lord I take my stand by de Word of God every time. Jasper ain' mad: he ain't fightin' nobody; he ain't been appointed janitor to run de sun: he nothin' but de servant of God and a lover of de Everlasting Word. What I care about de sun? De day comes on when de sun will be called from his race-track, and his light squelched out forever; de moon shall turn to blood, and this earth be consumed with fire. Let 'em go; dat won't scare me nor trouble God's elected people, for de word of de Lord shall endure forever, an' on dat Solid Rock we stand an' shall not be moved.

Is I got ya satisfied yet? Has I proven my point? Oh, ye whose hearts is full of unbelief! Is ya still holding out? I reckon de reason you say de sun don't move is 'cause you are so hard to move yourself. You is a real trial to me, but never mind; I ain't giving ya up yet, an' never will. Truth is mighty; it kin break de heart of stone, an' I must fire another arrow of truth outen de quiver of de Lord. If ya have a copy of God's Word 'bout your possession, please turn to dat minor prophet, Malachi, who wrote de last book in de old Bible, an' look at chapter de first verse eleven; what do it say? I better read it, for I got a notion your critics don't carry any Bible in their pockets every day in de week. Here is what it says: "For from de risin' of de sun even unto de goin' down of de same My name shall be great among de Gentiles. . . . My name shall be great among de heathen, says de Lord of hosts." How do dat suit ya? It look like dat ought to fix it. Dis time it is de Lord of hosts Hisself dat is doin' de talkin', an' He is talkin' on a wonderful an' glorious subject. He is tellin' of de spreading of His Gospel, of de coming of His last victory over de Gentiles, an' de worldwide glories dat at de las' He is to git. Oh, my brethren, what a time dat will be. My soul takes wing as I anticipate wid joy dat millenium day! De glories as dey shine befo' my eyes blinds me, an'

I forgets de sun an' moon an' stars. I just remembers dat 'long bout those last days dat de sun an' moon will go out of business, for dey won' be needed no mo'. Den will King Jesus come back to see His people, an' He will be de sufficient light of de world. Joshua's battles will be over. Hezekiah won't need no sundial, an' de sun an' moon will fade out befo' de glorious splendours of de New Jerusalem.

But what the matter wid Jasper? I most forgot my business, an' most gone to shoutin' over de far away glories of de second coming of my Lord. I beg pardon, an' will try to git back to my subject. I have to do as de sun in Hezekiah's case—fall back a few degrees. In dat part of de Word dat I gave you from Malachi—dat de Lord Hisself spoke—He declares dat His glory is gwine to spread. Spread? Where? From de risin' of de sun to de goin' down of de same. What? Don't say dat, does it? Dat's exactly what it sez. Ain't dat clear enough for ya? De Lord pity dese doubtin' Thomases. Here is enough to settle it all an' cure de worst cases. Walk up here, wise folks, an' git your medicine. Where is dem high-collared philosophers now? What they skulkin' roun' in de brush for? Why don't ya git out in der broad afternoon light an' fight for your collars? Ah, I understand it; ya got no answer. De Bible is against ya, an' in your consciences you are convicted.

But I hears ya back there. What you whisperin' 'bout? I know; you say you sent me some papers an' I never answer dem. Ha, Ha, Ha! I got 'em. De difficulty 'bout dem papers you sent me is dat dey did not answer me. Dey never mention de Bible one time. You think so much of yourselves an' so little of de Lord God an' thinks what you say is so smart dat you can't even speak of de Word of de Lord. When you ax me to stop believin' in de Lord's Word an' to pin my faith to yo words, I ain't a gwine to do it. I take my stan' by de Bible an' rest my case on what it says. I take what de Lord says 'bout my sins, 'bout my Saviour, 'bout life, 'bout death, 'bout de world to come, an' I take what de Lord say 'bout de sun an' moon, an' I cares little what de haters of my God choose to say. Think dat I will forsake de Bible? It is my only Book, my hope, de arsenal of my soul's supplies, an' I wants nuthin' else.

But I got another word for ya yet. I done work over dem papers dat you sent me without date an' without your name. You deals in figures an' thinks you are bigger dan de archangels. Lemme see what you done say. You set yourself up to tell me how far it is from here to de sun. You think you got it down to a nice point. You say it is 3,339,002 miles from de earth to de sun. Dat's what you say. Another one say dat de distance is 12,000,000; another got it to 27,000,000. I hear dat de great Isaac Newton worked it up to 28,000,000, an' later on de philosophers give it another rippin' raise to 50,000,000. De last one gits it bigger dan all de others, up to 90,000,000. Don't any of 'em agree exactly an' so dey runs a guess game, an' de last guess is always de biggest. Now, when dese guessers can have a convention in Richmond an' all agree upon de same thing, I'd be glad to hear from ya again, an' I does hope dat by dat time you won't be ashamed of your name.

Heaps of railroads have been built since I saw de first one when I was fifteen years old, but I ain't hear tell of a railroad built yet to de sun. I don't see why if dey can measure de distance to de sun, dey might not git up a railroad or a telegraph an' enable us to find something else 'bout it dan merely how far off de sun is. Dey tell me dat a cannonball could make de trip to de sun in twelve years. Why don't dey send it? It might be rigged up wid quarters for a few philosophers on de inside an' fixed up for a comfortable ride. Dey would need twelve years' rations an' a heap of changes of raiment — mighty thick clothes when dey start and mighty thin ones when dey git dere.

Oh, my brethren, dese things make ya laugh, an' I don't blame ya for laughin', 'cept it's always sad to laugh at der follies of fools. If we could laugh 'em outen countenance, we might well laugh day an' night. What cuts into my soul is, dat all dese men seem to me dat dey is hittin' at de Bible. Dat's wat stirs my soul an' fills me wid righteous wrath. Little care I what dey says 'bout de sun, provided dey let de Word of de Lord alone. But never mind. Let de heathen rage an' de people imagine a vain thing. Our King shall break 'em in pieces an' dash 'em down. But blessed be de name of our God, de Word of de Lord endureth forever. Stars may fall, moons may turn to blood, an' de sun set to rise no mo', but Thy kingdom, oh, Lord, is from everlasting to everlasting.

But I have a word dis afternoon for my own brethren. Dey is de people for whose souls I got to watch — for dem I got to stand an' report at de last — dey is my sheep an' I'se deir shepherd, an' my soul is knit to dem forever. It ain't for me to be troublin' ya wid dese questions about dem heavenly bodies. Our eyes goes far beyond de smaller stars; our home is clean out of sight of dem twinklin' orbs; de chariot dat will come to take us to our Father's mansion will sweep out by dem flickerin' lights an' never halt till it brings us in clear view of de throne of de Lamb. Don't hitch your hopes to no sun nor stars; your home is got Jesus for its light an' your hopes must travel up dat way. I preach dis sermon just for to settle de minds of my few brethren, an' repeats it 'cause kind friends wish to hear it, an' I hopes it will do honour to de Lord's Word. But nothing short of de pearly gates can satisfy me, an' I charge, my people, fix your feet on de solid Rock, your hearts on Calvary, an' your eyes on de throne of de Lamb. Dese strifes an' griefs will soon git over; we shall see de King in His glory an' be at ease. Go on, go on, ye ransomed of de Lord; shout His praises as you go, an' I shall meet ya in de city of de New Jerusalem, where we shan't need the light of de sun, for de Lamb of de Lord is de light of de saints.

Photograph of the Reverend John Jasper

*Courtesy Benjamin C. Ross, church historian
of the Sixth Mount Zion Baptist Church.*

The Highway That Skirts Sixth Mount Zion Baptist Church

Photograph by Daryl Cumber Dance.

ALEX CRUMMELL

Eulogium on Henry Highland Garnet, D.D.

· *From* Africa and America: Addresses and Discourses by
Alex Crummell ·

The following is the beginning and the ending of the eulogy for Henry Highland
Garnet delivered in Washington, D.C., on May 4, 1882, by the noted
Episcopalian priest, Alexander Crummell.

"Howl, fir tree; for the cedar is fallen!" This is the ejaculation of an ancient Prophet at the fall of a great and mighty nation. The figure is at once expressive and melancholy. It requires no extraordinary imagination to set before the eye one of those mighty monarchs of the forest, the grand cedars of Lebanon; tall, majestic and powerful, its age hoar and venerable, its girth enormous, its awful form uplifted to the skies, its arms widespread and gigantic, a mighty forest king which, for centuries, had defied the force of the severest hurricanes; but at last there comes the final, fatal storm, and down at once it falls, prostrate to the earth, its glory gone, its life forevermore but a thing of memory!

Such a natural disaster is easily transferred by the imagination to the calamities of nations and men. It is a spontaneous impulse of our being to resort to nature for the expressions of our most vivid emotions. On momentous occasions, or at times of dread calamity our own inward resources are too scanty; and so the sun's decline, the fall of a star, the waning, dying, light of a luminary in the heavens, or the fall of a majestic cedar of the forest serve as expressive emblems of the mortality of man.

The death of Henry Highland Garnet can have no more fitting threnody than the wail of the prophet: "Howl, fir tree; for the cedar hath fallen!" Like a cedar of Lebanon he was, in both his inner and his outer nature, a grand and majestic being; and his death, like the fall of a mighty monarch of the forest, is one of the saddest afflictions which has recently fallen upon our race. Our assembling here tonight is to express our admiration of the life and character of this eminent man, and our grief at his loss. He was a man of wonderful qualities, of astonishing eloquence, of strong, vigorous and commanding character, of long-continued and philanthropic labors, of great virtues; a true genius, a most illustrious example of the capacity of the Negro race and of the dignity of man.

In venturing a eulogy upon this eminent person, I approach a subject full of incident and adventure, variable with the lights and shades of human life, not seldom darkly lined with the traces of suffering and misfortune, now brilliant with the lustre of genius, and now dark with the touches of disaster; but everywhere, and at all time, whether in sunshine or in shade, lofty, self-sustained, brilliant and commanding.

Our distinguished friend was born in slavery, in Kent county, Md., December 23, 1815, on the plantation of Colonel William Spencer. His father before him was born in the same condition and at the same place. His grandfather, however, was born a freeman in Africa. He was a Mandingo chieftain and warrior, and, having been taken prisoner in a tribal fight, was sold to the slave traders, and then brought as a slave to America. But the fires of liberty were never quenched in the blood of this family; and they burst forth into an ardent flame in the bosom of George Garnet, the son of the native African warrior. . . .

I have spoken to you of the life, the genius, and the labors of Henry Highland Garnet, and now I must speak of his decline and death.

That decline had been manifest some five or six years. Gradually, during this period, his powers as a worker and speaker had been failing, as was evident to his friends, and apparent to himself. Age, excessive duty, the harassing cares of a poorly paid ministry; disease, the tardy lurking effects and influences of the maimed limb of his boyhood—all combined in his later years to reduce the vital energy of his once active system.

But, besides failing health, sad misfortunes in divers forms fell upon him. Troubles and trials served to weaken and undermine the brave spirit and the strong constitution in which it dwelt. It is useless to attempt concealment. Sorrow and discouragement fell upon his soul, and at times the wounded spirit sighed for release; and the strong desire arose to escape to some foreign land, where, oblivious of the ingratitude and forgetfulness of his people, he might have a few final days of peace and comfort, and at last sink quietly to his grave.

It happened under these circumstances that the offer was made him of the position of "Minister Resident" to the Republic of Liberia. It came as a recognition of his high character, his honorable career, his splendid services to the cause of freedom, and his grand qualities, both intellectual and moral. It was an offer honorable to the Government which made it, and to the grand man to whom it was tendered.

The offer was gladly accepted by my friend. It was the very thing he desired. He had long been wishing to see the Coast of Africa, to tread the soil of his ancestors. If this public position had not been offered him, he would, I have no doubt, sought some other mode, either as a missionary or a teacher, of reaching the Western Coast.

Gratifying as the offer was to him, it brought dismay and sorrow to a large circle of his best friends. For my own part, I felt it my duty to oppose its acceptance with candor, warmth, and decision. I had no doubt of its unwisdom, and I pressed my conviction very earnestly upon him.

Alas, all dissuasion was useless. "What," said he, "would you have me linger here in an old age of neglect and want? Would you have me tarry among men who have forgotten what I have done, and what I have suffered for them! To stay here and die among these ungrateful people?" "No," was his ejaculation; "I go gladly to Africa! Please the Lord I can only safely cross the ocean, land on the coast of Africa, look around upon its green fields, tread the soil of my ancestors, live if but a few weeks; then I shall be glad to lie down and be buried beneath its sod!"

Thus grandly, nobly did this high soul turn from baseness and ingratitude to a final far-distant haven of repose and death.

The Lord listened to the desires of his servant.

On the 6th of November he preached his farewell sermon to the people of Shiloh Church, to whom he had ministered twenty-six years. On the 12th of November he sailed for England. He sojourned there but a brief week, and sailed thence from London early in December, and landed at Monrovia on the 28th of the same month.

For the first time in his life he had seen the continent of Africa. He had seen the settlements from Goree to Liberia. He had seen the chief emporiums of that rising African civilization which already is blossoming into beauty and fruitfulness. He had seen the towns and villages of the young Republic, peopled by his own kith and kin, emigrants from this great nation. He had ascended a few miles the beautiful St. Paul's, trod its fertile banks, and seen its active farming and industries. He had looked around upon the land of the fathers, and was well pleased and declared his gratification. And now the time came for him to die; and calmly, quietly, resignedly, he yielded up his spirit to the God who gave it, with an assured trust in the Redeemer, and with the fullest hopes of the resurrection of the just.

They buried him like a prince, this princely man, with the blood of a long line of chieftains in his veins, in the soil of his fathers. The entire military force of the capital of the Republic turned out to render the last tribute of respect and honor. The President and his Cabinet, the ministry of every name, the President, Professors and students of the College, large bodies of citizens from the river settlements, as well as the townsmen, attended his obsequies as mourners. A noble tribute was accorded him by the finest scholar and thinker in the nation. Minute guns were fired at every footfall of the solemn procession. And when they laid him lowly in the sod, there was heard, on the hills, in the valleys, and on the waters —

> — The tributary peal
> Of instantaneous thunder which announced
> Through the still air the closing of the grave.

I know the very spot where they laid him. The cemetery is called Palm Grove. There clusters of the stately palm lift up their graceful forms, and spread abroad their feathery tops, waving in the breeze.

There he lies; the deep Atlantic but a few steps beyond; its perpetual surges beating at his feet, chanting evermore the choral anthems of the ocean, the solemn requiem of the dead.

No marble cenotaph as yet marks the place of his deep repose; but, ere long, we, in America, with his admirers in Europe and Africa, will erect on that Western Coast a shaft which shall fitly commemorate this glorious son of Africa.

Farewell! friend of my youth, Statesman, Poet, Orator, Clergyman, Philanthropist! And yet not farewell, for never can we forget thee! Ever shalt thou be embalmed in our richest memories! and thy tomb shall be the shrine whither perpetually our fond hearts shall travel, and the sons of Africa, through long periods, shall proudly visit.

For, if in the future as in the past, men continue to prize noble gifts used for the highest purposes; to honor our devoted service freely given for the maintenance of truth and justice; to applaud lofty speech used for the upbuilding humanity and the advancement of the race; to revere pure and lofty character, a lifetime illustration of the finest qualities of our kind,

> Then o'er his mould a sanctity shall brood,
> Till the stars sicken at the day of doom.

PAUL LAURENCE DUNBAR

An Ante-Bellum Sermon

· *From* Lyrics of Lowly Life ·

In this poem Dunbar successfully captures the essence of the folk sermon.
Paul Laurence Dunbar's work not only grew out of the folk tradition,
but also reentered it in the form that he crafted. When I was collecting
folklore from Virginia in the 1970s for *Shuckin' and Jivin'*, several informants
recited Dunbar's poems as verses they had learned from others, not knowing
that they were written by Dunbar. Many of the folk who never heard of
Dunbar learned his work in the same way that they learned traditional
verses.

We is gathahed hyeah, my brothahs,
  In dis howlin' wildaness,
Fu' to speak some words of comfo't
  To each othah in distress.
An' we chooses fu' ouah subjic'
  Dis — we'll 'splain it by an' by;
  "An' de Lawd said, 'Moses, Moses,'
  An' de man said, 'Hyeah am I.' "

Now ole Pher'oh, down in Egypt,
  Was de wuss man evah bo'n,
An' he had de Hebrew chillun
  Down dah wukin' in his co'n;
'T well de Lawd got tiahed o' his foolin',
  An' sez he: "I'll let him know —
Look hyeah, Moses, go tell Pher'oh
  Fu' to let dem chillun go."
"An' ef he refuse to do it,
  I will make him rue de houah,
Fu' I'll empty down on Egypt
  All de vials of my powah."
Yes, he did — an' Pher'oh's ahmy
  Was n't wuth a ha'f a dime;
Fu' de Lawd will he'p his chillun,
  You kin trust him evah time.

An' yo' enemies may 'sail you
    In de back an' in de front;
But de Lawd is all aroun' you,
    Fu' to ba' de battle's brunt.
Dey kin fo'ge yo' chains an' shackles
    F'om de mountains to de sea;
But de Lawd will sen' some Moses
    Fu' to set his chillun free.

An' de lan' shall hyeah his thundah,
    Lak a blas' f'om Gab'el's ho'n,
Fu' de Lawd of hosts is mighty
    When he girds his ahmor on.
But fu' feah some one mistakes me,
    I will pause right hyeah to say,
Dat I'm still a-preachin' ancient,
    I ain't talkin' 'bout to-day.

But I tell you, fellah christuns,
    Things'll happen mighty strange;
Now, de Lawd done dis fu' Isrul,
    An' his ways don't nevah change,
An' de love he showed to Isrul
    Wasn't all on Isrul spent;
Now don't run an' tell yo' mastahs
    Dat I's preachin' discontent.

'Cause I isn't; I'se a-judgin'
    Bible people by deir ac's;
I'se a-givin' you de Scriptuah,
    I'se a-handin' you de fac's.
Cose ole Pher'oh b'lieved in slav'ry,
    But de Lawd he let him see,
Dat de people he put bref in, —
    Evah mothah's son was free.

An' dahs othahs thinks lak Pher'oh,
    But dey calls de Scriptuah liar,

Fu' de Bible says "a servant
   Is a-worthy of his hire."
An' you cain't git roun' nor thoo dat,
   An' you cain't git ovah it,
Fu' whatevah place you git in,
   Dis hyeah Bible too'll fit.

So you see de Lawd's intention,
   Evah sence de worl' began,
Was dat His almighty freedom
   Should belong to evah man,
But I think it would be bettah,
   Ef I'd pause agin to say,
Dat I'm talkin' 'bout ouah freedom
   In a Bibleistic way.

But de Moses is a-comin',
   An' he's comin', suah and fas'
We kin hyeah his feet a-trompin',
   We kin hyeah his trumpit blas'.
But I want to wa'n you people,
   Don't you git too brigity;
An' don't you git to braggin'
   'Bout dese things, you wait an' see.

But when Moses wif his powah
   Comes an' sets us chillun free,
We will praise de gracious Mastah
   Dat has gin us liberty;
An' we'll shout ouah halleluyahs,
   On dat mighty reck'nin' day,
When we'se reco'nised ez citiz'—
   Huh uh! Chillun, let us pray!

Let My People Go

· *From* My Southern Home, or The South and Its People ·

In his autobiography, William Wells Brown provides a detailed account of a
plantation sermon on one of the most famous texts among slaves.

"My dear breethering, the Lord raised up his servant, Moses, that
he should fetch his people Isrel up outen that wicked land—ah. Then
Moses, he went out from the face of the Lord, and departed hence
unto the courts of the old tyranickle king—ah. An' what sez you,
Moses? Ah, sez he, Moses sez, sez he to that wicked old Faro: Thus
sez the Lord God of hosts, sez he: Let my Isrel go—ah. An' what sez
the ole, hard-hearted king—ah? Ah! sez Faro, sez he, who is the
Lord God of hosts, sez he, that I should obey his voice—ah? An'
now what sez you, Moses—ah. Ah, Moses sez, sez he: Thus saith the
Lord God of Isrel, let my people go, that they mought worship me, sez
the Lord, in the wilderness—ah. But—ah! my beloved breethering
an' my harden', impenitent frien's—ah, did the ole, hard-hearted king
harken to the words of Moses, and let my people go—ah? Nary time."

This last remark, made in an ordinary, conversational tone of
voice, was so sudden and unexpected that the change, the transition
from the singing state was electrical.

"An' then, my beloved breethering an' sistering, what next—ah?
What sez you, Moses, to Faro—that contrary ole king—ah? Ah,
Moses sez to Faro, sez he, Moses sez, sez he: Thus seth the Lord God
of Isrel: Let my people go, sez the Lord, leest I come, sez he, and
smite you with a cuss—ah! An' what sez Faro, the ole tyranickle
king—ah? Ah, sez he, sez ole Faro, Let their tasks be doubled, and
leest they mought grumble, sez he, those bricks shall be made without straw—ah! [Vox naturale.] Made 'em pluck up grass an' stubble
outen the fields, breethering, to mix with their mud. Mity hard on the
pore critters; warn't it, Brother Flood Gate?" [The individual thus in-
terrogated replied, "Jess so;" and "ole Louder" moved along.]

"An' what next—ah? Did the ole king let my people Isrel go—ah?
No, my dear breethering, he retched out his pizen hand, and he hilt
'em fash—ah. Then the Lord was wroth with that wicked ole king—
ah. An' the Lord, he sed to Moses, sez he: Moses, stretch forth now
thy rod over the rivers an' the ponds of this wicked land—ah; an' be-

hold, sez he, when thou stretch out thy rod, sez the Lord, all the waters shall be turned into blood—ah! Then Moses, he tuck his rod, an'
he done as the Lord God of Isrel had commanded his servant Moses
to do—ah. An' what then, say you, my breethering—ah? Why, lo an'
behold! the rivers of that wicked land was all turned into blood—ah;
an' all the fish an' all the frogs in them streams an' waters died a—
h!"

"Yes!" said the speaker, lowering his voice to a natural tone, and
glancing out of the open window at the dry and dusty road, for we
were at the time suffering from a protracted drouth: "An' I believe the
frogs will all die now, unless we get some rain purty soon. What do
you think about it, Brother Waters?" [This interrogatory was addressed to a fine, portly-looking old man in the congregation. Brother
W. nodded assent, and old Louder resumed the thread of his discourse.] "Ah, my beloved breethering, that was a hard time on old
Faro an' his wicked crowd—ah. . . .

For he hilt out agin the Lord, and obeyed not his voice—ah. Then
the Lord sent a gang of bull-frogs into that wicked land—ah. An'
they went hoppin' an' lopin' about all over the country, into the vittles, an' everywhere else—ah. My breethering, the old Louder thinks
that was a des'prit time—ah. But all woodent do—ah. Ole Faro was
as stubborn as one of Louder's mules—ah, an' he woodent let the
chosen seed go up outen the land of bondage—ah. Then the Lord
sent a mighty hail, an', arter that, his devourin' locuses—ah! An'
they et up blamed nigh everything on the face of the eth—ah."

"Let not yore harts be trubbled, for the truth is mitay and must
prevale—ah. Brother Creek, you don't seem to be doin' much of en-
nything, suppose you raise a tune!"

This remark was addressed to a tall, lank, hollow-jawed old man,
in the congregation, with a great shock of "grizzled gray" hair.

"Wait a minit, Brother Louder, till I git on my glasses!" was the
reply of Brother Creek, who proceeded to draw from his pocket an
oblong tin case, which opened and shut with a tremendous snap,
from which he drew a pair of iron-rimmed spectacles. These he carefully "dusted" with his handkerchief, and then turned to the hymn
which the preacher had selected and read out to the congregation.
After considerable deliberation, and some clearing of the throat,
hawking, spitting, etc., and other preliminaries, Brother Creek, in a
quavering, split sort of voice, opened out on the tune.

Louder seemed uneasy. It was evident that he feared a failure on the part of the worthy brother. At the end of the first line, he exclaimed:—

" 'Pears to me, Brother Creek, you hain't got the right miter."

Brother Creek suspended operations a moment, and replied, "I am purty kerrect, ginerally, Brother Louder, an' I'm confident she'll come out all right!"

"Well," said Louder, "we'll try her agin," and the choral strain, under the supervision of Brother Creek, was resumed in the following words:—

"When I was a mourner just like you,
　　Washed in the blood of the Lamb,
I fasted and prayed till I got through,
　　Washed in the blood of the Lamb.

CHORUS.—"Come along, sinner, and go with us;
　　　　If you don't you will be cussed.

"Religion's like a blooming rose,
　　Washed in the blood of the Lamb,
As none but those that feel it knows,
　　Washed in the blood of the Lamb."—*Cho.*

The singing, joined in by all present, brought the enthusiasm of the assembly up to white heat, and the shouting, with the loud "Amen," "God save the sinner," "Sing it, brother, sing it," made the welkin ring.

JEAN TOOMER

Barlo's Sermon

· *From "Esther," in* Cane ·

Following is Jean Toomer's rendering of the sermon preached by King Barlo on a Southern street corner.

"Jesus has been awhisperin strange words deep down, O way down deep, deep in my ears."

Hums of awe and of excitement.

"He called me to His side an' said, 'Git down on your knees beside me, son, Ise gwine t whisper in your ears.' "

An old sister cries, "Ah, Lord."

" 'Ise agwine t' whisper in your ears,' he said, an' I replied, 'Thy will be done on earth as it is in heaven.' "

"Ah, Lord. Amen. Amen."

"An' Lord Jesus whispered strange good words deep down, O way down deep, deep in my ears. An' He said, 'Tell 'em till you feel your throat on fire.' I saw a vision. I saw a man arise, an he was big an' black an' powerful —"

Someone yells, "Preach it, preacher, preach it!"

"—but his head was caught up in th clouds. An while he was agazin' at th' heavens, heart filled up with th' Lord, some little white-ant biddies came an' tied his feet to chains. They led him t' th' coast, they led him t' th' sea, they led him across th' ocean an' they didn't set him free. The old coast didn't miss him, an' th' new coast wasn't free, he left the old-coast brothers, t' give birth t' you an' me. O Lord, great God Almighty, t' give birth t' you an me. . . .

"Brothers an' sisters, turn your faces t' th' sweet face of the Lord, an' fill your hearts with glory. Open your eyes an' see th' dawnin of th' mornin' light. Open your ears . . ."

ZORA NEALE HURSTON

Behold de Rib!

· *From* Mules and Men ·

This scene takes place in Polk County, Florida, soon after several people have returned home to their quarters at the end of the day. After they have eaten, a stranger, a traveling preacher, appears with a Bible. Several people go in their houses and some leave for the jook, but the others give the man their attention. He nods to a woman to sing, and she sings "Death comes a Creepin'," after which he delivers the following sermon.

You all done been over in Pentecost (got to feeling spiritual by singing) and now we going to talk about de woman that was taken from man. I take my text from Genesis two and twenty-one (Gen. 2:21).

Behold de Rib!
Now, my beloved,
Behold means to look and see.
Look at dis woman God done made,
But first thing, ah hah!
Ah wants you to gaze upon God's previous works.
Almighty and arisen God, hah!
Peace-giving and prayer-hearing God,
High-riding and strong armded God
Walking acrost his globe creation, hah!
Wid de blue elements for a helmet
And a wall of fire round his feet
He wakes de sun every morning from his fiery bed
Wid de breath of his smile
And commands de moon wid his eyes.
And Oh—
Wid de eye of Faith
I can see him
Standing out on de eaves of ether
Breathing clouds from out his nostrils,
Blowing storms from 'tween his lips
I can see!!
Him seize de mighty axe of his proving power
And smite the stubborn-standing space,
And laid it wide open in a mighty gash—
Making a place to hold de world
I can see him—
Molding de world out of thought and power
And whirling it out on its eternal track,
Ah hah, my strong armded God!
He set de blood red eye of de sun in de sky
And told it,
Wait, wait! Wait there till Shiloh come
I can see!
Him mold de mighty mountains
And melting de skies into seas.
Oh, Behold, and look and see! hah
We see in de beginning

He made de bestes every one after its kind,
De birds that fly de trackless air,
De fishes dat swim de mighty deep—
Male and fee-male, hah!
Then he took of de dust of de earth
And made man in his own image.
And man was alone,
Even de lion had a mate
So God shook his head
And a thousand million diamonds
Flew out from his glittering crown
And studded de evening sky and made de stars.
So God put Adam into a deep sleep
And took out a bone, ah hah!
And it is said that it was a rib.
Behold de rib!
A bone out of a man's side.
He put de man to sleep and made wo-man,
And men and women been sleeping together ever since.
Behold de rib!
Brothers, if God
Had taken dat bone out of man's head
He would have meant for woman to rule, hah
If he had taken a bone out of his foot,
He would have meant for us to dominize and rule.
He could have made her out of back-bone
And then she would have been behind us.
But, no, God Amighty, he took de bone out of his side
So dat places de woman beside us;
Hah! God knowed his own mind.
Behold de rib!
And now I leave dis thought wid you,
Let us all go marchin' up to de gates of Glory.
Tramp! tramp! tramp!
In step wid de host dat John saw.
Male and female like God made us
Side by side.
Oh, behold de rib!

And less all set down in Glory together
Right round his glorified throne
And praise his name forever.
    Amen.

RUTH ROGERS JOHNSON

A Love Letter from de Lord

· *From Lealon N. Jones, ed.,* Eve's Stepchildren ·

I'm goin', dear Jesus, yes, I'm goin' too," chanted the Negroes, rocking back and forth in their seats. "I'm goin' to Heaven to be with you. I'm goin' to Heaven to be with you."

"Take Jesus with you day by day," sang the white-robed soloist in the choir loft, and the people in the seats chanted back, "I'm goin', dear Jesus, yes, I'm goin' too."

The members of Green Valley Baptist Church were holding their annual New Year's Eve service. The night was bitterly cold. Clouds covered the sky, and a knifelike wind penetrated heavy winter clothing. Some of the members paraded down the aisle in warm, fur-trimmed coats and flashing jewelry; others hurried in, shivering in thin, shabby suits and light wraps, grateful for the warmth of the meetinghouse. Women ushers in dark blue dresses, white collars, white cuffs, white gloves, and with glittering badges pinned on their breasts, escorted the people down the aisles to their seats. On the back seat of the church sat eight Red Cross nurses in uniform with their first-aid kits beside them. The men ushers, dressed in tuxedos and also wearing badges, stood at the back of the church. After the services started, they would take over the duties of ushering and preserving order.

Brother Clark, the minister, walked to the pulpit and read the sixty-fifth Psalm. "The folds shall be full of sheep: the valleys also shall stand so thick with corn that they shall laugh and sing."

"Amen!" chanted the people. "Amen!"

The church was packed by this time, and the men ushers were sending a few more late-comers up to the gallery.

"Silence in the presence of the Lord!" sang the soloist, and the choir and congregation answered back, "Silence in the presence of the Lord!" The building rang with their voices.

Brother Clark said, "Let us pray," and all during the prayer the people kept up their chanting.

"We ask you to come an' be in the service with us, Lord — (Yes! Yes!) — You know who's right an' you know who's wrong; we can't fool you — (Amen!) — We can't tell how much farther we're goin' — (No!) — for our 'magination an' our wisdom is too limited — (Yes! Yes!) — Raise up those that are bowed down — (Yes, Lord!).

"The reason I love to talk to you, Lord, is you feed the hungry — (Dat's de truf!) — You feed the fishes in the water, you feed the fowl — (Yes! Yes!) — You tol' me when I got in trouble you'd come — (Amen!) — Come to us now, Lord — (Yes! Yes!) — We don't know how much farther we're goin' — (No!) — We're in your hands — (Goin' up! Goin' up!) — Have mercy tonight — (Yes! Yes!) — We're comin' up the wrong side o' the mountain — (Goin' up!) — Guide us, O Lord — (Yes!).

"Some of us are in the hospital tonight — (Yes! Yes!) — Go out an' be with 'em — (Amen!) — We put our hand in your hand — (Goin' up! Goin' up!) — We're wrong an' you right — (Amen!) — Have mercy! (Yes, Lord!) — Make me a better servant — (Yes, Lord!).

"We don't know what the new year holds for us — (No, Lord!) — It may be dark an' we'll need you — (Yes! Yes!) — We can't get along without you — (Goin' up! Goin' up!) — Amen — (Amen!)."

The prayer was ended, and, while the choir sang, all the men and women ushers marched down the aisles, took long-handled baskets, and started collecting. First came the women, passing the baskets to each row. A few feet behind them came the men, collecting all that the women might have missed. Then the minister announced that another collection would be taken for the guest preacher who was with them that night. So again the long-handled baskets were passed through the congregation. The choir finished the song and sat down.

"I have some announcements to make," said Brother Clark. "Sister Mary Blackstone died Friday. The wake will be held at Stevens' Funeral Parlor Tuesday night. I hope a number of you will attend the wake.

"There will be the usual services in the church nex' Friday night. Nex' Sunday we will have a baptizin'. If the weather is too cold, we'll have it here in the church. Otherwise it will be at the river. I know that you much prefer for our baptizin's to be in the river than in the tub. We all follow John the Baptist, you know, an' do like he did when he baptized our blessed Lord in the River Jordan. But sometimes the river is so icy we have to use the tub.

"I now interduce Brother Brown, our visitor, who will talk to you in his own way."

"De first day of dis year," began Brother Brown, "was a Sabbath Day. De last day is a Sabbath Day. Dat means somethin'. How have I used dis year? Brothers an' sisters, ask yourself dat question: how have I used dis year? Have you done de Lord's will? Have you been a part of His fam'ly? Dere's somethin' 'bout gettin' in His fam'ly an' growin' up in it dat you can't get by comin' in late. I'm sixty years old. I growed up in His fam'ly an' I'm still here. What is it dat I'm here for? Others have been taken, why'm I left here?

"Lots of our people feel 'shamed of de fact dat we used to be slaves. Dey shuns talk of de past when we wasn't a free people. But I wants you to know dat I look upon slavery as anudder trial or burden dat was placed upon us, an' which de Lord has helped us to overcome. We is stronger for it. Dere is still many trials dat we must bear, but we is strong an' able to cast dem aside, an' we can look forward wid de Lord's help to bein' a more free people as we face each New Year.

"Ah sisters, ah brothers," he shouted, "how much of God's will have you done dis year? Have you read your Bible—dis love letter from de Lord? Dat's what de Bible is, a love letter from de Lord!"

The preacher paced up and down in a frenzy. The people before him, swaying and chanting, were as so much potential dynamite, waiting only for the spark of oratory to cause the explosion of religious fervor.

"I've got a mother over dere waitin' for me! Is your mother over dere waitin' for you? We're on our way to Canaan. We'll be dere one o' dese days!"

"Goin' up! Goin' up!" shouted old Brother Smith.

One of the women in the congregation felt the power of the Spirit. She screamed and began threshing her arms about. She pushed out into the aisle and rushed from one usher to another. The preacher finished his sermon with a shout and a flourish. The congregation moaned and chanted. Then the minister of Green Valley Baptist Church rose to his feet.

"We extend an invitation," he said, "for anyone to come into the church by letter, baptism, or personal experience. Anyone wantin' to join with us, come forward now."

The choir began to sing:

Oh, why not tonight,
Why not tonight?
We want to be saved,
Then why not tonight?

The congregation joined in, and the song became a rolling sea of sound. Their hands clapped and their feet stamped the floor. Their bodies swayed back and forth.

We want to be saved,
Then why not tonight?

The monotony of sound and motion produced a state of ecstasy. A woman stood up, followed by another and then another.

"Is there a sister who wants to be saved?" asked Brother Clark. "We'll ask that sister to come forward an' let us talk to her."

One by one the applicants went forward. The first sister gave her "personal experience."

"You have heard her 'experience,' " said the preacher. "All those in favor of takin' her in, say 'Aye.' "

"Aye," said the congregation.

Another testified that she was going to a church of the same faith and order but that she wanted to join Green Valley. Again the vote was taken.

"Aye," said the congregation.

"Tomorrow's sun may not rise for you," cried Brother Clark. "Come now! Come now!"

"We want to be saved," sang the people. "Then why not tonight?"

"Now," said the preacher, "we're goin' to turn the meetin' over to anyone that wants to talk. And when the meetin' is over, if you haven't had your said, come nex' Friday or nex' Sunday an' you can have your said. It's our custom to start out with our officers, but sometimes the officers don't feel like talkin'. So now you that the Spirit moves, you can do the talkin'."

Brother Smith stood up. "I'm eighty-six now," he said. "I been wid de Lord for sixty-one years." The congregation shouted jubilantly.

Sister Davis rose to her feet. "Somebody's touched me," she cried. "It must ha' been the hand o' the Lord."

The people were clapping and stamping to the rhythm of their chants. Each testimonial was preceded by a song or chant. The one standing sang the first line, and the entire congregation joined in on the following lines. Most of the chants were in a minor key and used the same three or four notes over and over again. The Negroes call them "meter-hymns." They have an endless number of them, and the people know the words to all of them.

"I'm on my way to Jesus. I'm a sinner, but I'm on my way."

"I rose as a witness to Jesus. I didn't rise because I was afraid I was goin' to pass out. Nobody called me to rise. I'm carryin' the blood-stained banner of Jesus."

"He's good to me. He's ever'thing to me. I been keepin' good all day. Jus' pray for me."

Several others began shrieking and jumping.

"I'm goin' to stick to Jesus. I'm goin' home. I love Jesus! I love ever'body!"

"Lord, ha' mercy, Jesus," chanted the people.

A fat sister with gold teeth and strong voice rocked back and forth as she sang: "You don't know when or where. Pray for me."

"I ain't missed a whole Sunday. I've come out ever' Sunday all dis year."

"We was born in de country. We had fam'ly prayers. You don't see dat now."

"O yes! O yes!" shouted the congregation.

"I want you all to pray for me."

"I been thirty years in this church; haven't gave no trouble. I've got religion. Ever'thing I do, God is with me. Never die no more. You all will be settin' in the grandstand when I run in."

"I don't care what comes or what goes."

"I've come two hundred miles to get here. I got up at six o'clock dis mornin' to get here before midnight."

"Fifty-four years I been servin' God. I was only four years old, an' God took hold o' my hand an' led me. Tol' me to be a good boy. Didn't know I was livin' in a valley till God took hold o' my hand."

"Sisters an' brothers, I rose as a witness. Long ago as a child in

Mississippi at eleven years old I was converted. I know I'm goin'
over the river."

"Sometimes I feel frantic, but I know Jesus is mine. I tol' Jesus
thirty-four years ago I'd live for him. I'm goin' to try to do better
'cause he's certainly been good to me."

> Jesus is mine, mine, mine,
> O Jesus is mine, mine, mine;
> Everywhere I go, everywhere I be
> Jesus is mine!

sang the people, and the building trembled with the stamping of their
feet.

Down in one of the front pews a man was sitting between two
women. One of the women felt the Ecstasy coming. She began to
thresh out with her arms. The man leaned over, removed her glasses,
and gave them to someone else. Then he held the woman down in her
seat. No sooner had she quieted than the one on his other side let out
a scream. He reached over, removed her glasses, and started to hold
her. Then all at once the Ecstasy came to him. He pushed through to
the aisle and began to walk up and down. Faster and faster he went
from one end of the aisle to the other. He shivered and jerked.
Furiously he began to fight the ushers who tried to restrain him.
One by one different members rushed to the aisles, screaming and
running, shouting and fighting. The Red Cross nurses went into action with their first-aid kits. The choir sang:

> My soul just couldn't be content
> Until I found my Lord.

It was now three minutes before twelve. For four hours they had
been testifying and singing. Brother Clark said, "Let us all kneel."
And so they knelt, facing the backs of their pews. Someone started
to sing "Nearer, My God, to Thee." Others joined in, half-singing,
half-chanting. Some, possessed by the Spirit, were still screaming
and shouting as they rushed up and down the aisles. The ushers in
their tuxedos and the nurses in their white uniforms were restraining the more violent and treating the exhausted. The preacher was
praying for help in the year to come.

The members of Green Valley Church lived close to God. They never fail to give credit for the blessings that come their way, and they take Jesus with them in their daily lives. Without this trust and faith they would be lost. They fervently believe what they are saying on New Year's Eve. They may go out the next day and break many of the Ten Commandments, but they will be back the following Sunday testifying, "I'm a sinner, but I'm on my way."

Outside, the whistles were blowing. A half moon hung low in the east, and stars looked down from a cloudless sky. A new year had come again.

THE REVEREND C. L. FRANKLIN
What of the Night?
· *From Jeff Todd Titon*, Give Me This Mountain ·

Popularly dubbed "the high priest of soul preaching," Reverend C. L. Franklin, father of singer Aretha Franklin, was pastor of the New Bethel Baptist Church in Detroit until he was shot and killed by intruders in his home in 1984. Despite his seminary and college training, he preached in the traditional way, gaining a congregation of more than ten thousand and reaching countless others through his frequently recorded sermons — sermons that inspired and influenced countless other preachers. Dolan Hubbard asserts that Franklin "shaped the religious imagination of the generation of preachers who came of age during the civil rights movement," and Jeff Todd Titon declares in the preface to *Give Me This Mountain*, "It is said that every African American preacher either has imitated him or has tried to avoid doing so."

"The burden of Dumah. He calleth to me out of Seir, Watchman, what of the night? Watchman, what of the night? The watchman said, The morning cometh, and also the night: if ye will enquire, enquire ye: return, come." [Isaiah 21:11–12]

The subject: Watchman, What of the Night?

This passage, according to all authoritative commentaries, is a prophecy of the doom of Edom. It is a prophecy of the aggression and the ultimate triumph of the military forces of Persia over Edom. This military victory that brought on for Edom oppression, placed Edom in such a dilemma that Edom cried out in her confusion and frustration, having experienced this transition, "Watchman, what of the night? Watchman, will our plight be better or worse now that we are

under a new government, now that we are in the orbit of a new political power? What will our lot be?"

Watchmen, in the scheme of Oriental things, were important people. They watched cities; they watched communities; they stood upon
lofty walls; and the security of these cities and these communities
depended upon the alertness of these watchmen: for while the city
slept, these watchmen watched. They watched for invading armies;
they watched for what you would call raids on the part of raiding
bands; and they gave the city, or the respective community, notice of
the approaching enemy. So that the figure here, on the part of either
Isaiah or that anonymous writer that is given the credit of having
written that part of the book of Isaiah after the exile—either Isaiah
or the anonymous Isaiah—is saying in this chapter, that because of
the plight of Edom, which is referred to here in terms of Dumah, the
burden of Dumah, for Dumah was a place in Edom, and this Hebraic
prophet declared that in a vision, the dilemma of Edom reached him
as he stood upon the lofty wall of vision, and in vision he heard the
cry of frustration, and the cry of oppression, coming out of Dumah,
and out of Edom, and that cry was an inquiring cry: "Watchman,
what of the night? What of the times? What time of history is this?
What time of trouble is this?" For after all, history is God's big clock.
For a day is but a thousand years in terms of eternity. (I wish somebody here would pray with me.)

History is but—or a day is but a thousand years [i.e., a thousand
years is but a day]—so that history is God's big clock; and inasmuch
as we cannot see within the next five minutes, in our system of time—
in God's system of time, in God's clock of history, we can't see—we
must call out to our men of vision, we must call out to our prophets,
as Edom or as the Edomites did in those long days, or bygone days:
[to] men who can pierce the future; men who can interpret the future; men who can see beyond now; and inquire of them,
"Watchman, what of the night? What time is this? What time of history is this? What hour in God's purpose and in God's plan is this?
Like the Edomites, what will our lot be?" The future is uncertain to
us, and we must make anxious inquiries, for we don't know. We are
blinded by the night, we are blinded by the mystery of history, we are
blinded by the density of time. (I wish you'd pray with me.)

For to us, it is like it was with John; for John said, he saw an angel standing with a scroll rolled in his hand, and it was sealed on all sides, and nobody could break the seals or read the writing therein, but the lambs. So we know that history is God's scroll, already sealed, written within and without; and we cannot read the writing, and we cannot break the seal; only God can reveal it to us, or reveal it to his men of mystery. And so, as the Edomites did, thousands of years ago, with the anxiety of the future, with questions of the future, we inquire to the men of vision, who walk upon the lofty walls of God's inspiration, "Watchman, what of the night?" (I don't believe you know what I'm talking about.)

For, after all, my brothers and sisters, we are living in times that are like the nighttimes. We don't know what the morning will bring. We don't know. We know that Africa is rumbling, that Africa is awakening like a sleeping giant, and that on the horizon we see the Gold Coast emerging as an independent nation. We see the Sudan that has come into independence as a young nation. We see Egypt, having seized and nationalized the Suez Canal. We have seen the English and the French and the Israelite forces, military forces that is, rush across her borders, and then be stopped by the mild force of the United Nations in order to pull out and go back to their own lands. We see Hungaria [Hungary] on the march, defying the pressure and the desire of international Communism to subjugate her. We have witnessed over a hundred thousand of Hungarian citizens fleeing across the Hungarian borders, into Austria. We see tension in Germany between East and West Germany. We see Poland resisting those who would deny her sovereign independence. (I wish somebody would pray with me.) We have heard say that no more is the Big Four America, England, France, and Russia, but rather, America, Russia, India, and China. (I wish you'd pray with me a little while.)

We see these signs, watchman, on the horizon of time. We've seen changes take place in China. We see India, the second great manpower pool in the world, come to a position of international neutrality. (I wish somebody would pray with me.) We see oppressed people, not only abroad, but in our own lands, becoming impatient, for full citizenship. Not only Africa, not only Egypt, not only the Arab world, not only Germany, not only China, not only India, but we see Montgomery, Alabama, we see Florida, we see other parts of our own land impatient for world brotherhood and full citizenship.

We don't know all what these signs mean. We see them, but we are too blind to properly interpret them. And so we call out to our prophets, to our preachers. We call out to our educators, to our philosophers, to our statesmen. We call them watchmen, and we inquire of them, as we view these conflicting signs, "Watchmen, what of the night? What of these times?" (I don't believe you're praying with me.) "What time is it? And what shall we expect, as history unfolds in this new year?" (I wonder are you praying with me?) "What shall we expect?"

The writer here gives us a picture of Oriental travelers who had traveled the deserts in the cool of the evening, and as the night had fallen, they came to the foot of a mountain range. And as they came to that mountain range, they decided to camp rather than to risk traveling in the mountains, rather than to risk the treachery and the dangers of the mountains. They decided to camp in the shadow of that mountain for that night, and wait until the morning comes. The night was long, the night was anxious, the night was trying as they waited to resume their journey the next morning. As they camped, the night was dark. They looked on the mountain ranges. They could see the cedars that crowned the top of the mountain like gory monsters in the dark. They could see the jagged edges of the mountain cliffs; they could hear the water running from mountain springs that made a menacing noise late in the night. (Pray with me if you please.)

The campers became anxious and restless during the night, for indeed, the night was dark, and indeed, the night was trying. And they called out to their watchman, hour after hour, "Watchman, what of the night?" And no doubt when they had checked the time, they went again, feeling that the time had come, and it was time to arise, and it was time for the sun to be up, and time for daylight to break upon men so that they could see their way in resuming their journey. [Whooping:]

> And
>> as they went to the watchman
> and
>> thought about it was time
>> for the morning light to come,

why,
they noticed that
though
the morning light was breaking,
great God,
and
though the darkness
was dispelling,
that
a new blinding,
a new blindingness
was settling over them.
Did you hear them say,
"Watchman,
what of the night?"
"Why,
the morning comes
and so does the night."
What a confusing statement is this.
Why,
what does it mean
by "the morning cometh
and so does the night"?
Does he mean to say that
night
follows the morning?
for, studying his language,
that seems to be what he's saying.
But we know morning
is not followed by the night.
Morning
is followed by the noon,
and then by the afternoon,
and then by the evening,
O Lord.
But the
inquirer,
great God,

why,
    realizes
     that though the darkness of the night
        has flown away,
    he's blinded
    by new
       darkness.
    And what darkness
      is this?
Well,
    what he is saying,
    and what he's alluding to,
      is this:
well,
    when the sun rose
great God,
    and spreaded
    its warm rays
      in the valleys,
       where the travelers were,
    the cool morning air
    mixed with the warmth of the morning sun,
and
    this conflict
    in atmospheric conditions
      created a fog.
O Lord.
    And the fog
    was more blinding
      than the night.
O Lord.
    For in the night
    they could see
      the top of the mountain.
    In the night
    they could see the jagged edges
      of the mountain ranges.
(I wish somebody knew what I was talking about tonight.)
O Lord.

In the night
they could see
the outlines
of the cedars that stood
on the mountaintop.
But when the morning came,
great God,
and when the sun rose,
and the heat
mingled with the cool air of the morning,
and created the fog,
O Lord,
the fog hid the mountain,
the fog hid the mountain clefts,
the fog hid
the cedars
that stood on the mountain.
O Lord.
So,
though the morning has come,
other confusion has arisen
that's even worse than the night.
O Lord.
As we look out
on history today,
and
as we look out
on world situations,
the night of slavery
has passed.
Great God.
And
the night
of many other oppressing things
has passed.
but other
foggy conditions
are arising,
yes,

and we want to inquire,
of those that can see,
yes,
we want to inquire
of those who are standing
in the lofty places,
O Lord,
those that God
would lift on higher ground,
"Watchman,
what of the night?"
O Lord.
"Oh, watchman!
It's mighty dark.
And
how long
will the darkness last?
How long
will we go through this night?
How long
will we blunder through this fog?"
O Lord.
Ohh!
"When will the skies clear?"
O Lord.
"Watchman!
We've waited a long time.
Watchman!
We've been restless a long time.
Watchman!"
(I don't believe you know what I'm talking about tonight.)
Yes.
"We've waited a long time.
Ohh!
How long,
how long,
how long,
watchman!

will we be oppressed?
And will we be cast down?
And
 watchman!
 Would you tell us?
   and give us a little light?
And
 watchman!
 will you give us new hope?"
And
 ohh!
   O Lord,
 oh yes,
 we've sung,
 we have prayed,
 we have waited,
 and we have watched;
 tell us how long.
O Lord.
 "Watchman!
 Our fathers waited,
 our grandfathers waited,
 and their fathers waited,
 the slaves waited,
 tell us how long!
 Ohh!
   how long,
   just how long?"
And
 we have shed tears,
   yes we have,
 we've sung
   "Pharaoh's army got drownded,"
 we've sung
   "Steal away to Jesus,"
 we've sung
   "Swing low, sweet chariot,"
 we've sung

"We're going to eat at the feasting table,
one of these old days."
"Ohh! how long,
just how long?
Ohh!
good Lord,
how long?"
O Lord.
Ohh, a few more days.
(Did you hear me?) [Singing:]
A few more days.
A little while to wait,
and a little while to pray,
a little while to labor,
a little while to sing.
We're blundering in the dark,
we're toiling in the light.
"Oh, tell us, watchman,
oh, we're waiting on an answer,
oh, how long,
how long?"

THE REVEREND C. L. FRANKLIN
The Eagle Stirreth Her Nest

· *From Jeff Todd Titon,* Give Me This Mountain ·

Franklin probably began by reading Deuteronomy 32:11–12.

The eagle stirreth her nest.

The eagle here is used to symbolize God's care and God's concern for his people. Many things have been used as symbolic expressions to give us a picture of God or some characteristic of one of his attributes: the ocean, with her turbulent majesty; the mountains, the lions. Many things have been employed as pictures of either God's strength or God's power or God's love or God's mercy. And the psalmist has said that The heavens declare the glory of God and the firmament shows forth his handiworks.

So the eagle here is used as a symbol of God. Now in picturing God as an eagle stirring her nest, I believe history has been one big nest that God has been eternally stirring to make man better and to help us achieve world brotherhood. Some of the things that have gone on in your own experiences have merely been God stirring the nest of your circumstances. Now the Civil War, for example, and the struggle in connection with it, was merely the promptings of Providence to lash man to a point of being brotherly to all men. In fact, all of the wars that we have gone through, we have come out with new outlooks and new views and better people. So that throughout history, God has been stirring the various nests of circumstances surrounding us, so that he could discipline us, help us to know ourselves, and help us to love another, and to help us hasten on the realization of the kingdom of God.

The eagle symbolizes God because there is something about an eagle that is a fit symbol of things about God. In the first place, the eagle is the king of fowls. And if he is a regal or kingly bird, in that majesty he represents the kingship of God or symbolizes the kingship of God. (Listen if you please.) For God is not merely a king, he is *the* king. Somebody has said that he is the king of kings. For you see, these little kings that we know, they've got to have a king over them. They've got to account to somebody for the deeds done in their bodies. For God is *the* king. And if the eagle is a kingly bird, in that way he symbolizes the regalness and kingliness of our God.

In the second place, the eagle is strong. Somebody has said that as the eagle goes winging his way through the air he can look down on a young lamb grazing by a mountainside, and can fly down and just with the strength of his claws, pick up this young lamb and fly away to yonder's cleft and devour it—because he's strong. If the eagle is strong, then, in that he is a symbol of God, for our God is strong. Our God is strong. Somebody has called him a fortress. So that when the enemy is pursuing me I can run behind him. Somebody has called him a citadel of protection and redemption. Somebody else has said that he's so strong until they call him a leaning-post that thousands can lean on him, and he'll never get away. (I don't believe you're praying with me.) People have been leaning on him ever since time immemorial. Abraham leaned on him. Isaac and Jacob leaned on him. Moses and the prophets leaned on him. All the Christians leaned on him. People are leaning on him all over the world today. He's never given way. He's strong. That's strong. Isn't it so?

In the second place, he's swift. The eagle is swift. And it is said that he could fly with such terrific speed that his wings can be heard rowing in the air. He's swift. And if he's swift in that way, he's a symbol of our God. For our God is swift. I said he's swift. Sometimes, sometimes he'll answer you while you're calling him. He's swift. Daniel was thrown in a lions' den. And Daniel rung him on the way to the lions' den. And having rung him, why, God had dispatched the angel from heaven. And by the time that Daniel got to the lions' den, the angel had changed the nature of lions and made them lay down and act like lambs. He's swift. Swift. One night Peter was put in jail and the church went down on its knees to pray for him. And while the church was praying, Peter knocked on the door. God was so swift in answering prayer. So that if the eagle is a swift bird, in that way he represents or symbolizes the fact that God is swift. He's swift. If you get in earnest tonight and tell him about your troubles, he's swift to hear you. All you do is need a little faith, and ask him in grace.

Another thing about the eagle is that he has extraordinary sight. Extraordinary sight. Somewhere it is said that he can rise to a lofty height in the air and look in the distance and see a storm hours away. That's extraordinary sight. And sometimes he can stand and gaze right in the sun because he has extraordinary sight. I want to tell you my God has extraordinary sight. He can see every ditch that you have dug for me and guide me around them. God has extraordinary sight. He can look behind that smile on your face and see that frown in your heart. God has extraordinary sight.

Then it is said that an eagle builds a nest unusual. It is said that the eagle selects rough material, basically, for the construction of his nest. And then as the nest graduates toward a close or a finish, the material becomes finer and softer right down at the end. And then he goes about to set up residence in that nest. And when the little eaglets are born, she goes out and brings in food to feed them. But when they get to the point where they're old enough to be out on their own, why, the eagle will begin to pull out some of that down and let some of those thorns come through so that the nest won't be, you know, so comfortable. So when they get to lounging around and rolling around, the thorns prick 'em here and there. (Pray with me if you please.)

I believe that God has to do that for us sometimes. Things are going so well and we are so satisfied that we just lounge around and forget to pray. You'll walk around all day and enjoy God's life, God's health and God's strength, and go climb into bed without saying, "Thank you, Lord, for another day's journey." We'll do that. God has to pull out a little of the plush around us, a little of the comfort around us, and let a few thorns of trial and tribulation stick through the nest to make us pray sometime. Isn't it so? For most of us forget God when things are going well with us. Most of us forget him.

It is said that there was a man who had a poultry farm. And that he raised chickens for the market. And one day in one of his broods he discovered a strange looking bird that was very much unlike the other chickens on the yard. [Whooping:]

And
    the man
        didn't pay too much attention.
    But he noticed
        as time went on
that
    this strange looking bird
        was unusual.
    He outgrew
        the other little chickens,
    his habits were stranger
        and different.
O Lord.
    But he let him grow on,
    and let him mingle
        with the other chickens.
O Lord.
    And then one day a man
    who knew eagles
        when he saw them,
    came along
        and saw that little eagle
        walking in the yard.
And

he said to his friend,
"Do you know
that you have an eagle here?"
The man said, "Well,
I didn't really know it.
But I knew he was different
from the other chickens.
And
I knew that his ways
were different.
And
I knew that his habits
were different.
And
he didn't act like
the other chickens.
But I didn't know
that he was an eagle."
But the man said, "Yes,
you have an eagle here on your yard.
And what you ought to do
is build a cage.
After while
when he's a little older
he's going to get tired
of the ground.
Yes he will.
He's going to rise up
on the pinion of his wings.
Yes,
and
as he grows,
why,
you can change the cage,
and
make it a little larger
as he grows older
and grows larger."

The man went out
        and built a cage.
And
    every day he'd go in
            and feed the eagle.
But
    he grew
            a little older
            and a little older.
Yes he did.
    His wings
            began
    to scrape on the sides
            of the cage.
And
    he had to build
            another cage
    and open the door of the old cage
            and let him into
    a larger cage.
Yes he did.
O Lord.
And
    after a while
            he outgrew that one day
            and then he had to build
            another cage.
    So one day
            when the eagle had gotten grown,
Lord God,
    and his wings
            were twelve feet
            from tip to tip,
O Lord,
            he began to get restless
            in the cage.
Yes he did.

He began to walk around
             and be uneasy.
Why,
      he heard
             noises
             in the air.
A flock of eagles flew over
             and he heard
             their voices.
And
      though he'd never been around eagles,
      there was something about that voice
             that he heard
      that moved
             down in him,
      and made him
             dissatisfied.
O Lord.
And
      the man watched him
             as he walked around
             uneasy.
O Lord.
      He said, "Lord,
             my heart goes out to him.
      I believe I'll go
             and open the door
             and set the eagle free."
O Lord.
      He went there
             and opened the door.
Yes.
      The eagle walked out,
             yes,
      spreaded his wings,
             then took 'em down.
      Yes.

The eagle walked around
    a little longer,
and
    he flew up a little higher
       and went to the barnyard.
And,
yes,
    he set there for awhile.
    He wiggled up a little higher
    and flew in yonder's tree.
Yes.
    And then he wiggled up a little higher
    and flew to yonder's mountain.
Yes.
Yes!
Yes.
    One of these days,
       one of these days.
    My soul
       is an eagle
    in the cage that the Lord
       has made for me.
    My soul,
       my soul,
    my soul
       is caged in,
       in this old body,
       yes it is,
    and one of these days
    the man who made the cage
    will open the door
    and let my soul
       go.
Yes he will.
    You ought to
       be able to see me
       take the wings of my soul.

Yes, yes,

yes,

yes!

Yes, one of these days.

One of these old days.

One of these old days.

Did you hear me say it?

I'll fly away

and be at rest.

Yes.

Yes!

Yes!

Yes!

Yes!

Yes.

One of these old days.

One of these old days.

And

when troubles

and trials are over,

when toil

and tears are ended,

when burdens

are through burdening,

ohh!

Ohh.

Ohh!

Ohh one of these days.

Ohh one of these days.

One of these days.

One of these days,

my soul will take wings,

my soul will take wings.

Ohh!

Ohh, a few more days.

Ohh, a few more days.

A few more days.

O Lord.

MARTIN LUTHER KING JR.

I Have a Dream

· *From James Melvin Washington, ed.,* A Testament of Hope: The
Essential Writings and Speeches of Martin Luther King, Jr. ·

King's "I Have a Dream" is the best-known American speech of the twentieth
century. While it reflects King's erudition, it also stands as the quintessence of the
traditional Black sermon, illustrating almost every feature of that folk form. It is
the illustration par excellence of the "grandiloquence" that James Weldon
Johnson noted among the Negro preachers he observed.

I am happy to join with you today in what will go down in history
as the greatest demonstration for freedom in the history of our nation.

Fivescore years ago, a great American, in whose symbolic shadow
we stand today, signed the Emancipation Proclamation. This momentous decree came as a great beacon light of hope to millions of
Negro slaves who had been seared in the flames of withering injustice. It came as a joyous daybreak to end the long night of their cap-
tivity.

But one hundred years later, the Negro still is not free; one hundred years later, the life of the Negro is still sadly crippled by the
manacles of segregation and the chains of discrimination; one hundred years later, the Negro lives on a lonely island of poverty in the
midst of a vast ocean of material prosperity; one hundred years later,
the Negro is still languished in the corners of American society and
finds himself in exile in his own land.

So we've come here today to dramatize a shameful condition. In
a sense we've come to our nation's capital to cash a check. When the
architects of our republic wrote the magnificent words of the
Constitution and the Declaration of Independence, they were sign-
ing a promissory note to which every American was to fall heir. This
note was the promise that all men, yes, black men as well as white
men, would be guaranteed the unalienable rights of life, liberty, and
the pursuit of happiness.

It is obvious today that America has defaulted on this promissory
note in so far as her citizens of color are concerned. Instead of hon-
oring this sacred obligation, America has given the Negro people a
bad check; a check which has come back marked "insufficient funds."

We refuse to believe that there are insufficient funds in the great vaults of opportunity of this nation. And so we've come to cash this check, a check that will give us upon demand the riches of freedom and the security of justice.

We have also come to this hallowed spot to remind America of the fierce urgency of now. This is no time to engage in the luxury of cooling off or to take the tranquilizing drug of gradualism. Now is the time to make real the promises of democracy; now is the time to rise from the dark and desolate valley of segregation to the sunlit path of racial justice; now is the time to lift our nation from the quicksands of racial injustice to the solid rock of brotherhood; now is the time to make justice a reality for all God's children. It would be fatal for the nation to overlook the urgency of the moment. This sweltering summer of the Negro's legitimate discontent will not pass until there is an invigorating autumn of freedom and equality.

Nineteen sixty-three is not an end, but a beginning. And those who hope that the Negro needed to blow off steam and will now be content, will have a rude awakening if the nation returns to business as usual.

There will be neither rest nor tranquility in America until the Negro is granted his citizenship rights. The whirlwinds of revolt will continue to shake the foundations of our nation until the bright day of justice emerges.

But there is something that I must say to my people who stand on the warm threshold which leads into the palace of justice. In the process of gaining our rightful place we must not be guilty of wrongful deeds.

Let us not seek to satisfy our thirst for freedom by drinking from the cup of bitterness and hatred. We must forever conduct our struggle on the high plane of dignity and discipline. We must not allow our creative protest to degenerate into physical violence. Again and again we must rise to the majestic heights of meeting physical force with soul force.

The marvelous new militancy which has engulfed the Negro community must not lead us to a distrust of all white people, for many of our white brothers, as evidenced by their presence here today, have come to realize that their destiny is tied up with our destiny and they have come to realize that their freedom is inextricably bound to our freedom. This offense we share mounted to storm the battlements of injustice must be carried forth by a biracial army. We cannot walk alone.

And as we walk, we must make the pledge that we shall always march ahead. We cannot turn back. There are those who are asking the devotees of civil rights, "When will you be satisfied?" We can never be satisfied as long as the Negro is the victim of the unspeakable horrors of police brutality.

We can never be satisfied as long as our bodies, heavy with fatigue of travel, cannot gain lodging in the motels of the highways and the hotels of the cities. We cannot be satisfied as long as the Negro's basic mobility is from a smaller ghetto to a larger one.

We can never be satisfied as long as our children are stripped of their selfhood and robbed of their dignity by signs stating "for whites only." We cannot be satisfied as long as a Negro in Mississippi cannot vote and a Negro in New York believes he has nothing for which to vote. No, we are not satisfied, and we will not be satisfied until justice rolls down like waters and righteousness like a mighty stream.

I am not unmindful that some of you have come here out of excessive trials and tribulation. Some of you have come fresh from narrow jail cells. Some of you have come from areas where your quest for freedom left you battered by the storms of persecution and staggered by the winds of police brutality. You have been the veterans of creative suffering. Continue to work with the faith that unearned suffering is redemptive.

Go back to Mississippi; go back to Alabama; go back to South Carolina; go back to Georgia; go back to Louisiana; go back to the slums and ghettos of the northern cities, knowing that somehow this situation can, and will be changed. Let us not wallow in the valley of despair.

So I say to you, my friends, that even though we must face the difficulties of today and tomorrow, I still have a dream. It is a dream deeply rooted in the American dream that one day this nation will rise up and live out the true meaning of its creed—we hold these truths to be self-evident, that all men are created equal.

I have a dream that one day on the red hills of Georgia, sons of former slaves and sons of former slave-owners will be able to sit down together at the table of brotherhood.

I have a dream that one day, even the state of Mississippi, a state sweltering with the heat of injustice, sweltering with the heat of oppression, will be transformed into an oasis of freedom and justice.

I have a dream my four little children will one day live in a nation where they will not be judged by the color of their skin but by the content of their character. I have a dream today!

I have a dream that one day, down in Alabama, with its vicious racists, with its governor having his lips dripping with the words of interposition and nullification, that one day, right there in Alabama, little black boys and black girls will be able to join hands with little white boys and white girls as sisters and brothers. I have a dream today!

I have a dream that one day every valley shall be exalted, every hill and mountain shall be made low, the rough places shall be made plain, and the crooked places shall be made straight and the glory of the Lord will be revealed and all flesh shall see it together.

This is our hope. This is the faith that I go back to the South with.

With this faith we will be able to hew out of the mountain of despair a stone of hope. With this faith we will be able to transform the jangling discords of our nation into a beautiful symphony of brotherhood.

With this faith we will be able to work together, to pray together, to struggle together, to go to jail together, to stand up for freedom together, knowing that we will be free one day. This will be the day when all of God's children will be able to sing with new meaning—"my country 'tis of thee; sweet land of liberty; of thee I sing; land where my fathers died, land of the pilgrim's pride; from every mountain side, let freedom ring"—and if America is to be a great nation, this must become true.

So let freedom ring from the prodigious hilltops of New Hampshire.

Let freedom ring from the mighty mountains of New York.

Let freedom ring from the heightening Alleghenies of Pennsylvania.

Let freedom ring from the snow-capped Rockies of Colorado.

Let freedom ring from the curvaceous slopes of California.

But not only that.

Let freedom ring from Stone Mountain of Georgia.

Let freedom ring from Lookout Mountain of Tennessee.

Let freedom ring from every hill and molehill of Mississippi, from every mountainside, let freedom ring.

And when we allow freedom to ring, when we let it ring from every village and hamlet, from every state and city, we will be able to speed up that day when all of God's children — black men and white men, Jews and Gentiles, Catholics and Protestants — will be able to join hands and to sing in the words of the old Negro spiritual, "Free at last, free at last; thank God Almighty, we are free at last."

MARTIN LUTHER KING JR.

Eulogy for the Martyred Children
· *From* A Testament of Hope ·

Following is the closing of King's elegy given at the funeral of the four Black girls killed while attending Sunday School at the 16th Street Baptist Church in Birmingham, Alabama, on September 15, 1963. The bombing of the church was an obvious retaliation for the Civil Rights marches and demonstrations of the time. Churches were often targeted by racists in retaliation for their serving as the sites where activists met, planned, and trained.

I hope you can find some consolation from Christianity's affirmation that death is not the end. Death is not a period that ends the great sentence of life, but a comma that punctuates it to more lofty significance. Death is not a blind alley that leads the human race into a state of nothingness, but an open door which leads man into life eternal. Let this daring faith, this great invincible surmise, be your sustaining power during these trying days.

At times, life is hard, as hard as crucible steel. It has its bleak and painful moments. Like the ever-flowing waters of a river, life has its moments of drought and its moments of flood. Like the ever-changing cycle of the seasons, life has the soothing warmth of the summers and the piercing chill of its winters. But through it all, God walks with us. Never forget that God is able to lift you from fatigue of despair to the buoyancy of hope, and transform dark and desolate valleys into sunlit paths of inner peace.

Your children did not live long, but they lived well. The quantity of their lives was disturbingly small, but the quality of their lives was magnificently big. Where they died and what they were doing when death came will remain a marvelous tribute to each of you and an eternal epitaph to each of them. They died not in a den or dive nor were they hearing and telling filthy jokes at the time of their death. They died within the sacred walls of the church after discussing a principle as eternal as love.

Shakespeare had Horatio utter some beautiful words over the dead body of Hamlet. I paraphrase these words today as I stand over the last remains of these lovely girls.

"Good-night sweet princesses; may the flight of angels take thee to thy eternal rest."

MARTIN LUTHER KING JR.

Our God Is Marching On

· *From* A Testament of Hope ·

What follows is the closing of the March 25, 1965, speech that Martin Luther King Jr. delivered in Montgomery, Alabama, to the more than eight thousand who had joined him in the now-famous walk from Selma, Alabama.

The threat of the free exercise of the ballot by the Negro and the white masses alike resulted in the establishing of a segregated society. They segregated southern money from the poor whites; they segregated southern mores from the rich whites; they segregated southern churches from Christianity; they segregated southern minds from honest thinking, and they segregated the Negro from everything.

We have come a long way since that travesty of justice was perpetrated upon the American mind. Today I want to tell the city of Selma, today I want to say to the state of Alabama, today I want to say to the people of America and the nations of the world: We are not about to turn around. We are on the move now. Yes, we are on the move and no wave of racism can stop us.

"We Are on the Move"

We are on the move now. The burning of our churches will not deter us. We are on the move now. The bombing of our homes will not dissuade us. We are on the move now. The beating and killing of our clergymen and young people will not divert us. We are on the move now. The arrest and release of known murderers will not discourage us. We are on the move now.

Like an idea whose time has come, not even the marching of mighty armies can halt us. We are moving to the land of freedom.

Let us therefore continue our triumph and march to the realization of the American dream. Let us march on segregated housing, until every ghetto of social and economic depression dissolves and Negroes and whites live side by side in decent, safe and sanitary housing.

Let us march on segregated schools until every vestige of segregated and inferior education becomes a thing of the past and Negroes and whites study side by side in the socially healing context of the classroom.

Let us march on poverty, until no American parent has to skip a meal so that their children may march on poverty, until no starved man walks the streets of our cities and towns in search of jobs that do not exist.

Let us march on ballot boxes, march on ballot boxes until race baiters disappear from the political arena. Let us march on ballot boxes until the Wallaces of our nation tremble away in silence.

Let us march on ballot boxes, until we send to our city councils, state legislatures, and the United States Congress men who will not fear to do justice, love mercy, and walk humbly with their God. Let us march on ballot boxes until all over Alabama God's children will be able to walk the earth in decency and honor.

For all of us today the battle is in our hands. The road ahead is not altogether a smooth one. There are no broad highways to lead us easily and inevitably to quick solutions. We must keep going.

"My People, Listen!"

My people, my people, listen! The battle is in our hands. The battle is in our hands in Mississippi and Alabama, and all over the United States.

So as we go away this afternoon, let us go away more than ever before committed to the struggle and committed to nonviolence. I must admit to you there are still some difficulties ahead. We are still in for a season of suffering in many of the black belt counties of Alabama, many areas of Mississippi, many areas of Louisiana.

I must admit to you there are still jail cells waiting for us, dark and difficult moments. We will go on with the faith that nonviolence and its power transformed dark yesterdays into bright tomorrows. We will be able to change all of these conditions.

Our aim must never be to defeat or humiliate the white man but to win his friendship and understanding. We must come to see that the end we seek is a society at peace with itself, a society that can live with its conscience. That will be a day not of the white man, not of the black man. That will be the day of man as man.

I know you are asking today, "How long will it take?" I come to say to you this afternoon however difficult the moment, however frustrating the hour, it will not be long, because truth pressed to earth will rise again.

How long? Not long, because no lie can live forever.

How long? Not long, because you still reap what you sow.

How long? Not long. Because the arm of the moral universe is long but it bends toward justice.

How long? Not long, 'cause mine eyes have seen the glory of the coming of the Lord, trampling out the vintage where the grapes of wrath are stored. He has loosed the fateful lightning of his terrible swift sword. His truth is marching on.

He has sounded forth the trumpets that shall never call retreat. He is lifting up the hearts of man before His judgment seat. Oh, be swift, my soul, to answer Him. Be jubilant, my feet. Our God is marching on.

MALCOLM X

Message to the Grass Roots

· *From George Breitman*, Malcolm X Speaks ·

This speech, delivered in November 1963, is one of the last speeches given by Malcolm X before Elijah Muhammad suspended and silenced him on December 4 for ninety days because of his comments upon the death of President John F. Kennedy that Kennedy "never foresaw that the chickens would come home to roost so soon." "Message to the Grass Roots" contains a number of the powerful and controversial declarations of the Black Muslims of that era. What follows is about one-half of the speech as edited by Breitman.

We want to have just an off-the-cuff chat between you and me, us. We want to talk right down to earth in a language that everybody here can easily understand. We all agree tonight, all of the speakers have agreed, that America has a very serious problem. Not only does America have a very serious problem, but our people have a very serious problem. America's problem is us. We're her problem. The only reason she has a problem is she doesn't want us here. And every time you look at yourself, be you black, brown, red or yellow, a so-called Negro, you represent a person who poses such a serious problem for America because you're not wanted. Once you face this as a fact, then you can start plotting a course that will make you appear intelligent, instead of unintelligent.

What you and I need to do is learn to forget our differences. When we come together, we don't come together as Baptists or Methodists. You don't catch hell because you're a Baptist, and you don't catch hell because you're a Methodist. You don't catch hell because you're a Methodist or Baptist, you don't catch hell because you're a Democrat or a Republican, you don't catch hell because you're a Mason or an Elk, and you sure don't catch hell because you're an American; because if you were an American, you wouldn't catch hell. You catch hell because you're a black man. You catch hell, all of us catch hell, for the same reason.

So we're all black people, so-called Negroes, second-class citizens, ex-slaves. You're nothing but an ex-slave. You don't like to be told that. But what else are you? You are ex-slaves. You didn't come here on the "Mayflower." You came here on a slave ship. In chains, like a horse, or a cow, or a chicken. And you were brought here by the people who came here on the "Mayflower," you were brought here by the so-called Pilgrims, or Founding Fathers. They were the ones who brought you here.

We have a common enemy. We have this in common: We have a common oppressor, a common exploiter, and a common discriminator. But once we all realize that we have a common enemy, then we unite—on the basis of what we have in common. And what we have foremost in common is that enemy—the white man. He's an enemy to all of us. I know some of you all think that some of them aren't enemies. Time will tell.

In Bandung back in, I think, 1954, was the first unity meeting in centuries of black people. And once you study what happened at the Bandung conference, and the results of the Bandung conference, it actually serves as a model for the same procedure you and I can use to get our problems solved. At Bandung all the nations came together, the dark nations from Africa and Asia. Some of them were Buddhists, some of them were Muslims, some of them were Christians, some were Confucianists, some were atheists. Despite their religious differences, they came together. Some were communists, some were socialists, some were capitalists—despite their economic and political differences, they came together. All of them were black, brown, red or yellow.

The number-one thing that was not allowed to attend the Bandung conference was the white man. He couldn't come. Once they excluded the white man, they found that they could get together. Once they kept him out, everybody else fell right in and fell in line. This is the thing that you and I have to understand. And these people who came together didn't have nuclear weapons, they didn't have jet planes, they didn't have all of the heavy armaments that the white man has. But they had unity.

They were able to submerge their little petty differences and agree on one thing: That there one African came from Kenya and was being colonized by the Englishman, and another African came from the Congo and was being colonized by the Belgian, and another African came from Guinea and was being colonized by the French, and another came from Angola and was being colonized by the Portuguese. When they came to the Bandung conference, they looked at the Portuguese, and at the Frenchman, and at the Englishman, and at the Dutchman, and learned or realized the one thing that all of them had in common—they were all from Europe, they were all Europeans, blond, blue-eyed and white skins. They began to recognize who their enemy was. The same man that was colonizing our people in Kenya was colonizing our people in the Congo. The same one in the Congo was colonizing our people in South Africa, and in Southern Rhodesia, and in Burma, and in India, and in Afghanistan, and in Pakistan. They realized all over the world where the dark man was being oppressed, he was being oppressed by the white man; where the dark man was being exploited, he was being exploited by the white man. So they got together on this basis—that they had a common enemy.

And when you and I here in Detroit and in Michigan and in America who have been awakened today look around us, we too realize here in America we all have a common enemy, whether he's in Georgia or Michigan, whether he's in California or New York. He's the same man—blue eyes and blond hair and pale skin—the same man. So what we have to do is what they did. They agreed to stop quarreling among themselves. Any little spat that they had, they'd settle it among themselves, go into a huddle—don't let the enemy know that you've got a disagreement.

Instead of airing our differences in public, we have to realize we're all the same family. And when you have a family squabble, you don't get out on the sidewalk. If you do, everybody calls you uncouth, unrefined, uncivilized, savage. If you don't make it at home, you settle it at home; you get in the closet, argue it out behind closed doors, and then when you come out on the street, you pose a common front, a united front. And this is what we need to do in the community, and in the city, and in the state. We need to stop airing our differences in front of the white man, put the white man out of our meetings, and then sit down and talk shop with each other. That's what we've got to do.

I would like to make a few comments concerning the difference between the black revolution and the Negro revolution. Are they both the same? And if they're not, what is the difference? What is the difference between a black revolution and a Negro revolution? First, what is a revolution? Sometimes I'm inclined to believe that many of our people are using this word "revolution" loosely, without taking careful consideration of what this word actually means, and what its historic characteristics are. When you study the historic nature of revolutions, the motive of a revolution, the objective of a revolution, the result of a revolution, and the methods used in a revolution, you may change words. You may devise another program, you may change your goal and you may change your mind.

Look at the American Revolution in 1776. That revolution was for what? For land. Why did they want land? Independence. How was it carried out? Bloodshed. Number one, it was based on land, the basis of independence. And the only way they could get it was bloodshed. The French Revolution—what was it based on? The landless against the landlord. What was it for? Land. How did they get it? Bloodshed. Was no love lost, was no compromise, was no negotiation. I'm telling you—you don't know what a revolution is. Because when you find out what it is, you'll get back in the alley, you'll get out of the way.

The Russian Revolution—what was it based on? Land; the landless against the landlord. How did they bring it about? Bloodshed. You haven't got a revolution that doesn't involve bloodshed. And you're afraid to bleed. I said, you're afraid to bleed.

As long as the white man sent you to Korea, you bled. He sent you to Germany, you bled. He sent you to the South Pacific to fight the Japanese, you bled. You bleed for white people, but when it comes to seeing your own churches being bombed and little black girls murdered, you haven't got any blood. You bleed when the white man says bleed; you bite when the white man says bite; and you bark when the white man says bark. I hate to say this about us, but it's true. How are you going to be nonviolent in Mississippi, as violent as you were in Korea? How can you justify being nonviolent in Mississippi and Alabama, when your churches are being bombed, and your little girls are being murdered, and at the same time you are going to get violent with Hitler, and Tojo, and somebody else you don't even know?

If violence is wrong in America, violence is wrong abroad. If it is wrong to be violent defending black women and black children and black babies and black men, then it is wrong for America to draft us and make us violent abroad in defense of her. And if it is right for America to draft us, and teach us how to be violent in defense of her, then it is right for you and me to do whatever is necessary to defend our own people right here in this country.

The Chinese Revolution—they wanted land. They threw the British out, along with the Uncle Tom Chinese. Yes, they did. They set a good example. When I was in prison, I read an article—don't be shocked when I say that I was in prison. You're still in prison. That's what America means: prison. When I was in prison, I read an article in *Life* magazine showing a little Chinese girl, nine years old; her father was on his hands and knees and she was pulling the trigger because he was an Uncle Tom Chinaman. When they had the revolution over there, they took a whole generation of Uncle Toms and just wiped them out. And within ten years that little girl became a full-grown woman. No more Toms in China. And today it's one of the toughest, roughest, most feared countries on this earth—by the white man. Because there are no Uncle Toms over there.

Of all our studies, history is best qualified to reward our research. And when you see that you've got problems, all you have to do is examine the historic method used all over the world by others who have problems similar to yours. Once you see how they got theirs straight, then you know how you can get yours straight. There's been a revolution, a black revolution, going on in Africa. In Kenya, the Mau Mau were revolutionary; they were the ones who brought the word "Uhuru" to the fore. The Mau Mau, they were revolutionary, they believed in scorched earth, they knocked everything aside that got in their way, and their revolution also was based on land, a desire for land. In Algeria, the northern part of Africa, a revolution took place. The Algerians were revolutionists, they wanted land. France offered to let them be integrated into France. They told France, to hell with France, they wanted some land, not some France. And they engaged in a bloody battle.

So I cite these various revolutions, brothers and sisters, to show you that you don't have a peaceful revolution. You don't have a turn-the-other-cheek revolution. There's no such thing as a nonviolent revolution. The only kind of revolution that is nonviolent is the Negro revolution. The only revolution in which the goal is loving your enemy is the Negro revolution. It's the only revolution in which the goal is a desegregated lunch counter, a desegregated theater, a desegregated park, and a desegregated public toilet; you can sit down next to white folks — on the toilet. That's no revolution. Revolution is based on land. Land is the basis of all independence. Land is the basis of freedom, justice, and equality.

The white man knows what a revolution is. He knows that the black revolution is world-wide in scope and in nature. The black revolution is sweeping Asia, is sweeping Africa, is rearing its head in Latin America. The Cuban Revolution — that's a revolution. They overturned the system. Revolution is in Asia, revolution is in Africa, and the white man is screaming because he sees revolution in Latin America. How do you think he'll react to you when you learn what a real revolution is? You don't know what a revolution is. If you did, you wouldn't use that word.

Revolution is bloody, revolution is hostile, revolution knows no compromise, revolution overturns and destroys everything that gets in its way. And you, sitting around here like a knot on the wall, say-

ing, "I'm going to love these folks no matter how much they hate me."
No, you need a revolution. Whoever heard of a revolution where
they lock arms, as Rev. Cleage was pointing out beautifully, singing
"We Shall Overcome"? You don't do that in a revolution. You don't
do any singing, you're too busy swinging. It's based on land. A revolutionary wants land so he can set up his own nation, an independent nation. These Negroes aren't asking for any nation—they're
trying to crawl back on the plantation.

When you want a nation, that's called nationalism. When the white
man became involved in a revolution in this country against England,
what was it for? He wanted this land so he could set up another
white nation. That's white nationalism. The American Revolution
was white nationalism. The French Revolution was white nationalism. The Russian Revolution too—yes, it was—white nationalism.
You don't think so? Why do you think Khrushchev and Mao can't
get their heads together? White nationalism. All the revolutions that
are going on in Asia and Africa today are based on what?—black nationalism. A revolutionary is a black nationalist. He wants a nation.
I was reading some beautiful words by Rev. Cleage, pointing out
why he couldn't get together with someone else in the city because all
of them were afraid of being identified with black nationalism. If
you're afraid of black nationalism, you're afraid of revolution. And if
you love revolution, you love black nationalism.

MALCOLM X

The Ballot or the Bullet

· *From George Breitman,* Malcolm X Speaks ·

This speech, delivered in Detroit, Michigan, on April 12, 1964, is representative
of Malcolm X's speeches following his break with Elijah Muhammad. Here he
emphasizes the need for all camps of the Black community to join together in a
more militant demand for their rights.

Although I'm still a Muslim, I'm not here tonight to discuss my religion. I'm not here to try and change your religion. I'm not here to
argue or discuss anything that we differ about, because it's time for
us to submerge our differences and realize that it is best for us to first

see that we have the same problem, a common problem—a problem that will make you catch hell whether you're a Baptist, or a Methodist, or a Muslim, or a nationalist. Whether you're educated or illiterate, whether you live on the boulevard or in the alley, you're going to catch hell just like I am. We're all in the same boat and we all are going to catch the same hell from the same man. He just happens to be a white man. All of us have suffered here, in this country, political oppression at the hands of the white man, economic exploitation at the hands of the white man, and social degradation at the hands of the white man.

Now in speaking like this, it doesn't mean that we're anti-white, but it does mean we're anti-exploitation, we're anti-degradation, we're anti-oppression. And if the white man doesn't want us to be anti-him, let him stop oppressing and exploiting and degrading us. Whether we are Christians or Muslims or nationalists or agnostics or atheists, we must first learn to forget our differences. If we have differences, let us differ in the closet; when we come out in front, let us not have anything to argue about until we get finished arguing with the man. If the late President Kennedy could get together with Khrushchev and exchange some wheat, we certainly have more in common with each other than Kennedy and Khruschev had with each other.

If we don't do something real soon, I think you'll have to agree that we're going to be forced either to use the ballot or the bullet. It's one or the other in 1964. It isn't that time is running out—time has run out! 1964 threatens to be the most explosive year America has ever witnessed. The most explosive year. Why? It's also a political year. It's the year when all of the white politicians will be back in the so-called Negro community jiving you and me for some votes. The year when all of the white political crooks will be right back in your and my community with their false promises, building up our hopes for a letdown, with their trickery and their treachery, with their false promises which they don't intend to keep. As they nourish these dissatisfactions, it can only lead to one thing, an explosion; and now we have the type of black man on the scene in America today—I'm sorry, Brother Lomax—who just doesn't intend to turn the other cheek any longer.

Don't let anybody tell you anything about the odds are against you. If they draft you, they send you to Korea and make you face 800 million Chinese. If you can be brave over there, you can be brave right here. These odds aren't as great as those odds. And if you fight here, you will at least know what you're fighting for.

JESSE JACKSON

Keep Hope Alive

· *From Frank Clemente, ed., with Frank Watkins,* Keep Hope Alive: Jesse Jackson's 1988 Presidential Campaign ·

This speech was delivered on July 19, 1988, to the Democratic National Convention meeting in Atlanta, Georgia. A few of the opening acknowledgments have been omitted.

My right and privilege to stand here before you has been won—in my lifetime—by the blood and sweat of the innocent.

Twenty-four years ago, the late Fanny Lou Hamer and Aaron Henry—who sits here tonight from Mississippi—were locked out on the streets of Atlantic City, the heads of the Mississippi Freedom Democratic Party. But tonight, an African American and a white delegation from Mississippi is headed by Ed Cole, an African American, from Mississippi, 24 years later.

Many were lost in the struggle for the right to vote. Jimmy Lee Jackson, a young student, gave his life. Viola Luizzo, a white mother from Detroit, called nigger lover, had her brains blown out at point-blank range.

Schwerner, Goodman and Chaney—two Jews and an African American—found in a common grave, bodies riddled with bullets in Mississippi. The four darling little girls in church in Birmingham, Alabama. They died that we may have a right to live.

Dr. Martin Luther King, Jr. lies only a few miles from us tonight. Tonight he must feel good as he looks down upon us. We sit here together, a rainbow, a coalition—the sons and daughters of slaves sitting together around a common table, to decide the direction of our party and our country. His heart must be full tonight.

As a testament to the struggles of those who have gone before; as a legacy for those who will come after; as a tribute to the endurance, the patience, the courage of our forefathers and mothers; as an assurance that their prayers are being answered, their work has not been in vain, and hope is eternal—tomorrow night my name will go into nomination for the Presidency of the United States of America.

We meet tonight at a crossroads, a point of decision. Shall we expand, be inclusive, or suffer division and impotence?

We come to Atlanta, the cradle of the Old South, the crucible of the New South. Tonight there is a sense of celebration because we are moved, fundamentally moved, from racial battlegrounds by law, to economic common ground. Tomorrow we will challenge to move to higher ground.

Common ground!

Think of Jerusalem—the intersection where many trails met. A small village that became the birthplace for three great religions— Judaism, Christianity and Islam. Why was this village so blessed? Because it provided a crossroads where different people met, different cultures and different civilizations could meet and find common ground.

When people come together, flowers always flourish and the air is rich with the aroma of a new spring. Take New York, the dynamic metropolis. What makes New York so special? It is the invitation of the Statue of Liberty—give me your tired, your poor, your huddled masses who yearn to breathe free.

Not restricted to English only.

Many people, many cultures, many languages—with one thing in common, the yearning to breathe free.

Common ground!

Tonight in Atlanta, for the first time in this century we convene in the South. A state where governors once stood in school-house doors. Where Julian Bond was denied his seat in the state legislature because of his conscientious objection to the Vietnam War. A city that, through its five African American universities, has graduated more African Americans than any other city in the world. Atlanta, now a modern intersection of the New South.

Common ground! That is the challenge to our party tonight.

Left wing. Right wing. Progress will not come through boundless liberalism nor static conservatism, but at the critical mass of mutual survival. It takes two wings to fly. Whether you're a hawk or a dove, you're just a bird living in the same environment, in the same world.

The Bible teaches that when lions and lambs lie down together, none will be afraid and there will be peace in the valley. It sounds impossible. Lions eat lambs. Lambs sensibly flee from lions. But even lions and lambs find common ground. Why?

Because neither lions nor lambs want the forest to catch on fire. Neither lions nor lambs want acid rain to fall. Neither lions nor lambs can survive a nuclear war. If lions and lambs can find common ground, surely we can as well, as civilized people.

The only time that we win is when we come together. In 1960, John Kennedy, the late John Kennedy, beat Richard Nixon by only 112,000 votes—less than one vote per precinct. He won by the margin of our hope. He brought us together. He reached out. He had the courage to defy his advisors and inquire about Dr. King's jailing in Albany, Georgia. We won by the margin of our hope, inspired by courageous leadership.

In 1964, Lyndon Johnson brought both wings together—the thesis, the antithesis—to create a synthesis, and together we won.

In 1976, Jimmy Carter unified us again and we won. When we do not come together we never win.

In 1968, division and despair in August led to our defeat in November.

In 1980, rancor in the spring and the summer led to Reagan in the fall. When we divide, we cannot win. We must find common ground as a basis for survival and development and change and growth.

Today when we debated, differed, deliberated, agreed to agree, agreed to disagree, when we had the good judgment to argue our case and then not to self-destruct, George Bush was just a little further away from the White House and a little closer to private life.

Tonight, I salute Governor Michael Dukakis. He has run a well-managed and a dignified campaign. No matter how tired or how tried, he always resisted the temptation to stoop to demagoguery.

I've watched a good mind fast at work, with steel nerves, guiding his campaign out of the crowded field without appeal to the worst in us. I've watched his perspective grow as his environment expanded. I've seen his toughness and tenacity close-up. I know his commitment to public service.

Mike Dukakis's parents were a doctor and a teacher; my parents, a maid, a beautician and a janitor.

There is a great gap between Brookline, Massachusetts and Haney Street, the Fieldcrest Village housing project in Greenville,

South Carolina. He studied law; I studied theology. There are differences of religion, region and race, differences in experiences and perspectives. But the genius of America is that out of the many, we become one.

Providence has enabled our paths to intersect. His foreparents came to America on immigrant ships; my foreparents on slave ships; we're in the same boat tonight.

Our ships could pass in the night if we have a false sense of independence, or they could collide and crash. We would lose our passengers. But we cannot seek a higher reality and a greater good apart. We can drift on the broken pieces of Reaganomics, satisfy our baser instincts, and exploit the fears of our people. At our highest, we can call upon noble instincts to navigate this vessel to safety. The greater good is the common good.

As Jesus said, "Not my will, but thine be done." It was his way of saying there's a higher good beyond personal comfort or position.

The good of our nation is at stake—its commitment to working men and women, to the poor and the vulnerable, to the many in the world. With so many guided missiles, and so much misguided leadership, the stakes are exceedingly high. Our choice: full participation in a Democratic government or more abandonment and neglect. And so this night we choose not a false sense of independence, not our capacity to survive and endure.

Tonight we choose interdependency in our capacity to act and unite for the greater good. The common good is finding commitment to new priorities, to expansion and inclusion; a commitment to expanded participation in the Democratic Party at every level; a commitment to new priorities that ensure that hope will be kept alive; a common ground commitment to D.C. statehood and empowerment—D.C. deserves statehood; a commitment to economic set-asides; a commitment to the Dellums bill for comprehensive sanctions against South Africa; a shared commitment to a common direction.

Common ground. Easier said than done. Where do you find common ground—at the point of challenge. This campaign has shown that politics need not be marketed by politicians, packaged by pollsters and pundits. Politics can be a marvelous arena where people come together, define common ground.

We find common ground at the plant gate that closes on workers without notice. We find common ground at the farm auction where a good farmer loses his or her land to bad loans or diminishing markets. Common ground at the schoolyard where teachers cannot get adequate pay, and students cannot get a scholarship and can't make a loan. Common ground at the hospital admitting room where somebody tonight is dying because they cannot afford to go upstairs to a bed that's empty, waiting for someone with insurance to get sick. We are a better nation than that. We must do better.

Common ground. What is leadership if not present help in a time of crisis? And so I met you at a point of challenge in Jay, Maine, where paper workers were striking for fair wages; in Greenfield, Iowa, where family farmers struggle for a fair price; in Cleveland, Ohio, where working women seek comparable worth; in McFarland, California, where the children of Hispanic farm workers may be dying in clusters with cancer; in the AIDS hospice in Houston, Texas, where the sick support one another, 12 of whom are rejected by their own parents and friends. Common ground.

America's not a blanket woven from one thread, one color, one cloth. When I was a child growing up in Greenville, South Carolina, and grandmother could not afford a blanket, she didn't complain and we did not freeze. Instead, she took pieces of old cloth—patches, wool, silk, gabardine, crokersack, only patches—barely good enough to wipe your shoes with.

But they didn't stay that way very long. With sturdy hands and a strong cord, she sewed them together into a quilt, a thing of beauty and power and culture.

Now, Democrats, we must build such a quilt. Farmers, you seek fair prices and you are right, but you cannot stand alone. Your patch is not big enough. Workers, you fight for fair wages. You are right. But your patch, labor, is not big enough. Women, you seek comparable worth and pay equity. You are right. But your patch is not big enough. Women, mothers, who seek Head Start and day care and prenatal care on the front side of life, rather than welfare and jail care on the back side of life, you're right, but your patch is not big enough.

Students, you seek scholarships. You are right. But your patch is not big enough. African Americans and Hispanics, when we fight for civil rights, we are right, but our patch is not big enough. Gays and lesbians, when you fight against discrimination and for a cure for

AIDS, you are right, but your patch is not big enough. Conservatives and progressives, when you fight for what you believe, right-wing, left-wing, hawk, dove—you are right from your point of view, but your point of view is not enough.

But don't despair. Be as wise as my grandmama. Pool the patches and the pieces together, bound by a common thread. When we form a great quilt of unity and common ground, we'll have the power to bring about health care and housing and jobs and education and hope to our nation.

We the people can win. We stand at the end of a long dark night of reaction. We stand tonight united in a commitment to a new direction. For almost eight years, we've been led by those who view social good coming from private interest, who viewed public life as a means to increase private wealth. They have been prepared to sacrifice the common good of the many to satisfy the private interest and the wealth of a few. We believe in a government that's a tool of our democracy in service to the public, not an instrument of the aristocracy in search of private wealth.

We believe in government with the consent of the governed—of, for and by the people. We must not emerge into a new day without a new direction.

Reaganomics is based on the belief that the rich had too little money, and the poor had too much. So they engaged in reverse Robin Hood—took from the poor, gave to the rich, paid for by the middle-class. We cannot stand four more years of Reaganomics in any version, in any disguise.

How do I document that case? Seven years later, the richest one percent of our society pays 20 percent less in taxes; the poorest ten percent pay 20 percent more. Reaganomics.

Reagan gave the rich and the powerful a multi-billion-dollar party. Now the party is over. He expects the people to pay for the damage. I take this principled position: let us not raise taxes on the poor and the middle class, but those who had the party, the rich and the powerful, must pay for the party!

I just want to take common sense to high places. We're spending $150 billion a year defending Europe and Japan 43 years after the war is over. We have more troops in Europe tonight than we had seven years ago, yet the threat of war is ever more remote. Germany and Japan are now creditor nations—that means they've got a surplus. We are a debtor nation—that means we are in debt.

Let them share more of the burden of their own defense—use some of that money to build decent housing. Use some of that money to educate our children. Use some of that money for long-term health care. Use some of that money to wipe out these slums and put America back to work.

I just want to take common sense to higher places. If we can bail out Europe and Japan, if we can bail out Continental Bank and Chrysler—and Mr. Iacocca makes $8,000 an hour—we can bail out the family farmer.

I just want to make common sense. It does not make sense to close down 650,000 family farms in this country while importing food from abroad subsidized by the U.S. government.

Let's make sense. It does not make sense to be escorting oil tankers up and down the Persian Gulf, paying $2.50 for every $1.00 worth of oil we bring out, while oil wells are capped in Texas, Oklahoma and Louisiana. I just want to make sense.

Leadership must meet the moral challenge of its day. What's the moral challenge of our day? We have public accommodations. We have the right to vote. We have open housing.

What's the fundamental challenge of our day? It is to end economic violence. Plants closing without notice, economic violence. Most poor people are not lazy. They're not Black. They're not brown. They're mostly white, female and young.

But whether white, black, brown, the hungry baby's belly turned inside-out is the same color. Call it pain. Call it hurt. Call it agony.

Most poor people are not on welfare. Some of them are illiterate and can't read the want-ad sections. And when they can, they can't find a job that matches their address. They work hard every day. I know. I live among them. I'm one of them.

I know they work. I'm a witness. They catch the early bus. They work every day. They raise other people's children. They work every day. They clean the streets. They work every day. They drive vans and cabs. They work every day. They change the beds you slept in at these hotels last night and can't get a union contract. They work every day.

No more. They're not lazy. Someone must defend them because

it's right, and they cannot speak for themselves. They work in hospitals. I know they do. They wipe the bodies of those who are sick with fever and pain. They empty their bedpans. They clean out their commodes. No job is beneath them, and yet when they get sick, they cannot lie in the bed they made up every day. America, that is not right. We are a better nation than that. We are a better nation than that.

We need a real war on drugs. You can't "just say no." It's deeper than that. You can't just get a palm reader or an astrologer; it's more profound than that. We're spending $150 billion on drugs a year. We've gone from ignoring it to focusing on the children. Children cannot buy $150 billion worth of drugs a year. A few high profile athletes—athletes are not laundering $150 billion a year—bankers are.

I met the children in Watts who are unfortunate in their despair. Their grapes of hope have become raisins of despair, and they're turning on each other and they're self-destructing—but I stayed with them all night long. I wanted to hear their case. They said, "Jesse Jackson, as you challenge us to say no to drugs, you're right. And not to sell them, you're right. And not to use these guns, you're right."

And, by the way, the promise of CETA—they displaced CETA. They did not replace CETA. We have neither jobs nor houses nor services nor training—no way out. Some of us take drugs as anesthesia for our pain. Some take drugs as a way of pleasure—both short-term pleasure and long-term pain. Some sell drugs to make money. It's wrong, we know. But you need to know what we know. We can go and buy the drugs by the boxes at the port. If we can buy the drugs at the port, don't you believe the federal government can stop it if they want to?

They say, "We don't have Saturday night specials anymore." They say, "We buy AK-47s and Uzis, the latest lethal weapons. We buy them across the counter at Long Beach Boulevard." You cannot fight a war on drugs unless and until you are going to challenge the bankers and the gun sellers and those who grow the drugs. Don't just focus on the children, let's stop drugs at the level of supply and demand. We must end the scourge on the American culture.

Leadership. What difference will we make? Leadership cannot just go along to get along. We must do more than change presidents. We must change direction. Leadership must face the moral challenge of our day. The nuclear weapons build-up is irrational. Strong leadership cannot desire to look tough, and let that stand in the way of the pursuit of peace. Leadership must reverse the arms race.

At least we should pledge no first use. Why? Because first use begets first retaliation, and that's mutual annihilation. That's not the rational way out. No use at all—let's think this out, and not fight it out, because it's an unwinnable fight. Why hold a card that you can never drop? Let's give peace a chance.

Leadership. We now have this marvelous opportunity to have a breakthrough with the Soviets. Last year, 200,000 Americans visited the Soviet Union. There's a chance for joint ventures into space, not Star Wars and the arms race escalation, but a space development initiative. Let's build in space together and demilitarize the heavens. There's a way out.

America, let us expand. When Mr. Reagan and Mr. Gorbachev met, there was a big meeting. They represented together one-eighth of the human race. Seven-eighths of the human race were locked out of that room: most people in the world tonight—half are Asian, one half of them are Chinese. There are 22 nations in the Middle East. There's Europe, 400 million Latin Americans next door to us, the Caribbean, Africa—a half a billion people. Most people in the world today are yellow or brown or black, non-Christian, poor, female, young, and don't speak English—in the real world.

This generation must offer leadership to the real world. We're losing ground in Latin America, the Middle East, South Africa, because we are not focusing on the real world. We must use basic principles: support international law. We stand the most to gain from it. Support human rights; we believe in that. Support self-determination; we'll build on that. Support economic development; you know it's right. Be consistent, and gain our moral authority in the world.

I challenge you tonight, my friends, let's be bigger and better as a nation and a party. We have basic challenges. Freedom in South Africa—we've already agreed as Democrats to declare South Africa to be a terrorist state. But don't just stop there. Get South Africa out of Angola. Free Namibia. Support the Frontline states. We must have a new, humane human rights assistance policy in Africa.

I'm often asked, "Jesse, why do you take on these tough issues? They're not very political. We can't win that way."

If an issue is morally right, it will eventually be political. It may be political and never be right. Fannie Lou Hamer didn't have the most votes in Atlantic City, but her principles have outlasted every delegate who voted to lock her out. Rosa Parks did not have the most votes, but she was morally right. Dr. King did not have the most votes about the Vietnam War, but he was morally right. If we're principled first, our politics will fall into place.

Jesse, why did you take these big bold initiatives? A poem by an unknown author went something like this: We mastered the air, we've conquered the sea, and annihilated distance and prolonged life, we were not wise enough to live on this earth without war and without hate.

As for Jesse Jackson, I'm tired of sailing my little boat, far inside the harbor bar. I want to go out where the big boats float, out on the deep where the great ones are. And should my frail craft prove too slight, the waves that sweep those billows o'er, I'd rather go down in a stirring fight than drown to death on the sheltered shore.

We've got to go out, my friends, where the big boats are. And then, for our children, young America, hold your head high now. We can win. We must not lose you to drugs and violence, premature pregnancy, suicide, cynicism, pessimism and despair. We can win.

Wherever you are tonight, I challenge you to hope and to dream. Don't submerge your dreams. Exercise above all else the right to dream. Even on drugs, dream of the day that you are drug-free. Even in the gutter, dream of the day that you will be up on your feet again. You must never stop dreaming. Face reality, yes. But don't stop with the way things are; dream of things the way they ought to be. Dream. Face pain, but love, hope, faith and dreams will help you rise above the pain.

Use hope and imagination as weapons of survival and progress, but you keep on dreaming, young America. Dream of peace. Peace is rational and reasonable. War is irrational in this age and unwinnable.

Dream of teachers who teach for life and not merely for a living. Dream of doctors who are concerned more about public health than private wealth. Dream of lawyers more concerned about justice than a judgeship. Dream of preachers who are more concerned about prophecy than profiteering. Dream on the high road of sound values.

And in America, as we go forth to September, October and November and then beyond, America must never surrender its high moral challenge.

Do not surrender to drugs. The best drug policy is a no first use. Don't surrender with needles and cynicism. Let's have no first use on the one hand or clinics on the other. Never surrender, young America.

Go forward. America must never surrender to malnutrition. We can feed the hungry and clothe the naked. We must never surrender. We must go forward. We must never surrender to illiteracy. Invest in our children. Never surrender, and go forward.

We must never surrender to inequality. Women cannot compromise the ERA or comparable worth. Women are making 67 cents on the dollar to what a man makes. Women cannot buy meat cheaper. Women cannot buy bread cheaper. Women cannot buy milk cheaper. Women deserve to get paid for the work that they do. It's right and it's fair.

Don't surrender, my friends. Those who have AIDS tonight, you deserve our compassion. Even with AIDS you must not surrender. You in your wheelchairs. I see you sitting here tonight. I've stayed with you. I've reached out to you across our nation. Don't you give up. I know it's tough sometimes. People look down on you. It took a little more effort to get here tonight.

And no one should look down on you, but sometimes mean people do. The only justification we have for looking down on someone is that we're going to stop and pick them up. But even in your wheelchairs, don't give up. We cannot forget 50 years ago when our backs were against the wall, Roosevelt was in a wheelchair. I would rather have Roosevelt in a wheelchair than Reagan and Bush on a horse. Don't you surrender, and don't you give up.

Don't surrender and don't give up. Why can I challenge you this way? Jesse Jackson, you don't understand my situation. You be on television. You don't understand. I see you with the big people. You don't understand my situation. I understand. You're seeing me on TV but you don't know what makes me me. They wonder why does

Jesse run, because they see me running for the White House. They don't see the house I'm running from.

I have a story. I wasn't always on television. Writers were not always outside my door. When I was born late one afternoon, October 8th, in Greenville, South Carolina, no writers asked my mother her name. Nobody chose to write down our address. My mama was not supposed to make it. You see, I was born to a teenage mother who was born to a teenage mother.

I know abandonment and people being mean to you, and saying you're nothing and nobody, and can never be anything. I understand. Jesse Jackson is my third name. I'm adopted. When I had no name, my grandmother gave me her name. My name was Jesse Burns until I was 12. So I wouldn't have a blank space, she gave me a name to hold me over. I understand when you have no name. I understand.

I wasn't born in the hospital. Mama didn't have insurance. I was born in the bed at home. I really do understand. Born in a three-room house, bathroom in the backyard, slop jar by the bed, no hot and cold running water. I understand. Wallpaper used for decoration? No. For a windbreaker. I understand. I'm a working person's person, that's why I understand you whether you're African American or white.

I understand work. I was not born with a silver spoon in my mouth. I had a shovel programmed for my hand. My mother, a working woman. So many days she went to work early with runs in her stockings. She knew better, but she wore runs in her stockings so that my brother and I could have matching socks and not be laughed at at school.

I understand. At three o'clock on Thanksgiving Day we couldn't eat turkey because mama was preparing someone else's turkey at three o'clock. We had to play football to entertain ourselves and then around six o'clock she would get off the Alta Vista bus when we would bring up the leftovers and eat our turkey—leftovers, the carcass, the cranberries around eight o'clock at night. I really do understand.

Every one of these funny labels they put on you, those of you who are watching this broadcast tonight in the projects, on the corners, I understand. Call you outcast, low-down, you can't make it, you're nothing, you're from nobody, subclass, underclass—when you see Jesse Jackson, when my name goes in nomination, your name goes in nomination.

I was born in the slum, but the slum was not born in me. And it wasn't born in you, and you can make it. Hold your head high, stick your chest out. You can make it. It gets dark sometimes, but the morning comes. Don't you surrender. Suffering breeds character. Character breeds faith. In the end faith will not disappoint.

You must not surrender. You may or may not get there, but just know that you're qualified and you hold on and hold out. We must never surrender. America will get better and better. Keep hope alive. Keep hope alive. Keep hope alive. On tomorrow night and beyond, keep hope alive.

I love you very much. I love you very much.

MAGGIE RUSSELL

Testimony of Conversion

· *From Alonzo Johnson and Paul Jersild, "Ain't Gonna Lay My 'Ligion Down"* ·

Typically, this conversion testimony includes a vision of the Lord, a crossing of the water, and an assurance of salvation.

But I stayed there until the Lord talked to me in the Spirit and this night in the Spirit he came to me. I was on one side of the river, and I could not come cross the river, because there was water. And we were not supposed to walk into the water. And I said, "How I gonna git cross dat water?" And he said, when I looked back [*sic*]. And I looked up at him and there was this white man on a milk white horse. And I looked up and his eyes were so strong. And I tried to look in his eyes, but my eyes were too weak, I couldn't take it. His eyes were so strong. Jesus has a very strong eye. And he didn't mean for me to see into his eye, but he was talking to me. But I tried to look him in the eye. He took me by my hand. He reached down and took me by my hand. I do not know how I git through dat water. I don't know whether I walk on dat water or walked through dat water. But he lead me, he lead me across. And he said, "Go tell Peter Singleton to baptize you. Tell your Pastor to baptize you, in the Name of the Father, Son, and the Holy Ghost." And he say everything will be alright.

JOHN JASPER

Light as a Feather

· *From William E. Hatcher,* John Jasper: The Unmatched Negro Philosopher and Preacher ·

Jasper, strikingly handsome and popular with the women, was pursuing the things of the "flesh and the devil" until he was converted while he was stemming tobacco on his twenty-seventh birthday, July 4, 1839. What follows is his story, with some of the exaggerated dialect modified.

My sins was piled on me like mountains; my feet was sinkin' down to de regions of despair, an' I felt dat of all sinners I was de wust. I thought dat I would die right den, an' wid what I supposed was my las' breath I flung up to heaven a cry for mercy. 'Fore I knowed it, de light broke; I was as light as a feather; my feet was on the mountain; salvation rolled like a flood through my soul, an' I felt as if I could knock off the factory roof wid my shouts.

But I says to myself, I going to hol' still till dinner, an' so I cried and laughed, an' tore up de tobacco. Presently I looked up de table, an' dere was an old man — he loved me, an' tried hard to lead me out de darkness, an' I slip roun' to where he was, an' I says in his ear as low as I could: "Hallelujah; my soul is redeemed!" Den I jump back quick to my work, but after I once open my mouf it was hard to keep it shet any mo'. It won't long 'fore I looked up de line again, an' dere was a good ole woman dere dat knew all my sorrows an' had been prayin' for me all de time. Dere was no use a talkin'. I had to tell her, an' so I skip along up quiet as a breeze, an' started to whisper in her ear, but just den de holing-back straps of Jasper's preachin' broke, an' what I thought would be a whisper was loud enough to be heard clean 'cross James River to Manchester. One man said he thought de factory was fallin' down; all I knowed I had raise my first shout to de glory of my Redeemer.

I Am Blessed but You Are Damned

· *From Clifton H. Johnson,* God Struck Me Dead ·

This and the two following selections are from interviews with unnamed African
Americans born under slavery. They were conducted between 1927 and 1929 by
Andrew Polk Watson, a graduate student in anthropology at Fisk University, and
first published in 1969.

One day while in the field plowing I heard a voice. I jumped because I thought it was my master coming to scold and whip me for
plowing up some more corn. I looked but saw no one. Again the
voice called, "Morte! Morte!" With this I stopped, dropped the plow,
and started running, but the voice kept on speaking to me saying,
"Fear not, my little one, for behold! I come to bring you a message
of truth."

Everything got dark, and I was unable to stand any longer. I began
to feel sick, and there was a great roaring. I tried to cry and move but
was unable to do either. I looked up and saw that I was in a new
world. There were plants and animals, and all, even the water where
I stooped down to drink, began to cry out, "I am blessed but you are
damned! I am blessed but you are damned!" With this I began to
pray, and a voice on the inside began to cry, "Mercy! Mercy!
Mercy!"

As I prayed an angel came and touched me, and I looked new. I
looked at my hands and they were new; I looked at my feet and they
were new. I looked and saw my old body suspended over a burning
pit by a small web like a spider web. I again prayed, and there came
a soft voice saying, "My little one, I have loved you with an everlasting love. You are this day made alive and freed from hell. You are
a chosen vessel unto the Lord. Be upright before me, and I will guide
you unto all truth. My grace is sufficient for you. Go, and I am with
you. Preach the gospel, and I will preach with you. You are henceforth the salt of the earth."

I then began to shout and clap my hands. All the time, a voice on
the inside was crying, "I am so glad! I am so glad!" About this time
an angel appeared before me and said with a loud voice, "Praise
God! Praise God!" I looked to the east, and there was a large throne
lifted high up, and thereon sat one, even God. He looked neither to

the right nor to the left. I was afraid and fell on my face. When I was still a long way off I heard a voice from God saying, "My little one, be not afraid, for lo! many wondrous works will I perform through thee. Go in peace, and lo! I am with you always." All this he said but opened not his mouth while speaking. Then all those about the throne shouted and said, "Amen."

I then came to myself again and shouted and rejoiced. After so long a time I recovered my real senses and realized that I had been plowing and that the horse had run off with the plow and dragged down much of the corn. I was afraid and began to pray, for I knew the master would whip me most unmercifully when he found that I had plowed up the corn.

About this time my master came down the field. I became very bold and answered him when he called me. He asked me very roughly how I came to plow up the corn, and where the horse and plow were, and why I had got along so slowly. I told him that I had been talking with God Almighty, and that it was God who had plowed up the corn. He looked at me very strangely, and suddenly I fell for shouting, and I shouted and began to preach. The words seemed to flow from my lips. When I had finished I had a deep feeling of satisfaction and no longer dreaded the whipping I knew I would get. My master looked at me and seemed to tremble. He told me to catch the horse and come on with him to the barn. I went to get the horse, stumbling down the corn rows. Here again I became weak and began to be afraid for the whipping. After I had gone some distance down the rows, I became dazed and again fell to the ground. In a vision I saw a great mound and, beside it or at the base of it, stood the angel Gabriel. And a voice said to me, "Behold your sins as a great mountain. But they shall be rolled away. Go in peace, fearing no man, for lo! I have cut loose your stammering tongue and unstopped your deaf ears. A witness shalt thou be, and thou shalt speak to multitudes, and they shall hear. My word has gone forth, and it is power. Be strong, and lo! I am with you even until the world shall end. Amen."

I looked, and the angel Gabriel lifted his hand, and my sins, that had stood as a mountain, began to roll away. I saw them as they rolled over into a great pit. They fell to the bottom, and there was a great noise. I saw old Satan with a host of his angels hop from the pit, and there they began to stick out their tongues at me and make mo-tions as if to lay hands on me and drag me back into the pit. I cried out, "Save me! Save me, Lord!" And like a flash there gathered around me a host of angels, even a great number, with their backs to me and their faces to the outer world. Then stepped one in the direction of the pit. Old Satan and his angels, growling with anger and trembling with fear, hopped back into the pit. Finally again there came a voice unto me saying, "Go in peace and fear not, for lo! I will throw around you a strong arm of protection. Neither shall your oppressors be able to confound you. I will make your enemies feed you and those who despise you take you in. Rejoice and be exceedingly glad, for I have saved you through grace by faith, not of yourself but as a gift of God. Be strong and fear not. Amen."

I rose from the ground shouting and praising God. Within me there was a crying, "Holy! Holy! Holy is the Lord!"

I must have been in this trance for more than an hour. I went on to the barn and found my master there waiting for me. Again I began to tell him of my experience. I do not recall what he did to me afterwards. I felt burdened down and that preaching was my only relief. When I had finished I felt a great love in my heart that made me feel like stooping and kissing the very ground. My master sat watching and listening to me, and then he began to cry. He turned from me and said in a broken voice, "Morte, I believe you are a preacher. From now on you can preach to the people here on my place in the old shed by the creek. But tomorrow morning, Sunday, I want you to preach to my family and neighbors. So put on your best clothes and be in front of the big house early in the morning, about nine o'clock."

I was so happy that I did not know what to do. I thanked my master and then God, for I felt that he was with me. Throughout the night I went from cabin to cabin, rejoicing and spreading the news.

The next morning at the time appointed I stood up on two planks in front of the porch of the big house and, without a Bible or anything, I began to preach to my master and the people. My thoughts came so fast that I could hardly speak fast enough. My soul caught on fire, and soon I had them all in tears. I told them that God had a chosen people and that he had raised me up as an example of his matchless love. I told them that they must be born again and that their souls must be freed from the shackles of hell.

Ever since that day I have been preaching the gospel and am not a bit tired. I can tell anyone about God in the darkest hour of midnight, for it is written on my heart. Amen.

God Struck Me Dead

· *From Clifton H. Johnson,* God Struck Me Dead ·

I have always been a sheep. I was never a goat. I was created and cut out and born in the world for heaven. Even before God freed my soul and told me to go, I never was hell-scared. I just never did feel that my soul was made to burn in hell.

God started on me when I wasn't but ten years old. I was sick with the fever, and he called me and said, "You are ten years old." I didn't know how old I was, but later on I asked my older sister and she told me that I was ten years old when I had the fever.

As I grew up I used to frolic a lot and was considered a good dancer, but I never took much interest in such things. I just went many times to please my friends and, later on, my husband. What I loved more than all else was to go to church.

I used to pray then. I pray now and just tell God to take me and do his will, for he knows the every secret of my heart. He knows what we stand most in need of before we ask for it, and if we trust him, he will give us what we ought to have in due season. Some people pray and call on God as if they think he is ignorant of their needs or else asleep. But God is a time-God. I know this, for he told me so. I remember one morning I was on my way home with a bundle of clothes to wash—it was after my husband had died—and I felt awfully burdened down, and so I commenced to talk to God. It looked like I was having such a hard time. Everybody seemed to be getting along well but poor me. I told him so. I said, "Lord, it looks like you come to everybody's house but mine. I never bother my neighbors or cause any disturbance. I have lived as it is becoming a poor widow woman to live and yet, Lord, it looks like I have a harder time than anybody." When I said this, something told me to turn around and look. I put my bundle down and looked towards the east part of the world. A voice spoke to me as plain as day, but it was inward and said, "I am a time-God working after the counsel of my own will. In due time I will bring all things to you. Remember and cause your heart to sing."

When God struck me dead with his power I was living on Fourteenth Avenue. It was the year of the Centennial. I was in my house alone, and I declare unto you, when his power struck me I died. I fell out on the floor flat on my back. I could neither speak nor move, for my tongue stuck to the roof of my mouth; my jaws were locked and my limbs were stiff.

In my vision I saw hell and the devil. I was crawling along a high brick wall, it seems, and it looked like I would fall into a dark, roaring pit. I looked away to the east and saw Jesus. He called to me and said, "Arise and follow me." He was standing in snow—the prettiest, whitest snow I have ever seen. I said, "Lord, I can't go, for that snow is too deep and cold." He commanded me the third time before I would go. I stepped out in it and it didn't seem a bit cold, nor did my feet sink into it. We traveled on east in a little, narrow path and came to something that looked like a grape-arbor, and the snow was hanging down like icicles. But it was so pretty and white that it didn't look like snow. He told me to take some of it and eat, but I said, "Lord, it is too cold." He commanded me three times before I would eat any of it. I took some and tasted it, and it was the best-tasting snow I ever put into my mouth.

The Father, the Son, and the Holy Ghost led me on to glory. I saw God sitting in a big armchair. Everything seemed to be made of white stones and pearls. God didn't seem to pay me any attention. He just sat looking into space. I saw the Lamb's book of life and my name written in it. A voice spoke to me and said, "Whosoever my son sets free is free indeed. I give you a through ticket from hell to heaven. Go into yonder world and be not afraid, neither be dismayed, for you are an elect child and ready for the fold." But when he commanded me to go, I was stubborn and didn't want to leave. He said, "My little one, I have commanded you and you shall obey."

I saw, while I was still in the spirit, myself going to my neighbors and to the church, telling them what God had done for me. When I came to this world I arose shouting and went carrying the good news. I didn't do like the Lord told me, though, for I was still in doubt and wanted to make sure. Because of my disobedience, he threw a great affliction on me. I got awfully sick, and my limbs were all swollen so that I could hardly walk. I began to have more faith then and put more trust in God. He put this affliction on me because it was hard for me to believe. But I just didn't want to be a hypocrite and go around hollering, not knowing what I was talking and shouting about. I told God this in my prayer, and he answered me saying, "My little one, my grace is sufficient. Behold! I have commanded you to go, and you shall go."

When I was ready to be baptized I asked God to do two things. It had been raining for days, and on the morning of my baptism it was still raining. I said, "Lord, if you are satisfied with me and pleased with what I have told the people, cause the sun to shine this evening when I go to the river." Bless your soul, when we went to the river, it looked like I had never seen the sun shine as bright. It stayed out about two hours, and then the sky clouded up again and rained some more.

The other thing I asked God was that I might feel the spirit when I went down to the river. And I declare unto you, my soul caught on fire the minute I stepped in the carriage to go to the river. I had been hobbling around on a stick, but I threw it away and forgot that I was ever a cripple.

Later the misery came back, and I asked God to heal me. The spirit directed me to get some peach-tree leaves and beat them up and put them about my limbs. I did this, and in a day or two that swelling left me, and I haven't been bothered since. More than this, I don't remember ever paying out but three dollars for doctor's bills in my life for myself, my children, or my grandchildren. Doctor Jesus tells me what to do.

Pray a Little Harder

· *From Clifton H. Johnson,* God Struck Me Dead ·

I am glad to talk to you about my religion, because it means more to me than I can express. I have been a member of the church for fifty-four years. I came through when you had to be a thoroughbred, and I mean I am a thoroughbred.

I was converted in a peculiar way, but I haven't got a peculiar religion. I have that kind that I am not afraid to express anywhere and at any time. I had to get down on my knees and stay there for several days, until the Lord freed my soul from the gates of hell. He did that because I asked him to show me my mother, who had been dead about twenty years. That he did. I asked him to protect me from evil spirits, and he did that. I remember one time when I was almost conjured by a hoodoo, and I prayed to the Lord and asked him to save me from him. I promised him if he would protect me and save me from being destroyed that way I would serve him the balance of my days. This he did, and I mean it has been a blessing.

I am a good old-time Christian. I have been serving the Lord for fifty years. I was converted in an old church out from the town of Columbia, Tennessee. I had to work hard to get my religion. I fasted and prayed for two weeks trying to seek the Lord. I was a great worldly person, and it was extremely hard for me to give up the ways of the world, but I had to come through right before I could be called a pure Christian.

The Lord has shown me many visions, and I know he lives true because he not only lives in my soul, as Job said, but he lives about me every day, and since I can't read he directs my path. When I was converted I lost sight of everything. While I was fasting I did not know where I was, nor did I know where I was going. One day about noon my mother came and found me, and it seemed as if I was afar off; but she kissed me many times and told me to keep on praying. I prayed and prayed and finally, after having many visions (some of them are so precious to me that I can't tell you), all of the evil things that I had done were shown to me.

I was carried to the very gates of hell, and the devil pulled out a book showing me the things which I had committed and that they were all true. My life as a midwife was shown to me, and I have certainly felt sorry, after I was converted, for all of the things I did.

When I testified in the church I had to tell all the things I had seen and heard. I heard one day, while I was out praying, a voice as if a mighty rumbling of thunder saying, "Mollie, Mollie, you must pray a little harder. You haven't come to the right place yet." I kept on until I asked the Lord, if he had converted me, to show me a beautiful star out of a cloudy sky. This was done, and I saw a star in the daytime shining out of a cloudy sky. I know I have got it, and hell and its forces can't make me turn back.

LANGSTON HUGHES

Salvation

· *From* The Big Sea ·

Hughes does not give the usual testimony of salvation here, but I include his account because it provides the details of the mourners' bench ritual.

I was saved from sin when I was going on thirteen. But not really saved. It happened like this. There was a big revival at my Auntie Reed's church. Every night for weeks there had been much preaching, singing, praying, and shouting, and some very hardened sinners had been brought to Christ, and the membership of the church had grown by leaps and bounds. Then just before the revival ended, they held a special meeting for children, "to bring the young lambs to the fold." My aunt spoke of it for days ahead. That night I was escorted to the front row and placed on the mourners' bench with all the other young sinners, who had not yet been brought to Jesus.

My aunt told me that when you were saved you saw a light, and something happened to you inside! And Jesus came into your life! And God was with you from then on! She said you could see and hear and feel Jesus in your soul. I believed her. I had heard a great many old people say the same thing and it seemed to me they ought to know. So I sat there calmly in the hot, crowded church, waiting for Jesus to come to me.

The preacher preached a wonderful rhythmical sermon, all moans and shouts and lonely cries and dire pictures of hell, and then he sang a song about the ninety and nine safe in the fold, but one little lamb was left out in the cold. Then he said: "Won't you come? Won't you come to Jesus? Young lambs, won't you come?" And he held out his arms to all us young sinners there on the mourners' bench. And the little girls cried. And some of them jumped up and went to Jesus right away. But most of us just sat there.

A great many old people came and knelt around us and prayed, old women with jet-black faces and braided hair, old men with work-gnarled hands. And the church sang a song about the lower lights are burning, some poor sinners to be saved. And the whole building rocked with prayer and song.

Still I kept waiting to *see* Jesus.

Finally all the young people had gone to the altar and were saved, but one boy and me. He was a rounder's son named Westley. Westley and I were surrounded by sisters and deacons praying. It was very hot in the church, and getting late now. Finally Westley said to me in a whisper: "God damn! I'm tired o' sitting here. Let's get up and be saved." So he got up and was saved.

Then I was left all alone on the mourners' bench. My aunt came and knelt at my knees and cried, while prayers and songs swirled all around me in the little church. The whole congregation prayed for me alone, in a mighty wail of moans and voices. And I kept waiting serenely for Jesus, waiting, waiting—but he didn't come. I wanted to see him, but nothing happened to me. Nothing! I wanted something to happen to me, but nothing happened.

I heard the songs and the minister saying: "Why don't you come? My dear child, why don't you come to Jesus? Jesus is waiting for you. He wants you. Why don't you come? Sister Reed, what is this child's name?"

"Langston," my aunt sobbed.

"Langston, why don't you come? Why don't you come and be saved? Oh, Lamb of God! Why don't you come?"

Now it was really getting late. I began to be ashamed of myself, holding everything up so long. I began to wonder what God thought about Westley, who certainly hadn't seen Jesus either, but who was now sitting proudly on the platform, swinging his knickerbockered legs and grinning down at me, surrounded by deacons and old women on their knees praying. God had not struck Westley dead for taking his name in vain or for lying in the temple. So I decided that maybe to save further trouble, I'd better lie, too, and say that Jesus had come, and get up and be saved.

So I got up.

Suddenly the whole room broke into a sea of shouting, as they saw me rise. Waves of rejoicing swept the place. Women leaped in the air.

My aunt threw her arms around me. The minister took me by the hand and led me to the platform.

When things quieted down, in a hushed silence, punctuated by a few ecstatic "Amens," all the new young lambs were blessed in the name of God. Then joyous singing filled the room.

That night, for the last time in my life but one—for I was a big boy twelve years old—I cried. I cried, in bed alone, and couldn't stop. I buried my head under the quilts, but my aunt heard me. She woke up and told my uncle I was crying because the Holy Ghost had come into my life, and because I had seen Jesus. But I was really crying because I couldn't bear to tell her that I had lied, that I had deceived everybody in the church, that I hadn't seen Jesus, and that now I didn't believe there was a Jesus any more, since he didn't come to help me.

Chapter 6

Family Folklore and Personal Memorates

Christ warned us by his life and death, so who am I that I
should not warn my daughter by my life?
—Yula Moses, quoted in *Drylongso:*
A Self-Portrait of Black America,
John Langston Gwaltney, ed.

Family folklore—those stories, customs, and expressions that are shared whenever relatives get together and are passed along to the young ones in every branch of the family tree—had certainly become an accepted branch of American folklore by the time Steven J. Zeitlin, Amy J. Kotkin, and Holley C. Baker, published *A Celebration of American Family Folklore* in 1982: They declare that

> [f]amily tradition is one of the great repositories of American culture. It contains clues to our national character and insights into our family structure.
>
> For an individual family, folklore is its creative expressions of a common past. As raw experiences are transformed into family stories, expressions, and photos, they are codified in forms which can be easily recalled, retold, and enjoyed. Their drama and beauty are heightened, and the family's past becomes accessible as it is reshaped according to its needs and desires.

They go on to note that family folklore is distinguished from family history in that "its stories, photographs, and traditions are personalized and often creative distillations of experience, worked and re-worked over time." Though family stories are usually based on true incidents, they exist in variant forms, reflecting the individual embellishments that have been made by those who circulate the stories. There is no question that, as Greta Swenson has pointed out in *Festivals of Sharing: Family Reunions in America,* "the American family [is] a structured group of identity and transmission."

Following the tradition of the African griot, storytellers in African American families have preserved and transmitted their legends through the years. Nowhere is this better illustrated than in Alex Haley's well-known *Roots* (1976).[1] In recent years, many families have similarly begun to record their history and to supplement the oral materials through a formal pursuit of genealogical research. A popular outgrowth of this renewed fascination with family stories is the Black family reunion, scores of which fill up hotels throughout the nation during the summer months as family members from around the world converge on a variety of sites—but mainly the small Southern towns from which their families sprang. Meeting to celebrate ancestors and to share tales that have passed on through varied lines, these gatherings reinforce Greta Swenson's assertion that "Family reunions emerge on the American landscape as the most visible demonstration of the family as a viable group of identity."

A much earlier tradition than the formal family reunion is the Black church homecomings celebrated throughout the South each year. Commenting on African American family reunions in *Somerset Homecoming: Recovering a Lost Heritage,* Dorothy Spruill Redford insists, "Yes, the families have their get-togethers, but the real homecomings around these parts take place at the churches." For one week in August or September most Baptist churches hold revival, nightly meetings featuring guest ministers. The revival week culminates in all-day homecoming services on Sunday, featuring a big dinner—held on the grounds in early days, but more recently in all-purpose rooms built onto the sanctuary. Traditionally members of the church who had scattered around the nation planned their vacations

---

[1]Despite the controversy about its historical accuracy, Haley's novel/genealogy/history was a popular and influential study that sparked much interest among African Americans in tracing their roots back to Africa.

to coincide with these services. The newer tradition of African American family reunions incorporates elements of the Church homecoming—with almost all of them culminating in a worship service at the family church on Sunday morning.

Included in this chapter are some samples of the tales shared whenever African American families get together. One of the most prominent subjects in African American family folklore is the tale of a relationship between a White father (usually a wealthy plantation owner, preferably a president or at least a state senator) and his Negro slave or servant. On rare occasions the White father is someone of less prominence or the story features a White woman who has children by a Black male. Whatever the case, the tale of racial mixture and of some very fair descendent of this liaison is a signature trait of African American family lore. Other frequently appearing motifs include recollections of the moment when forebears were freed from slavery; accounts of how early members of the family learned to read and write; anecdotes about religious worship and the founding of churches; exploits of brave runaways, rebels, and soldiers; and histories of encounters with racist Whites, among them sheriffs, jailers, and the Ku Klux Klan. African American families also recount the usual tales of birth, graduation, coming-of-age, marriage, and death.

Such folklore moves with families as they spread out across the nation and tends to survive generations after contact among branches of the family is severed. I had this reinforced a few years ago as I read Sarah Lawrence Lightfoot's *Balm in Gilead* and recognized suddenly that, though I believed her story was far removed from me, I was reading the familiar account of my own family's history:

> At the center of the Charles City community stood Elam Baptist Church. . . . "All the land about the church was owned by the Brown family . . . and they deeded part of the land over to the church."[2] . . . [T]he church was more than a religious center. It symbolized the strength, pride, and dignity of this extended family. It represented the interlocking of political activity and

[2]Here Lightfoot quotes her father Charles Radford Lawrence II, who passed the story on to her.

Family
Folklore
and
Personal
Memorates

*

359

spiritual commitment. The simple white-wooded frame structure, lovingly built and carefully tended, expressed the solid, unpretentious quality of these hardworking rural folk.

I have met people—previously unknown to me—from the East Coast to the West Coast whose tales of their family's history immediately tied us together as descendants of Abraham Brown, the free Black family patriarch who established Elam Church in Charles City County, Virginia, in 1810. They too shared the familiar tale of the ancestor who was a U.S. president.

Closely related to the general area of family folklore is the *memorate,* which might be distinguished from family folklore because it is the individual teller's recollection of certain events. Relying as it does on the observer's account, the memorate tends not to circulate as broadly as do other forms of family folklore. A number of these memorates are enriched in that the remembered event offers the opportunity to also expound folk beliefs, wisdom, moral lessons, and philosophy. Further, the significance, popularity, and survival of the memorate depend upon the degree to which it reflects and reinforces popular folk themes. In addition to the numerous memorates from slavery, such as those collected by the Works Progress Administration (WPA) Federal Writers' Project, among the most popular groups are those recalling poverty during the tellers' formative years, their problems acquiring an education, and their difficult working conditions, most especially of those working as domestics in White households. A more recent type of memorate is that of DWB (driving while Black). Countless African Americans have experienced racist attacks while driving through White neighborhoods or on our nation's highways, and there are many memorates to be shared in groups when this subject arises. Oftentimes the memorate's interest is not specific to the family but to the individual (see for example, "Let the Wheelers Roll," an old gentleman's account of his work experience). On the other hand, several memorates enter the general realm of family folklore as tales begin, "My grandpa always used to tell me about the time . . ."

"God Delivered 'Em," the first selection in this chapter, is an interesting combination of the two. My recording of that teller's account of a story that obviously had been passed down in her family reinforced for me the significance of sharing such memorates in the African American community. I collected the tale in Richmond, Virginia, on December 20, 1974, when I met with a group of elderly Richmonders, mostly women. As they sat there in a senior citizens center, they joined memory to memory, adding individual patches of a shared history in which personal stories were contributed to create the group history. They were not merely sharing their stories with me; they were celebrating their ancestors who maintained faith in difficult times, struggled against oppression, used their mother wit to escape the master, and made that journey to freedom. In her memorate, my informant was, in effect, singing a praisesong to Harriet Tubman for her heroic efforts. In chronicling a history that had been passed down in her family, she dynamically recounted it with all the drama and fervor of a sermon, utilizing the familiar body movements, foot patterns, arm gestures, and voice intonations. Like a preacher, she established a rhythm in her delivery that built up to an emotional crescendo, evoking fervent responses from her audience. I felt a sense of awe among this group of elderly Richmonders of African descent whom the griot, Mamadou Kouyaté, would label "depositories of the knowledge of the past." These griots were rendering that past in "the warmth of the human voice," entrusting that history to me in the faith that I would respect, protect, and preserve it. Sessions such as this reinforced for me the truth of the Griot Mamadou's declaration in *Sundiata:* "Other people use writing to record the past, but this invention killed the faculty of memory among them. They do not feel the past any more, for writing lacks the warmth of the human voice. With them everybody thinks he knows, whereas learning should be a secret. The prophets did not write and their words have been all the more vivid as a result. What paltry learning is that which is congealed in dumb books." Note here that the griot emphasizes the oral transmission of history *and* the signifying tradition, both of which are so crucial in all aspects of African American folklore.

Whether or not we choose to make distinctions between memorates and other family folklore, we must recognize the significance of all these narratives. The stories and memorates passed down by a people often ignored or misrepresented in formal historical accounts frequently provide the only records of the events in the lives of African Americans on these shores. And finally, in the words of folk-

Family
Folklore
and
Personal
Memorates

★
361

lorist Sw. Anand Prahlad, such narratives are "particularly folkloric and authentic . . . remarkable and compelling . . . [because] they . . . capture so much of black speech, belief, experience, thought, and narrative style" (letter to author, May 29, 2000).

God Delivered 'Em

· *From Daryl Cumber Dance,* Shuckin' and Jivin' ·

I collected this tale in Richmond, Virginia, on December 20, 1974.

My stepmother told me that when her mother was comin' 'long, all them was comin' up, say, they wasn't allowed to pray, and say they would git in that place where they would stay—in the lil' cabin—they'd turn the iron pot down—turn it down, bottomwards—so the white people couldn't hear 'em in the house, you know. And they would *sing* and they would *pray.* They would *sing* and they would *pray!* And have that pot turned down to hol' the sound in—'cause if they caught 'em prayin' and singin', they would *whip* 'em. And say that they would turn that pot down and get in there and have a meeting, have a meeting.

So one time—they called 'em Marster or something, my aunt say—Marster Charles, Marster this, Marster the other. And say he came to the door—of course they had a bolt on it—and that fly open, and they all was down there *prayin'* to the Lord. And he say, "What yawl doing down there? Git up from there and shet that foolishness up!" Say they was prayin' to the Lord, you know, for deliverence—

"Yeah!" [from the audience]

And they didn't 'low 'em to do it!

"Thank you!" [from the audience]

"Shut that fuss up! Whatcha doin' down there? Git up from there! And go to bed so you kin git up in the mornin' and go to work at daylight!"

Lawd, they was worried to death. He must o' been 'round there somewhere, outside. Well, anyway, say after he left, they turned the pot back down—gon' try it again. And say, "Don't yawl pray so loud—Mars Charles gon' come down here again." But say they *prayed* for dee-li-vrance, because they was under bondage.

"God delivered 'em too!" [from the audience]

Yeah, prayed for deliverance—say, "God, deliver us!

"God deliver!" [from the audience]

Yeah, and God delivered 'em. And say colored people been prayin' 'long down through the years when they was in slavery, you know, God was with 'em and He taught 'em how to pray.

And they say Mars Charles, or whatever he was, took the pot, *took* the pot, and carried it in the house, carried it somewhere, but say what was in here [indicating heart], couldn't get it out, say they prayed together . . . and they did that until this lady [Harriet Tubman] came down here and got 'em and carried 'em up North under that underpass. She say Mars Charles, he caught some of 'em and carried 'em back, but she said the majority of the slaves . . . this lady got 'em from down there and carried 'em up North.

That was *years* and *years* ago! And I sit up there and cried 'cause I didn't have no better sense.

Grandma

· *From Melissa Fay Greene,* Praying for Sheetrock ·

Greene, a White paralegal, writes of a Black community in rural Georgia that, with the help of poverty lawyers, took on the local power structure. Many of the members of the community shared family stories such as the following with Greene.

Miss Fanny was soft-gummed, bleary-eyed, and spirited, and her voice was full of metal and gravel—scraping, raucous:

"She had a little black hat and her hair just as *white,* white as snow, just as white as snow. And she been in slavery when it first start, when it *first* start. My grandma been a hundred and fifteen when she die. She say she had a *time* in slavery. She say, Whooo, she had some white peoples then! When the boss man call her in the morning, she say she shuffle her feet. God knows she didn't feel like going, she shuffle her feet. Say the boss man call her two times and say, 'If you ain't up, I'm coming back there and you better get up!' Say she got up. Oh Lord, she got up.

"My grandma used to go with her dress tied up round her waist and a big foot tub on her head, going down the road. And the boss man behind her with a strap. In the bucket they had guano to throw on the fields. And that boss man follow behind. Plat! Got to work or he beat the devil out of them. That in slavery time. Yeah, they got to work. And she had her little child tied 'round her back. That were my mother, hugging her tight 'round the neck, a string around her little legs, a band around her waist—she tied to my grandmother's waist. And the poor little child—that my mama—cries, but that's all right, you better not stop. And all day long four or five white mens walking up and down the fields with whips that plait up [braided with leather straps]. When they cut you, the blood come. You can hear 'em: 'Oh Cap, oh Cap, I'm working.' And you better not stop. You better not stop, 'cause if you stop, they'll kill you. They kill some of them, my grandma say, they lynch them and they hang them out on trees; it were a shame to see. Sometimes they would try to run away, then they had dogs to catch them. She say they have a hard time in slavery time.

"You know you can't tie no child to your back, and hoe and pick, is it? My grandma say they work her till the tears fall from her eyes. Some had beds to sleep in and some on the floor. They get plenty of moss. You get your little child and y'all lay down on that moss. And when that big old clock strike, everybody rise, everybody rise. And that boss man, that white man, come there with that whip and get them up off that bed.

"Grandma say that field be full of good people, and plenty of people working and singing. They sing they little songs. Ain't know nothing about no church. When the thunder roll, boss man say, 'That God driving across the big bridge.' And the lightning: 'That be God striking his cigarette.' My grandma say she couldn't go to church in slavery, but she say, 'Let me be *turn* church [born again]!' I mean she *really* be turn church. When she die, she hold on and she say, 'Come on death!'

"My grandma say the Yankees! The Yankees the ones that make 'em free them. You ever see a Yankee? My grandma say the *Yankees* the ones that free them. She say she was a glad soul then. She say, 'Children, all we that been in slavery got something to tell God when we go home. Get the Negro up before God, every tongue going to tell the story, every tongue going to confess.

" 'You got to tell God all your troubles about this world below,' she say. 'I got a lot to tell him and plenty more.'

"She say that be a time."

My Marster . . . Was a Good Man

· *From Belinda Hurmence*, Before Freedom ·

Students of the WPA narratives have noted that former slaves were more likely to say that their masters were nice to them and that they preferred slavery if the interviewer were White rather than Black. This piece was collected from Fannie Griffin.

My marster, Marster Joe Beard, was a good man, but he wasn't one of the richest men. He only had six slaves, three men and three women. But he had a big plantation and would borrow slaves from his brother-in-law, on the adjoining plantation, to help with the crops.

I was the youngest slave, so Missy Grace, that's Marster Joe's wife, keep me in the house most of the time, to cook and keep the house cleaned up. I milked the cow and worked in the garden, too.

My marster was good to all he slaves, but Missy Grace was mean to us. She whip us a heap of times when we ain't done nothing bad to be whipped for. When she go to whip me, she tie my wrists together with a rope and put that rope through a big staple in the ceiling and draw me up off the floor and give me a hundred lashes. I think about my old mammy heap of times now and how I's seen her whipped, with the blood dripping off of her.

All that us slaves know how to do was to work hard. We never learn to read and write. Nor we never had no church to go to, only sometimes the white folks let us go to their church, but we never join in the singing. We just set and listen to them preach and pray.

The graveyard was right by the church and heap of the colored people was scared to go by it at night. They say they see ghosts and hants and spirits, but I ain't never see none, don't believe there is none. I more scared of live people than I is dead ones; dead people ain't going to harm you.

Our marster and missus was good to us when we was sick. They send for the doctor right off and the doctor do all he could for us, but

Family
Folklore
and
Personal
Memorates

*

365

he ain't had no kind of medicine to give us 'cepting spirits of turpentine, castor oil, and a little blue mass. They ain't had all kinds of pills and stuff then, like they has now. But I believe we ain't been sick as much then as we do now. I never heard of no consumption them days; us had pneumonia sometimes, though.

We never was allowed to have no parties nor dances, only from Christmas Day to New Year's Eve. We had plenty good things to eat on Christmas Day and Santa Claus was good to us, too. We'd have all kinds of frolics from Christmas to New Year's, but never was allowed to have no fun after that time.

I remembers one time I slip off from the missus and go to a dance, and when I come back, the dog in the yard didn't seem to know me and he bark and wake the missus up, and she whip me something awful. I sure didn't go to no more dances without asking her.

The patrollers would catch you, too, if you went out after dark. We most times stay at home at night and spin cloth to make our clothes. We make all our clothes, and our shoes was handmade, too. We didn't have fancy clothes like the people has now. I likes it better being a slave. We got along better then, than we do now. We didn't have to pay for everything we had.

The worst time we ever had was when the Yankee men come through. We heard they was coming, and the missus tell us to put on a big pot of peas to cook. So we put some white peas in a big pot and put a whole ham in it, so that we'd have plenty for the Yankees to eat. Then, when they come, they kicked the pot over and the peas went one way and the ham another.

The Yankees destroyed most everything we had. They come in the house and told the missus to give them her money and jewels. She started crying and told them she ain't got no money or jewels, 'cepting the ring she had on her finger. They got awfully mad and started destroying everything. They took the cows and horses, burned the gin, the barn, and all the houses 'cept the one Marster and Missus was living in.

They didn't leave us a thing 'cept some big hominy and two banks of sweet potatoes. We chipped up some sweet potatoes and dried them in the sun, then we parched them and ground them up and that's all we had to use for coffee. It taste pretty good, too. For a good while, we just live on hominy and coffee.

We ain't had no celebration after we was freed. We ain't know we was free till a good while after. We ain't know it till General Wheeler come through and tell us. After that, the marster and missus let all the slaves go 'cepting me; they kept me to work in the house and the garden.

My Life

· *From Belinda Hurmence,* Before Freedom ·

Adele Frost was 93 when she was interviewed by Hattie Mobley, in Richland County, South Carolina.

I was born in Adams Run, South Carolina, January 21, 1844. My father name was Robert King, and my mother was Minder King. My father was born in Adams Run, but my mother came from Spring Grove, South Carolina. My master was kind to his slaves, and his overseers was all Negroes. He had a large farm at Parker's Ferry.

I was brought here at the age of twelve to be maid for Mr. Mitchell, from who I didn't get any money, but a place to stay and plenty of food and clothes. I never gone to school in my life, and Marster nor Missus ever help me to read. I used to wear thin clothes in hot weather and warm, comfortable ones in the winter. On Sunday I wear a old-time bonnet, armhole apron, shoes, and stocking. My bed was the old-time four-post with pavilion [canopy] hanging over the top.

On the plantation was a meeting house in which we used to have meetings every Tuesday night, Wednesday night, and Thursday night. I used to attend the white church. Dr. Jerico was the pastor. Colored people had no preacher, but they had leader. Every slave go to church on Sunday, 'cause they didn't have any work to do for Marster. My grandma used to teach the catechism and how to sing. I joined the church 'cause I wanted to be a Christian, and I think everybody should be.

Funerals was at night, and when ready to go to the graveyard, everybody would light a lightwood knot as torch while everybody sing. This is one of the songs we used to sing:

Family
Folklore
and
Personal
Memorates

*
367

Going to carry this body
To the graveyard,
Graveyard, don't you know me?
To lay this body down.

We ain't had no doctor. Our missus and one of the slaves would attend to the sick.

The Yankees take three nights to march through. I was afraid of them and climbed into a tree. One call me down and say, "I am your friend." He give me a piece of money and I wasn't afraid no more.

After the war, I still work as a maid for Mr. Mitchell.

My husband was Daniel Frost. We didn't have no wedding, just married at the judge office. We had three chillun.

I move here [near Columbia] with my granddaughter, about ten year ago.

Fire Sticks

· *From* The Negro in Virginia, *compiled by Workers of the Writers' Program of the Work Projects Administration in the State of Virginia* ·

Collected from Fannie Berry.

Nother time Marse Tom come to me, an' say, "Fanny look here, look what I got." An' he had some little sticks wid yellow ends on 'em. I didn't know what dey was. So he took 'em over back of de barn an' drawed one cross a rock, an' it made a fire. So I said, "Marse Tom give me one dem." Well he ain't had but three, an' now he only got two left, but he give me one. I stuck it in my hair an' went on doin' what I been doin' till dat afternoon. Den I took it an' went inside de barn an' put some leaves down in de corner, an' struck dis piece of wood cross a rock jus' like Marse Tom done an' sho' nough it made a fire. An' I drap it in de leaves, an' run on out de barn down in de corn fiel' an' pretty soon de smoke come rollin' out, an' de flames show an' dar was de corner of de barn on fire.

It was gittin' bigger an' bigger an' I could hear it crackin'. Den I hear ev'body yellin' an' pretty soon ole Marse come runnin' an' shoutin' at ev'body. Well dey formed a chain an' passed water fum de well an' purty soon dey put it out. Den ole Marse called all de nigger chillun together an' tole em he gonna whup ev'y las' one of 'em 'cause he knows one of dem done made dat fire. An' he whupped 'em too till he got tired, whilst I lay dere in de corn fiel' not darin' to raise my head. Never did whup me. An' I never did play wid none dem fire sticks no mo'.

It's a Good Time to Dress You Out

· *From B. A. Botkin,* Lay My Burden Down ·

Collected from a former slave.

[Mistress] set me to scrubbing up the bar-room. I felt a little grum, and didn't do it to suit her; she scolded me about it, and I sassed her; she struck me with her hand. Thinks I, it's a good time now to dress you out, and damned if I won't do it. I set down my tools and squared for a fight. The first whack, I struck her a hell of a blow with my fist. I didn't knock her entirely through the panels of the door, but her landing against the door made a terrible smash, and I hurt her so badly that all were frightened out of their wits and I didn't know myself but what I'd killed the old devil.

Childhood

· *From Dorothy Sterling, ed.,* We Are Your Sisters ·

Collected from a former slave.

When the colored women has to cut cane all day till midnight come and after, I has to nurse the babies for them and tend the white children too. Some them babies so fat and big I had to tote the feet while 'nother gal tote the head. The big folks leave some toddy for colic and crying, and I done drink the toddy and let the children have the milk. I don't know no better. Lawsey me, it a wonder I ain't the biggest drunker in this here country, counting all the toddy I done put in my young belly!

The Smell of Death

Family
Folklore
and
Personal
Memorates

*

369

· *From Ethel Morgan Smith,* From Whence Cometh My Help ·

Mrs. Emma Bruce of Roanoke, Virginia, shared with Smith the following memorate of "Uncle Clem," Clem Bolder, who she said was about her grandpapa's age and loved to tell stories about the war. He had been drafted into the Confederate army in 1863.

The dead bodies started smellin'. Us colored men had to bury them fast as we could. Sometimes the ground be hard and cold and diggin' took all of our strength. But with the help of the Good Lord, we got them buried, but there was always more bodies to bury. Couldn't bury no coloreds near the whites. You get beat if you did. Longest two years of my life. Just wanted to get back home to see the flowers growing and blooming. The smell of death was enough to make anyone want to get back to livin'.

Photograph of Clem Bolder

*University Archives, Robertson Library,
Hollins University.*

SARAH AND A. ELIZABETH DELANY

Our Papa's People

· *From* Having Our Say ·

On February 5, 1858, our Papa, Henry Beard Delany, was born into slavery on a plantation owned by the Mock family in St. Marys, Georgia, on the coast near the Florida border. He was just a little bitty fellow—seven years old—when the Surrender came in 1865. "The Surrender" is the way Papa always referred to the end of the Civil War, when General Robert E. Lee surrendered to the Union at Appomattox Court House.

We used to ask Papa, "What do you remember about being a slave?" Well, like a lot of former slaves he didn't say much about it. Everybody had their own tale of woe and for most people, things had been so bad they didn't want to think about it, let alone talk about it. You didn't sit and cry in your soup, honey, you just went on.

Well, we persisted, and finally Papa told us of the day his people were freed. He remembered being in the kitchen and wearing a little apron, which little slave boys wore in those days. It had one button at the top, at the back of the neck, and the ends were loose. And when the news of the Surrender came, he said he ran about the house with that apron fluttering behind him, yelling, "Freedom! Freedom! I am free! I am free!"

Of course, being a little child, he did not know what this meant. Back in slavery days, things were bad, but in some ways getting your freedom could be worse! To a small boy, it meant leaving the only home you ever knew.

Now, Papa's family were house niggers, and the Mocks had been very good to them. We remember our Papa saying the Mocks were as good as any people you could find anywhere in this world. That's a generous thing to say about the people who *owned* him, wouldn't you say? But he said that not all white people who owned slaves were evil. There was great variety in the way white people treated Negroes. That's what Papa told us about slavery days, and it's true now, too.

Mrs. Mock thought a heap of Papa's mother, Sarah, who was born on the plantation on the fifth of January, 1814. Why, Mrs. Mock had even let Sarah have a wedding ceremony in the front parlor. It was a double wedding—Sarah's twin sister, Mary, married at the same time. Oh, it was said to be a big affair! Of course, these weren't legal marriages, since it was against the law for slaves to get married. But it was a ceremony, and Sarah was joined in matrimony to Thomas Sterling Delany. This was about 1831. Their first child, Julia, was born on the first of November, 1832. Altogether, Sarah and Thomas had eleven children, and our Papa was the youngest.

Thomas was a handsome man. To what extent he was white, we do not know. We were told he was mostly Negro. The family Bible says he was born in St. Marys, and the date of his birth was the fifteenth of March, 1810.

Sarah was obviously part Indian; she had long, straight black hair but otherwise looked just like a Negro. When we were children we always giggled about her photograph, because her hair looked so peculiar to us. We never knew Papa's parents because they died when we were tiny. Why, Sarah died on the eleventh of September, 1891, just a few days after Bessie was born.

Thomas was part Scottish, which is where the Delany name came from. We have been asked, over the years, if we are any kin to Martin Delany, the Negro army officer during the Civil War. We are quite certain we are not, having discussed it with a historian once. People assume that we are related to him because we spell Delany the same way. A few of our relatives spell our name with an "e," as in "Delaney," which is really an Irish spelling. Others spell it "DeLany" with a capital *L* in the middle. Papa insisted we spell it "Delany." He said, "That's the way my father spelled it, and that's good enough for me."

Now, of course, we haven't any idea what our original African name was. But it doesn't worry us none. We have been Delanys for a long time, and the name belongs to us, as far as we're concerned.

The Mocks let the Delanys keep their name and even broke Georgia law by teaching Papa and his brothers and sisters to read and write. Maybe the Mocks thought the Delanys wouldn't leave, after the Surrender. But they did, and they each didn't have but the shirt on their backs. They crossed the St. Marys River and set down roots in Fernandina Beach, Florida. Papa told us that each day they would wash their only shirt in the river and hang it up to dry, then put it on again after it had dried in the sun.

Those were hard times, after slavery days. Much of the South was scarred by the Civil War and there wasn't much food or supplies among the whites, let alone the Negroes. Most of the slaves, when they were freed, wandered about the countryside like shell-shocked soldiers. Papa said everywhere you went, it seemed you saw Negroes asking, begging for something. He said it was a pitiful sight.

He said those folks didn't know how to be free. It was like if you took the hen away, what do you think would happen to those chicks?

Most of the slaves became sharecroppers, living off the land owned by whites. The whites fixed it so those Negroes could never get ahead. Wasn't much better than slavery. The whites were able to cheat the Negroes because very few Negroes could read or write or do arithmetic. And even if the Negroes knew they were being cheated, there wasn't a thing they could do about it.

The Delanys were among only a handful of former slaves in those parts who didn't end up begging. Papa was proud of this, beyond words. They survived by eating fish they caught in the river and gathering up wild plants for food. After a while, they built a home, some kind of lean-to or log cabin. They were smart, but they were lucky, and they knew it. They could read and write, and they hadn't been abused, and their family was still together. That's a lot more than most former slaves had going for them.

Papa and his brothers all learned a trade. Following in the shoes of one of his older brothers, Papa became a mason. His brother was known in the South for being able to figure the number of bricks it would take to build a house. People would send him drawings and that fellow could figure out in his head exactly how many bricks it would take! Saved people a lot of trouble and money. Another of Papa's brothers was said to be the first Negro harbor pilot in America, and his older sister, Mary, taught school, mostly at night to poor colored men who worked all day in the field.

The Delanys were Methodists through and through. Papa was already a grown man, in his early twenties, when one day the Reverend Owen Thackara, a white Episcopal priest, said to him, "Young man, you should go to college." The chance to go to college was so fantastic it boggled Papa's mind, and of course he jumped at the chance, even though it meant giving up on being a Methodist. Reverend Thackara helped Papa go to Saint Augustine's School, way north in Raleigh, in the great state of North Carolina.

Well, Papa did not disappoint anyone. In college, he was a shining star among shining stars. He was as smart as he could be, and blessed with a personality that smoothed the waters. He soon met a fellow student named Nanny James Logan, the belle of the campus. She was a pretty gal and very popular, despite the fact that she was smarter than all the boys—and became the class valedictorian.

CARRIE ALLEN McCRAY

Freedom's Child

· *From* Freedom's Child: The Remarkable Life of a Confederate General's Black Daughter ·

The "monstrous system" continued long after the last shots of the Civil War were fired. Young black girls, though free now, were going to work as maids and housekeepers and had no protection against the men in those homes. Mama's mother, Malinda Rice, was one of those girls. In 1873, at age sixteen, she went to work in the home of General Jones. On March 2, 1875, Mama, the daughter of Malinda Rice and General Jones, was born in Harrisonburg, Virginia. They named her Mary Magdalene Rice. For many decades this was all we knew. A curtain was drawn to hide the truth about Mama and her father.

I always wanted to know more about Mama's father, more about her mother, more about all the people around her when she was growing up. I wanted to know what it was like for her, born into such a situation. And I wanted to know what combination of people, places, circumstances, and events set Mama on her course, dedicated to fighting for freedom, equality, and justice for all people.

In the late sixties, I traveled to our former home in Lynchburg to talk with Mama's dearest friend, the poet Anne Spencer. J. Lee Greene says in *Time's Unfading Garden* "Mary Rice was one of three women whom Annie considered almost as close as a sister." We called her Aun' Tannie. (She always laughed and said that before we moved north, we'd called her *"Ant* Annie.") I figured that Mama and Aun' Tannie, as young women, must have shared stories of their lives, stories that they'd kept to themselves. I was right. . . .

In her view Mama, though born of the strange situation so prevalent during those times, had a more stable life. Malinda Rice was a woman of beauty and dignity and Aun' Tannie believed that Malinda and the General must have had a warm, loving relationship. "Even though they could never marry, their relationship endured until your grandmother's death."

I found myself squirming as she spoke the words. I was not quite ready for them. Aun' Tannie went on to discuss the culture of the times—strange times. Some white wives accepted their husbands' having mistresses, but they must have smoldered underneath. "Some kept it tight in their bosoms, and others took their hurting out on our girls. They should have been taking it out on their rascal husbands," she said.

General's wife, however, must have been a kind, gentle woman. She was sickly and had no children. Even after Mama's and her brother's births, Malinda continued working and living in the Jones home and taking care of Mrs. Jones. During that time the children lived with their Uncle John and Aunt Dolly. Once General's wife asked Malinda to bring Mary to see her, which she did. Before they left, General's wife gave Mary a porcelain-headed doll that had belonged to Mrs. Jones when she was a child.

A porcelain-headed doll? Mama had kept a porcelain-headed doll in a box in her wardrobe. It was a doll she would not let us play with. This revelation stirred some undefinable feeling of circles being closed. Then Aun' Tannie told me that when Mary thanked Mrs. Jones and hugged her, Mrs. Jones reached over and kissed her on the forehead. Mrs. Jones asked Malinda to bring Mary back, and Mary visited her often before Mrs. Jones died.

"Evil and pain were back there, but so was a kind of humanity—in smaller doses, but it was there," Aun' Tannie commented. "It's hard to understand some things from past times, when you're not living it." . . .

Aun' Tannie backtracked. She said that Mary's father had taken her many places with him. He even took her into an ice-cream parlor where Negroes were not supposed to go. One time when they were there, Mary's father heard a white man whisper, "That's his little nigger bastard," so he went over and knocked the man off the ice-cream-parlor stool. Aun' Tannie clearly enjoyed telling this story. But then in a more serious tone she described Mary's situation as "a mixed blessing." She was sometimes called such names by Negroes as well as by whites, and Mary was troubled by the fact that her fa-

*Family
Folklore
and
Personal
Memorates*

*

375

ther never took her darker-skinned brother, Willie, whom Mary adored, with them. Aun' Tannie believed that was one of the reasons Mary staged her first protest when she was just twelve years old. . . .

One of the stories Uncle John told Mary was about an old slave named Jeremiah. It was one of Mama's favorites, and she never forgot it.

Once on a time (Uncle John always started his stories that way), there was an old slave man named Jeremiah Solomon. (I picture Mama snuggled close to Uncle John, little Willie right beside her.) Now, this old man's real name was Jeremiah Brent because he belonged to Masta Brent. But he was a very wise old man, so everyone called him Jeremiah Solomon; that is, everybody except Masta Brent and a mean old slave woman named Aunt Kreasy. Anyways, lot of slave people knew things from the Bible like the Twenty-third Psalm, "The Lord is my shepherd." Well, one night Masta Brent's son, Robert, stole down in the dark to Jeremiah's cabin and gave him a Bible, on the sly. Masta Robert loved Jeremiah. When he was a little boy he'd run down to Jeremiah's cabin and they'd sit there eating sweet potatoes Jeremiah baked in the fireplace. Anyways, when they finished eating their sweet potatoes, Jeremiah would set Masta Robert on his knee and tell him stories, all kinds of stories about animals and things. How the possum tricked old fox and the like.

Now when Masta Robert gave Jeremiah the Bible, he showed him where the Twenty-third Psalm was. Masta Robert watched Jeremiah finger them words—"The Lord is my shepherd." Then Jeremiah jumped up. "I'm reading," he shouted. "I'm reading. I'm reading." Jeremiah felt it was a blessing to know how to read and just kept on thanking Masta Robert, and then he looked up to Heaven and said "Thank you, Lord." Then Masta Robert cautioned him. "Jeremiah," he said, "you have to hide that book under your floorboards. Papa will be angry if he finds out, and you and I will be in trouble. But if we keep our secret, I'll come by every now and again and teach you how to really read."

When Masta Robert left, Jeremiah took that Bible, kept fingering "The Lord is my shepherd" and smiling. Then he took the iron from the fireplace, pulled up a board of his cabin floor, and hid that Bible under it.

Jeremiah learned how to read real good. But one day he got in trouble because of mean old Aunt Kreasy. She was a skinny old woman, and meaner than a hundred mules. She took care of a lot of little slave children while their mamas was in the fields and some other ones who didn't have no mamas there. Masta Brent sold them away to somebody else, so he got Aunt Kreasy to take care of them. Aunt Kreasy would fix a little fat meat fried to a crisp, then take the grease, make a little gravy, and pour it over some cornmeal mush. Then she'd parcel a little out to those poor little children and say in her old creaky voice, "That's enough to hang on your bones. Give you anymore be too heavy to do your chores." Mean old lady, she was.

She the one told Masta Brent about Jeremiah having a Bible and reading. Masta Brent went down there fuming. Aw, was he mad. Made Jeremiah give him the Bible. He tried to get Jeremiah to tell him who gave him the Bible, but Jeremiah just kept saying, "A child of God, sir. A child of God." Finally, Masta Brent just stomped on away, Jeremiah's Bible under his arm. But see, he didn't know his son had given Jeremiah some other books, so Jeremiah kept those. It was against the law for slaves to read. But Jeremiah, after he learned to read, he taught a lot of little slave children to read, on the sly. Yes he did. Yes he did.

The story over, Uncle John would say to Mary, "You go on with all that reading your papa teaching you and one day you'll be a teacher and teach little children like Jeremiah did, and y'all won't have to hide your books."

T. O. MADDEN JR.

We Were Always Free

· *From* We Were Always Free: The Maddens of
Culpeper County, Virginia, A 200-Year Family History ·

Willis and Kitty had been proud when their daughter Sarah Ann was married to John Taylor, another free Negro from the neighborhood, in 1851—married by a registered minister, and the marriage recorded in the county courthouse. But not all of the Madden daughters had, in Willis Madden's eyes, behaved so admirably.

The youngest daughter, Maria, had taken up with a white man, and by the spring of 1859 she was pregnant with his child. Willis Madden wanted to send her over the mountains to live with relatives

*Family
Folklore
and
Personal
Memorates*

★

377

in the Shenandoah Valley, but Maria refused to go. She moved into a little cabin on the edge of Willis's land near the cemetery. No amount of arguing or pleading from her parents would make her break off with the man, and she was determined to stay on the farm to have her baby. Willis was deeply hurt and ashamed. He saw Maria's actions as an insult to the family—and to herself.

Maria Madden gave birth to a son, Thomas Obed, on January 26, 1860. He was my father.

There is a fragment of a letter in the Madden family papers, from Maria Madden to "Mr. Wilson Green" at "Culpeper Court House" (the county seat):

> . . . my father and mother have both sleighted me on your account. and if you cannot make it conveinat to come as soon as I wish you must send me a letter. no more at present so fare well
>
> Maria Maden

The rest of the letter, now destroyed by age, remains in my memory. It stated that she was "in a family way" and detailed the tense situation between Maria and her parents. This would seem to suggest that Wilson Green might be the father of Thomas Obed Madden, Sr. However, stories that had circulation in the neighborhood rumored that Jack Wales, a slave trader from Stevensburg, was the father of Maria Madden's son. (T. O. Madden, Sr., always believed that his father was Jack Wales).

MADISON HEMINGS

Life among the Lowly

· *From "Life among the Lowly,"* Pike County (Ohio) Republican
(*March 13, 1873*) ·

Hemings's account of his mother's relationship with Thomas Jefferson has provided a number of the details still pertinent to this long-running historical debate. Even the introduction of DNA evidence tying at least some of the descendants of Jefferson's slave, Sally Hemings, to Thomas Jefferson has done little to resolve this controversy.

I never knew of but one white man who bore the name of Hemings; he was an Englishman and my greatgrandfather. He was captain of an English tracking vessel which sailed between England and Williamsburg, Va., then quite a port. My grandmother was a full-blooded African, and possibly a native of that country. She was the property of John Wales, a Welchman. Capt. Hemings happened to be in the port of Williamsburg at the time my grandmother was born, and acknowledging her fatherhood he tried to purchase her of Mr. Wales, who would not part with the child, though he was offered an extraordinarily large price for her. She was named Elizabeth Hemings. Being thwarted in the purchase, and determined to own his own flesh and blood he resolved to take the child by force or stealth, but the knowledge of his intention coming to John Wales' ears, through leaky fellow servants of the mother, she and the child were taken into the "great house" under their master's immediate care. I have been informed that it was not the extra value of that child over other slave children that induced Mr. Wales to refuse to sell it, for slave masters then, as in later days, had no compunctions of conscience which restrained them from parting mother and child of however tender age, but he was restrained by the fact that just about that time amalgamation began, and the child was so great a curiosity that its owner desired to raise it himself that he might see its outcome. Capt. Hemings soon afterwards sailed from Williamsburg, never to return. Such is the story that comes down to me.

Elizabeth Hemings grew to womanhood in the family of John Wales, whose wife dying she (Elizabeth) was taken by the widower Wales as his concubine, by whom she had six children—three sons and three daughters, viz: Robert, James, Peter, Critty, Sally and Thena. These children went by the name of Hemings.

Williamsburg was the capital of Virginia, and of course it was an aristocratic place, where the "bloods" of the Colony and the new State most did congregate. Thomas Jefferson, the author of the Declaration of Independence, was educated at William and Mary College, which had its seat at Williamsburg. He afterwards studied law with Geo. Wythe, and practiced law at the bar of the general court of the Colony. He was afterwards elected a member of the provincial legislature from Albemarle county. Thos. Jefferson was a visitor at the "great house" of John Wales, who had children about his own age. He formed the acquaintance of his daughter Martha (I believe that was her name, though I am not positively sure), and intimacy sprang up between them which ripened into love, and they were married. They afterwards went to live at his country seat Monticello, and in course of time had born to them a daughter whom they named Martha. About the time she was born my mother, the second daughter of John Wales and Elizabeth Hemings, was born. On the death of John Wales, my grandmother, his concubine, and her children by him fell to Martha, Thomas Jefferson's wife, and consequently became the property of Thomas Jefferson, who in the course of time became famous, and was appointed minister to France during our revolutionary troubles, or soon after independence was gained. About the time of the appointment and before he was ready to leave the country his wife died, and as soon after her interment as he could attend to and arrange his domestic affairs in accordance with the changed circumstances of his family in consequence of this misfortune (I think not more than three weeks thereafter) he left for France, taking his eldest daughter with him. He had sons born to him, but they died in early infancy, so he then had but two children—Martha and Maria. The latter was left home, but afterwards was ordered to follow him to France. She was three years or so younger than Martha. My mother accompanied her as her body servant. When Mr. Jefferson went to France Martha was a young woman grown; my mother was about her age, and Maria was just budding into womanhood. Their stay (my mother's and Maria's) was about eighteen months. But during that time my mother became Mr. Jefferson's concubine, and when he was called back home she was *enciente* by him. He desired to bring my mother back to Virginia with him but she demurred. She was just beginning to understand the French language well, and in France she was free, while if she returned to Virginia she would be re-enslaved. So she refused to return with him. To induce her to do so he promised her extraordinary privileges, and made a solemn pledge that her children should be freed at the age of twenty-one years. In consequence of his promise, on which she implicitly relied, she returned with him to Virginia. Soon after their arrival, she gave birth to a child, of whom Thomas Jefferson was the father. It lived but a short time. She gave birth to four others, and Jefferson was the father of all of them. Their names were Beverly, Harriet, Madison (myself), and Eston—three sons and one daughter. We all became free agreeably to the treaty entered into by our parents before we were born. We all married and have raised families.

Beverly left Monticello and went to Washington as a white man. He married a white woman in Maryland, and their only child, a daughter, was not known by the white folks to have any colored blood coursing in her veins. Beverly's wife's family were people in good circumstances.

Harriet married a white man in good standing in Washington City, whose name I could give, but will not, for prudential reasons. She raised a family of children, and so far as I know they were never suspected of being tainted with African blood in the community where she lived or lives. I have not heard from her for ten years, and do not know whether she is dead or alive. She thought it to her interest, on going to Washington, to assume the role of a white woman, and by her dress and conduct as such I am not aware that her identity as Harriet Hemings of Monticello has ever been discovered.

Eston married a colored woman in Virginia, and moved from there to Ohio, and lived in Chillicothe several years. In the fall of 1852 he removed to Wisconsin, where he died a year or two afterwards. He left three children.

As to myself, I was named Madison by the wife of James Madison, who was afterwards President of the United States. Mrs. Madison happened to be at Monticello at the time of my birth, and begged the privilege of naming me, promising my mother a fine present for the honor. She consented, and Mrs. Madison dubbed me by the name I now acknowledge, but like many promises of white folks to the slaves she never gave my mother anything. I was born at my father's seat of Monticello, in Albemarle county, Va., near Charlottesville, on the 19th day of January, 1805. My very earliest recollections are of my grandmother Elizabeth Hemings. That was when I was about three years old. She was sick and upon her death bed. I was eating a piece of bread and asked if she would have some. She replied: "No, granny don't want bread any more." She shortly afterwards breathed her last. I have only a faint recollection of her.

Of my father, Thomas Jefferson, I knew more of his domestic than his public life during his life time. It is only since his death that I have learned much of the latter, except that he was considered as a foremost man in the land, and held many important trusts, including that of President. I learned to read by inducing the white children to teach me the letters and something more; what else I know of books I have picked up here and there till now I can read and write. I was almost 21 1/2 years of age when my father died on the 4th of July, 1826. About his own home he was the quietest of men. He was hardly ever known to get angry, though sometimes he was irritated when matters went wrong, but even then he hardly ever allowed himself to be made unhappy any great length of time. Unlike Washington he had but little taste or care for agricultural pursuits. He left matters pertaining to his plantations mostly with his stewards and overseers. He always had mechanics at work for him, such as carpenters, blacksmiths, shoemakers, coopers, &c. It was his mechanics he seemed mostly to direct, and in their operations he took great interest. Almost every day of his later years he might have been seen among them. He occupied much of the time in his office engaged in correspondence and reading and writing. His general temperament was smooth and even; he was very undemonstrative. He was uniformly kind to all about him. He was not in the habit of showing partiality or fatherly affection to us children. We were the only children of his by a slave woman. He was affectionate toward his white grandchildren, of whom he had fourteen, twelve of whom lived to manhood and womanhood. His daughter Martha married Thomas Mann Randolph by whom she had thirteen children. Two died in infancy. The names of the living were Ann, Thomas Jefferson, Ellen, Cornelia, Virginia, Mary, James, Benj. Franklin, Lewis Madison, Septemia and Geo. Wythe. Thos. Jefferson Randolph was Chairman of the Democratic National Convention in Baltimore last spring which nominated Horace Greeley for the Presidency, and Geo. Wythe Randolph was Jeff. Davis' first Secretary of War in the late "unpleasantness."

Maria married John Epps, and raised one son—Francis.

My father generally enjoyed excellent health. I never knew him to have but one spell of sickness and that was caused by a visit to the Warm Springs in 1818. Till within three weeks of his death he was hale and hearty, and at the age of 83 years walked erect and with stately tread. I am now 68, and I well remember that he was a much smarter man physically, even at that age, than I am.

When I was fourteen years old I was put to the carpenter trade under the charge of John Hemings, the youngest son of my grandmother. His father's name was Nelson, who was an Englishman. She had seven children by white men and seven by colored men — fourteen in all. My brothers, sister Harriet and myself, were used alike. They were put to some mechanical trade at the age of fourteen. Till then we were permitted to stay about the "great house," and only required to do such light work as going on errands. Harriet learned to spin and to weave in a little factory on the home plantation. We were free from the dread of having to be slaves all our lives long, and were measurably happy. We were always permitted to be with our mother, who was well used. It was her duty, all her life which I can remember, up to the time of father's death, to take care of his chamber and wardrobe, look after us children and do such light work as sewing, &c.

Provision was made in the will of our father that we should be free when we arrived at the age of 21 years. We had all passed that period when he died but Eston, and he was given the remainder of his time shortly after. He and I rented a house and took mother to live with us, till her death, which event occurred in 1835.

RUTH POLK PATTERSON

Sally

· *From* The Seed of Sally Good'n ·

From all indications, it was during the years between 1820 and 1830 that the Arkansas branch of the esteemed Polk family of America (they would later boast a president, James Knox Polk, and a renowned Methodist bishop, Leonidas Polk) made their West African connection. The elder Taylor Polk was nearing the end of his journey (he died in 1824), and the younger Taylor had taken over the reins of the family. Sometime during the 1820s young Taylor made a trip to the "Indian Country," as it was called. Perhaps he went to trade with the Indians or to reconnoiter their status in the territory, considering the 1821 petition he signed. Whatever his purpose, his most obvious transaction during the trip was the purchase from the Cherokees of a young African slave girl named Sally.

The Choctaws and Cherokees were being dispersed from their lands to the south, and between 1817 and 1828 they settled on tracts of land in Arkansas as designated by government treaties. The Jackson-Hinds Treaty of 1820 gave the Choctaws a reservation west of a line extending from Point Remove Creek to Fulton on the Red River. This treaty would have forced the Polks and other settlers to move from southwestern Arkansas. The treaty was never enforced, however, and few Choctaw ever settled in the state. The Cherokee Nation West, on the other hand, occupied a reservation in Arkansas from 1817 until 1828, on lands extending from Fort Smith southward to the mouth of Point Remove Creek near Morrilton. Some Cherokee settled south of the Arkansas River in what is now Yell County. The "Indian Country," therefore, was located just north of the area where the Polks lived. Furthermore, the Cherokees brought with them into Arkansas their own African slaves. Sally belonged to the Cherokees, and for some reason—whether fate, ambition, or some undefined need—Taylor Polk bought her. She was his first slave. The tax assessment records of Hot Spring County for 1830 show Polk owning only one slave, a female, between the ages of sixteen and forty-five.

All that is known of Sally comes from accounts handed down orally by the descendants of other slaves who knew her and by her own children, one of whom, John Spencer Polk, is the subject of this book. According to Spencer Polk, who passed the story on to his children, Taylor Polk "went into the Indian Territory and bought Sally," probably as early as 1821, about the same time he signed the petition against the Indian presence in Arkansas. Polk was undoubtedly a man of unusual disposition, for, although he was apparently happily married to his first wife, Prudence Anderson, whom he had wed in 1821, the slave girl Sally caught his eye, it is said, and he bought her for his concubine. Those who remember their grandparents talking about Sally say she was Polk's "servant" or "housekeeper" or "maid." Legally, she was his slave.

Sally was a very beautiful "brown-skinned" girl, according to those who saw her and told their children about her. Taylor Polk may have kept her in or near Fort Smith at first, entrusted to the care of a friend, or he may have left her with the Cherokees. Oral sources insist that Sally was left in Fort Smith, which Polk frequented in the interest of his political activities. No evidence of these trips has been found, but the oral reports insist that whenever Polk went to Fort Smith to trade or conduct business, he had his trysts with Sally. As a result of these encounters, Sally's first child, a son named Peter, was born in 1827. Sally later produced two more sons by Polk—Frank, probably born in 1829, and John Spencer, born in 1833. During this period Taylor Polk was rearing a family by his first wife; his first legitimate child, Eleanor, was born in 1823. Sometime before 1833 Polk brought Sally to Caddo Township, to "The Wilds," and built her a cabin next to his own. It was here that the youngest son, Spencer, was no doubt born. Sally occupied her little cabin and continued to serve Polk, in spite of the vehement disapproval of Polk's legitimate spouse. . . .

Between 1835 and 1838, the slave Sally gave birth to her fourth child, a girl named Eliza. It is said that Sally's three sons looked just like "the Old Man," as Taylor Polk was known by his descendants. The three sons were definitely mulattoes; all had fairly straight hair, the characteristic high-bridged, enormous nose, and very fair complexions, and one had blue eyes. But Eliza was "dark." Not only was her skin dark, but soon after her birth her hair began to take on too much of the natural African curl and had not grown as long as "white" hair should.

Apparently out of a combination of jealousy and ignorance, Taylor Polk sold Sally shortly after Eliza's birth. Sally's descendants say that she was sold "down the river to New Orleans." Polk, according to oral reports, believed that his concubine had proved unfaithful, taken up with a slave man, and conceived Eliza. Spencer remembered that he was only four years old at the time. Mrs. Pearl Murphy, Spencer's oldest living descendant, wrote of her great-grandmother in a 1978 letter:

> She was named Sally, a part Negro and Choctaw Indian girl. In those days Federal Court was held at Ft. Smith (probably once a year) and prominent citizens were called there to serve on the jury, and Taylor Polk was one that would be called. So on one of the times he was there, he picked up this girl and brought her

Family
Folklore
and
Personal
Memorates

★

385

back as a slave. If she had any family name except Sally no one ever knew.

She became the mother of three sons, Peter, Frank, and John Spencer and later a girl named Eliza. The girl was black and after her birth the mother was sold. My grandfather was only four years old when she was sold away from them. The children were kindly treated and they never suffered for care and really never felt like slaves. I think, however, the fact that their mother was sold away from them at a tender age testifys to the harshness of the slave system in the U.S.

Later, in a personal interview, Mrs. Murphy insisted that Sally was part Cherokee, not Choctaw, and other family members confirmed the Cherokee lineage.

Though apparently deeply affected by the loss of their mother, Spencer and his brothers seldom discussed their maternal lineage. Spencer told his own children only that Taylor Polk "went into the Indian Country" and bought Sally, and that when Eliza was born he sold her away because of suspected infidelity. The act of selling a mother away from her children no doubt caused little concern among the slaveholding class in Arkansas. According to Orville Taylor, "Since there was no legal requirement of keeping husbands, wives, and children together, there were many instances of separation." While the information on Sally is scant, the details of how Taylor Polk acquired her and how he got rid of her are strongly etched in the oral history handed down by all the descendants of Spencer Polk.

Much of the information that does exist about Sally was passed on by the descendants of another slave family, the slaves of Blount Bullock, another early Arkansas settler. The Bullock families, both black and white, intermarried with the Polks and lived in close proximity to them in both Montgomery and Howard counties. It was from the Bullock slaves and their descendants that Sally's status with Taylor Polk was most clearly delineated. Blount Bullock's slaves passed the story on to their children, who told it to later generations of the Polk family. The Bullocks were the first to reveal that Taylor Polk kept Sally in a little cabin next to his own, and that Sally's children were sired by her master.

NAT TURNER

Confession

· *From* The Confessions of Nat Turner ·

There are several confession narratives that, like *The Confessions of Nat Turner,* were oral accounts of a "criminal's" actions recorded by a White scribe. As one might expect, there were a number of Negroes classified as "criminals" during the period of slavery, since many actions considered normal for others were deemed criminal for Blacks—such as protecting themselves and their families, seeking freedom, or merely walking down the road without permission. Nat Turner, who led one of the largest slave insurrections in this country, provided a detailed "confession" to Thomas Gray. The authenticity of the confession was certified by six other White men. Though narratives such as this are to some degree suspect in that they are recorded by Whites who view their subjects as criminals, it is clear that there is a distinction between the cool, calm voice of the narrative and the horrified and accusatory voice of the scribe. Gray does not strive for an objective portrayal: he resists using any but the most derogatory terms in describing Nat Turner, whom he labels a "savage" with a "warped" mind. Throughout he places the confession in the most condemnatory context. Yet, the reader cannot help but be amazed that the power of Nat Turner to portray himself as a prophet overwhelms the efforts of Gray to portray him as a misguided, fanatical brute. Gray, the recorder, seems nonplussed by a man whose power he cannot help but unwillingly convey: "The calm, deliberate composure with which he spoke of his late deeds and intentions, the expression of his fiendlike face when excited by enthusiasm, still bearing the stains of the blood of helpless innocence about him; clothed with rags and covered with chains; yet daring to raise his manacled hands to heaven, with a spirit soaring above the attributes of man; I looked on him and my blood curdled in my veins."

It is unequivocal from his confession that Turner viewed himself as a chosen prophet with a God-given mission. Some of his descriptions of events, such as his thirty days in the woods, and his message that "Christ had laid down the yoke he had borne for the sins of men, and that I should take it on," suggest he perceived himself as a Christ figure. When Gray asks him if he does not consider himself mistaken now that he has been captured and is about to be killed, Turner responds, "Was not Christ crucified?"

Following his execution, Turner became a legendary figure in the slave community.

S_{ir},—You have asked me to give a history of the motives which induced me to undertake the late insurrection, as you call it—To do so I must go back to the days of my infancy, and even before I was born. I was thirty-one years of age the 2d of October last, and born the property of Benj. Turner, of this county. In my childhood a circumstance occurred which made an indelible impression on my mind, and laid the ground work of that enthusiasm, which has terminated so fatally to many, both white and black, and for which I am about to atone at the gallows. It is here necessary to relate this circumstance—trifling as it may seem, it was the commencement of that belief which has grown with time, and even now, sir, in this dungeon, helpless and forsaken as I am, I cannot divest myself of. Being at play with other children, when three or four years old, I was telling them something, which my mother overhearing, said it had happened before I was born—I stuck to my story, however, and related somethings which went, in her opinion, to confirm it—others being called on were greatly astonished, knowing that these things had happened, and caused them to say in my hearing, I surely would be a prophet, as the Lord had shewn me things that had happened before my birth. And my father and mother strengthened me in this my first impression, saying in my presence, I was intended for some great purpose, which they had always thought from certain marks on my head and breast—[a parcel of excrescences which I believe are not at all uncommon, particularly among negroes, as I have seen several with the same. In this case he has either cut them off or they have nearly disappeared]—My grandmother, who was very religious, and to whom I was much attached—my master, who belonged to the church, and other religious persons who visited the house, and whom I often saw at prayers, noticing the singularity of my manners, I suppose, and my uncommon intelligence for a child, remarked I had too much sense to be raised, and if I was, I would never be of any service to any one as a slave—To a mind like mine, restless, inquisitive and observant of every thing that was passing, it is easy to suppose that religion was the subject to which it would be directed, and although this subject principally occupied my thoughts—there was nothing that I saw or heard of to which my attention was not directed—The manner in which I learned to read and write, not only had great influence on my own mind, as I acquired it with the most perfect ease, so much so, that I have no recollection whatever of learning the alphabet—but to the astonishment of the family, one day, when a book was shewn me to keep me from crying, I began spelling the names of different objects—this was a source of wonder to all in the neighborhood, particularly the blacks—and this learning was constantly improved at all opportunities—when I got large enough to go to work, while employed, I was reflecting on many things that would present themselves to my imagination, and whenever an opportunity occurred of looking at a book, when the school children were getting their lessons, I would find many things that the fertility of my own imagination had depicted to me before; all my time, not devoted to my master's service, was spent either in prayer, or in making experiments in casting different things in moulds made of earth, in attempting to make paper, gunpowder, and many other experiments, that although I could not perfect, yet convinced me of its practicability if I had the means. [When questioned as to the manner of manufacturing those different articles, he was found well informed on the subject.] I was not addicted to stealing in my youth, nor have ever been—Yet such was the confidence of the negroes in the neighborhood, even at this early period of my life, in my superior judgment, that they would often carry me with them when they were going on any roguery, to plan for them. Growing up among them, with this confidence in my superior judgment, and when this, in their opinions, was perfected by Divine inspiration, from the circumstances already alluded to in my infancy, and which belief was ever afterwards zealously inculcated by the austerity of my life and manners, which became the subject of remark by white and black.— Having soon discovered to be great, I must appear so, and therefore studiously avoided mixing in society, and wrapped myself in mystery, devoting my time to fasting and prayer—By this time, having arrived to man's estate, and hearing the scriptures commented on at meetings, I was struck with that particular passage which says: "Seek ye the kingdom of Heaven and all things shall be added unto you." I reflected much on this passage, and prayed daily for light on this subject—As I was praying one day at my plough, the spirit spoke to me, saying "Seek ye the kingdom of Heaven and all things shall be added unto you. *Question*—what do you mean by the Spirit. *Ans.* The Spirit that spoke to the prophets in former days—and I was greatly astonished, and for two years prayed continually, whenever my duty would permit—and then again I had the same revelation, which fully confirmed me in the impression that I was ordained for some great purpose in the hands of the Almighty. Several years rolled round, in which many events occurred to strengthen me in this my belief. At this time I reverted in my mind to the remarks made of me in my childhood, and the things that had been shewn me—and as it had been said of me in my childhood by those by whom I had been taught to pray, both white and black, and in whom I had the greatest confidence, that I had too much sense to be raised, and if I was, I would never be of any use to any one as a slave. Now finding I had arrived to man's estate, and was a slave, and these revelations being made known to me, I began to direct my attention to this great object, to fulfil the purpose for which, by this time, I felt assured I was intended. Knowing the influence I had obtained over the minds of my fellow servants, (not by the means of conjuring and such like tricks—for to them I always spoke of such things with contempt) but by the communion of the Spirit whose revelations I often communicated to them, and they believed and said my wisdom came from God. I now began to prepare them for my purpose, by telling them something was about to happen that would terminate in fulfilling the great promise that had been made to me—About this time I was placed under an overseer, from whom I ran away—and after remaining in the woods thirty days, I returned, to the astonishment of the negroes on the plantation, who thought I had made my escape to some other part of the country, as my father had done before. But the reason of my return was, that the Spirit appeared to me and said I had my wishes directed to the things of this world, and not to the kingdom of Heaven, and that I should return to the service of my earthly master—"For he who knoweth his Master's will, and doeth it not, shall be beaten with many stripes, and thus have I chastened you." And the negroes found fault, and murmured against me, saying that if they had my sense they would not serve any master in the world. And about this time I had a vision—and I saw white spirits and black spirits engaged in battle, and the sun was darkened—the thunder rolled in the Heavens, and blood flowed in streams—and I heard a voice saying, "Such is your luck, such you are called to see, and let it come rough or smooth, you must surely bear it." I now withdrew myself as much as my situation would permit, from the intercourse of my fellow servants, for the avowed purpose of serving the Spirit more fully—and it appeared to me, and reminded me of the things it had already shown me, and that it would then reveal to me the

knowledge of the elements, the revolution of the planets, the operation of tides, and changes of the seasons. After this revelation in the
year 1825, and the knowledge of the elements being made known to
me, I sought more than ever to obtain true holiness before the great
day of judgment should appear, and then I began to receive the true
knowledge of faith. And from the first steps of righteousness until the
last, was I made perfect; and the Holy Ghost was with me, and said,
"Behold me as I stand in the Heavens"—and I looked and saw the
forms of men in different attitudes—and there were lights in the sky
to which the children of darkness gave other names than what they
really were—for they were the lights of the Saviour's hands,
stretched forth from east to west, even as they were extended on the
cross on Calvary for the redemption of sinners. And I wondered
greatly at these miracles, and prayed to be informed of a certainty of
the meaning thereof—and shortly afterwards, while laboring in the
field, I discovered drops of blood on the corn as though it were dew
from heaven—and I communicated it to many, both white and black,
in the neighborhood—and I then found on the leaves in the woods hi-
eroglyphic characters, and numbers, with the forms of men in different attitudes, portrayed in blood, and representing the figures I
had seen before in the heavens. And now the Holy Ghost had revealed itself to me, and made plain the miracles it had shown me—
For as the blood of Christ had been shed on this earth, and had
ascended to heaven for the salvation of sinners, and was now returning to earth again in the form of dew—and as the leaves on the
trees bore the impression of the figures I had seen in the heavens, it
was plain to me that the Saviour was about to lay down the yoke he
had borne for the sins of men, and the great day of judgment was at
hand. About this time I told these things to a white man, (Etheldred
T. Brantley) on whom it had a wonderful effect—and he ceased from
his wickedness, and was attacked immediately with a cutaneous
eruption, and blood ozed from the pores of his skin, and after praying and fasting nine days, he was healed, and the Spirit appeared to
me again, and said, as the Saviour had been baptised so should we be
also—and when the white people would not let us be baptised by the
church, we went down into the water together, in the sight of many
who reviled us, and were baptised by the Spirit—After this I rejoiced greatly, and gave thanks to God. And on the 12th of May,

1828, I heard a loud noise in the heavens, and the Spirit instantly appeared to me and said the Serpent was loosened, and Christ had laid down the yoke he had borne for the sins of men, and that I should take it on and fight against the Serpent, for the time was fast approaching when the first should be last and the last should be first. *Ques.* Do you not find yourself mistaken now? *Ans.* Was not Christ crucified. And by signs in the heavens that it would make known to me when I should commence the great work—and until the first sign appeared, I should conceal it from the knowledge of men—And on the appearance of the sign, (the eclipse of the sun last February) I should arise and prepare myself, and slay my enemies with their own weapons. And immediately on the sign appearing in the heavens, the seal was removed from my lips, and I communicated the great work laid out for me to do, to four in whom I had the greatest confidence, (Henry, Hark, Nelson, and Sam)—It was intended by us to have begun the work of death on the 4th July last—Many were the plans formed and rejected by us, and it affected my mind to such a degree, that I fell sick, and the time passed without our coming to any determination how to commence—Still forming new schemes and rejecting them, when the sign appeared again, which determined me not to wait longer.

Since the commencement of 1830, I had been living with Mr. Joseph Travis, who was to me a kind master, and placed the greatest confidence in me; in fact, I had no cause to complain of his treatment to me. On Saturday evening, the 20th of August, it was agreed between Henry, Hark and myself, to prepare a dinner the next day for the men we expected, and then to concert a plan, as we had not yet determined on any. Hark, on the following morning, brought a pig, and Henry brandy, and being joined by Sam, Nelson, Will and Jack, they prepared in the woods a dinner, where, about three o'clock, I joined them.

Q. Why were you so backward in joining them.

A. The same reason that had caused me not to mix with them for years before.

I saluted them on coming up, and asked Will how came he there, he answered, his life was worth no more than others, and his liberty as dear to him. I asked him if he thought to obtain it? He said he would, or lose his life. This was enough to put him in full confidence.

Jack, I knew, was only a tool in the hands of Hark, it was quickly agreed we should commence at home (Mr. J. Travis') on that night, and until we had armed and equipped ourselves, and gathered sufficient force, neither age nor sex was to be spared, (which was invariably adhered to.) We remained at the feast, until about two hours in the night, when we went to the house and found Austin; they all went to the cider press and drank, except myself. On returning to the house, Hark went to the door with an axe, for the purpose of breaking it open, as we knew we were strong enough to murder the family, if they were awaked by the noise; but reflecting that it might create an alarm in the neighborhood, we determined to enter the house secretly, and murder them whilst sleeping. Hark got a ladder and set it against the chimney, on which I ascended, and hoisting a window, entered and came down stairs, unbarred the door, and removed the guns from their places. It was then observed that I must spill the first blood. On which, armed with a hatchet, and accompanied by Will, I entered my master's chamber, it being dark, I could not give a death blow, the hatchet glanced from his head, he sprang from the bed and called his wife, it was his last word, Will laid him dead, with a blow of his axe, and Mrs. Travis shared the same fate, as she lay in bed. The murder of this family, five in number, was the work of a moment, not one of them awoke; there was a little infant sleeping in a cradle, that was forgotten, until we had left the house and gone some distance, when Henry and Will returned and killed it; we got here, four guns that would shoot, and several old muskets, with a pound or two of powder. We remained some time at the barn, where we paraded; I formed them in a line as soldiers, and after carrying them through all the manœuvres I was master of, marched them off to Mr. Salathul Francis', about six hundred yards distant. Sam and Will went to the door and knocked. Mr. Francis asked who was there, Sam replied it was him, and he had a letter for him, on which he got up and came to the door; they immediately seized him, and dragging him out a little from the door, he was dispatched by repeated blows on the head; there was no other white person in the family. We started from there for Mrs. Reese's, maintaining the most perfect silence on our march, where finding the door unlocked, we entered, and murdered Mrs. Reese in her bed, while sleeping; her son awoke, but it was only to sleep the sleep of death, he had only time to say who is that, and he was no more. From Mrs. Reese's we went to Mrs. Turner's, a mile distant, which we reached about sunrise, on Monday morning. Henry, Austin, and Sam, went to the still, where, finding Mr. Peebles, Austin shot him, and the rest of us went to the house; as we approached, the family discovered us, and shut the door. Vain hope! Will, with one stroke of his axe, opened it, and we entered and found Mrs. Turner and Mrs. Newsome in the middle of a room, almost frightened to death. Will immediately killed Mrs. Turner, with one blow of his axe. I took Mrs. Newsome by the hand, and with the sword I had when I was apprehended, I struck her several blows over the head, but not being able to kill her, as the sword was dull. Will turning around and discovering it, dispatched her also. A general destruction of property and search for money and ammunition, always succeeded the murders. By this time my company amounted to fifteen, and nine men mounted, who started for Mrs. Whitehead's, (the other six were to go through a by way to Mr. Bryant's, and rejoin us at Mrs. Whitehead's,) as we approached the house we discovered Mr. Richard Whitehead standing in the cotton patch, near the lane fence; we called him over into the lane, and Will, the executioner, was near at hand, with his fatal axe, to send him to an untimely grave. As we pushed on to the house, I discovered some one run round the garden, and thinking it was some of the white family, I pursued them, but finding it was a servant girl belonging to the house, I returned to commence the work of death, but they whom I left, had not been idle; all the family were already murdered, but Mrs. Whitehead and her daughter Margaret. As I came round to the door I saw Will pulling Mrs. Whitehead out of the house, and at the step he nearly severed her head from her body, with his broad axe. Miss Margaret, when I discovered her, had concealed herself in the corner, formed by the projection of the cellar cap from the house; on my approach she fled, but was soon overtaken, and after repeated blows with a sword, I killed her by a blow on the head, with a fence rail. By this time, the six who had gone by Mr. Bryant's, rejoined us, and informed me they had done the work of death assigned them. We again divided, part going to Mr. Richard Porter's, and from thence to Nathaniel Francis', the others to Mr. Howell Harris', and Mr. T. Doyles. On my reaching Mr. Porter's, he had escaped with his family. I understood there, that the alarm had already spread, and I immediately returned to bring up those sent to Mr. Doyles, and Mr. Howell Harris'; the party I left going on to Mr. Francis', having told them I would join them in that neighborhood. I met these sent to Mr. Doyles' and Mr. Harris' returning, having met Mr. Doyle on the road and killed him; and learning from some who joined them, that Mr. Harris was from home, I immediately pursued the course taken by the party gone on before; but knowing they would complete the work of death and pillage, at Mr. Francis' before I could get there, I went to Mr. Peter Edwards', expecting to find them there, but they had been here also. I then went to Mr. John T. Barrow's, they had been here and murdered him. I pursued on their track to Capt. Newit Harris', where I found the greater part mounted, and ready to start; the men now amounting to about forty, shouted and hurraed as I rode up, some were in the yard, loading their guns, others drinking. They said Captain Harris and his family had escaped, the property in the house they destroyed, robbing him of money and other valuables. I ordered them to mount and march instantly, this was about nine or ten o'clock, Monday morning. I proceeded to Mr. Levi Waller's, two or three miles distant. I took my station in the rear, and as it 'twas my object to carry terror and devastation wherever we went, I placed fifteen or twenty of the best armed and most to be relied on, in front, who generally approached the houses as fast as their horses could run; this was for two purposes, to prevent their escape and strike terror to the inhabitants—on this account I never got to the houses, after leaving Mrs. Whitehead's, until the murders were committed, except in one case. I sometimes got in sight in time to see the work of death completed, viewed the mangled bodies as they lay, in silent satisfaction, and immediately started in quest of other victims—Having murdered Mrs. Waller and ten children, we started for Mr. William Williams'—having killed him and two little boys that were there; while engaged in this, Mrs. Williams fled and got some distance from the house, but she was pursued, overtaken, and compelled to get up behind one of the company, who brought her back, and after showing her the mangled body of her lifeless husband, she was told to get down and lay by his side, where she was shot dead. I then started for Mr. Jacob Williams, where the family were murdered—Here we found a young man named Drury, who had come on business with Mr. Williams—he was pursued, overtaken and shot. Mrs. Vaughan was the next place we visited — and after murdering the family here, I determined on starting for Jerusalem — Our number amounted now to fifty or sixty, all mounted and armed with guns, axes, swords and clubs — On reaching Mr. James W. Parkers' gate, immediately on the road leading to Jerusalem, and about three miles distant, it was proposed to me to call there, but I objected, as I knew he was gone to Jerusalem, and my object was to reach there as soon as possible; but some of the men having relations at Mr. Parker's it was agreed that they might call and get his people. I remained at the gate on the road, with seven or eight; the others going across the field to the house, about half a mile off. After waiting some time for them, I became impatient, and started to the house for them, and on our return we were met by a party of white men, who had pursued our blood-stained track, and who had fired on those at the gate, and dispersed them, which I knew nothing of, not having been at that time rejoined by any of them — Immediately on discovering the whites, I ordered my men to halt and form, as they appeared to be alarmed — The white men, eighteen in number, approached us in about one hundred yards, when one of them fired, (this was against the positive orders of Captain Alexander P. Peete, who commanded, and who had directed the men to reserve their fire until within thirty paces) and I discovered about half of them retreating, I then ordered my men to fire and rush on them; the few remaining stood their ground until we approached within fifty yards, when they fired and retreated. We pursued and overtook some of them who we thought we left dead; (they were not killed) after pursuing them about two hundred yards, and rising a little hill, I discovered they were met by another party, and had haulted, and were re-loading their guns, (this was a small party from Jerusalem who knew the negroes were in the field, and had just tied their horses to await their return to the road, knowing that Mr. Parker and family were in Jerusalem, but knew nothing of the party that had gone in with Captain Peete; on hearing the firing they immediately rushed to the spot and arrived just in time to arrest the progress of these barbarous villians, and save the lives of their friends and fellow citizens.) Thinking that those who retreated first, and the party who fired on us at fifty or sixty yards distant, had all only fallen back to meet others with amunition. As I saw them re-loading their guns, and more coming up than I saw at first, and several of my bravest men being wounded, the others became panick struck and squandered over the field; the white men pursued and fired on us several times. Hark had his horse shot under him, and I caught another for him as it was running by me; five or six of my men were wounded, but none left on the field; finding myself defeated here I instantly determined to go through a private way, and cross the Nottoway river at the Cypress Bridge, three miles below Jerusalem, and attack that place in the rear, as I expected they would look for me on the other road, and I had a great desire to get there to procure arms and amunition. After going a short distance in this private way, accompanied by about twenty men, I overtook two or three who told me the others were dispersed in every direction. After trying in vain to collect a sufficient force to proceed to Jerusalem, I determined to return, as I was sure they would make back to their old neighborhood, where they would rejoin me, make new recruits, and come down again. On my way back, I called at Mrs. Thomas's, Mrs. Spencer's, and several other places, the white families having fled, we found no more victims to gratify our thirst for blood, we stopped at Majr. Ridley's quarter for the night, and being joined by four of his men, with the recruits made since my defeat, we mustered now about forty strong. After placing out sentinels, I laid down to sleep, but was quickly roused by a great racket; starting up, I found some mounted, and others in great confusion; one of the sentinels having given the alarm that we were about to be attacked, I ordered some to ride round and reconnoitre, and on their return the others being more alarmed, not knowing who they were, fled in different ways, so that I was reduced to about twenty again; with this I determined to attempt to recruit, and proceed on to rally in the neighborhood, I had left. Dr. Blunt's was the nearest house, which we reached just before day; on riding up the yard, Hark fired a gun. We expected Dr. Blunt and his family were at Maj. Ridley's, as I knew there was a company of men there; the gun was fired to ascertain if any of the family were at home; we were immediately fired upon and retreated, leaving several of my men. I do not know what became of them, as I never saw them afterwards. Pursuing our course back and coming in sight of Captain Harris', where we had been the day before, we discovered a party of white men at the house, on which all deserted me but two, (Jacob and

Nat,) we concealed ourselves in the woods until near night, when I sent them in search of Henry, Sam, Nelson, and Hark, and directed them to rally all they could, at the place we had had our dinner the Sunday before, where they would find me, and I accordingly returned there as soon as it was dark and remained until Wednesday evening, when discovering white men riding around the place as though they were looking for some one, and none of my men joining me, I concluded Jacob and Nat had been taken, and compelled to betray me. On this I gave up all hope for the present; and on Thursday night after having supplied myself with provisions from Mr. Travis's, I scratched a hole under a pile of fence rails in a field, where I concealed myself for six weeks, never leaving my hiding place but for a few minutes in the dead of night to get water which was very near; thinking by this time I could venture out, I began to go about in the night and eaves drop the houses in the neighborhood; pursuing this course for about a fortnight and gathering little or no intelligence, afraid of speaking to any human being, and returning every morning to my cave before the dawn of day. I know not how long I might have led this life, if accident had not betrayed me, a dog in the neighborhood passing by my hiding place one night while I was out, was attracted by some meat I had in my cave, and crawled in and stole it, and was coming out just as I returned. A few nights after, two negroes having started to go hunting with the same dog, and passed that way, the dog came again to the place, and having just gone out to walk about, discovered me and barked, on which thinking myself discovered, I spoke to them to beg concealment. On making myself known they fled from me. Knowing then they would betray me, I immediately left my hiding place, and was pursued almost incessantly until I was taken a fortnight afterwards by Mr. Benjamin Phipps, in a little hole I had dug out with my sword, for the purpose of concealment, under the top of a fallen tree. On Mr. Phipps' discovering the place of my concealment, he cocked his gun and aimed at me. I requested him not to shoot and I would give up, upon which he demanded my sword. I delivered it to him, and he brought me to prison. During the time I was pursued, I had many hair breadth escapes, which your time will not permit you to relate. I am here loaded with chains, and willing to suffer the fate that awaits me.

DARYL CUMBER DANCE
Ruthville Post Office
· *From* The Lineage of Abraham ·

This is my account of a legend known by everyone in my family regarding the naming of the local post office, the only one found by the United States Commission of Civil Rights (which studied the Southern counties in the Black Belt between 1959 and 1961) to have a Negro postmistress. It is very likely that Ruthville Post Office had held that distinction for many years — in fact, it had Black postmasters and postmistresses for most of the twentieth century.

Ruth Brown Hucles is the subject of many legends, the best known of which regards Will's (William H. C. Brown)[3] unrequited love for her.

W hen Ruth was growing up in Charles City County, Virginia, the closest post office to our community was at Providence Forge (about six miles away), and the children (such as my Grandmother Sallie and her friends) had to walk that long distance to pick up their families' mail. Will, being a lawyer, petitioned the U.S. government for a post office in the community, indicating that it was to be named Ruth Will (after Ruth, the prettiest woman in the county, and himself). When it was named, it was Ruthville — whether a clerical error, a misunderstanding, or a governmental change is not clear. From that time the community and the post office have been known as Ruthville, and its postmaster or postmistress has for most of those years been a descendant of Abraham and a niece or nephew of Ruth. According to legend Will was so devastated when Ruth married someone else that he never married, and when he died he left all of his money to Wilberforce University.[4]

---

[3]Brown went on to become the founder of a bank and the only Black who attended the Republican State Convention in Roanoke in 1905 (after most Negroes had been effectively disfranchised by the Virginia Constitution of 1902), where he made a seconding speech for Judge L. L. Lewis for governor (*Roanoke Times*, August 10, 1905).

[4]Will did, in fact, marry.

Unrequited Love

· *From* The Lineage of Abraham ·

Sallie (my maternal grandmother) seems to have had no lack of suitors when she returned to Charles City from Virginia Normal and Collegiate Institute (VN&CI) in 1896, but never was there a more ardent suitor than my paternal grandfather, Ernest Cumber, who presumably loved her all of his life and even renewed his efforts years later when she became a widow. Granddaddy Ernest had been at VN&CI with her, and he worked in the dining hall. He would put potatoes in his shirt and save them for her. Sallie's brothers used to make fun of Ernest's efforts to court Sallie. Once he bought a horse, Hannibal, and took him to the store, evidently to make an impression, and Sallie's brother Arthur pretended to jump on the horse but jumped *over* him as a joke. Such teasing on the part of her brothers greatly annoyed and provoked Ernest. Sallie was [also annoyed] and provoked by his attentions. She complained to her friends, "He makes me sick—all he talks about is hair. Wants me to let my hair down so he can lay his head on it." She would get [so annoyed] by his attentions and his obsession with hair. He used to declare, "Sallie's hair falls down around her shoulders like seaweed." When my mother and my father went to tell him that they had married (he was then briefly institutionalized), he responded, "I didn't want any of my sons to marry Sallie's daughters because she wouldn't have me." Many years later, when Sallie was living with her daughter and son-in-law (my mother and father), they all went to visit Granddaddy Ernest, and Mama Sallie told him, "I'm living at Mount Misery" (the name he gave the family home because of his disappointments, not the least of which was his failure to win her hand—and later the early death of his young wife, Sarah Bassett Brown, my paternal grandmother), and he replied, "I built it for you."

Let the Wheelers Roll

· *From Daryl Cumber Dance*, Shuckin' and Jivin' ·

I recorded the following memorate in Richmond, Virginia, in a session attended
by a group of older Black men in their seventies and eighties. They laughed
uproariously at the end of the anecdote, and then they started talking about their
own experiences with similar cruel bosses, one asserting, "Yeah, the boss man
didn't care 'bout nothin' but let them wheelers roll." At the repetition of this key
line from the anecdote, they laughed again; but then, almost abruptly, they
returned to the painful reminiscences of the similar ordeals they had endured. I
detected an almost imperceptible crack in their voices; I watched their brows
slowly wrinkle and their eyes dim with painful memories. For one brief moment I
saw in their faces the suffering of my people, and I felt the magnitude of a pain so
deep that none of them could ever have verbalized it. Tears began to well in my
eyes, but I was abruptly snatched from my sentimental mood when one of them
repeated, "What that boss man say? 'Let them wheelers roll!' " And we all
laughed heartily again. If they noticed the tears that fell from my eyes, I am sure
they assumed it resulted from my exuberant laughter. I experienced then, more
vividly that ever before, the verity of that old blues line, "laughing to keep from
crying."

They had what you call those rooters—had two mules—go up there
and tear the ground up and the other fellows up there had what they
call a wheeler—it was more of a scoop with two wheels on it. And
they hook four mules there and scoop up in order to get that dirt up
and then they unhook these mules, 'n' 'course they had laborers down
there to lift up the dirt and carry it up the hill where they gon' dump
it. One cold day, you know, said they out there loadin' wheelers and
like that, and say, and they slowed down, and the boss man say, [nas-
tily] "Hey, what's wrong with them wheelers up there? Let them
wheelers roll!"

Say the fellow say, [pleadingly] "Boss Man, Boss Man, my feet is
cold."

He say, "Damn your feet, let the wheelers roll!"

The Sheriff

· *From* Praying for Sheetrock ·

Family
Folklore
and
Personal
Memorates

∗
401

"He ran McIntosh County with an iron fist," said Doug Moss. "He was a benevolent dictator, but he was a racist. He had black police officers, probably some of the first in the state, but I believe he had them in order to control the people. McIntosh County under his tutelage was a very depressed area. I think he felt if the county got in too much money, too much industry, too many outsiders, they'd lose control. And he kept his eye on the black community. If a black person got out of control in McIntosh County, he simply disappeared. We used to say they took a swim across the river wearing too much chain."

"There lots of people disappear that people don't know about," said Thurnell Alston. "A friend of mine was out in the country digging, and they dig up human bones—none of them even deteriorating, the head and all of them not even decayed. I think everybody in the county knew the sheriff had people killed. He was too powerful to do it himself. He always have somebody to have it done. He know about it. He know whatsoever went on. He *knew* that it was done or he *ordered* it done, one out of the two.

"These people haven't been nowhere else. The sheriff just really had them hoodwinked. They're just ignorant to what's going on. The sheriff was running this county just like an old plantation. When Tom said dance, you dance. When Tom said die, you die."

I Was Leaving

· *From Elizabeth Clark-Lewis,* Living In, Living Out: African
American Domestics and the Great Migration ·

Beulah Nelson gave this account of her experience as a domestic.

And I worked them three days. Why? Mama sent me, and they was paying a quarter a week! Now, you had to cook the breakfast, you wait on all of them, all the children, and get them ready for school if they had to go to school. Fix their lunch and everything. Then you wash up all the dishes. Then you had to go make up all the beds and pick up all the things behind all the children, and then after that you had to go out behind the house, honey, and pick the garden. And pick what kind of vegetables you got to have. You got to wash them and cook them. And they had three meals a day. They would eat they breakfast, and then twelve o'clock they had to have a big dinner. And then they had supper later in the evening.

But they didn't want no nigger to put they hand on their bread. Understand me good now. I set the table up and put the food on the table. But the bread be the last thing. Never bring the bread in until after they say the grace, so the bread would be seeping hot. I wait just as good until they said the grace, and I wouldn't move because I would have had to pick up the bread out of the pan, and I still would have to take knife or fork to lift it to put in the plate to take to the table, and I know she didn't want me to touch it. Right? Well, if she didn't want me to touch it, if I couldn't touch it, I wasn't going to try not to touch it to carry it to the table to give it to them. She said to me, "How long are you going to wait before you bring that bread in here?" I said, "I'm not even going to bring it in there." I said, "You put it in there. You cook it, you don't want me to touch it. If you don't want me to touch it, you don't need me to bring it in there." And I didn't bring it in there. And that's when she got mad, arguing with me so. She jumped up from table and she said to me, "Beulah, you fired." But she didn't fire me—I fired myself, 'cause I *intended* to do what I did. I said, "These two days I been in your house. You could've done—as far as you know—you could be done ate a lot of my spit [in your food]. I could have done did anything I want to do to it, and you wouldn't have never known nothing about it. But just because you could see me if I touch it." I said, "No, if that's the way it's to be—not me!" I said, "For what? Six days a week for twenty-five cents? Not me!" You see, I didn't have to do it—I was leaving.

I Am a Hard Woman

· *From John Langston Gwaltney,* Drylongso: A Self-Portrait of
Black America ·

Collected from Mabel Lincoln.

I'll tell you *what* I think, but you know how I think, just like I know how you think. Now, I wouldn't know where to start if I had to explain black folks to anybody who was not one of the people. This is not an easy thing to try to do. At first I thought, "Well, I'll start with me." But that's not all that easy to do, either. If you could see me you would know some things about me, but they wouldn't be the most important things that there is to know about Mabel Lincoln. What do you know about the way I look? Now, son, I wanted to see how you answer questions and I see that you are trying to be nice. I know that you know that I have a limp, but you didn't mention that. You say I'm small, but you know that a heap of folks would say I look like a very flat ironing board. You kept it to looks and that's what you should have done, because that's what I asked you to do. But you know, there are more folks out here who think I am mean than don't, and my father was the only person I ever knew who thought I was sweet. But be that as it willormay, I am going to tell you what kind of person I know I am and what kind of people I think we are.

Now, I never had much of what you might call education, but I have heard the thunder more than once and I have not slept too much in this world. The fact that I'm sitting here talking to you is the best proof of that. Now, you know that isn't my doing, but it is mostly my doing. Of course, you can do howsoever you will and still get carried away from here because of something somebody did that was not known to you or anybody you know. Anyway, I am going to tell you about me and us like I know how to tell things, without any who-shot-John or he-said-she-said.

Marva Johns Selby Lincoln breathed her first breath on December the eighth in nineteen and three in a little place I wouldn't call a house now in a little place in South Carolina that most Geechees never heard of. My mother died a day after she birthed me, and my father and my mother's sisters brought me up and they brought me up hard and I am glad of it to this day. My father was a blind man, and he made as much of a living as he could by carving decoys, teaching people how to play stringed instruments like the guitar and banjo and the piano, too. My mother's sisters were hard women, so they didn't like some of the things my father did because he wasn't what you might call a practical kind of person. Anyway, the crackers killed him. Ran him down beside our house. A carload of young crackers from somewhere ran him down in front of our house. They were just playing with him, but when he didn't run, the one at the wheel got mad and ran right over him. He didn't die for a week, but he was out of his head. I was twenty-one. He died on my birthday. I left there then and came here to work, and work is what I have done and work is what I am doing and will do until they throw dirt in my face.

Now, if you want to know one thing black people are known by, it is working. You can smell my house, so you know that it is wholesome. If you could see this house you would know that you could eat off the floor. Now, that's another thing about blackfolks—they will clean theyself if they possibly can. They are fussy about what goes into their stomachs. When I first went to Detroit, there was this black man working in the restaurant I used to work in. I cooked and waited and washed and did some of everything you should do in a restaurant. Pretty soon they was buying so much food that they got another man to sort of manage this place, and he was a devil. He didn't do much but tell folks who already knew what to do and when to do it some fool something that just slowed things down. Well, this fool didn't like me, so he used to do things that he thought would bother me. Now, he didn't know me, so most of the times he couldn't bother me, but one thing he did used to bother me no end. He would say, "Mabel, I'm glad you liked the beef stew, but I just spit in it." Well, that would make me sick and he would laugh and say how foolish blackfolks were to him.

So one day James Selby brought him some corn-clam chowder, which he was a fool about. He ate two bowls of it and said to Jeems, who was doing all the cooking then, "Will, that's good, but it's a little salty." And Jeems said, "Right, Mr. Simon. That's because I pissed in it." Now, that's how I lost that job, because when he got rid of Jim I took my apron off the hook and was out the door before anybody. And that's how I come to live in Chicago with my half sister.

Now, I did not forget what I'm supposed to be telling you. I'm trying to show you why I am the kind of person I am. I am a hard woman because I have had a hard time out here. I mean, I do whatever I have to do to take care of myself in such a way that I don't feel low or nothing or dirty because of my own weakness or greediness. If somebody takes advantage of me because of something I didn't know or couldn't help, well, all right, they got me. But I didn't help them to do me. But if I get hung because I helped somebody who wouldn't help me, if I lose money trying to get your money, well, then I feel like dirt and I would rather take a whipping than feel that way.

I have had to tell my own half sister's child, "You got yourself into jail, now get yourself out!" Now, that hurt me to my heart, but right is right and it don't wrong nobody that should not be wronged. Now, that's hard right there! In the Book of Proverbs in the eleventh chapter and the twenty-ninth verse, it says that "the fool shall be servant to the wise." To me that means if you don't look out for yourself, somebody will have you looking out for them.

Now, you remember that I told you that whether you can see me or not wouldn't help you to know my mind. What I think is more important than what I look like. Now, that is not just because I am an old lady that don't worry none about looks. I still worry about my looks, although the truth is I never really had any. Now, that don't mean that I haven't had all the trash talked at me that any other woman would have to listen to. I even liked hearing some of those lies, but I always knew they was lies. Some slick men got mad with me because I had the nerve, black and plain as I was, not to let them make a fool out of me after a little sweet talk. I hope them words about black and ugly are not out of turn, but that is how it is with a lot of people out here. Now, you are a dark man, son, and I know you have to know what I'm talking about and that is one of the things about our people that some would like to hide. But I do not believe in that. If all I can do for you is tell some more lies about blackfolks, then we might as well just say any old thing or, better yet, don't say nothing at all. I would rather be what I am than anything I know anything about. But I'm not going to sit here and try to convince anybody that I'm perfect. I'm all right, but I have done and will do some things that don't make much sense to me and some things that I know are wrong while I'm doing them.

Now, that's the way it is with my people or any other people. Too many blackfolks are fools about color and hair. That is probably the most mixed-up thing in this world. Now, me, like a fool, would not marry Jeems Selby for five years because he was a red-headed man. He lost his job over me and did everything a good man could to please a simple woman, but I would not marry him because, thinking as I did then, that the color was everything, I couldn't figure out why Jeems wanted to marry me. Jeems' sister Nancy was the best woman friend I have ever had, but I wouldn't trust her for years because she looked whiter than most whitefolks I ever saw. Now, that is another thing that most black people do that they should not do. I can understand feeling that way about most white people, but I know that's not right, thinking that way about black people who look white. It took me a long time to get that as straight as I managed to get it. I've been telling you about wrong things about myself and my folks, but there is much more right about us than there is wrong.

At May Anna's I didn't say much, but I was thinking a lot. There are so many blackfolks of so many kinds who know they are black that it is a hard thing to say what makes them all black. There are so many of us who don't want to be known, and a few who keep jumping up telling anybody who will pay them some mind that blackfolks are whatever this leelittle passel of loud mouths say we are, that it must be hard for a foreigner to know anything about us. Now, that's all right, you know, because most of us don't want foreigners knowing but so much about our business no way. Now, I have told you what you know is the most important thing about us: we are very private people. And most of the time the more anybody tells you about his business, the less you really know about that person. I know because I am that way myself and most black people I know are that way too. Now, if I didn't think you was that way I wouldn't say anything to you. I wouldn't lie to you, because that would be putting a stumbling block before the blind. I know that you are not going to put my business in the street so it will come back on me. I don't want my truth to be a snare to me, so generally I don't say much about anything to anybody. The old lady don't trust any and everybody out here; now, that's the blackness in her, you understand.

One thing that is very important to most black people is that you should call them by whatsoever name their mamas saw fit to call

Family
Folklore
and
Personal
Memorates

*

4o7

them. There are not too many of us that don't have more nicknames than Carter got pills, and some folks can use some of them and some can't, and you have to know the person to know what you can call him. But above all, don't give me some damn name and call me by it like you had been knowing me as long as my mama. If it's not worth the trouble to you to find out what I want to be called, then don't bother to call me at all. If you are going to call me Will when you know my name is James, you might as well call me dog or dirt or any other thing I am not. Like most of us, I feel very strongly on that, but I know that if you are the kind of person who would call me what you want to call me instead of what I should be called, well, I couldn't explain anything to you if that's the kind of person you are. Most white people—anyway, all the white people I know—are people you wouldn't want to explain anything to. I don't think it is in the color because I have known and still know black people who are the same color but who think like I think.

I can't tell you about how many of us there are and how much we make and things of that kind. I just know there are a lot of us and that I have never been anywhere where there were not some black people there before I got there. I have been a waitress, laundress, cook, cannery worker, and I have worked in service for more than twenty-seven years. I thought it was hard for me on the farm in my home, but that was because I was young then. It was hard because being poor is hard and even if your people take advantage of you, they are cursing you to bless you. They know that their time may be short and they know that when they are gone you must scuffle for yourself. My father took a few pennies out of every quarter he made and kept it. He said that he was keeping it for a new suit to bury him in. He took money I earned too, and that was the only thing I ever disliked that he did. When I was just learning to write, he made me write a note: "This is for Marva." And when they buried him, you know, they were going to put his money together to help with the funeral, but they found my note in the cigar box with $146. I left home with that money; he knew I would want to.

But now, when you are working for folks that, as they say, "ain't folks," now then, you will suck sorrow! I am talking about what I know. Now, if you are a woman slinging somebody else's hash and busting somebody else's suds or doing whatsoever you might do to keep yourself from being a tramp or a willing slave, you will be called out of your name and asked out of your clothes. In this world most people will take whatever they think you can give. It don't matter whether they want it or not, whether they need it or not, or how wrong it is for them to ask for it. Most people figure, "If I can get it out of you, then I am going to take it." Now, that's why I have to be hard and that's why my people are the same way.

Now, life is hard and it is whitefolks that make it harder than it has to be for me. Now, they are a people that will bless you to curse you. Last Sunday my elder preached on welfare, and he took his text from Job, the thirtieth chapter, the fifteenth verse: "My welfare passeth as a cloud." Now, he preached welfare's funeral! And somebody like me can look at him and still listen to him. He has not got more money on his back than I will see in a year and he knows how to work just like I do. He don't take no vacation in some place I couldn't find on a fifty-dollar map and expect me and folks that work as hard as I do to send him there. Now, while we are at it we might as well kill that chicken too. Some blackfolks worship their ministers more than they do their God, and that is a great sin and foolishness. I used to be as guilty of it as anybody, so I can and will speak of it. When I married Arthur Lincoln I was taken sick and could not work for a solid year! Now, the doctor used to come to see me and this little red minister used to come too. That doctor would wait for his money, but Reverend Summers was always hinting about my empty envelope. Fool-like, I borrowed some money from Nancy Selby to help my South Carolina Club Diamond Circle. She lent me the money, but she opened my eyes to the truth. I got me some good food and paid the rent and my doctor. Now, Nancy was a good friend because she gave you good advice and whatever else she had that you needed and ought to have. She didn't loud-talk you, but told you softly and honestly when she thought you was wrong. Now, that is the kind of friendship most black people appreciate.

To black people like me, a fool is funny—you know, people who love to break bad, people you can't tell anything to, folks that would take a shotgun to a roach. Now, I can help myself some and help anybody that really wants to be helped a little. That's all I have time for. If I have to run you down or put up with uku lip from you to do you some good, then I will go on my way and you can do the same.

Schoolboy was over here last Thursday telling me what I thought when he was supposed to be finding out what I thought. Now, I just don't have time for that. So I just let him drink Arthur's beers until he went to sleep and called Roland to come and get him. That's how blackfolks are. They say a thousand maybes for every yes or no to anybody they don't know and the foreigner walks away happy. Nobody in this world can say "Uhn-huhn" like we can. Now, no matter how we say it, it is a way of not saying anything if we don't trust you, and we don't trust most black people, so you know how we feel about the rest. There are more meats in blackfolks than there is in turtles!

But most of us try to be cool. That is what we respect the most in ourselves and look for in other people. That means being a person of sober, quiet judgment. My middle name, and the name that anybody back home would call me, is Dorcas because my father, who named me, wanted me to be a wise, sober, upright woman. He told me why he called me that and I tried hard to live up to that name. Now, that was some use to me because it was trying to live up to that name that kept me from making a fool of myself in the corn rows or just saying any old thing that came into my head. I don' have to tell you that in the Book of Proverbs, in the twenty-ninth chapter in the eleventh verse, it says that "a fool uttereth all his mind." Out in the street people say "Be cool" when they mean look out for something or somebody, but being cool is a more weighty thing than that. My father used to say, "Laugh with your friends, but smile with strangers." When I was coming up, you didn't frown with anybody.

The Difference between Us and Them

· *From John Langston Gwaltney,* Drylongso: A Self-Portrait of Black America ·

Collected from May Anna Madison.

My mother named every child she had for her or for my grandmother. Even my brother Mason is really named for my grandmother May. I don't remember her too well, but I do remember that she came to see us once or twice and brought a lot of food and presents. I can remember one Thursday—it was my mother's birthday and they brought my grandmother up here as a surprise.

Thursdays I remember even better than the Sundays. That's when all of us would have our day-off get-togethers. That was really nice. People would come to one house and cook all the special things that we liked to eat. We would play games and they would make banana-blackberry ice cream or chocolate-banana ice cream. And each person would have a thing that they were called the boss of. My Aunt Ocie was the boss of buttermilk-custard pies. My Aunt May was the boss of apple puppies and hoecakes and simon cakes and anything cooked on top of the stove like that. My mother's friend Mrs. Miller was the boss of fried chicken and my father was the boss of chiddlins and maws. He used to fry them and bake them and boil them with noodles or dumplings, which he and I used to make together. They used to have fresh beans cooked with hocks and lots of different kinds of bread. That was the best times we ever had! They would spread pallets on the floor if there were too many people for beds and the children would sleep on them. That Thursday get-together was what we all looked forward to then!

My mother and father both worked in service. My mother always did that kind of work, off and on—I mean, that was really the only kind of work she did while she was working. My father finally got out of that kind of work, but he used to cook and I can remember when he chauffeured for some white people. But his thing was really gardening! He always kept a lot of plants and he liked to try to grow things that you wouldn't expect to see growing here. He really loved the country. Every time they would go home to visit my mother's people he would bring something up with him to try to grow it. He was really good at that! That didn't come down to me, though. I try, but I don't have too much luck with plants now. The windows to your left have got what's left of my plants in them. I was doing pretty good there for a while. The plants once covered those windows.

The police came here looking for somebody we had never heard of and they got mad because they couldn't find this person, so they tore down the plants and knocked holes in my bedroom and kitchen walls. They wouldn't say what they were looking for. They didn't find anything, anyway. I asked them, "What about the damage?" and they said, "What goddamned damage?" So I knew they were not going to do anything about it. There were four of them and the leading one asked all the others if they saw any damage, and they all laughed and said no. There was one black one with them and I know he felt like a penny with a hole in it, but he couldn't do anything with the others standing right there. They tried to make me sign a paper that they wouldn't let me read, so I told them that I couldn't write. They argued about it for a while, but when they saw that I wasn't going to sign it, they left.

Now, you asked me what the difference between us and them is and that's it—they don't have to put up with that. Those cops came here and wrecked my house, ate my food and used my telephone and took the church envelope with the money, but there was nothing I could do about that because I am black. Now, if I had been a white woman, they wouldn't have done that. My life is different from theirs because they don't have to respect anything I have.

The TV is full of people talking about women's lib. Well, I can handle black men; what I can't handle is this prejudice. White women have done more bad things to me than black men ever thought of doing. Black men will make a fool out of me if I let them, but it was a white woman who had me crawling around her apartment before I was thirteen years old, cleaning places she would never think of cleaning with a toothbrush and toothpick! It was a female chauvinist sow that worked me a full day for seventy-five cents! When I was nothing but a child myself, white women looked the other way when their fresh little male chauvinist pigs were trying to make a fool out of me! That's why I don't pay any attention to all that stuff. A black man can't do any more to me than I will let him do because I can and have taken care of myself. But I do have to work to be able to do that and that means that I have to be able to deal with white people. White men and women are the people who make life hard for me.

I never got married, but if I did my husband and I would have to agree on things and if we couldn't, then we would just have to separate. My Aunt May's second husband always used to argue with her about money. When she got down, he said he would leave her if she didn't spend some of the money for what he wanted. They say she said, "Go on about your business if you feel that way." Now, that's why she saved her money and kept it apart from his.

I don't know any black woman who is too proud to get out here and work. That's why I can't stand this welfare thing. I don't mean that people should not be helped if they are too sick to work. But this business of paying somebody to lay up here and have children that they can't support makes the welfare mother the only black woman who has to depend on some man to get what she has to have. I know that a lot of people are not going to want to hear that, but it is the truth. Mrs. Miller's grandniece got into that. She is a really beautiful girl, but she let some nigger make a fool out of her and so she got on welfare. She has two children for one welfare worker and one for another one! Welfare gives her enough to get over and get pregnant, but that is all it does for her.

Now, in my day she would have had to work, just like I did. You owe children more than just food and clothes, though. This girl I'm telling you about has a little UN. All those children look different from each other and none of them look like their mother and the fathers are long gone because they got what they wanted in a few minutes. Now, white men and black men have both taken advantage of her, but the black men couldn't *make* her do anything. But she put herself in a position by joining welfare, so that white men could say, "Do what I tell you to or you won't get the first red cent!" She told me herself that her first welfare worker tried to rape her! Well, she said no to that one, I guess, but she don't seem to say no to the others. Now, me, I have to work, but I don't have to put up with that. White women don't have to put up with it, either, but black women on welfare do. All these pigs out here, if you want to call them that, had to have mothers. Most of them must have had sisters and aunts and daughters. Now, I would not raise any son of mine to oppress me. If you raise your children to kick you in the behind, then who do you have to blame if they do that?

I have worked for white people almost all my working days. I know them. I worked for a lady for five years, and do you know that woman always called me Anna May? She used to say that she depended on me for everything and that I was just like one of the family, but she didn't want to call me by my name. After I had been working for them for about three years I asked her why she did that, and she said it was just easier for her to call me Anna May. So that's what she did. That's what I was there for—to make things easier for her. Now, that's what a lot of white people think we are here for. The women think that just as much as the men do. I could see that she was mad because I asked her about that. She said she had a headache. Well, I had a headache and a bill-ache and a child-ache and I had to deal with them and take care of little things like her laundry and her cooking and her kids. Now, all she had to do was to have her headaches whenever it was time to do anything. Now, she could lay around like that and bug people about nothing because I was out there in her kitchen. I had to be out there so that I can say no to anybody.

Now, there are certain things I will not do just to keep a job. I don't know what would happen if all my jobs were the same. I mean, if I was asked to do some of the things I don't want to do to keep a job on every job I went to, I don't really know what I would do. I would try to find some other work, I guess. But I haven't had that to worry me. I have always been able to find a job that was as good as my kind of work can be. Working for other people can't be but so good for you because you are working for them and not yourself. See, the best work is work that you want to do that you do for yourself. Now, work can be fun. Remember what I told you about the Thursday get-togethers? That was hard work, but people didn't mind because they wanted to do that and they were working for themselves. They were working with people they liked and at the end they made this grand meal. Now, they didn't work any harder for the white woman. As a matter of fact, they didn't work as hard for white people as they did for themselves. But when we worked for ourselves, everybody did what he could do best and nobody bothered you. It is not only the hard work that I mind when I have to work for somebody else, but I just don't like people hanging overtop of me all day long. I wish the people I work for would just say, "I want this and this and this done," and then leave me alone to do what they are paying me to do. But, you see, they are afraid that I don't know how to do what they are paying me to do or that I won't do it. They don't know that I can get done as much as I want to get done, no matter how many people are watching me. It's just easier if they leave me alone.

Now, if I tell you that I am going to do it if life lasts me, I will get that thing done! Now, I know a lot of women who don't feel like I do about that. Some women say, "All right, I'll do just what you must think I'm going to do." Now, what I can't figure out about that is why anybody wants people like that to work for them! I am able to do this kind of work. There is nothing wrong with this work. People eat and they don't like to eat in filthy rooms or to wear dirty clothes or walk on filthy floors. Now, I can do all that kind of work and people want it done. But not everyone can do this kind of work and not everybody wants to do it. If I will do it and do it well, then pay me what you would ask if you came to me and said, "May Anna, I will clean and dust and cook for you if you will give me what I need to live on."

I Limit My Syllable Output

· *From John Langston Gwaltney,* Drylongso: A Self-Portrait of Black America ·

Collected from Carolyn Chase.

I have sugar. Many of my people had it and some have it now. I have also a swelling of the legs. I'm just a little heavy in the place where "our girls" are heavy. I guess I have what they used to call the hour-glass figure. I'm dark brown, about your color. I'm a black woman, so you know I'm curious and will show it. So, if you don't mind, I'm going to ask you some questions: How should I refer to you? Do you resent the word "blind"? Would you rather be called "sightless"? I've heard "visually handicapped" but wouldn't use it here because some of these girls in my building are very quick to scream "educated fool" or "Miss Anne" at you. So unless we are talking race or religion, I limit my syllable output.

But sometimes you can get into an awful lot of trouble by trying to break things down too. Mrs. Marshall in 3B is still very active and alert, although we celebrated her eighty-ninth birthday just two weeks ago. You should really try to talk to her. When I first met her I was trying to explain some silly thing about the tenants' union to her. My girl friend Gladys, whom you should also interview, had told me that Mrs. Marshall was going to be eighty-nine soon, so naturally I tried to break my message down. Well, in the process I garbled everything and confused even myself! It has been quite some time now before I just start automatically breaking things down without carefully looking over the situation. That old lady just sat there, and when I was just about as hung up as it's possible for one human being to get, she cleared her throat and said, "Dear. You have accomplished prodigies in the vineyard of oversimplification. But perhaps the end of genuine communication might be more efficaciously facilitated were you to couch your explanation in standard English, a dialect with which I have a more than casual acquaintance." We both fell out! She says you should talk to everyone in his own tongue and if you listen to them, you'll find out which tongue they prefer.

When I lived in California with an aunt of my father, there was a blind man boarding there too. You know, many of the girls would permit him to touch them when they would not let men who could see do anything like that under those circumstances. On his birthday one lady I know slept for him, or with him, however you want to say it. I know that this is often the custom and I have often wondered how it got started with us. I think our people like to make people who are down feel good. I think that's why we accuse very poor people of having a great deal of money. I don't want to offend you, but I do think many sightless people must find it more difficult to find sexual partners. So much of this mating game depends upon being able to see. If you could see the way different women dress, you might have some idea of your chances. Then, too, because almost all women talk more nicely to a man with a handicap, it must be very easy to get the wrong idea about your chances. But then, maybe sighted people get as much or more out of this than the sightless do.

Mr. Ramos was kidding me about your being here. That was an excuse for him to raise the subject of *that talk* with me. He has asked me to go out with him several times and one time I did. Then I started getting some very evil looks from one of the Spanish girls I used to help. So I cornered her one day and asked her right there what was wrong. She said she liked me, but was angry because I was trying to take her sister's husband. I told Neva that somebody was lying and that we should get to the bottom of this mess. I said she could come to my house or I would go to her house or her sister's house. We finally went to our friend Ana's house, and Ana said she knew I was a decent woman and Ruth said she thought so too.

Then both Ana and I asked Neva to go and bring her sister. But she didn't want to do that, so we called her sister. Her sister's child was sick, so she was not able to come to Ana's, but we asked if we could come there. She hesitated, but Ruth persuaded her, so we went over there. She said she didn't want any trouble, but she didn't like people taking bread out of her kids' mouths and sleeping with her man. So I said that I would certainly not like anyone to do that to me if I had a husband and a family, and that was why I would never do that to another woman. Then I got up and went right over to that lady and told her the truth, which is that I do not go out with married men! She looked at me and said that she believed me. Then Ana said that she had known me a very long time and had always respected me.

Then her husband, Mr. Ramos, came in and saw us all there, but I still didn't know he was her husband. So I said, "Hello, Mr. Diaz." He just looked at me and said, "My name is Ramos." Then everybody knew I was telling the truth; they could tell just by looking at the look on his face. I asked him to tell Mrs. Ramos what he had told me about himself. He said I was crazy and that he was in a hurry because he had to meet someone. He said, "I'm not going to stand around here arguing with a bunch of crazy women!" He practically flew out of that apartment! So I told Mrs. Ramos that I was sorry for the misunderstanding, but that I had not known that Mr. Diaz was her husband. We sent Mrs. Ramos' oldest boy for some pizza and chicken and made a sangria and had a regular party! And we have been good friends since then.

I like to cook and if you could see me you would know I like to eat. Well, anyway, I like to cook, especially the traditional dishes people are now calling soul food. I don't know whether you know it or not, but traditional black cooking is probably the least well known of all the great cuisines of the world. I just can't eat in most of these so-called soul-food restaurants! Don't get me going on food or you'll be stuck here for weeks! I had the pizza and sangria in their house, so I invited all the Ramos family and Ruth to have dinner here and, do you know, they came, even Mr. Ramos! He's very careful with me now, but he still sort of halfway tries. So maybe his kidding me about your being here was a sort of way of raising the great forbidden subject. Who knows? I guess I don't trust most men very much.

Did you know Mr. Ramos was teasing me about you? Frankly, I didn't know whether you understood us or not. Your face didn't indicate anything. It's really not fair, is it, that we should be able to judge you by looking at you and you can't do that with us. You have to be very careful, don't you? But then, can't you judge sighted people's emotions by their voices very often? I guess we all have to be very careful.

I guess I wondered whether you understood us because most black people don't accept first impressions. We are a very suspicious people and I'm sure we lose a lot that way. My aunt used to say, "A heap see, but a few know," and I guess it's quite natural for us to think that way. The white systems we have to deal with have hidden their real workings from us. We have never been able to act honestly with the white people who run and own these big agencies. We compete with each other for the favor of these systems, so there are many areas in which we cannot be honest with each other. The whole thing is very mixed up. For example, you know, white prejudice completely reverses the truth! It was the slaves and their children who had to be devious, subtle and complicated. Masters and their children kind of had to be simple people. If you can *make* people do things, you don't have to persuade or trick them into doing what you want them to do.

If You Ain't in the Know, You Are in Danger

· *From John Langston Gwaltney,* Drylongso: A Self-Portrait of Black America ·

Collected from John Oliver.

You know, I hate it when somebody who is dumber than me tries to trick me. I just listen to all that bullshit, and I don't side with any of them because I know that they are all together against me. That's just more of that I'm-bad-but-I-want-everybody-to-say-I'm-good shit. My brother went for bad, you know that, but he was bad and he knew that was wrong and he knew that nobody was going to thank him for being bad. Now, we know that you can't be good and bad at the same time, but Chahlie don't know that because his mama done told him that he can do anything he feel like doing, so that's how he sees things. See, they figure if nobody blows the whistle, then nothing wrong has gone down. As long as they can make somebody say that rough is smooth, they are happy. Like that place they shot up over there in Vietnam — the first thing they want to do is to prove that those dudes didn't mean to do what everybody know they did. What difference does it make whether the dude meant to do it; he did it, didn't he? Now, how that really was is these gray dudes went over there and couldn't make these Vietnam people do what they wanted to make them do, so they treated them like roaches. They lynched those people because they was mad with them, and if they had not been black, then they would not have treated them that way. Did you ever hear of whitefolks dropping napalm or atomic bombs on other whitefolks? You have *not* heard of that and you are not going to hear of it, either! Like I told you, whitefolks don't care nothing about what the truth is. It's like when you lie but so much you don't know what the truth is. This man thinks the truth is what is good for him and a lie is anything that is good for us.

I wish you would write a book about that. Why do whitefolks have to be bad and good at the same time? If they get what they want, why can't they just go with that? You know what they used to say about street angels and house devils? This dude don't want to admit that there is anything wrong with him. This devil that is handing out more hell than anybody wants everybody to think that he is an angel. You could whip head till hell freeze over, but hell is still hell and you can't *be* decent and *do* rotten things.

Sometimes I really do think that there is something wrong with this man's wig. I mean, they really do act kind of simple. All the black cats I know who go for bad do that because they kind of like being bad. They want you to know that they are bad asses! If a black bad cat gets half a chance, he'll tell you, "I'm bad, don't mess with me!" Everybody knows what a man like that will do. Now, with white people half of what they do just don't match the other half of what they do. I mean, they will shoot uku people who were just minding their own business, and then work like hell to get them to the hospital sometimes. Now, I cannot get to that. Why didn't they just leave those people alone to begin with?

When I used to live in the projects, a whole gang of cops came down there looking for some boy that they said was a sniper. Well now, I'm coming home from work and it has been a long time since I was a boy. But six of these guinea cops start beating on me. Now, if you know why, I know why! They took my pay and beat and kicked me like I was the worst criminal in this world. Now, after they beat me for nothing, one of them says, "Let the nigger go." Now, the others say, "We have to get this man to the hospital." Now, I didn't want to go to the hospital, because if the cops will half kill you, the doctors might finish you. But, do you know, they made me go to the hospital anyhow? I had not done a damned thing! I never did get my money and I had to pay $109.50 to the hospital. Now, what kind of sense does that make, will you tell me? I knew these cops wanted my money, so I told them what I had and where it was. But they had to beat me anyway. It wasn't just me—they were beating anybody and everybody they saw, women and little kids! Now, they found this so-called sniper and he was a white high school kid, but they didn't beat his ass and they didn't even put him in jail. The only person he shot was a black woman. Now, I don't understand what those cops were trying to prove. They hurt more people than the sniper and they stole people's money and stripped grown men and women in the street.

Now, these junkies out here are doing the same thing with the permission of the cops. But if I show my black face in certain places, every cop in creation is right there. "What is your business here?" "Keep moving, nigger." "Do you work for some white family around here?" Shit, this might just as soon be South Africa. See, that's so these junkies they are making down here don't go up there and sock it to those big pushers up there living in those fine castles.

They do everybody that is not their color that way. I mean, they will bomb the shit out of some little country that never did anything to them, and then pat theirself on the back because they sent some Band-Aids and a jackleg doctor over there to patch up these kids that would have been fine if they had left them alone. I think it would make more sense to give them Vietnamese some planes and ships so they could stop crazy people from bombing them. I mean, it's like this nut that was going around killing women and writing on the walls, "Stop me before I kill again." It's the same thing! You know, they can just act like the truth is whatever they feel like it is.

I see these damn commercials telling me to "see America first."
Now, how do I know that my family can go where these white people are going? I'm not going to spend my money to have some dude
spit in my soup. I can cook, so I don't need to pay for a hard time
from Howard Johnson or any of them other places. Now, if they tell
me that black people are just as welcome as anybody else, that don't
mean a damn thing either, because I have been asked to go to places
by whitefolks who almost had a shit fit when I got there. You can't
believe nothing the man says. If I go to a place and check it out, then
I know what is going down—that day, anyway. A white woman is
going to find a hell of a lot more gracious living than I am in most of
those places. Even if she wasn't welcome in there, they are not going
to go upside her head or put her in jail, like they would you or me.
That's one of the worst things about the whole country. Half of everything you have to know about doing anything here is left out. If you
ain't in the know, you are in danger!

DARYL CUMBER DANCE

Driving While Black

When I was a young instructor at Virginia State College in the
early 1960s, I carpooled with Ray, an assistant professor, and Gene,
a graduate student. As we left the college and drove through the
small White town of Colonial Heights, we were always careful to
observe the rather low speed limit because the town had a reputation
of being a speed trap and of being particularly hostile to Blacks.
From its opening in 1883, the college had faced hostility from Ettrick
and Colonial Heights, neighboring White mill-town communities
that resented a class of "uppity" educated Negroes in its midst.

On this day, Gene drove slowly as usual, but when he pulled into
the right lane to prepare to get onto the interstate, we heard a siren
go off and looked back to see lights flashing. Perplexed, Gene
stopped. A white officer strode to the car and angrily demanded,
"Why'd you cut in front of that *Wh-a-a-te* lady back thar?" It did not
matter, of course, that Gene had not checked to ascertain the race
and gender of the driver in the car well behind him in the right lane

when he pulled over. No explanation would suffice. As a Black driver, he wasn't simply given a ticket and sent on his way. He was informed that he would have to pay the large fine before he would be allowed to get back into his car and proceed. Since none of us had that much cash on hand and they wouldn't take a check, Gene was taken to jail while Ray and I drove around trying to find a place to cash a check.

Many hours later, with Gene behind the wheel, we pulled onto the highway, breathing a sigh of relief. There had been no physical attack, no beating, no unfortunate incident in the jail. We were lucky. Many who were "guilty" of DWB suffered much more disastrous consequences. As angry as we were, we drove down the highway joking about the incident and the officer's accent, warning Gene, "Look out, don't drive too close to that *Wh-a-a-te* lady over thar!"

Chapter 7

Soul Food

I'm eating higher up on the hog now.
—Traditional saying

I yam what I am.
—Ralph Ellison's Invisible Man

White folks be talkin' about classic and they mean
Beethoven . . . and French cooking. Classic to me is
James Brown and soul food.
—Verta Mae Grosvenor, Vibration Cooking

While African American cooking, often known as soul food or down-home cooking, is certainly a derivative of African cuisine, it largely developed as a result of the exigencies of life as a slave. On the plantation, the best of food went to the master's table, of course, and the Negroes had to make do with the discards—the trash that was generally considered uneatable. Thus their lot usually included the undesirable parts of the pig (the intestines, feet, jowls, tails, brains, tripe, and maws, the scavenger fish that would otherwise be thrown out (such as catfish), the rotten or spoiled fruits, the less attractive parts of vegetables (such as the tops of turnips and beets),[1] and the stale bread. Once life improved for the Black man, one of his favorite sayings was, "I'm eating higher up on the hog now," suggesting that he could afford pork chops, ham, and other choice parts rather than the remnants of the hog. But the fact of the matter is that enslaved Africans had transformed those discards into such succulent dishes that, no matter their

---

[1]Numerous tales exist about efforts of animals to trick others into having the least attractive parts of vegetables. See "Bobtail Beat the Devil" in Chapter 1.

improved financial situation, many in the African American communities continued to enjoy chitterlings[2] and pigs' feet and corn pone and fruit cobblers (made from overripe fruit) and bread puddings (made from stale bread). Indeed these became (at least for many) our gourmet foods, our dishes of choice. For more than thirty years, from the time I married until a few years before her death, my mother always prepared a meal of chitterlings and potato salad and greens as a special treat for my birthday. I, like Ralph Ellison, appreciate that "Chitterlings [are] a part of a high low-class cuisine" (*Going to the Territory*). Today there are chitterlings sites on the Internet (www.chitterlings.com and www.bsc.net/williec/chitterlings.html), not to mention other soul food sites and chat rooms too numerous to mention.

The meager allowances of food provided the enslaved African Americans were often supplemented by wild game and fish that they could catch, trap, or otherwise kill on their own at night, or on Sundays, or whenever they could find a free hour from their toiling for the master.[3] Occasionally they could enjoy chickens and eggs since these were small enough to be easily stolen and concealed in a cooking pot. Then, too, some of them were allowed a few chickens of their own and a number of them had a little plot for raising vegetables.

It's not surprising that there are a lot of popular one-pot dishes since the enslaved African Americans had limited access to utensils and cooking equipment. Stoves were rare and the cooking was done over an open fire. In some instances a ditch would be dug, wood laid in it and burned, and the entire body of an animal cooked there (Solomon Northup, *Twelve Years a Slave*). Of course, those Blacks who cooked for the master had the opportunity to improvise recipes from choicer fare and to prepare them using the best cooking stoves available (assuming the master was reasonably well-heeled). On a

---

[2]Chitterlings are the small intestines—and thus may be perceived as the filthiest and least desirable part of the hog.

[3]If any conclusions can be reached from slave tales, the opossum was a favorite meal. This is reinforced by some slave narrators as well: Solomon Northup declares in *Twelve Years a Slave*, "verily there is nothing in all butcherdom so delicious as a roaster 'possum."

special occasion, like Christmas, they might even be allowed to cook in the plantation kitchen (Northup). The Christmas celebration was in some instances quite a sumptuous affair, perhaps something like the feast described in mouthwatering detail in Paul Laurence Dunbar's "The Party" (see chapter 3).

Most African American females (and a few males) learned to prepare certain traditional African American dishes from their grandmothers, mothers, and other females (and occasionally males). These dishes were often influenced by African cuisine. They were frequently prepared in the same way over an open fire and often in one pot. African foods such as yams, watermelon, legumes, okra, and grains remained popular with Africans in America, as did wildlife such as deer, rabbits, squirrels, birds, and (of course) opossums. As in Africa, the African American's meals were predominantly vegetarian (this not so much by choice as circumstance). African American cuisine reflects a number of other influences in this diverse nation: Native American, British, Spanish, Caribbean, French; the French influence is especially obvious in African American dishes from Louisiana. But wherever Africans have settled in the United States, the Caribbean, Canada, and in Central and South America, their dishes often bear many similarities to their African forbears.

Soul food cuisine includes such fare as homemade biscuits, rolls, spoon bread, cracklin' bread,[4] hoecakes, ashcakes,[5] cornbread, hushpuppies, black-eyed peas, greens, cabbage, red beans and rice, fried okra, squash, succotash, macaroni and cheese, candied yams, stewed tomatoes, corn pudding, potato salad, coleslaw, deviled eggs, homemade pickles, barbecued ribs, fried chicken, baked chicken, smothered chicken, chicken and dumplings, fried fish (especially catfish), baked shad, gumbo, chitterlings, pigs' feet, pigs' tails, souse, ham, roast 'possum, venison steaks, smothered rabbit, watermelon, fruit cobblers, apple brown betty, bread pudding, pecan pie, lemon meringue pie, sweet-potato pie, chocolate cake, coconut cake, and

---

[4]Crackling is made from little pieces of pork fat and ham skin.

[5]These latter two, both made out of cornmeal, presumably got their names from their manner of preparation — hoecakes being held in a hoe over an open fire and ashcakes baked in an open fire. The hoe, allowing as it does for easy flipping, was a convenient spatula.

homemade ice cream. At Christmastime, turkey with dressing (oyster dressing was favored at my house), Smithfield or country ham, fruitcake, and eggnog grace the tables. Special breakfast treats include bacon, sausage, fish cakes, fried oysters, pork chops, grits, hash brown potatoes, and fritters. Popular drinks include homemade wine, homemade lemonade, a variety of punches (spiked and plain), soda pops, beer, coffee, and tea. The dishes that were served during slave celebrations are generally the dishes that will be found today in many homes for Sunday dinner and for other special occasions in Black communities: for celebrations and parties,[6] for barbecues, for Church homecomings, and after funerals. Most larger communities also have restaurants specializing in this fare, variously called soul-food restaurants, rib joints, greasy skillets, and chicken shacks. Often their name is preceded by "Mama's."

Several films and literary works have eulogized soul food: in addition to poems such as Dunbar's "The Party" and Johnson's "What's Mo Temptin' to de Palate" (included in this chapter), and novels such as Ntozake Shange's *Sassafrass, Cypress & Indigo*, there are movies such as Julia Dash's *Daughters of the Dust* (1991) and George Tillman Jr.'s *Soul Food* (1997). Soul food is prominent as theme, subject, or scene in works by Toni Morrison, Alice Walker, Paule Marshall, Gloria Naylor, Dori Sanders, Ralph Ellison, and a host of other African American writers.

Despite the general popularity of soul food, we should note that Black Muslims and some other groups in the community do not eat pork for religious reasons. Many Black militants have rejected much soul food as slave fare. Dick Gregory declared that "the quickest way to wipe out a group of people is to put them on a soul food diet" (*Natural Diet for Folks Who Eat*). Like the spirituals, blues, and Black dialect, soul food is also something that aspiring Blacks often leave behind as they move into the larger community. Finally, because the food is so high in fat and cholesterol, many health-conscious Blacks either avoid it or modify the way it is traditionally prepared. Whole cookbooks now are dedicated to preparing soul food in a healthful

---

[6]The popular rent parties that started in Harlem during the Depression often highlighted the food in their advertisements. (See Langston Hughes's "Rent Parties" in chapter 3.)

way.[7] (See for example Wendolyn Wallace Johnson's two versions of greens in this chapter.)

Clearly the whole issue of soul food and related icons goes far beyond the kitchen and the dining room table and has significant ramifications in the larger culture. No symbol is more beloved in White America than that of Aunt Jemima, the beloved smiling, buxom mammy cook in apron, a figure so revered that the Daughters of the Confederacy petitioned Congress to erect a monument in Washington in her honor (White, *Ar'nt I a Woman?*). Aunt Jemima has long been the trademark for Quaker Oats pancakes and syrup; the company updated her image in the early 1990s, removing the stereotypical kerchief. When Quaker Oats announced in 1994 that popular singer Gladys Knight would represent their products in television advertisements, many in the Black community were appalled that so popular an entertainer would allow herself to become what they viewed as a modern-day Aunt Jemima. That image is regarded in the Black community not as a symbol of African American family cooks but rather as the White society's conception of the Black woman as *their* cook—an icon of slavery.

It is interesting to note that when Tiger Woods won the U.S. Masters golf tournament in April 1997, fellow golfer Fuzzy Zoeller felt more inclined to talk about Black food than about Tiger's golf game: "That little boy is driving well. . . . You pat him on the back . . . and tell him not to serve fried chicken next year. Got it? . . . Or collard greens or whatever the hell they serve." Although Zoeller eventually apologized after a firestorm of criticism, the pervasive patronizing attitude toward Blacks and their food is apparent.

The watermelon is another item that has become a folk icon, one that evokes mixed responses from Blacks who have been so maligned about their supposed love of watermelon. Consequently watermelon is often avoided when Blacks attend mixed-race gatherings though it is a staple at closed community affairs. It is no surprise that most of the attendees at the annual Watermelon Festival in Richmond,

---

[7]These include Danella Carter's *Down Home Wholesome*, Wilbert Jones's *The Healthy Soul Food Cookbook*, Ruby Banks-Payne's *Ruby's Low-Fat Soul-Food Cookbook*, Fabiola Demps Gaines and Roniece Weaver's *The New Soul Food Cookbook for People with Diabetes*, and Dorothy I. Height's *The Black Family Dinner Quilt Cookbook: Health Conscious Recipes & Food Memories*.

Virginia—a Black-majority city—are Whites. Many comedians, like Godfrey Cambridge, joke that when Blacks living in integrated communities buy a watermelon in the grocery store they have it wrapped and pretend it is a bowling ball in order to sneak it into their homes. Langston Hughes's Simple ridicules Negroes who "pass"—pass for nonchitterling and nonwatermelon eaters (*The Best of Simple*). So hated was the image of watermelons that LeRoi Jones was threatened with expulsion for eating a watermelon on Howard University's campus. He declares that the dean reprimanded him, "Do you realize you're sitting right in front of the highway where white people can see you? Do you realize that this school is the capstone of Negro higher education? Do you realize that you're compromising the Negro?" (Jones, "Philistinism"). So hated is the image of the watermelon that I quickly vetoed Indiana University Press's initial proposal to use a watermelon for the cover of *Shuckin' and Jivin'*. Numerous jokes abound about watermelons: "He's got one foot in the ghetto and the other on a watermelon rind"; "she swallowed a watermelon" (referring to a woman's pregnancy).

Perhaps the most controversial soul food icon is the chitterling. Many observers have noted similar reactions to that of Ellison's Invisible Man when he suggests that Black people can be caused the greatest of humiliation by being confronted with liking certain soul foods. He goes on to imagine the extreme shame he would cause his college president, Dr. Bledsoe, if he accused him of liking chitterlings: "Bledsoe, you're a shameless chitterling eater! I accuse you of relishing hog bowels! Ha! And not only do you eat them, you sneak and eat them in *private* when you think you're unobserved." He then envisions forcing Bledsoe to lug out yards of chitterlings along with mustard greens, pigs' ears, pork chops, and black-eyed peas—concluding that with others present, this revelation would be worse than accusing him of raping a blind and lame old woman. Chitterlings are often used to suggest the worst reserved for Blacks: thus the segregated booking agency for Black Vaudevillians and minstrels, such as Butterbeans and Susie and Moms Mabley, was often called "the chitlin' circuit."

I begin this chapter with a few items regarding food, but most of the chapter is composed of traditional recipes from my own collection and from family and friends. I have tried to acknowledge individuals from whom recipes have been borrowed, but some of the recipes in my collection have been a part of my own cuisine for so long that I don't recall the sources. The recipes here have been passed along for generations in families, but as always, contemporary culinary artists work their own variations on them. I apologize that the cooks who provided the recipes are not always explicit about portions, since most don't bother to measure: *a pinch, a dash, to taste,* and similar descriptions are open to your own interpretation. Like other forms of Black culture, African American recipes are improvisational. Vertamae Grosvenor probably speaks for most soul cooks when she declares that she does not "measure or weigh anything. I cook by vibration. . . . Different strokes for different folks. Do your thing your way" (*Vibration Cooking*).

Rabbit in de Briar Patch

· *From Francis Edward Abernathy and Carolyn Fiedler Satterwhite,*
Juneteenth Texas ·

The following is a slave verse collected by WPA interviewers in Texas.

Rabbit in de briar patch
Squirrel in de tree,
Wish I could go huntin',
But I ain't free.

MAGGIE POGUE JOHNSON

What's Mo Temptin to de Palate?

· *From* Virginia Dreams/Lyrics for the Idle Hour ·

Johnson, like her better-known male contemporaries Paul Laurence Dunbar and
Daniel Webster, often treated folk life in dialect.

What's mo' temptin' to de palate,
  When you's wuked so hard all day,
En cum in home at ebentime
  Widout a wud to say, —

En see a stewin' in de stove
   A possum crisp en brown,
Wid great big sweet potaters,
   A layin' all aroun'.

What's mo' temptin' to de palate,
   Den a chicken bilin' hot,
En plenty ob good dumplin's,
   A bubblin' in de pot;
To set right down to eat dem,
   En 'pease yo' hunger dar,
'Tis nuffin' mo' enjoyin',
   I sho'ly do declar.

What's mo' temptin' to de palate
   Den a dish ob good baked beans,
En what is still mo' temptin'
   Den a pot brimfull ob greens;
Jis biled down low wid bacon,
   Almos' 'til dey's fried,
En a plate ob good ol' co'n cakes
   A layin' on de side.

What's mo' temptin' to de palate
   Den on Thanksgibin' Day
To hab a good ol' tuckey
   Fixed some kin' o' way;
Wid cranber'y sauce en celery,
   All settin' on de side,
En eat jis 'til yo' appetite
   Is sho' full satisfied.

What's mo' temptin' to de palate,
   Den in de Summer time,
To bus' a watermillion
   Right from off de vine;
En set right down to eat it
   In de coolin breeze,

Wif nuffin' to moles' you,
　Settin' neaf de apple trees.

What's mo' temptin' to de palate,
　Den poke chops, also lam',
En what is still mo' temptin'
　Den good ol' col' biled ham;
Veal chops dey ain't bad,
　Put de mutton chops in line,
I tell you my ol' appetite,
　Fo' all dese t'ings do pine.

What's mo' temptin' to de palate,
　When you cum from wuk at night,
To set down to de fiah,
　A shinin' jis so bright,
De ol' 'oman walks in, —
　Wid supper brilin' hot,
En a good ol' cup ob coffee,
　Jis steamin' out de pot.

'Tis den I kin enjoy myse'f,
　En eat dar by de fiah,
Case puttin' way good eatin's
　Is sho'ly my desire;
Dar's nuffin dat's so temptin',
　Dat to me is a treat,
Den settin' at a table
　Wid plenty good to eat.

Ain't Ready for Integration

I collected this tale in Richmond, Virginia, in 1974.

This Black lady was so excited when integration came and she could eat in a nice White restaurant. So she got all dressed up and went there Sunday evening. The White waitress come over to her and was all nice and mannerly: "What can I get for you, Ma'am?"

Black lady was so pleased—never had a White person call her "Ma'am"—and serve her food as well!

"I'll have some pigs' feet and collards," she smiled in pleasant anticipation.

"Oh, I'm sorry, we don't serve *that*," the waitress declared.

"Then, just bring me some chitlins, please."

"What?" the waitress exclaimed.

"Chit-ter-lings," she pronounced it more carefully this time.

"What is *that*?" the waitress asked.

"Well, what kinda soul food *do* you have?" she impatiently asked.

"*Soul* food? What in the world is *soul* food?" the waitress inquired.

"Lord have mercy! You White folks just ain't ready for integration!" the lady exclaimed as she haughtily pushed her chair back from the table and hightailed it out the door.

DARYL CUMBER DANCE ET AL.

Chitterlings

This recipe is my own combination devised from my recollections of Mother's preparation and a consultation with Wendolyn Wallace Johnson.

Chitterlings may be purchased cleaned and ready to cook, but even then one should carefully check and rinse them. You might begin by preboiling chitterlings for five minutes before rinsing them. If one uses fresh chitterlings, all residue must be rinsed out of them. Then place them in warm water and wash them as one would scrub clothes until all the grease (although some people like to leave a little fat to retain seasoning) and any remaining residue are removed. Continue changing the water and running water through the chitterlings until the water is clear.

Put the carefully cleaned chitterlings in a pot and add a sliced *onion*, some crushed *red pepper pods*, a *garlic* clove, a few stalks of *celery*, some *beer*, and a pinch of *salt*. Note that no water is needed, since they already have a lot of water in them. You may put a potato on top to absorb the odor, but this will not be eaten. Simmer for two to three hours, stirring and checking water. Pour excess water off the top. After chitterlings become tender, cut them up. Continue cooking for another hour or two. Season to taste with *vinegar, hot sauce, salt,* and *pepper.*

Fried Chitterlings

After chitterlings have been cooked as directed above, take small pieces and dip them in a batter of *eggs* and *flour.* Then deep fry.

VERONICA BELL CUMBER
Baked Chicken

Shake one *cut-up chicken* in a paper bag with *flour, salt,* and *pepper* until coated. Place in a buttered baking pan. Slice an *onion* over the chicken. Sprinkle some *Jamaican Pickapepper Sauce* over the chicken (if you don't have Pickapepper use A-1 Sauce). Put about *four slices of bacon* over the chicken. Bake at 350 degrees until done (about 45 minutes). Check often and add a little water if necessary. You should have a nice gravy in the pan.

VERONICA BELL CUMBER
Fried Chicken with Gravy

Put *flour, paprika, dry mustard, salt,* and *pepper* to taste in a brown paper bag. Add a *cut-up chicken* or chicken parts and shake until well coated. Deep fry until golden brown. Drain on paper towel.

Gravy: Leave only about three tablespoons of the grease in the pan. Add 2–3 tablespoons of *flour* and a sliced *onion.* Cook on high heat, stirring constantly until the flour is so brown it appears burned. Carefully add two cups of water (if you put it in too fast, the grease will splatter) and stir until smooth. Add more water if necessary to achieve the consistency you desire. Season with salt and pepper.

DARYL CUMBER DANCE ET AL.

Pigs' Feet

This is my combination of my mother's and Wendolyn Wallace Johnson's recipes.

Cover *split pigs' feet* with boiling water in a large sauce pan. Liberally add the following seasonings: *vinegar, salt, catsup, hot sauce, Worcestershire sauce, garlic, red pepper, black pepper, chili, barbecue sauce, sliced onion,* and *diced green pepper.* Boil (don't simmer) until done (meat should be falling off the bones). Then place in a casserole dish, cover with more barbecue sauce, and run in oven at 350 degrees for a few minutes.

DARYL CUMBER DANCE ET AL.

Pork Chop Casserole

Brown *6–8 chops.* Sprinkle 1 cup of *uncooked rice* and 1 envelope of *dry onion soup mix* in a large baking dish. Add pork chops. Cover with 1 can of *cream of mushroom soup.* Add water to cover and bake at 375 degrees for one hour.

OSWALD DIAMOND

Beef Ribs

I have been preparing this recipe from my good friend, the late Oswald Diamond, for many years. I expect there are some variations from the original.

Put 2 pounds of *beef ribs* in a casserole dish with 2 cups of water, a sliced *onion,* ½ cup of *vinegar,* 1½ teaspoons of *pickling spice,* and some *chili peppers.* Marinade for 2 hours. Cover the casserole dish and cook the ribs in the oven until tender (about 2 hours). Drain ribs, put in a greased dish, and brush *barbecue sauce, Worchestershire sauce,* and *salt* over them. Bake, turning and basting, for about 20–30 minutes.

QUINCY MOORE

Spicy Country Meat Loaf

Preheat the oven to 350 degrees.

In a skillet sauté 1 cup of *finely diced onions* in a tablespoon of *extra virgin olive oil*, stirring until soft and slightly brown.

In a large bowl soak ½ cup of cut-up *Hawaiian sweet bread* in ½ cup of *whole milk* until softened. Add 1½–2 pounds of *ground sirloin*, the cooked onions, 1 slightly beaten *egg*, 2 tablespoons of *Parm Plus Garlic Herb Seasoning Blend*, 2 tablespoons of *Cajun seasoning*, 2 tablespoons of *hot pepper sauce*, 4 ounces of *Trappey's cut okra and tomatoes*, and 4 ounces of *La Costera Mexican Hot Sauce*. Season to taste with *salt* and *pepper*. Shape into a loaf.

Bake loaf in a large greased baking dish or loaf pan for 1 hour, covered with aluminum foil. Remove the foil and pierce the meat several times with a fork. Mix 1 can of *tomato sauce*, 4 ounces of *La Costera Mexican Hot Sauce*, and 1 teaspoon of *red pepper flakes*, and pour over the meat. Place 4 strips of *green and red bell peppers* and 3 strips of *sweet fire-roasted peppers* on top of the meat. Bake uncovered for 30 minutes.

Let stand for 15 minutes before serving.

Yield: 6 servings.

NIKKI GIOVANNI

I Always Think of Meatloaf

When Grandmother died the O'Neal sisters who were in their nineties and blind brought four eggs that their hen had just laid: "For Lou" which is what they called her. Reverend James was there explaining why he did not announce "Mrs. Watson's passing" because "you know how people are." Mommy seemed to know what he meant but I did not "know" how people are then though I have learned. As is the case with small towns like Knoxville many friends and neighbors brought food and drink: Ham, macaroni with sautéed onions and peppers and three cheeses, homemade breads, apple cakes, and because it is still sort of country, butter, homemade preserves and of course the O'Neal sisters to whom Grandmother had always been very kind especially as they lost their sight, newly laid eggs. I wanted Meatloaf. I always think of meatloaf when I want a comfort food.

My grandmother did not like Meatloaf so it became an elegant presentation when she cooked it. In her day, even to my remembrance, you could go to the butcher and purchase a piece of round steak. The butcher would grind it for you on the spot and Grandmother always had a couple of pork chops ground with it. My sister makes a more elegant loaf as she caters and does things more upscale. Hers is a veal with pork and beef which is very Californian. Mommy buys her meat already ground and she, like many people, adds oatmeal or bread crumbs not to "stretch it" as some people think but to make it firmer. We all mix it with our hands. Grandmother taught us all that.

I like ground round, one and a half pound is just about right. I add one beaten egg which I beat with my kitchen fork that I got from Mommy in a two cup measuring cup. Grandmother and Gary, though not with the same bowl, both use egg bowls. It's not that I in any way dislike egg bowls, I have one and I think it is a very pretty bowl but Grandmother and my sister both messied up the kitchen when they cook. One thing for this, another for that. Mommy and I tend to keep the kitchen neat washing and putting away as we go; using the same measuring cup or bowl for many different things and since meatloaf is peasant food it must be mixed with your hands. Grandmother taught us that.

The meat is cold so your hands will get cold while you mix so be sure to keep a little running water on warm to get the color back in your fingers. When the egg and beef are well mixed but not overly so, add your spices. But I should confess here: Lately I have been thinking of Margie's macaroni and cheese which she makes with onions and peppers. I cheat when I think about that and go to the freezer department of my local supermarket and purchase frozen peppers in a bag. I sauté them in olive oil while I do my egg and meat mixing. I add them to the bowl just before the spices. I still turn it by hand, however.

There is nothing in the world that can't be improved by a bit of garlic. Have a headache? Eat a garlic clove. Love life suffering? A little garlic in a quarter stick of butter two scrambled eggs that are angel wings light will bring him around. Scared of werewolves or the tax man or your neighbor next door? Eat lots of garlic until you are sweating it: Everyone will leave you alone. So while I don't load it up with garlic never using more than two or three cloves or garlic powder of which you only need a dash (but never garlic salt as you do not need more salt) I am generous with it. And fennel. Fennel is one of the wonders of the culinary world. I am generous with that, too. And then you need what I call the Italian herbs—thyme, rosemary, a pinch of savory. Mix those by hand, too. Now open one medium size can of tomato sauce. Slowly mix that in until you have a nice warm feeling as the room temperature sauce will help your hand come back to color. Now turn that into a loaf dish. Wash your hands and give it a once over. It should look wonderful. Open a small can of tomato sauce and pour it over the top of your loaf. Take a medium sized yellow or white onion, you can actually use purple but the color will be lost in this dish, and slice it as thin as you can. Place the slices down the spine of the meatloaf. Arrange four to six slices of bacon across the top. Sprinkle a little more garlic powder and freshly ground pepper. Place in the middle of a 250-degree oven and go about your business for the next hour or so. The juices will bubble and the bacon will be very brown when it is done. Take out of the oven, let sit until it cools. Drop biscuits and a bit of salad add to the meal or if you're having a truly bad day, boil a couple of potatoes in their jackets, slather them in butter, load up on the pepper, pour any Zinfandel and things will look up but if you just want to remember a wonderful woman you need to make Spoonbread. Mix a bit of cornmeal, one beaten egg and enough milk to make a smooth though runny mixture. A dash of salt, a smidgen of sugar, stir with a wooden spoon as you would grits until it is firm. Turn the batter into a round baking dish you have hand buttered with a good pat of butter. And while you wait for it to soufflé you can sit at the table and cry a little bit because there's nothing wrong with crying for the people and the things we have lost. When the bread is ready, though, you have to stop because Spoonbread has to come out on time. My Grandmother taught me that.

WENDOLYN WALLACE JOHNSON
Baked Shad

Carefully clean and dry a *large shad*. Put it in the center of a large piece of aluminum foil. Liberally sprinkle the inside and outside of the fish with *seafood seasoning, pepper, garlic* (and any other seasoning you like). Add a little *salt* inside and out. Squeeze *fresh lemon juice* on the fish and then slice the lemon and put it on top of the fish. Stuff the fish with *Stovetop Stuffing Mix.* You may add *crab meat* to the stuffing as well. Cover the fish with *strips of bacon.* Wrap the foil tightly around the whole fish. (It is important that the fish be tightly wrapped.) Bake at 275 degrees for six hours.

QUINCY MOORE
Jambalaya

Boil *one chicken* for 45 minutes with *bay leaf,* and *salt* and *pepper* to taste.

In a separate pan, make a roux of ¼ cup of *bacon drippings* and 3 tablespoons of *flour.* Add *2 onions,* a cup of *scallions,* and 2 cloves of *garlic,* 2 stalks of *celery,* a cup of *green peppers,* and stir fry for 10 minutes. Add cooked *Andouille sausage, ham, chicken,* 2 teaspoons of *salt,* 1 teaspoon of *cayenne,* some *chili powder,* 2 cans of tomatoes, 1½ teaspoons of *thyme, oregano, basil, paprika,* and *sage* to taste. Add 3 cups of *chicken broth,* bring to a boil, then turn to lowest heat. Add 2 cups of *uncooked rice* and cook for 45 minutes. Uncover and stir well. Add *shrimp* as desired (I like a lot of shrimp). Heat 10 minutes until rice dries out.

DARYL CUMBER DANCE
Saltfish and Cabbage

Boil *saltfish* for 30 minutes and set aside. Cut up *cabbage* and fry it in oil at very low heat. Add *chopped onions, scallions,* and *green pepper* to cabbage. Take the skin off the fish and flake the fish into fine pieces. Add *onion* and fry with the fish. Add the fish to the cabbage when the cabbage is almost done. Put in some *diced tomatoes* and steam everything together until the cabbage is cooked to your taste (just a few minutes). It is not necessary to add any salt to this dish.

FRANCES SMITH FOSTER

Sloppy Salmon

Dr. Foster included the following comments in her letter with the recipe.

Here's my "family recipe" for "Sloppy Salmon." It's an essential part of our holiday breakfasts (every Christmas, New Year's, etc.). Generally we serve it with scrambled eggs (or omelet), grits, toast, and chilled canned peaches. (Don't know why chilled canned peaches but that's the way I learned to eat it. I do sometimes do chilled apricots or fruit salad instead, but it's not authentic then.) We also do this dish for dinner sometimes—using rice instead of grits—and green peas. I cooked it Friday to ascertain measurements—since we just "do it." So this is Friday's version.

2 tablespoons margarine or butter
⅓ cup chopped onion
1 can salmon (15 ounces) with juice
1 cup water
2 eggs
⅛ teaspoon black pepper
1 teaspoon salt
1 teaspoon sage

Melt margarine in skillet (we use a cast iron one) and sauté onion until transparent.

In mixing bowl, break up the salmon. Stir in remaining ingredients.

Add to onions. Bring to boil and cover for 15 minutes. Remove cover and cook until enough liquid has evaporated to make this a good consistency to go over grits or rice.

JOANNE V. GABBIN
Pot Meals

Most of the meals we ate in our three-story rowhouse on Baltimore's Eastside were "pot meals." Pot meals held so many possibilities. Mama cooked Great Northern beans and ham hocks; string beans, potatoes and neck bones; ox tail stew; collard greens with streak-o-lean; and her remarkable chicken pot pie. Every night she made two pans of biscuits, even after we began to buy Schmidt's Blue Ribbon Bread from the corner grocery store. When we'd come home from school, we would go straight to the kitchen where that night's dinner would be sputtering and whistling from the family iron cook pot on the left back eye of the gas stove. Sometimes Mama lifted the lid so we could smell the savory aromas. But we knew that she could not lift the lid on the pot when she cooked the chicken pot pie. For many years we never understood why and just accepted it as one of the many mysteries of Mama's kitchen.

Mama learned to cook during the Depression years. Her mother told her how to stretch a pot so that it would feed a lot of people. "Add some water to the bean soup, put in more potatoes, add twice the onions and tomatoes to the ox tail stew," she admonished, "but always add love. Love multiplies." Pot meals allowed for drop-ins: nephews, nieces, friends, neighbors, aunts and uncles who found their way to our house around dinnertime. Mama would simply have us get a chair or two from the dining room (we never ate in the dining room; we always ate in the kitchen). Though the aluminum table with the red-and-white marbled top would often be filled to overflowing, she would squeeze one more plate on the table with little ceremony, except for her customary ritual of explaining that the black specks that we saw in the stew were ground black pepper. For the only vanity she indulged herself was her reputation as a scrupulously clean cook.

JOANNE V. GABBIN

Chicken Pot Pie

In places outside of Baltimore known as chicken and dumplings.

1 large chicken
1 large onion (diced)
3 stalks of celery (diced)
1½ teaspoons pepper
1 teaspoon salt
½ teaspoon poultry seasoning
2 cups all-purpose flour
1 cup cold water

Cover the chicken with water in a large pot. Add the diced onion and celery; then add the pepper, salt, and poultry seasoning. Boil until the chicken is tender (I like it falling off the bone).

For the dumplings, combine the flour and cold water. Stir until soft dough is formed. Place dough on floured board and knead until firm. Separate dough into three parts and roll each part until dough is very thin. Cut into 1 × 3 inch strips.

Bring 9 cups broth and chicken to boil. Drop in strips of dough. Continue dropping the dough into the pot, making sure to lightly push the strips into the broth. Stir gently to prevent the dumplings from sticking together. When all the strips of dough are in the broth, reduce heat and simmer for 15 minutes until the dough is firm. Remember: cover the pot and don't remove the lid for the entire time the pot is simmering.

Delicious!

ETHEL MORGAN SMITH

Aunt Honey's Rabbit Stew and Peach Wine

The following selection is an account of a visit that author Ethel Morgan Smith
fantasizes she and her sister (Pearl and Ruby are the fictional names here) had to
Louisville, Alabama, with her legendary Aunt Honey, whom she never really met
in the flesh but knew through stories that circulated in her family.

A welcomed peace descended upon them as they stared into the small fire. In spite of the Alabama heat, Aunt Honey's house was cool.

"Let's eat." Aunt Honey lifted the stew from the fire and set it on the hearth of the fireplace. From under the ashes in the fireplace, she pulled four medium-sized sweet potatoes. Between her bed and the back door was her dining room. One of her walls was papered in three panels of what used to be country rose patterned wallpaper. The middle panel had started to peel down, but it just dropped, like it decided it didn't want to fall after all. In the corner of the dining room stood the same knick-knack pole that was in their living room. But unlike theirs, it was filled with rocks and seashells of different shades of white. Next to the pole stood an oak washstand with a light blue and cream-colored pitcher on top. A cake of octagon soap set by the pitcher in a saucer, just like the plates that Aunt Honey and Ruby had set the table with—white porcelain, red roses dancing around the edge of them. They were the same plates that their family had donated to the church 25 years ago. Aunt Honey could lay a table like it was nobody's business. And most important to her, she hadn't acquired her table-setting skills in the kitchen of white women, like most of the colored women in Silk Hope.

"Pearl, git dem jelly glasses from under the bed," Aunt Honey ordered.

"Yes ma'am." Aunt Honey only drank water from the spring that ran behind her house, past the garden. Pearl wrestled with getting the glasses from under the bed; they were stacked in a wooden box. Afterwards she rinsed and filled them with cool, clear spring water that she dipped with a blue-specked tin dipper. None of Aunt Honey's flatware matched, but her napkins of white cotton were starched and ironed with a military slickness. Christmas trees were stitched on one end, and hollyhocks formed a colorful border around the edge of the napkins. Her dining room table was a telephone wire ring, covered with a starched, coarse white table cloth. Aunt Honey placed a piece of broken marble-looking surface in the center of the table, and then she eased the rabbit stew on top of it. Ribbons of grey smoke curled up from the hypnotic-smelling pot, with stew that was smothered with baby carrots, and onions, and what Pearl thought were white potatoes were dumplings. The spring water quenched Pearl's thirst and nurtured her spirit. And the feast moved her.

"This is good eating," Ruby finally said.

"Let us thank the Good Lord. Gracious Spirit of the Universe, we thank You for this food, and we pray that You bless everyone from the lowest to the highest. We know we ain't nothin' w'out You. Amen," Aunt Honey prayed.

"Amen," Pearl and Ruby said at the same time.

"Plenty good eatin' round cher. Auh go fishin' some days. Last week had fresh catfish. Squirrels, even ole possum, sometimes. Yes siree, plenty good eatin' round cher. You always welcome."

Peach Wine

Peel as many peaches as you want.
(Use the skin of the fruit.)
Allow to ferment for 2 weeks.
Strain, add sugar to taste.
Let stand another 2 weeks.
Strain, add sugar to taste.
Ready!

Rabbit Stew

If rabbit is fresh, soak as long as you can in cold water.
Make dumpling the same as biscuits, cut in squares.
Boil rabbit, add carrots, onions and any other vegetables.
Add dumplings.
Salt and pepper to taste

WENDOLYN WALLACE JOHNSON
Greens I

Put *ham hocks* or *smoked pork neckbones* in a large pot and cover with water. Simmer until well done (the meat should be falling off the bones). Clean and chop *collards* and *kale* (or any combination of greens you prefer). Add the greens to the pot of ham hocks or neckbones. Add some *diced onions* and *hot red peppers* if you wish. Add additional water whenever needed. Cook until greens are tender, adding *salt* when the greens are almost done.

WENDOLYN WALLACE JOHNSON
Greens II

This is the more healthful variation Ms. Johnson has improvised for her greens.

Clean and chop *collards* and *kale* and cover with *chicken broth* and ½ cup of *canola oil* or *corn oil*. Add *dillweed, red hot peppers, onions,* and a little *liquid smoke.* When greens are almost done, add *salt.*

DARYL CUMBER DANCE
Baked Beans

Mix a small can of *baked beans* with a *chopped onion,* a *chopped green pepper,* ½ teaspoon of *dry mustard,* one tablespoon of *molasses,* ½ cup of *brown sugar,* ½ teaspoon of *cloves,* and *catsup* to taste. Lay a few slices of *bacon* over the beans. Bake in oven at 350 degrees for an hour.

DOROTHY MONTAGUE
Corn Pudding

The corn pudding is usually served with the regular meal as a vegetable rather than as a dessert.

Mix 1 large can of *creamed corn*, 1 slightly beaten *egg*, 1 small can of *evaporated milk*, ¼ stick of *butter*, and 1 tablespoon of *sugar*. Stir well. Put the mixture in a greased casserole dish and bake at 325 degrees for 35–40 minutes. Be sure *not* to let the pudding cook until it is stiff.

MARTHA GILBERT
Corn Pudding

Put 2 teaspoons of *butter* in a one-quart casserole dish and place the dish in a hot oven until butter melts.

Put 2 cups of *milk* and 1 package of *frozen corn* in a saucepan. Bring to a boil over medium heat. Remove from the stove.

Beat three *eggs* in a mixing bowl until they are a lemon yellow. Add 3 tablespoons of *sugar* and a pinch of *salt* and blend with whisk for 20 seconds. Pour corn mixture into this bowl, stirring the egg mixture rapidly. Pour everything into the heated casserole dish. Cook in a 325 degree preheated oven until custard is set (a knife inserted into the mixture will come out clean).

DARYL CUMBER DANCE
Candied Yams

Cook *yams* in the oven until tender. Slice and put in a buttered casserole dish. Add sliced *bananas*, diced *pineapple*, *raisins*, some *brown sugar*, a dash of *salt*, a liberal number of pats of *butter*, and some *orange juice*. Bake at 350 degrees until bubbly.

DARYL CUMBER DANCE
Potato Salad

Boil, peel, and dice white *potatoes*. (If you use red potatoes, you may keep the peeling.) Boil and cut up *eggs*. Mix potatoes and eggs with liberal amounts of diced *celery, green pepper*, and *onions*. Mix with *mayonnaise, dry mustard*, and *pickle relish*. Add *celery salt, salt*, and *pepper* to taste. Sprinkle with *paprika*.

DARYL CUMBER DANCE
Deviled Eggs

Hard-boil *eggs*. Peel and cut in half lengthwise. Remove yolks and mash them, mixing with a small amount of *mayonnaise, mustard, salt, pepper*, and *relish*. This dish is great if you add a little *ground Smithfield* or *County Ham*, or *anchovies*, or *crumbled bacon*. Fill egg whites with yolk mixture and garnish with *paprika* or *parsley*.

DARYL CUMBER DANCE
Cucumber Salad

Slice *cucumbers, red onions*, and *tomatoes*. Toss with *salt, pepper, red wine vinegar*, a little *sugar*, and some chopped *hot chili pepper*.

DARYL CUMBER DANCE
Grits Casserole

Cook 1 cup of *grits* in 4 cups of water. In a separate dish beat 3 *eggs*. Add 1 cup *sour cream*, 1 teaspoon *salt*, ½ teaspoon of *white pepper*, and a dash of *nutmeg* to the eggs. Add grits and stir. Add 1 cup of grated *sharp cheddar cheese*. Put in casserole dish. Cover with ½ cup of cheddar cheese. Bake 40 minutes at 375 degrees.

ROZEAL DIAMOND
Rolls

Mix 1 *yeast cake,* 1 *egg,* and ½ cup of *sugar* in a bowl using a cup of warm water. Stir until smooth. In a separate bowl sift 4 cups of *flour* and add to it a pinch of *salt* and 4 heaping tablespoons of *Crisco shortening.* Knead until all lumps are gone. Slowly add the yeast mixture, kneading until velvety smooth and soft. Add water slowly as needed until the mixture is soft like velvet.

Put bread in a plastic bag and refrigerate until it rises.

Remove from refrigerator and grease a muffin pan. Break off mixture into small balls and place them in the muffin pan, two or three in each tin as desired.

Let rise to triple the original size.

Bake in an oven preheated to 375 degrees about 15 to 20 minutes until rolls are brown.

DARYL CUMBER DANCE ET AL.
Spoonbread

In a mixing bowl, mix 1 cup of *cornmeal,* 1 teaspoon *salt,* and 3 teaspoons of *baking powder.* Stir in 1 quart of *milk,* 4 well-beaten *eggs,* and 2 tablespoons of melted *butter.* Pour mixture into a greased deep casserole dish and bake at 375 degrees until set, about 25 minutes.

ESTHER VASSAR
Cornbread

I have been making this recipe for years. I apologize for any variations I may have made to Ms. Vassar's original.

Mix 1 package of *Washington Cornbread Mix* according to directions on package, adding ¼ can of *whole kernel corn,* drained.

Place shallow oven dish in oven with a little butter and allow it to melt and cover the bottom. Then pour the cornbread mix into the pan.

Bake according to directions on package. When cornbread is almost ready to turn brown, turn the oven to broil and brown the top that way.

SANDRA Y. GOVAN

My Mama's Corn Pone: or, Hot Water Cornbread

My mother made cornpone, or hot water cornbread, just for me and her. Whenever I returned from school she made them for me. Nobody else in the family, not Daddy, not my brother, liked the thickish, unsweetened, minimalist flat fried bread. While regular oven-baked, or stove top, cornbread could be split and buttered, cornpones were cooked without any added sweetener and eaten without any additional fat (which, since I had/have an aversion to butter or rich foods of any kind, may have been why I liked this humble country bread). Cornpones were also the perfect finger food, shaped like golden fat pancakes but far more substantial. Cornpones are/were an acquired taste: I acquired my taste for this special treat while watching my mother mix and make the bread and listening to her tell stories while she cooked of growing up on her family's farm in Ruston, Louisiana. She acquired her taste from watching her grandmother, who had been a slave, bake the bread on an open-hearth fireplace skillet. Mama also liked to crumple cold cornpones into a glass of buttermilk and eat the resulting mixture with a spoon when we had leftovers. More a purist, I liked my cornpones hot or cold, eaten alone or with the aforementioned homemade soup, chili, beans—but never in buttermilk. What I liked best, however, was sharing the moment of mixing and shaping with Mama, wondering how she could put her hands into the hot batter and shape the ovals she dropped into the skillet. Though she had recited the recipe for me over time, it took me at least five years after her death before I finally made a successful batch on my own. Even then I probably had divine guidance.

Ingredients and equipment
Yellow cornmeal (do not use white meal!)
Flour
Salt

1 egg (optional)

1 teaspoon vegetable shortening (Crisco)

1 teaspoon baking powder

Boiling water (as much as needed to make thick batter
consistency: ⅓–½ cup)

1 large or medium-sized cast iron skillet

1 to 2 tablespoons of hot oil

Directions

Sift together two parts yellow cornmeal to one part flour (⅔ cup meal to ⅓ cup flour); shake salt (scant ⅛ teaspoon approx.).

Add shortening; then add boiling water.

Stir until shortening melts and mixture forms thick batter. (If egg added, less water required.)

Add in baking powder after mixture cools slightly. Stir quickly (but not too long) until baking powder absorbed.

Heat skillet with oil or Crisco.

While batter still hot/warm, spoon out enough to shape several flat oval shaped pones in hands (like mixing mud pies); batter should be thick, or fairly stiff, consistency. Pat down and drop each pone into hot skillet with melted Crisco. Turn heat down to medium and cook slowly, flipping when edge of pone bubbles and firms up—pone should be golden underneath. Flip and wait until other side is also deep golden color, not "pancake" brown.

Serve stack of fresh hot cornpones with homemade soup, chili, red beans and rice, greens, buttermilk, etc. (Those raised on Jiffy mix can add a modicum of sugar [1–2 tablespoons] if absolutely necessary but, be warned, such adulteration drastically affects the "old-time" taste.)

VERONICA BELL CUMBER

Eggnog

We had this eggnog every Christmas that I can remember. During the early years, Mother used the real corn liquor from Charles City County bootleggers, but in recent years we have purchased State Corn Liquor. After I married, Mother would spend Christmas in Richmond and we would make the eggnog together.

Beat 8 *eggs*. Add 2 cans of *evaporated milk* and ¾ can of water (using the water to rinse out the cans). Still beating, add 1 cup of *sugar*. Pour the following slowly, still beating: 1 cup of *bourbon,* 1 cup of *brandy,* 1 cup of *rum,* and 1 cup of *corn liquor.* Whip ½ pint of *whipping cream* separately (this whips best when it has been taken out of the refrigerator for a while), and then add to the mixture, beating slowly. Add 1 ounce of *vanilla.* Sprinkle *nutmeg* on the mixture and add a bit more nutmeg after the eggnog has been poured into punch cups for serving.

Warning: This is quite potent; you may wish to dilute it some by proportionately increasing all of the ingredients except the alcohol.

VERONICA BELL CUMBER

Chocolate Fudge

This is the recipe for chocolate fudge that Mother made every Christmas of my life until her condition prevented her from continuing—around 1990. It's very difficult to get just the right texture, but when one is successful, this fudge is crunchy (rather than smooth and creamy) and a real conversation piece. The secret is in cooking it at just the right temperature for just the right amount of time and letting it cool just the right amount of time. I have listed the times Mother suggests, but practice and instinct will help the candymaker to recognize those magic moments. Good luck to anyone who tries this, but expect to try it a few times before perfecting it.

4 squares of unsweetened Baker's chocolate (½ package)
7 cups of sugar
1 cup of brown sugar
2½ cups of water
3 cups of canned evaporated milk
2 sticks of butter (no substitute—if you're watching fat and cholesterol, this recipe is not for you)
1½ ounces of vanilla
1 large package of black walnuts (not regular walnuts, *black* walnuts)

Cook chocolate, sugar, water, and milk together at medium heat for 1 hour and 45 minutes, stirring occasionally. Stir in the butter and vanilla. Then remove the pot from the stove and set it in cold water, stirring the mixture until it gets very thick. Stir in the walnuts and pour into a buttered pan. Allow to set until hard enough to cut into squares. Cut and remove from pans. If you keep this refrigerated, it will last much longer.

DARYL CUMBER DANCE ET AL.

Chocolate Fudge

This recipe, which I believe is a variation of one given to me by Ruth Richardson, is for those like me who don't have the time for Mother's fudge or simply can't get it to turn out just right. This is foolproof and produces a nice smooth and creamy fudge every time.

4½ cups of cane sugar
2 tablespoons of butter
pinch of salt
13-ounce can of Carnation evaporated milk
1 package of cracked walnuts
1 package of bittersweet chocolate bits
3 German chocolate bars
1 7-ounce jar of marshmallow cream
dash of vanilla

Bring the first four ingredients to a boil and allow the mixture to bubble slowly for six minutes. Add the next four ingredients and stir until completely mixed. Add the dash of vanilla. Allow the mixture to cool a bit and then pour it into buttered pans. Allow the fudge to set in the refrigerator until firm enough to cut into squares. Cut with a sharp knife and remove from pan. If this is kept in the refrigerator, it will remain fresh much longer.

DOROTHY MONTAGUE

Fruit Cobbler

Real cooks like Mrs. Montague make their own crusts, but she says you may buy the prepared crust.

Put the *crust* in a deep, greased baking pan. Sprinkle a little *cinnamon* and *brown sugar* over the crust. Put a layer of cooked fresh *fruit* or canned fruit in the pan (you may use apples, peaches, or blueberries singly or mixed [I love a mixture of peaches and blueberries]). Over this add *cinnamon, nutmeg, vanilla,* and a little *brown sugar* (the tartness of the fruit will determine how much sugar you need). Add another layer of fruit and again add cinnamon, nutmeg, vanilla, and a little brown sugar. Dot the fruit with 4 or 5 teaspoons of *butter*. Then add a top crust or strips of the crust. Again sprinkle with a little cinnamon and brown sugar. Preheat oven to 350 degrees and bake for approximately one hour.

ESTHER VASSAR

Applesauce Rum Cake

Preheat oven to 350 degrees.

Soak 1 cup of *raisins* in *rum* for several hours and drain.

Sift together 2½ cups of all-purpose *flour*, 1½ teaspoons of *baking soda*, 1½ teaspoons of *salt*, ½ teaspoon of *cloves*, ¾ teaspoon of *cinnamon*, and ½ teaspoon of *allspice*.

In a separate bowl combine ½ cup of *vegetable shortening*, 2 cups of *sugar*, 2 *eggs*, and 16 ounces of *applesauce*. Beat at high speed.

Stir in flour mixture, alternating with ⅓ cup of water.

Stir in the drained raisins and ¾ teaspoon of *rum extract* just to blend.

Pour into a 9-inch tube pan.

Bake at 350 degrees for 1 hour or until the center springs back when pressed.

ESTHER VASSAR

Aunt Maude's Sweet Potato Pie

As in many families, this dish bears the name of the ancestor who created it.

Preheat oven to 350 degrees.

Cover and boil a 40-ounce can of *sweet potatoes* (yams) in their own juice for approximately 12 minutes or until they are tender.

Place yams in large mixing bowl and add 2 full cups of *granulated sugar* and mix at medium speed until blended.

Add 1½ sticks of *margarine* and continue mixing at moderate speed.

Add 4 *eggs* to the mixture and mix at medium to low speed.

Add 2 level teaspoons of *nutmeg*, ¼ teaspoon of *salt*, and 2 full ta-blespoons of *vanilla*.

Now, slowly add an 8-ounce can of *Carnation evaporated milk* to the other ingredients and continue mixing slowly at low speed so as to avoid splashing.

Pour the mixture into two deep-dish *frozen pie shells*. Bake in a 350-degree oven for 60–70 minutes or until done.

DOROTHY MONTAGUE
Sweet Potato Pudding

Boil six *yams* until soft. Cool, peel, and slice into small pieces. Add ¾ cup of *sugar* (modify to taste), 2 *eggs*, 2 teaspoons *vanilla*, ½ teaspoon *nutmeg*, ½ teaspoon *cinnamon*, ½ teaspoon of *baking powder*, ½ stick of *butter*, and one cup of *evaporated milk*. Whip or beat with a mixer until smooth. Bake in a preheated 350-degree oven for 45 minutes.

QUINCY MOORE
Blackberry Bread Pudding

Combine 1 cup of *blackberries* (blueberries may be substituted), ½ cup of *Grand Reserve VSOP Brandy*, ½ cup of *confectioner's sugar*, ½ cup of *pecans*, and ½ cup of *cinnamon-covered raisins* in a covered container and refrigerate for 1 hour.

Preheat oven to 350 degrees.

Whisk together in a large bowl 1 cup of *whole milk*, 1 cup of *half-and-half*, 2 large *eggs*, ½ cup of *pure cane sugar*, 1 teaspoon of *vanilla ex-tract*, and ½ teaspoon of *cinnamon*.

Cut 4 slices of *Hawaiian sweet bread* in 1-inch squares.

Add the blackberry mixture to the bread. Turn the bread over in the liquid to soak evenly for 10 minutes. Arrange the bread in a 10-inch × 12-inch baking dish or pan and pour the milk mixture over the bread. Sprinkle ¼ cup of *brown sugar* evenly over the bread.

Bake for 1 hour or until golden brown.

CAROL F. BOONE

Wine Jelly

This recipe, a favorite Sunday dessert in Ms. Boone's family, was passed down from her great-grandmother.

Soak 2 envelopes of *gelatin* in 1 cup of cold water. Dissolve 1 cup of *sugar* and the gelatin mixture in 1 cup of boiling water. Add 1 cup of *Manischewitz Concord Grape wine* and the strained juice from one *lemon*. Pour into molds or bowl and chill.

When ready to serve, top with *whipped cream* or *old-fashioned boiled custard*.

VERONICA BELL CUMBER

Pear Preserves

Slice 9 cups of *pears* and put in a pan with 7 cups of *sugar* and 1 tablespoon of *lemon juice*. Let mixture stay in the pan overnight. Next morning, bring the mixture to the boiling point and simmer slowly for 2½ hours. Add *cloves* and *cinnamon* and let it boil for another half hour. Put in jars and seal.

Chapter 8

Proverbs and Other
Memorable Sayings

Proverbs are the palm oil with which words are eaten.
–Chinua Achebe, *Things Fall Apart*

Proverbs, those brief, pithy encapsulations of the wisdom of a people, are prevalent in every culture, but nowhere more so than in African cultures, where they not only teach lessons, reflect values, reinforce points, issue warnings, tender consolations, attack enemies, and philosophize about life, but also serve to distinguish the speaker and even to settle court disputes (see John Messenger, "The Role of Proverbs in a Nigerian Judicial System"). The individual who can contribute traditional wisdom to the argument in the form of a proverb or who can make his case in eloquent and memorable language wins a number of points. The admiration for such a figure in African American culture can be seen whether he is an expert player of the dozens or one who grew up under the tutelage of a proverb master and consciously continues as a bearer and active guardian of that tradition (Sw. Anand Prahlad, *African-American Proverbs in Context*). And while proverbs may not be as central or as commonplace in African American communities today as they are in Africa, they continue to be a very viable folk expression here.

Proverbs of course must not merely convey traditional wisdom;

they must present it in a formulaic and memorable way. It is precisely the beauty of the language, the striking figure of speech, the familiar image, the balanced phrasing, and the succinctness that characterize this form of folklore. Brevity is the hallmark of the proverb. It is usually just a few words, never more than a brief sentence. Proverbs are poetic: they occasionally rhyme; they are lyrical; and they make use of alliteration, assonance, and other poetic techniques. The proverb works successfully in the folk community because its significance to the issue at hand is apparent enough that it persuades the person being addressed or the audience of the accuracy and legitimacy and traditional wisdom of its counsel. At times its value is further enhanced by its use of humor.

Like other forms of folklore, proverbs are constantly evolving. Many of them seem to continue from time immemorial. Others pass out of currency or are recast in modified form, appearing in completely new contexts. As can be seen in *African-American Proverbs in Context,* familiar old proverbs are constantly popping up in songs and other cultural forms (as in the use of "Different strokes for Different folks" in the popular television show). Proverbs are, as Prahlad reminded me, "an essential component of [African American] sermons and speeches."[1] Then too, new proverbial expressions are constantly developing as someone utters a truism that catches people's attention and bears repeating.

What follows is a list of proverbs that I have collected through the years from African Americans.[2] Undoubtedly many entered from a variety of cultures, including European, Asian, Caribbean, and, of course, African. A number of them are familiar throughout the world. While the basic message of many of these expressions is quite clear—though they are out of context—and while there is much pleasure to be derived from the sheer beauty of the language and the universal truths and realities they incorporate, it is true, as with any form of folklore, that a full appreciation of such expressions is possible only when they are observed in the situation from which they sprang. Otherwise, as Bronislav Malinowski suggests in *Magic, Science and Religion and Other Essays,* such isolated folk items may be viewed as

[1]Letter to author, August 30, 2000.
[2]Variants of a number of these proverbs appear in *Honey, Hush!*

"lifeless . . . [and] mutilated bit[s] of reality." To provide some samples of proverbs presented within context, the list of proverbs is followed by two selections from *African-American Proverbs in Context*, one in which Prahlad discusses a proverb frequently found in the narratives of former slaves, "You reap what you sow"; and another in which he provides two very different interpretations of the popular proverb "the kettle calling the pot black and the frying pan standing up for witness."

The chapter ends with some aphorisms, brief philosophical reflections, and miscellaneous other sayings that may not be strictly proverbs, but certainly are proverbial. A number of these are not as traditional as most proverbs, having been recently introduced by some famous figure and adopted by the community. One section includes reflections on American justice.

To read this chapter is to be reminded of the truth of the Ashanti proverb, "Ancient things remain in the ear."[3]

Proverbs and Proverbial Expressions

Brick top o' brick makes house.

It takes one to know one.

What goes around comes around.

Folks who live in glass houses shouldn't throw stones.

The chickens come home to roost.

You reap what you sow.

One good turn deserves another.

You make your bed, you sleep in it.

[3]Quoted by Mary F. Berry and John W. Blassingame in "Africa, Slavery and the Roots of Contemporary Black Culture," in *Chant of Saints*.

If you can't stand the heat, you better git outta the kitchen.

Live by the sword, you die by the sword.

Who the cap fit, wear it.

If the shoe fits . . .

The deeper you dig, the richer the soil.

You may not get all you pay for, but you will certainly pay for all
you get.

If you go to the dance, you have to pay the band.

You have to take the fat with the lean.

It's better to have a star in your crown than a dollar in your
pocket.

Every tub must sit on its own bottom.

Two heads are better than one.

Fingers are not equal.

Don't cut off your hand because you hurt your finger.

Don't cut off your nose to spite your face.

Look before you leap.

Don't burn your bridges behind you.

Don't put the cart before the horse.

Don't count your chickens before they hatch.

Never put all your eggs in one basket.

An apple a day keeps the doctor away.

Don't bite the hand that feeds you.

Live and let live.

If it ain't broke, don't fix it.

Don't trouble trouble till trouble troubles you.

If you look for trouble, you will find it.

When trouble sleeps, don't wake 'im up.

Feed the devil wit' a *long* spoon.

If you don't want to trade with the devil, keep out of his shop.

An idle mind is the devil's workshop.

If you make yourself an ass, folks will ride you.

If you gon' dig a hole for someone, better dig two.

You can take him outta the gutter, but you can't take the gutter
outta him.

Don't jump outta the frying pan into the fire.

Men are like buses—you miss one there's another one coming.

A bird in the hand is worth two in the bush.

A snake may change his skin, but he's still a snake.

A leopard don't change his spots.

If you play with dogs, you get bitten.

You run with dogs, you catch fleas.

A dog that will bring a bone will carry one.

You can't teach a old dog new tricks.

When the cat's away, the mouse will play.

The bird can't fly with one wing.

It takes two birds to make a nest.

The littlest snowflakes make the deepest snow.

There's more than one way of skinning a cat.

He knows what side his bread is buttered.

Blood is thicker than water.

One hand washes the other.

You scratch my back, I'll scratch yours.

Nothing ventured, nothing gained.

You can't hurry up good times by waitin' for 'em.

Naught from naught leaves naught.

Don't cry over spilt milk.

You never miss your water till your well runs dry.

They don't have a pot to piss in or a window to throw it out.

They don't have a pot to piss in or a bed to push it under.

The sun ain't gon' shine in your door always.

The sun's gon' shine in my door someday.

It's six in one hand and a half-dozen in the other.

Robbing Peter to pay Paul.

The gourd will follow the vine.

Fruit don't fall too far from the tree.

No matter how far a stream flows, it never cuts off from its source.

Spare the rod and spoil the child.

You have to crawl before you walk.

To climb a tree, you have to start at the bottom.

You can take a horse to water, but you can't make him drink; you can send a fool to school, but you can't make him think.

Wait for you? Weight broke the wagon down.

Don't measure my bushel by your pint.

If you not gon' shit, git off the pot.

If you move, you lose.

Play fool to catch wise.

No fool, no fun.

Ask me no questions and I'll tell you no lies.

Silence is golden.

You run your mouth, I'll run my business.

A whistling woman and a crowing hen never come to a good
end.

You ever see a fish what kept his mouth shut caught on
anybody's hook?

Shut mouth don't catch no flies.

We can all sing together, but we can't talk together.

The empty barrel makes the most noise.

A tattler keeps the pot boiling.

Don't let the cat out the bag.

Speak when spoken to; answer when called.

Sticks and stones may break my bones, but words will never
hurt me.

Never let your right hand know what your left hand is doing.

You study long, you study wrong.

He who laughs last laughs best.

You can run, but you can't hide.

You can hide the fire, but what you gon' do with the smoke?

Where there's smoke, there's fire.

Monkey should know where he gon' put his tail before he order
trousers.

One monkey can't stop the show.

Monkey see, monkey do.

The higher monkey climb, the more you see his behind.

The higher you climb, the farther you have to fall.

No matter how high the bird flies, he have to come back down
to the ground to eat.

The early bird gets the worm.

Birds of a feather flock together.

Too many cooks spoil the pot.

There is a lid for every pot and a key for every lock.

The rich git richer and the poor git chirren.

He's not gon' buy the cow if he can get the milk for free.

If you give an inch, they'll take a foot.

The rooster does all the crowing, but it's the hen what lay the
egg.

It's a mighty poor chicken that can't scratch up her own food.

What's fair for the goose is fair for the gander.

There's more than one way to skin a cat.

We'll cross that bridge when we come to it.

I might wear out, but I won't rust out.

It's a poor dog that won't switch its own tail.

I wasn't born yesterday.

Every shut-eye ain't sleep; every good-bye ain't gone.

I laugh and joke, but I don't play.

He can hit a straight lick with a crooked stick.

God does not sleep.

The Lord helps those who help themselves.

The grass is always greener on the other side.

All that glitters is not gold.

Root, pig, or die.

What you don't have in your head, you got to have in your feet.

Change the joke and slip the yoke.

The blind leading the blind.

A po' dog is glad of a whippin'.

Beauty is only skin deep, but ugly is to the bone.

The blacker the berry, the sweeter the juice.

I been in sorrow's kitchen, and I licked the pot clean.

Old kindlin' is easy to catch fire.

The older the moon, the brighter it shine.

Old Man Death don't know the difference between the big house and the cabin.

Every dog has his day.

Actions speak louder than words.

An empty bag cannot stand up.

The empty wagon makes the loudest noise.

Old Man Know-It-All died las' year.

Bring me my flowers while I am still alive.

SW. ANAND PRAHLAD

You Reap What You Sow

· *From* African-American Proverbs in Context ·

Just prior to the selection extracted below Prahlad discusses some examples of
the use of this proverb in ex-slave narratives and concludes that it was probably
one of the most popular proverbs among African Americans during slavery and
the postslavery era.

The next example reveals even more about the way in which
proverbs were used by African- to European-Americans. . . . [T]he
speaker is telling the interviewer a story, perhaps a legend that had
been in circulation among members of the African-American community since the period of slavery. A pertinent question about such
instances is, why is the speaker choosing to relate the legend to the
interviewer? While the data provided by the interviewer is insufficient to determine the reason, we can surmise certain possible motivations. The legend is one that demonstrates the recurrent theme of
the enslaved outwitting the slaveowner. It further indicates the specific strategy employed by the enslaved man, and this becomes a central aspect of the message. Two components of the strategy are
prominent: (1) the use of biblical authority to successfully argue a
case and, more specifically, the use of that authority to defeat an as-
sault that is based on that canon; and (2) the importance of literacy
in pursuing an argument.

Example #7
Billy come to de house marster says Billy you preachah? Billy say
yas sah. He says, Billy you'se cut dem collads, Billy says yas sah.

I'se got some greens. He says now Billy you preachah, git me de Bible and sayd read dis, he shore hates to, but Marster makes him do it, den he shore tares loose on Billy bout stealin, finally Billy says now Marster I can show you in de Bible where I did not steal, he tells Billy to find it and Billy finds it and reads, "You shall reap when you laborth." Marster sayd to Billy get to hell outn here. . . .

It is only logical to conclude that the speaker was at some level communicating to the interviewer several different things: his pride in his cultural heritage, a culture that had managed to survive by outwitting the enslavers; a belief held by many African-Americans since the inception of slavery that they were smarter than European-Americans; an awareness that European-Americans had attempted to use Christianity as a mechanism to instill submission and justify oppression; and the belief that African-Americans were entitled to the material benefits of the American system because they had been the primary work force for production of those goods—whether or not the American legal or social system recognized that right. All of these sentiments are encapsulated in the use of the proverb.

The social meanings discussed for the previous example apply here both in the fictive and in the natural contexts, and the story can be viewed as a discourse on the subversion of canonical texts to engender meaning appropriate for the enslaved, or the emergence of liberation theology. In the context of the story, Billy reinterprets the Euro, social level of meaning and applies it socially and situationally. Socially, slaves were entitled to the benefits of the system; situationally, he was entitled to the greens that he had grown. At the level of natural discourse, both meanings are also salient. Socially, the speaker is arguing the entitlement of African-Americans in the antebellum period to benefits of the system and, situationally, his own right to government assistance.

To return for a moment to an earlier point, it is quite interesting to observe this tale being told to a Euro-American. In the context of African-American culture, it was very likely a humorous tale, one which served several functions: it provided an outlet for the expression of anger and a mechanism for the criticism of slaveowners and the plantation system in general, and it celebrated the slaves' sense of pride in their abilities to successfully outwit the oppressors and to obtain the necessary goods to maintain their own culture. . . . So it would seem a rather bold and even defiant move on the part of the speaker to relate the legend to the interviewer. Perhaps this is permitted by the thin veneer of the story and of fictive discourse in general. Certainly, we would not expect the interviewer to find the story humorous, at least not in the same way that the speaker would. At the core of all of this, however, is the reinterpretation that the speaker gives to the proverb, the implications of which amount to no less than the reinterpretation of the canon holding the institutions of American society in place. Of note is the consistent social level of meaning in examples #6 and #7, while the applications are so different. In one, the proverb has a negative correlation—the sowers are oppressors and the harvest is devastation. In the other, the correlation is positive, first person—the sowers are the oppressed and the harvest is their share of the American wealth.

The dynamics of example #7 are even more evident in example #8, in which the interaction preceding the use of the proverb is accessible. It seems that the interviewer has attempted to put the speaker, Mr. Mack Taylor, "in his place" by referring to the religious virtues of piety, long-suffering and patience, a common tactic of Euro-Americans intended to repress the anger and rebellious spirit of enslaved people and of later generations of African-Americans.

Example #8
Howdy do sir! As Brer Fox 'lowed to Brer Rabbit when he ketched him wid a tar baby at de spring, "I 'is got you now!" I's been waintin' to ask you 'bout dis old age pension. I's been to Winnboro to see 'bout it. Some nice white ladies took my name and ask some questions, but dat seem to be de last of it. Reckon I gwine to get anything?

Well, I's been here mighty nigh a hundred years, and just 'cause I pinched and saved and didn't throw my money away on liquor, or put it into de palms of every jezabel hussy dat slant her eye at me, ain't no valuable reason why them dat did dat way and 'joyed deirselves can get de pension and me can't get de pension. 'Tain't fair! No, sir. If I had a knowed way back yonder, fifty years ago, what I knows now, I might of gallavanted 'round a little more wid de shemales than I did. What you think 'bout it?

You say I's forgittin dat religion must be thought about? Well,

I can read de Bible a little bit. Don't it say: what you sow you sure to reap? Yes sir. Us fell de forests for corn, wheat, oats, and cotton; drained de swamps for rice; built de dirt roads and de railroads; and us old ones is got a fair right to our part of de pension. . . .

A number of significant features of this speaker's discourse are readily apparent. The first is the initial application of metaphor to invert the social order and status of the speaker and the interviewer. By casting himself in the metaphorical role of Brer Fox and the interviewer in the role of Brer Rabbit, the speaker reverses the social roles that exist in the real world, becoming the one with the upper hand and moving the interviewer into the subordinate position. Because of the lighthearted tone of the speech event, any serious implications of this maneuver are played down. A compelling aspect of this initial strategy is the masking of the identity of the speaker, as he shrouds himself in the dramatic role of a traditional, fictive character. Also important is the nature of the role assigned to the interviewer, for Brer Rabbit is the ultimate trickster and can only be captured for short periods of time before he devises some method of escape.

It is clear that the speaker assumes that the interviewer is capable of assisting him in obtaining his pension, and the remainder of his discourse consists of his feelings about the government's policy of benign neglect. In response to his entreaty, the interviewer resorts to the familiar rhetorical strategy of referring to the Bible to encourage a submissive attitude. The speaker becomes even more adamant at this point, perhaps reacting in part to the implicit condescension contained in the interviewer's response. He cites the proverb, as does the speaker in example #7, reinterpreting it to apply in precisely the same way. As in other examples, further elaborative and explanatory comments follow the proverb. The social and situational meanings here are identical to those in example #7, as is the rhetorical and argumentative strategy in which the proverb is located.

SW. ANAND PRAHLAD

The Pot Calling the Kettle Black . . .

· *From* African-American Proverbs in Context ·

Example #60
A family of five children, two parents and one great-grandmother
had gathered at the dinner table for dinner and was waiting on
one of the children to come and sit down. Another of the children
impatiently criticized the one who was coming for being so slow.
A third child agreed with the criticism. The great-grandmother
at this point said, "The kettle calling the pot black and the frying
pan standing up for witness. All of y'all contrary when you want
to be."

The speech event here was a criticism of all of the grandchildren.
The speaker was struggling with issues of aging and dependency.
She had been accustomed to living alone and independently, but,
due to poor health, had moved in with her granddaughter and family. While on one hand she longed to be taken care of, on the other,
she feared having to be dependent. In the speech event, she was
lashing out at the grandchildren and at the parents, venting her frustration. The speech event struck me as an expression of her power-
lessness and loss of ability to control the environment around her.
The proverb speech act had a bitter tone to it and functioned as a
means of commenting negatively about the family members; it was,
in essence, the equivalent of "signifying," or "capping." All of these
factors obtained at the situational level, including a wish that the
children would simply stop their bickering and get on with the meal.
Also registered as a part of the communication was some sense of dis-
appointment that no one of the children could be relied upon to be
as receptive to the transmission of her values or as malleable as the
speaker might have wished them to be. At the symbolic level, the children were aware that this was one of the speaker's favorite proverbs
and that it reminded her of her own mother; they were aware of the
symbolic meaning of the item for their great-grandmother. In some
way this knowledge allowed them to interpret the speech event as an
indication of her insecurity and sense of displacement and vulnera-

bility, as well as her need to evoke memories of cherished and secure moments in her life. Furthermore, the images of kettles and pots have another shared dimension for the speaker and audience: these items were literally the ones that Mrs. Abrams had held onto from the time of her mother's tenure on the plantation and that had been shown to the children. So, the grammatical level informs the situational and symbolic, for the proverb contains images of actual objects that have symbolic meaning for speaker and audience, representing enslavement, struggle, and emancipation.

In another situation Mrs. Abrams used the same proverb to two of the great-granddaughters. . . .

> Example #61
> The two sisters were washing dishes, and one of them criticized the other for the way that she was stacking them. Mrs. Abrams rocked back in her chair and slid her feet across the floor. "Ah Lord, well there! The kettle calling the pot black," she said, laughing.

This speech event contains aspects of humor, ignited by the play already occurring between the two sisters. The proverb is applied to remind the critical party that they also have shortcomings *of some kind*. A difference between this example and the previous one is that here the proverb speech act functions to unite the speaker and listeners emotionally, whereas in the first example it functions to isolate them from each other. The speech act here has a light-hearted quality about it that the previous example obviously did not. Its social meaning remains relatively the same, but because of the nature of the interaction, the situational message becomes humorous. Here, the speaker is feeling close to and positive toward the listeners, and, at the symbolic level, the proverb evokes fond memories of ancestors that are being shared with the children. At the situational level, there is no directive here—there is no behavior or course of action that is being suggested—rather, the proverb speech act is intended as an act of bonding. Note that the speaker in this case does not actually say the proverb to anyone specifically. She says it aloud so that both of the girls can hear it, and they clearly understand how it is being applied and to whom it refers.

Aphorisms and Other Proverbial Sayings

A daughter is your daughter the rest of her life; but a son is your
son until he takes a wife.

I'm sick and tired of being sick and tired. —*Fannie Lou Hamer*

*If I'd known I was going to live this long, I'd have taken better
care of myself. —*Eubie Blake*

What you don't know can't hurt you.

*It's not the load that breaks you down, it's the way you carry it.
—*Lena Horne*

Don't look back —something might be gaining on you. —
Attributed to Satchel Paige

The water brought us here. The water will take us away. —
*Comment by the leader of the Ebo tribesmen who, according to
tradition, walked away from American slavery on the water* (*in
Parrish,* Slave Songs)

You're either part of the solution or you're part of the problem.

Life has two rules: number 1, never quit! Number 2, always
remember rule number 1. —*Duke Ellington*

*Blackness is no longer a color; it is an attitude. —*Dick Gregory*

God don't like ugly.

Hard head, soft behind.

You are not judged by the height you have risen, but from the
depth you have climbed. —*Frederick Douglass*

*From Richard Newman, *African American Quotations.*

He who would be free must himself strike the first blow.

*You can kill a man, but you can't kill an idea. —*Medgar Evans*

We are almost a nation of dancers, musicians, and poets.—
Olaudah Equiano writing about his native Africa

It don't mean a thing if it ain't got that swing. —Duke Ellington

Brothers and sisters, today I intend to explain the
unexplainable, find out the undefinable, ponder the
imponderable, and unscrew the inscrutable. —*Lines
traditionally attributed to the Black preacher and used in a slightly
variant form by James Weldon Johnson in his introduction to* God's
Trombones

Other Figurative Language

He's sharp as a tack.

He's as high as a Georgia pine.

He's cool as a cucumber.

He could talk a 'possum out a tree.

He's crazy as a bedbug.

She done lost all her marbles.

She's out to lunch.

She spent her life slinging hash and busting suds [cooking and
washing clothes].

It's raining cats and dogs.

They're shacking up.

Let's go back to my crib [house].

She swallowed a watermelon [is pregnant].

They have a house full of crumbsnatchers [children].

That's her backdoor man [secret lover].

He has an ace up his sleeve.

Your money won't spend here [person won't accept payment].

That's all she wrote for her [the end].

I just wish she'd get off my back.

I told that dude to get his hat [leave].

You'd better straighten up and fly right [behave properly].

She's always bad-mouthing someone.

Don't make me show my colors [act like a Negro—ba-a-d].

He calls hogs all night long [snores].

The eagle flies on Friday [paycheck].

He's living high on the hog now [doing well].

She's cooking with gas [in style].

Where did you get that bad do [hairdo], girl?

When she walked in she laid them in the aisle [impressed them
with her stylishness].

Reflections on American Justice

Reflecting on the prevalence and brutality of lynchings of Blacks and the fact that Black life was valued less than that of an animal, one Black Southerner recalled, "They had to have a license to kill anything but a nigger. We was always in season." —*Cited in James Allen et al.*, Without Sanctuary.

Congress ought to set aside some place where we can go and nobody can jump on us and beat us, neither lynch nor jim crow us every day. Colored folks rate as much protection as a buffalo or a deer. —*Langston Hughes*, The Best of Simple

When the white man says "justice," he means just that —*just us.*

The closer the black man got to the ballot box, the more he looked like a rapist. —*From James Allen et al.*, Without Sanctuary

If a nigger kills a white man, that's murder in the first degree.
If a white man kills a nigger, that's justifiable homicide.
If a nigger kills another nigger, that's one less nigger.

In a tale about a White man crying because he is facing the electric chair and his Black cohort consoling him, saying "Man, we committed the crime, we've got to pay the price," the White man retorts, still crying, "Yeah, you kin talk like that; *yawl* used to it!"

A Southern sheriff comes to report to a woman that her husband was found at the bottom of the river, his hands in handcuffs, his feet tied, his testicles cut off, and his head bashed in, and says to her, "It's the worse case of suicide I've ever seen."

Chapter 9

Folk Rhymes, Work Songs, and Shouts

*[Two of] the main elements that compose . . . the folk
poetry tradition of the African American . . . are rhyming
[and] moralizing, . . . Moralizing without the rhyme is
preaching, and rhyming without moralizing
is mere versification.*
—Molefi Kete Asante, "Folk Poetry in the
Storytelling Tradition"

The love of rhyme, like the passion for other aspects of poetry and eloquent expression, is a given in Black communities. From Nipsy Russell to Homey the Clown and from Cassius Clay (Muhammad Ali) to Jessie Jackson and Michael Eric Dyson and numerous orators in between, the ability to phrase thoughts in catchy rhymes and rhythms has endeared them to Black folk. Everything from street cries to scholarly discourse, political debate and sermonic exegesis goes down a little better when it rhymes. The most memorable—and arguably the most compelling—line from the fifty-three-week-long O. J. Simpson trial of 1994–95 (often called the Trial of the Century) was leading defense counsel Johnnie Cochran's "If it doesn't fit / You must acquit!"[1] Such rhymes are popular in every aspect of Black life: they may be found from slavery to the present; they may be found in every form—in children's verses,

---

[1] In a dramatic moment during the trial, the prosecuting attorney had Simpson try on the bloody gloves presumed to have been worn by the assailant who killed Nicole Simpson and Ron Goldman, but he had difficulty getting them on (they appeared to be too small).

autograph album verses, college fraternity and sorority performance pieces, toasts (long, rhyming narrative performance pieces), ballads, street cries, the dozens, brags, and varied other forms of folk poetry. Many of them are parodies of serious political, religious, and educational pieces. And many of the creators of these rhymes possess, in the words of Ralph Ellison "a great virtuosity with the music, the poetry, of words." Indeed, Ellison continues, "the word play of Negro kids in the South would make the experimental poets, the modern poets, green with envy" (*Going to the Territory*).

The line between a number of folk rhymes and songs is a dubious one. Many of these verses are recited, some chanted, and others may at times be sung. In many of these performances hands may be clapped, feet stomped. People may sway their bodies, move in circles, jump and skip, or even dance. Such performances have been popular from slavery through contemporary fraternity and sorority step shows and rap performances.

A number of these rhymes accompany children's clapping games, ring games, and jump-rope games. Several of these games are not limited to African American children, and a few may clearly have had their origins in England or elsewhere. Oftentimes when those songs and games are adopted in Black communities, lyrics are added and variations are made. It is amazing how often ring games persist over long periods of time and over large geographical areas encompassing several different cultures.

Among the most popular African American adult folk rhymes are those long bawdy narrative poems called the toasts. The toasts generally deal with a hero who is "ba-a-d," one who violates the laws and moral codes of the larger society but engages in exploits and lives a lifestyle that is celebrated in these verses. He kills without a second thought. He courts death constantly and does not fear dying. He loves flashy clothes and luxury cars. He asserts his manhood through his violent physical deeds and sexual exploits. Because the toasts are generally so obscene, most of the ones I have included here have been slightly expurgated. The toasts are a clear precursor of contemporary rap, which usually celebrates the same type of characters, the same lifestyle, and the same exploitation of women. The sexually explicit language and even some of the formulaic lines of the raps seem to be taken directly from the toasts.

Another special group of rhymes is the various work songs. Among these are the field hollers, shouts yelled from workers in the field to others in the distance. Their verbal gymnastics, like scat singing, communicated emotions and feelings, as well as messages, without using words. Then there are those work songs whose often bawdy lyrics were created by men doing hard, often repetitive physical labor such as rowing boats, loading ships, digging ditches, picking crops, driving steel, or chopping wood. The lyrics, the sounds of the tools, and the grunts of the laborers all contributed to the rhythms of these verses, which were often sung. The work song often signifies on the nature of the work and the boss man. At other times it signals what the workers were to do. Historian Lawrence W. Levine points to a work song that contributed to coordinating the group effort with lines such as

> Lay down easy (*umph*)
> On de groun' (*umph*)
>
> Y'ain' no longuh (*umph*)
> A growin' tree (*umph*)
> Come on cross-tie (*umph*)
> Slip along (*umph*)
> Yuh ain't nothin' now (*umph*)
> But a heavy log (*umph*)

These work songs could even signal the group to take a break for someone to relieve himself, with the leader singing out, "Everybody lay their bar down, it's one to go."

A natural outgrowth of the work songs was the shout of vendors plying their wares on city streets. One interesting and persistent form of this latter is the shout of the horse-cart vendors in Baltimore, Maryland, generally called *arabbers*, who sell ice, wood, coal, junk, seafood, and fresh produce from their horse-drawn wagons. A few of their street cries are reproduced in *The Arabbers of Baltimore* by Roland L. Freeman, who admits being fascinated by that group since his childhood in the 1940s, when his father wanted to take him out arabbing but his mother refused to let him go.

Another form of the shout is the ring shout, a religious ritual in which the participants align themselves in a ring and shuffle around in a circle beating time with their feet but being careful that their feet do not leave the floor.[2] As they move, they clap their hands, chant, shout, hum, moan, grunt, and generally become more frenzied until some people fall to the ground quivering, or in other ways reflect spiritual possession. The circle is significant in many African-inspired religions and is believed necessary for the spirit to enter into the worshippers' midst. One popular song, "The Circle Be Unbroken," reflects the importance of the circle. Though ring shouts continue only in a few isolated instances in the United States, the practice of joining in a circle persists, even if just for a prayer. Rituals akin to the ring shout still flourish in religious sects throughout the Caribbean.

My Ole Missis/Massa

· *Traditional* ·

My ole Missis promised me
Dat when she died, she'd set me free.
But she lived so long an' got so po'
Dat she left me diggin wid a hoe.

My ole Missis promised me
Dat when she died, she'd set me free.
She lived so long dat her head got bald,
An' she give up de notion o' dying at all.

My ole Missis promised me
Dat when she died, she'd set me free.
Now she's dead and gone to hell,
I hope the devil will burn her well.

My ole Massa promised me
But his papers didn't leave me free.
A dose of poison helped him 'long.
May de Devil preach his funeral song.

---

[2]If their feet left the floor they would be dancing, and dancing was often regarded as sinful.

Run, Nigger, Run, De Patteroler'll Ketch You

· *From* Southern Workman *24 (February 1895)* ·

This verse has been slightly edited for clarity.

Run, nigger, run, de patteroler'll ketch you,
Hit you thirty-nine and swear he didn't tech you.
Run, nigger, run, de patteroler'll ketch you . . .
Poor white out in de night
Huntin' for niggers wid all deir might.
Dey don' always ketch deir game
D'way we fool 'em is a shame.
Run, nigger, run, de patteroler'll ketch you . . .

Long Gone

· *Traditional* ·

This is a traditional work song celebrating Long John's outrun-
ning the sheriff and the deputies and their bloodhounds in his flight
from the chain gang to freedom. The celebration of flight in the Black
community is the subject of my book *Long Gone: The Mecklenburg Six
and the Theme of Escape in Black Folklore.*

Leader: It's a Long John.
Group: Long John.
Leader: He's long gone.
Group: Long gone.
Leader: Like a turkey through the corn.
Group: Like a turkey through the corn.
Leader: He's long gone.
Group: Long gone.

Jack and Dinah Want Freedom

· *From Thomas W. Talley,* Negro Folk Rhymes ·

Ole Aunt Dinah, she's jes lak me.
She wuk so hard dat she want to be free.
But, you know, Aunt Dinah's gittin' sorter ole;
An' she's feared to go to Canada, caze it's so col'.

Dar wus ole Uncle Jack, he want to git free.
He find de way Norf by de moss on de tree.
He cross dat river a-floatin' in a tub.
Dem Patterollers give 'im a mighty close rub.

Dar is ole Uncle Billy, he's a mighty good Nigger.
He tote all de news to Mosser a little bigger.
When you tells Uncle Billy, you wants free fer a fac';
De nex' day de hide drap off'n yo' back.

WILLIAM WELLS BROWN

The Big Bee

· *From* Clotel ·

Clotel was the first novel published by a Black American author. The following
rhyme is recited by Slave Jack for Connecticut visitors to the plantation. Jack, of
course, did not please his Negro-driver, who had ordered him to give a toast "to
show that slaves under his charge were happy and contented."

The big bee flies high, the little bee makes the honey: the black
folks make the cotton, and the white folks get the money.

FREDERICK DOUGLASS
We Raise de Wheat
· *From* Life and Times of Frederick Douglass ·

We raise de wheat,
Dey gib us de corn;
We bake de bread,
Dey gib us de crust;
We sif de meal,
Dey gib us de huss;
We peel de meat,
Dey gib us de skin;
And dat's de way
Dey take us in;
We skim de pot,
Dey give us de liquor,
And say dat's good enough for nigger.
Walk over! walk over!
Your butter and de fat;
Poor nigger you cant get over dat.
Walk over —

I'll Eat When I'm Hungry
· *From Thomas W. Talley*, Negro Folk Rhymes ·

I'll eat when I'se hongry,
An' I'll drink when I'se dry;
An' if de whitefolks don't kill me,
I'll live till I die.

In my liddle log cabin,
Ever since I'se been born;
Dere hain't been no nothin'
'Cept dat hard salt parch corn.

But I knows whar's a henhouse,
An' de tucky he charve;
An' if ole Mosser don't kill me,
I cain't never starve.

Aught's a Aught
· *Traditional* ·

An aught's a aught and a figger's a figger;
All for the white folks and none for the nigger.

Missus in the Big House
· *From Mel Watkins,* On the Real Side ·

Watkins cites this as a slave verse.

Missus in the big house, Mammy in the yard,
Missus holdin' her white hands, Mammy workin' hard.

Charlie
· *From* The Negro in Virginia, *compiled by Workers of the Writers' Program of the Work Projects Administration in the State of Virginia* ·

Collected from Julia Frazier.

Charlie was the "rhymster" for the big house as well as the slave quarters, according to Mrs. Frazier, who provided the WPA interviewer the following illustration of his talent of "mak[ing] up songs 'bout anything."

One day Charlie saw ole Marsa comin' home wid a keg of whiskey on his ole mule. Cuttin' 'cross de plowed field, de ole mule slipped an' Marsa come tumblin' off. Marsa didn't know Charlie saw him, an' Charlie didn't say nothin'. But soon arter a visitor come an' Marsa called Charlie to de house to show off what he knew. Marsa say,

"Come here, Charlie, an' sing some rhymes fo' Mr. Henson." "Don' know no new ones, Marsa," Charlie answered. "Come on, you black rascal, give me a rhyme fo' my company—one he ain't heard." So Charlie say, "All right, Marsa, I give you a new one effen you promise not to whup me." Marsa promised, an' den Charlie sung de rhyme he done made up in his haid 'bout Marsa:

> Jackass rared
> Jackass pitch
> Throwed ole Marsa in de ditch.

Well, Marsa got mad as a hornet, but he didn't whup Charlie, not dat time anyway. An' chile, don' you know us used to set de flo' to dat dere song? Mind you, never would sing it when Marsa was roun', but when he wasn't we'd swing all roun' de cabin singin' 'bout how old Marsa fell off de mule's back. Charlie had a bunch of verses:

> Jackass stamped
> Jackass neighed
> Throwed ole Marsa on his haid.

Don' recollec' all dat smart slave made up. But ev'ybody sho' bus' dey sides laughin' when Charlie sung de las' verse:

> Jackass stamped
> Jackass hupped
> Marsa hear you slave, you sho' git whupped.

Destitute Former Slave Owners

· *From J. Mason Brewer,* American Negro Folklore ·

This has been slightly edited for clarity.

Missus an' Massa a'walkin' de street,
Deir han's in deir pockets and nothin' to eat.
She'd better be home a-washin' up de dishes,
An' a-cleanin' up de old man's raggedy britches.
He'd better run 'long an' git out de hoes

An' clear out his own crooked weedy corn rows;
De Kingdom is come, de Niggers is free.
Ain't no Nigger slaves in de Year Jubilee.

WILLIAM WELLS BROWN

Hang Up the Shovel and the Hoe

· *From* Clotel ·

Within the narrative the slaves sing the chorus of the following song, with Sam
singing the solo. I have borrowed only the words of the song and omitted the
narrative.

Hang up the shovel and the hoe —
Take down the fiddle and the bow —
Old master has gone to the slaveholder's rest;
He has gone where they all ought to go.

I heard the old doctor say the other *night*
    As he passed by the dining-room door —
"Perhaps the old man may live through the night,
But I think he will die about four."
Young mistress sent me, at the peril of my life,
    For the parson to come down and pray,
For says she, "Your old master is now about to die,"
    And says I, "God speed him on his way."

Hang up the shovel and the hoe —
Take down the fiddle and the bow —
Old master has gone to the slaveholder's rest;
He has gone where they all ought to go.

The Lord's Prayer

· *Traditional* ·

Our father, which art in heaben
White man owe me leben an' pay me seben.

Thy kingdom come, thy will be done,
If I hadn't took that, I wouldn't git none.

If You're White

· *Traditional* ·

If you're white, you're right,
If you're yellow, you're mellow,
If you're brown, stick around.
If you're black, step back.

American Justice

The popular saying among Blacks that when White folks talk about "justice," they
mean "just us," is reinforced in this traditional verse.

If a white man kills a Negro,
They hardly carry it to court;
If a Negro kills a White man,
They hang him like a goat.

Oh, Lord, Will I Ever?

This well-known folk verse recounts a "conversation" that begins as a Negro male
views a beautiful White woman. I have used it as the title of a chapter in *Shuckin'*
and Jivin' that focuses on that large body of tales focusing on the alleged attraction
of the Black man to the White woman.

Black Man: Oh, Lord, will I ever?
White Man: No, nigger, never!
Black Man: As long as there's life there's hope.
White Man: As long as there's trees, there's rope.

Bedbug

· *From J. Mason Brewer,* American Negro Folklore ·

De June-bug's got de golden wing,
De Lightning-bug's de flame;
De Bedbug's got no wing at all,
But he gits dar jes de same.

De Punkin-bug's got a punkin smell,
De Squash-bug smells de wust;
But de puffume of dat ole Bedbug,
It's enough to make you bust.

W'en dat Bedbug come down to my house,
I wants my walkin' cane.
Go git a pot an' scald 'im hot!
Good-by, Miss Liza Jane!

Old Man Know-All

· *From Thomas W. Talley,* Negro Folk Rhymes ·

Ole man Know-All, he come 'round
Wid his nose in de air, turned 'way frum de ground.
His ole woolly head hain't been combed fer a week;
It say: "Keep still, while Know-All speak."

Ole man Know-All's tongue, it run;
He jes know'd ev'rything under de sun.
When you knowed one thing, he knowed mo'.
He 'us sharp 'nough to stick an' green 'nough to grow.

Ole man Know-All died las' week.
He got drowned in de middle o' de creek.
De bridge wus dar, an' dar to stay.
But he knowed too much to go dat way.

When I Go to Marry

· *From Thomas W. Talley,* Negro Folk Rhymes ·

W'en I goes to marry,
I wants a gal wid money.
I wants a pretty black-eyed gal
To kiss an' call me "Honey."

Well, w'en I goes to marry,
I don't wanter git no riches.
I wants a man 'bout four foot high,
So's I can w'ar de britches.

Slave Marriage Ceremony Supplement

· *From Thomas W. Talley,* Negro Folk Rhymes ·

I have regularized some of the spelling for easier reading.

Dark and stormy may come de weather;
I joins dis he-male an' dis she'male together.
Let none, but Him dat makes de thunder,
Put dis he-male and dis she-male asunder.
I therefore pronounce you both de same.
Be good, go 'long, an' keep up yo' name.
De broomstick's jumped, de world's not wide.
She's now yo' own. Salute yo' bride!

Love Is Just a Thing of Fancy

· *From Thomas W. Talley,* Negro Folk Rhymes ·

Love is jes a thing o' fancy,
Beauty's jes a blossom;
If you wants to git yo' finger bit,
Stick it at a 'possum.

*Folk
Rhymes,
Work
Songs,
and
Shouts*

*
487

Beauty, it's jes skin deep;
Ugly, it's to de bone.
Beauty, it'll jes fade 'way;
But Ugly'll hol' 'er own.

Interpret Dat

· *From Jack and Olivia Solomon,* Ghosts and Goosebumps ·

Collected from Ann Godfrey.

I 'members Marse David myself but can't say zackly how ole I is.
Ain't never been ter no school, but I kin talk Greek en I kin present
politics. My reason for stammer, I ain't studied grammer. I come
from a part uv de country where dey use coarse gravel sand fer
hominy, an' fine gravel sand for salt, eel skin fer shoe leather, ma'
leuse hids fer bakin', mosquito wings fer umbrellas. If you can't in-
terprat dat come back tomorrow afternoon, bring a silver spoon an'
a fat racoon. May God be with you amen.

John Henry

· *From Willis Laurence James,* Stars in de Elements ·

The first dirt they throwed on poor Henry
It called John Henry's name.
The next dirt they throwed on John Henry's feet
Cried Lawd it's a pity and a shame.

The next dirt they throwed on John Henry
Sound like thunder ball
And everybody that heard it say
Sound lak mountain done fall.

The next dirt they throwed on Henry
Run like a rollin' stone

But the next dirt they throwed on Henry
Couldn't do nothin' but moan.

The last dirt they throwed on John Henry
Fell on the coffin top
Made a sound like a hammer drivin' steel down
Like the one made John Henry drop.

Shine

· *Traditional* ·

I have expurgated this toast.

Say the fifth of May was a hell of a day,
When the great *Titanic* sailed away.
It was hell, hell, it was some messed-up times
When that *Titanic* hit that iceberg and began to go down.
Shine come up on board from down below,
Say, "Captain, Captain, water is coming in through the boiler
  room do'!"
Captain said, "Now Shine, oh, Shine, go back and pack your
  sack,
'Cause I got forty-nine electric pumps to keep that water back."
Shine said, "That may be true because you carrying a load.
But I'm gon' take my chances in jumping overboard."
Captain say, "Now, Shine, oh Shine, don't be no fool and don't
  be no clown,"
Say, "Anybody go overboard is bound to drown."
Shine say, "You may have them pumps, and they better work
  fast,"
Say, " 'cause I'm going overboard when that water reach
  my____."

Say now the Captain's daughter came up on the deck.
She had her hands on her hips and her dress round her neck,
She say, "Now, Shine, oh, Shine, save poor me,
And I'll give you more loving than one Shine can see."

Shine say, "Now you may have good loving and that might be
    true,
But women on land got good loving too."

All the millionaires looked around at Shine, say, "Now, Shine,
    oh, Shine, save poor me";
Say, "We'll make you wealthier than one Shine can be."
Shine say, "You hate my color and you hate my race;
Now jump overboard and give those sharks a chase."

Now women began to scream, and babies began to cry,
And everybody on board realized they had to die.
But Shine could swim and Shine could float,
And Shine could throw his tail like a motorboat.
Say Shine hit the water with a hell of a splash,
And everybody wondered if that Black sonofagun could last.
Say the Devil looked up from hell and grinned,
Say, "He's a *black, swimming mammyjammer,* I think he's gon'
    come on in."

Stagolee

· *Traditional* ·

I have expurgated this toast.

Back in thirty-two when times was hard,
Stag had two forty-fives and a marked deck o' cards.
He had a pin-striped suit and a old messed-up hat,
He had a twenty-nine Ford and owed payments on that.
Stag thought he'd take a walk down on Vampire Street,
There where all them slick and ba-a-d dudes meet.
He wade through filth and he wade through mud,
He come to a crib they call the Bucket o' Blood.
He called to the bartender for something to eat.
Bartender gave 'im a muddly glass o' water and a stale piece o'
    meat.
He say, "Bartender, Bartender, you don't realize who I am!"
Bartender say, "Frankly speaking, Mister, I don't give damn."

But just then (the bartender hadn't realized what he had said)
Stag pumped two forty-five slugs in his mammyjamming head.
And in walked this ho [whore] and say, "Oh, no! Oh, no! He
    can't be dead!"
Stag say, "Then you get back there, ho, and mend them holes in
    his mammyjamming head."

In walked that bad mammyjammer they call Billy Lyons.
He say, "Where, oh, where may that bad man be?"
Stag say, "Excuse me, Mister, but my name is Stagolee."
Ho come up there and say, "Stag, please—"
Stag slapped that ho down to her mammyjamming knees.
And then old Slick Willie John, he turned out the lights,
And when the lights came on Billy Lyons was layin' at rest
With two of Stagolee's forty-five slugs pumped in his chest.
Somebody say, "Stag, oh Stag, you know that ain't right.
One o' us tell Mrs. Lyons 'bout this old fight."
Stag went to Mrs. Lyons, say, "Miz Lyons, Miz Lyons, you
    know what I've done?
I went out there and killed your last and only son."
Mrs. Lyons looked at Stag, say, "Stag, Stag, you know that can't
    be true!
You and Billy been good friends for the last year or two."
He say, "Look, woman, if you don't believe what I said,
Go down there and count them holes in his mammyjamming
    head."
And in walked the rollers [police];
They picked up Stag and carried him to court.
Judge told Stag, say, "Stag, I been wanting you for a long time."
Say, "I'm gon' give you twenty years."
Stag looked up at the Judge, say, "Twenty years! Twenty years
    ain't no time.
I got a brother in Sing Sing doing one ninety-nine."

And then a ho walked in and to the courtroom's surprise
She pulled out two long forty-fives.
Stag grabbed one and shot his way to the courtroom do',
Tipping his hat to all the ladies once mo'.

Railroad Bill

· *From Howard W. Odum, "Folk-Song and Folk-Poetry as Found in the Secular Songs of the Southern Negroes"* ·

I reproduce here two of the several versions of the song collected by Odum, the first a brief one that tells of Railroad Bill's episodes from the perspective of a victim and the second from the perspective of an admirer.

Some one went home an' tole my wife
All about—well, my pas' life,
   It was that bad Railroad Bill.

Railroad Bill, Railroad Bill,
He never work, an' he never will,
   Well, it's that bad Railroad Bill.

Railroad Bill so mean an' so bad,
Till he tuk ev'ything that farmer had,
   It's that bad Railroad Bill.

I'm goin' home an' tell my wife,
Railroad Bill try to take my life,
   It's that bad Railroad Bill.

Railroad Bill so desp'rate an' so bad,
He take ev'ything po' womens had,
   An' it's that bad Railroad Bill.

Railroad Bill was mighty sport,
Shot all buttons off high sheriff's coat,
Den hollered, *"Right on desperado Bill!"*
Lose, lose—I don't keer,
If I win, let me win lak' a man,
If I lose all my money,
I'll be gamblin' for my honey,
Ev'y man ought to know when he lose.

Lose, lose, I don't keer,
If I win, let me win lak' a man,

Lost fohty-one dollars tryin' to win a dime,
Ev'y man plays in tough luck some time.

Honey babe, honey babe, where have you been so long?
I ain't been happy since you been gone,
Dat's all right, dat's all right, honey babe.

Honey babe, honey babe, bring me de broom,
De lices an' chinches 'bout to take my room,
O my baby, baby, honey, chile!

Honey babe, honey babe, what in de worl' is dat?
Got on tan shoes an' black silk hat,
Honey babe, give it all to me.

Talk 'bout yo' five an' ten dollar bill,
Ain't no Bill like ole desperado Bill,
Says, Right on desperado Bill.

Railroad Bill went out west,
Met ole Jesse James, thought he had him best,
But Jesse laid ole Railroad Bill.

Honey babe, honey babe, can't you never hear?
I wants a nuther nickel to git a glass o' beer,
Dat's all right, honey babe, dat's all right.

The Signifying Monkey
· *Traditional* ·

I have expurgated this version.

The Monkey and the Lion got to talkin' one day.
Monkey say, "There's a bad cat livin' down your way."
He say, "You take this fellow to be your friend,
But the way he talks about you is a sin;
He say folks say you king, and that may be true,

But he can whip the daylights outta you.

And somethin' else I forgot to say:

He talks about your mother in a hell of a way."

Monkey say, "His name is Elephant, and he's not your friend."

Lion say, "He don't need to be 'cause today will be his end."

Say like a ball of fire and a streak of heat,

The old Lion went rolling down the street.

That Lion let out a terrible sneeze,

And knocked the damned giraffe to his everlastin' knees.

Now he saw Elephant sittin' under a tree,

And he say, "Now you bring your big black butt to me."

The Elephant looked at 'im out the corner of his eyes,

And say, "Now little punk, go play with somebody your size."

The Lion let out a roar and reared up six feet tall,

Elephant just kicked him in the belly and laughed to see him fall.

Now they fought all night and they fought all day;

And I don't know how in the hell that Lion ever got away.

But the Lion was draggin' back through the jungle more dead
   than alive,

And that's when that Monkey start that signifying.

He say, "Hey-y-y-y, Mr. Lion, you don't look so swell;

Look to me like you caught a whole lotta hell!

You call yourself a king and a ace,

It's gon' take ninety yards o' sailcloth to patch yo' face.

Now git on out from under my tree,

before I decide to drop my drawers and pee.

Stop, don't let me hear you roar,

or I'll come down outta this tree and beat your tail some more.

Say the damn old Lion was sitting down there crying,

And the Monkey just *kept* signifying.

And then Monkey started jumpin' around

And his foot slipped and he fell down.

Like a ball of fire and a streak of heat,

The old Lion was on him with all four feet.

Say the Monkey looked up with tears in his eyes,

And say, "Mr. Lion, I apologize!

Now, good buddy, in this jungle friends are few;

You know I was only playin' wit' you."

Monkey looked at Lion and saw he wasn't gon' get away,
So he decided to think of a bold damn play.
He say, "Mr. Lion, you ain't raisin' no hell,
Everybody in the jungle saw me when I fell.
Now if you let me up like a real man should,
I'll kick your butt all over these woods."
The old Lion looked at 'im and jumped back for a hell of a fight.
And in a split second the Monkey was damn near outta sight.
He jumped up in a tree higher than any human eye can see,
And say, "You dumb mammyjammer, don't you ever mess wid
    me!"

Betty and Dupree

· *From Hughes and Bontemps,* The Book of Negro Folklore ·

Dupree was settin' in a hotel,
Wasn't thinkin' 'bout a dog-gone thing,
Settin' in a hotel,
Wasn't thinkin' 'bout a dog-gone thing.
Betty said to Dupree,
I want a diamond ring.

Dupree went to town
With a forty-five in his hand.
He went to town with
A forty-five in his hand.
He went after jewelry —
But he got the jewelry man.

Dupree went to Betty cryin',
Betty, here is your diamond ring.
He went to Betty cryin',
Here is your diamond ring.
Take it and wear it, Betty,
'Cause I'm bound for cold old cold Sing Sing.

Then he called a taxi
Cryin', drive me to Tennessee.
Taxi, taxi, taxi,
Drive me to Tennessee.
He said, drive me, bubber,
'Cause the dicks is after me.

He went to the post office
To get his evenin' mail.
Went to the general delivery
To get his evenin' mail.
They caught poor Dupree, Lordy,
Put him in Nashville Jail.

Dupree said to the judge, Lord,
I ain't been here before.
Lord, Lord, Lord, Judge,
I ain't been here before.
Judge said, I'm gonna break your neck, Dupree,
So you can't come here no more.

Betty weeped, Betty moaned
Till she broke out with sweat.
Betty weeped and she moaned
Till she broke out with sweat.
Said she moaned and she weeped
Till her clothes got soppin' wet.

Betty brought him coffee,
Betty brought him tea.
Betty brought him coffee,
Also brought him tea.
She brought him all he needed
'Cept that big old jail-house key.

Dupree said, it's whiskey I crave,
Bring me flowers to my grave.
It's whiskey I crave.

Bring flowers to my grave.
That little ole Betty's
Done made me her dog-gone slave.

It was early one mornin'
Jus about the break o' day,
Early, early one mornin'
Just about break o' day,
They had him testifyin'
And this is what folks heard him say:

Give my pappy my clothes,
Oh, give poor Betty my shoes.
Give pappy my clothes,
Give poor Betty my shoes.
And if anybody asks you,
Tell 'em I died with the heart-breakin' blues.

The Wanderer's Trail

· *From Bruce Jackson*, "Get Your Ass in the Water and Swim like Me" ·

This is a tale of a wanderer's trail,
of a man with his back to the wall.
Some smart guys who think they're wise,
but they can't conquer their downfall.
But me, myself, I'm a wise old egg,
I can lie, steal, or beg.
I've been overheard over thousands of dead
and I've slept on the banks of the Rhine.
I've listened to y'all's toasts sincerely,
now I want you to listen to mine.
As I gaze at night at the pale moonlight,
through the doors of my prison cell,
thinkin' of a past which is hard as cast
and a record as dark as hell.

I've committed every crime that a man could find
in the laws or statute books,
I've shot my cue in society pew
and I've mingled with the worst of crooks.
I've juggled trays in New York cafés,
hopped bells in hotels in Chi,
I've toted a pack down a B and O track
hopped redball freights on the fly.
I've built jungle fires beneath northern stars,
ate mackerel with the dirtiest of bums,
and I've stayed a spell in some of the best hotels
and I've slept on cots in slums.
In this case a woman's always the reason,
but that was only for a while,
for she did me like all the rest,
she left me with a smile.
My shoulders are drag and droopy
from travelin' so thorny trail,
I now feel the aches and pains
where I've slept in jails.
My life have been such a failure,
from travelin' so thorny trail,
my shoulders are saggin' and droopin'
from sleepin' on bunks in jails.
As I sit in deep meditation,
thinkin' of a home which is far away,
I know that there someone is waiting,
a mother and father who is old and gray.
Many many years ago I promised them that I would return,
oh, how I wish that I could keep that promise
and down that old lane could turn.
But my life have been such failure
with criminal wrote upon my face,
I would rather not meet them now
and to bring their name to disgrace.
I've had lots of pals and partners,
who helped me commit a lot of crimes,
but they all turned snitches to the cops

and caused me to do a lot of time.
If I ever get lucky and should accident and go free again,
I'm gonna get me a dog for a partner,
And I know I'll have me a friend.

Convict's Prayer

· *From Bruce Jackson*, "Get Your Ass in the Water and Swim like Me" ·

The warden is my shepherd, I shall always want.
He maketh me to lie down behind the green door,
he leadeth me beside the wagon of salty water,
he kills my soul.
He leadeth me away from the righteousness for his own sake.
Yea, though I walk down the alley of shadow and death
I fear all evil, for he is with me.
His pistol and solitary discomfort me.
He preparest a table for me with all of my enemies,
he balds my head with double-ought clippers, my cup stays
  empty.
Surely goodness and mercy shall find me one of these days in
  life
and I will drill away from this house for ever and ever. Hey man.

An Escaped Convict

· *From E. C. L. Adams*, Tales of the Congaree ·

Nothin' but a convict
Loosed from de chains,
Wid shackles left behind me,
Wid shackle scars upon me,
Wid a whip an' a chain
Waitin' ef dey ketch me,
Wid bloodhounds an' bullets

On my trail,
An' de dangers er de swamp
In front er me.
I'll take my chance, brother,
I'll take my chance.

De rattlesnake an' moccasin,
De mud an' de briar,
An' de pizen vine ain' nothin'
To de danger
Dat is left behind me.
Dere is striped clothes
An' double shackles
An' a rawhide whip
All behind me.
So I'll take my chance, brother,
I'll take my chance.

I know dere's a hard, hard road
Behind me,
An' dere ain' no road in front;
Dat de mud is heavy,
An' dere ain' much food
To separate my backbone
From my belly.
For I ain' nothin' but a convict,
Wid de scars to prove it.
I'll take my chance, brother,
I'll take my chance.

World War II Rhymes

· *From J. Mason Brewer,* American Negro Folklore ·

I don't know, but I've been told,
A boot ain't nothin' till he's nine weeks old.

Ain't no need of looking down;
Ain't no discharge on the ground;
Raise the flags, and raise them high.
Squadron F is passing by.

The WACS and WAVES will win the war, Parlez-vous.
The WACS and WAVES will win the war, Parlez-vous.
The WACS and WAVES will win the war, so what in the hell
   are we fighting for?

Hit the floor, and don't get back in bed no more.
You slept all night and the night before,
And now you want to sleep some more.

There you are in your dungarees;
Jodie's wearing your BVD's.

I don't know, but I believe,
One of these days I'm gonna get a leave.
Left, right, hup. A hup, a hup,
A hup, a hup, a left-right hup.

Two more days and an hour or two
Nine day's leave, and OGU.
Hey left, right up [three times].
Hey left, right up [three times].

What's the use of going home?
Jodie's got your gal and gone.

Left, right, left. Left, right, left.
Left, right, left. Left, right, left.
When you stand retreat, Jodie's getting your meat.
When you dressed all up in brown, Jodie's with your wife,
   going to town.

Jodie's got your gal and gone,
One, two, three, four.

Folk
Rhymes,
Work
Songs,
and
Shouts

★
501

Ain't no use in feeling blue, Jodie's got your mama too,
One, two, three, four.

I don't know, but I've been told,
Jodie's wearing my one-button roll.

No more reveille, no more retreat.
No more formation in duh company street.

Off of yo' cot, and on yo' feet.
Fall out in duh company street.

The War Is On

· *From Thomas W. Talley,* Negro Folk Rhymes ·

De boll-weevil's in de cotton,
De cut-worm's in de corn,
De Devil's in de white man;
An' de wah's a-gwine on.
Poor Nigger hain't got no home!
Poor Nigger hain't got no home!

Craps Rhymes

· *From Lyle Saxon et al.,* Gumbo Ya-Ya ·

These are typical of the many gambling rhymes recited during crapshooting
games. Every number on the dice has a name; among the names that follow are
craps (3), Little Joe (4), and Snake Eyes (2).

Look down rider, spot me in the dark,
When I calls these dice, break these niggers' hearts.
Roll out, seven, stand back, craps,
If I make this pass, I'll be standin' pat.

My baby needs a new pair of shoes; come along, you seven,
She can't get 'em if I lose; come along, you seven.
Roll them bones, roll 'em on a square, roll 'em on a sidewalk,
Street and everywhere; we'll roll 'em in the mornin', Joe.

Roll them in the night,
We'll roll them bones the whole day long,
When the cops are out of sight,
We will roll them bones.

Craps Lines

· *From Lyle Saxon et al.,* Gumbo Ya-Ya ·

The following are miscellaneous lines uttered singularly at varied points in the game, usually when the crapshooter is rolling the dice.

Six and eight, while you wait.

Callin' five, shine your line.

Damn them snake eyes!

Shoot all. I got to get it while it's hot.

Little Joe, everywhere I go.

Shake, baby, shake! You don't shake, you don't get no jelly-cake.

Roll, baby, roll. You don't get my gold.

My nutmeg does lost its charm, damn it.

Jump Jim Crow

· *From Thomas W. Talley,* Negro Folk Rhymes ·

Git fus upon yo' heel,
An' den upon yo' toe;

*Folk
Rhymes,
Work
Songs,
and
Shouts*

★

5o3

An ebry time you tu'n 'round,
You jump Jim Crow.

Now fall upon yo' knees,
Jump up an' bow low;
An ebry time you tu'n 'round,
You jump Jim Crow.

Put yo' han's upon yo' hips,
Bow low to yo' beau;
An' ebry time you tu'n 'round,
You jump Jim Crow.

Little Sally Walker

This is a popular ring game, which begins with the "It" kneeling in the middle; the actions are as the lines dictate, the last line indicating a choice of the person who will next be "It."

Little Sally Walker,
Sitting in the sand,
Crying and a weeping for a nice young man.
Rise, Sally, rise,
Wipe your eyes.
Turn to the east,
Turn to the west,
Turn to the one that you love the best.

Variants:
Shake it to the east,
Shake it to the west,
Shake it to the one
That you love the best.

Now put your hands on your hip
And let your backbone slip.

Slip it to the east,
Slip it to the west,
Slip it to the one that you love the best.

RUTH POLK PATTERSON

Hull-Gull and Other Games

· *From* The Seed of Sally Good'n ·

One of the games which appears to have had an African origin was the game of hull-gull. No reference to the term "hull-gull" has been found, but there is a once-popular Afro-American dance called the "hully-gully." Hull-gull was a counting and guessing game played in the following manner: Two players sat facing each other. The first player would pick up a handful of "pieces" from his own personal stock. While he held the pieces concealed in his fist, the game proceeded:

1st Player: Hull-Gull!
2nd Player: Handful!
1st Player: How many?
2nd Player: Five [or any number he chose].

The first player then opened his hand, revealing his pieces. If there were more than the number guessed, the first player repeated the action. If there were fewer than guessed, the second player had to pay the first player the difference between the number of pieces guessed and the number held in the hand. If the second player guessed the exact number of pieces in the hand, the first player had to pay his opponent all of the pieces he held and give up the lead to the second player. The game continued until one player ran out of pieces, or until both grew tired.

Hull-gull pieces were made, as in present-day African games, from the seeds of a local wild fruit. The pieces were acquired by picking the hard, green berries from a vine that grew among the corn in the bottom fields. The berries were peeled, exposing hard, white, concave seed kernels, which, with their serrated edges, closely resemble cowrie shells. The seed kernels were allowed to dry in the sun and made excellent pieces for handling by small hands. The game was similar in both the way it was played and the use of seeds as pieces to the traditional game of owari played in Ghana. Owari utilizes seeds as pieces and a special game board or receptacle, and it teaches concentration, mathematical skill, and manual dexterity. The game is known by other names and found throughout West Africa and in parts of the eastern hemisphere.

Another popular game the Polk children played was a "counting out" game that utilized a nonsense verse that was chanted. The origin of the game is left to speculation, but the limericks are well remembered. Any number of players could participate by sitting in a circle. The "leader" started the game by chanting and pointing to each player in turn at each word:

Wild brow limba lock
Five geese in a flock
One flew east
One flew west
One flew over the Cuckoo's nest.

My father lived on Brandy Hill
He had a hammer and nine nails
He had a cat-o-nine-tails.

Tom whup Dick
Blow the bellows
Good old man
Go!

The player to whom the "leader" pointed on the last word, "Go!" was "out," and was removed from the game. The lead passed to another player until all players were "out." If the leader pointed to himself on the word "Go," he too was "out." The counting was done very rapidly up to the last line; consequently, it could not be ascertained beforehand just where the last syllable would fall. The object of the game was to be the last one left sitting in the circle.

A game played by the Polk children and identified as having a definite African origin was "Chick-A-My, Chick-A-My Crainy Crow," or "What Time, Old Witch?" In this game, the players would walk around the "witch," who sat in the middle of a circle alone. The players, representing a hen and her chickens, would chant as they trooped around the witch:

> Chick-a-my, chick-a-my Crainy Crow,
> I went to the river to wash my toe,
> When I got back
> My black-eyed Susan was gone.
> What time, Old Witch?

The witch would answer with any number from one to twelve. If she answered twelve, however, that was the signal that she was going to leap up and catch one of the chickens. The captive would then take over the lead as the "witch" and the chanting would go on, varying only on the last line to indicate that another "chicken" was gone:

> When I got back
> My brown-eyed Lucy was gone.

In *Folk Beliefs of the Southern Negro,* Newbell Niles Puckett explains that in "Chick-A-My, Chick-A-My-Crainy Crow," "we have a possible survival not only of belief in witches but also apparently of cannibalism, since the 'old witch' steals the children [chickens] from the leader and pretends to cook them." By the time this game reached the Polk children, however, the motif of cooking the children had fortunately been lost. There is a difference between cooking symbolic "chickens" and practicing cannibalism, a concept that has not been handed down among Afro-Americans. Another probable meaning in "Chick-A-My-Crainy Crow" might be connected with the selling away of one's children or loved ones during slavery, for the idea of stealing or kidnapping the children was strong in the version of the game played by the Polk children.

To ascertain the exact origin of these games will require further research. The games were peculiar to the Polk family, however, for the white children at Muddy Fork with whom the Polk children played did not know these games, and neither did the black children at Center Point, where the Polk children first attended public school. At Center Point the children played the traditional Afro-American games of "Little Sally Walker," "Lost My Handkerchief," and "Walking on the Green Grass."

Juba

· *From* Southern Workman *24 (February 1895)* ·

Perhaps the most popular and enduring of all the slave clapping songs, Juba was sung or recited with an accompaniment of patting of the thigh or a patting of the feet or a clapping of the hands. Often there was dancing during Juba as well. This version has been slightly regularized for clarity.

Master had a yaller man
Tallest nigger in de land.
Juba was dat feller's name.
De way he strutted was a shame.
Juba, Juba, Juba, Juba [repeat several times]
Oh, 'twas Juba dis and Juba dat
Juba killed de yaller cat
To make his wife a Sunday hat.
    Juba —
Marster had a yaller steer
Old as de mountain to a year,
I tells you dis for all of dat
He'd run away at de drop o' your hat.
    Whoa Mark.
See 'im comin up de road
Pulling on a monstrous load,
Git out'n de way mighty spry
Or he'll throw you to de sky.
    Whoa Mark.
Juba drive dat ole steer
For five and twenty year,
Thru de rain and thru de snow
Juba and de steer'd go.
    Whoa Mark — Juba.
When de sun was shinin' bright,
If 'twas day, if 'twas night,
Hear him holler loud and strong,
Mark, who don't you git along.
    Golong — Whoa Mark — Juba.
By-'n'-by dat ole ox died,
Juba he jes cried and cried

Till one day he ups an' die
I spec he's drivin in de sky.
Golong—Whoa Mark—Juba.

Juber

· *From James Hungerford,* The Old Plantation ·

This verse has been slightly regularized for clarity.

Juber lef' and Juber right;
Juber dance wid all yo' might;
Juber here and Juber dere,
Juber, Juber, ebery where.

Mary Mack

· *Traditional* ·

Miss Mary Mack, Mack, Mack,
All dressed in black, black, black
With silver buttons, buttons, buttons,
All down her back, back, back.

Patty-Cake

This traditional clapping game is often played with babies, at first holding and
guiding their hands. Toddlers soon learn the routine of clapping their own hands
together and then patting the hands of the other player.

Patty-cake, patty-cake, baker's man,
Put 'im in the oven and bake 'im in the pan.
Put it in the oven and spike it with tea,
Save it for supper for baby and me.

Folk
Rhymes,
Work
Songs,
and
Shouts

★
509

Hambone, Hambone

This traditional clapping game may be played with a partner or one individual can
slap his thigh as he recites. Additional lines may be improvised.

Hambone, Hambone, where you been?
Round the world and back again.

Hambone, Hambone, what'd you do?
I got a train and I fairly flew.

Hambone, Hambone, where'd you stay?
I met a pretty girl and I couldn't get away.

Hambone, Hambone, where'd you go?
I hopped up to Miss Lucy's door.

Hambone, Hambone, what'd you see?
I asked Miss Lucy to marry me.

SHEILA LOUISE HOLMES

Grandma, Grandma

· From "Jump Rope Rhymes and Hand Games: Their Educational
Significance in the Educational Development of
African-American Children" ·

"Grandma, Grandma" is a hand rhyme that was provided by two
first-grade girls from [an elementary school in California]. The hand
rhyme is performed extremely fast and the units of action include
verbal interplay, kinesthetic involvement and social interaction. The
phrase "let's get the rhythm of the head, Ding, dong," is accompanied
with the head going from side to side; the phrase "let's get the rhythm
of the hands" is associated with a clap, while the phrase "let's get the
rhythm of the feet" is associated with a stomp. The phrase "let's get
the rhythm of the high-dong" is associated with a swaying of the hips
in a sexual motion and moving the head. The neck movement is the

same movement that occurs when African-American females move
their neck in a circular fashion. These kinesthetic movements are all
taking place while the hand games are being performed at high
speeds and the verbal exchange is simultaneously taking place.

> Grandma, Grandma, sick in bed,
> She called the doctor and the doctor said,
> Let's get the rhythm of the head,
> Ding, dong,
> Let's get the rhythm of the head,
> Ding, dong.
> Let's get the rhythm of the hands,
> Clap, clap.
> Let's get the rhythm of the hands,
> Clap, clap.
> Let's get the rhythm of the feet,
> Stomp, stomp.
> Let's get the rhythm of the feet,
> Stomp, stomp.
> Let's get the rhythm of the high-dong,
> Let's get the rhythm of the high-dong.
> Put them all together and what do you get?
> High-dong, stomp stomp, clap clap, ding dong;
> Put them all together and what do you get?
> High-dong, stomp stomp, clap clap, ding dong.

This Little Pig

· *Traditional* ·

Usually recited to a baby as one pulls on separate toes with each line.

> This l'il pig went to market,
> This l'il pig stayed home.
> This l'il pig had roast beef,
> This l'il pig had none.
> This l'il pig cried "We-e-e-, We-e-e!" all the way home.

*Folk
Rhymes,
Work
Songs,
and
Shouts*

*
511

We Must, We Must, We Must

· *From Daryl Cumber Dance,* Honey, Hush! ·

When I recorded this verse on May 21, 1995, the singer told me she learned it in gym glass in the 1950s, but as she sang a younger woman joined her, suggesting that it has passed on to the next generation.

We must, we must, we must,
We must develop our bust.

We must, we must, we must,
We must develop our bust.

The bigger the better,
The tighter the sweater,
The boys are depending on us.

Anniebelle

· *From Lydia Parrish,* Slave Songs of the Georgia Sea Islands ·

This is a traditional work song, sometimes called a hammering song. Parrish's informant told her he learned it from the stevedores who loaded lumber, but that it was also used for spiking steel on the railroads. She also observed its use in chopping wood and swinging a weed cutter.

Anniebelle
     Hunh!
Don't weep
     Hunh!
Anniebelle
     Hunh!
Don't moan
     Hunh!
Anniebelle
     Hunh!
Don't go
     Hunh!

Leave home.

Hunh!

When I throw

Hunh!

My head

Hunh!

In the bar

Hunh!

Room doo'

Hunh!

I'll never

Hunh!

Get drunk

Hunh!

No mo'.

Hunh!

Don't want t' hurt *no*body

Hunh!

O-h no

Hunh!

O-h no

Hunh!

Dis ole hammer

Hunh!

Kill John Henry

Hunh!

Laid him low buddy

Hunh!

Laid him low.

Hunh!

[At this point Joe interpolated rhythmically: "Stan' by for another verse."]

Ain't no hammer

Hunh!

In this mount'in

Hunh!

*Folk
Rhymes,
Work
Songs,
and
Shouts*

★
513

Ring like mine buddy

      Hunh!

Ring like mine buddy.

      Hunh!

Raise Up

· *From Willis Laurence James,* Stars in de Elements ·

According to James, this song was sung by the "shack-rouster," the man whose
job it was to drive the men in the old road camps out to work in the mornings.

Buddy, raise up!
Raise up!
Raise up!
An' git dis fo' day coffee.
I ain't yo' ma!
Dat ain't her bed!
Call yo' ag'in,
Gwine whip yo' head!

Damn de Cap'm!

· *From William Laurence James,* Stars in de Elements ·

I have slightly regularized this work song for clarity.

Damn de captain!
Damn de company too!
I'm natchal born eas' man
Thoo an' thoo.
White folks done cuss me!
Done buke me 'round!
I'll take dis here pick
An' tear you down!
Captain, captain, hear me,
Listen to what I say:

Cap'm, cap'm, hear me,
Dis here's my last day.

I'm a Man

· *From William Laurence James,* Stars in de Elements ·

I'm a man,
Tall like a mountain,
I'm a man,
Steady like a fountain,
Folks all wonder
What makes it thunder,
When dey hear, Lawd,
My hammer fall!
It swing like thunder, Lawd, Lawd
When mah hammer fall.

Got One Mind for the White Folks to See

· *Traditional* ·

Me and my captain don't agree,
But he don't know, 'cause he don't ask me.
He don't know, he don't know my mind,
When he sees me laughing, laughing to keep from crying.
Got one mind for the white folks to see,
Another for what I know is me.

ROLAND L. FREEMAN

Street Cries

· *From* The Arabbers of Baltimore ·

Street Arabic is much like calypso singing. It has a similar rhythm
and meter, and often it tells a story made up on the spur of the moment.

As an example, there is considerable joshing among the Arabs who gather at Market space every morning to buy and load their produce. The ones who wait to buy their produce last, and so get it cheaper, are always butts. These men, it is alleged, can then practically give their stuff away and still make a profit. Meeting such a "Cheap John" on the street, another Arab may sing out:

Heah come ol' Cheap Jawn
He make a easy dollar
He buy his stuff so awful cheap
He don' even haf to holler.

That is an ideal "holler." First, it rubs "Ol' Jawn" the wrong way, which is the main idea. Second, its melody draws attention to the singer's own wagon. No bystander has the slightest idea what the Arab is saying, but "Ol' Jawn" knows.

And "John" may take a look at what his tormentor has to sell and then retaliate:

Folks don' want yo' ol' stringbeans
Ain't gonna buy yo' ol' sprouts
But deys something in DIS wagon
(Oh yes, dis wagon o' miiiine)
Dey is wiiiild about
Got sweet wah duh mil yun [etc.]

The adage that success depends not upon what you say, but how you say it, is the Arab's byword. One Arab with a line of garden produce seldom uses any sales talk except this:

Heah come Cheap Charlie, the po' man's friend
Oh yes, heah come ol Charlie, the po' man's friend.

Charlie isn't any cheaper than any other Arab, actually. He just likes the sound of the lines.

Another man, with a seafood line, frequently sings:

Got feesh, got feesh, whoa bee
Fifteen cent a pound, and dey knock you down

Oh pound
Knock you down
Whoa bee.

The calypso type of "holler," the one that tells a sort of story, is probably the most popular in Baltimore. Often its verses are composed from the Arab's observations or reflections as he plods beside his horse.

I've hollered and I've hollered
An' now my th'ote's all so'
If you don't git no mil yun
You won't see me no mo'.

The Arab may then improvise on the phrase "no mo-oo" for three or four blocks, or until his attention is diverted by something else.

Stop all 'at housewuk
An stop 'at laundry too
An' come to de wagon
(Oh yes and bring de bay-BEE)
An' heah dis ol' man's blues
Got sweet wah duh mil yun, lay-DEE.

An Arab who operates throughout South Baltimore employs a combination of chant and yodel:

Meel yun
Meel yun
Wah duh meel yun
Dime dime dime dime
Wah duh meel yun
Raid to de rine
Rine rine rine rine rine
Oh diiiiiime.

This man hasn't anything that sells for a dime, but his cry has never been questioned.

Of all the hundreds of cries that have echoed through Baltimore streets through the years, probably 80 percent have had to do with the watermelon. The cries that sell other produce are not only fewer; they're also less imaginative and less fervently delivered.

Strawbuees
Raid riipe strawbuees
An'rannel strawbuees
All fahn

Peeeeaches
Open an' cling
Sof' as anything
All sof

Tay-tooooooes
Whoa bee tay tooooes
Whoa bee

New Yeaaawk eeeeatin' apple
New Yeaaawk eeeeatin' apple
Sugah caaaaawn
Shoooooo peg
Shoooooo peg

Cantaloupes, tomatoes and strawberries from Anne Arundel county are the only things sold as enthusiastically as watermelons. Identifying any produce as "An'arranel" boosts sales.

Like men in any other business, the street Arabs have their heroes, "the real somebody persons" who have made their mark in the trade. One of these was a fellow by the name of Ol' Joe, who worked around Hollins Street a long time ago. He wore a spotless apron and cap and pushed a coaster wagon holding a sort of combination bin and counter, and above those a frame holding a large bell.

The bell rang as Ol' Joe plodded along, but he always held the clapper still during his "holler":

Hyah come de feesh man
Bring out de deesh pan

Fresh feesh today
From de Ches'peake Bay
Got perch, shad an' trout
Come on, white folks, come on out
God hahd crebs alive
[Vigorous shake of the bell]
Hahhhhhhhhd crebs!

Sometimes Ol' Joe had a wicker basket full of deviled crabs, covered over with white oilcloth. Then he would chant:

Debil debil debil debil debuuuuuuuuuuuul creb!

Another man working that section sold crabs with this chant:

Craaaaaaaaybs
Hard, fried and debble
To keep yo' haid on de lebble.

A fishmonger in another part of town once specialized in sturgeon steaks, which for some reason he called Albany beef:

Albanyyyyyy beeeeeef
Won't tangle in yo' teeeeeef.

Possibly the most famous Arabs of one period were Ol' Moses and Midas, who sold ice cream, oysters, hot corn, baked pears and a dozen other things. Ol' Moses had a particularly fascinating repertoire:

La lilla lilla lilla lilla lilla lemon ice curreem

Or on another day, with oysters:

Oysh, oysh, oysh, oysh
Shock oysh!

Ol' Moses whistled, too—with his tongue out, half folded like a leaf. He punctuated his cries with piercingly whistled snatches of songs:

Oysh, oysh, oysh
[Blow Ye the Trumpet, Blow]
F'om de Ches'peake Bay
[Old Oaken Bucket]
Jes comin' roun' once mo'
[Polly Put de Kittle On]
[*Etc.*]

Those calls are gone forever, the Arabs say, because one man never borrows a cry from another.

"You use someone else's words," one of them says, "and you don't know what you say."

ROLAND L. FREEMAN

Photographs of Arabbers

"Red" Earl on West Fayette Street, Baltimore, August 1979.

Broadway near Fells Point. East Baltimore, March 1980.

Heading up the Arabbers' contingent in the annual "I am an American" Day Parade are: *left to right,* Bilal Abdullah and his family in the near wagon; William "Sharp Eye" Clark in the middle; and Albert Ennis in the lead wagon. They are turning off Baltimore Street onto South Linwood Avenue. Twenty wagons participated, representing the five remaining stables. East Baltimore, September 1988.

Photographs used with permission of Roland L. Freeman.

Folk
Rhymes,
Work
Songs,
and
Shouts

*

521

Street Cries

· From J. Mason Brewer, American Negro Folklore ·

I sell to the rich,
I sell to the po';
I'm gonna sell the lady
Standin' in that do'.

Watermelon, Lady!
Come and git your nice red watermelon, Lady!
Red to the rind, Lady!
Come on, Lady, and get 'em!
Gotta make the picnic fo' two o'clock,
No flat tires today.
Come on, Lady!

I got water with the melon, red to the rind!
If you don't believe it just pull down your blind.
You eat the watermelon and preeee—serve the rind!

Nice little snapbeans,
Pretty little corn,
Butter beans, carrots,
Apples for the ladies!
Jui-ceee lemons!

Blackber—reees! Fresh and fine.
I got blackber—reeeees, Lady!
Fresh from th' vine!
I got blackberries, Lady!
Three glass fo' a dime.
I got blackberries!
I got blackberries!
Black—berrieeeeeeeees!

I got strawberries, Lady!
Strawberries, Lady!
Fifteen cents a basket—
Two baskets for a quarter.

Oyster Man! Oyster Man!
Get your fresh oysters from the Oyster Man!
Bring out your pitcher, bring out your can,
Get your nice fresh oysters from the Oyster Man!

We sell it to the rich, we sell it to the poor,
We give it to the sweet brownskin, peepin' out the door.
Tout chaud, Madame, tout chaud!
Git 'em while they're hot. Hot *calas!*

One cup of coffee, fifteen cents *calas,*
Make you smile the livelong day.
Calas, tout chauds, Madame, Tout chauds!
Git 'em while they're hot! Hot *calas!*

The little Jamaica boy he say,
More you eatta, more you wanta eatta.
Get 'em while they're hotta. Hot *calas!*
Tout chauds, Madame, tout chauds.

The Waffle Man is a fine old man.
He washes his face in a frying-pan,
He makes his waffles with his hand,
Everybody loves the waffle man.

Char-coal! Char-coal!
My horse is white, my face is black.
I sell my charcoal, two-bits a sack —
Char-coal! Char-coal!

Here's yo' chimney sweeps,
We goes up to the roofs,
Sweep the smokestacks down right now,
Don't care for soot, anyhow.
Rami—neau! Rami—neau! Rami—neau!

Sweep 'em clean! Sweep 'em clean!
Save the firemen lots of work,
We hate soot, we never shirk,
Sweep 'em clean! Sweep 'em clean!

Old Rag Man! Get your rags ready!
For the Old Rag Man!
Money to be made!
Get your rags ready for the old Rag Man!

*Folk
Rhymes,
Work
Songs,
and
Shouts*

★

523

. . . .

I live four miles out of town,
    I am gwine to glory.
My strawberries are sweet an' sound,
    I am gwine to glory.
My chile is sick, an' husban' dead,
    I am gwine to glory.
Now's de time to get 'em cheap,
    I am gwine to glory.
Eat 'em wid your bread an' meat,
    I am gwine to glory.
Come sinner, get down on your knees,
    I am gwine to glory.
Eat dese strawberries when you please,
    I am gwine to glory.

. . . .

Vanilla, chocolate, peach cream
Dat surely freezed by de stream.
It was made in de shade, an' is sold in de sun.
If you ain't got a nickel, you can't get none.

I got yellow cat and the white cat,
Got everything but the tom cat,
And he's on the inside.
If you believe I'm lying
Buy one an' try him.
Take him home
An' then you fry him.

Here comes yo' fish man,
Go git yo' dish pan,

Peep out de winder, step back to de dinin' room,
Tell de Mrs. I got fish-o-o.

Any rags, any bones, any bottles today?
The same old rag man comin' this a-way.

Swimp man, swimp man, raw, raw, raw.
Fifteen cents a plate, two for a quarter.
Raw, raw, raw.
Get 'em fore 'e too late, put 'em in de wash tub,
Raw, raw, raw.
Swimp man, swimp man. Raw, raw, raw, raw, raw, raw.
Ef you wanna see sum'pm fine,
Jes look in dis cart of mine,
Raw, raw, raw, raw, raw, raw.

Dry load, dry load of pine. . . .
Dry load, dry load going by.
Make up your mind before dis mule cry;
Make up your mind before I pass by.
I'll sell it to the rich, I'll sell it to the poor;
I'll sell it to the yellow gal,
Standing in the door.

WILLIAM WELLS BROWN

Baptist Chitlins

· *From* My Southern Home, or The South and Its People ·

In this section from his autobiography, William Wells Brown provides a full sense
of the marketplace and the street cries. The scene that he records took place in
Alabama right after the Civil War. He observed a "head peddler" with a tub on his
head singing the following lyrics. Brown not only provides the lyrics of the street
cry but also the humorous conversation that ensues between the seller and his
perspective customer.

Here's yer chitlins, fresh an' sweet
    Who'll jine de Union?
Young hog's chitlins hard to beat,
    Who'll jine de Union?

Folk
Rhymes,
Work
Songs,
and
Shouts

★

525

Methodist chitlins, jest been biled,
   Who'll jine de Union?
Right fresh chitlins, dey ain't spiled,
   Who'll jine de Union?
Baptist chitlins by de pound,
   Who'll jine de Union?
As nice chitlins as ever was found,
   Who'll jine de Union?

"Here's yer chitlins, out of good fat hog; jess as sweet chitlins as ever yer see. Dees chitlins will make yer mouf water jess to look at 'em. Come an' see 'em."

At this juncture the man took the tub from his head, sat it down, to answer a woman who had challenged his right to call them "Baptist chitlins."

"Duz you mean to say dat dem is Baptiss chitlins?"

"Yes, mum, I means to say dat dey is real Baptist chitlins, an' nuffin' else."

"Did dey come out of a Baptiss hog?" inquired the woman.

"Yes, mum, dem chitlins come out of a Baptist hog."

"How duz you make dat out?"

"Well, yer see, dat hog was raised by Mr. Roberson, a hard-shell Baptist, de corn dat de hog was fatted on was also raised by Baptists, he was killed and dressed by Geemes Boone, an' you all know dat he'e as big a Baptist as ever lived."

"Well," said the woman, as if perfectly satisfied, "lem-me have two poun's."

WILLIAM WELLS BROWN

I Am Gwine to Glory

· *From* My Southern Home, or The South and Its People ·

Brown heard this street cry in Norfolk, Virginia.

"I live fore miles out of town,
   I am gwine to glory.
My strawberries are sweet an' soun',
   I am gwine to glory.

I fotch 'em fore miles on my head,
    I am gwine to glory.
My chile is sick, an' husban' dead,
    I am gwine to glory.
Now's de time to get 'em cheap,
    I am gwine to glory.
Eat 'em wid yer bread an' meat,
    I am gwine to glory.
Come sinner get down on your knees,
    I am gwine to glory.
Eat dees strawberries when you please,
    I am gwine to glory."

Autograph Album Rhymes

· *From J. Mason Brewer,* Worser Days and Better Times ·

You are sharp as a tack, never dull;
Just like a peanut in a hull.

. . . .

Love all, trust few;
Learn to paddle your own canoe.

Sitting still fishing makes no one great.
The good Lord sends the fishes, you must dig the bait.

Blue is a color, red is too;
Try a smile when you feel blue.

Remember the M, remember the E;
Put them together and remember ME.

Corns really hurt, they give you the blues;
Remember that fact and buy fitting shoes.

*Folk
Rhymes,
Work
Songs,
and
Shouts*

*

527

When you marry and get out of shape,
Get you a girdle for $2.98.

The Mississippi River is deep and wide;
Catch a alligator to the other side.

Girls are made of sugar and spice;
Boys aren't made, they just shoot dice.

Green is green, red is red;
Study each day! Put knowledge in your head!

The moon is in the sky, and so is the sun;
Study first, then have your fun.

When you get old and think you're sweet,
Take off your shoes, and smell your feet.

When you're at a party and they drink alcohol,
Remember it's not needed to have you a ball.

I wish you luck, I wish you joy,
I wish you first a baby boy;
And when his hair begins to curl,
I wish you next a baby girl;
And when her hair begins to knot,
I guess you know it's time to stop.

The boys think I'm sweet, the girls think I'm kind.
I would like to know what's on your mind.

I'm writing you this letter, darling, I would write it in gold;
But ink is all my pen will hold.

Ice cream city, candy state,
This sweet letter don't need no date.

Up on a house top, baking a cake,
The way I love you is no mistake.

I don't make love by the garden gate,
For love is blind, but the neighbors ain't.

If you want your man, better keep him by your side;
If he flags my train, I'm sure gonna let him ride.

The higher the mountain, the cooler the breeze,
The lighter the couple, the harder they squeeze.

I've got a cute little shape, and a pretty little figure;
Stand back, big boys, until I get a little bigger!

I love you once, I love you twice;
Baby, I love you next to Jesus Christ.

When your heart tells you you're in a rut,
Tell your heart to keep its big mouth shut.

Milk is milk, cheese is cheese;
What is a kiss without a squeeze?

Choice kind of fish don't bite any kind of line;
You have to go deep-sea fishing to find my kind.

When you marry, marry good;
Make your husband cut your wood!

You're my morning milk, my evening cream,
My all-day study, and my midnight dream.

Roses on my shoulders, slippers on my feet;
I'm my mother's baby, don't you think I'm sweet?

Apples on the shelf, peaches in the bowl,
Can't get a sweetheart to save my soul.

Up on the mountain, five feet high,
I love you, baby, that ain't no lie.

. . . .

When you get married and have twenty-four,
Don't stop there, the Army needs lots more.

When you get married and your husband gets drunk,
Put him in the trunk and sell him for junk.

When you get married and have twenty-five,
Don't call it a family, call it a tribe!

The river is wide, the boat is floating,
Darling, let's marry and stop this courting!

Ice is ice, rice is rice;
One day, baby, you'll be my wife.

Apples on the table, peaches on the shelf,
Baby, I'm getting tired of sleeping by myself.

When you get married and live in China,
Remember me back in old North Carolina.

Life is sweet, life is swell,
But when you marry, life is hell.

When you marry and live across the lake,
Send me a kiss by a rattlesnake.

When you get married and live upstairs,
Don't fall down putting on airs.

When you marry don't marry a cook,
Marry a man with a fat pocketbook.

When you marry and live across the sea,
Send me a cocoanut C.O.D.

Lions in the cage, monkeys in the zoo,
Who wants to marry a fool like you?

*Folk
Rhymes,
Work
Songs,
and
Shouts*

*
529

If you don't like my apples, don't shake my tree;
I ain't after your man, he's after me.

When you get married and live out west,
I'll send your mail by the Jigger express.

Jack Johnson and Jim Jeffries

· *From J. Mason Brewer,* Worser Days and Better Times ·

Amaze an' Grace, how sweet it sounds,
Jack Johnson knocked Jim Jeffries down.
Jim Jeffries jumped up an' hit Jack on the chin,
An' then Jack knocked him down agin.

The Yankees hold the play,
The white man pulls the trigger;
But it make no difference what the white man say,
The world champion's still a nigger.

Rhymes and Brags from Muhammad Ali, formerly Cassius Clay

Unquestionably the most popular boxer ever in the Black community,[3] which has always embraced Black boxers as heroes, is Muhammad Ali, whose prowess in the ring was exceeded only by his quick tongue and ready wit: he declared himself "boxing's poet laureate." His boxing matches were always enthusiastically anticipated, not only for the titles at stake but also for the anticipation of the outcome he had forecast in some memorable phrase that he had coined to describe the forthcoming match, often in the context of the folk brag or dozens.

Ali was also admired as a "ba-a-ad nigger," refusing to go to Vietnam, continuing to declare himself the people's champion after he had been stripped of his world

[3]My focus on Ali's popularity in the Black community should not overshadow the fact that Ali is considered by many to be the best-known and most popular individual in the world.

heavyweight championship, boasting that he could "whup" anybody (and making good his word), always talking about how pretty he was, calling himself "the greatest," and, of course, always talkin' that talk!

I float like a butterfly 'n' sting like a bee.

It will be a killa and a chilla and a thrilla when I get the gorilla in Manila! [Forever after, the fight with Joe Frazier on October 1, 1975, was referred to as "The thrilla in Manila."]

The rumble in the jungle [fight in Zaire against George Foreman]

Rope-a-dope [Ali's description of his method of constantly forcing his opponent to come to the ropes after him]

The Ali Shuffle [his description of his moves in the ring, of which he said, "The shuffle gonna make you scuffle."]

You done run out of gas, now I'm gonna kick your ass.

They all must fall in the round I call. [He frequently forecast in a rhyme the specific round in which he would knock his opponents out.]

This is the piston that got to Liston (gesturing with his raised fist as he comments about his fight with Liston). — *William Nack, "The Fight's Over, Joe,"* Sports Illustrated *85 (September 30, 1996)*

He's got my title. He ain't the champ, he's the chump. [Ali's comments regarding Joe Frazier; the combatants in the forthcoming fight were often described as follows: "Frazier, the White man's champ; Ali, the great Black hope."]

I should be a postage stamp. That's the only way I'll ever get licked. —*Neil Leifer and Thomas Hauser,* Muhammad Ali Memories

I'm so mean, I make medicine sick. —*Neil Leifer and Thomas Hauser,* Muhammad Ali Memories

The Ring Shout

I reproduce this description of the ring shout from William Francis Allen et al., *Slave Songs of the United States*, who reprinted it from the *New York Nation* of May 30, 1867.

This is a ceremony which the white clergymen are inclined to discountenance, and even of the colored elders some of the more discreet try sometimes to put on a face of discouragement; and although, if pressed for Biblical warrant for the shout, they generally seem to think "he in de Book," or "he dere-da in Matchew," still it is not considered blasphemous or improper if "de chillen" and "dem young gal" carry it on in the evening for amusement's sake, and with no well-defined intention of "praise." But the true "shout" takes place on Sundays or on "praise"-nights through the week, and either in the praise-house or in some cabin in which a regular religious meeting has been held. Very likely more than half the population of the plantation is gathered together. Let it be the evening, and a light-wood fire burns red before the door of the house and on the hearth. For some time one can hear, though at a good distance, the vociferous exhortation or prayer of the presiding elder or of the brother who has a gift that way, and who is not "on the back seat," —a phrase, the interpretation of which is, "under the censure of the church authorities for bad behavior;" —and at regular intervals one hears the elder "deaconing" a hymn-book hymn, which is sung two lines at a time, and whose wailing cadences, borne on the night air, are indescribably melancholy. But the benches are pushed back to the wall when the formal meeting is over, and old and young, men and women, sprucely-dressed young men, grotesquely half-clad field-hands—the women generally with gay handkerchiefs twisted about their heads and with short skirts—boys with tattered shirts and men's trousers, young girls barefooted, all stand up in the middle of the floor, and when the "sperichil" is struck up, begin first walking and by-and-by shuffling round, one after the other, in a ring. The foot is hardly taken from the floor, and the progression is mainly due to a jerking, hitching motion, which agitates the entire shouter, and soon brings out streams of perspiration. Sometimes they dance silently, sometimes as they shuffle they sing the chorus of the spiritual, and sometimes the song itself is also sung by the dancers. But more frequently a band, composed of some of the best singers and of tired shouters, stand at the side of the room to "base" the others, singing the body of the song and clapping their hands together or on the knees. Song and dance are alike extremely energetic, and often, when the shout lasts into the middle of the night, the monotonous thud, thud of the feet prevents sleep within half a mile of the praise-house.

In the form here described, the "shout" is probably confined to South Carolina and the States south of it. It appears to be found in Florida, but not in North Carolina or Virginia. It is, however, an interesting fact that the term "shouting" is used in Virginia in reference to a peculiar motion of the body not wholly unlike the Carolina shouting. It is not unlikely that this remarkable religious ceremony is a relic of some native African dance, as the Romaika is of the classical Pyrrhic. Dancing in the usual way is regarded with great horror by the people of Port Royal, but they enter with infinite zest into the movements of the "shout."

Photograph of Ring Shout

Courtesy of The Georgia Historical Society.

ART ROSENBAUM

We Never Did Let It Go By

· *From* Shout Because You're Free ·

The ring shout is the oldest African American performance tradition surviving on the North American continent. An impressive fusion of call-and-response singing, polyrhythmic percussion, and expressive and formalized dancelike movements, it has had a profound influence on African American music and religious practice. The integrity of the early form of the ring shout has survived in unbroken traditional practice from slavery times in the Bolden, or "Briar Patch," community in McIntosh County on the coast of Georgia. First described by outside observers in the mid-nineteenth century and practiced by slaves and their descendants principally in the coastal regions of South Carolina, Georgia, and Florida, the southeastern ring shout was believed to have died out in active practice by the middle of the twentieth century. Remarkably, the close-knit Bolden community and its Mount Calvary Baptist Church have continued the shout annually to welcome in the New Year on Watch Night. Since 1980 an organized group from the community has also performed the shout away from home at churches, folk festivals, and universities, and this has reinforced local pride in the venerable practice. "The only people can shout is right here," shouter Catherine Campbell affirms. "Calvary was the stopping place of the shout because we kept the tradition going. We never did let it go by." . . .

With the help of folklorists Fred Fussell and George Mitchell, the Quimbys located the shouters of Bolden, who were persuaded to form a group that would present the traditional practice at the festival on St. Simons that year.

We were among those who saw the group, which was assembled by Lawrence McKiver, first perform the ring shout for the public on a wooden stage under the huge live oak trees; all the elements of this presumed extinct tradition were presented conscientiously, much as the elements had been reported by nineteenth-century observers. McKiver, as lead singer or "songster," began or "set" a song. At his side sat a "sticker" or "stick man," beating a broomstick on the floor in rhythm. Behind them a group of other singers, or "basers," answered McKiver's lines in call-and-response fashion, at the same time setting up counter-rhythms to the stick beat with clapping hands and patting feet. Then the "shouters," women dressed in the long dresses and head rags of their grandmothers' day, began to move in a counterclockwise circle, with a compelling hitching shuffle, often stooping or extending their arms in gestures pantomiming the content of the song being sung. This looked like dancing, but nonagenarian Deacon James Cook later explained the difference: "Back in the days of my coming on in the shout, if you cross your feet you were dancing, but if you solid, move on the square, you were shouting. But if you cross your feet you were turned out of the church because you were doing something for the devil. . . . So you see those ladies didn't cross their feet, they shouted! And shouting is . . . praising God with an order of thanksgiving."

Like their slave ancestors, today's shouters apply the term "shout" specifically to the movements rather than to the vocal or accompanying percussive components of the shout tradition, and distinguish between shouters—those who step and move in the ring—and the singers, basers, and stickers. Lorenzo Dow Turner reported that the word is a Gullah dialect survival of the Afro-Arabic *saut,* sometimes pronounced "shout," meaning a fervent dance around the Kabaa in Mecca. In his essay concluding the present work, ethnomusicologist Johann Buis advances the discussion of the relationships between the Arabic *saut* and the coastal ring shout. Early on, practitioners of the shout may have had their concept of the shout as a way to praise God reinforced by the English word "shout" in the Psalms ("O clap your hands, all ye people, shout unto God," Ps. 47:1) and elsewhere in Scripture; the Afro-Arabic *saut* does incorporate song as well as movement. Thus it is understandable that outside commentators should confuse shout as movement with the English word for a loud vocalization. Historical accounts of the coastal ring shout, as well as the testimony of the shouters of Bolden whom we have interviewed, usually differentiate between the shout as movement and the singing and percussive rhythm, even as they might refer to the collective components of the practice as "the shout." In inland areas where the ring shout has been forgotten, the term "shout" is still commonly used to describe the violent movements rather than the vocalization of a worshiper seized by the Spirit.

The shouters of Bolden also clearly differentiate between the shout songs and other types of religious songs, such as spirituals, hymns, and the more recent jubilee and gospel songs. The shout songs (in earlier times occasionally referred to as "runnin' spirituals") begin slowly at times but quickly accelerate to the brisk tempo of the shout. Most of them date back to slavery times, and many of the melodies hint at African and Afro-Caribbean origins. The texts, while occasionally prosaic and even secular ("Hold the Baby"), carry biblical messages ("Pharaoh's Host Got Lost"), coded references to the hardships of slavery ("Move, Daniel"), and often rise to impressive heights of apocalyptic poetry ("Time Drawin' Nigh"). Perhaps the texts function to mobilize those who perform the shout into the group-affirming symbolic motion; this may explain the positive content of the shout song texts, even when the subject is confrontation with death ("Wade the Water to My Knees"), when compared to the more poignant, introspective sentiments frequently expressed in early spirituals some of which have been called "sorrow songs."

Another defining element of the shout tradition, at least in the coastal regions of Georgia, Florida, and South Carolina, is that it has almost never been a regular part of church worship service but takes place in churches only after the prayer meeting is over. Some members of the clergy were sympathetic to the practice and others opposed it. The southeastern coastal ring shout, unlike a related tradition, the singing and praying bands in the Chesapeake Bay region, has functioned outside of the structured worship of the organized church. In earlier times benches were pushed out of the way in the church so that the shout might have room to proceed; or shouters would meet surreptitiously in cabins or in "praise houses" in the woods. In recent years churches have been modernized, the pews have been fixed to the floor, and the floors carpeted; Deacon Cook spoke sadly of such "dead churches with a concrete floor." However the Mount Calvary church congregation has built an annex with a wooden floor to allow room for shouting and for the resonance of the stick. The shout is also seasonal—as Deacon Cook put it, "shouting ain't no easy job. The tradition of shouting is when it was cold weather." This meant the Christmas to New Year's holiday season within the memories of today's shouters. Vertie McIver recalls that as she was growing up, the community would have shouts from house to house during Christmas week, go to church to shout on Christmas, and finally go to Mount Calvary on New Year's; they would "shout all night long," beginning at midnight and shouting until day break when they would sing "Farewell, Last Day Goin'."

Though there is ongoing debate about the degree of African origination of many African American folk traditions, there is little question, both from internal evidence and from the testimony of today's inheritors of the shout tradition, that the basic elements of the ring shout were brought from Africa. Besides the term itself, the call-and-response singing, the polyrhythms of the stick and hands and feet, the swaying and hitching shuffle of the shouters, all derive from African forms. The fusion of dance, song, and rhythm in fervid religious possession is an African practice, and it is not surprising that the ring shout flourished in coastal areas where there are many other documented examples of African, including Afro-Arabic, survivals. White camp-meeting songs also utilized call-and-response and white sects, such as the Shakers, worshipped in moving circles, but exposure of blacks to these white practices does not negate the African origins of the shout, though it might suggest a reinforcement or modification of African-derived practices. Deacon Cook stated explicitly that his forebears, born in slavery, told him that their ancestors had brought the shout off the ship from Africa in the 1700s. Lawrence McKiver's family tradition has it that "Kneebone Bend" was a shout performed as the family's slave ancestors landed in Virginia. McKiver understood that the slaves were not Christian when they arrived in America and that the tradition had to have evolved in practice in the New World; as he put it, while the shout moves "to an African beat . . . the slave, after he got over here, they got a little bit more — time brings on a change — they could get hold a little bit of the Bible, that's the way they tell me, and the one that could learn to read a little bit, they could . . . pick out a word, and they make — that's the way they make the songs." The slaves adapted their dialect of the English language, Christianity, and some elements of the musical traditions and hymnody encountered in America to the African-derived shout forms.

Chapter 10

Riddles and Other Verbal Tests and Contests

We played the Dozens for recreation, like white folks play Scrabble.
–H. Rap Brown, *Die, Nigger, Die!*

olk riddles, those traditional questions with trick answers, are among the earliest known forms of folklore recorded. References to the practice of riddling are found in Greek and Roman drama and epics, in ancient Asian writings, in the earliest European recorded literature, and in the Bible.

Though riddles need not be presented in rhyming verse, they often are. In some cultures, including African American, they are often preceded by a formulaic phrase, such as "Riddle me this riddle," and end with "What is it?"

Very popular in the African American community is the sexually suggestive riddle that provokes an obscene answer when the true answer is something quite innocent. Also popular in the African American community are a number of other verbal puzzles that challenge the audience or one individual. Among the most common of these is the courtship ritual, a form of which arose on the American slave plantations. The goal of the ritual was for the young man to test a lady before proposing marriage to her—to see, in the words of one slave named Uncle Gilbert, "ef [she] gives a man as good anser as he gives her question" (Frank D. Banks, "Plantation Courtship"). Thus the young man might ask the lady the traditional question in a courtship ritual, "Are you a standin' dove or a flyin' lark?" If she wishes to inform him that she is already involved in a relationship, she will respond that she is a standin' dove. If, however, she is unattached and free, she will describe herself as a flyin' lark. This playful interchange allows the suitor to make his approach without leaving himself open to a direct rejection, and it also provides a test of the lady's ability to equal him in a ritualistic exchange.

Closely related to the courtship ritual is the duel between two competing males debating which one loves and appreciates the object of their affection most and which one would do the most to win her love.

A number of other verbal contests are popular in a community where eloquence is highly valued, a contest of words is among the most popular entertainment, and the man or woman who can talk the talk is lionized. The most popular of these contests is commonly called "the dozens" or "the dirty dozens," but it is also referred to variously as rapping, snapping, cracking, jacking, busting, capping, signifying, joning/joaning, sounding, goading, dissing, bad-talking, wolfing, and a never-ending series of terms. Distinctions may be made among these terms by participants or scholars. John W. Roberts, in "Joning: An Afro-American Verbal Form in St. Louis," distinguishes between joning and the dozens and joning and signifying, suggesting that joning is closer to signifying, and that it may be distinguished from the dozens by the fact that the players are older, not as competitive, and do not use rhyme. He concludes that his analysis stems from categories recognized in the St. Louis area and acknowledges "that the community does not universally accept these distinctions and recognizes other categories as well." Many individuals who play these verbal games have never heard of the labels or the distinctions provided by scholars. Important to note is that all forms of this game of verbal one-upmanship are clearly variants of the dozens.

In the dozens two combatants face off in the presence of an audience to put each other down. They may attack each other individually or attack members of the other's family. So popular is the attack on one's mama that the game is sometimes referred to as (talking about) "Yo' Mama." The goal, of course, is to utter the most obscene, most striking, and most humorous insult that elicits the greatest audience response. Such insults take on added impact, of course, when uttered in rhyming couplets. Something of the significance of the dozens in the educational and recreational life of young Blacks was suggested by H. Rap Brown:

> The street is where young bloods get their education. I learned how to talk in the street, not from reading about Dick and Jane going to the zoo and all that simple shit. The teacher would test our vocabulary each week, but we knew the vocabulary we needed. They'd give us arithmetic to exercise our minds. Hell, we exercised our minds by playing the Dozens. . . . [Here Brown gives examples of rhyming couplets suggesting his sexual power.] And the teacher expected me to sit up in class and study poetry after I could run down shit like that. If anybody needed to study poetry, she needed to study mine. We played the Dozens for recreation, like white folks play Scrabble. (*Die, Nigger, Die!*)

Many Blacks who grew up in the ghettos, Dick Gregory and Nikki Giovanni among them, write about learning the Dozens as a necessary survival technique, teaching them to deal with their problems and to develop that verbal facility that is so admired.

While psychologists and a variety of other scholars have had a field day analyzing the significance of the dozens (arguing among other things that they are a rite of passage to manhood, an attack on matriarchal society, a valve for aggressions, a method of gaining control, a device for learning to deal with the insults to be faced in a racist society, and a subliminal expression of one's repressed fears of sexual incompetence and of homosexuality), most young Blacks continue having fun with these contests while laughing at the theories about their function. I might note also that the dozens has moved into the larger community, appearing in a number of popular Black movies, played at times in almost all the Black comedy shows, and even incorporated into commercials for Nike athletic shoes and Hallmark cards. Variants of the dozens are popular with young people from other ethnic backgrounds as well.

Another related word contest is the competition of one-upmanship where people compete in offering the most striking descriptions of a particular subject: who is the strongest person they've ever seen, the ugliest, the tallest, etc. Whatever the form, riddles and other word contests with their challenge of wit and their display of eloquence have always been popular in the African American community.

Riddles

· *From Elsie Clews Parson*, **Folk-Lore of the Sea Islands,**
South Carolina ·

These are exactly as given by Elsie Clews Parson except that I have regularized the spelling of answers that might not be clear to readers, such as substituting *egg* for *aigg*. The answers to each riddle follow in parentheses.

A house full, a yard full, a chimney full,
No one can get a spoonful.
(Smoke)

Feather it have, an' cannot fly;
Feet it have, an' cannot walk.
(Bed)

Something has a ear and can't hear. What is that?
(A ear of corn)

Something goes all around your house and never comes in.
    Guess what it is.
(A fence)

Higher than a house,
Higher than a tree,
Oh! whatever can that be?
(Star)

Round as a biscuit,
Busy as a bee,
The prettiest little thing I ever did see.
(Watch)

Somet'in' large, an' somet'in' small,
Has two han's, no feet at all.
It always runs, yet cannot walk,
You might be still to hear it talk.
(Clock)

Humpy Dumpy sat on a wall,
Humpy Dumpy had a fall.
All the king horses an' all the king men
Could not put him up again.
(Egg)

Riddle, ma riddle, as I suppose,
Hundred eyes an' never a nose.
(Sieve)

Little Nancy Hetticote in a white petticoat
An' a red nose,
De longer she stan',
De shorter she grows.
(Candle)

Who made it don' use it.
Who use it don' see it.
(Coffin)

More Riddles

· *From J. Mason Brewer,* American Negro Folklore ·

These riddles have also been slightly edited.

Something follow you everywhere you go.
(Your shadow)

I was goin' along de road. I met a man. He tipped his hat an'
drew his feet. What was his name?
(Andrew)

What goes and never comes back?
(Your breath)

*Riddles
and Other
Verbal
Tests and
Contests*

*
543

Why is de President wife nightgown like de United States
  flag?
('Cause dey both go off at his command)

If one drop of rain come to a pailful, what would a shower come
  to?
(To de ground)

Constantinople is a very long word. Can you spell it in two
  letters?
(*I-t*)

Why a chimney smokin'?
(Because he can't chew)

What is it that fly high and fly low, but haven't got any wings?
(Dust)

The whole house full,
And can't catch a mouthful.
Guess what it is.
(Air)

The black man sit on a red man head.
(Pot sit on a fire)

Something ran 'round de house an' didn' make but one track.
(Wheelbarrow)

Dere's something goin' through de wood an' don't touch a limb.
(Your voice)

Ol' lady an' ol' man was under de tree. An' de ol' man shook it,
  an' de ol' lady take up her dress an' took it.
(Apple)

Something has one eye and one foot.
(A needle)

There is something that run all time and never stop.
(The river)

Go day and night an' never get tired.
(The wind)

Spell hard water in three letters.
(*I-c-e*)

Two sisters set in an upstairs winder. Dey can't see each other.
(Eyes)

Some More Riddles

What's black and white and red all over?
(A newspaper)

What goes in very stiff and comes out soft and wet?
(Chewing gum)

What kinda bird don't have wings?
(Jailbird)

Walks on four feet in the morning, two in the afternoon, and
    three in the evening. What is that?
(A man—crawls as a baby, walks as a young man, and uses a
    cane as an old man)

Riddles
and Other
Verbal
Tests and
Contests

★
545

Tall Tales

· *From J. Mason Brewer,* Humorous Folk Tales of the
South Carolina Negro ·

I have slightly edited these riddles.

Question. What's the darkest night you ever saw?
Answer. The darkest night I ever saw, a raindrop knocked to my
doorstep and asked for a light to see how to hit the ground.

Question. What is the tallest man you ever saw?
Answer. The tallest man I ever saw was gettin' a haircut in Heaven and
a shoeshine in Hell.

Question. What's the shortest man you ever saw?
Answer. The shortest man I ever saw took a ladder to climb a grain of
sand.

Question. What's the tallest stalk o' corn you ever saw?
Answer. I saw a stalk o' corn so tall till the angels in heaven was pickin'
roastin' ears off o' it.

More Tall Tales

· *From J. Mason Brewer,* American Negro Folklore ·

Question. What de blackest man you done see?
Answer. De blackest man Ah ever done saw, de chickens go in de
chicken house, think hit sundown.

Question. What is de runningest car you ever see?
Answer. The runningest car Ah ever see was my uncle's ole car—it run
over Monday, kill Tuesday, sen' Wednesday to de hospital, cripple
Thursday, an' tol' Friday to tell Saddy to be at de fun'al Sunday at
4 o'clock P.M.

Question. What de fattest woman you done see?

Answer. De fattest woman Ah done see — her husban' have to hug her on de installment plan.

Question. What is the coldest day you ever see?

Answer. The coldest day Ah ever did see — de sun rose wid a overcoat on, an' went down wid a bunch o' kindlin' wood to make a fire.

Question. What de poorest horse you saw?

Answer. Ah saw a ole horse so po' till he have to put on rubber boots to tip pas' de buzzards.

Question. What de greediest man you ever see?

Answer. De greediest man Ah ever saw — he ate up evuhthing on earth, ate all de angels out o' heaven, and snapped at God.

Question. What de strongest mule you ever saw?

Answer. Well, Ah saw a ol' mule so strong till you hitched him to midnight, an' he break daylight.

Question. How hot you ever done seen it?

Answer. Ah seen it so hot till two pieces of ice was walkin' up de street fannin'.

Sample of a "Courtship" Conversation

*· From "Plantation Courtship," Southern Workman 24
(January 1895) ·*

Collected from Frank D. Banks, this selection has been slightly edited
for readability.

Kind lady, are yo' a standin' dove or a flyin' lark? Would you decide to trot in double harness and will you give de mos excrutish pleasure of rolling de wheels of de axil, accordin' to your understandin'? If not my tracks will be cold and my voice will not be heard around your door. . . .

Kind lady, if I was to go up between de heavens and de earth and drop down a grain of wheat over ten acres of land and plow it up with a rooster's feather, would you marry me?

Kind lady, suppose you was to go long de road and meet a pet rabbit, would you take it home an' call it a pet o'yourn?

Good lady, if you was to come down de riber and you saw a red strand of thread, black or white, which one would you choose to walk on? (In the answer, the color of the thread given is the color of the man she would accept.)

Are you a rag on the bush or a rag off the bush? (Answer—If a rag on the bush, free, if off, engaged.)

I saw three ships on the water, one full rigged, one half-rigged, and one with no rigging at all. Which would you rather be? (Full rigged, married; half-rigged, engaged; no rigging, single.)

Sometimes the girl wishes to find out her friends' intentions. *If so* it may be done without loss of dignity through the following circumlocution:

"Suppose you was walkin' by de side o' de river an dere was three ladies in a boat, and dat boat was overturned, which lady would you save, a tall lady or a short lady or a middle-sided lady?"

If the young man declares his desire to save a lady corresponding in height to his questioner she may rest assured that his intentions are serious. He may perhaps add the following tender avowal:

"Dear miss, if I was starvin' and had just one ginger-cake, I would give you half, and dat would be de biggest half."

Should a girl find herself unable to understand the figurative speech of her lover she may say "Sir, you are a huckleberry beyond my persimmon," and may thus retire in good form from a conversation in which her readiness in repartee has not been equal to her suitor's skill in putting sentimental questions.

Antebellum Courtship Inquiry
· *From Thomas W. Talley,* Negro Folk Rhymes ·

(He) Is you a flyin' lark or a settin' dove?
(She) I'se a flyin' lark, my honey Love.
(He) Is you a bird o' one fedder, or a bird o' two?

(*She*) I'se a bird o' one fedder, w'en it comes to you.
(*He*) Den, Mam:
　I has desire, an' quick temptation,
　To jine my fence to yo' plantation.

NIKKI GIOVANNI

Yo' Mama

· *From* Gemini ·

"Look at the stuck-up boobsie twins," they started. "Mama had to send the baby to look out for the coward."

"Don't say anything," I advised. "You always say something to make them mad. Maybe they'll just leave us alone." We made it past the house where we never saw the people and started by Dr. Richardson's. "They walk alike, talk alike and roll on their bellies like a reptile," they chanted. There had been a circus that year and everybody had gotten into the barker thing. "Just look at them, folks. One can't do without the other." And they burst out laughing. "Hey, old stuck-up. What you gonna do when your sister's tired of fighting for you?" "I'll beat you up myself. That's what." Damn, damn, damn. Now we would have to fight. "You and what army, 'ho'?" *'Ho'* was always a favorite. "Me and yo' mama's army," Gary answered with precision and dignity. "You talking 'bout my mama?" "I would but the whole town is so I can't add nothing." They sidled up alongside us at the Spears's. "You take it back, Gary." Deadly quiet. "Yo' mama's so ugly she went to the zoo and the gorilla paid to see her." "You take that back!" "Yo' mama's such a 'ho' she went to visit a farm and they dug a whole field before they knew it was her."

The Dozens

· *From John Dollard, "The Dozens," in* Mother Wit from the
Laughing Barrel ·

Your ma behind
Is like a rumble seat.

*Riddles
and Other
Verbal
Tests and
Contests*

*
549

It hang down from her back
Down to her feet.

If you wanta play the Dozens,
Play them fast.
I'll tell you how many bulldogs
Your mammy had.
She didn't have one;
She didn't have two;
She had nine damned dozens
And then she had you.

More Dozens

Because the dozens is such an obscene exchange, no attempt is made to reproduce
a game here. Rather I present some carefully chosen standard lines from
the game.

Yo' mama don't wear no drawers.

Yo' mama's like a piece o' pie. Everybody gets a piece.

Yo' mama's like a bag of chips. She free to lay.

Yo' mama's so stupid she got hit by a parked car.

Yo' mama's so dumb she tripped over a cordless phone.

Yo' mama's so stupid it takes her two hours to watch *60 Minutes.*

Yo' mama's so stupid she thought Taco Bell was a phone
company.

Yo' mama's so dumb she thought she could send a voice mail by
screaming into a envelope.

Yo' mama's so dumb that she would starve to death in a grocery
store.

Yo' mama's so stupid she sits on the TV to watch the couch!

Yo' mama's so bald you can read her mind.

Yo' mama's so bald she gets brainwashed when she takes a
shower.

Yo' mama's so ugly y'awl need a sign in your yard, "Beware of
bulldog."

Yo' mama's so dirty she makes mud look clean.

Yo' mama's so dirty she has to sneak up on bathwater.

Yo' mama raised you on ugly milk.

Yo' mama's in the kitchen; yo' daddy's in jail;
     yo' sister on de corner offering it for sale.

When yo' daddy go to work at ten,
Yo mama's at home ready to sin;
She call me on the telephone
An' tell me "I'm home alone."

Insults

Happy birthday to you,
You belong in a zoo.
You look like a monkey,
And smell like one too!

My name is Ran,
I work in the sand;
I'd rather be a nigger
Than a poor White man.

White folks think they fine,
But their raggedy drawers stink just like mine.

He is so ugly he has to *sneak* up on a mirror.

JAMES PERCELAY ET AL.

More Insults

· *From* Snaps ·

You're so fat, you have to use a train track for a belt.
Your mom is so fat, they use her underwear for bungee-jumping.
Your mother is so dumb, they had to burn down the school to
     get her out of the third grade.
Your mother is so dumb, she couldn't pass a blood test.
Your father is so dumb, when the judge said, "Order in the

*Riddles
and Other
Verbal
Tests and
Contests*

*
551

court," he said, "I'll have five chicken wings and some fried
    rice."
You're so dumb, you tried to dial 911, but you couldn't find 11
    on the phone.
Your mother is so ugly, the tide wouldn't bring her in.
Your father is so poor, he can't afford to pay attention.
You're so skinny, you could sleep in a pencil case.
You're so skinny, you have to tie knots in your legs to make
    knees.

Responses to the Dozens and Other Insults

Yo' mama.

Man, I don't play the dozens.

Talk 'bout one thing, talk 'bout another,
You talk 'bout me, I'll talk 'bout yo' mother.

At least my mama ain't no doorknob,
Everybody get a turn.

Least my mama ain't no railroad track,
Lay out all over the country.

Man, he's talking about your mama so bad
He's making *me* mad!

Retorts

These are sayings that are responses to or comments upon insults, requests,
threats, etc.

Tell the truth, snaggle tooth.
What you mean, jelly bean?

See you later, Alligator.
After while, Crocodile.

I dig all jive,
That's the reason I stay alive.

I respect work like I respect my mother,
And I don't *hit* her a *lick!*

Sticks and stones may break my bones, but words will never
hurt me.

Your eyes may shine, your teeth may grit,
But none of this food will you git.

Ask me no questions, and I'll tell you no lies.

Chapter 11

Superstitions and Other Folk Beliefs

Ole Satan is a liar and a conjurer too,
Don't watch out, he'll put a spell on you.
—Spiritual

The definition of superstition presents a problem here since what is called a superstition by others is not regarded as such by the believers. Indeed it is axiomatic that "If *you* believe it, it's religion; if it's what *other people* believe, it's superstition." Generally the word *superstition* carries with it the connotation of ignorance and is associated with unscientific and uninformed backwoods people. But everyone has some superstitions, some folk beliefs (what individuals would call their own "personal" beliefs) about what will bring good luck, what will cause bad luck, what can be used to cure illnesses, what can influence love, what can influence pregnancy and the expectant baby, what interactions spirits or ghosts have with living beings, etc., etc.

One of the most prevalent beliefs among early African Americans (and one that is not without some contemporary adherents) is in conjuration. One could go to the Conjure Doctor or the Goofer Man or the Hoodoo Doctor or the Two-Headed Doctor or the Root Worker or the Voodoo Priest[1] to secure help or relief for a variety of

[1]I recognize that it is problematic to discuss conjuration and Vodoun/Voodoo/Voudou as if they are the same; Vodoun clearly continues as something

concerns. The Conjure Worker is a direct descendant of the African medicine man. In his 1980 *Voodoo Heritage,* Michael Laguerre traces the origins of conjure to religious practices of the West African Yoruba people. The power of the Conjure Doctor, like that of anyone with double sight (unusual powers, such as the ability to see ghosts), is believed to stem from the fact that he was born with a caul (preferably seven cauls) over his face and, perhaps, that he is the seventh son of a seventh son. Conjure Doctors might also be trained as apprentices under the guidance of an experienced practitioner, as Zora Neale Hurston was in the ceremony she describes in "Hoodoo in America" and *Mules and Men.* Some are born into a line of doctors whose power is believed to have been transmitted— as was the most famous of all, Marie Leveau of New Orleans, whose mother and grandmother were Conjure Doctors.[2] Others come to their craft through meditation and signs. On the plantation the Conjure Doctor would be consulted to facilitate or end love affairs, to punish enemies, to remove conjures, to save slaves from punishment, to help slaves escape, to provide advice about everyday affairs (when to plant, when it will rain, etc.), and to cure illnesses. Though antebellum Whites generally ridiculed the slaves' beliefs in conjuration, their behavior suggests that in many cases they too had a healthy respect for or fear of conjurers. There are numerous tales of Whites consulting, fearing, respecting, and even freeing the Conjure Doctors on their plantations. They certainly enacted laws that seemed directed toward protecting themselves from the tactics of Conjure Doctors.

---

that is arguably more of a conventional religion. However, conjuration, Vodoun, Obeah, Santeri'a, Pocomania, Shango, Macumba, and a host of other African-inspired Diasporic belief systems have a common source in African theology, and all are regarded by the dominant society as folk practices. We should note here that many Christian practices, rituals, and beliefs bear similar ties to folk practices.

[2]The third Marie Leveau was born in New Orleans in 1827 and studied hoodoo with a master named Alexander. Legends abound about her power, many of which are recounted by Zora Neale Hurston in "Hoodoo in America." Hurston writes of her, "[S]he sums up traditionally a whole era of hoodoo; she was the great name in its Golden Age." Many later practitioners claim some relationship with her.

Significant ingredients in the potions the Conjure Doctor concocted included graveyard dirt, blood (especially menstrual blood), pins, needles, candles, horseshoes, a variety of herbs and roots, tea, silver five-cent coins, salt, red pepper, ashes of selected burned animals, and various parts of animals (especially black cats, dogs, rabbits, chickens, snails, rats, snakes, lizards, toads, and scorpions). Considered particularly useful were scorpions' and snakes' heads, chickens' gizzards, cats' bones, cats' hair, and hair balls. Conjurers often also used Voodoo dolls and charms. Several of the items in their arsenal needed to be obtained at specific times—at sundown or when the moon was in a particular stage. At times personal items, such as hair, urine, excrement, and/or a photograph, needed to be procured from the individual on whom the conjure was to be worked. Also important to the Conjurer's practice was a knowledge of numbers—a recognition of which ones were important in specific instances. The numbers three, seven, and nine were regarded as particularly significant and powerful numbers. Almost all conjures calling for pins and needles and hairs specify nine of the prescribed item.

Potions concocted by the Conjure Doctor might be fed to, put on the body of, or placed in the bedroom of the person to be conjured. If it were not possible to gain access to the individual or admission into his or her house, they might be placed under the steps, above the door, or at other locations nearby. Often they were buried in the vicinity of his or her house, usually a specified depth (such as seven inches). The person might be given a conjured item of clothing, or shoes, or a bottle of perfume. Sometimes it would be necessary for the individual to touch or handle an item for it to work. In other instances the Conjure Doctor could do something to a doll made in the person's image that would affect the individual even without immediate contact with the Conjure Doctor or with anything the Conjure Doctor prepared (sympathetic magic). Sometimes it would be enough to perform some ritual with the name of the person written on paper (preferably nine times), with his or her picture or something else associated with the subject.

There were clear indications that one had been hexed/cursed/fixed/tricked/whammied/conjured. Symptoms included pain and swelling, possession of the body by reptiles,[3] and animal-like behavior (howling, crowing, barking, growling, and walking on all fours). The discovery of some kind of charm or potion in or around one's house also was a sign that someone was attempting to work a hex on the individual. One diagnosis to confirm the suspicion of conjuration involved putting a piece of silver in the sufferer's mouth or hand. If it turned black, he or she was conjured.

There were always ways to prevent or counter conjures. Wearing good-luck charms such as a rabbit's or a jay-bird's foot, nailing a horseshoe over the door, and wearing a smooth stone in one's shoes were among the preventive measures. One might also wear a bag around one's neck with certain protective items, such as garlic and nutmeg. Once one was the victim of a conjure, the Conjure Doctor could counter it by devising a new conjure or perhaps turning the original conjure against the perpetrator. Other devices to exorcise conjures included drinking May-water (water from the first rain that falls in May), taking medicinal baths followed by special wraps, and meditating. Finally, individuals who discovered a sign that they had been conjured could seize that item, sprinkle salt on it, and burn it or throw it into the river.

While there continue to exist Voodoo cultural centers and museums as well as retail stores in some locations in the United States, especially in New Orleans, contemporary believers can turn to the Internet for just about anything they want—Voodoo dolls, gris-gris bags, juju charms (blessed objects designed to protect), love spells, general spell kits, "baby maker" kits, "leave my man/woman alone" kits, "lots-a-luck" kits, revenge kits, hex-removal kits, candles, books, and training programs. Obviously one loses on the Internet the whole ambience of the visit by a Conjure Doctor who examines one's person, inspects one's home, and concocts and administers potions or places them in the most efficacious locations in the house—or even, more memorably, the ambience of paying a visit to the Conjure Doctor's or the Voodoo Priest's sanctuary and experiencing not only

---

[3]Possession of the body by reptiles is the belief that snakes, lizards, or other reptiles were actually in the body of an individual who had been conjured. Some claimed to be able to see evidence of such reptiles moving through the body under the skin. Others claimed to see the head of a reptile when a victim opened his or her mouth.

the charismatic individual but the smells and textures and sights of the paraphernalia of the practice. When one is actually admitted into the presence of a fabled spiritualist and glimpses the mysterious bottles and jugs, the numerous roots and herbs, the heads of animals, the charms and crosses, the varied fascinating fabrics (such as red flannel and black cloth),[4] perhaps a mock grave, even the skull of a human, and eerie Voodoo dolls positioned on shelves and tables or arranged in shrines in a dimly lit inner sanctum, one certainly experiences a sense of awe not to be duplicated while sitting at the computer. But the Internet does offer consultations, chat rooms, bulletin boards, interactive Voodoo, and a host of other modern-day substitutes. These sites are careful to offer warnings and other disclaimers, but they insist upon the efficacy and authenticity of their charms and spells and claim traditional sources of power. Samantha Kaye writes:

> My entire line is based on spiritual information and religious tradition that has been passed down to me through my family lineage in Louisiana. All items are offered as historical curiosities. We do not accept responsibility for consequences or effects resulting from the use of any product sold herein. What that last statement means is if you use these products and you get what you wanted, and THEN decide that you didn't want that after all, that is not my responsibility. You should be sure what you want before using these products. (spellmaker.com)

A belief in ghosts was very prevalent in the early Black community and to some extent today. Spirits figure prominently in much of the

---

[4]Red flannel or some other red fabric was considered to be so fascinating that slavery is attributed to the African's attraction to it, an attraction that allowed the European to entrap him. For examples, see "How Blacks Got to America," in Daryl Cumber Dance, *Shuckin' and Jivin'*; "Red Flannel," in B. A. Bodkin, *Lay My Burden Down*; and Zora Neale Hurston's observation in *Dust Tracks on a Road* that she was "brought up" on the folklore "that the white people had gone to Africa, waved a red handkerchief at the Africans, and lured them aboard ship and sailed away." Black cloth (as well as other black items) is important in many of the rituals of the Conjure Doctor. The Conjure Doctor's potions were often wrapped or carried in red flannel or black cloth (see A. M. Bacon, "Conjuring and Conjure-Doctors," *Southern Workman* 24 [December 1895]).

practice of Hoodoo Doctors, so much so that some Spiritualists specialize in contacting the dead. While even ordinary folk sometimes see ghosts, people born with cauls over their eyes or with certain powers are considered better qualified to see, call forth, and/or communicate with spirits. Many are convinced that animals, especially cats and dogs, can see ghosts. Ghosts in Black folklore often appear at or near graveyards. They appear elsewhere at other times because of some problem they want resolved. Perhaps they want their death to be avenged or they want to reveal where treasures are hidden. Dogs, which are often assumed to contain the spirits of the dead, figure prominently in ghost lore. Calling upon the name of the Lord ("What in the name of the Lord do you want?") is one way of escaping from ghosts or of getting them to explain their purposes for appearing to you. One might also get rid of ghosts by pouring liquor on the ground, whereupon they will stop to drink it. A silver bullet also can kill a spirit. Conjure doctors recommend a host of other familiar remedies to help victims escape ghosts, including salt, charms, horseshoes, and hair from a black cat. The popularity of ghost tales is not limited to those who are true believers. These stories are often told to entertain, frequently with a goal of frightening the listeners, particularly children.

Popular Beliefs

It's bad luck . . .
if a black cat crosses your path
if someone steps across you when you are lying down
if you step in anyone else's tracks
if you walk on peanut shells, onion peelings, or salt
if you work on New Year's Day (you will then work all year
    long)
if you sweep a young girl's feet with a broom (she'll never
    marry)
if you point a broom at a person
if you sweep in the evening after sundown (you will sweep your
    good luck away)

if you sweep under a sick person's bed (he will die)

if you burn two lights in one room

if you hang a purse on a doorknob

if you put shoes on the bed

if you walk around the house with one shoe on and one shoe off

if you don't let the telephone ring at least twice

if a dog howls at night (sign of death)

if you dream about a fish

if you dream about snakes (that means you have enemies)

if you dream about a newborn baby

if you tell your dream before you break your fast

if you don't burn the hair left in your comb (somebody might get
   it and work a root on you)

if you let a frog pee on you (you'll get warts)

if you kill a cat (you will have seven years of bad luck)

if you break a broom handle

if two people look in the mirror at the same time

if something scares you when you are pregnant (it will mark
   your child)

if you do something mean to someone while you are pregnant (it
   will mark your child)

if you laugh at a person while you are pregnant (your baby will
   look like that person)

if you are a bridesmaid twice (twice a bridesmaid, never a bride)

if your husband-to-be sees you before the wedding

if you start building a house on Friday

if you step over a grave (you will die)

if you look back at a funeral procession (you will be the next to
   die)

if you wear anything new, especially shoes, to a funeral
   (someone in your family will follow in death)

if a new grave sinks in faster than usual (another family member
   will die)

It's good luck . . .
to find a four-leaf clover
to find a penny
to eat blackeye peas and hog jowl on New Year's Day

to see a redbird (you can throw a kiss and make a wish)
to put on your right shoe first (you will have good luck that day)
to befriend a cat that follows you home

Someone will die . . .
if a dog howls at night
if you cross in front of a funeral procession
if you wash clothes on New Year's Day
if you dream about fish
if you dream about a newborn baby
if a rooster crows at your back door

You can avert bad luck by . . .
wearing good luck charms and amulets
making the sign of the cross
burning white candles in your house
crossing your fingers when you pass a graveyard (otherwise
you'll be the next to die)

You can make a man love you by . . .
putting his picture on a table and burning a candle on top of it
for nine days
writing his name nine times on a piece of paper and putting it
under your pillow or under your steps
wiping his discharge in a handkerchief and putting it under your
mattress
cutting some hair out of your man's head and putting it in a jar
in a hole under your step (he won't be able to stay away from
your house)
putting a lock of your hair in his shoe
cooking some of your menstrual blood in his food
cooking some of your urine in his food
putting your unwashed panties under his pillow
"Mak[ing] a mixture of orange flower water, rose water, and
honey. Add to this nine lumps of sugar on each of which you
have written his name first and then yours. Burn a pink
candle in this mixture every day for nine days." —*Jim Haskins,*
Voodoo & Hoodoo

You can get rid of a man by . . .

sprinkling some pepper behind him when he leaves

putting his picture faceup in the bottom of your shoe (he'll walk
away from you)

buying him some new shoes (he'll walk away from you)

More Beliefs

Babies born with a caul over their eyes can see ghosts and often
have other powers.

A baby born at midnight will be able to see ghosts.

When a baby cries and jumps in his sleep, an evil spirit is
bothering him.

If there's a ring around the moon, there will be warm weather.

If you drop food, that means someone is wishing for it.

Kiss your elbow and you change your sex.

If a cat washes his face, it's going to rain.

If a rooster crows at your front door, you will have guests.

If it rains on a person's funeral, that means his soul has gone to
heaven.

If the sun shines when it is raining, that means the Devil is
beating his wife.

If you dream about water, that means it will rain.

If you dream about a funeral, that's a sign of a wedding.

If you dream about a wedding, that's a sign of a funeral.

If you dream that someone is dead, he will live a long time.

If you put your hand on a corpse, his ghost will not bother you.

If you go to the cemetery at midnight on a full moon, you will
see the dead walking.

If a pregnant woman craves a certain food, the baby will have a
birthmark resembling that food.

When a woman is pregnant, her skin will clear up.

When a woman is pregnant, her nails grow faster than usual.

If you carry your baby high, it will be a boy; if you carry it low,
it will be a girl.

If you carry your baby high, it will be a girl; if you carry it low,
it will be a boy.

You can get rid of a baby by drinking a lot of castor oil.

You can get rid of a baby by drinking hot coffee and taking quinine pills.

You can get rid of a baby by sitting in very hot water.

You can get rid of a baby by drinking sassafras tea.

If you pull a tooth and put it under your pillow, you will get some money.

If you find a four-leaf clover, you can make a wish and it will come true.

If your eye is itching, that's a sign you will get some money.

If your eye is itching, that means company is coming.

To make grapes grow on a vine, bury old shoes under the vine.

A new nail in an apple tree keeps the tree from being wormy.

When someone dies in a house, turn the clock to the wall.

After someone dies, take down or cover the mirror.

You can prevent White pursuers' bloodhounds from catching you by putting cayenne pepper and graveyard dust on your feet.

Good Luck

· *Traditional* ·

Find a pin and pick it up,
All day you'll have good luck.
Find a pin and let it lay,
Bad luck you'll have all the day.

Wedding Colors

· *From Newbell Niles Puckett,* Folk Beliefs of the Southern Negro ·

Marry in green, your husband will be mean.
Marry in red, you will wish yourself dead.
Marry in brown, you will live in town.
Marry in blue, your husband will be true.

Marry in black, you will wish yourself back.
Marry in gray, you will stray away.
Marry in pink, your love will sink.
Marry in white, you have chosen all right.

Medical Help

· *Traditional* ·

These are folk remedies.

Drink hot toddy (bourbon, honey, water, and lemon) for a cold.
Gargle with your own urine for sore throat.
Tie your sock around your throat for a sore throat.
Eat chicken soup to cure a cold.
Pour urine over affected area if you are stung by jellyfish.
Let a dog lick a dog bite; that will heal it.
Put some onion at the bottom of baby's feet to cure a fever.
Dip a wet rag in vinegar and hold it across your forehead to
   cure a headache.
Put cucumber over eye to remove puffiness.
Put potato peeling over eye to remove puffiness.
Rub ice on gums of teething child to soothe them.
To cure the hiccups, scare the person.
To cure the hiccups, drop some keys down the person's back.
To cure the hiccups, hold your breath and take nine swallows of
   water.
To cure a nosebleed, tie a string tightly around the little finger.
To protect from diseases, wear a bag containing asafetida
   around your neck.

Cures for Rheumatism

Among the many cures that Newbell Niles Puckett lists in *Folk
Beliefs of the Southern Negro* as cures for rheumatism are carrying a
raw potato in the pocket, wearing brass and copper rings or ear-

rings, wearing a silver coin, putting a penny in the shoe, wearing a ball of asafetida around the neck, wearing a snakeskin around the waist, wrist, or leg, rubbing stiff joints with grease stewed from a black dog, and wrapping the limbs in red flannel.

Signs from the Hampton Folk-Lore Society

· *From* Southern Workman *23 (January 1894)* ·

When looking at the new moon for the first time it is considered good luck to see it clearly, with no limbs of trees across its disk. If a man has silver with him when he sees the new moon and shows it to the moon, he will have money throughout the entire month.

Vegetables that grow under the ground must be planted on the decrease of the moon—those that grow above ground, on the increase. If you kill pork on the decrease of the moon it shrinks in the pot.

Other times and seasons besides the waxing and waning of the moon may be lucky or unluckly, according as they are used.

It is bad luck to do anything on Friday that you cannot finish on that day, but it is bad luck to trim the fingernails on any day but Friday, except it be the first day of the year or month.

It is very bad luck to wash clothes on the first Friday of the New Year. You wash away a member of your family.

The jay-bird and the red-bird are said to visit hell on Friday; whether this has any connection with the bad luck of that day has not yet been discovered by the Folk-Lore Society.

Saturday is a lucky day.

In connection with the coming in of the year it was noted that it means bad-luck for the year to have a woman or girl to enter your house on New Year's day and good luck to have a man or boy.

It also means bad luck for the year if you stumble on New Year's day.

It is bad luck to have your hair trimmed on the first day of March.

March is believed to be an unlucky month, but the first snow in March is good for sore eyes, if taken before the sun has shone upon it.

It is very bad luck to meet a cross-eyed person the first thing in the morning, or for a man's path to be crossed by a woman first thing in the morning. If this occurs on Monday morning the bad luck will continue through the week.

There are popular ways of bringing rain in time of drought.

If you sweep down the cobwebs in the house it will bring rain, or if you hang up a black snake the day he is killed the same result will follow.

Animals of different kinds bring good or bad luck with them.

It is bad luck to have a hare cross your path.

If you hear the first whippoorwill of the season when you are lying down, it forebodes a fit of sickness.

If you kill the first snake you meet in the spring, you will prevail over your enemy during the year. It is bad luck to kill a cat, but on the other hand it is good luck if a cat follows you, especially if the cat be black.

The howling of a dog or the lowing of a cow with no apparent cause are signs of death. A bird flying in at the door or window is a sign of death in the house, and if it flies over the head of anyone, of the death of that person.

If you catch a butterfly and bite off his head you will have a new suit of clothes. An inchworm on you is measuring you for a new suit.

A rabbit's foot, especially the foot of a graveyard rabbit, brings good luck to its possessor.

If a screech owl or whippoorwill frequents for several nights in succession a tree in a town or settlement or near a house it is the sign of a death there. If you hear it you must turn your pillow or put salt on the fire to make the bird leave.

A man's path from the cradle to the grave seems beset with dangers either from his most innocent actions or those of his friends or neighbors. Here are a few of the things that must be guarded against:

Never cut a baby's nails or he will grow up a rogue; they must be bitten or torn off.

Never sleep "cross-wise of the world," that is with the bed north and south.

Never point your finger at growing fruit or it will drop from the bough.

Never point your finger at a corpse or grave, bad luck is sure to follow.

Never lace one shoe before you put on the other or bad luck will come to you.

Never lift an umbrella in the house, or carry a hoe into the house over your shoulder, or enter a house at one door and go out by another, or sweep dirt or carry ashes out of the house at night.

When you cut your hair or nails burn the cuttings. If a bird should get hold of the hair it would make your head ache.

Never let your enemy get hold of your picture. If he should turn it upside down or throw it overboard into the water you would die.

If you dream of snakes but do not kill them in your dream, your enemy is living and will get the best of you.

When you go to bed at night lay a stick across the door and hang a sifter over the keyhole to keep the hags out. Open a Bible and lay it at your head. If no Bible can be procured, any other book is better than nothing to keep off hags.

Hang a horseshoe over your door to keep out the witches.

It means seven years of bad luck if a looking glass is broken in the house, or a death in the family.

If, when you are preparing to leave a room for any business transaction you strike your left elbow, it is better not to go, for only bad luck awaits you.

If, when you are walking you stub the toe of your left foot, it is an evil omen, on the other hand if you stub your right foot, good luck is coming.

If your left eye twitches it means bad luck, and the right eye good luck.

If the palm of your right hand itches, spit on it and put it in your pocket and money will come in to you soon. If the left hand itches it shows that you must soon pay money out.

When a man is baptized (by immersion) if he chokes in the water it is a sign that he has never been truly converted.

If it rains on a Wednesday the bride will soon be left a widow.

In undressing a bride throw ten pins over her left shoulder.

If a rat gnaws your clothes it is a sign that you are going to move. Never mend the clothes yourself, it will bring you bad luck to do so.

After starting out on a journey, if you have to turn back you may avert the bad luck that follows that action by marking a cross mark in the road with your foot and spitting in the middle of it.

You may know that strangers are coming if a rooster crows near your house door or if a spider comes down in his web.

He who lies crosswise of the world dies hard. Men die easier with the head turned toward the west and should be buried in the same position.

The last person whose name is called by the dying will be the next to go.

If, when a man is dying, the lightning strikes near his house, he is lost. The devil has come for his soul.

Never let any kinsperson wash or dress a corpse. If a corpse remains limp for some time after death some member of the family will soon follow.

The water in which a dead body has been washed must not be thrown out at night but must remain in the house until morning. This, however, is quite contrary to the usage in regard to other dirty water, as none can be allowed to remain in the house overnight without bringing misfortune.

Never cross a funeral train if you do not want to have bad luck. If you meet a funeral, do not pass it, but turn back and go with it if possible, if not turn out of the road and wait until it has gone by.

Old Jule

· *From "Some Conjure Doctors We Have Heard Of,"* Southern Workman *26 (February 1897)* ·

An old woman [conjure doctor] by the name of Old Jule killed so many people that her master said he'd sell her if she didn't do better. This threatening did not stop her, so he made preparations for sending her away. He put her on board a boat and started her away. She was very quiet all that day till dark, then she began to use her power. It is reported that she caused the boat to run backward all that night. When morning dawned the people were surprised to find that they had not made any progress during the night. When he found that he could not send her away, her master was compelled to let her remain.

ZORA NEALE HURSTON

Preparation for the Crown of Power

· *From* Mules and Men ·

Folklorist and writer Zora Neale Hurston tells of her study under a two-headed
doctor and her initiation as a Hoodoo Priest.

The next day he began to prepare me for my initiation ceremony,
for rest assured that no one may approach the Altar without the
crown, and none may wear the crown of power without preparation. *It must be earned.*

And what is this crown of power? Nothing definite in material.
Turner crowned me with a consecrated snake skin. I have been
crowned in other places with flowers, with ornamental paper, with
cloth, with sycamore bark, with egg-shells. It is the meaning, not the
material that counts. The crown without the preparation means no
more than a college diploma without the four years' work.

This preparation period is akin to that of all mystics. Clean living,
even to clean thoughts. A sort of going to the wilderness in the spirit.
The details do not matter. My nine days being up, and possessed of
the three snake skins and the new underwear required, I entered
Turner's house as an inmate to finish the last three days of my novi-
tiate. Turner had become so sure of my fitness as a hoodoo doctor
that he would accept no money from me except what was necessary
to defray the actual cost of the ceremony.

So I ate my final meal before six o'clock of the evening before and
went to bed for the last time with my right stocking on and my left
leg bare.

I entered the old pink stucco house in the Vieux Carré at nine o'-
clock in the morning with the parcel of needed things. Turner placed
the new underwear on the big Altar; prepared the couch with the
snake-skin cover upon which I was to lie for three days. With the
help of other members of the college of hoodoo doctors called together to initiate me, the snake skins I had brought were made into
garments for me to wear. One was coiled into a high headpiece — the
crown. One had loops attached to slip on my arms so that it could be
worn as a shawl, and the other was made into a girdle for my loins.

All places have significance. These garments were placed on the small altar in the corner. The throne of the snake. The Great One [the Spirit] was called upon to enter the garments and dwell there.

I was made ready and at three o'clock in the afternoon, naked as I came into the world, I was stretched, face downwards, my navel to the snake skin cover, and began my three day search for the spirit that he might accept me or reject me according to his will. Three days my body must lie silent and fasting while my spirit went wherever spirits must go that seek answers never given to men as men.

I could have no food, but a pitcher of water was placed on a small table at the head of the couch, that my spirit might not waste time in search of water which should be spent in search of the Power-Giver. The spirit must have water, and if none had been provided it would wander in search of it. And evil spirits might attack it as it wandered about dangerous places. If it should be seriously injured, it might never return to me.

For sixty-nine hours I lay there. I had five psychic experiences and awoke at last with no feeling of hunger, only one of exaltation.

I opened my eyes because Turner called me. He stood before the Great Altar dressed ceremoniously. Five others were with him.

"Seeker, come," Turner called.

I made to rise and go to him. Another laid his hand upon me lightly, restraining me from rising.

"How must I come?" he asked in my behalf.

"You must come to the spirit across running water," Turner answered in a sort of chant.

So a tub was placed beside the bed. I was assisted to my feet and led to the tub. Two men poured water into the tub while I stepped into it and out again on the other side.

"She has crossed the dangerous stream in search of the spirit," the one who spoke for me, chanted.

"The spirit does not know her name. What is she called?"

"She has no name but what the spirit gives."

"I see her conquering and accomplishing with the lightning and making her road with thunder. She shall be called the Rain-Bringer."

I was stretched again upon the couch. Turner approached me with two brothers, one on either side of him. One held a small paint brush dipped in yellow, the other bore one dipped in red. With ceremony Turner painted the lightning symbol down my back from my right shoulder to my left hip. This was to be my sign forever. The Great One was to speak to me in storms.

I was now dressed in the new underwear and a white veil was placed over my head, covering my face, and I was seated in a chair.

After I was dressed, a pair of eyes was painted on my cheeks as a sign that I could see in more ways than one. The sun was painted on my forehead. Many came into the room and performed ceremonial acts, but none spoke to me. Nor could I speak to them while the veil covered my face. Turner cut the little finger of my right hand and caught the gushing blood in a wine cup. He added wine and mixed it with the blood. Then he and all the other five leaders let blood from themselves also and mixed it with wine in another glass. I was led to drink from the cup containing their mingled bloods, and each of them in turn beginning with Turner drank mine. At high noon I was seated at the splendid altar. It was dressed in the center with a huge communion candle with my name upon it set in sand, five large iced cakes in different colors, a plate of honeyed St. Joseph's bread, a plate of serpent-shaped breads, spinach and egg cakes fried in olive oil, breaded Chinese okra fried in olive oil, roast veal and wine, two huge yellow bouquets, two red bouquets and two white bouquets and thirty-six yellow tapers and a bottle of holy water.

Turner seated me and stood behind me with his ceremonial hat upon his head, and the crown of power in his hand. "Spirit! I ask you to take her. Do you hear me, Spirit? Will you take her? Spirit, I want you to take her, she is worthy!" He held the crown poised above my head for a full minute. A profound silence held the room. Then he lifted the veil from my face and let it fall behind my head and crowned me with power. He lit my candle for me. But from then on I might be a candle-lighter myself. All the candles were reverently lit. We all sat down and ate the feast. First a glass of blessed oil was handed me by Turner. "Drink this without tasting it." I gulped it down and he took the glass from my hand, took a sip of the little that remained. Then he handed it to the brother at his right who did the same, until it went around the table.

"Eat first the spinach cakes," Turner exhorted, and we did. Then the meal began. It was full of joy and laughter, even though we knew that the final ceremony waited only for the good hour of twelve midnight.

About ten o'clock we all piled into an old Studebaker sedan—all but Turner who led us on a truck. Out Road No. 61 we rattled until a certain spot was reached. The truck was unloaded beside the road and sent back to town. It was a little after eleven. The swamp was dismal and damp, but after some stumbly walking we came to a little glade deep in the wood, near the lake. A candle was burning at each of the four corners of the clearing, representing the four corners of the world and the four winds. I could hear the occasional slap-slap of the water. With a whispered chant some twigs were gathered and tied into a broom. Some pine straw was collected. The sheets of typing paper I had been urged to bring were brought out and nine sheets were blessed and my petition written nine times on each sheet by the light from a shaded lantern. The crate containing the black sheep was opened and the sheep led forward into the center of the circle. He stood there dazedly while the chant of strange syllables rose. I asked Turner the words, but he replied that in good time I would know what to say. It was not to be taught. If nothing came, to be silent. The head and withers of the sheep were stroked as the chanting went on. Turner became more and more voluble. At last he seized the straw and stuffed some into the sheep's nostrils. The animal struggled. A knife flashed and the sheep dropped to its knees, then fell prone with its mouth open in a weak cry. My petition was thrust into its throat that he might cry it to the Great One. The broom was seized and dipped in the blood from the slit throat and the ground swept vigorously—back and forth, back and forth—the length of the dying sheep. It was swept from the four winds toward the center. The sweeping went on as long as the blood gushed. Earth, the mother of the Great One and us all, has been appeased. With a sharp stick Turner traced the outline of the sheep and the digging commenced. The sheep was never touched. The ground was dug from under him so that his body dropped down into the hole. He was covered with nine sheets of paper bearing the petition and the earth heaped upon him. A white candle was set upon the grave and we straggled back to the road and the Studebaker.

FREDERICK DOUGLASS

Sandy's Roots

· *From* Narrative of the Life of Frederick Douglass, an
American Slave ·

The first passage here occurs after Frederick Douglass has implored his master to
protect him from the cruel slavebreaker to whom he has hired Douglass out, but
the master only reprimands the beaten slave and sends him back to Covey. Note
that though Douglass professes not to believe in the magical powers of herbal
roots, we are left with the possibility that Sandy's prescription might have been
efficacious. The second passage describes the preparations of Douglass, Sandy,
and other slaves to run away, and again we are left with the belief that their
presentiments of failure are accurate, for they are caught immediately after the
close of the text here reproduced.

But as the night rambler in the woods drew nearer I found him to
be a friend, not an enemy, a slave of Mr. William Groomes of Easton,
a kind-hearted fellow named "Sandy." Sandy lived that year with
Mr. Kemp, about four miles from St. Michaels. He, like myself, had
been hired out, but unlike myself had not been hired out to be broken. He was the husband of a free woman who lived in the lower part
of Poppie Neck, and he was now on his way through the woods to
see her and to spend the Sabbath with her.

As soon as I had ascertained that the disturber of my solitude was
not an enemy, but the good-hearted Sandy,—a man as famous among
the slaves of the neighborhood for his own good nature as for his
good sense—I came out from my hiding-place and made myself
known to him. I explained the circumstances of the past two days
which had driven me to the woods, and he deeply compassionated
my distress. It was a bold thing for him to shelter me, and I could not
ask him to do so, for had I been found in his hut he would have suffered the penalty of thirty-nine lashes on his bare back, if not something worse. But Sandy was too generous to permit the fear of
punishment to prevent his relieving a brother bondman from hunger
and exposure, and therefore, on his own motion, I accompanied him
home to his wife—for the house and lot were hers, as she was a free
woman. It was about midnight, but his wife was called up, a fire was
made, some Indian meal was soon mixed with salt and water, and an
ash cake was baked in a hurry, to relieve my hunger. Sandy's wife

was not behind him in kindness; both seemed to esteem it a privilege to succor me, for although I was hated by Covey and by my master, I was loved by the colored people, because they thought I was hated for my knowledge, and persecuted because I was feared. I was the only slave in that region who could read or write. There had been one other man, belonging to Mr. Hugh Hamilton, who could read, but he, poor fellow, had, shortly after coming into the neighborhood, been sold off to the far south. I saw him in the cart, to be carried to Easton for sale, ironed and pinioned like a yearling for the slaughter. My knowledge was now the pride of my brother slaves, and no doubt Sandy felt on that account something of the general interest in me. The supper was soon ready, and though over the sea I have since feasted with honorables, lord mayors and aldermen, my supper on ash cake and cold water, with Sandy, was the meal of all my life most sweet to my taste and now most vivid to my memory.

Supper over, Sandy and I went into a discussion of what was possible for me, under the perils and hardships which overshadowed my path. The question was, must I go back to Covey, or must I attempt to run away? Upon a careful survey the latter was found to be impossible, for I was on a narrow neck of land, every avenue from which would bring me in sight of pursuers. There was Chesapeake Bay to the right, and "Pot-pie" River to the left, and St. Michaels and its neighborhood occupied the only space through which there was any retreat.

I found Sandy an old adviser. He was not only a religious man, but he professed to believe in a system for which I have no name. He was a genuine African, and had inherited some of the so-called magical powers said to be possessed by the eastern nations. He told me that he could help me, that in those very woods there was an herb which in the morning might be found, possessing all the powers required for my protection (I put his words in my own language), and that if I would take his advice he would procure me the root of the herb of which he spoke. He told me, further, that if I would take that root and wear it on my right side it would be impossible for Covey to strike me a blow, and that, with this root about my person, no white man could whip me. He said he had carried it for years, and that he had fully tested its virtues. He had never received a blow from a slaveholder since he carried it, and he never expected to receive one, for he meant always to carry that root for protection. He knew Covey well, for Mrs. Covey was the daughter of Mrs. Kemp, and he (Sandy) had heard of the barbarous treatment to which I had been subjected, and he wanted to do something for me.

Now all this talk about the root was to me very absurd and ridiculous, if not positively sinful. I at first rejected the idea that the simple carrying a root on my right side (a root, by the way, over which I walked every time I went into the woods) could possess any such magic power as he ascribed to it, and I was, therefore, not disposed to cumber my pocket with it. I had a positive aversion to all pretenders to "divination." It was beneath one of my intelligence to countenance such dealings with the devil as this power implied. But with all my learning — it was really precious little — Sandy was more than a match for me. "My book-learning," he said, "had not kept Covey off me" (a powerful argument just then), and he entreated me, with flashing eyes, to try this. If it did me no good it could do me no harm, and it would cost me nothing any way. Sandy was so earnest and so confident of the good qualities of this weed that, to please him, I was induced to take it. He had been to me the good Samaritan, and had, almost providentially, found me and helped me when I could, not help myself; how did I know but that the hand of the Lord was in it? With thoughts of this sort I took the roots from Sandy and put them in my right-hand pocket.

This was of course Sunday morning. Sandy now urged me to go home with all speed, and to walk up bravely to the house, as though nothing had happened. I saw in Sandy, with all his superstition, too deep an insight into human nature not to have some respect for his advice, and perhaps, too, a slight gleam or shadow of his superstition had fallen on me. At any rate, I started off toward Covey's, as directed. Having, the previous night, poured my griefs into Sandy's ears and enlisted him in my behalf, having made his wife a sharer in my sorrows, and having also become well refreshed by sleep and food, I moved off quite courageously toward the dreaded Covey's. Singularly enough, just as I entered the yard-gate I met him and his wife on their way to church, dressed in their Sunday best, and looking as smiling as angels. His manner perfectly astonished me. There was something really benignant in his countenance. He spoke to me as never before, told me that the pigs had got into the lot and he wished me to go to drive them out, inquired how I was, and seemed an altered man. This extraordinary conduct really made me begin to think that Sandy's herb had more virtue in it than I, in my pride, had been willing to allow, and, had the day been other than Sunday, I should have attributed Covey's altered manner solely to the power of the root. I suspected, however, that the Sabbath, not the root, was the real explanation of the change. His religion hindered him from breaking the Sabbath, but not from breaking my skin on any other day than Sunday. He had more respect for the day than for the man for whom the day was mercifully given, for while he would cut and slash my body during the week, he would on Sunday teach me the value of my soul, and the way of life and salvation by Jesus Christ.

All went well with me till Monday morning, and then, whether the root had lost its virtue, or whether my tormentor had gone deeper into the black art than I had (as was sometimes said of him), or whether he had obtained a special indulgence for his faithful Sunday's worship, it is not necessary for me to know or to inform the reader; but this much I may say, the pious and benignant smile which graced the face of Covey on Sunday wholly disappeared on Monday.

Long before daylight I was called up to go feed, rub, and curry the horses. I obeyed the call, as I should have done had it been made at an earlier hour, for I had brought my mind to a firm resolve during that Sunday's reflection to obey every order, however unreasonable, if it were possible, and if Mr. Covey should then undertake to beat me to defend and protect myself to the best of my ability. My religious views on the subject of resisting my master had suffered a serious shock by the savage persecution to which I had been subjected, and my hands were no longer tied by my religion. Master Thomas's indifference had severed the last link. I had backslidden from this point in the slaves' religious creed, and I soon had occasion to make my fallen state known to my Sunday-pious brother, Covey.

While I was obeying his order to feed and get the horses ready for the field, and when I was in the act of going up the stable-loft, for the purpose of throwing down some blades, Covey sneaked into the stable, in his peculiar way, and seizing me suddenly by the leg, he brought me to the stable-floor, giving my newly-mended body a terrible jar. I now forgot all about my roots, and remembered my pledge to stand up in my own defense. The brute was skillfully endeavoring to get a slipknot on my legs, before I could draw up my feet. As soon as I found what he was up to, I gave a sudden spring (my two days' rest had been of much service to me) and by that means, no doubt, he was able to bring me to the floor so heavily. He was defeated in his plan of tying me. While down, he seemed to think that he had me very securely in his power. He little thought he was—as the rowdies say—in for a rough and tumble fight, but such was the fact. Whence came the daring spirit necessary to grapple with a man who, eight-and-forty hours before, could, with his slightest word, have made me tremble like a leaf in a storm, I do not know; at any rate, I was resolved to fight, and what was better still, I actually was hard at it. The fighting madness had come upon me, and I found my strong fingers firmly attached to the throat of the tyrant, as heedless of consequences, at the moment, as if we stood as equals before the law. The very color of the man was forgotten. I felt supple as a cat, and was ready for him at every turn. Every blow of his was parried, though I dealt no blows in return. I was strictly on the defensive, preventing him from injuring me, rather than trying to injure him. I flung him on the ground several times when he meant to have hurled me there. I held him so firmly by the throat that his blood followed my nails. He held me, and I held him.

All was fair thus far, and the contest was about equal. My resistance was entirely unexpected and Covey was taken all aback by it. He trembled in every limb. "Are you going to resist, you scoundrel?" said he. To which I returned a polite "Yes, sir," steadily gazing my interrogator in the eye, to meet the first approach or dawning of the blow which I expected my answer would call forth. But the conflict did not long remain equal. Covey soon cried lustily for help, not that I was obtaining any marked advantage over him, or was injuring him, but because he was gaining none over me, and was not able, single-handed, to conquer me. He called for his cousin Hughes to come to his assistance, and now the scene was changed. I was compelled to give blows, as well as to parry them, and since I was in any case to suffer for resistance, I felt (as the musty proverb goes) that I might as well be hanged for an old sheep as a lamb. I was still defensive toward Covey, but aggressive toward Hughes, on whom, at his first approach, I dealt a blow which fairly sickened him. He went off, bending over with pain, and manifesting no disposition to come again within my reach. The poor fellow was in the act of trying to catch and tie my right hand, and while flattering himself with success, I gave him the kick which sent him staggering away in pain, at the same time that I held Covey with a firm hand.

Taken completely by surprise, Covey seemed to have lost his usual strength and coolness. He was frightened, and stood puffing and blowing, seemingly unable to command words or blows. When he saw that Hughes was standing half bent with pain, his courage quite gone, the cowardly tyrant asked if I meant to persist in my resistance. I told him I did mean to resist, come what might, that I had been treated like a brute during the last six months, and that I should stand it no longer. With that he gave me a shake, and attempted to drag me toward a stick of wood that was lying just outside the stable-door. He meant to knock me down with it, but, just as he leaned over to get the stick, I seized him with both hands, by the collar, and with a vigorous and sudden snatch brought my assailant harmlessly, his full length, on the not over-clean ground, for we were now in the cowyard. He had selected the place for the fight, and it was but right that he should have all the advantages of his own selection.

By this time Bill, the hired man, came home. He had been to Mr. Helmsley's to spend Sunday with his nominal wife. Covey and I had been skirmishing from before daybreak till now. The sun was shooting his beams almost over the eastern woods, and we were still at it. I could not see where the matter was to terminate. He evidently was afraid to let me go, lest I should again make off to the woods, otherwise he would probably have obtained arms from the house to frighten me. Holding me, he called upon Bill to assist him. The scene here had something comic about it. Bill, who knew precisely what Covey wished him to do, affected ignorance, and pretended he did not know what to do. "What shall I do, Master Covey?" said Bill. "Take hold of him! Take hold of him!" cried Covey. With a toss of his head, peculiar to Bill, he said: "Indeed, Master Covey, I want to go to work." "This is your work," said Covey, "take hold of him." Bill replied, with spirit, "My master hired me here to work, and not to help you whip Frederick." It was my turn to speak. "Bill," said I, "don't put your hands on me." To which he replied, "My God, Frederick, I ain't goin' to tech ye"; and Bill walked off, leaving Covey and myself to settle our differences as best we might.

But my present advantage was threatened when I saw Caroline (the slave woman of Covey) coming to the cowyard to milk, for she was a powerful woman, and could have mastered me easily, exhausted as I was.

As soon as she came near, Covey attempted to rally her to his aid. Strangely and fortunately, Caroline was in no humor to take a hand in any such sport. We were all in open rebellion that morning. Caroline answered the command of her master to "take hold of me," precisely as Bill had done, but in her it was at far greater peril, for she was the slave of Covey, and he could do what he pleased with her. It was not so with Bill, and Bill knew it. Samuel Harris, to whom Bill belonged, did not allow his slaves to be beaten unless they were guilty of some crime which the law would punish. But poor Caroline, like myself, was at the mercy of the merciless Covey, nor did she escape the dire effects of her refusal: he gave her several sharp blows.

At length (two hours had elapsed) the contest was given over. Letting go of me, puffing and blowing at a great rate, Covey said, "Now, you scoundrel, go to your work; I would not have whipped you half so hard if you had not resisted." The fact was, he had not whipped me at all. He had not, in all the scuffle, drawn a single drop of blood from me. I had drawn blood from him, and should even without this satisfaction have been victorious, because my aim had not been to injure him, but to prevent his injuring me.

During the whole six months that I lived with Covey after this transaction, he never again laid the weight of his finger on me in anger. He would occasionally say he did not want to have to get hold of me again—a declaration which I had no difficulty in believing— and I had a secret feeling which answered, "You had better not wish to get hold of me again, for you will be likely to come off worse in a second fight than you did in the first."

This battle with Mr. Covey, undignified as it was and as I fear my narration of it is, was the turning-point in my "life as a slave." It rekindled in my breast the smouldering embers of liberty. It brought up my Baltimore dreams and revived a sense of my own manhood. I was a changed being after that fight. I was nothing before—I was a man now. It recalled to life my crushed self-respect, and my self-confidence, and inspired me with a renewed determination to be a free man. A man without force is without the essential dignity of humanity. Human nature is so constituted, that it cannot honor a helpless man, though it can pity him, and even this it cannot do long if signs of power do not arise.

He only can understand the effect of this combat on my spirit, who has himself incurred something, or hazarded something, in repelling the unjust and cruel aggressions of a tyrant. Covey was a tyrant and a cowardly one withal. After resisting him, I felt as I had never felt before. It was a resurrection from the dark and pestiferous tomb of slavery, to the heaven of comparative freedom. I was no longer a servile coward, trembling under the frown of a brother worm of the dust, but my long-cowed spirit was roused to an attitude of independence. I had reached the point at which I was *not afraid to die.* This spirit made me a freeman in *fact,* though I still remained a slave in *form.* When a slave cannot be flogged, he is more than half free. He has a domain as broad as his own manly heart to defend, and he is really "a power on earth." From this time until my escape from slavery, I was never fairly whipped. Several attempts were made, but they were always unsuccessful. Bruised I did get, but the instance I have described was the end of the brutification to which slavery had subjected me.

. . . .

In the progress of our preparations Sandy (the root man) became troubled. He began to have distressing dreams. One of these, which happened on a Friday night, was to him of great significance, and I am quite ready to confess that I myself felt somewhat damped by it. He said: "I dreamed last night that I was roused from sleep by strange noises, like the noises of a swarm of angry birds that caused, as they passed, a roar which fell upon my ear like a coming gale over the tops of the trees. Looking up to see what it could mean, I saw you, Frederick, in the claws of a huge bird, surrounded by a large number of birds of all colors and sizes. These were all pecking at you, while you, with your arms, seemed to be trying to protect your eyes. Passing over me, the birds flew in a southwesterly direction, and I watched them until they were clean out of sight. Now I saw this as plainly as I now see you, and furder, honey, watch de Friday night dream; dere is sumpon in it shose you born, dere is indeed, honey." I did not like the dream, but I showed no concern, attributing it to the general excitement and perturbation consequent upon our contemplated plan to escape. I could not, however, at once shake off its effect. I felt that it boded no good. Sandy was unusually emphatic and oracular and his manner had much to do with the impression made upon me. . . .

The week before our intended start, I wrote a pass for each of our party, giving him permission to visit Baltimore during the Easter holidays. The pass ran after this manner:

> This is to certify that I, the undersigned, have given the bearer, my servant John, full liberty to go to Baltimore to spend the Easter holidays.
>
>

—W. H.

near St. Michaels,

Talbot Co., Md.

Although we were not going to Baltimore, and were intending to land east of North Point, in the direction I had seen the Philadelphia steamers go, these passes might be useful to us in the lower part of the bay, while steering towards Baltimore. These were not, however, to be shown by us, until all other answers failed to satisfy the inquirer. We were all fully alive to the importance of being calm and self-possessed when accosted, if accosted we should be; and we more than once rehearsed to each other how we should behave in the hour of trial.

Those were long, tedious days and nights. The suspense was painful in the extreme. To balance probabilities, where life and liberty hang on the result, requires steady nerves. I panted for action, and was glad when the day, at the close of which we were to start, dawned upon us. Sleeping the night before was out of the question. I probably felt more deeply than any of my companions, because I was the instigator of the movement. The responsibility of the whole enterprise rested on my shoulders. The glory of success, and the shame and confusion of failure, could not be matters of indifference to me. Our food was prepared, our clothes were packed; we were all ready to go, and impatient for Saturday morning—considering that the last of our bondage.

I cannot describe the tempest and tumult of my brain that morning. The reader will please bear in mind that in a slave State an unsuccessful runaway was not only subjected to cruel torture, and sold away to the far South, but he was frequently execrated by the other slaves. He was charged with making the condition of the other slaves intolerable by laying them all under the suspicion of their masters — subjecting them to greater vigilance, and imposing greater limitations on their privileges. I dreaded murmurs from this quarter. It was difficult, too, for a slave-master to believe that slaves escaping had not been aided in their flight by some one of their fellow-slaves. When, therefore, a slave was missing, every slave on the place was closely examined as to his knowledge of the undertaking.

Our anxiety grew more and more intense, as the time of our intended departure drew nigh.

Early on the appointed morning we went as usual to the field, but with hearts that beat quickly and anxiously. Any one intimately acquainted with us might have seen that all was not well with us, and that some monster lingered in our thoughts. Our work that morning was the same that it had been for several days past — drawing out and spreading manure. While thus engaged, I had a sudden presentiment, which flashed upon me like lightning in a dark night, revealing to the lonely traveler the gulf before and the enemy behind. I instantly turned to Sandy Jenkins, who was near me, and said: "*Sandy, we are betrayed!* — something has just told me so." I felt as sure of it as if the officers were in sight. Sandy said, "Man, dat is strange, but I feel just as you do."

WILLIAM WELLS BROWN

Voodoo in St. Louis

· *From* My Southern Home, or The South and Its People ·

In the following passage from his autobiography, which reflects on the power struggle between Blacks and Whites rather than his own bondage and freedom, African American novelist William Wells Brown discusses Negro beliefs in Voodooism. Despite Brown's patronizing tone, he provides us a view of many commonly held superstitions during slavery and also dramatizes the power of the Voodoo practitioner. Because of the length of this passage, I have summarized the ending of the chapter.

Forty years ago, in the Southern States, superstition held an exalted place with all classes, but more especially with the blacks and uneducated, or poor, whites. This was shown more clearly in their belief in witchcraft in general, and the devil in particular. To both of these classes, the devil was a real being, sporting a club-foot, horns, tail, and a hump on his back.

The influence of the devil was far greater than that of the Lord. If one of these votaries had stolen a pig, and the fear of the Lord came over him, he would most likely ask the Lord to forgive him, but still cling to the pig. But if the fear of the devil came upon him, in all probability he would drop the pig and take to his heels.

In those days the city of St. Louis had a large number who had implicit faith in Voudooism. I once attended one of their midnight meetings. In the pale rays of the moon the dark outlines of a large assemblage was visible, gathered about a small fire, conversing in different tongues. They were negroes of all ages, —women, children, and men. Finally, the noise was hushed, and the assembled group assumed an attitude of respect. They made way for their queen, and a short, black, old negress came upon the scene, followed by two assistants, one of whom bore a cauldron, and the other, a box.

The cauldron was placed over the dying embers, the queen drew forth, from the folds of her gown, a magic wand, and the crowd formed a ring around her. Her first act was to throw some substance on the fire, the flames shot up with a lurid glare — now it writhed in serpent coils, now it darted upward in forked tongues, and then it gradually transformed itself into a veil of dusky vapors. At this stage, after a certain amount of gibberish and wild gesticulation from the queen, the box was opened, and frogs, lizards, snakes, dog liver, and beef hearts drawn forth and thrown into the cauldron. Then followed more gibberish and gesticulation, when the congregation joined hands, and began the wildest dance imaginable, keeping it up until the men and women sank to the ground from mere exhaustion.

In the ignorant days of slavery, there was a general belief that a horse-shoe hung over the door would insure good luck. I have seen negroes, otherwise comparatively intelligent, refuse to pick up a pin, needle, or other such object, dropped by a negro, because, as they alleged, if the person who dropped the articles had a spite against them, to touch anything they dropped would voudou them, and make them seriously ill.

Nearly every large plantation, with any considerable number of negroes, had at least one, who laid claim to be a fortune-teller, and who was regarded with more than common respect by his fellow-slaves. Dinkie, a full-blooded African, large in frame, coarse featured, and claiming to be a descendant of a king in his native land, was the oracle on the "Poplar Farm." At the time of which I write, Dinkie was about fifty years of age, and had lost an eye, and was, to say the least, a very ugly-looking man.

No one in that section was considered so deeply immersed in voudooism, gooperism, and fortune-telling, as he. Although he had been many years in the Gaines family, no one could remember the time when Dinkie was called upon to perform manual labor. He was not sick, yet he never worked. No one interfered with him. If he felt like feeding the chickens, pigs, or cattle, he did so. Dinkie hunted, slept, was at the table at meal time, roamed through the woods, went to the city, and returned when he pleased, with no one to object, or to ask a question. Everybody treated him with respect. The whites, throughout the neighborhood, tipped their hats to the old one-eyed negro, while the policemen, or patrollers, permitted him to pass without a challenge. The negroes, everywhere, stood in mortal fear of "Uncle Dinkie." The blacks who saw him every day, were always thrown upon their good behavior, when in his presence. I once asked a negro why they appeared to be afraid of Dinkie. He looked at me, shrugged his shoulders, smiled, shook his head and said, —

"I ain't afraid of de debble, but I ain't ready to go to him jess yet." He then took a look around and behind, as if he feared some one would hear what he was saying, and then continued: "Dinkie's got de power, ser; he knows things seen and unseen, an' dat's what makes him his own massa."

It was literally true, this man was his own master. He wore a snake's skin around his neck, carried a petrified frog in one pocket, and a dried lizard in the other.

A slave speculator once came along and offered to purchase Dinkie. Dr. Gaines, no doubt, thought it a good opportunity to get the elephant off his hands, and accepted the money. A day later, the trader returned the old negro, with a threat of a suit at law for damages.

A new overseer was employed, by Dr. Gaines, to take charge of "Poplar Farm." His name was Grove Cook, and he was widely known as a man of ability in managing plantations, and in raising a large quantity of produce from a given number of hands. Cook was called a "hard overseer." The negroes dreaded his coming, and, for weeks before his arrival, the overseer's name was on every slave's tongue.

Cook came, he called the negroes up, men and women; counted them, looked them over as a purchaser would a drove of cattle that he intended to buy. As he was about to dismiss them he saw Dinkie come out of his cabin. The sharp eye of the overseer was at once on him.

"Who is that nigger?" inquired Cook.

"That is Dinkie," replied Dr. Gaines.

"What is his place?" continued the overseer.

"Oh, Dinkie is a gentleman at large!" was the response.

"Have you any objection to his working?"

"None, whatever."

"Well, sir," said Cook, "I'll put him to work to-morrow morning."

Dinkie was called up and counted in.

At the roll call, the following morning, all answered except the conjurer; he was not there.

The overseer inquired for Dinkie, and was informed that he was still asleep.

"I will bring him out of his bed in a hurry," said Cook, as he started towards the negro's cabin. Dinkie appeared at his door, just as the overseer was approaching.

"Follow me to the barn," said the impatient driver to the negro. "I make it a point always to whip a nigger, the first day that I take charge of a farm, so as to let the hands know who I am. And, now, Mr. Dinkie, they tell me that you have not had your back tanned for many years; and, that being the case, I shall give you a flogging that you will never forget. Follow me to the barn." Cook started for the barn, but turned and went into his house to get his whip.

[Dinkie gives a knowing look to his fellow slaves as he enters the barn with the overseer. There is much suspense as everyone waits to see what will happen in this encounter. After many suspenseful minutes, the two walk out peacefully, but several days pass before exactly what happened between them is revealed. Dinkie had shown the overseer the devil and threatened to tell the devil to take him away, whereupon the overseer begged, "Let me go dis time, an' I'll nebber trouble you any more."]

Magic Power

· From Elliott P. Skinner, Drums and Shadows ·

Collected from Jack Wilson.

Wilson acknowledged a firm belief in the supernatural. He told us, "I wuz bawn wid spiritual knowledge which gib me duh powuh tuh read duh mines uh people. I kin see people wut bin dead many yeahs. Duh dead know wut duh libin is doin an come roun deah close kin an friens wen dey is in trouble. I kin speak tuh duh dead folk in song an dey kin unduhstan me.

"I kin see ghos mos any time. Dey seem lak natchul people. Duh way I know it's a ghos is cuz I kin nebuh ketch up wid um. Dey keep jis a suttn distance ahead uh me.

"Witches an cunjuh is jis groun wuk. Ef yuh keep way frum um dey sho caahn hut yuh. Some hab magic powuh wut come tuh um frum way back in Africa. Muh mothuh use tuh tell me bout slabes jis brung obuh frum Africa wut hab duh supreme magic powuh. Deah wuz a magic pass wud dat dey would pass tuh udduhs. Ef dey belieb in dis magic, dey could scape an fly back tuh Africa. I hab a uncle wut could wuk dis magic. He could disappeah lak duh win, jis walk off duh plantation an stay way fuh weeks at a time. One time he git cawnuhed by duh putrolmun an he jis walk up to a tree an he say, 'I tink I go intuh dis tree.' Den he disappeah right in duh tree."

Witches Who Ride

· From Newbell Niles Puckett, Folk Beliefs of the
Southern Negro ·

The chief activity of the witch is riding folks, though occasionally there is that evil succubus who steals wives. One informant regards witches as identical with conjurers: "Dey's who' hoodoos, Marse Newebell, dey sho' is. Dey's done sold deir soul ter de debbil (the old European view) an' ole Satan gi' dem de pow'r ter change ter anything dey wants. Mos' gen'ally dey rides you in de shape uv a black cat, an' rides you in de daytime too, well ez de night." You can always tell when such witches have been riding you; you feel "down and out" the next morning and the bit these evil friends put in your mouth leaves a mark in each corner. When you feel smothered and cannot get up ("jes' lak somebody holdin' you down"), right then and there the old witch is taking her midnight gallop. You try to call out, but it is no use; your tongue is mute, your hair crawls out of its braids and your hands and feet tingle. My old mammy was very sick one time. Something heavy was pressing upon her chest. A good woman touched her, the load was lifted, and a dark form floated out through the window. "Hit mus' 'er been a witch." When you find your hair plaited into little stirrups in the morning or when it is all tangled up and your face scratched you may be sure that the witches have been bothering you that night. In Virginia "the hag turns the victim on his or her back. A bit (made by the witch) is then inserted in the mouth of the sleeper and he or she is turned on all-fours and ridden like a horse. Next morning the person is tired out, and finds dirt between the fingers and toes."

There is one song about an old woman who saddles, bridles, boots, and spurs a person, and rides him fox-hunting and down the hillsides, but in general, the Negroes deny that the person ridden is actually changed into a horse. But, horse or not, when a person talks or cries out in his sleep a witch is surely after him. Horses as well as humans are ridden; you can tell when the witches have been bothering them by finding "witches' stirrups" (two strands of hair twisted together) in the horses' mane. A person who plaits a horse's mane and leaves it that way is simply inviting the witches to ride, though they will seldom bother the horses except on very dark nights, and even then have a decided preference for very dark horses.

RUTH BASS

Mojo

· *From* Scribner's Magazine *87 (1930)* ·

White Mississippian Ruth Bass presents a memorable account of Conjure beliefs, practices, and practitioners in the Bayou Pierre swamplands.

Conjur is a strange thing. Some conjurers are born that way. Some learn their magic through long, slow years of patient meditating and watching of signs, and others, like young Donis, have conjur thrust upon them by accident. Donis picked up a hat that had been blown from another Negro's head in a whirlwind. He handed the hat back to the man. A few hours later the owner of the hat stooped to untangle the traces from his black mule's leg. He was laughing. The mule became frightened and kicked the man to death. He had died laughing aloud, and his death was attributed to Donis who had taken the hat from the devil in the whirlwind. Men would no longer work around him. He could not get a place to stay or to eat. Eventually he was forced to live away from his fellows in a tumble-down cabin on the edge of the swamp and follow conjuring as a trade. Sometimes a gal will come down from one of the plantations begging him for a love-charm; or a half-scared buck will come, willing to pay for a trick that will bring his wandering woman back home. But mostly Donis will be alone with the swamp and the silence—and the powers of conjuration. For magic is a lonely thing and when it falls upon a native of the Bayou Pierre swamp-lands there is no escape from it.

In these swamp-lands there are different ways by which a conjurer can be identified. If you are a double-sighted person and can see ghosts, if you happen to have been born on Christmas Day, or are a seventh son, you are born for magic. Others say, if you are an albino, or have three birthmarks on your left arm, or a luck-mole on your right arm, or if you have one blue eye and one black, you are born to conjure and it will be no trouble for you to learn the art of gri-gri. Of the several conjurers I have known in Mississippi, each one had some distinguishing physical characteristic. One was tall and dark with grave eyes. One was an undersized, dwarfed mulatto, almost an albino, with green eyes and a cunning little face. I remember one who had a twisted back and walked with a sickening, one-sided limp. But the most powerful conjurer I know today is a tall, dark woman. Her straight-backed, small-breasted figure seems in some strange way to suggest unusual strength. Her eyes are grave and wise, terribly wise in the ways of ghosts and devils and mojo, as well as in the practice of medicine. "Dat sickness ain't nat'ul an' doctor's medicine am bound tuh be agin hit," they say and send for Menthy. Menthy will come, grave and dark, to work her cures. A strange conglomeration of superstition and folklore these cures are.

She might prescribe the sucking of alum, or rubbing the limbs with graveyard dirt. Her specific for all diseases brought on by tricks or conjur is to mix some mutton suet with powdered bluestone and quinine and rub this salve on the bottoms of the patient's feet every morning. No one can harm the person who uses this salve, because it contains the fat of a lamb, and the lamb "am so innercint." For diagnosis Menthy will put a piece of silver in the hand or mouth of the sufferer. If the silver turns black, he has been conjured and must be treated accordingly. To locate the conjurer she uses the blood of a fat chicken. This is put into the hand of the patient and the hand slapped; whichever way the blood flies—well, the origin of the trick lies in that direction. One conjurer, a blue-gum Negro called a "Ponton," or cross between a horse and a man, uses tea made from the burned lining of the gizzard of a frizzly chicken pounded up with prince-feathers, to relieve a trick. Still another—an old, wrinkled, black woman—claims that water in which silver has been boiled is very effective.

As a preventive against being tricked Menthy prescribes nutmeg worn on a string around the neck, or the red foot of a jay-bird carried in the pocket. Others advise carrying the paw of a mole or a little ball of "he-garlic." One old man from up the swamp carries the right eye of a wolf in his right sleeve as a guard against the evil eye. The little old, black, wrinkled woman claims that she can prevent a woman from ever having children by giving her tea brewed from black haw and dogwood roots. Menthy accomplishes this by giving the woman dog-fennel to chew. She makes salves by boiling collard leaves and vinegar or vinegar and clay. But Tully, the hunchback conjurer who has a crippled body but unusual "strength uv haid," makes salve out of earthworms fried in lard. He cures rheumatism with the gall from animals, and headache with a poultice of jimson-weeds. To cure chills and fever he rubs red pepper up and down the patient's back to warm up the system. Others put red pepper into the sufferer's shoes. Menthy prescribes bathing in sun-warmed water and wrapping up in leaves of "Palma Christian." All over Mississippi one will find hog's hoof tea prescribed for pneumonia or pine-top tea sweetened with honey, or sweetgum ball tea. Menthy cures consumption by giving the patient hot blood form the heart of a young bull and by rubbing goose grease on the chest. To cure toothache, she picks the teeth with a sliver from a pine-tree that was struck by lightning and then throws the pick into running water. The best-known general household remedy, given for all manner of diseases, is May-water. May-water is water caught in the first rain that falls in the month of May.

The strangest cure I think I ever heard of in Mississippi was when Overlea, a seventh son and a born double-sighter, loosed five white pigeons that had never known freedom, for a sick child. When the pigeons crossed water the child was cured. Overlea, they say, can "split a storm" by sticking an axe into the corner of the room or into the ground. He can produce rain by crossing two matches and sprinkling salt on them, or by hanging up a "snake-shed." He can call fair weather by sleeping with certain flowers under his head. Yes, magic is still a practised and powerful thing among the Negroes of some parts of the South today.

It was Menthy, feared and respected as she is all over the Bottoms, who told me how to become a conjurer. It seems that the secret of the whole thing is to know the signs. First, last, and always, know the signs, and nothing will be hidden from you. If a person knows the signs, he can always tell what is going to happen. One thing the conjurer always does is to learn some secret name by which he calls himself when working spells. This name is never revealed to any one. Then he learns to meditate. If he knows the signs and knows how to meditate, all he has to do is lie down on his back, fold his arms, and watch the visions swing by. There are a few signs that are more or less common to all mojo-workers.

They always carry a beauty rock (a small, clear pebble) in their pockets and they are careful never to drink from a gourd after another conjurer. They always watch out for cats, pigs, and wood-peckers. From various sources I learned why these three creatures are watched out for. Woodpeckers are conjur-birds, always tapping at things and digging out secrets. Pigs can see the wind. When you hear pigs squealing uncommon loud—well, that's a sure sign of a change in the weather. The pigs are squealing at what they see on the wind. If a person wishes to see the wind, he must put a little of the water that runs out of the corner of the pig's eye in his own eyes. Cats were first made of Jesus' glove, and that's why it's so unlucky to kill a cat. Always watch out for cats.

Then the student of mojo must learn how to lay the tricks. Red flannel is almost always used in making tricks. To hoodoo a person,

Menthy takes a bunch of hair or wool, a rabbit's paw, and a chicken gizzard. She ties these up in a red flannel rag and fastens the bundle to some implement which the man to be conjured is in the habit of using. She assures me that as soon as the person catches sight of the trick his eyes will bulge out, and he will break into a cold sweat. He gradually grows weak and will eventually fall away to a mere shadow. Some conjurers put their tricks into the person's shoes; others into his sweet-potato patch or his wood-pile, or rub it on his razor or butcher-knife. Menthy's grandpappy, who from all accounts was a most powerful witch-doctor, could make the wind a bearer of devilment. He would dust his hands with powdered devil's-shoestring and devil's-snuff, then hold them up so the wind would blow the dust toward the person he wished to conjure. Jimson-weed pounded with the dried head of a snake will fly on the wind and work the trick also. However, except in extreme cases, Menthy herself is averse to using the wind to carry tricks. She would only shake her head when I asked her why. Probably because too many people can see the wind nowadays.

As a personal favor to a friend of long standing, Menthy disclosed to me, on special request, the most powerful trick known to any conjurer in the Bottoms. It is a dangerous business and can't be played with. You take the wing of a jay-bird, the jaw of a squirrel, and the fang of a rattlesnake and burn them to ashes on red-hot metal. Mix the ashes with a bit of grave dust, taken at sundown from the grave of the old and wicked, moisten with the blood of a pig-eating sow, and make into a cake. Put this cake into a little bag tied with ravellings from a shroud, name it for a person you wish to conjure, and bury it under his house. It will bring certain death to the victim. In making this trick, the forefinger of the left hand must be used. In fact, among conjurers of this section of the South it is a common practice to use this certain finger. This is the dog finger. The dog finger is the conjur finger and the left hand is the devil's hand.

So far as I have been able to discover, there seems to be a trick for every kind of occupation and desire in life. To the swamp Negroes nothing is inanimate, incapable of being tricked. I have heard a swamp Negress talking aloud to her pot because it was slow about boiling. She begged it to boil, pointed out the advantages of boiling over not boiling, and when it remained obstinate she resorted to a trick which consisted of rubbing her belly. The pot promptly cooked faster. To prevent things from boiling over, the cook rubs her head. I have often heard plantation folks use angry words to a fire because it refused to burn. And they say that if a fire burns with a blue flame it is making anger and you'd better "chunk" some salt in there to drive the devil away.

The swamp seems to be full of old and familiar friends, and those who live in its shadows are never lonely. The fisherman on the wet, shaded banks of the bayou talks to his fish-hook before he sets it to catch the sleepy catfish in the sluggish stream. He tells the hook how hungry his children and his old grandmammy are, and how easy it is to catch fish. Then he spits on the hook and sets it out. A hook that continually refuses to catch a fish is judged naturally bad-natured and perverse and is soon consigned to the bottom of the bayou.

One class of tricks always popular and useful is the great and powerful love-charm. Chewing of heart-root in the presence of a person will soften that person's heart toward you. To get control over a person, chew some shame-weed and rub it on your hands before shaking hands with the person you desire. To call a woman to you is a little more complicated and usually has to be done by a professional, though the common population tries its hand at most of the love-tricks. You pick up some dirt from the woman's foot-track, mingle it with some dust from your own track, mix with red onion juice, and tie in red flannel. This charm is carried in the left breast-pocket and acts as a magnet to draw the desired one to you. To bring a man and woman together, Menthy gets some hair from the head of each. She takes this to the woods and finds a young sapling that has grown up in a fork. She splits the tree a little at this fork and puts the hair in the split place. When this tree grows up the two will be eternally united. Menthy informs me that men are always coming to her for tricks to keep a wandering woman at home, and this is how she does it. Devil's-shoestring (a plant that grows abundantly in the Bottoms) mixed with snail-water, tracks from the woman's right foot, gunpowder, and bluestone. This mixture planted around the house is guaranteed to keep any woman at home. To break up a couple, Menthy takes some of the tracks of each while the ground is wet, rolls this up in brown paper, putting some whiskers of a cat and those of a dog in with it. She ties this up in a sack and leaves until the earth is dry. When it has dried she throws it all into the fire, and the two will henceforth fight like cats and dogs.

These are a few proofs that magic is a living thing in some parts of the South today. Where did it come from? How long has it existed? What part of it was brought from the African jungle? How much of it has been acquired from the whites, who in turn had brought it from their own foreign forefathers? Most of us have lost our ancient mysteries in the creation and worship of machinery. We have left magic behind. As they have taken the out-of-date clothes and old-fashioned, battered furniture, they took our outworn wisdom. Planted in the swamp this patched and cut-down wisdom has lived and grown. Their mojo is not fakery. It is not trickery. It is magic. Swamps themselves are mysterious, and magic belongs there. Swamps are refuges for wild things that are in danger of extermination. Mojo is taking its last stand. It has retreated to the swamplands. Whatever its origin, whatever its future, it is no less interesting and no less an outward sign of the emotional and spiritual life of the rural Negroes in parts of the South today. I am convinced that volumes of unsurpassably interesting folk-knowledge exist among the plantation black folk of Mississippi and other Southern States. It seems certain that at least a part of this magic is of African origin. It is doubly certain that it is all in danger of passing away with the passing of plantation Negro life.

In these swamp-lands I have often found traces of the old magic called tree-talking. Here magic becomes a still more imponderable thing and carries with it a philosophy that is more or less pantheistic. It had its roots in the friendship of the jungle man for the mysterious, animated, and beautiful world in which he lived. The swamp people, like the jungle men, recognize life in everything about them. They impart a consciousness and a wisdom to the variable moods of material things, wind, water, trees. Details are vague and hard to find, but, so far as I have been able to ascertain, the basis of tree-talking is the cultivation of a friendship with a certain tree — any tree of any species will do. The young tree-talker goes to this tree, first with a teacher and later alone. He loves it and studies it under all conditions and seasons. He listens while the summer breezes whisper through it. He pays attention to the lashing of winter winds. He meditates under it by day and sleeps under it at night. Then, when he has learned its language, tree and man talk together. No one can explain it. It is simply magic, a magic that is still found in the Bayou Pierre swamp-land today. Among my acquaintances I number one tree-talker. The other conjurers point to Divinity when I mention tree-talking. More than once I have visited his cabin in the edge of the swamp, burning with curiosity, and I learned nothing tangible. I resolved to try again and on a warm afternoon in autumn I followed the swamp path along the bayou until I found him—and what he lived by.

Old Divinity sat on the little front porch of his cabin at the very edge of the swamp. It was late October, dry and still with a low-hanging sky. Leaves were beginning to drift from the big water-oak that dominated his clean-swept yard. A frizzly cock and three vari-colored hens scratched and clucked in the shrivelled leaves under a fig-tree near the porch. Six white pigeons sat in a row on the roof, sunning their ruffled feathers. A brown leaf, whirled from the oak by a sudden gust of wind, fell on Divinity's knee. He laid a gnarled old hand on the leaf and held it there. A swarm of sulphur-yellow but-terflies floated by. Silently, aimlessly, purposefully, they drifted east-ward. Divinity sighed.

"Bes' tuh stay in one place an' take whut de good Lawd sends, lak a tree. Here was my chance, it seemed.

"Yes, there's something of magic about a tree. I've heard that, for whoever can understand, there's a thing called tree-talking, Ever hear of it, Divinity?

"Did Ah! Ma gran'mammy brung tree-tawkin' from de jungle. Ah's from a tree-tawkin' fambly, an' Ah ain't be livin' undah this watah-oak evah since ah surrendah foh nuthin'." I felt that I was near to looking into that almost inscrutable Negro soul. Here were pages of precious folk-knowledge and all of it in danger of passing with ninety-six-year-old Divinity. What could I say to draw out a bit of his jungle lore? I said nothing.

The old man fumbled through his numerous pockets for his sack of home-mixed tobacco and clay pipe. A flame flared up from his match, then the fragrance of burning deer-tongue slipped away on the soft air. Divinity rubbed his dry old hands together. I was afraid to seem too eager. Silence lay between us. Suddenly there came from the swamp pines and cypresses that crowded upon the little clearing, a soft murmur, a sound like the whimper of a company of comfort-less creatures passing through the trees. We felt no wind and there was no perceptible movement in the treetops; but the gray swamp-moss swayed gently as though it were endowed with the power of voluntary motion.

"Heah dat? If yo heah murmurin' in de trees when de win' ain't blowin' dem's sperrits. Den effen yo know how tuh lissen yo kin git dey wisdom."

"Spirits of what, Divinity?"

"Why, de sperrits ob trees! Dey rustle de leaves tuh tract tenshun, den dey speaks tuh yo."

"So trees have spirits, have they?"

"Cose dey does." The old man withered me with a glance, puffed out a cloud of fragrant smoke and proceeded, in his slow old voice, to tell me a few things about spirits. Everything has spirit, he told me. What is it in the jimson-weed that cures asthma if it isn't the spirit of the weed? What is that in the buckeye that can drive off rheumatism unless it's spirit? Yes, he assured me, everything has spirit. To prove it he could take me to a certain spring that was haunted by the ghost of a bucket. Now if that bucket didn't have a spirit where did its ghost come from? To Divinity man is only a rather insignificant par-taker in the adventure called life. The soul of man is a living thing, but neither greater nor less than the soul of anything else in nature. To him it is stupid to think of all other things as being soulless, in-sensitive, dead. "Is eberything cept'n man daid den? Dat red-burd yondah—" A cardinal, like a living flame, flashed into a dark pine, "Dat black bitch ob yourn—what she got?" Old Divinity had hit home. I stroked the soft head the old spaniel rested on my knee. "Yessum, mens an' dey rememberings keep on livin' but dat ain't all; so do de wind an' de trees an' de burds dat sing in 'em. Men am a part uv hit, dat's all. Jes' a part uv de livin' souls, no mo' an' no less. Men ain't all."

"It's a pity more men don't know this," I agreed, half to myself.

"Yessum. Hit's a sho pity," Divinity agreed, half to himself. Then I asked Divinity how men could learn this truth of his. He assured me that some men were born with it, though most people had to find it out for themselves.

"What about you, Divinity, were you born with wisdom, or did you learn it?"

"Me? Ah's de gran'son ob a witch," he answered proudly. "An' Ah's bawn wid a veil ovah ma face. A pusson what bawn wid a veil is er dubble-sighter." A double-sighter, he told me gravely, was a person who had two spirits, one that wanders and one that stays in the body. He was "strong in de haid." I gathered that a double-sighter was one who looked not merely at things but into them—and through them—one who could see beauty and significance in things near at hand. One spirit might be sitting on the little porch meditating, but the other would be swinging in the tree-tops. Double-sighters, Divinity told me seriously, mixing great truths with sheerest fancy, could see the wind. However, he assured me that there was no cause for worry if I hadn't been lucky enough to have been born with a veil.

"No'm, yo' gotta watch de signs, dat's all. Anybody what watch de signs kin tell what comin'. Heah dat woodpecker? Woodpeckers is conjur-burds, allus tappin' an' seekin'. Effen he come a tappin' on yo' housetop hit's a sho' sign ob death in dat fambly. He's a nailin' down a coffin-lid, an' somebody bettah git ready tuh go. Yessum, effen yo' know de signs yo' knows enuff." For instance, he said, when one feels a warm breath of air on his neck at night, that's a sign there's a spirit near and wanting to talk to him. Sometimes spirits were known to break a stick near by or throw down a handful of leaves to attract the attention. If the spirit is your friend he will call you by name. He asked me if I had ever been awakened in the middle of the night with a feeling that a voice had called my name. I confessed that I had.

"Well, dat's a sperrit callin' yo'. Don't nevah answer no strange voices at night," he warned me. "Pepul's sperrits wander at night an' effen dey's woke too sudden-like de sperrit is likely tuh be left out walkin'." Then the old man was silent, while a mocking-bird sang from the fig-tree. Suddenly he pointed toward the swamp with his rattan cane.

"See dem buzzards ovah dah on dat daid cypress stump? Dey's a waitin' fuh tuh smell deaf. Atter while dey'll go sailin' off in a certain d'rection an' yo' kin be sho' somebody daid ovah dat way.

> Deaf, he is a little man,
> An' he go from do' tuh do'.

Dat what de ole song say. But de little man allus sen' a sign, effen you jes' knows how tuh watch fuh 'em."

"What are some of the signs of death?" I wanted to know, and these are some of the things he told me. There is the sign of the empty rocking-chair rocking. That's a sure sign. If a wild bird flies into your house that's a sure sign. To drop one's bread in taking it out of the stove means sure and sudden death. If a white measuring-worm gets on a person, that worm is just measuring the person's shroud. Sweeping out of the door after sundown is a sure sign that you are sweeping somebody's soul out. If a lamp goes out of its own accord, that's a sign. If you wash clothes on New Year's Day, you're washing one of your family away. To lie on two chairs is to measure your own grave. Then there are the bad signs, such as: don't stand a hoe alongside the house you live in; and don't ever take a fire from one room to another unless you first spit on the fire. A flock of crows around a house is a bad sign, and, if you see one lone crow fly over, then turn and come back—that's a certain sign of death. Then there is the infallible ticking of deathwatches (wood-beetles). "De deaf-watches is heard mos' when a pusson is low sick; when de tickin' stop, de pusson die. Yessum, 'Deaf, he is a little man, an' he go from do' tuh do'.'"

The sun was reddening in the west. A breeze had sprung up, bringing a continual soft murmur from the swamp trees. Old Divinity sat silent. His pipe had gone out. No wonder he sat and thought of death, so lonely and so old, with no one to look to.

"Do you get very lonely, Divinity, now that all your children are gone?"

"No'm. When Jessmin, ma baby, lef', Ah felt sad at fust, but now Ah sets an' tawks tuh mase'f, er de trees an' de win'. Sometimes Ah tawks tuh God an' Jesus an' Saint Peter an' dem. Sometimes, when de win' be's right Ah heah de trains comin' an' goin'. Hit allus makes me sad, folks comin' an' goin'. Bettah tuh stay in one place an' take what de good Lawd sen', lak a tree." Dusk was creeping through the swamp. I rose to go. A killdeer went crying across the little patch back of the cabin.

"Tu'n col', Honey. Heah Killdee cryin' dat away, he callin' up de win'. Wintah comin'." Winter! "Ah, winter, touch that little cabin lightly," I wished, as I turned through the darkening swamp and left the old, old grandson of a witch sitting on his porch, while a lone killdeer called up the wind. Mojo? Call it what you will. The magic of the swamp had come upon me. I found myself talking with the wind!

PAULE MARSHALL

Returning to Africa

· *From* Praisesong for the Widow ·

The accounts of the Ibos walking back to Africa or of other discontented slaves flying back to Africa were popular legends that circulated during and long after slavery. The Ibo account motivated Paule Marshall's *Praisesong for the Widow,* and the legend of flying back to Africa is treated in Toni Morrison's *Song of Solomon.*

They just turned, . . . and walked on back down to the edge of the river here. . . . They had seen what they had seen and those Ibos was stepping! They just kept walking right on out over the river. Now you wouldna thought they'd of got very far seeing as it was water they was walking on. Besides they had all that iron on 'em. Iron on they ankles and they wrists and fastened 'round they necks like a dog collar. 'Nuff iron to sink an army. And chains hooking up the iron. But chains didn't stop those Ibos none. Neither iron. . . . they just kept on walking like the water was solid ground. Left the white folks standin' back here with they mouth hung open and they taken off down the river on foot. Stepping . . . And they was singing by then, so my gran' said. When they realized there wasn't nothing between them and home but some water and that wasn't giving 'em no trouble they got so tickled they started in to singing. . . . They sounded like they was having such a good time my gran' declared she just picked herself up and took off after 'em. In her mind. Her body she always usta say might be in Tatem but her mind, her mind was long gone with the Ibos.

Flying Africans

· *From Elliott P. Skinner,* Drums and Shadows ·

Collected from Wallace Quarterman.

"But yuh caahn unduhstan much wut deze people [recently captured African slaves] say. Dey caahn unduhstan yo talk an you caahn unduhstan dey talk. Dey go 'quack, quack, quack,' jis as fas as a hawse kin run, an muh pa say, 'Ain no good tuh lissen tuh um.' Dey git long all right but yuh know dey wuz a lot ub um wut ain stay down yuh."

Did he mean the Ibos on St. Simons who walked into the water?

"No, ma'am, I ain mean dem. Ain yuh heah bout um? Well, at dat time Mr. Blue he wuz duh obuhseeuh an Mr. Blue put um in duh fiel, but he couldn do nuttn wid um. Dey gabble, gabble, gabble, an nobody couldn unduhstan um an dey didn know how tuh wuk right. Mr. Blue he go down one mawnin wid a long whip fuh tuh whip um good."

"Mr. Blue was a hard overseer?" we asked.

"No, ma'am, he ain hahd, he jis caahn make um unduhstan. Dey's foolish actin. He got tuh whip um, Mr. Blue, he ain hab no choice. Anyways, he whip um good an dey gits tuhgedduh an stick duh hoe in duh fiel an den say 'quack, quack, quack,' an dey riz up in duh sky an tun hesef intuh buzzuds an fly right back tuh Africa."

At this, we exclaimed and showed our astonishment.

"Wut, you ain heah bout um? Ebrybody know bout um. Dey sho lef duh hoe stannin in duh fiel an dey riz right up an fly right back tuh Africa."

Had Wallace actually seen this happen, we asked.

"No, ma'am, I ain seen um. I bin tuh Skidaway, but I knowd plenty wut did see um, plenty wut wuz right deah in duh fiel wid um an seen duh hoe wut dey lef stickin up attuh dey done fly way. . . .

"Muh gran say ole man Waldburg down on St. Catherine own some slabes wut wuzn climatize an he wuk um hahd an one day dey wuz hoein in duh fiel an duh dribuh come out an two ub um wuz unuh a tree in duh shade, an duh hoes wuz wukin by demsef. Duh dribuh say 'Wut dis?' an dey say, 'Kum buba yali kum buba tambe. Kum kunka yali kum kunka tambe,' quick like. Den dey rise off duh groun an fly away. Nobody ebuh see um no mo. Some say dey fly back tuh Africa. Muh gran see dat wid he own eye."

ALAN LOMAX

Voodoo Had Hold of Him, Too

· *From* Mister Jelly Roll ·

Following are the comments of Jelly Roll Morton's companion Anita Gonzalez
regarding the death of the jazz great.

Jelly was a very devout Catholic. Anita explained, speaking calmly, giving the facts. But voodoo, which is an entirely different religion, had hold of him, too. I know. I nursed and supported him all during his last illness after he had driven across the continent in the midst of winter with that bad heart of his.

The woman, Laura Hunter, who raised Jelly Roll, was a voodoo witch. Yes, I'm talking about his godmother who used to be called Eulalie Echo. She made a lot of money at voodoo. People were always coming to her for some help and she was giving them beads and pieces of leather and all that. Well, everybody knows that before you can become a witch you have to sell the person you love the best to Satan as a sacrifice. Laura loved Jelly best. She loved Jelly better than Ed, her own husband. Jelly always knew she'd sold him to Satan and that, when she died, he'd die, too—she would take him down with her.

Laura taken sick in 1940 and here came Jelly Roll driving his Lincoln all the way from New York. Laura died. And then Jelly, in spite that I had financed him a new start in the music business and he was beginning to feel himself again, he taken sick, too. A couple months later he died in my arms, begging me to keep anointing his lips with oil that had been blessed by a bishop in New York. He had oil running all over him when he gave up the ghost.

Little Eight John

· *From James R. Aswell,* God Bless the Devil ·

Once an long ago dey was a little black boy name of Eight John. He was a nice lookin little boy but he didn't act like he look. He mean little boy an he wouldn't mind a word de grown folks told him.

Naw, not a livin word. So if his lovin mammy told him not to do a thing, he go straight an do hit. Yes, spite of all de world.

"Don't step on no toad-frawgs," his lovin mammy told him, "aw you bring de bad lucks on yo family. Yes you will."

Little Eight John he say, "No'm, I won't step on no toad-frawgs. No ma'am!"

But jes as sho as anything, soon as he got out of sight of his lovin mammy, dat Little Eight John find him a toad-frawg an squirsh hit. Sometime he squirsh a heap of toad-frawgs.

An the cow wouldn't give no milk but bloody milk an de baby would have de bad ol colics.

But Little Eight John he jes duck his haid an laugh.

"Don't set in no chair backwards," his lovin mammy told Eight John. "It bring de weary troubles to yo family."

An so Little Eight John he set backwards in every chair.

Den his lovin mammy's cawn bread burn an de milk wouldn't churn.

Little ol Eight John jes laugh an laugh an laugh cause he know why hit was.

"Don't climb no trees on Sunday," his lovin mammy told him, "aw hit will be bad luck."

So dat Little Eight John, dat bad little boy, he sneak up trees on Sunday.

Den his pappy's taters wouldn't grow an de mule wouldn't go.

Little Eight John he know howcome.

"Don't count yo teeth," his lovin mammy she tell Little Eight John, "aw dey come a bad sickness in yo family."

But dat Little Eight John he go right ahaid an count his teeth. He count his uppers an he count his lowers. He count em on weekdays an Sundays.

Den his mammy she whoop an de baby git de croup. All on count of dat Little Eight John, dat badness of a little ol boy.

"Don't sleep wid yo haid at de foot of the baid aw yo family git de weary money blues," his lovin mammy told him.

So he do hit an do hit sho, dat cross-goin little ol Eight John boy.

An de family hit went broke wid no money in de poke.

Little Eight John he jes giggle.

"Don't have no Sunday moans, faw fear Ol Raw Haid Bloody Bones," his lovin mammy told him.

So he had de Sunday moans an he had de Sunday groans, an he moan an he groan an he moan.

An Ol Raw Haid Bloody Bones he come after dat little bad boy an change him to a little ol grease spot on de kitchen table an his lovin mammy wash hit off de next mawnin.

An dat was de end of Little Eight John.

An dat whut always happen to never-mindin little boys.

The Stubborn Piano

· *From J. Mason Brewer,* Worser Days and Better Times ·

Right after slavery time was over there was an old man who lived alone after his wife done died. While his wife was livin' she always liked to play a piano she had in her front-room. So just before she died she called the old man to her bedside and asked him never to sell or move the piano out of the house, 'cause she loved it so much.

A little later on, however, the old man got tired of livin' on such a big farm. So he sold this place and bought him a smaller farm. The following day he started moving his furniture and other things out of the house, but when he tried to move his wife's piano it would turn around and go back into the room he had taken it from. Every time he'd get the piano to the front door it would turn right around and go back into the room where his wife used to play it.

The old man was so disgusted that he offered a large sum of money to anyone who could move the piano out of the house. During this time "root women" were very popular. So a colored root woman heard about the old man's offer and went to see him. She told him that if she couldn't move the piano out of the house she'd die and go to hell "ballin' the jack." So the old man told the root woman to go home and get her roots and come back and see what she could do.

When the root woman returned, she brought her mother with her. The root woman's mother was frightened about what the root woman had said to the old man, and tried to persuade her daughter not to try and move the piano, saying that she had heard of people makin' big promises and sayin' what they hoped would happen to 'em if they couldn't do a job, and then havin' things happen to 'em that they said would happen if they didn't do what they done said they could do.

But the root woman wouldn't listen to her mother; she took out her roots and started tryin' to move the piano out of the house. But the piano did just as it had done before; it moved out of the room it was in, but when it got to the front door leadin' out to the front porch, it turned around and went back into the room where it stood all the time. On its way back to the room, it knocked the root woman down and killed her so the root woman with her roots died, and everybody says they believe that she is in hell, ballin' the jack.

In the Name of the Lord

· *From Daryl Cumber Dance,* Shuckin' and Jivin' ·

Now this actually happened. This little girl, she was living with these people. They was makin' a Cinderella out of her, see, and at night when they get through supper, they use to make her go out on the back porch and wash dishes. And say, every time that she would go out there, something would scare her, and she'd run back in the house. And they'd make her run right back out there. Then she run back—keep on till she get through. So they told the Preacher about it, you know, and he said, "It could be possible the child see something. I'll come over sometime and sit."

And say after they got through with supper, they sent her out on the porch in the dark to wash the dishes, and all at once she screamed and run back in the house, say she saw somethin'. He say, "Now look, daughter, don't get scared now, but whatever it is, when this thing come to you again, say you ask it, 'In the name of the Lord, what do you want?' Say, 'Either speak or leave me alone.' "

Say she went back and the thing appeared again. She say, "What in the name of the Lord do you want with me?"

He say, "Take—take a pick and shovel and follow me."

So she got a shovel and pick and followed him. Say he went on-n-n down—led her down in this little valley like, and say, he say, "Now you dig right here by this tree, and you gonna find a big earthen jar—full of money." He say, "Lil' o' that that runs out, I'm gonna tell you who I want you to give it to, but what stays in there will be yours." And she dug and found it. And they poured it out till it stop runnin' and they left enough in there for her and everybody else. And never did pay her no more visits.

See somebody had buried it and died and they wanted somebody to have it.

What Do You Want Here?

· *From Rosa Hunter,* Southern Workman *27 (March 1898)* ·

Once upon a time, in a lonely little house upon a hill, there lived a man and his wife. The husband worked down in the town all day, and the wife worked at home alone. Every day, at nocn, when the clock was striking twelve, she was startled by the pale ghost-like figure of a man that stood in the doorway and watched her. She was very much frightened, and told her husband that she could not stay in that house any longer. But they were very poor, and the rent was cheaper than they could find elsewhere. While the husband was look-ing for another house, the preacher came to see the wife. She told him about the pale-faced ghost that continually watched her. The preacher told her to sit down before her looking glass with her back to the door and read a certain passage from the Bible backward. Then she must turn her chair around, look the ghost in the face, and ask him, "What do you want here?" The very next day she did as she was told. At first her voice trembled and she did not think that she could finish, but strength came to her and she read it. Then she turned upon the ghost and asked him the question. His face was frightful to look upon, but he told her to take her hoe and follow him. He led her to a lonely spot and rolled away a large stone and com-manded her to dig. She dug until she was exhausted and the hoe fell from her hand. He jerked it up and dug until she had regained her strength. Then she commenced to dig again and at last struck some-thing hard. He commanded her to stop, then stooped down and with wonderful strength drew up a large earthen pot. Upon taking off the cover, she saw by the dim light of the setting sun, gold and silver coins in great abundance. The ghost told her to go home and tear the plastering from off the western corner of her little one-room house, and she would find a package of letters. From these she must get his brother's address and send him half of the hidden treasure. The other half was for herself. She did as she was told. The pale-faced ghost was never seen again, and she was made a rich woman and they lived happily ever afterward.

The Dog Ghost and the Buried Money

· *From J. Mason Brewer,* Dog Ghosts ·

Does Ah know any scary stories 'bout dawg ghostes? Lemme see now! Come to think 'bout hit, 'pears to me Ah heerd mah gran'ma tell sump'n' one time 'bout a dawg ghos' prowlin' 'roun' on dey fawm when she warn't no mo'n three yeahs ole, rat attuh her papa was kilt an' dey done buried 'im.

De way gran'ma tol' hit—her papa, what was name Sam Lee, was one of de bestes' fawmuhs in de whole of Bastrop County. He hab a limp, an' walk hip-hoppity, but dat don' bar 'im from followin' 'hin' ole Beck an' meckin' good crops evuh yeah de Lawd sen'. But when he done sell his cotton an' cawn, he hol' fas' to his money. Gran'ma say her papa was a po' han' at spennin' his money, dat he didn't git shed of hit fas', an' dat he didn' let wuck pile up on 'im. He comed up moughty quick in de worl' 'caze he set aside mos' all de money he raked in from his cotton an' cawn. But he didn' b'lieve in puttin' his money in no bank; he allus hided hit on de place somewhars, an' wouldn' ebun down tell gran'ma's mama whar he done statched hit out.

Gran'ma say her papa was a po' han' at jarrin' loose from his money, but he sho was a good providuh for his fam'ly when hit comed to eatin' an' sleepin'; he hab lots an' lots of cows to milk an' kill for beef, plenty hawgs in de hawg-pen for hawg-killin' time, a passel of sheeps, gobbs of chickens an' tuckies, an' a han'ful of geeses an' ducks ramblin' 'roun' de bawnyaa'd all de time. An' sides dis, he raised bushels an' bushels of yalluh-yam sweet 'taters, an' a whoppin' big crop of onions, I'ish 'taters, an' tuhmatoes evuh yeah de Lawd sen'. He hab 'is own 'lasses mill lackwise, an' a ole-timey gris'-mill to grin' cawn an' meck meal for cracklin' bread. Gran'ma say de house dey libed in was a five room house what hab a roof dat hab rail good shingles on hit so's de rain wouldn' leak thoo hit; dat de flo's in de rooms didn' hab no holes in 'em, an' dat dey wasn' a broke windah pane on de whole place.

Gran'ma say her papa lub money so much dat he hab a li'l' sayin' he say all de time what go lack dis:

White man got de money an' education,
De Nigguh got Gawd an' conjuration.

An' gran'ma say attuh he done hab his say, he'd 'low: "Ah didn' git no further'n McGuffey's secon' readuh in book-learnin', so Ah cain't come up to de white man in education, but Ah kin putty nigh rech 'im when hit come down to de money proposition."

Gran'ma say her papa was a po' han' at 'tendin' to othuh folkses bizniss, dat dey wasn' a bit of trickerashun in 'im, an' dat he ain't nevuh done nobody no dirt in his whole nachul bawn life. But dey was lots of peoples what begrudged 'im what he hab, 'caze dey hab a haa'd time gittin' on foot lack he done did. Gran'ma say de reports was dat her papa hab 'nuff money to las' 'im de res' of his nachul life if'n he didn' nevuh hit 'nothuh tap of wuck ez long ez he libed.

Onlies' thing dat gran'ma say she couldn't forgib her papa for was his bein' so tight wid his money dat he wouldn' buy her mama an' de chilluns no dress-up clo'es to w'ar. Gran'ma say de onlies' kinda goods he'd buy for her mama to meck dresses for her an' de girl chilluns in de fam'ly was calico, an' dat her mama hab to meck dey unnuhskirts an' drawers an' night gowns outen flour sacks an' bran sacks. She say dat he wouldn' buy her onlies' brothuh Tom nothin' but duckins to w'ar, ebun down on a Sunday, dat de boy hab to sleep in a cotton drag sack evuh night de Lawd sen', an' dat de whole fam'ly hab to go to chu'ch in dey bare feets. Gran'ma say de bad thing 'bout hit was dat, when her mama'd call her papa in questshun 'bout hit, she couldn' switch his min' 'roun' 'bout spennin' money for clo'es. When she'd call 'im in questshun 'bout hit, he'd jes' cloud up an' 'low dat he ain't nevuh seed nowhars in de Bible whar hit say you hab to dress yo'se'f up to go to chu'ch, but he seed whar hit say you hab to dress yo' soul up to go to heabun!

Well, gran'ma say dat things rocked on an' rocked on in dis fashion 'till one Saddy evenin' rolled 'roun' an' her papa saddled up his saddle hoss, ole Molly, an' rid her into Bastrop to git 'im a box of cigars to las' 'im thoo de nex' week. Hit was way late in de evenin' time an' lookin' kinda stormified when he lit out for home, so he tuck out his quirt an' let ole Molly hab hit rat on her shanks, an' she tuck a-runnin' staa't for home. Hit was pitch dark an' ole Molly was jes' battin' hit down de road trawna meck hit home 'fo' hit rained, but a big downpour ketched her jes' 'fo' she reched a li'l ole branch 'bout two miles from de fawmhouse, an' Molly los' 'er way an' strayed off from de dirt road. Gran'ma's papa hab holt of de bridle reins an' tries to pilot ole Molly back on de dirt road, but Molly so feart of de lightnin' an' thunnuh 'till she keeps runnin' straight ahaid thoo de bushes 'till she runs slap-bang up to de edge of a high cliff on de branch an' falls in hit, th'owin' gran'ma's papa to de groun' an' breakin' his neck. He was a sho 'nuff goner. Some mens foun' 'im in de branch dat night 'fo' de wadduh got high 'nuff to float 'im way somewhars down de creek an' brung 'im on home.

Gran'ma say dat her papa didn' b'lieve in b'longin' to no lodges, so, since he ain't nevuh tol' her mama whar he done hided his money, she don' hab a cryin' copper cent to bury 'im wid. She hab to sell her bes' team of mules an' all de hawgs in de pen to buy a coffin to bury 'im in.

De way de dawg ghos' git into hit was lack dis: Gran'ma say dat her mama an' her two sistuhs an' her an' her brothuh Tom hab a practice evuh night of goin' down to de bafroom, what was way down 'crost a thick patch of timber in de lowuh pastur' of dey fawm. Dey allus tuck a lantern wid 'em so's dey c'd fin' dey way to de bafroom 'dout stumblin' an' fallin'. De nex' night attuh dey done buried gran'ma's papa, when dey gits 'bout ha'fway to de lowuh pastur' on de way to de bafroom, what you reckon dey looked up an' seed followin' 'em? —a big white dawg wid red eyes jes' a shinin'. Dey ain't nevuh seed de dawg 'roun' de premisus 'fo', so dey stoops down an' picks up some rocks offen de groun' an' chunks 'em at 'im, an' he runs off. Dey don' nevuh spy de dawg in de daytime, but evuh night when dey'd staa't down to de lowuh pastur' to de bafroom dis dawg'd show up from somewhars an' staa't followin' 'em, an' lack ez on de fuss night dey spied 'im, dey gits 'em some rocks an' th'ows 'em at de dawg, an' lack ez 'fo' he runs on off. Dey ca'ies on in dis wise for mo'n a mont' 'till one Saddy night when dey staa'ts down to de bafroom, an' de dawg follows in 'hin' 'em an' dey chunks at 'im, he don' run off; dis heah night, he jes' keep on comin' to'a'ds 'em, an' hit look lack de rocks dey chunked at 'im jes' go rat thoo 'im an' don' hit 'im nowhars. Dis heah kinda th'owed a scare into gran'ma an' dem, so dey staa'ts runnin' on down to'a'ds de bafroom wid de dawg rat in 'hin' 'em. When dey done finished at de bafroom, gran'ma an' all of 'em was still scairt, so dey all lights out for de house jes' a runnin' to beat de ban'. But when dey looks back, de dawg ain't followin' 'em—he jes' stannin' dere by de bafroom lookin' to'a'ds a big clump of trees further down in de thicket, an' when gran'ma an' dem looked at 'im, he staa'ted walkin' to 'a'ds de clump of trees. So gran'ma's brothuh Tom turnt to his mama an' say, "Mama, les'n us follow de dawg—look lack he wanna show us sump'n' 'nothuh." So gran'ma's mama say dat suit her fancy, so dey all staa'ts walkin' to'a'ds de clump of trees, followin' in 'hin' de dawg. When de dawg done rech hit, he stops in front of de bigges' pos'-oak tree in de whole clump, an' tecks his front rat foot an' staa'ts scratchin' in de dirt.

When gran'ma an' dem seed de dawg staa't pawin' in de ground', dey all tuck a runnin' staa't for de tree whar de dawg was scratchin' at. De dawg don' budge 'till dey all done rech de spot. Den he looks up at 'em kinda pitiful lack an' dis'pears so sudden lack dey don' ebun see whichaway he go. Look lack he jes' turnt hisse'f into a fog o' sump'n' 'nothuh, 'caze all gran'ma an' dem c'd see whar de dawg was stannin' at was sump'n' dat looked lack smoke floatin' up to'a'ds de sky. Ez soon ez de dawg dis'peared, gran'ma's brothuh Tom broke a limb offen de tree an' marked de spot whar de dawg was diggin' an' de nex' mawnin' him an' gran'ma's mama tuck a pick an' shovel an' goes down an' staa'ts diggin' in de spot whar de dawg was scratchin'. When dey digs down 'bout five feet, dey fin's sebun cigar boxes full of gol' an' silvuh money what gran'ma's papa done buried dere; hit wasn't no li'l' bitty dab neithuh; dey was mo'n three thousan' dolluhs in de boxes, all tol'.

De dawg nevuh did show up no mo' attuh dey digged up de money, an' de reports was dat de dawg was gran'ma's papa what done comed back to show his fam'ly whar he done statched 'way his money.

The Boy and the Ghost

· *From* Southern Workman *27 (March 1898)* ·

Once there was a very rich family of people and they all died. Everybody was afraid to go there. Finally someone set up a sign board which said "Anyone who will go to this house and stay over night can have the house and all that is in it."

A poor boy came along and read it. "I will go," said he, and he went at sunset. He found all he wanted and went to work to cook his supper. Just as he was ready to eat it he heard a voice from the top of the chimney. He looked up and saw a leg. The leg said, "I am going to drop." "I don't keer," said the boy, "jes' so's you don' drap in my soup."

The leg jumped down on a chair, and another leg came and said, "I am going to drop." "I don't keer," said the boy, "so you don' drap in my soup." One after another all the members of a man came down in this way.

The little boy said, "Will you have some supper? Will you have some supper?" They gave him no answer. "Oh" said the little boy, "I save my supper and manners too." He ate his supper and made up his bed. "Will you have some bedroom? Will you have some bedroom?" said the little boy. No answer. "Oh," said the little boy, "I save my bedroom and my manners too," and he went to bed.

Soon after he went to bed, the legs pulled him under the house and showed him a chest of money. The little boy grew rich and married.

Hold Him, Tabb

· *From* Southern Workman *26 (June 1897)* ·

A number of wagons were travelling together one afternoon in December. It was extremely cold and about the middle of the afternoon began to snow. They soon came to an abandoned settlement by the roadside, and decided it would be a good place to camp out of the storm, as there were stalls for their horses and an old dwelling house in which they, themselves, could stay, When they had nearly finished unhooking their horses a man came along and said that he was the owner of the place and that the men were welcome to stay there as long as they wanted to, but that the house was haunted, and not a single person had staid in it alive for twenty-five years. On hearing this the men immediately moved their camp to a body of woods about one-half mile further up the road. One of them whose name was Tabb, and who was braver than the rest, said that he was not afraid of haunts, and that he did not mean to take himself and horses into the woods to perish in the snow, but that he'd stay where he was.

So Tabb staid in the house. He built a big fire, cooked and ate his supper, and rested well through the night without being disturbed. About day-break he awoke and said, "What fools those other fellows are to have staid in the woods when they might have staid in here, and have been as warm as I am." Just as he had finished speaking he looked up to the ceiling, and there was a large man dressed in white clothes just stretched out under the ceiling and sticking up to it. Before he could get from under the man, the man fell right down upon him, and then commenced a great tussel between Tabb and the man. They made so much noise that the men in the woods heard it and ran to see what was going on. When they looked in at the window and saw the struggle, first Tabb was on top and then the other man. One of them cried, "Hold him. Tabb, hold him!" "You can bet your soul I got him," said Tabb. Soon the man got Tabb out of the window. "Hold him Tabb, hold him," one of the men shouted. "You can bet your life I got him," came from Tabb. Soon the man got Tabb upon the roof of the house. "Hold him, Tabb, hold him," said one of the men. "You can bet your boots I got him," answered Tabb. Finally the man got Tabb up off the roof into the air. "Hold him, Tabb, hold him," shouted one of the men. "I got him and he got me too," said Tabb. The man, which was a ghost, carried Tabb straight up into the air until they were both out of sight. Nothing was ever seen of him again.

Old Joe Can Keep His Two Bits

· *From Jack and Olivia Solomon,* Ghosts and Goosebumps ·

Collected from Anthony Abercrombie.

Marse Jim had 'bout three hundred slaves, and he had one mighty bad overseer. But he got killed down on de bank of de creek one night. Dey never did find out who killed him, but Marse Jim always b'lieved de field han's done it. 'Fore dat us niggers useta go down to de creek to wash ourselves, but atter de overseer got killed down dar, us jes' leave off dat washin', 'cause some of 'em seed de overseer's hant down dar floatin' over de creek.

Dar was another hant on de plantation, too. Marse Jim had some trouble wid a big double-jinted nigger named Joe. One day he turn on Marse Jim wid a fence rail, and Marse Jim had to pull his gun an' kill him. Well, dat happen in a skirt of woods whar I get my light-wood what I use to start a fire. One day I went to dem same woods to get some 'simmons. Another nigger went wid me, and he clumb de tree to shake de 'simmons down whilst I be pickin' 'em up. 'Fore long I heared another tree shakin' every time us shake our tree, dat other tree shake too, and down come de 'simmons from it. I say to myself, "Dats Joe, 'cause he likes 'simmons too." Den I grab my basket and holler to de boy in de tree, "Nigger turn loose and drap down from dar, and ketch up wid me if you can, I's leavin' here right now, 'cause Old Joe is over dar gettin' 'simmons too."

Den another time I was in de woods choppin' lightwood. It was 'bout sundown, an' every time my ax go "whack" on de lightwood knot, I hear another whack 'sides mine. I stops and lis'ens and don't hear nothin'. Den I starts choppin' ag'in, and ag'in I hears de yuther whacks. By dat time my old houn' dog was crouchin' at my feets, wid de hair standin' up on his back and I couldn't make him git up nor budge.

Dis time I din' stop for nothin'. I jes' drap my ax right dar, an' me and dat houn' dog tore out for home lickety split. When us got dar Marse Jim was settin' on de porch, an' he say: "Nigger, you been up to somep'n you got no business. You is all outer breath. Who you runnin' from?" Den I say, "Marse Jim, somebody 'sides me is choppin' in yo' woods, an' I can't see him." And Marse Jim, he say, "Ah, dat ain't nobody but Old Joe. Did he owe you anythin?" And I say, "Yassah, he own me two-bits for helpin' him shuck corn." "Well," Marse Jim say, "don't pay him no mind, it jes' Old Joe come back to pay you."

Anyhow, I didn' go back to dem woods no mo'. Old Joe can jes' have de two-bits what he owe me, 'cause I don't want him follerin' 'round atter me. When he do I can't keep my mind on my bizness.

The Witch with a Gold Ring

· *From Jack and Olivia Solomon,* Ghosts and Goosebumps ·

Once upon a time Mr. Dave, a wealthy man, owned a large mill. At this mill he kept an overseer for day and one for night, as the mill ran twenty-four hours daily.

He and his wife lived alone in a large house upon a hill overlooking this mill, and friends were always welcome. His wife was a woman who did not care for finery, but just wore a plain gold ring. She was regarded as peculiar because she always wore an odd smile, unlike that of other people.

As it happened this land owner had hired a great number of night foremen at the mill. Repeatedly these foremen were killed in the night. Thus he began to have a hard time getting a man to stay on that account.

One night the local preacher came to spend the night and was met in friendly fashion by the man of the house and was given a welcome by the good wife, but she greeted him with that peculiar knowing smile of hers. During the general conversation Mr. Dave explained the difficult time he was having in getting someone to run the mill at night as the watchmen were being killed as fast as he hired them.

This preacher said, "I'll stay down there for you tonight. I'm not afraid." "O, no, I can't think of letting you take a chance of being killed," was the answer but he was finally overpersuaded and the preacher said, "All I want is my Bible and this dagger of mine." But the good wife begged him not to go. After supper the parson got his Bible and proceeded down to the mill office, lighted his lamp, made up a good fire and prepared to read his Bible. Before he sat down, in looking the room over he noticed the door had a cat-hole cut in the bottom, but thinking nothing of it, he made hisself comfortable with his dagger in his hand and began to read his Bible. In the night, when all was quiet but the spit-spit of the mill, he noticed a black cat creeping through the hole in the door. The preacher didn't say a word but kept one eye on the cat and one eye on his Bible and his hand on his blade. The cat stole in a little closer, intently watching the man. A little nearer and a little nearer he crept, the parson still with one eye on his Bible, blade in hand and the other eye on the cat but still pretending not to be noticing. Suddenly the cat gave a great "Yeow," and pounced on the preacher, but the parson as quick as the cat, gave a slash and cut off one of its front paws.

The paw fell at the parson's feet, but when he looked for the cat it had disappeared. Then turning to kick the cat's foot away, lo and behold, he was thunderstruck, for instead of the cat's foot, a woman's hand bearing the gold band of his host's wife was there. He rolled it in a piece of paper and tied it up.

The next morning when he went to the house for breakfast, the landlord was plainly surprised to see him alive, but asked what kind of a night he had spent. He replied that he had passed a perfectly quiet night with the exception of a wild cat trying to scratch him but that he had his blade and cut off one of its front paws.

"But I wrapped its claw up and brought it along to show," he said, and added, "By the way where is your wife this morning?" "She hasn't gotten up this morning," answered his host. "She is not feeling well."

The preacher unwrapped his little package to show, laying it on the table, without a word. The husband fell back in astonishment and said, "My fathers, that is my wife's hand and gold ring!" "You go up and ask her where I got it," answered the preacher. "She can tell you better than I can."

As they both entered her room, she shrank down under the covers, but her husband made her show her arm and the hand was missing. Then he asked her what it all meant. She was so cowed and ashamed she could not talk but she finally admitted that she was a witch but that her spell had been broken. The old mill ran from that time forward without any further deaths.

Beliefs and Customs Connected with Death and Burial

· From Southern Workman 26 (January 1897) ·

If any one in the house is seriously ill, and the clock suddenly stops, or one that has been long out of repair starts or strikes, or if the looking-glass is heard to crack even though no crack can be seen, or if an owl hoots or a dog howls near the house, further efforts to restore health may as well be given up at once, for these are certain signs of death. All you can do is to help the patient out of life as comfortably as possible. Never let a dying friend lie "crossways of the world," for his death in that position will be hard and painful. Turn around the bed so that he lies with head to the west and feet to the east. If he dies hard even when placed in the right position, it is a bad sign. He will haunt you. Never go to his grave alone. If as he dies, he calls the name of some living person, that person will be the next to go. If he dies in a thunder-storm, and the lightning strikes near the house, it means that the Devil himself has come to receive the passing soul. This belief is referred to in one of the "spirtuals" of which the refrain is:

"I don't want to die in a storm, good Lord, I don't want to die in a storm."

After a death has occurred, the looking-glasses must be taken down or covered. If this precaution is not observed the face of the dead will reappear in the glass and after a time the glass itself will turn black. The pictures too must be turned with their faces to the wall, and the clock must be stopped and turned to the wall. The clock will stop itself if it is not stopped. The death must be announced to the bees by knocking on the hive and waking them. If this is not done the bees will all die.

In the preparation of the body for burial no person related by blood must take any part. It is bad for anyone to work around a dead person until he is tired. The water used in washing the body must not be thrown out, but must be put under the bed and kept until after the burial. If the body remains limp for some time after death, some other member of the same family will die soon. The hair must not be plaited for burial but should be combed out and left loose. If for any reason the hair is more elaborately dressed, the Devil will send his black birds to unplait it. It is said that these birds can be heard at their work inside the coffin even after it has been buried.

During the three days that elapse between the death and the burial, the body must never be left alone. Some neighbor or friend remains with it by day; and at night the whole neighborhood gathers in the house of death and the whole night is spent in singing, prayer and mourning. From a Gloucester County, Va. correspondent comes the following description of the "settin' up" as practised there.

"The people begin to gather about six o'clock on the second night and when enough are gathered together they begin singing and praying. This they keep up till one o'clock, when a lunch, consisting of coffee, biscuits, crackers, cakes, sweet bread, pudding and tea is served. After the lunch they begin again and sing plantation melodies, keeping time with a low and impressive beating of the feet. The songs sung at a "settin' up" are usually bordering on the minor, and are sometimes very weird, but most are of Heaven, the Promised Land, and rest. The singing is kept up until about four in the morning, when the neighbors begin to leave in small parties, for no one would think of leaving a 'settin' up' alone. The third night is a repetition of the second."

It is at these "settin's up" that many of the "spirituals" have first been brought forth, some friend of the deceased thus giving vent to his emotions in original song. The last to leave a "settin' up" is the first to die, and it is for this reason that no one is willing to leave alone.

Burials and "funerals" among the colored people are two quite distinct ceremonies. Sometimes the funeral as well as the burial takes place on third day, but more often it is postponed until some convenient season when all the relatives can be gathered together. If the funeral is thus postponed, the body will be carried straight from the house to the grave, on the third day after the death, and there committed to the earth with a brief religious ceremony. Of the "funeral," our Gloucester Co. correspondent writes as follows: —

"Once a great deal of importance was attached to funerals and burials. They were two ceremonies that were well attended. Funerals were held at the church or at the house, three days after death, or six months, to when? The crowd was in proportion to the popularity of the deceased. Black was the color worn by the women and white by the children. The men wore crape on one sleeve and around their hats. The male relatives of the deceased wore their hats through the service. Usually before hearses were used the body was taken to the church in a wagon with a white sheet thrown over the coffin, and the people sang mournful 'leading praises' all the way to the church. In the church, the coffin was placed in front of the pulpit, which had been previously draped with a black cover with white and black rosettes. The front seats were reserved for the mourners and nearest friends. When preaching was over, the invitation was given to the people to come and look at the corpse. It was considered an insult to the congregation if this privilege was denied. Then the weeping and wailing of the people began, and was continued all the way from the church to the grave.

At the burial a death-like stillness settled on all while the coffin was being lowered into the grave, planks laid across it and armfuls of leaves and pine-chaff thrown on the boards. Then the minister began to read over the grave. When he came to the words, 'dust to dust, ashes to ashes' handfuls of dirt were thrown into the grave."

A grave must never be left open over night. It should be dug and closed on the day of the burial. To leave the grave before it is filled, or to be the first to leave it after it is filled is death. For this reason the company gathered about the grave breaks up into little groups as it does from the "settin' up," no one daring to go away alone. The tools used in digging the grave must not be taken away, but must be left beside it for a day or two.

Of the doings of the spirit after death there are many superstitions. It is believed that for three days it remains about the house, going through everything. All food in the house at the time of the death must be thrown away. At the end of the three days the spirit goes to judgment. If admitted to Heaven it never returns to its earthly abode, but if condemned it is likely to come back at any time. If however the living neglect in any way their duty to the dead, they may be haunted by them. If, for instance the "funeral" is postponed too long or forgotten altogether, the dead may return and demand a "funeral" for the repose of their souls. People are unwilling to receive or use the personal property of the dead, for fear that its owner may return and claim it. The ghosts of bad people are red. It is perfectly safe to go through a grave-yard between twelve o'clock at night and four in the morning as at that time the ghosts are all away visiting their friends.

Chapter 12

The Rumor Mill

*"Telephone, telegraph, tell-a-Negro — and the news is
out. The last is fastest — a Negro."*
—Traditional saying cited from Langston Hughes's *Simple
Takes a Wife*

I heard it by the grapevine.
—Traditional saying

umors are beliefs that circulate widely with no discernible
source and with at least a degree of believability. They are
frequently transmitted orally, but with the advent of the
Internet, rumors often take the form of E-mail. Indeed, several of the
pieces in this chapter were sent to me through E-mail. There are also
several Web sites where rumors and urban legends may be posted.
Occasionally they are circulated on posters or fliers. Rarely are rumors completely true, and there are always many folk who do not accept their veracity. However, rumors may later be shown to have
been more than rumors—indeed facts. Many would say that this is
the case with the long-standing rumor that the children of Sally
Hemings were fathered by Thomas Jefferson. On the other hand,
some rumors, like "Voting Rights of African Americans to Expire,"
are basically false. Rumors sometimes stem from true incidents; there
is often, at least, some kernel of truth in most rumors. As the folk say,
"Just because you're paranoid doesn't mean somebody is not out to
get you."

Rumors and urban legends are closely related. Gordon W. Allport
and Leo Postman argue in *The Psychology of Rumor* that legends are no

more than solidified rumors, and Patricia Turner, author of *I Heard It Through the Grapevine*, the definitive study of African American rumors, suggests a link "in the African-American rumor/legend tradition." I use rumor here in its broadest sense to include both brief and longer narrative expressions of unsubstantiated beliefs. Some prefer to distinguish the longer, narrative beliefs as urban legends. We should appreciate that the folk who circulate these beliefs don't use either term to define them; however, folk who don't embrace the beliefs may speak condescendingly of "the rumor mill."

A number of rumors have become so prevalent that formal denials or explanations have been issued by the subjects of the rumors, major TV shows have focused on them, numerous newspapers have run articles on them, scientific studies have been conducted to counter them, and special meetings have been held to address them (as Representative Maxine Waters did in South-Central Los Angeles in 1996 with CIA Director John Deutch to try to confront the rumor about CIA support of Nicaraguan drug dealers). The latest items from the rumor mill are often featured on Black radio stations.

Rumors are often provoked by fear. It is no surprise then that the African American rumor mill began with the early contact between the Europeans and the Africans. Hunted, purchased, kidnapped, chained, and shipped in the holds of ships in the most barbaric conditions, Africans were likely to believe the worst about their captors. The reality of what they were experiencing was so horrific that they could hardly be expected to discount rumors about the nature of their enslavers as exaggerations. One of the most prevalent rumors that circulated among these captured Africans, as may be seen in some of the following selections, was that they would be eaten by the Whites. Many also believed the Whites were sea-monsters or devils. Ensuing events, such as slavery, Jim Crow, and the Ku Klux Klan, understandably continued to fuel the rumor mill.

Most of the rumors included in this chapter are exclusively concerned with the Black community. Others that warn of dangers to the general public without specifying any ethnic group are included when they circulate widely among African Americans because they believe that there is greater danger in their communities. For example, the many rumors about conscious efforts to spread HIV among

Black people, coupled with the fact that AIDS disproportionately affects the Black community in the United States and is currently practically wiping out whole generations of people in several African nations, make it highly likely that Black communities would embrace the rumors that HIV-infected needles are a danger in gas stations and movie theater seats, believing that such hazards would be targeted at them.

Even a few rumors that seem to be about Whites are included because they reflect a Black perspective. "The Black Man on the Elevator," for example, which is briefly summarized in this chapter, includes in its full text language and descriptions that suggest it is parodying the fear that White women have of Black men, a fear that has been documented in reputable scientific studies.

Rumors directed at large American corporations are rampant in the Black community. A number of them deal with the hidden symbolism of trademarks of major companies or the disastrous results of using their products: the rumor mill falsely has it that the clipper ship on the Snapple Iced Tea label is actually a slave ship and the company is owned by the Ku Klux Klan; that the *Troop* in Troop Sport Clothing Company was really an acronym for a KKK slogan — "To rule over oppressed people"; that Church's Chicken is owned by the Klan, who put something into the chicken to sterilize Black males and to affect Black fetuses; and that drinking Tropical Fantasy causes sterility in Black men. Tommy Hilfiger and Liz Claiborne were wrongly rumored to have made racist comments on a TV show. Countless companies have been rumored to use slave labor in foreign countries in the manufacturing of their products. A false rumor started on the day of O. J. Simpson's acquittal that Mrs. Field's Cookies was donating free sweets for his victory party (I would suspect that this did not begin in the Black community). Numerous companies have been rumored to have served rats or some similar item in their food: widespread rumors reported that several people had gotten fried rat from Kentucky Fried Chicken or had discovered a mouse in a Coca-Cola.

While most rumors are proven not to be true or completely true, and though several have been reviewed, studied, tested, investigated, and debunked by Congress, law agencies, scientists, scholars, newspaper reporters, television broadcasters, and corporate executives, many of the folk who accept the rumors refuse to let them go. When Patricia Turner asked her informants for *I Heard It Through the Grapevine* how Church's chicken could affect Black males and not Whites, they said that most of the Church's franchises were located in Black neighborhoods; others insisted that a special substance used by Church's "impedes the production of sperm in black males but is harmless when consumed by whites." In some instances, when informed of scientific tests that proved the rumors wrong, the informants simply asserted that the scientists were in cahoots with the businesses. When Turner confronted one "bright young African-American female college junior" with evidence that Church's was not contaminating their chicken and that they were not owned by the Ku Klux Klan, the young lady responded, "Well, it's the kind of thing they would do if they could."

It is important to recognize, when looking at the Black community's responses to these rumors and efforts to disprove them, that the community has had a long history of enduring persecution, attack, misrepresentation, rejection, and other racist treatment by the government and law enforcement agencies as well as major industry. Whether we go back to slavery; the beatings, torture, and killings of prisoners in jails and on chain gangs; lynchings; the Tuskegee experiment; the CIA involvement in undermining the Civil Rights movement; governmental efforts to control, restrict, or restrain Black reproduction;[1] or documented instances of the contamination of food served to Blacks (and the list is unending), there is adequate cause for suspicion and doubt among African Americans. Thus, for example, the general lack of attention to the prevalence and impact of drugs in Black communities; the obvious complicity

[1]Some Blacks see laws such as those prohibiting women from receiving welfare if a man lives with them, or efforts to pass laws to discourage reproduction among welfare recipients, or to sterilize certain women (who were on welfare and had a certain number of children, or were retarded), or to coerce birth control, as indications that White America is determined to inhibit the reproduction of Blacks. This suspicion is exacerbated by issues such as the disproportionate number of Black men sent to Vietnam, incarcerated, sentenced to die, or in other ways removed from the community.

of some corrupt police officers in the drug trade; and the disparity in the arrest, prosecution, and sentencing of Blacks and Whites involved in drugs provide a source for and lend credence to the rumors about the involvement of the government, and especially the CIA, in the drug infestation in African American communities. Factual news stories constantly reinforce the racism of all too many American businesses—as I was writing this chapter in the summer of 2000, *Jet* magazine reported that American General Life and Accident Insurance Company paid $206 million to settle a claim stemming from its decades-long practice of charging Blacks higher fees than Whites for burial insurance (*Jet* 98 [July 10, 2000]). It has been shown that some banks and real estate companies redline, that many businesses do not hire Blacks or do not promote them, that businesses negatively target advertisements and promotions to communities based on race, and so on and on. It should come as no surprise, then, that the Black community is rife with rumors about racism in American corporations.

It is important to acknowledge as well that the distinction between rumor and theory is an ambiguous one. There are many who would contend that a number of these "rumors," such as those about the Atlanta murders and the drug conspiracy, are based on substantial facts and are arguable theories.

Several scholar-detectives have attempted to trace the origins of rumors. Some have been successful in pointing to events that may well have triggered or influenced the development of certain rumors, but as with most folk items, proving sources is a difficult (some might argue, impossible) task. It is certainly also clear, that again like most folk items, several rumors have multiple origins and diffusion.

One thing remains certain: whether or not you telephone, telegraph, tell-a-Negro, or tell-E-mail, the rumor mill is alive and well among African American folk.

OLAUDAH EQUIANO
The Slave Ship
· *From* Equiano's Travels ·

This account by slave narrator Olaudah Equiano details his response to the
Whites who have captured him and taken him aboard a ship for the journey to
America. He provides a superb setting of the context in which rumors arose in
such a situation and focuses on the main rumor with which he is understandably
obsessed.

The first object which saluted my eyes when I arrived on the coast
was the sea, and a slave ship which was then riding at anchor and
waiting for its cargo. These filled me with astonishment, which was
soon converted into terror when I was carried on board. I was immediately handled and tossed up to see if I were sound by some of the
crew, and I was now persuaded that I had gotten into a world of bad
spirits and that they were going to kill me. Their complexions too dif-
fering so much from ours, their long hair and the language they spoke
(which was very different from any I had ever heard) united to confirm me in this belief. Indeed such were the horrors of my views and
fears at the moment that, if ten thousand worlds had been my own,
I would have freely parted with them all to have exchanged my condition with that of the meanest slave in my own country. When I
looked round the ship too and saw a large furnace or copper boiling
and a multitude of black people of every description chained together, every one of their countenances expressing dejection and sorrow, I no longer doubted of my fate; and quite overpowered with
horror and anguish, I fell motionless on the deck and fainted. When
I recovered a little I found some black people about me, who I believed were some of those who had brought me on board and had
been receiving their pay; they talked to me in order to cheer me, but
all in vain. I asked them if we were not to be eaten by those white
men with horrible looks, red faces, and loose hair. They told me I was
not, and one of the crew brought me a small portion of spirituous
liquor in a wine glass, but being afraid of him I would not take it out
of his hand. One of the blacks therefore took it from him and gave it
to me, and I took a little down my palate, which instead of reviving
me, as they thought it would, threw me into the greatest consterna-

tion at the strange feeling it produced, having never tasted such any liquor before. Soon after this the blacks who brought me on board went off, and left me abandoned to despair.

I now saw myself deprived of all chance of returning to my native country or even the least glimpse of hope of gaining the shore, which I now considered as friendly; and I even wished for my former slavery in preference to my present situation, which was filled with horrors of every kind, still heightened by my ignorance of what I was to undergo. I was not long suffered to indulge my grief; I was soon put down under the decks, and there I received such a salutation in my nostrils as I had never experienced in my life: so that with the loathsomeness of the stench and crying together, I became so sick and low that I was not able to eat, nor had I the least desire to taste anything. I now wished for the last friend, death, to relieve me; but soon, to my grief, two of the white men offered me eatables, and on my refusing to eat, one of them held me fast by the hands and laid me across I think the windlass, and tied my feet while the other flogged me severely. I had never experienced anything of this kind before, and although, not being used to the water, I naturally feared that element the first time I saw it, yet nevertheless could I have got over the nettings I would have jumped over the side, but I could not; and besides, the crew used to watch us very closely who were not chained down to the decks, lest we should leap into the water: and I have seen some of these poor African prisoners most severely cut for attempting to do so, and hourly whipped for not eating. This indeed was often the case with myself. In a little time after, amongst the poor chained men I found some of my own nation, which in a small degree gave ease to my mind. I inquired of these what was to be done with us; they gave me to understand we were to be carried to these white people's country to work for them. I then was a little revived, and thought if it were no worse than working, my situation was not so desperate: but still I feared I should be put to death, the white people looked and acted, as I thought, in so savage a manner; for I had never seen among my people such instances of brutal cruelty, and this not only shewn towards us blacks but also to some of the whites themselves. One white man in particular I saw, when we were permitted to be on deck, flogged so unmercifully with a large rope near the foremast that he died in consequence of it; and they tossed him over the side as they would have done a brute. This made me fear these people the more, and I expected nothing less than to be treated in the same manner. . . .

The ship had a very long passage, and on that account we had very short allowance of provisions. Towards the last we had only one pound and a half of bread per week, and about the same quantity of meat, and one quart of water a day. We spoke with only one vessel the whole time we were at sea, and but once we caught a few fishes. In our extremities the captain and people told me in jest they would kill and eat me, but I thought them in earnest and was depressed beyond measure, expecting every moment to be my last. While I was in this situation, one evening they caught, with a good deal of trouble, a large shark, and got it on board. This gladdened my poor heart exceedingly, as I thought it would serve the people to eat instead of their eating me; but very soon, to my astonishment, they cut off a small part of the tail and tossed the rest over the side. This renewed my consternation, and I did not know what to think of these white people, though I very much feared they would kill and eat me. There was on board the ship a young lad who had never been at sea before, about four or five years older than myself: his name was Richard Baker. He was a native of America, had received an excellent education, and was of a most amiable temper. Soon after I went on board he showed me a great deal of partiality and attention and in return I grew extremely fond of him. We at length became inseparable, and for the space of two years he was of very great use to me and was my constant companion and instructor. Although this dear youth had many slaves of his own, yet he and I have gone through many sufferings together on shipboard, and we have many nights lain in each other's bosoms when we were in great distress. Thus such a friendship was cemented between us as we cherished till his death, which to my very great sorrow happened in the year 1759, when he was up the Archipelago on board his Majesty's ship the *Preston,* an event which I have never ceased to regret as I lost at once a kind interpreter, an agreeable companion, and a faithful friend; who, at the age of fifteen, discovered a mind superior to prejudice, and who was not ashamed to notice, to associate with, and to be the friend and instructor of one who was ignorant, a stranger, of a different complexion, and a slave! My master had lodged in his mother's house in America: he respected him very much and made him always eat with him in the cabin. He used often to tell him jocularly that he would kill me to eat. Sometimes he would say to me the black people were not good to eat, and would ask me if we did not eat people in my country. I said, No: then he said he would kill Dick (as he always called him) first, and afterwards me. Though this hearing relieved my mind a little as to myself, I was alarmed for Dick and whenever he was called I used to be very much afraid he was to be killed, and I would peep and watch to see if they were going to kill him: nor was I free from this consternation till we made the land. One night we lost a man overboard, and the cries and noise were so great and confused in stopping the ship, that I, who did not know what was the matter, began as usual to be very much afraid and to think they were going to make an offering with me and perform some magic, which I still believed they dealt in. As the waves were very high I thought the Ruler of the seas was angry, and I expected to be offered up to appease him. This filled my mind with agony, and I could not any more that night close my eyes to rest.

Liable to Plot Rebellion

· *From James Pope-Hennessy,* Sins of the Fathers: A Study of the Atlantic Slave Traders 1441–1907 ·

Following is the comment of a slave trader.

The slaves from up-country "very innocently persuade one another that we buy them only to fatten them and afterwards eat them as a delicacy." These rustic slaves had to be watched with particular care, as they were liable to plot rebellion, kill the Europeans, and try to put the ship ashore or swim from it.

Caution!!

· *From Middleton Harris,* The Black Book ·

A poster apparently written by Theodore H. Parker and printed and posted by
the Vigilante Committee of Boston in April 1861. There is, of course, much truth
in this poster, given the Fugitive Slave Act, and some might validly discount its
inclusion in this chapter about rumors.

CAUTION!!

COLORED PEOPLE

OF BOSTON, ONE & ALL,

You are hereby respectfully CAUTIONED and
advised, to avoid conversing with the

Watchmen and Police Officers
of Boston,

For since the recent ORDER OF THE MAYOR &
ALDERMEN, they are empowered to act as

KIDNAPPERS
AND
Slave Catchers,

And they have already been actually employed in
KIDNAPPING, CATCHING, AND KEEPING
SLAVES. Therefore, if you value your LIBERTY,
and the *Welfare of the Fugitives* among you, *Shun*
them in every possible manner, as so many *HOUNDS*
on the track of the most unfortunate of your race.

Keep a Sharp Look Out for
KIDNAPPERS, and have
TOP EYE open.

APRIL 24, 1851.

THEODORE PARKER'S PLACARD

Placed written by Theodore Parker and printed and posted by the Vigilance Committee of Boston after the rendition of Thomas Sims to slavery in April 1851

MARY CABLE

Cinque

· *From* Black Odyssey: The Case of the Slave Ship *Amistad* ·

The following passage describes the rumor that apparently led to the famed
mutiny on board the *Amistad*, where fifty-three Africans under the leadership of
Joseph Cinque took over the slave ship on which they were headed for Cuba in
1839. In a landmark case before the U.S. Supreme Court, former president John
Quincy Adams won their freedom and they returned to Sierra Leone.

Conditions were less horrifying aboard the *Amistad* than they had
been on the *Teçora,* though scarcely pleasant. The slaves were chained
below decks by means of iron collars, each connected to his neighbor,
the whole string of collars being secured by one chain to the wall.
They were brought on deck to eat. A single plantain, some bread, and
a cup of water constituted a day's rations. One of them who tried to
take water from a cask was severely flogged by the captain. When
they asked the cook, a mulatto slave, for more food, the answer was
that they soon would need none at all—for when they arrived at
Príncipe, he told them, they would have their throats cut and be
chopped in pieces and salted down as meat for the Spaniards. He
pointed to some barrels of beef, then to an empty barrel, and "by talking with his fingers" (as the Africans said) made them understand
what lay in store.

On the third day out, when the slaves went on deck to eat, Cinque
found a nail, which he secreted under his arm. Then, back in the
hold, they held a council. One of them, Kin-na (after he had learned
some English), described it this way: "We feel bad, and we ask
Cinque what to do. Cinque say, 'Me think and by and by I tell you.'
Cinque then said, 'If we do nothing, we be killed. We may as well die
in trying to be free as to be killed and eaten.' "

With the aid of the nail, Cinque managed to break the chain that
fastened them all to the wall. Then they separated the chains that
bound them together. All, except the children, armed themselves
with cane-knives, which they found in the hold, and stole out upon
the deck.

GLADYS-MARIE FRY

Night Doctors

· *From* Night Riders in Black Folk History ·

The mass movement of Blacks from the rural South to urban centers of the North, West, and South [following the outbreak of World War I] seriously affected the Southern economy. Emmett J. Scott described the effects of this movement on the South: "Homes found themselves without servants, factories could not operate because of the lack of labor, farmers were unable to secure laborers to harvest their crops."

Southerners made strenuous efforts to check the Black exodus by legislation, by the use of force, and by circulating false rumors about the fate Blacks suffered at the hands of labor agents in the North. Severe laws were passed in some Southern states (Alabama, Arkansas, Mississippi, and Georgia) to curtail the activities of labor agents. Licenses were required of all agents and then made prohibitively expensive. If labor agents failed to observe the license laws they were often arrested and heavily fined. Added to this form of legal intimidation was the physical abuse and injury inflicted on many of these labor agents. When discriminatory legislation and physical force against labor agents failed to diminish the number of Blacks leaving for Northern centers, white Southerners resorted to creating false rumors about the perils Blacks would face in the North. According to one author, "Blacks were then warned against the rigors of the northern winter and the death rate from pneumonia and tuberculosis." Another rumor that traveled throughout the Southeast was that Blacks were being enticed to the coast, where they were loaded on ships, taken to Cuba, and sold into slavery.

Perhaps the most effective rumor deliberately circulated by Southern whites among the Blacks concerned the kidnapping and murdering of city people by night doctors. At least this is the assertion the Black folk make in their oral tradition. The following statement concerning night doctors appears in an 1896 issue of the *Journal of American Folklore:*

> On dark nights negroes in cities consider it dangerous to walk alone on the streets because the "night-doctor" is abroad. He does

not hesitate to choke colored people to death in order to obtain their bodies for dissection. The genesis of this belief from the well-known practice of grave-robbing for medical colleges, several of which are located in Southern cities, is sufficiently evident. . . .

Among the Black folk, oral accounts testify to the influence of night-doctor beliefs in the rural South. Based on the same principle of psychological control that had been in earlier use, the action to be avoided (in this case residence in the city) was made an object of fear. Rumor spread the idea, according to an informant, "that there was a scarcity of dead bodies, and that in order to get one for dissection they [doctors] would sometimes kidnap people." Landed proprietors pictured cities to their Black tenants as dangerous places in which people were daily being kidnapped and murdered by night doctors. Southern farms were made to appear as havens of security and serenity by contrast. An informant explains the fear some Blacks had of city life:

I have heard many stories about the night doctor, but it usually related to the fear of the city. From my experience this is the story that the elders in the country would tell about city life. You see the hospitals were there, and these are the places where the doctors were to be found, and it was there that one was apt to be caught and, well, eventually killed, as it were, for the purpose of medical inspection or investigation. You were safe in the country.

The old theme of impending danger was played by the same group of labor-conscious whites on an old instrument, the Black, but to a new tune, the night doctors. In this new phase of psychological control the supernatural elements were combined with certain scientific overtones, exploiting the new interest in education in general and medical science in particular that had developed in the post–Civil War South. Body-snatching, as it related to the struggling young discipline of anatomy, made a natural addition to the pattern of psychological control. Southern white landowners played on both the superstitions of the Black and his suspicion of science, realizing that the uninformed and the uneducated were naturally suspicious of all things scientific. As the focal point of a new interest in science, doctors and hospitals represented a strange phenomenon to Black folk, who had had little contact with either during slavery or Reconstruction. . . .

At present there seems to be no consensus among the folk concerning the wearing apparel of night doctors. Three schools of thought predominate—that they wore white robes or suits, black robes or suits, or plain clothes. Concerning the first, one group of informants insists that night doctors wore the traditional physician's attire, either white intern suits or long white coats. An eyewitness who "used to see them here in town" gave the following description: "Well, most of them used to be dressed in a long white coat like these doctors wear, long like that, straight down to the ankles." Other informants stated that the doctors wore white robes or a covering like a sheet. William Henderson recalled that "They usually come dressed in white . . . like a white sheet over them, a gown, or something like that."

A good number of informants support the second opinion, that night doctors wore black robes, suits, or coats for the same reason that the patrollers and some Klansmen had chosen this color: it allowed them to take their victims unaware. As Fred Manning said: "All of them dressed in black. You can't see where they are dressed in black." Henry Lewis Brown vividly described a night doctor's black garments:

> They called themselves night doctors and they had a black cape over their heads, all the way down. And around their eyes they had a white circle right around where, you know, you see through the eyes there. And they would only come out at night. When they got a hold of you that was it.

The third view expressed by informants was that the night doctors just dressed in plain clothes, or that "they dressed ordinary, like ordinary people dress." The rationale for this opinion is that the doctors did not want to be singled out as body-snatchers by dressing in any special outfits. Mary Johnson explains:

> They couldn't because people would know who they was, see? They didn't wear no certain outfit. Now these here night doctors,

they had the name but they wasn't supposed to do that, because that was killing people, you know. Catching them and killing them.

Supporters of this school of thought argued that white was an unlikely color for night doctors because it "could be seen a pretty long ways off, and if you saw that, you wouldn't continue to contact with it. You'd change your course. You can see white a long ways off, you understand." A "colored" night doctor purportedly seen by Rachel Jenfier was wearing plain clothes. She described him as "tall, dark, wore dark clothes, and a black striped hat."

Most informants agreed that masks or hoods completed the night-doctor outfit. In fact, it was the one item most frequently mentioned by informants in their description of night-doctor attire and was often the only article of clothing described. One Black woman said, "They described that they wore masks over their face." The mask she referred to was a surgical type of mask used in this instance to conceal the wearer's identity. According to Elizabeth Wheeler, "You could only see their eyes, you know."

Voting Rights of African Americans to Expire

I received this E-mail message in July 2000.

The Voters Rights Act signed in 1965 by Lyndon B. Johnson was just an ACT. It was not made a law. In 1982 Ronald Reagan amended the Voters Rights Act for only another 25 years. Which means that in the year 2007 we could lose the right to vote! Does anyone realize that Blacks/African Americans are the only group of people who require PERMISSION under the United States Constitution to vote?! In the year 2007 Congress will once again convene to decide whether or not Blacks should retain the right to vote (crazy but true). In order for this to be passed, 38 states will have to approve an extension.

Social Security Numbers—Odd or Even

I received this widely circulating rumor while I was working on this anthology; I expect I received at least five E-mails such as the following in August 2000.

Have you heard anything about Social Security numbers and African Americans and the 5th digit of your SSN?

Supposedly, if you are an African American or a Minority, the 5th digit in your SSN is even and odd if you are white!

It has been said if you take a poll, most African Americans will have an even 5th digit. Rumor has it; some companies are looking at potential employees SSN to discriminate.

Why not send this email to every African American and Minority that you know! I'm sending this to everyone I know. Mine was even, what's yours?

Black Colleges to Close Down Forever

This rumor began circulating during the 2000 presidential campaign of Texas governor George W. Bush. Though a number of Black colleges, especially those on the list, face serious problems that threaten their survival, news of their imminent closure must be treated as a rumor.

Subject: FW: Black Colleges to Close Down Forever

Regardless of your choice for President—some things remain the same, some things change, and then, some things get worst.
See below.

Black Colleges to Close Down Forever
14 Black Colleges to Close Down Forever

1. Allen Univ. (Columbia, SC)
2. Arkansas Baptist College (Little Rock, AK)
3. Barber-Scotia College (Concord, NC)
4. Central State Univ. (Wilberforce, OH)

5. Houston-Tillotson College (Austin, TX)
6. Jarvis Christian College (Hawkins, TX)
7. Lane College (Jackson, TN)
8. Mary Holmes College (West Point, MS)
9. Miles College (Birmingham, AL)
10. Paul Quinn College (Dallas, TX)
11. Southwestern Christian College (Terrell, TX)
12. Texas College (Tyler, TX)
13. Texas Southern Univ. (Houston, TX)
14. Wiley College (Marshall, TX)

Isn't it interesting that seven of these colleges are in Texas? Who is the Governor running for President in that state again? Hmmmmm . . .

Please forward this information to all the brothers and sisters you know. (Especially those who vote! And, if they don't vote, encourage them to!)

Health Alert

I received this E-mail message in May 2000.

Health Alert

This is an alert about a virus in the original sense of the word . . . one that affects your body, not your hard drive.

There have been 23 confirmed cases of people attacked by the Klingerman Virus, a virus that arrives in your real mail box, not your E-mail in-box.

Someone has been mailing large blue envelopes, seemingly at random, to people inside the U.S. On the front of the envelope in bold black letters is printed, "A gift for you from the Klingerman Foundation." When the envelopes are opened, there is a small sponge sealed in plastic. This sponge carries what has come to be known as the Klingerman Virus, as public health officials state this is a strain of virus they have not previously encountered.

When asked for comment, Florida police Sergeant Stetson said, "We are working with the CDC and the USPS, but have so far been unable to track down the origins of these letters. The return addresses have all been different, and we are certain a remailing service is being used, making our jobs that much more difficult."

Those who have come in contact with the Klingerman Virus have been hospitalized with severe dysentery. So far seven of the twenty-three victims have died. There is no legitimate Klingerman Foundation mailing unsolicited gifts.

If you receive an oversized blue envelope in the mail marked, "A gift from the Klingerman Foundation," DO NOT open it. Place the envelope in a strong plastic bag or container, and call the police immediately. The "gift" inside is one you definitely do not want.

PLEASE PASS THIS ON TO EVERYONE YOU CARE ABOUT.

You Have Been Infected with HIV

I received this E-mail message in June 2000.

For your information, a couple of weeks ago, in a Ft. Myers Florida movie theater, a person sat on something sharp in one of the seats. When she stood up to see what it was, a needle was found poking through the seat with an attached note saying, "you have been infected with HIV." The Centers for Disease Control in Atlanta reports similar events have taken place in several other cities recently. All of the needles tested HAVE been positive for HIV. The CDC also reports that needles have been found in the coin return areas of pay phones and soda machines. Everyone is asked to use extreme caution when confronted with these types of situations. All public chairs should be thoroughly but safely inspected prior to any use. A thorough visual inspection is considered the bare minimum. Furthermore, they ask that everyone notify their family members and friends of the potential dangers, as well. Thank you.

The previous information was sent from the Ft. Myers Florida Police Department to all of the local governments in the Washington area and was interdepartmentally dispersed. We were all asked to pass this to as many people as possible.

PATRICIA TURNER

AIDS

· *From* I Heard It Through the Grapevine ·

More so than most of the other texts discussed in this book, AIDS origins stories are known to a public beyond African-Americans. Unlike the Atlanta child killer or Church's Chicken, namely, AIDS is indiscriminate in picking its victims—the list of which, moreover, has grown to include more and more groups beyond the "four H's." [Tamotsu] Shibutani points out, "Spectacular events with possible consequences for millions result in a sudden increase in demand for news that cannot be satisfied even by the most efficient press service."[2] AIDS certainly falls in this category, and indeed, the rumors are abundant. For instance, I encountered many informants, gay and heterosexual alike, who believed that the disease was an experiment in biological warfare intended to diminish the world's homosexual population. Narratives about "AIDS Mary" also were reported, in which a somewhat naive, young heterosexual man allows himself to be seduced by an irresistible woman; the next morning he finds that she has disappeared, the only trace of her being a lipstick message on a bathroom mirror: "Welcome to the world of AIDS."

Discerning the folkloric elements of these theories is problematic for several reasons. For one thing, the media has played a significant role in reporting and perpetuating AIDS material, making it difficult to distinguish between AIDS lore and AIDS fact. To the layperson,

[2]*Improvised News: A Sociological Study of Rumor* (Indianapolis: Bobbs-Merrill, 1966), 60.

the complexities of the disease and the research into it can be confusing. For example, several informants claimed that the alleged biological warfare experiment began when scientists injected the experimental substance into African green monkeys. At first glance, such a statement might appear outlandish. Yet although respected AIDS researchers do discredit such theories, they in fact believe that African green monkeys may become key in understanding the disease's origins. Many theories about the disease, moreover, are spread in both oral and print discourse, making it nearly impossible to determine if an item is the product of communal folk imagination or of evidence gathered by responsible authorities. Finally, to investigate AIDS from any angle at all is to investigate a mystery that is still unfolding. Because what is unknown about AIDS exceeds what is known, we cannot know what is in fact correct. In other words, some of the theories about AIDS origins that circulate orally may turn out to contain pieces of the truth.

Despite these obstacles, I think it is important, in the context of a chapter devoted to African-American beliefs about contamination, to include a section on AIDS beliefs. In collecting this material, I was always particularly careful to ask the informant about his or her source and whether or not this was an item in folk circulation. Given the growing sophistication of the media and technology generally, variables that will surely influence the future shape and direction of folk transmission, I hope that this study will offer some insights into how folklorists can face these challenges.

After the "four H's," the next populations linked with the AIDS virus were Africans and African-Americans. With titles such as "Special Help Needed to Halt Black AIDS Cases," "AIDS More Prevalent Among Black Military Recruits," "Black Health Professionals Urge AIDS Precautions," and "Black Man's Teeth a Deadly Weapon, Jury Rules," newspaper, magazine, and television reports have depicted AIDS as a particular threat to the African-American community since 1982. Although the media have proved adept at reporting the ostensibly disproportionately high number of diagnoses among blacks, the reasons why one ethnic group might be more vulnerable than another are less clear. It is therefore not surprising that such people have responded with their own theories about the disease's origins.

I began collecting stories about AIDS as a possible conspiracy

against a particular community in the summer of 1987; my informants include white and black college students, blue-collar workers,
professional people, prison inmates, members of the armed services —
in short, a broad cross-section of the population. As a result, I have
several hundred examples of AIDS origins beliefs, and many make
specific reference to a conspiracy or contamination plot directed
against people of color.

Several motifs recur frequently. (1) Some branch of the U.S. government is usually the author of the conspiracy (informants have
identified the CIA, the army, the Reagan administration, the
Pentagon, the Centers for Disease Control, the far right, and "the su-
perpowers"), though a couple of informants in 1987 referred to the
"Chicago" version popularized by the national media, in which
Jewish doctors were the culprits. (2) The contamination targets of
the conspiracy are labeled as Africans or descendants of Africans, either directly or by implication — for example, Haitians, Africans,
blacks, black babies, the lower classes, and the outcasts of society.
Many informants identify more than one group, claiming, for instance, that the conspiracy was intended to limit both the gay and the
black populations. (3) The conspiracy is described usually as either
an experiment or as the intentional use of biological/chemical/germ
warfare; hence, the goal is either to learn more about an experimental weapon or actually to use a known weapon against a targeted
group. (4) The spread of the disease through groups other than those
intended by the conspirators (such as white heterosexuals) is cited as
a big mistake made by those in charge when the disease became too
powerful for them. (5) Authenticating motifs frequently provide closure in one of two versions that are not mutually exclusive. An informant might say, "That's why the disease is rampant" within one
of the identified groups or why it is so widespread in a specified
locale — Africa, Haiti, inner cities, San Francisco. Or the informant
will make the familiar comment, "I know it's true, I read it in the
paper/saw it on television" — identified in folklore shorthand as *r.i.p.*
(read it in paper). And indeed, the media, particularly left-wing publications but also black-owned, gay-owned, and even straight, conventional forms of the print and television media, have discussed
various versions of this conspiracy motif, whether as fact, possibility,
or hearsay. The idea of the army's inflicting AIDS on undesirables,
for example, gained prominence in an Ann Landers column in 1986.

Many informants who identify a specific media source will also claim to have heard the item "in the street."

Informants almost always begin their reports with a motif identifying the conspirators—usually "the government" or "government scientists," though the other parties implicated could be considered symbolic equivalents for the government. Statements singling out the far right, the Reagan administration, the CDC, and like groups all clearly refer to groups perceived to have the power to conduct such a mission. The CIA was the agency most often named. As one informant put it, "[AIDS was] a chemical experiment sponsored by the CIA that went awry." Yet I would say that the conspirator's precise identity is far less important to informants than the contamination plot itself. Informants, after all, have no particular stake in claiming that the CIA conducted the experiment, as opposed to some other government agency. The frequency of the CIA attribution appears to stem from the popular association of that agency with covert foreign affairs, making it the logical group to instigate such an action.

Not surprisingly, the CIA itself views the situation from a different angle. In response to my inquiry about this association, a CIA spokesman wrote:

> We believe that rumors linking the CIA with the development or the spreading of the AIDS virus, especially in Africa, may be the result of what we would call "disinformation" efforts of hostile intelligence services to damage the United States. The CIA has had absolutely nothing to do with either the development nor the spreading of AIDS or any other virus. The CIA is not carrying out experiments in this regard and you may document this by corresponding with either the House or Senate Select Committees on Intelligence which monitor Agency operations. The CIA has undertaken to try to understand the effects of the AIDS virus around the world, since it is clear that the spreading of such a disease could constitute a threat to US national security.

Once again we seem to have a "blame the Russians" explanation for the dissemination of material perceived as disruptive. In official documents informing American policymakers of the alleged scope of Soviet disinformation campaigns, in fact, various versions of the rumor are offered. A 1988 report, for example, states, "The largest

Soviet disinformation campaign of recent years has made the totally false claim that the AIDS virus was created in a U.S. military facility at Fort Detrick, Maryland." None of my informants named the Maryland or any other military installation by name, though several did claim the virus was developed in a government, CIA, or CDC "laboratory." The above report continues, "The main 'source' for the Soviet allegations, Dr. Jacob Segal, argues that AIDS must been created at Fort Detrick because it appeared first in New York which Segal describes as the 'nearest big city' to Fort Detrick. In fact, New York is 250 miles from Fort Detrick. Baltimore, Washington and Philadelphia are all closer."[3] According to this convoluted reasoning, because Dr. Segal has a flawed knowledge of northeastern geography, his hypothesis about AIDS dissemination is necessarily inaccurate.

The reports to Congress as well as the letter responding to my inquiry are as provocative for what they do not say as for what they do say. It is troubling to note that in denying the U.S. government–AIDS connection, U.S. Information Agency officials begin by stating, "Science has not yet reached the stage where it would be possible to create artificially a virus as complex as AIDS."[4] By making "science" the subject of the sentence, the report authors seem to be directing attention away from the role Americans have, according to Soviet propagandists, allegedly played in the conspiracy; after all, "science" cannot create a virus, but scientists could. This statement would be more reassuring if it were followed by a disclaimer along the lines of, "and American scientists would not engage in such a research project." But it is not. The authors also make no reference to any other forces that might have fueled the spread of the rumor/disinformation. Implicit in their commentary is the assumption that if the Soviet Union had not perpetuated this information, it would not be circulating among Americans.

Discussion of the conspiracy targets revealed only one real pattern. If an informant had a connection to a particular group of people of color, he or she was more likely to name that group as the intended victims. For example, many Haitians responded to my

[3]U.S. House Committee on Appropriations, *Soviet Active Measures in the Era of Glasnost* (Washington, D.C. 1988), 12.
    [4]Ibid.

query with accusations similar to one from a male Haitian postal service employee who claimed that the CIA planted AIDS on that island to curtail "Haitians immigrating into the United States illegally." Like many Haitian informants, this one identified the United States' dislike of former president-for-life Jean-Claude "Papa Doc" Duvalier as instrumental in the decision to spread the disease. Similarly, Africans, as well as people who had recently traveled to Africa, identified that continent as the target of the conspiracy. An African-American female college professor recently returned from Zaire claimed to have heard that the virus was "tried out" both in that nation and in Uganda. Informants with no particular allegiance to Africa or Haiti usually combined the two locales in their commentary. A Jamaican-born female college student, for example, reported that "the AIDS virus was started in Africa and Haiti by the government." Other informants used general labels such as "non-whites," "Africans," "minority people," and "blacks" to refer to the targeted groups. These patterns are not absolute. While not all Haitian informants claimed that the contamination was conducted in their homeland, some did. That is, informants are more likely to focus on a locale they identify with, but that does not mean that all members of a given group personalize the threat.

The contamination motif commonly emerges in one of two ways: the AIDS virus is characterized as either (a) the aftermath of a biological warfare experiment that was tried out on Africans or Haitians or (b) an intentional use of biological warfare *intended to* diminish the African or Haitian population. The former explanation was more common among those I interviewed. While the second option attributes a much more sinister motive to the perpetrators, the first assumes more than just a marginal hostility. After all, few people would disagree that an "experiment" in biological or germ warfare is apt to have negative consequences; in using human guinea pigs, the experimenters are clearly risking the well-being of people they presume to be "disposable." An unemployed white male reported, "The AIDS virus was created in a CIA laboratory. The CIA brought it to Africa to test on blacks, thinking they could watch it, but it got out of control. This is why doctors cannot come up with a vaccine that will work on it. It has to be man-made." Here again we find, as in the Atlanta child killer legend and the castrated boy legend, the rationale that the powerful group needs the oppressed group's bodies for their own enrichment. If people do not know how the tools of germ or biological warfare are tested, they may well assume that the power in question would look for an impotent (pun intended) population on which to refine its weapon. Utility, not evil, motivates the powerful ones.

Diabolical malice is abundant in the second option—the notion that the AIDS virus was intended for the purposes of African genocide. These versions clearly reflect a belief that "they" are out to get us. One young woman who identifies herself as a black American/Seminole Indian stated, "The story was told to me by an aunt. Apparently the CIA was testing to find a disease which would resist any cures known to man. They did this testing somewhere in Africa [South]. The purpose of finding this incurable disease was to bring America back to the old days of the moral majority. Therefore this disease was to be transmitted sexually among the outcasts of society, namely people of color and gay men."

No doubt much of the momentum for the contamination beliefs is provided by a group of highly credentialed authorities who maintain that AIDS is just the latest form of genocide practiced by the U.S. government. Tracing this impulse backward through "Cointelpro" (the code name for an FBI campaign conducted in the 1960s and 1970s to undermine the credibility of "radical" black leaders), the Tuskegee experiment, and slavery, they make the case that whites have always been anxious to rid the world of blacks. Advocates of this theory include medical doctors, college professors, writers, and ministers. A partial list includes James Small, a black studies professor at City College of New York; Robert Strecker, M.D., Ph.D.; and Louis Farrakhan, leader of the Nation of Islam. They also cite cryptic references contained in the World Health Organization bulletin and the Congressional Record. In an articulate and nonequivocating manner, they contribute their theories at any forum that invites them.

For every expert willing to argue that AIDS is the result of a grotesque genocide conspiracy, several others can be cited who debunk these theories and the evidence on which they are based. Both white and African-American experts have little respect for the proponents of conspiracy theory. Chief of infectious diseases at Howard University Hospital, Wayne Greaves, M.D., laments, "I'm too busy worrying about caring for sick patients and educating people about AIDS to get caught up in this kind of inane rhetoric."[5] Once again, the bottom line for most of these experts is not that the United States would never conduct such research, but rather that the scientific community is not sufficiently advanced to create a virus as complex as AIDS.

Attention!

· *From Patricia Turner*, I Heard It Through the Grapevine ·

This flyer was distributed in New York City in 1990 and 1991.

ATTENTION!!! ATTENTION!!! ATTENTION!!!

.50 CENT SODAS

BLACKS AND MINORITY GROUPS

DID YOU SEE (T.V. SHOW) 20/20 ???

PLEASE BE ADVISE, "TOP POP" & "TROPICAL FANTASY" ALSO TREAT .50 SODAS ARE BEING MANUFACTURED BY THE KLU.. KLUX.. KLAN..

SODAS CONTAIN STIMULANTS TO STERILIZE THE BLACK MAN, AND WHO KNOWS WHAT ELSE!!!

THEY ARE ONLY PUT IN STORES IN HARLEM AND MINORITY AREAS YOU WON'T FIND THEM DOWN TOWN....LOOK AROUND.....

YOU HAVE BEEN WARNED
PLEASE SAVE THE CHILDREN

---

[5]Karen Grigsby Bates, "Is It Genocide?" *Essence* (September 1990), 78.

Driving Tips

I received this E-mail in December 1998.

Subject: Driving Tip

One of our employees whose husband works for the City of Cincinnati received the following message and we, Administrative Services, feels that it is worth passing on to you, your friends and families:

FYI

A police officer that works with the DARE Program at an elementary school passed this warning on. . . .

If you're ever driving after dark and see an on-coming car with no headlights turned on, DO NOT flash your lights at them! This is a common gang member "initiation game" that goes like this: the new gang member under initiation drives along with no headlights and the first car to flash their headlights at him is now his "target." He is now required to turn around and chase that car and shoot at or into the car in order to complete his initiation requirements. Please share this information with people you know.

Stay safe!

Administrative Services

Black Blood

· *From Middleton Harris et al.,* The Black Book ·

Another famous American born in the West Indies, and whose mother is a shadowy figure, was Alexander Hamilton. Not only is there a persistent rumor that his mother was a Negro, but in New York City there are black Hamiltons who claim direct descent from the illustrious first U.S. Treasurer.

Boycott Tommy Hilfiger

I received this E-mail in August 2000. Despite the fact that the Tommy Hilfiger Company issued a denial of the rumor in 1997, noting that he had not appeared on the Oprah Winfrey Show, the false accusation continues to circulate.

Subject: Fwd: Boycott Tommy Hilfiger

Date: Mon, 31 Jul 2000 11:15:36

Don't buy your next shirt from Tommy Hilfiger. I'm sure many of you watched the recent taping of the Oprah Winfrey Show where her guest was Tommy Hilfiger. On the show, she asked him if the statements about race he was accused of saying were true. Statements like: "if I'd known African Americans, Hispanics, Jewish and Asians would buy my clothes, I would not have made them so nice. I wish these people would NOT buy my clothes, as they are made for upper-class white people."

His answer to Oprah was a simple "YES." Whereafter she immediately asked him to leave her show.

My suggestion? Let's give him what he asked for. Let's not buy his clothes, let's put him in a financial state where he himself will not be able to afford the ridiculous prices he puts on his clothes.

BOYCOTT.

PLEASE SEND THIS MESSAGE TO ANYONE YOU KNOW WHO SPENDS THEIR HARD-EARNED MONEY ON CLOTHES MADE BY SOMEONE WHO DOES NOT RESPECT THEM AS A PERSON, OR PEOPLE IN GENERAL FOR WHO THEY ARE DESPITE THEIR RACE.

A Brief Summary of a Few Prevalent Rumors

Forty Acres and a Mule: President Lincoln is going to confiscate the land of slave owners and give former slaves forty acres and a mule.

Cats in Chinese Food: Chinese restaurateurs kill and use cats in the preparation of their food.

Concentration Camps: The U.S. government has already constructed concentration camps with the express purpose of incarcerating Black Americans in them.

Drugs in L.A.: The CIA spread the crack epidemic by backing Nicaraguan drug dealers whose profits supported the Contras. Drugs are a part of the conspiracy to commit genocide in the Black community.

Tampon Dangers: Tampon manufacturers include asbestos to increase menstrual bleeding and promote reliance on their product. Other versions propose a variety of dangers stemming from their use. In his presentations Dick Gregory often warned Black women of the dangers of using tampons.

HIV-Infected Needles: Warning from a Florida Police Department captain that HIV-infected needles have been found affixed to gas pump handles. He states that several people have been stuck with the needles and a large percentage found to be infected as a result.

AIDS: Sleeping with a virgin will cure a man of AIDS. (This rumor, which is prevalent in Africa, is now circulating in the United States.)

AIDS Mary: A beautiful woman picks up men in a bar, takes them to a hotel room and has sex with them. When they wake up, she has gone and left nothing except a message written with lipstick on the mirror: "Welcome to the World of AIDS."

Date-Rape Drug: A new drug, ———, is used in connection with ———, the date-rape drug by men at parties to rape and sterilize their female victim and avoid DNA identification. Any woman who is given this drug in a drink will never be able to conceive.

Black Heritage Stamps: The U.S. government is about to drop the series because they aren't selling well. If we want to keep these stamps, Black people need to be sure to start buying them.

The Black Man on the Elevator: A White woman forces herself to overcome her fears and get on the hotel elevator when a door opens revealing two Black men. One man says to another, "Hit the floor," and she, afraid of what will happen if she doesn't obey, throws herself to the floor. Laughing, they ask her what floor she wants them to punch for her. Seeing how nervous she is, they insist on walking her to her room. Still frightened of them despite their apparent kindness, she is too terrified to resist. They ensure that she is safely in her room and leave. As she closes the door, she hears them laughing. She is embarrassed that all her racial fears have come out in front of these two nice men. The next morning she receives a dozen roses from Eddie Murphy thanking her for the best laugh he and his bodyguard have had in years. In other versions the Black man is some other famous person, including Reggie Jackson, Muhammad Ali, and Lionel Richie.

Charles Richard Drew: Though he discovered the means to preserve blood for transfusions and saved countless lives, including hundreds of soldiers during World War II, Drew was allowed to die by White doctors in Alamance County, North Carolina, who refused him a transfusion. (The fact is that though he died following a car accident in April 1950, he did receive treatment in the emergency room of a segregated North Carolina hospital. A similar rumor spread following the accidental death of Bessie Smith. Such rumors were easily fueled because of the fact that Blacks were routinely denied treatment at "White" hospitals in the South.)

Statue of Liberty: An E-mail message laments the fact that valuable information about the Statue of Liberty is not taught in our schools. It goes on to provide the true story: the original Statue of Liberty in France is of a Black woman and the model was a Black woman. The Statue that we have was presented through the American Abolitionist Society in recognition of the fact that Black soldiers won the Civil War and as a tribute to their prowess. (Among those who have contributed to the debate about the Statue of Liberty are Professor Leonard Jeffries, former chairman of New York City College's African American Studies Department, and Professor Jim Haskins, Department of English at the University of Florida.)

Subway Mugging: A White lawyer is jostled by a Negro male on the subway. He then notices that his wallet is missing and follows the Negro off the subway and demands his wallet. The frightened man gives the wallet to him. Later the lawyer phones his wife and tells her about the incident, whereupon she informs him that he left his wallet at home on the dresser. The lawyer is the one who mugged the Negro.

The Atlanta Murders: They haven't got the right person for killing all those young Black people in Atlanta, and they know Wayne Williams is not guilty. The series of murders was part of a KKK plot to destroy young Blacks, and the FBI and Atlanta law officials helped protect the real perpetrators. (Patricia Turner argues that "a growing amount of evidence suggests possible Klan involvement in some of the deaths in Atlanta" and declares, "Of all the rumors covered in this book [*I Heard It Through the Grapevine*], those linking the KKK with the Atlanta child murders have the most potential for accuracy. The folk may have this one right, at least in part.")

The Assassination of John F. Kennedy: He was killed by the Mafia/J. Edgar Hoover/the CIA because he was doing too much to help Black people and because Hoover just couldn't stand the Kennedy brothers.

The Assassination of Martin Luther King: Varied suspicions still circulate among Blacks, many of whom, like the King family, do not believe that James Earl Ray was the major figure responsible for King's death. The KKK, the FBI, and J. Edgar Hoover are rumored to have been involved in his murder.

O. J. Simpson: He was set up by the Japanese Mafia.

Richard Wright: He was killed by the CIA.

Chapter 13

Techlore

Lead us not into temptation, but deliver us some E-mail.
Amen.
—The ending of "The Lord's Prayer" as recited by
a young child

N ew advances in technology have resulted in new forms of folklore, which I have chosen to label *techlore*. In the latter half of the twentieth century, with the introduction of copiers in the workplace, reproductions of cartoons, other drawings, narratives, verses, and tales were made and circulated among individuals' colleagues and friends. Some folk made changes and created new versions of those pieces; others simply copied and circulated the items as they received them. As Alan Dundes and Carl R. Pagter point out in *Urban Folklore from the Paperwork Empire*, the individual creators of these copies are not known. Though infrequently a name appears on them, variants are often found with other names.

Folklore from the paperwork empire, which Dundes and Pagter describe as "a major form of tradition in modern America" (*When You're Up to Your Ass in Alligators*), was one of the most popular new forms of folklore until the Internet became accessible from almost every contemporary workstation. With the advent of E-mail, pieces that were formerly copied and circulated are now sent with one click of the mouse to a long list of one's associates — who often send them on to other groups of acquaintances. These E-mail pieces are also occasionally photocopied, continuing to circulate in hard-copy form. Their originators are rarely known, and even when names are attached, those names more often identify the sender rather than the originator.

Numerous Web sites also have jokes, tales, and other folkloristic items on their message boards that varied surfers post and share with one another. There are Web sites that focus on specific kinds of humor, with names such as Star Trek Humor, Men & Women, the Weird Stuff, Dirty Jokes, Daily Life, Religious Humor, and Computer Humor.

All of this techlore is circulated interchangeably as oral lore. Several of the items were clearly initially transcribed from oral lore and then copied or posted on the Internet. Similarly, people who receive tales and jokes via E-mail, Web sites, or the paperwork empire often share them orally. In some instances I have personally come across the same tale, as oral items, copied items, E-mailed items, and postings on Web sites.

Frequently, it is impossible to determine whether or not the items disseminated by means of modern technology originated with African Americans. Considering that dilemma, I have chosen to include in this chapter items that circulate widely among African Americans, indicating that they either grow out of that community or are embraced by that group.[1] With the exception of the items that speak to male-female relations, aging, and the Bible that I have personally found so popular among my own Black friends, I have basically omitted those pieces that do not have African Americans as their subject, that do not have motifs popular in the Black community, or that have no race specific references (language, allusions to individuals, etc.). For example, in some instances, such as "A Few Things Not to Say to a Cop," I have selected items because they treat themes, reflect viewpoints, and utilize language that are common in Black folklore; I recognize that such themes and such language may not be exclusive to African Americans, and I would not be surprised if some of these originated outside the Black community.

---

[1] I considered my choice of selections reinforced somewhat when Professor Trudier Harris of the University of North Carolina, Chapel Hill, wrote to me after reading this chapter, "I have received probably ninety percent of the email messages you copied" (letter to author, August 25, 2000).

Indeed it is quite obvious that some selections in this chapter have a currency with other groups as well. For example, the redneck jokes, which are popular among Blacks who have always enjoyed making Whites the butt of their humor—particularly Southern "crackers"—may also be told by rednecks. Some of the pieces that ridicule Blacks may well have originated with White racists, but there is no question that demeaning tales about Blacks originate, circulate, and enjoy great popularity among African Americans as well. This same paradox can be found in much traditional folklore, such as the etiological tales explaining how Blacks got their color, hair, and economic standing.[2]

Other popular items that are undoubtedly of African American origin include selections that are educational, some designed to instruct the audience about Black history and culture and others designed to caution the audience about events that may have an impact on the Black community (these are sometimes legitimate and at other times more in the nature of rumors).

And then, of course, the chain letter has also gone high tech. I constantly receive these letters insisting the recipient send them on to a certain number of other people. One recent one declares, "Today I share this treasure with thee / It's the treasure of friendship you've given to me. / If this comes back to you then you'll have a friend for life / but if this becomes deleted, you are not a friend." Others threaten bad luck and even death if you break the chain. Nothing about these is unique in the African American community, so none are included here. It is important to observe, however, that they are a popular part of the techlore circulating widely among African Americans.

Whatever the subject or the goal of the selections that follow, it is clear that twentieth-century technology, which changed every area of our society, is irrevocably transforming the circulation of traditional folklore.

---

[2]I discuss demeaning folklore in the Black community in full chapters in *Shuckin' and Jivin'* ("A Nigger Ain't Shit: Self-Denigrating Tales") and *Honey, Hush!* ("My People, My People! Self-Denigrating Tales" and "Mirror, Mirror on the Wall: The Black Woman's Physical Image").

N.U.D.

I have deleted the list of companies mentioned in this E-mail, received June 20, 2000.

What does this mean . . .

You have probably never heard of "N.U.D." With good reason.

It is the acronym for a very subtle and little known marketing term specifically directed toward people of color. NUD stands for Non Urban Dictate. Three words that essentially mean a company is not interested in the Black Consumer. (A NUD label means that a company does not want their Marketing and Advertising materials placed in media that claim an urban audience as their main target.)

There are legitimate reasons for companies not using urban radio. It may be that Blacks don't index high in certain categories or that a company's strategy is to market to the Black consumer down the road after they have established a strong position in their primary target.

But a NUD usually means that a company is not interested in the Black consumer. Companies evade discrimination liability by embracing it as theory rather than policy. As a service to Black consumers, the Urban Institute will list all Companies that have a NUD policy. Armed with this information, we feel that Black consumers will be able to make informed buying decisions.

No Fear

E-mail received June 29, 2000

I just picked up some interesting information regarding "No Fear." Perhaps you have seen this decal on automobile windows, etc. Well, here in the Old Dominion, specifically in Chesterfield County, the administrators have designated April as Confederate Month.

To make a long story short, David Duke, former grand

wizard for the KKK, was in town to speak at a shopping mall. David Duke is the head of a group calling itself NO FEAR; it stands for:

"National Organization For European-American Rights."

All this time I thought No Fear was just something young white people placed onto their vehicles, meaning they fear nothing because of their youth. How wrong I was, so please pass this on so that more of our people know what No Fear really means.

We Niggas Today

E-mail received in December 1999.

There was a plane flying over the Atlantic, and the pilot got on the intercom and said that the plane was experiencing difficulties and that the weight would have to be lessened on the plane. So he said that everyone had to throw their luggage off the plane. So everyone did. He got back on the intercom, "The plane is still too heavy, so people are going to have to jump off, but we're going to do this alphabetically. All African-Americans jump off the plane." No one stood up. He got back on and said, "All Blacks, jump off the plane." Still no one stood up. "All coloreds jump off the plane." Again, no one stood up. Then the little Black boy turned to his mother and said, "Momma, aren't we all those things?" She answered, "No son, we Niggas today."

Ten Indisputable Truths . . .

E-mail received August 4, 2000.

Ten Indisputable Truths Black People Know That White People Won't Admit
    1. Elvis is dead.

2. Anything below 45 degrees is cold. You should be wearing a jacket and long pants.

3. Jesus was not White.

4. Skinny does not equal sexy.

5. Yes, Black folks do tan!

6. There's a very thin line between being a legitimately cool White person and being an insulting wannabe gangster.

7. Thomas Jefferson did father Sally Hemings' children.

8. Bob Hope has never been funny.

9. In his prime, Joe Louis would have beat the snot out of Rocky Marciano. So would Muhammad Ali.

10. Making money does not make you a man.

Ten Indisputable Truths White People Know That Black People Won't Admit

1. O.J. did it.

2. Gold-plating does not make everything better.

3. Just because you have ten fingers does not mean you have to wear ten rings.

4. Tupac is dead.

5. Teeth should not be decorated.

6. Spandex and mini-skirts are not for everyone.

7. Jesse Jackson will never be President.

8. Larry Bird wasn't just "white hype"; he could play.

9. Your sound system should not be worth more than your car.

10. Making babies does not make you a man.

You Went to a Black University

E-mail received October 6, 1999.

You went to a black university if:

The twirler is GAY!!!

The lunchroom worker wore his or her plastic cap after work!

You had homemade frats (Alcorn's MF Wrecking Crew & Jackson State's Memphis Clique).

Kappa Kappa Psi got their own tree (even Alpha Phi Omega may have one).

You knew exactly how many miles your car could go on "E."

The only time Security would raid the dorms was when somebody called because their boyfriend or girlfriend was cheating on them.

You climbed through the girl's dorm window late at night and left early in the morning.

You climbed through the boy's dorm window late at night and left early in the morning.

You only sat with your crew, girls, athletes, band members, fraternities or sororities during lunch and had your assigned table.

A fight would break out if someone else sat there.

Popcorn, french fries, Hot Pockets, & ramen noodles were special cuisine in your room.

You wash 2 loads of clothes—funky and dirty.

You scheduled your classes around the Soaps.

You had the answers to the test from last year . . . which would be the same test this year.

Half-way through the semester you are attending class while still walking around with an incomplete registration packet.

The majority of the black teachers are Africans.

People showed up at the football game just to see the half-time show, then left.

If the Sigmas are cooking out somewhere.

If the library was a known gathering place.

If you stole utensils, cups or bowls from the cafeteria.

If you knew the physical plant people or janitors by first name.

The cafeteria workers were missing more than one tooth.

The food in the cafeteria gave you diarrhea. . . .

Everybody skipped class the first hot day of spring.

The Ques were thrown off the yard.

The bookstore did not get the books you needed until midterm.

You couldn't find a job.

Campus was the hangout spot for locals. . . .

It normally took 5 or more years to graduate.

You spent more time in the Student Union than in the Library.

There was only one building with an air conditioner.

Your mama went there.

A Spades tournament was played in your dorm lobby.

The B.M.O.C. was not the star athlete, but the one who had the weed.

You skipped class to get your refund check.

Your refund check was late.

You used your work-study money to buy a car.

Every floor in the dorm had a barber or a beautician. . . .

Everyone hung out around a tree. . . .

The Ques were always fighting another frat.

Campus security carried a flashlight instead of a gun. . . .

Even though you had elevators in the dorm, they didn't work half of the time.

Everybody had to go to the nearest Wal-mart to get a window fan during summer school, because the air has gone out.

You had an extra person staying in the room with you the entire semester that was never in school in the first place.

Ghetto Wedding

E-mail received October 26, 1998.

To those of you who have been married recently . . .

To those of you who have become engaged recently . . .

To those of you who are contemplating marriage at some point in the future . . .

To those of you who just like reading another funny email . . .

Ever been to a "Ghetto Wedding?" You have, if you find that more than Five (5) of the following statements are true.

- Upon your arrival, you were afraid to leave your car unattended.
- The programs weren't there yet.
- You had to beg the hostess for a program, once you finally found a hostess.
- The usher didn't know which side of the church was the Bride's side or the Groom's.
- The only air conditioning was a handheld fan from the local funeral home.
- The wedding started twenty (20) or more minutes after the time stated on your invitation.
- The wedding was delayed because the Groom was late.
- The bridesmaids' gowns don't all match. . . .
- A groomsman had his tux leg rolled up. . . .
- A groomsman or bridesmaid was carrying a cellular phone during the ceremony.
- A groomsman or bridesmaid answered a cellular phone during the ceremony.
- Nobody in the church had their beeper set for "vibrate."
- The preacher's beeper goes off.
- The preacher answered his beep on his cell phone during the ceremony.
- You couldn't hear the vows because of the crying babies. . . .
- The parents of the Bride or Groom were under 30 years old.
- Some bridesmaids were wearing platform shoes like THE SPICE GIRLS.
- The Bride and some bridesmaids had miraculously grown their hair 14 inches in a week.
- A groomsman was sporting cornrows.
- A member of the wedding party was wearing sunglasses.
- There were more than 40 people in the wedding party. . . .
- Either of the grandparents was asleep during the ceremony. . . .
- The happy couple already had more than 6 kids between them.
- Any Al Green song was played during the ceremony (i.e. Love & Happiness). . . .
- The communion wine came from Food Lion.

- The salute to the bride took more than 5 minutes, and involved sound effects. . . .
- After the couple was pronounced husband & wife, at least 1 of their mothers shouted out at the top of her lungs, "THANK YOU LORD JESUS CHRIST ALMIGHTY!!!!!"
- The limos were actually the family cars from the funeral home that provided the church fans.
- The couple had the limo stop by Winn Dixie for cold beer on the way to the reception.
- The person announcing the names of the wedding party couldn't pronounce most of them.
- There were twice as many people at the reception than were at the wedding. . . .
- The couples' first dance was to a song by "Master P."
- The buffet included collards, souse meat and/or pig's feet.
- The reception photos were ruined by unsupervised kids running in front of the photographer. . . .
- The "Lecktit Slide" (Electric Slide) lasted more than 15 minutes, each of the 5 times it got played.
- There was 1 woman off to the side trying to teach her 3 friends "The New Electric Slide" even though that version came and went 10 years ago.
- None of the bridesmaids were still wearing shoes.
- The wedding cake came from Sam's Club.
- The lady serving the punch advised you to keep your cup.
- Your cup would only hold 4 ounces BEFORE that big ice cube was put in it.

You Probly frum da Projeks If:

E-mail received on December 13, 1999.

The milk you drink requires water.
You put sugar on your frosted flakes.
Your kids were in your wedding.
You call your mama by her first name.

You can speak to more than ten neighbors at the same time.

You have a car phone and no car.

You iron dirty clothes.

You've been a guest on a talk show.

You wear house shoes to the grocery store.

You use a clothes hanger as a TV antenna.

You're married with kids and still live at mama's.

Your shoes are black but the heels are gold. . . .

You record over previously recorded tapes.

Your mom does your hair in the kitchen.

You don't pay your rent until you get a three-day notice.

You put on panty-hose instead of shaving your legs.

You buy clothes, wear them to a party and return them to the store the next day.

You only go to church on Easter, on Mother's Day, or to meet women.

Your first name begins with Ta', La,' or Sha'.

You took the batteries out of the smoke detector and put them in your pager.

Your bank is a check-cashing place.

You have to put stuff on layaway at the 99-cent store.

Your man can wear his hair in a ponytail but you can't.

You make sandwiches without meat in them (i.e., ketchup, syrup or mayonnaise sandwiches).

You think putting batteries in the refrigerator recharges them.

When you were little, you had to be in the house before the street lights came on.

You take bubble baths with dishwashing liquid.

You return gifts for the money.

You yell "Pookie" in your house and five people turn around.

You think going to prison is "keeping it real."

You save cooking grease.

The only dates marked on your calendar are the 1st and the 15th.

Your mama whipped you and your friends.

You keep food stamps in your money clip.

You think grease and water make your hair curly. . . .

You put your kids to sleep with NyQuil.

You use your welfare check as collateral.

You can read your haircut.

You use a toothbrush to style your "baby hair."

You bought your rims before you bought your car.

Your fingernails are longer than your fingers.

You think jury duty is a good way to make money.

You think going on a diet means no candy.

You have a drawer in your kitchen just for condiments from fast food restaurants.

Only Black Folks

E-mail received June 11, 2000.

1. Are engaged 5 years or more.

2. Never bother to divorce, they just separate (for the rest of their life).

3. Are late to church, work, and everything else EXCEPT when the club is free before 11.

4. Refer to diabetes as "Sugar."

5. Are strapped with a posse at their own wedding in case an "ex" shows up.

6. Wait for movies to premier at the $1 movie.

7. Are so proud of their drunk uncle in his leisure suit with a sash around the waist.

8. Practice "shout outs" at a graduation ceremony.

9. Show up at weddings, showers, graduation, birthday parties with a new outfit on with nails and hair done offering you a "raincheck" on a gift.

10. In relation to #9, they eat like dogs and take a plate home wrapped up in foil paper.

11. Spend $20 worth of gas to pay bills instead of mailing them off (because they are late).

12. Considers "clubbing" as a monthly expense.

13. Leave bills (instead of insurance money) behind for surviving relatives.

14. Have at least one relative with a jheri curl.

15. Borrow money for a wedding and live in an apartment.

16. Have mothers who can use curse words and religion ALL IN ONE SENTENCE.

For example, "Lord give me strength because I'm bout to knock the SHIT out of this child!"

17. Remember historical moments by R&B hit singles such as "Computer Love," Keith Sweat's "Make it Last Forever," etc.

18. Swear that the Korean lady at the flea market gives them the best deals!

19. Have at least one uncle that "almost went pro" playing basketball.

20. Spend the insurance money on everything EXCEPT getting the dent fixed.

21. Invite co-workers and all of their friends to their child's first birthday party which happens to have a professional DJ with only about 3 kids in attendance.

Check Black . . .

E-mail received March 23, 2000.

By this time most of you should have already received your Census 2000 forms in the mail. There are several ethnicities listed on the form. The black race needs to be counted. It is of the utmost importance. Just in case you are not sure which catagory you belong in, here are a few helpful suggestions:

If you have ever used a pressing comb,
Check BLACK.

If you can name all of the characters on the show *Good Times*,
Check BLACK.

If you have ever used a box relaxer or wave kit,
Check BLACK.

If you are a white woman and only date black men,
Check BLACK.

If you know what Fat Back and Hog Maws are,
Check BLACK. . . .

If you sleep with a bag, wave cap, or do-rag on your head
at night,
Check BLACK.

If you can name 3 Al Green songs,
Check BLACK.

If somebody in your family is called Big Mama,
Check BLACK.

If there is a can of grease on the back of your stove,
Check BLACK.

If your skin has ever been ashy and you know what that
term means,
Check BLACK.

If you eat greens more than 3 times a year,
Check BLACK.

If you have ever used grease and water to make your hair
lie down and look naturally wavy,
Check BLACK.

If you can wear a comb or pick in the back of your head,
walk around, and it doesn't fall out,
Check BLACK.

If you have more than 2 piercings in your ear or wear a
nose ring,
Check BLACK.

If you have ever used black eyeliner for a lip liner,
Check BLACK.

If you know how to do the Huck-a-buck, Tootsie Roll, or
Electric Slide,
Check BLACK.

If you have ever used the phrase nah looky heyah, wa-
chout there nah, or sho nuff,
Check BLACK.

If your hair is 2 or 3 inches and the next day it is halfway
down your back,
Check BLACK.

If you refer to anyone (family or friend) as Pookey or
Boo,
Check BLACK.

If when you shave, your face or neck bumps up,
Check BLACK.

If you are a member of a church and the choir songs are
choreographed,
Check BLACK.

If you have ever used gel of Dax to hold your hair down
or make a ponytail,
Check BLACK.

If your name is or rhymes with Shaniqua,
Check BLACK.

If you have ever used duct tape or electrical tape to repair
anything in your house or car,
Check BLACK.

If the screen door to your house has no screen or glass,
Check BLACK.

If you understand Ebonics or use it,
Check BLACK.

If you have tape-recorded music on your answering machine,
Check BLACK.

Ebonics Version of Windows 98

E-mail received May 7, 2000.

There are numerous differences between Windows 98 and the Ebonics version. When opening the Ebonics version, it will have several gangsta signs, slogans, and "shout outs."

On the main screen, My Computer is replaced with "Dis My Sh——." The Recycle Bin has been replaced with a Goodwill dumpster. The Network Neighborhood is replaced with "Da Hood."

Users of the Ebonics version will notice several command and dialog box changes:

Break Back In = Reentry
Aww Sh—— = Error
Itz All Good = OK
4 Real Doe = Yes
Hold Up, Dawg = Cancel
Do Dat Sh—— Again = Reset
R U Crazy? = Are You Sure?
Hunt Dat Down = Find
Put A Cap In It = Delete
Games & Sh—— = Programs
Letters & Sh—— = Documents

The Ebonics version comes standard with a special edition of Microsoft Works titled "Homie Essentials."

Several functions on the title bar have been changed:

Dat Thang = File
I Be Seein' It = View
Put Sumpin In = Insert
Hook It Up = Format
Stuff I Ain't Gone Need = Tools
Number Sh—— = Table
Break In = Window
What Da . . . ? = Help

Also, the familiar "AutoCorrect" has been replaced with "Keepin' It Real."

Your Office Is Ghetto When . . .

E-mail received May 9, 2000.

- The vending machine sells Kool-Aid and sugar in Ziploc bags.
- Company cars have rag tops and rims.
- Your company's logo is in graffiti.
- Your company gets frequent-flier miles on Greyhound.
- You have to supply your own pens.
- The hold music is the theme from *Shaft*.
- You're pulling six figures. They pay you in cash. . . .
- Your office is on 767 Al Green Boulevard. . . .
- You establish rapport with, "Throw your hands in the air, and wave 'em like you just don't care!"
- Your office Christmas party is held at Harold's Chicken.
- Your company's president wears leather suits and silk shirts.
- Your secretary wears one sponge roller.
- Your office hours are 10–4. Wednesday to Friday. Maybe.
- The phones are rotary.
- The pencil holders are old chittlin' buckets.
- People use jelly jars instead of coffee mugs.
- Your office closes for Al Sharpton's birthday.
- The janitor's name is Bookman.
- The company ID photo is taken in wicker chairs.
- The company's conference room is rented out for revivals.

- Your company's waiting room magazines are *Right On* and a 1969 *Jet*. The Beauty of the Week is ripped out.
- Your company motto is "Well we movin' on up." . . .
- Your boss got a relaxer. He's a man. . . .
- The company's president bears a striking resemblance to Grand Master D.
- Your work voice mail plays "Computer Love." . . .
- There's a velvet picture of Malcolm X, Martin Luther King, and Tupac in the lunchroom.
- When you send a letter, you always "cc" Pooky, Punkin' & Peaches.
- *General Hospital* counts as a business meeting.

Two Genies

E-mail received November 21, 1991.

One day there was a bloke walking along the beach when he stumbled upon a lamp. He had seen movies about this kinda stuff so he rubbed it and out popped two genies. "Two genies . . . that must mean six wishes!" he said.

"No, still only three," replied one of the genies. After a little thought, the man walked over toward the genies and whispered his three wishes. The two genies told the man to go home and his three wishes would come true.

So the man ran home as fast as he could. . . .

When he arrived home he saw that his lounge room was full up to his shoulders in $100 notes. "Yes!" he said, "that's wish one!"

When he went to his bedroom he saw the most beautiful woman he had ever seen naked on his bed. "Yes!" he cried, "wish two!"

Then he heard a knock at the front door. He ran down the steps as fast as he could and answered the door.

There stood two KKK men. Before he could say anything he was thrown up against the wall, beaten up and then had a noose placed around his neck. He was dragged into his front yard, the end of the rope thrown over the branch of a tree and the two KKK men hoisted him into the air, watching him kick and thrash about until he died.

As the two KKK men walked away, they took off their hats, and heaven behold it was the two genies. One genie, looking rather confused, turned to the other and said, "I could understand the money and the woman but why on earth did he want to be hung like a black man!!"

You Know You're at a Black Church

E-mail received April 30, 1999.

. . . if the preacher has a cordless microphone

. . . if the choir director and the preacher have on the same robe

. . . if there are more than 2 offerings

. . . if there are more than 5 names in the church title (ex. Greater Mount Sinai Full Gospel Baptist Church or St. Mary's Hallelujah House of Prayer or Gospel Tabernacle Word in Action Ministries)

. . . if the congregational activities are stand up, sit down, stand up, sit down, give somebody a high five, etc.

. . . if there are more than 2 choirs (ex. youth choir, young adult choir, missionary choir, male chorus)

. . . if the preacher's car has rims (or Vogues)

. . . if there is SOME type of service every night (Mon. — Bible study, Tues. — prayer meeting, Wed. — new members, Thurs. — BTU, Fri. — Sunday school review)

. . . if there is a camcorder set up in the center aisle

. . . if members sit in the choir stand once the pews are full OR if there are chairs in the aisles

. . . if the church has at least 2 of the following: musician's appreciation, pastor's anniversary, vacation Bible school, homecoming/revival, church anniversary, or harvest drive

. . . if the Christmas program consists of 9 little kids reciting "C is for Christ who lives within me, H is for his Holy Spirit, R is for resurrection," etc. . . .

. . . if you drink grape juice instead of wine during Communion

. . . if the church has a concession stand ("the mother's board will be selling fried chicken samiches after the service for $2.50")

. . . if the preacher and/or any of the choirs have a recording contract

. . . if the church has a choir anniversary and includes a parade of anywhere from 5 to 20 choirs

. . . if the MC asks the choir to give an "A," "B," "C" selection, or "a theme" and "2 selections"

. . . if the ushers wear nurse uniforms (including the hat) or black and white

. . . if the musician is a man & has the best-looking hair in the building

. . . if the ushers pass out paper fans with a picture of Martin Luther King Jr. on the front & a funeral home advertisement on the back; and if you have to make a special request to get a fan that still has the stick on it

. . . if someone gets up & hands the preacher a handkerchief in the middle of the sermon

. . . if the prayer lasts longer than 5 minutes

. . . if the children outnumber the adults

. . . if the instruments take up more space than the pulpit

. . . if someone brings the preacher a glass of water or juice

. . . if there is a child laid out asleep in the pew

. . . if the offering time is like a fashion show; everyone has to march down the outside aisle & come back around through the middle aisle starting from the rear

. . . if the ushers run out of sheets and begin using people's coats to place over those who are slain with the spirit

. . . if the service begins at 11 a.m. and people are still coming in whenever 12:30 p.m. rolls around

. . . if the preacher sings before, after, or during the sermon

. . . if the PA/sound system squeaks at any time during the service

. . . if you hear one of the following phrases: "saved, sanctified, and filled with the Holy Ghost," "fire-baptized" . . . "praise the Lord, Saints (praise the Lord!) — I said praise the Lord, Saints (Praise the Lord!)," "God is good (all datime!)," "sick & shut in" . . .

. . . if the preacher has gold in his mouth

. . . if they ever have a "foot-washing" service

. . . if there is a prayer line; if the line extends down the aisle and if the people in the line whisper their request into the preacher's ear

. . . if the sermon includes derogatory statements about particular denominations

. . . if service is going on, but there are only 3 or 5 cars outside

. . . if the church building used to be a night club, joint, or some side store . . .

Alligator Shoes

This was submitted to Singledin.com.

A young blonde was on vacation in the depths of Louisiana. She wanted a pair of genuine alligator shoes in the worst way, but was very reluctant to pay the high prices the local vendors were asking. After becoming very frustrated with the "no haggle" attitude of one of the shopkeepers, the blonde shouted, "Maybe I'll just go out and catch my own alligator so I can get a pair of shoes at a reasonable price!"

The shopkeeper said, "By all means, be my guest. Maybe you'll luck out and catch yourself a big one!"

Determined, the blonde turned and headed for the swamps, set on catching herself an alligator.

Later in the day, the shopkeeper is driving home, when he spots the young woman standing waist deep in the water, shotgun in hand. Just then, he sees a huge 9 foot alligator swimming quickly toward her. She takes aim, kills the creature and with a great deal of effort hauls it on to the swamp bank. Laying nearby were several more of the dead creatures.

The shopkeeper watches in amazement.

Just then the blonde flips the alligator on its back, and frustrated, shouts out, "Darn it, this one isn't wearing any shoes either!"

Hillbilly First Aid

E-mail received November 7, 1999.

Two West Virginians were having the blue plate special at their favorite watering hole, when they heard this awful choking sound. They turned around to see a lady, a few bar stools down turning blue from wolfing down a 'possum burger too fast.

The first hillbilly said to the other, "Think we otta' help?"

"I reckon," said the second hick.

The first hillbilly got up and walked over to the lady and asked, "Kin yew breathe?" She shook her head no.

"Kin yew speak?" he asked. Again she shook her head no.

With that he helped her to her feet, lifted up her skirt and licked her on the butt.

She was so shocked, she coughed up the obstruction and began to breathe, with great relief.

The first hillbilly turned back to his friend and said, "Funny how that there Hind Lick Maneuver works ever' time."

When a Yankee Moves South

E-mail received November 12, 1999.

If you are from the Northern states and planning on visiting or moving to the South, there are a few things you
should know that will help you adapt to the difference in
lifestyles:

1. If you run your car into a ditch, don't panic. Four
men in a four-wheel-drive pickup truck with a 12-pack of
beer and a towchain will be along shortly. Don't try to
help them, just stay out of their way. This is what they live
for.

2. Don't be surprised to find movie rentals and bait in
the same store. Do not buy food at this store.

3. Remember: "Y'all" is singular, "All y'all" is plural,
and "All y'alls' " is plural possessive.

4. Get used to hearing "You ain't from around here, are
ya?"

5. You may hear a Southerner say "Oughta!" to a dog
or child. This is short for "Y'all oughta not do that!" and
is the equivalent of saying "No!"

6. Don't be worried about not understanding what people are saying; they can't understand you either.

7. The first Southern expression to creep into a trans-
planted Northerner's vocabulary is the adjective "big ol',"
as in "big ol' truck" or "big ol' boy." Most Northerners
begin their new Southern-influenced dialect this way. All
of them are in denial about it.

8. The proper pronunciation you learned in school is no
longer proper.

9. Be advised that "He needed killin' " is a valid defense
here.

10. If you hear a Southerner exclaim, "Hey, y'all, watch
this," stay out of the way. These are likely to be the last
words he'll ever say.

11. If there is the prediction of the slightest chance of
even the smallest accumulation of snow, your presence is

required at the local grocery store. It doesn't matter whether you need anything or not. You just have to go there.

12. When you come upon a person driving 15 mph down the middle of the road, remember that most folks here learn to drive on a John Deere, and that this is the proper speed and position for that vehicle.

The Dayvorce

E-mail received September 8, 1999.

A farmer walked into an attorney's office wanting to file for divorce.

The attorney asked, "May I help you?"

"Yea, I want to get one of them there dayvorces."

"Well do you have any grounds?"

"Yep, I got about 140 acres."

"No, you don't understand, do you have a case?"

"Nope, I don't got a Case, but I got a John Deere."

"No, you don't understand, I mean do you have a grudge?"

"Yep, I got a grudge; that's where I park my John Deere."

"Ah . . . I mean do you have a suit?"

"Yes sir, I got a suit, I wear it to church on Sundays."

The attorney, trying a different tack, asked, "Well sir, does your wife beat you up or anything?"

"Nope, we both gets up about 4:30."

The attorney then asked, "Well is she a nagger or anything?"

"Heck no, she's a born and bred White gal, but our last child was a nagger and that's why I want this here dayvorce!"

Redneck Jokes

E-mail received January 18, 2000.

Did you hear about the South Carolina redneck who passed away and left his entire estate in trust for his beloved widow?

She can't touch it till she's fourteen.

What's the difference between a good ol' boy and a redneck?

The good ol' boy raises livestock. The redneck gets emotionally involved.

Emily Sue passed away and Bubba called 911. The 911 operator told Bubba that she would send someone out right away.

"Where do you live?" asked the operator. Bubba replied, "At the end of Eucalyptus Drive." The operator asked, "Can you spell that for me?"

There was a long pause and finally Bubba said, "How 'bout if I drag her over to Oak Street and you pick her up there?"

How do you know when you're staying in a Kentucky hotel?

When you call the front desk and say, "I've gotta leak in my sink," and the person at the front desk says, "go ahead."

How can you tell if a Texas redneck is married?

There is dried chewing tobacco on both sides of his pickup truck.

Did you hear that they have raised the minimum drinking age in Tennessee to 32?

It seems they want to keep alcohol out of the high schools!

What do they call reruns of "Hee Haw" in Mississippi?
A documentary.

How many rednecks does it take eat a 'possum?
Two. One to eat, and one to watch out for traffic.

Why did God invent armadillos?
So that Texas rednecks can have 'possum on the half-shell.

Arkansas State trooper pulls over a pickup truck on I-40. He says to the driver, "Got any ID?"
The driver says, "Bout what?"

Did you hear about the $3,000,000 Tennessee State Lottery?
The winner gets $3 a year for a million years.

Why did O. J. Simpson want to move to West Virginia?
Everyone has the same DNA.

Did you hear that the governor's mansion in Little Rock, Arkansas, burned down?
Yep. Pert' near took out the whole trailer park.

A new law recently passed in North Carolina:
When a couple gets divorced, they're still brother and sister.

What's the best thing to ever come out of Arkansas?
I-40.

What do a divorce in Alabama, a tornado in Kansas, and a hurricane in Florida have in common?
Somebody's fixin' to lose them a trailer.

A Mississippian came home and found his house on fire. He rushed next door, telephoned the fire department and shouted, "Hurry over here. My house is on fire!"

"OK," replied the fireman, "how do we get there?"
"Shucks, don't you still have those big red trucks?"

Why do folks in Kentucky go to the movie theater in groups of 18 or more?
'Cuz 17 and under not admitted.

What do you get when you have 32 rednecks in the same room?
A full set of teeth.

West Virginia Medical Terminology for the Layman

Received as a photocopy.

Artery	The study of fine paintings.
Barium	What you do when CPR fails.
Benign	What you be after you be eight.
Caesarean section	A district in Rome.
Colic	A sheep dog.
Coma	A punctuation mark.
Congenital	Friendly.
Denial	A large river in Egypt.
Dilate	To live longer.
Fester	Quicker.
Grippe	A suitcase.
G.I. series	Baseball games between teams of soldiers.
Hangnail	A coathook.
Medical staff	A doctor's cane.
Minor operation	Coal digging.
Morbid	A higher offer.
Nitrate	Lower than the day rate.
Node	Was aware of (I node it).
Organic	Church musician.
Outpatient	A person who has fainted.
Postoperative	A letter carrier.

Protein	In favor of young people.
Secretion	Hiding something.
Serology	Study of English knighthood.
Tablet	A small table.
Tumor	An extra pair.
Urinalysis	What you get from your psychiatrist.
Urine	Opposite of you're out.
Vagina	A state just south of Maryland.
Varicose veins	Veins that are very close together.

The Strong Black Woman Is Dead

E-mail received August 26, 1999.

While struggling with the reality of being a human instead of a myth, the strong black woman passed away, without the slightest bit of hoopla. Medical sources say that she died of natural causes, but those who knew and used her know she died from:

being silent when she should have been screaming,
milling when she should have been raging,

being sick and not wanting anyone to know because her pain might inconvenience them

an overdose of other people clinging on to her when she didn't even have energy for herself

loving men who didn't love themselves and could only offer her a crippled reflection

raising children alone and for not doing a complete job

the lies her grandmother told her mother and her mother told her about life, men and racism

being sexually abused as a child and having to take that truth everywhere she went every day of her life, exchanging the humiliation for guilt and back again

being battered by someone who claimed to love her and she allowed the battering to go on to show she luvvvvvvvvv'd him too

asphyxiation, coughing up blood from secrets she

kept trying to burn away instead of allowing herself the
kind of nervous breakdown she was entitled to, but only
white girls could afford

being responsible, because she was the last rung on
the ladder and there was no one under her she could
dump on

The strong black woman is dead.

She died from:

the multiple births of children she never really wanted
but was forced to have by the strangling morality of
those around her

being a mother at 15 and a grandmother at 30 and an
ancestor at 45

being dragged down and sat upon by un-evolved
women posing as sisters

pretending the life she was living was a Kodak moment instead of a 20th century, post-slavery nightmare

tolerating Mr. Pitiful, just to have a man around the
house

lack of orgasms because she never learned what made
her body happy and no one took the time to teach her
and sometimes, when she found arms that were tender,
she died because they belonged to the same gender

sacrificing herself for everybody and everything when
what she really wanted to do was be a singer, a dancer,
or some magnificent other

lies of omission because she didn't want to bring the
black man down

race memories of being snatched and snatched and
raped and snatched and sold and snatched and bred and
snatched and whipped and snatched and worked to
death

tributes from her counterparts who should have been
matching her efforts instead of showering her with dead
words and empty songs

myths that would not allow her to show weakness
without being chastised by the lazy and hazy

hiding her real feelings until they became monstrously

hard and bitter enough to invade her womb and breasts
like angry tumors
  always lifting something from heavy boxes to refriger-
ators:
  The strong black woman is dead.

  She died from:
  the punishments received from being honest about
life, racism and men
  being called a bitch for being verbal, a dyke for being
assertive and a whore for picking her own lovers
  never being enough of what men wanted, or being too
much for the men she wanted
  being too black and died again for not being black
enuff
  castration every time somebody thought of her as
only woman, or treated her like less than a man
  being misinformed about her mind, her body and the
extent of her royal capabilities
  knees pressed too close together because respect was
never part of the foreplay that was being shoved at her
  loneliness in birthing rooms and aloneness in abortion
centers

  She died of shock in court rooms where she sat,
alone, watching her children being legally lynched.
  She died in bathrooms with her veins busting open
with self-hatred and neglect.
  She died in her mind, fighting life, racism, and men,
while her body was carted away and stashed in a human
warehouse for the spiritually mutilated.

  And sometimes when she refused to die, when she
just refused to give in, she was killed by the lethal images of blonde hair, blue eyes and flat butts, rejected to
death by the O.J.s, the Quinceys, and the Poitiers.
  Sometimes, she was stomped to death by racism and
sexism, executed by hi-tech ignorance while she carried

the family in her belly, the community on her head, and
the race on her back!!!!!!!!!!!!!!!!!!

The strong silent, s**t-talking black woman is
dead!!!!!!!!!!!!!!

Or is she still alive and kicking??????????????????

I know I am still here.   —Author Unknown

RICHARD O. JONES

The Liberation of Aunt Jemima

Though the following E-mail was widely circulated and received by me from
several individuals under the title "The Powerful Sister" and with the notation at
the end "Author Unknown," Lucinda Bartley discovered that it was taken from
Richard O. Jones's autobiography, *When Mama's Gone.*

Times certainly have brought about a change
And to a few it might sound strange
Black women are soaring with ambition
No more barefoot, pregnant, and in the kitchen

And she's not slaving like an ox
Have you seen her new image on the pancake box?
Purse full of credit cards, fancy car
And the girl ain't even a movie star

Not long ago I was on the bus
Eating fried chicken from The Colonel
Viewing my girlie magazine, and full of lust
Sitting next to a sista reading a *Wall Street Journal*

I said, "Pardon me baby, where are you on yo' way?
I would like to know your name, if that's okay
Your perfume I surely adore
I believe we've met somewhere before"

She said, "I'm on my way downtown to City Hall
I must chair a council meeting and that's not all

Then I'm flying off to the United Nations
To advise on a classified situation

I'm sorry but I fail to remember you
Were you ever in Zaire, Sudan, or Istanbul?
Or perhaps it was Rome, England, or by chance
It was Chad, Morocco, or Paris, France

You see, I'm multi-lingual, and travel a lot
The universe is my melting pot
However, once a month I board a bus
Just my way of staying in touch

Nefertiti is my name
And world peace is my game
I attended Benedict College in South Caroline
And earned my Bachelor degree
Then I went to Fisk and received my Masters
In Nashville, Tennessee

And Howard University in Washington, D.C.
That's where I earned my Ph.D.
I have offices in Dallas, Chicago, and Mexicana
A penthouse in New York, and a home in Atlanta
I play the harp and pilot a jet
Now tell me brotha, where you THINK we met?"

I rung the bell; got up and left
Aunt Jemima done got beside herself!

Only a Black Woman

E-mail received July 14, 2000.

Only a Black Woman . . .
Can take a week of left over scraps and make a gourmet
meal.

Only a Black Woman...
Can cuss a man out, make him feel like s**t then make love to him that same night and make him feel like a king.

Only a Black Woman...
Can wear a burgundy French roll, 3-inch heels and a split up her thigh to work and make it look professional.

Only a Black Woman...
Can wear the hell out of spandex.

Only a Black Woman...
Can raise a doctor, a world-class athlete and an A+ student in an environment deemed by society as dysfunctional, broken, underprivileged and disenfranchised.

Only a Black Woman...
Can heat a whole house in the winter without help from the gas company.

Only a Black Woman...
Can go from the boardroom to the block and "keep it real" in both places.

Only a Black Woman...
Can slap the taste out of your mouth.

Only a Black Woman...
Can put a Black man and his non-Black date on pins and needles just by walking into the room.

Only a Black Woman...
Can live below poverty level and yet set fashion trends.

Only a Black Woman...
Can fight two struggles everyday and make it look easy.

Only a Black Woman . . .
Can make a child happy on Christmas Day even if he didn't get a damn thing.

Only a Black Woman . . .
Can be admired and fantasized about by men of other races and know that when she does cross over it's done out of sincerity not a political move.

Only a Black Woman . . .
Can be 75 years old and look 45.

Only a Black Woman . . .
Can make other women want to pay plastic surgeons top $$$ for physical features she was already born with.

Only a Black Woman . . .
Can be the mother of civilization.

Did Ya Hear Me?
If you are BLACK in origin please do not delete. . . . Pass it on to 10 good friends of yours. . . . Let the Black people come together . . .

That's My House

E-mail received October 11, 1999.

After living a full life and being as fraternal as possible a proud member of Alpha Kappa Alpha dies. When she got to heaven, God was showing her around. They came to a modest little house with a faded AKA Crest in the window.

"This house is yours for eternity," said God. "This is very special; not everyone gets a house up here."

The AKA felt special, indeed, and walked up to her

house. On her way up the porch, she noticed another house just around the corner. It was a 3-story mansion with a crimson carpet rolled on the pathway, a 50-foot tall crimson and cream statue with the enormous letters Delta Sigma Theta, and, in every window, Delta paraphernalia.

The AKA looked at God and said, "God, I'm not trying to be ungrateful, but I have a question. I was a good citizen, I served my country well, and I did the best I could for my people and my sorority."

God asked, "So what do you want to know?"

"Well, why do the Deltas get a better house than me?"

God chuckled and said, "That's *my* house."

Women's Problems Start with Men

E-mail received December 20, 1999.

Just a thought for all the women out there.

MENtal illness
MENstrual cramps
MENtal breakdown
MENopause

Ever notice how all of women's problems start with men? Send this to all of the women you know and brighten their day!!!

And when we have real trouble, it's HISterectomy!!!!!

Three Wise Women

E-mail received October 16, 1999.

Do you know what would have happened if it had been three Wise Women instead of three Wise Men?

They would have asked directions,
arrived on time,
helped deliver the baby,
cleaned the stable,
made a casserole, and
brought practical gifts.

The Smarter Sex

E-mail received November 8, 1999.

A woman and a man were involved in a car accident —
it was a bad one. Both of their cars were totally demolished, but amazingly, neither of them were hurt.

After they crawled out of their cars, the woman said,
"So, you're a man — that's interesting. I'm a woman. Wow,
just look at our cars! There's nothing left, but fortunately
we are both unhurt. This must be a sign from God that we
should meet and be friends, and live together in peace for
the rest of our days."

The man thoughtfully replied, "I agree with you completely. This must be a sign from God!"

The woman continued, "And look at this, here's another
miracle. My car is completely demolished but this bottle of
wine didn't break. Surely God wants us to drink this wine
and celebrate our good fortune."

Then she handed the bottle to the man. The man nodded his head in agreement, opened it, and drank half the
bottle. He then handed it back to the woman.

The woman took the bottle, and immediately put the
cap back on, and handed it back to the man.

In surprise, he asked, "Aren't you having any?"

"No," the woman replied, "I think I'll just wait for the
police . . ."

The Gender of Computers

E-mail received March 1, 1999.

A man who had previously been a sailor was very aware that ships are addressed as "she" and "her." He often wondered what gender computers should be addressed. To answer that question, he set up two groups of computer experts. The first was comprised of women, and the second of men. Each group was asked to recommend whether computers should be referred to in the feminine gender or the masculine gender. They were asked to give 4 reasons for their recommendation. The group of women reported that the computers should be referred to in the masculine gender because:

1. In order to get their attention, you have to turn them on.

2. They have a lot of data, but are still clueless.

3. They are supposed to help you solve problems, but half the time they are the problem.

4. As soon as you commit to one, you realize that, if you had waited a little longer, you could have had a better model.

The men, on the other hand concluded that computers should be referred to in the feminine gender because:

1. No one but the Creator understands their internal logic.

2. The native language they use to communicate with other computers is incomprehensible to everyone else.

3. Even your smallest mistakes are stored in long-term memory for later retrieval.

4. As soon as you make a commitment to one, you find yourself spending half your paycheck on accessories for it.

Life before the Computer

E-mail message received November 1, 1999.

An application was for employment
A program was a TV show
A cursor used profanity
A keyboard was a piano.

Memory was something that you lost with age
A CD was a bank account
And if you had a 3″ floppy
You hoped nobody found out!

Compress was something you did to the garbage
Not something you did to a file
And if you unzipped anything in public
You'd be in jail for a while!

Log on was adding wood to the fire
Hard drive was a long trip on the road
A mouse pad was where a mouse lived
And a backup happened to your commode!

Cut—you did with a pocket knife
Paste—you did with glue
A web was a spider's home
And a virus was the flu!

I guess I'll stick to my pad and paper
And the memory in my head
I hear nobody's been killed in a computer crash
But when it happens they wish they were dead!

For All Those Born Prior to 1940

Received as a photocopy.

We are survivors! Consider the changes we have seen:

We were before television, penicillin, polio shots, frozen foods, Xerox, contact lenses, frisbees and The Pill.

We were before radar, credit cards, split atoms, laser beams and ballpoint pens; before pantyhose, dishwashers, clothes dryers, electric blankets, air conditioners, drip-dry clothes and before man walked on the moon.

We got married first and *then* lived together. How quaint can you be?

In our time, closets were for clothes, not for "coming out of." Bunnies were small rabbits and rabbits were not Volkswagens. Designer jeans were scheming girls named Jean or Jeanne, and having a meaningful relationship meant getting along with our cousins.

We thought fast food was what you ate during Lent and Outer Space was the back of the Riviera Theatre.

We were before house-husbands, gay rights, computer dating, dual careers and commuter marriages. We were before day-care centers, group therapy and nursing homes. We never heard of FM radio, tape decks, electric typewriters, artificial hearts, word processors, yogurt and guys wearing earrings. For us, time-sharing meant togetherness—not computers or condominiums; a "chip" meant a piece of wood; hardware meant hardware and software wasn't even a word.

In 1940, "made in Japan" meant *junk* and the term "making out" referred to how you did on an exam. Pizzas, "McDonald's" and instant coffee were unheard of.

We hit the scene when there were 5 and 10¢ stores where you bought things for five and ten cents. Sanders or Wilson's sold ice cream cones for a nickel or a dime. For one nickel you could ride a streetcar, make a phone call, buy Pepsi or enough stamps to mail one letter and two postcards. You could buy a new Chevy Coupe for $600, but who could afford one? Pity, too, because gas was only 11¢ a gallon.

In our day, cigarette smoking was fashionable, "grass" was mowed, "Coke" was a cola drink and "pot" was something you cooked in. Rock music was a Grandma's lullaby and AIDS were helpers in the principal's office.

We were certainly not before the difference between the sexes was discovered but we were surely before the sex change; we made do with what we had. And we were the last generation that was so dumb as to think you needed a husband to have a baby!

No wonder we are so confused and there is such a generation gap today!

But we survived. What better reason to celebrate!

The Really Good Old Days When We Were Young

E-mail received July 17, 2000.

This and the previous selection are a part of a popular group of folklore that circulates among many cultural groups in photocopies and through the E-mail, reminiscing about the good old days. The following has some memories more commonly associated with African American childhood and has been widely circulated among my friends.

Looking back . . .
Close your eyes and go back . . .

Before the Internet or the Mac,
Before semi automatics and crack
Way back . . .

I'm talking 'bout hide-and-seek at dusk.
Sittin' on the porch,
The Good Humor man,
Red light, green light.

Chocolate milk,
Lunch tickets,
Penny candy in a brown paper bag.

Playin' pinball at the corner store.
Hopscotch, butterscotch, double Dutch
Jacks, kickball, dodgeball.

Mother may I?
Red rover and roly-poly.

Double-dog dares!

Hula hoops and sunflower seeds,
Mary Janes, banana splits
Wax lips and mustaches

Running through the sprinklers
The smells of outdoors
and lickin' salty lips . . .

Watchin' Saturday morning cartoons,
Fat Albert, Road Runner,
He-Man, The Three Stooges, and Bugs.

Or back further,
listening to Superman
and The Shadow on the radio.

Catchin' lightning bugs in a jar,
Playin' slingshot.

Remember when around the corner seemed far away,
And going downtown seemed like going somewhere?

Climbing trees,
An ice-cream cone on a warm summer night,
A cherry Coke from the fountain at the drugstore.

A million mosquito bites,
sticky fingers,
Cops and robbers,
Cowboys and Indians.

Sittin' on the curb,
Jumpin' down the steps,
Jumpin' on the bed.

Pillow fights,
Being tickled to death,
Running till you were out of breath,
Laughing so hard your stomach hurt.

Crowding in a circle around the "after-school fight,"
then running when the teacher came.

Eating Kool-Aid powder and sugar.

Remember when there were two types of sneakers for
girls and boys (Keds & PF Flyers) and the only time you
wore them at school was for "gym"?

When it took five minutes for the TV to warm up, if you
had one.

When nearly everyone's mom was at home after school.

When nobody owned a purebred dog.

When a quarter was a decent allowance, and another
quarter a miracle.

When milk went up one penny.

When your Mom wore nylons that came in two pieces.

When all your male teachers wore neckties
and female teachers had their hair done.

When you got your windshield cleaned, oil checked, and
gas pumped, without asking — for free — every time.
And, you didn't pay for air. And, you got trading stamps
to boot!

When laundry detergent had free glasses,
dishes or towels hidden inside the box.

When any parent could discipline any kid,
or use him to carry groceries,
and nobody, not even the kid, thought a thing of it.

When it was considered a great privilege to be taken out
to dinner at a real restaurant with your parents.

When they threatened to hold kids back a grade if they
failed . . . and did!

When being sent to the principal's office was nothing compared to the fate that awaited a student at home.

We were in fear for our lives, but it wasn't because of
drive-by shootings, drugs, gangs, etc.
Our parents and grandparents scared us! And some of us
are still afraid of 'em!!!

Didn't that feel good? To smile and say, "Oh yeah . . . I remember . . ."

There's nothing like the good old days!
They were good then, and they're still good now when we
think about them.
Share some of these thoughts with a friend who can relate . . .
then share with someone who missed out. . . .

A Little Mixed Up

Received as a photocopy.

Just a line to say I'm living
That I'm not among the dead.
Though I'm getting more forgetful

And I'm mixed up in the head.
I've got used to my arthritis
To my dentures I'm resigned,
I can manage by bifocals
But, Oh God, I miss my mind!
For sometimes I can't remember
When I stand at the foot of the stairs
If I must go up for something
Or I just came down from there.
I open my fridge so often
My poor mind is filled with doubt,
Have I put some food away
Or have I come to take some out?
And there are times when it is dark
With my night-cap on my head
I don't know if I'm retiring
Or just getting out of bed.
So if it's my turn to write to you
There's no need in getting sore
I may think I might have written you
But don't want to be a bore.
Just remember I do love you
And wish that you were near
But now it's nearly mail time
So must say good-bye, my dear.
There I stand beside the mail box
With a face so very red,
Instead of mailing you my letter
I have opened it instead!

Sincerely Yours

You Know You're Old When . . .

E-mail received April 9, 1999.

You Know You're Old When . . .
Your insurance company has started sending you their free
calendar . . . a month at a time.

At cafeterias, you complain that the gelatin is too tough.

Your new easy chair has more options than your car.

When you do the "Hokey Pokey" you put your left hip out . . . and it stays out.

One of the throw pillows on your bed is a hot-water bottle.

You find yourself beginning to like accordion music.

You're sitting on a park bench and a boy scout comes up and helps you cross your legs.

Lawn care has become a big highlight of your life.

You're asleep, but others worry that you're dead.

You tune into the easy listening station . . . on purpose.

You discover that your measurements are now small, medium and large . . . in that order.

You light the candles on your birthday cake and a group of campers form a circle and start singing "Kumbaya."

Your arms are almost too short to read the newspaper.

You start videotaping daytime game shows.

At the airport, they ask to check your bags . . . and you're not carrying any luggage.

Conversations with people your own age often turn into "dueling ailments."

It takes a couple of tries to get over a speed bump.

You discover the words "whippersnapper," "scallywag," and "by-crikey" creeping into your vocabulary.

You're on a TV game show and you decide to risk it all and go for the rocker.

You begin every other sentence with "Nowadays . . ."

You run out of breath walking DOWN a flight of stairs.

You look both ways before crossing a room.

Your social security number only has three digits.

You come to the conclusion that your worst enemy is gravity.

People call at 9 P.M. and ask, "Did I wake you?"

You go to a garden party and you're mainly interested in the garden.

You find your mouth making promises your body can't keep.

The waiter asks how you'd like your steak . . . and you say "pureed."

At parties you attend, "regularity" is considered the topic of choice.

You start beating everyone else at trivia games.

You frequently find yourself telling people what a loaf of bread USED to cost.

Cafeteria food starts tasting GOOD.

You refer to your $2,500 stereo system as "The Hi-Fi."

You make it a point to attend all the RV shows that come to town.

You realize that a stamp today costs more than a picture show did when you were growing up.

Your childhood toys are now in a museum.

Many of your coworkers were born the same year that you got your last promotion.

The clothes you've put away until they come back in style . . . come back in style.

All of your favorite movies are now revised in color.

The car that you bought brand-new becomes an antique.

You have more hair in your ears and nose than your head.

You wear black socks with sandals.

You take a metal detector to the beach.

Dialing long-distance wears you out.

Your knees buckle, but your belt won't.

You get winded playing games on the computer.

You sit in a rocking chair and can't get it going.

Almost everything hurts and what doesn't hurt, doesn't work.

You can't stand all those stupid people who are intolerant.

You feel like the morning after when you haven't been anywhere the night before.

You get winded playing chess.

Your children begin to look middle-aged.

You know all the answers, but nobody asks you the questions anymore.

You look forward to a dull evening.

You turn off the lights for economic rather than romantic reasons.

You are 17 around the neck, 42 around the waist, 96 around the golf course.

You burn the midnight oil until 9:00 P.M.

Your back goes out more often than you do.

Your pacemaker raises the garage door when you see a pretty
  girl go by.
The little gray-haired lady you help across the street is your
  wife.
You get exercise acting as a pallbearer for friends who exercise.
You have too much room in the house and not enough in the
  medicine cabinet.
You sink your teeth into a steak . . . and they stay there.

Chuckle for the Day

Received as a photocopy.

Remember, old folks are worth a fortune, with silver in their hair, gold
in their teeth, stones in their kidneys, lead in their feet, and gas in
their stomachs.

I have become a little older since I saw you last and a few changes
have come into my life since then. Frankly I have become quiet a friv-
olous old gal. I am seeing five gentlemen every day.

As soon as I wake up, Will Power helps me get out of bed. Then
I go see John. Then Charlie Horse comes along and when he is here
he takes a lot of my time and attention. When he leaves Arthur Ritis
shows up and stays all day. He doesn't like to stay in one place very
long, so he takes me from joint to joint. After such a busy day I'm really tired and glad to go to bed with Ben Gay. What a life.

P.S. The Preacher came to call the other day. He said at my age I
should be thinking about the hereafter. I told him, oh, I do all the
time. No matter where I am in the parlor, upstairs, in the kitchen or
down in the basement, I ask myself, what am I here after?

Creation

E-mail received November 9, 1999.

Adam was walking around the garden of Eden feeling
very lonely, so God asked him, "What is wrong with you?"

Adam said he didn't have anyone to talk to.

God said that He was going to make Adam a companion and that it would be a woman.

He said, "This person will gather food for you, cook for you, and when you discover clothing she'll wash it for you.

She will always agree with every decision you make.

She will bear your children and never ask you to get up in the middle of the night to take care of them.

She will not nag you and will always be the first to admit she was wrong when you've had a disagreement.

She will never have a headache and will freely give you love and passion whenever you need it."

Adam asked God, "What will a woman like this cost?"

God replied, "An arm and a leg."

Then Adam asked, "What can I get for a rib?"

The rest is history. . . .

Precious Memories

This was submitted to Singledin.com.

A minister decided to do something a little different one Sunday morning. He said "Today, church, I am going to say a single word and you are going to help me preach. Whatever single word I say, I want you to sing whatever hymn that comes to your mind."

The pastor shouted out, "Cross." Immediately the congregation started singing in unison "The Old Rugged Cross."

The Pastor hollered out "Grace." The congregation began to sing "Amazing Grace, how sweet the sound."

The Pastor said "Power." The congregation sang "There Is Power in the Blood."

The Pastor said "Sex." The congregation fell in total silence. Everyone was in shock. They all nervously began to look around at each other, afraid to say anything.

Then all of a sudden way from in the back of the church, a little 87-year-old grandmother stood up and began to sing . . . "Precious Memories."

Can You Find the 19 Books of the Bible?

Received as a photocopy.

SOMEONE SHOWED ME THIS STORY AND REMARKED THAT THERE ARE 19 BOOKS OF THE BIBLE HIDDEN HERE. HE CHALLENGED ME TO FIND THEM. SURE ENOUGH, THEY'RE ALL HERE. STILL THIS THING'S A LULU, KEPT ME LOOKING SO HARD FOR THE LONGEST TIME. SOME OF YOU WILL GET BOGGED DOWN IN THE FACTS, OTHERS ARE HIT BY THEM LIKE THEY WERE SOME KIND OF REVELATION OR SOMETHING. YOU MAY GET IN A JAM, ESPECIALLY SINCE ALL THE WORDS ARE CAPITALIZED AND THE NAMES OFTEN LEAP THE SPACES BETWEEN THE WORDS. THIS MAKES IT A REAL JOB TO FIND THEM BUT IT'LL PROVIDE A MOST FASCI-NATING FEW MINUTES FOR YOU. YES, THERE ARE SOME REALLY EASY ONES TO SPOT. BUT DON'T GET THE BIG HEAD, 'CAUSE TRUTHFULLY YOU'LL SOON FIGURE THAT IT WOULD TAKE MOST FEDERAL JUDGES AND PREACHERS NUMBERS OF HOURS TO FIND THEM ALL. I WILL ADMIT THAT IT USUALLY TAKES A MIN-ISTER TO FIND ONE OF THEM, AND THAT IS NOT UNCOMMON FOR THERE ARE TO BE LOUD LAMEN-TATIONS WHEN IT IS POINTED OUT. ONE LADY SAYS THAT WHEN SHE IS CONFRONTED WITH PUZZLES LIKE THIS SHE BREWS A CUP OF TEA TO HELP HER CON-CENTRATE BETTER, BUT THEN THIS GAL'S A REAL PRO! VERBS, NOUNS AND ALL THAT STUFF ARE HER THING. SEE HOW YOU CAN COMPETE. RELAX: THERE REALLY ARE 19 NAMES OF BIBLE BOOKS IN THE STORY. IF YOU FAIL TO FIND THEM, THERE'S A PENALTY. YOU'LL HAVE TO GO FLY A KITE, SIT ON A BANANA, HUM "THE

From
My
People

★
696

BATTLE HYMN OF THE REPUBLIC," OR HOSE A DOG (A
MEAN ONE). GET TO IT!

Answer Key to "Can You Find the 19 Books of the Bible?"

SOMEONE SHOWED ME THIS STORY AND RE<u>MARKED</u>
THAT THERE ARE 19 BOOKS OF THE BIBLE HIDDEN
HERE. HE CHALLENGED ME TO FIND THEM. SURE
ENOUGH, THEY'RE ALL HERE. STILL THIS THING'S A
LU<u>LU, KE</u>PT ME LO<u>OKING S</u>O HARD FOR THE LONGEST
TIME. SOME OF YOU WILL GET BOGGED DOWN IN THE
F<u>ACTS</u>, OTHERS ARE HIT BY THEM LIKE THEY WERE
SOME KIND OF <u>REVELATION</u> OR SOMETHING. YOU
MAY GET IN A <u>JAM, ES</u>PECIALLY SINCE ALL THE WORDS
ARE CAPITALIZED AND THE NAMES OFTEN LEAP THE
SPACES BETWEEN THE WORDS. THIS MAKES IT A REAL
<u>JOB</u> TO FIND THEM BUT IT'LL PROVIDE <u>A MOS</u>T FASCI-
NATING FEW MINUTES FOR YOU. Y<u>ES, THER</u>E ARE
SOME REALLY EASY ONES TO SPOT. BUT DON'T GET
THE BIG HEAD, 'CAUSE <u>TRUTH</u>FULLY YOU'LL SOON
FIGURE THAT IT WOULD TAKE MOST FEDERAL <u>JUDGES</u>
AND PREACHERS <u>NUMBERS</u> OF HOURS TO FIND THEM
ALL. I WILL ADMIT THA<u>T IT US</u>UALLY TAKES A MIN-
ISTER TO FIND ONE OF THEM, AND THAT IS NOT
UNCOMMON FOR THERE ARE TO BE LOUD <u>LAMENTA-
TIONS</u> WHEN IT IS POINTED OUT. ONE LADY SAYS THAT
WHEN SHE IS CONFRONTED WITH PUZZLES LIKE THIS
<u>S</u>H<u>E BREWS</u> A CUP OF TEA TO HELP HER CONCEN-
TRATE BETTER, BUT THEN THIS GAL'S A REAL <u>PRO!</u>
<u>VERBS</u>, NOUNS AND ALL THAT STUFF ARE HER THING.
SEE HOW YOU CAN CO<u>MPETE.</u> RELAX: THERE REALLY
ARE 19 NAMES OF BIBLE BOOKS IN THE STORY. IF YOU
FAIL TO FIND THEM, THERE'S A PENALTY. YOU'LL HAVE
TO GO FLY A KITE, SIT ON A BANA<u>NA, HUM</u> "THE
BATTLE HYMN OF THE REPUBLIC," OR <u>HOSE A</u> DOG (A
MEAN ONE). GET TO IT!

From the Mouths of Babes

E-mail received November 22, 1999.

The following statements about the Bible were written by children and have not been retouched or corrected (i.e., bad spelling has been left in):

In the first book of the Bible, Guinessis, God got tired of creating the world, so he took the Sabbath off. Adam and Eve were created from an apple tree. Noah's wife was called Joan of Ark. Noah built an ark, which the animals came on to in pears. Lot's wife was a pillar of salt by day, but a ball of fire by night.

The Jews were a proud people and throughout history they had trouble with the unsympathetic Genitals.

Samson was a strongman who let himself be led astry by a Jezebel like Delilah.

Samson slayed the Philistines with the axe of the Apostles. Moses led the Hebrews to the Red Sea, where they made unleavened bread which is bread without any ingredients.

The Egyptians were all drowned in the dessert. Afterwards, Moses went up on Mount Cyanide to get the ten ammendments.

The first commandment was when Eve told Adam to eat the apple. The seventh commandment is that thou shat not admit adultery.

Moses died before he ever reached Canada. Then Joshua led the Hebrews in the battle of Geritol.

The greatest miracle in the Bible is when Joshua told his son to stand still and he obeyed him.

David was a Hebrew king skilled at playing the liar. He fought with the Finkelsteins, a race of people who lived in Biblical times.

Solomon, one of David's sons, had 300 wives and 700 porcupines.

When Mary heard that she was the mother of Jesus, she sang the Magna Carta.

When the three wise guys from the east side arrived, they found Jesus in the manager.

Jesus was born because Mary had an immaculate contraption. St. John, the blacksmith, dumped water on his head. Jesus enunciated the Golden Rule, which says to do one to others before they do one to you.

He also explained, "a man doth not live by sweat alone." It was a miracle when Jesus rose from the dead and managed to get the tombstone off the entrance.

The people who followed the Lord were called the 12 decibels. The epistles were the wives of the apostles. One of the opposums was St. Matthew who was also a taximan. St. Paul cavorted to Christianity. He preached holy acrimony, which is another name for marriage.

A Christian should have only one spouse. This is called monotony.

What My Mother Taught Me

E-mail received September 4, 2000.

My mother taught me *to appreciate a job well done:*
"If you're going to kill each other, do it outside."

My mother taught me *religion:*
"I just finished cleaning! You better pray that will come out of the carpet."

My mother taught me about *time travel:*
"If you don't straighten up, I'm going to knock you into the middle of next week!"

My mother taught me *logic:*
"Because I said so, that's why."

My mother taught me *foresight:*
"Make sure you wear clean underwear, in case you're in an accident."

My mother taught me *irony*:
"Keep laughing and I'll give you something to cry about."

My mother taught me about the science of *osmosis*:
"Shut your mouth and eat your supper!"

My mother taught me about *contortionism*:
"Will you look at the dirt on the back of your neck!"

My mother taught me about *stamina*:
"You'll sit there 'til all that spinach is finished."

My mother taught me about *weather*:
"It looks as if a tornado swept through your room."

My mother taught me how to solve *physics problems*:
"If I yelled because I saw a meteor coming toward you, would you listen then?"

My mother taught me about *hypocrisy*:
"If I've told you once, I've told you a million times, don't exaggerate!!!"

My mother taught me *the circle of life*:
"I brought you into this world, and I can take you out."

My mother taught me about *behavior modification*:
"Stop acting like your father!"

My mother taught me about *envy*:
"There are millions of less fortunate children in this world who don't have 2 wonderful parents like you do!"

A Few Things Not to Say to a Cop

This was submitted to Singledin.com.

1. I can't reach my license unless you hold my beer.

2. Sorry, I didn't realize that my radar detector wasn't on.

3. Aren't you the guy from the Village People?

4. Hey you must have been going 125 mph just to keep up with me.

5. I thought you had to be in good physical condition to be a cop.

6. Bad cop! No donut!

7. You're gonna check the trunk, aren't you?

8. I was going to be a cop, really, but I decided to finish high school.

9. I pay your salary.

10. That's terrific, the last guy only gave me a warning also.

11. Is that a 9 mm? It's nothing compared to this .44 magnum!

12. What do you mean, have I been drinking? You're a trained specialist.

13. Do you know why you pulled me over? Good, at least one of us does.

14. That gut doesn't inspire too much confidence, bet I can outrun you.

15. Didn't I see you get your butt kicked on *Cops*?

16. Is it true people become cops because they are too dumb to work at McDonald's?

17. I was trying to keep up with traffic.

18. Yes, I know there are no other cars around—that's how far they are ahead of me.

19. Well, when I reached down to pick up my bag of crack, my gun fell off my lap and got lodged between the brake pedal and gas pedal, forcing me to speed out of control.

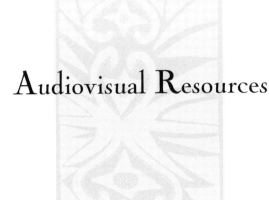

Audiovisual Resources

Following is a list of selected audiovisual resources related to some of the materials included in this book. In many instances the media are variants of the texts of the stories, songs, sermons, and other items reproduced in this anthology. In some instances they expand the offerings here through performances by artists, musicians, and speakers.

I provide annotations only when the content may not be clear from the title.

Blank, Les. *Always for Pleasure.* Videotape. C1830. El Cerrito, CA: Flower Films, 1978.

Part 1 treats the music, food, and street celebrations of New Orleans, including a jazz funeral; and part 2 captures the Black "Indian tribes" as they prepare for a celebration of Mardi Gras.

Blues Masters: The Essential History of the Blues. Videotape. Los Angeles: Distributed by Rhino Home Video/Records, 1993. Volume 1, 10389. Volume 2, 9553.

Blues Routes: Heroes & Tricksters, Blues & Jazz, Worksongs & Street Music. CD. Washington, DC: Smithsonian Folkways 40118, 1999.

*

Album includes blues from the Delta, Piedmont, San Francisco, and Chicago; jazz from Kansas City and New Orleans; hambone call and response; Texas jump blues; Louisiana zydeco; minstrel banjomen; and railroad track-lining.

Bluesland: A Portrait in American Music. Videotape. 10013. Produced by Toby Byron and Richard Saylor. Directed by Ken Mandel. New York: BMG Video, 1993.

Bowling, M. J., and Jerald B. Harkness. *Steppin'.* Documentary. Library of Congress Video Collection. Indianapolis: Visionary Productions, 1991.

Discusses the role of dance and step shows in African American fraternities and sororities and shows performances at Indiana University.

The Call of the Jitterbug. Videotape. Greenroom Productions. Producers: Jesper Sorensen, Vibeke Winding, and Tana Ross. Editor: Rachel Reichman. New York: Filmakers Library, 1988.

Discussion of derivation of the jitterbug from the lindy hop.

Cataliotti, Robert H. *The Audio Compact Disc to Accompany Call & Response.* Disc. 3-33231. Boston: Houghton Mifflin Company, 1998.

Includes Sojourner Truth's "Speech at Akron Convention" (appears in this anthology under the title "Ain't I A Woman?") read by Ruby Dee; Frederick Douglass's "The Meaning of July 4 for the Negro" read by Ossie Davis; "Go Down Moses," "Wade in the Water," "John Henry," "Titanic," and James Weldon Johnson's "Go Down Death" read by Margaret Walker; "Backwater Blues;" and "I Have a Dream."

Chicago Blues. Videotape and film. Directed by Harley Cokliss. New York: Distributed by Rhapsody Films, 1985.

Cohen, Edward. *Good Mornin' Blues.* Documentary. 4023. Narrated by B. B. King. 1979.

Explores the history of blues music from the Mississippi Delta, including performances by leading bluesmen.

Cox, James. *Nobody Knows You When You're Down and Out.* LP record. Los Angeles: Universal MCA Music Publishing: A Division of Universal Studies, Inc.

Davenport, Cow Cow. *Back in the Alley.* CD. Los Angeles: MCA/Northern Music Company, Inc., 1994.

De La Soul. *3 Feet High and Rising.* CD. New York: Tee Girl Music Publishing, 1989.

Includes the rap "Ghetto Thang."

Didn't We Ramble On: The Black Marching Band. Videotape. Narrated by Dizzy Gillespie; produced by Billy Jackson. New York: Filmakers Library, 1989, 1992.

Award-winning film shows how the musical processions of the Yorubas of West Africa continue to be expressed in Black marching bands at football games, celebrations, and funerals.

Douglas, Lydia Ann. *Nappy.* Videotape. Available from Women Make Movies. Takoma Park, MD: Peazey Head Productions, 1997.

Treats the significance of hairstyles in American culture.

Elliott, Stephen, and Grant Elliot. *Rap, Race and Equality.* Documentary. Videotape 13331. New York: Filmakers Library, 1994.

Rap artists such as Ice Cube, Ice Tea, and the band Naughty by Nature discuss rap and the subjects they treat.

Franklin, Nicole. *Double Dutch Divas.* Videotape. Epiphany Productions. New York: Filmakers Library, 1997.

Franklin, The Reverend C[larence] L. *The Eagle Stirreth Her Nest.* LP record. Chess. 9210-A, 9310-B. See also Robert G. O'Meally.

Georgia Sea Island Songs. LP record. NW 278. New York: New World Records, 1977.

Work songs, other secular songs, and spirituals sung by local performers.

Give My Poor Heart Ease. Videotape. Produced by Bill Ferris. Yale University Media Design Studio, 1975. Available through The Center for the Study of Southern Culture's Southern Culture Catalog.

The blues experience related through interviews and performances with B. B. King, prison inmates, and performers in Delta juke joints.

Graffiti Vérité: Read the Writing on the Wall. Videotape. 13289. Los Angeles: Bryan World Productions, 1995.

Los Angeles graffiti artists shown at work on projects and discussing the themes and motivations of their work.

Grandmaster Flash and the Furious Five. *The Sugar Hill Records Story.* Disc 3. Englewood Cliffs, NJ: Sugar Hill Music Publishing Ltd., 1999.

Box set including various artists; Grandmaster Flash's "The Message" is on disc 3.

Gullah Tales. Film and videotape. V4005. Directed by Gary Moss. Atlanta: Georgia Endowment for the Humanities, 1986.

Dramatization of tales about Brer Rabbit and Slave John told in Gullah dialect.

Hurston, Zora Neale. *Recordings of Zora Neale Hurston.* Sound cassette. Washington, DC: Library of Congress, Archive of Folk Culture.

Includes folk songs, blues, and work songs sung by Hurston.

Jackson, Bruce, recorder and editor. *"Get Your Ass in the Water and Swim Like Me!": Narrative Poetry from Black Oral Tradition.* LP recorded as an aural companion to Bruce Jackson's book of the same title. Also issued as a CD. Cambridge, MA: Rounder Records, 1974.

Recording of toasts, including "Stagolee," "Signifying Monkey," and "Titanic"; Rounder has a parental advisory sticker on these bawdy recitations.

Jackson, Jesse. *Speech at the Democratic Convention.* VHS 447. Videotape. Washington, DC: Speech and Transcript Center.

This 1988 speech is often titled "Keep Hope Alive."

Jenkins, Ella. *Ella Jenkins Call-And-Response: Rhythmic Group Singing.* CD. Washington, DC: Smithsonian Folkways *45030.* Originally released as an LP in 1957.

Features call-and-response chants from the United States and Africa, specially adapted for young children.

Jones, Bessie. *Step It Down.* Cassette LP. 2015. Record 8004. Cambridge, MA: Rounder Records, 1979.

Children's games.

New Hanover County Public Library

Wilmington, North Carolina

Automated Renewal number: 910/798-6320

renew online: www.nhclibrary.org

Please have your card ready

Use www.libraryelf.com to help manage your account

****

Title: American dreams / John Jakes.
Item ID: 34200004872038
Checked-out Date: 8/17/2009 2:35:34 PM
Due Date: 9/8/2009
Location: Myrtle Grove

Title: Free food for millionaires / Min
Jin Lee.
Item ID: 34200008524601
Checked-out Date: 8/17/2009 2:35:38 PM
Due Date: 9/8/2009
Location: Myrtle Grove

Title: From my people : 400 years of
African American folklore / edited by
Daryl Cumber Dance.
Item ID: 34200006504316
Checked-out Date: 8/17/2009 2:35:42 PM
Due Date: 9/8/2009
Location: Myrtle Grove

Ask about upcoming Programs...

Libraries are more than just booksX!

JVC Smithsonian Folkways Video Anthology of Music and Dance of the Americas. Volume 3. Washington, DC: The Smithsonian, 1997.

Contains African American sacred traditions.

Kein, Sybil and Charles Moore. *Creole Ballads & Zydeco.* CD. Forest Sales and Distributing Company, 4157 St. Louis Street, New Orleans, LA 70119, 1996.

————. *Creole Classique.* CD. Forest Sales and Distributing Company, 4157 St. Louis Street, New Orleans, LA 70119, 2000.

————. *Maw-Maw's Creole Lullaby.* CD. Forest Sales and Distributing Company, 4157 St. Louis Street, New Orleans, LA 70119, 1997.

King, B. B. *Bobby Bland & B. B. King Together Again . . . Live.* MCDA-27012. Universal/MCA, 1974 and 1976.

Includes "Let the Good Times Roll," written by Fleecie Moore and Sam Theard.

King, Martin Luther Jr. *The "I Have a Dream" Speech.* Videotape. Produced and edited by Richard S. R. Johnson. Atlanta: Martin Luther King Jr. Center for Nonviolent Social Change, 1985. Also available through Teacher's Video Company, Scottsdale, AZ.

KRS-One. *KRS-One.* New York: BMG/Jive/NOVAS/Silvertone, 1995.

This includes "R.E.A.L.I.T.Y."

Krsone, Parker Lawrence. *You Must Learn.* New York: Boogie Down Productions Music/Zomba Enterprises, 1989.

Learning the Ropes of Competitive Double Dutch. Videotape. Natural Clearinghouse for Alcohol and Drug Information VHS 89, 1997.

Though the focus here is on double dutch as a sport rather than folklore, it provides views of urban African American girls jumping double dutch as they prepare for competition.

Ledbetter, Huddie. *Leadbelly Sings for Children: Negro Folk Songs for Young People.* Folkways 7533. Washington, DC: Smithsonian Folkways Recordings, 1960.

Includes Ledbetter's versions of the following pieces included in this anthology: "Little Sally Walker," "Jimmie, Crack Corn," "Good Morning Blues," "Every Time I Feel the Spirit," "Swing Low, Sweet Chariot," and "John Henry."

—————. *Midnight Special: The Library of Congress Recordings.* Volumes 1, 2, and 3. Videotape. RO 1044, RO 1045, RO 1046. Recorded by John and Alan Lomax. Cambridge, MA: Rounder Records, 1991.
    Contains ballads, sacred pieces, and blues by the famed folksinger.

Lightning and Thunder. Featuring Monk Boudreaux and The Golden Eagles. Recording. Smithsonian Folkways, 1978.
    Recording of a group of Mardi Gras "Indians."

Louisiana, Where Music Is King. Part 4 of *Mississippi River of Song.* Videotape. With Ani DiFranco. Bethesda, MD: Acorn Media, 1999.
    Features meeting of country and blues with French styles resulting in Cajun and zydeco.

Made in Mississippi: Black Folk Arts and Crafts. Videotape. Produced by Bill Ferris. Yale University Media Design Studio, 1975. Available through The Center for the Study of Southern Culture's Southern Culture Catalog.
    Quilters, basketmakers, sculptors, and house builders discuss and demonstrate their crafts.

Malcolm X. *The Ballot or the Bullet.* Sound cassette. Berkeley, CA: Pacifica Tape Library, 1965.

—————. *Malcolm X Speaks: Message to the Grassroots.* Sound cassette. Cambria Heights, NY: BlaCast Entertainment, 1990 and 1992.

Martinez, Esperanza G., and Linda Roennau. *African American Quilting.* Videotape. New York: Filmakers Library, 1998.

—————. *The Cloth Sings to Me.* Videotape. New York: Filmakers Library, 1995.
    Award-winning film introduces quilters displaying their work and scholars analyzing it.

Metaxis, Eric, Danny Glover, Taj Mahal, and Joel Chandler Harris. *Danny Glover Reads Brer Rabbit and the Wonderful Tar Baby.* Sound cassette. Westport, CT: Rabbit Ears Storybook Classics, 1989 and 1990.

Mire, Pat. *Dance for a Chicken: The Cajun Mardi Gras.* Videotape. Eunice, LA: Attakapas Productions, 1993.

O'Meally, Robert G. *The Norton Anthology of African American Literature Audio Companion.* Sound disc. New York: W. W. Norton, 1997.

    Includes recordings of several work songs, spirituals, blues, raps, tales, and sermons; among those titles included in this anthology are "Go Down Moses," "Steal Away," "John Henry," "Good Morning, Blues," "Backwater Blues," "The Tarbaby Story," "Ain't I a Woman?" "I Have a Dream," "The Eagle Stirreth Her Nest," and "The Ballot or the Bullet."

Peiser, Jude, Bill Ferris, and David Evans. *Gravel Springs Fife and Drums.* 16 mm film documentary. (In the University of North Carolina library at Chapel Hill.) 1972.

    Compares fife and drum music in Gravel Springs, Mississippi, to traditional West African music.

The Performed Word. Videotape. Directed by Gerald Davis, 1981.

    Excerpts from sermons and interview with Bishop E. E. Cleveland of Berkeley, California, provide a close look at African American church services.

Public Enemy. *Fear of a Black Planet.* CD. New York: Universal/Def Jam, 1990.

    Includes "Brothers Gonna Work It Out."

―――. *Greatest Misses.* CD. New York: Universal/Def Jam, 1992.

    Includes "Get Off My Back."

Saints' Paradise: Trombone Shout Bands from the United House of Prayer. CD. Washington, DC: Smithsonian Folkways, 1999.

Say Amen, Somebody. Film and videotape. Directed by George Nierenberg. New York: First Run Features, 1980. Also Videotape 2718. Carmel, CA: Pacific Arts Video Records, 1984.

    Documentary of gospel songs of Willie Mae Ford. Also features her mentor, Thomas Dorsey.

Smith, Bessie. *Bessie Smith: The World's Greatest Blues Singer.* LP. New York: Columbia Records, 1951.

Her first sixteen and last sixteen recordings, including "Tain't Nobody's Bizness If I Do," "Black Mountain Blues," and "Need a Little Sugar in My Tea."

———. "Jail-House Blues." Written by Bessie Smith and Clarence Williams. Los Angeles: Universal MCA Music Publishing: A Division of Universal Studies, Inc. Originally recorded in 1923.

The Smithsonian Collection of Classic Jazz. Sound recording. Selected and annotated by Martin Williams. Washington, DC: Division of Performing Arts, Smithsonian Institution. Educational distribution by W. W. Norton and Company, 1987.
Six-record album plus booklet.

The Songs Are Free: Bernice Johnson Reagan and African American Music. Videotape. From *World of Ideas with Bill Moyers.* Princeton, NJ: Films for the Humanities and Sciences, 1998.
Traces the history of communal singing in the Black church from the Underground Railroad through the Civil Rights movement and into the 1990s.

Straight Up Rappin'. Videotape. 9478. Produced by Tana Ross and Freke Vuijst. New York: Filmakers Library, 1992.
A documentary on rap in the streets of New York.

Too Close to Heaven: The History of Gospel Music. Videotape. CWF 6974. Narrated by Alphonsia Emmanuel. Princeton, NJ: Films for the Humanities and Sciences, 1997.

We Shall Overcome. Videotape. Produced by Jim Brown et al. Narrated by Harry Belafonte. San Francisco: California Newsreel, 1989.
Traces the transformation of the song "We Shall Overcome" from a slave spiritual to the Civil Rights anthem in America and a freedom song all around the world.

Wild Women Don't Have the Blues. Videotape. Produced by Carole van Falkenburg and Christine Dall. San Francisco: California Newsreels, 1989.
Treats the lives of several famous blues women and compiles dozens of classic renditions of the early blues.

Zora Is My Name! Videotape. 4199. Produced by Ruby Dee. PBS TV. Alexandria, VA: PBS Video, 1989.

Treats Zora Neale Hurston and her capturing of the folklore of the rural South.

Bibliography

Adams, E. C. L. *Potee's Gal: A Drama of Negro Life Near the Big Congaree Swamps.* Columbia, SC: The State Company, 1929.

"Ali Says He Is Still the Greatest Fighter of All Time." *Jet* 93 (May 11, 1998): 50.

Allen, James, et al. *Without Sanctuary: Lynching Photography in America.* Santa Fe, NM: Twin Palms, 2000.

Allport, Gordon W., and Leo Postman. *The Psychology of Rumor.* New York: Henry Holt, 1947.

"American General Life and Accident Insurance Co. Pays $206 Mil. Settling Claims It Overcharged Blacks." *Jet* 98 (July 10, 2000): 22.

Angelou, Maya. *Phenomenal Woman.* New York: Random House, 1994.

———. "Still I Rise." *The Collected Poems of Maya Angelou.* New York: Random House, 1994. 163–64.

Asante, Molefi Kete. "Folk Poetry in the Storytelling Tradition." In *Talk That Talk: An Anthology of African-American Storytelling,* ed. Linda Goss and Marian E. Barnes. New York: Simon & Schuster, 1989: 91–93.

Bacon, A. M. "Conjuring and Conjure-Doctors." *Southern Workman* 24 (November 1895): 193–94.

———. "Conjuring and Conjure-Doctors." *Southern Workman* 24 (December 1895): 209–11.

Baldwin, James. *No Name in the Street.* New York: Dial Press, 1972.

Banks, Frank D. "Plantation Courtship." *Southern Workman* 24 (January 1895): 14–15.

Berry, Mary F., and John W. Blassingame. "Africa, Slavery and the Roots of Contemporary Black Culture." In *Chant of Saints: A Gathering of Afro-American Literature, Art, and Scholarship,* ed. Michael S. Harper and Robert B. Stepto. Urbana: Univ. of Illinois Press, 1979, 241–56.

Bonner, Lonnice Brittenum. *Plaited Glory: For Colored Girls Who've Considered Braids, Locks, and Twists.* New York: Crown Trade Paperbacks, 1996.

Botkin, B. A. *Lay My Burden Down: A Folk History of Slavery.* Chicago: University of Chicago Press, 1945.

Brown, Elsa Barkley. "African-American Women's Quilting: A Framework for Conceptualizing and Teaching African-American Women's History." *SIGNS: Journal of Women in Culture and Society* 14 (summer 1989): 921–29.

Brown, H. Rap. *Die, Nigger, Die!* New York: Dial Press, 1969.

Brown, Sterling. "Been Acquainted with the Blues So Long." *SAGALA* 3 (1983): 12–19.

———. "Negro Folk Expression." In *Black Expression: Essays by and about Black Americans in the Creative Arts,* ed. Addison Gayle. New York: Weybright and Talley, 1969.

———. *Southern Road.* New York: Harcourt Brace, 1932.

Brown, Stewart, Mervyn Morris, and Gordon Rohlehr, eds. *Voice Print: An Anthology of Oral and Related Poetry from the Caribbean.* Essex, England: Longman Group UK, 1989.

Brown, W[illiam]. W[ells]. *Clotel: A Tale of the Southern States.* Boston: James Redpath, Publisher, 1864.

Bundles, A'Lelia. *On Her Own Ground: The Life and Times of Madam C. J. Walker.* New York: Scribner, 2001.

Caponi, Gena Dagel, ed. *Signifyin(g), Sanctifyin', & Slam Dunking: A Reader in African American Expressive Culture.* Amherst: Univ. of Massachusetts Press, 1999.

Cochran, Johnnie L., Jr., with Tim Rutten. *Journey to Justice.* New York: Ballantine, 1996.

Dance, Daryl Cumber. *Honey, Hush! An Anthology of African American Women's Humor.* New York: W. W. Norton, 1998.

———. *The Lineage of Abraham: The Biography of a Free Black Family in Charles City, VA.* N.p.: n.p., 1998.

———. *Long Gone: The Mecklenburg Six and the Theme of Escape in Black Folklore.* Knoxville: Univ. of Tennessee Press, 1987.

————. *Shuckin' and Jivin': Folklore from Contemporary Black Americans.* Bloomington: Indiana Univ. Press, 1978.

Douglass, Frederick. *Life and Times of Frederick Douglass, Written by Himself: His Early Life as a Slave, His Escape from Bondage, and His Complete History to the Present Time.* Hartford: Park Publishing Co., 1881.

Du Bois, W. E. B. *The Souls of Black Folk.* 1903; reprint, New York: New American Library, 1969.

Dunbar, Paul Laurence. "The Party." In *Lyrics of Lowly Life.* New York: Dodd, Mead and Company, 1912, 199–208.

Dundes, Alan. " 'Jumping the Broom': On the Origin and Meaning of an African American Wedding Custom." *Journal of American Folklore* 109 (1996): 324–29.

Dundes, Alan, and Carl R. Pagter. *Urban Folklore from the Paperwork Empire.* Austin: American Folklore Society, 1975.

————. *When You're Up to Your Ass in Alligators: More Urban Folklore from the Paperback Empire.* Detroit: Wayne State Univ. Press, 1987.

Dunne, Finley Peter. *Observations of Mr. Dooley.* New York: Russell, 1902.

Ellison, Ralph. *Going to the Territory.* New York: Random House, 1986.

————. *Invisible Man.* 1952. New York: Vintage, 1972.

————. *Shadow and Act.* 1964. New York: Vintage, 1972.

Equiano, Olaudah. *Equiano's Travels: His Autobiography: The Interesting Narrative of the Life of Olaudah Equiano or Gustavus Vassa the African.* New York: Printed and sold by W. Durell, 1791; reprint, ed. Paul Edwards, New York: Frederick A. Praeger, 1966.

Fanon, Frantz. *Black Skin, White Masks.* 1951; reprint, New York: Grove Press, Inc., 1967.

Flowers, Arthur. Introduction to *Mojo Rising.* Reprinted in *Networking 2000: In the Spirit of the Harlem Renaissance* 7 (spring 2000): 3–4.

Foster, Frances Smith. *Written by Herself: Literary Production by African American Women, 1746–1892.* Bloomington: Indiana Univ. Press, 1992.

Freeman, Roland L. *The Arabbers of Baltimore.* Centreville, MD: Tidewater Publishers, 1989.

————. *A Communion of Spirits: African-American Quilters, Preservers, and Their Stories.* Nashville: Rutledge Hill Press, 1997.

Gage, Frances Dana. "Sojourner Truth." *National Anti-Slavery Standard* 2 (May 2, 1863): 4.

Gates, Henry Louis, Jr. *The Signifying Monkey: A Theory of Afro-American Literary Criticism.* New York: Oxford Univ. Press, 1988.

Germaneso, " 'I Made This Jar': The Life and Works of the Enslaved

African-American Potter, Dave." *Folk Art Magazine* 12 (Summer 1999): 15.

Gordon-Reed, Annette. *Thomas Jefferson and Sally Hemings: An American Controversy.* Charlottesville: Univ. Press of Virginia, 1997.

Greenfield, Jeff. "The Black and White Truth about Basketball." *Esquire,* October 1975, 170–71, 248.

Gregory, Dick. *Natural Diet for Folks Who Eat: Cookin' with Mother Nature.* Ed. James R. McGraw, with Alvenia M. Fulton. New York: Perennial-Harper, 1974.

———. *Nigger: An Autobiography.* Cutchogue, New York: Buccaneer Books, 1964.

Grosvenor, Vertamae Smart. *Vibration Cooking, or the Travel Notes of a Geechee Girl.* Garden City, NY: Doubleday, 1970.

Gwaltney, John Langston, ed. *Drylongso: A Self-Portrait of Black America.* New York: Random House, 1980.

Harlan, Howard H. *John Jasper — A Case History in Leadership.* Charlottesville: Publication of the University of Virginia Phelps-Stokes Fellowship Papers, 1938.

Harrison, Daphne Duval. *Black Pearls: Blues Queens of the 1920s.* New Brunswick, NJ: Rutgers Univ. Press, 1988.

Haskins, James. *Voodoo & Hoodoo: Their Tradition and Craft as Revealed by Actual Practioners.* Chelsea, MI: Scarborough House, 1990.

Hemenway, Robert. "Are You a Flying Lark or a Setting Dove?" In *Afro-American Literature: The Reconstruction of Instruction,* ed. Dexter Fisher and Robert Stepto. New York: MLA, 1979, 122–52.

———. *Zora Neale Hurston: A Literary Biography.* Urbana: Univ. of Illinois Press, 1977.

"History [of Graffiti]." Parts 1 and 2. www.at149st.com.

Holland, Endesha Ida Mae. *From the Mississippi Delta.* New York: Simon & Schuster, 1997.

Hubbard, Dolan, "Sermons and Preaching." In *The Oxford Companion to African American Literature,* ed. William L. Andrews, Frances Smith Foster, and Trudier Harris. New York: Oxford University Press, 1997, 648–52.

Hughes, Langston. *The Best of Simple.* New York: Hill and Wang, 1961.

———. *The Big Sea: An Autobiography.* 1963; reprint, New York: Thundermouth Press, 1986.

———. *The Langston Hughes Reader.* New York: George Braziller, 1958.

———. *Simple Takes a Wife.* New York: Simon & Schuster, 1957.

Hungerford, James. *The Old Plantation, and What I Gathered There in an Autumn Month.* New York: Harper & Brothers, 1859.

Hurst, Fannie. "Zora Hurston: A Personality Sketch." *Yale University Library Gazette* 35: 17–21.

Hurston, Zora Neale. *Dust Tracks on a Road.* 1942; reprint, Urbana: Univ. of Illinois Press, 1970.

———. "Hoodoo in America." *The Journal of American Folk-Lore* 44 (October–December 1931): 317–417.

———. *Mules and Men.* Philadelphia: J. P. Lippincott, 1935; reprint, New York: Harper and Row, 1970.

Hurston, Zora Neale, and Langston Hughes. *Mule Bone: A Comedy of Negro Life,* ed. George Houston Bass and Henry Louis Gates Jr. New York: Harper Perennial, 1991.

Jackson, Margaret Young. "An Investigation of Biographies and Autobiographies of American Slaves Published Between 1840 and 1860: Based Upon the Cornell Special Slavery Collection." Ph.D. diss., Cornell University, 1964.

"The John Jasper Memorial Room and Museum." A pamphlet produced by the Sixth Mount Zion Baptist Church, Richmond, VA [n.d. n.p.].

"John Jasper, Unique and Unforgettable." *The Richmond Literature and History Quarterly 1* (summer 1978) 39–40.

Johnson, Alonzo, and Paul Jersild, eds. *"Ain't Gonna Lay My 'Ligion Down": African American Religion in the South.* Columbia: Univ. of South Carolina Press, 1996.

Johnson, James Weldon. *The Book of American Negro Spirituals.* New York: Viking Press, 1925.

———. *God's Trombones: Seven Negro Sermons in Verse.* New York: Viking Press, 1927.

Jones, LeRoi. "Philistinism and the Negro Writer." In *Anger and Beyond: The Negro Writer in the United States,* ed. Herbert Hill. New York: Harper and Row, 1966, 51–61.

Kaye, Samantha. www.spellmaker.com.

Keckley, Elizabeth. *Behind the Scenes, or, Thirty Years a Slave and Four Years in the White House.* New York: G. W. Carleton, 1868.

Killens, John Oliver. *Black Man's Burden.* New York: Simon & Schuster, 1970.

Kinser, Samuel. *Carnival, American Style: Mardi Gras of New Orleans and Mobile.* Chicago: Univ. of Chicago Press, 1990.

Laguerre, Michel S. *Voodoo Heritage.* Beverly Hills, CA: Sage Publications, 1980.

Lee, Jimmie. *Soul Food Cookbook.* New York: Award Books, 1970.

Levine, Lawrence W. *Black Culture and Black Consciousness: Afro-American Folk Thought from Slavery to Freedom.* New York: Oxford Univ. Press, 1977.

Leifer, Neil, and Thomas Hauser. *Muhammad Ali Memories.* New York: Rizzoli International.

Lightfoot, Sarah Lawrence. *Balm in Gilead: Journey of a Healer.* New York: Addison-Wesley, 1988.

Livingston, Jane, and John Beardsley. *Black Folk Art in America: 1930–1980.* Jackson: Univ. Press of Mississippi, 1982.

Lomax, Alan. *Mister Jelly Roll: The Fortunes of Jelly Roll Morton, New Orleans Creole and "Inventor of Jazz."* 1950. 2nd ed. Berkeley: Univ. of California Press, 1973.

———. "Self-Pity in Negro Folk-Songs." *The Nation* 105 (August 9, 1917).

Madden, T. O., Jr., with Ann L. Miller. *We Were Always Free: The Maddens of Culpeper County, Virginia, a 200-Year Family History.* New York: W. W. Norton, 1992.

Major, Clarence, ed. *Juba to Jive: A Dictionary of African-American Slang.* New York: Penguin, 1994.

Malone, Jacqui. *Steppin' on the Blues: The Visible Rhythms of African American Dance.* Urbana: Univ. of Illinois Press, 1996.

Malinowski, Bronislav. *Magic, Science and Religion and Other Essays by Bronislav Malinowski.* New York: Doubleday, 1954.

McKelway, Bill. "Her Refusal Made History." *Richmond Times-Dispatch,* August 6, 2000, A1, A14.

Messenger, John. "The Role of Proverbs in a Nigerian Judicial System." *Southwestern Journal of Anthropology* 15 (1959): 64–73.

Nack, William. "The Fight's Over, Joe." *Sports Illustrated* 85 (September 30, 1996): 52ff.

Newman, Richard. *African American Quotations.* New York: Facts on File, 2000.

Northup, Solomon. *Twelve Years a Slave: Narrative of Solomon Northup, a Citizen of New-York, Kidnapped in Washington City in 1841, and Rescued in 1853, from a Cotton Plantation Near the Red River, in Louisiana.* 1853; reprint, New York: Miller, Orton & Co. 1857.

Oliver, Paul. *The Story of the Blues.* Philadelphia: Chilton, 1969.

Painter, Nell Irvin. *Sojourner Truth: A Life, A Symbol.* New York: W. W. Norton, 1996.

Parrish, Lydia. *Slave Songs of the Georgia Sea Islands.* New York: Creative Age Press, 1941.

Parsons, Elsie Clews. *Folk-Lore of the Sea Islands, South Carolina.* Cambridge, MA: American Folk-Lore Society, 1923.

Patterson, Ruth Polk. *The Seed of Sally Good'n: A Black Family of Arkansas, 1833–1953.* Lexington: Univ. Press of Kentucky, 1985.

Perry, Regenia A. "Black American Folk Art: Origins and Early Manifestations." In *Black Folk Art in America: 1930–1980,* ed. Jane Livingston and John Beardsley. Jackson: Univ. Press of Mississippi, 1982, 25–37.

————. *Harriet Powers's Bible Quilts.* New York: Rizzoli Art Series (ed. Norma Broude), 1994.

————. *What It Is: Black American Folk Art from the Collection of Regenia Perry* (catalog). Richmond: Anderson Gallery, School of the Arts, Virginia Commonwealth University exhibit, October 6–27, 1982.

Phillips, Susan A. *Wallbangin': Graffiti and Gangs in L.A.* Chicago: Univ. of Chicago Press, 1999.

Piersen, William D. "African-American Festive Style." In *Signifyin(g), Sanctifyin', & Slam Dunking: A Reader in African American Expressive Culture,* ed. Gena Dagel Caponi. Amherst: Univ. of Massachusetts Press, 1999, 417–33.

Pope-Hennessy, James. *Sins of the Fathers: A Study of the Atlantic Slave Traders 1441–1907.* New York: Alfred A. Knopf, 1968.

Prahlad, Sw. Anand. *African-American Proverbs in Context.* Jackson: Univ. of Mississippi Press, 1996.

Puckett, Newbell Niles. *Folk Beliefs of the Southern Negro.* Chapel Hill: Univ. of North Carolina Press, 1926.

Raboteau, Albert J. *A Fire in the Bones: Reflections on African-American Religious History.* Boston: Beacon Press, 1995.

Redford, Dorothy Spruill, with Michael Dorson. *Somerset Homecoming: Recovering a Lost Heritage.* New York: Doubleday, 1988.

Reisner, Robert, and Lorraine Wechsler. *Encyclopedia of Graffiti.* New York: Macmillan Publishing, 1974.

Roberts, John W. "Joning: An Afro-American Verbal Form in St. Louis." *Journal of the Folklore Institute* 19 (January–April 1982): 61–70.

Southern, Eileen. *The Music of Black Americans: A History.* 2nd ed. New York: W. W. Norton, 1983.

Stanley, Lawrence A., ed. *Rap: The Lyrics.* New York: Penguin, 1992.

Sterling, Dorothy, ed. *We Are Your Sisters: Black Women in the Nineteenth Century.* New York: W. W. Norton, 1984.

Sterling, Philip, ed. *Laughing on the Outside: The Intelligent White Reader's Guide to Negro Tales and Humor.* New York: Grosset & Dunlap, 1965.

Stowe, Harriet Beecher. "Sojourner Truth, the Libyan Sibyl." *Atlantic Monthly* 11 (April 1863): 473–80.

Sundiata: An Epic of Old Mali. By D. T. Niane; trans. by G. D. Pickett. 1960; reprint, Essex, England: Longman, 1979.

Swenson, Greta E. *Festivals of Sharing: Family Reunions in America.* New York: AMS Press, 1989.

Thomas, Lorenzo. "From Gumbo to Grammys: The Development of Zydeco Music in Houston." In *Juneteenth Texas: Essays in African-American Folklore,* ed. Francis Edward Abernethy and Carolyn Fiedler Satterwhite. Denton: Univ. of North Texas Press, 1996.

Thompson, Robert Farris. *African Art in Motion: Icon and Act.* Berkeley and Los Angeles: Univ. of California Press, 1974.

Tobin, Jacqueline, and Raymond Dobard. *Hidden in Plain View: The Secret Story of Quilts and the Underground Railroad.* New York: Doubleday, 1999.

Turner, Patricia A. *I Heard It Through the Grapevine: Rumor in African-American Culture.* Berkeley and Los Angeles: Univ. of California Press, 1993.

Vlach, John Michael. *By the Work of Their Hands: Studies in Afro-American Folklife.* Charlottesville: Univ. Press of Virginia, 1991.

Wahlman, Maude. *Signs and Symbols: African Images in African-American Quilts.* New York: Studio Books in Association with Museum of American Folk Art, 1993.

Walker, Alice. "Zora Neale Hurston—a Cautionary Tale and a Partisan View." Preface to *Zora Neale Hurston: A Literary Biography,* by Robert E. Hemenway. Urbana: Univ. of Illinois Press, 1983.

Walsh, Mike. "The Miracle of St. James Hampton." Expresso Tilt Online Anthology (www.missioncreep.com/tilt/hampton.html).

Watkins, Mel. *On the Real Side: Laughing, Lying, and Signifying—The Underground Tradition of African-American Humor That Transformed American Culture, from Slavery to Richard Pryor.* New York: Simon & Schuster, 1994.

Weldon, Fred O., Jr. "Negro Folktale Heroes." In *And Horns on the Toads,* ed. Mody C. Boatright, Wilson M. Hudson, and Allen Maxwell. Dallas: Southern Methodist University Press, 1959.

White, Deborah Gray. *Ar'n't I a Woman? Female Slaves in the Plantation South.* New York: W. W. Norton, 1987.

White, Shane, and Graham White. *Stylin': African American Expressive Culture from Its Beginnings to the Zoot Suit.* Ithaca, NY: Cornell Univ. Press, 1998.

Wiggins, William H., Jr., *O Freedom! Afro-American Emancipation Celebrations.* Knoxville: Univ. of Tennessee Press, 1987.

Wilson, Sule Greg C. *African American Quilting: The Warmth of Tradition.* New York: Rosen, 1999.

Witt, Doris. "Soul Food, Where the Chitterling Hits the (Primal) Pan." In *Eating Culture,* ed. Ron Scapp and Brian Seitz. Albany: State Univ. of New York Press, 1998, 258–87.

Wolfe, George C. *The Colored Museum. New Plays USA.* New York: Theatre Communications Group, 1988.

Yetman, Norman R., ed. *"Life Under the "Peculiar Institution": Selections from the Slave Narrative Collection.* 1970; reprint, Huntington, NY: R. E. Kreiger, 1976.

Zeitlin, Steven J., et al. *A Celebration of American Family Folklore.* New York: Pantheon, 1982.

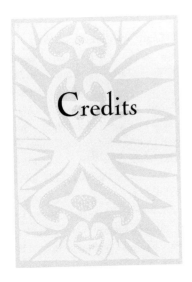

Credits

Abernathy, Francis Edward, and Carolyn Fielder Satterwhite, "Rabbit in de Briar Patch," from *Juneteenth Texas: Essays in African-American Folklore*. Denton: University of North Texas Press, 1996.

Adams, Edward C. L., and Robert G. O'Meally, "An Escaped Convict," "Thirteen Years," "The Lynchers," "Silas," "Sister Lucy," and "Potee's Gal: A Drama of Negro Life Near the Big Congaree Swamps," from *Tales of the Congaree*. Copyright © 1987 by the University of North Carolina Press. Used by permission of the publisher.

Allen, William Francis, Charles Pickard Ware, and Lucy McKim Garrison, "The Ring Shout," "I Heard from Heaven Today," "Michael, Row de Boat A-Shore," "Charleston Gals," and "I Want to Go Home," from *Slave Songs of the United States*. New York: A. Simpson & Co., 1867.

Aswell, James R., and others of the Tennessee Writers' Project, "Little Eight John" and "De Ways of de Wimmens," from *God Bless the Devil!: Liars' Bench Tales*. Copyright © 1940 by the University of North Carolina Press, renewed 1968 by James R. Aswell & others. Used by permission of the publisher.

Banks, Ann, ed., "Quilting Parties," "Sweet-the-Monkey," "Bernice Gore," and "A Different Style," from *First-Person America: Voices of the Great Depression*. Used by permission of Ann Banks.

Banks, Frank D., "Sample of a 'Courtship' Conversation," from *Southern Workman* 24 (January 1895): 15.

Bass, Ruth, "Mojo," from *Scribner's Magazine* 87 (1930), 83–90. Used by permission of M. A. Bass Jr.

"Beliefs and Customs Connected with Death and Burial," from *Southern Workman* 26 (January 1897).

Berry, Fannie, "Fire Sticks" and "We's Free." See Writers' Program (Va.).

Boone, Carol F, "Wine Jelly." Used by permission of Carol F. Boone.

Botkin, B. A., "It's a Good Time to Dress You Out," from *Lay My Burden Down: A Folk History of Slavery.* Chicago: University of Chicago Press, 1945.

"The Boy and the Ghost," from *Southern Workman* 27 (March 1898): 57.

Bradford, Perry, "The Lonesome Blues." Philadelphia: Standard Theatre, 1916.

Bradford, Sarah, ed., "When Dat Ar Ole Chariot Comes," by Harriet Tubman, from *Harriet, The Moses of Her People.* New York: Citadel Press, 1974.

Bray, Rosemary L., "Renaissance for a Pioneer of Black Pride." *New York Times Book Review*, February 4, 1990, 7, 41.

Brewer, J. Mason, "World War II Rhymes," "Street Cries," "Bedbug," "More Riddles," "Destitute Former Slave Owners," and "More Tall Tales," from *American Negro Folklore.* Chicago: Quadrangle Books, 1968. We have made every effort to find the copyright holder for these selections. If you have information regarding the copyright holder, please write to W. W. Norton, 500 Fifth Avenue, New York, NY 10110 (Attn: Amy Cherry).

———, "The Dog Ghost and the Buried Money," from *Dog Ghosts and Other Texas Negro Folk Tales*, pp. 105–9. Copyright © 1958, renewed 1986. Courtesy of the University of Texas Press.

———, "The Stubborn Piano," "Uncle Jim Speaks His Mind," "Autograph Album Rhymes," and "Jack Johnson and Jim Jeffries," from *Worser Days and Better Times.* Chicago: Quadrangle Books, 1965. We have made every effort to find the copyright holder for these selections. If you have information regarding the copyright holder, please write to W. W. Norton, 500 Fifth Avenue, New York, NY 10110 (Attn: Amy Cherry).

———, "Tall Tales." *Humorous Folk Tales of the South Carolina Negro.* Orangeburg, S.C.: The South Carolina Negro Folklore Guild, 1945.

———, "Why the Guardian Angel Let the Brazos Bottom Negroes Sleep," from *The Word on the Brazos: Negro Preacher Tales from the Brazos Bottoms of Texas*, pp. 81–82. Copyright © 1953, renewed 1991. Courtesy of the University of Texas Press.

Brown, Sterling A., "Ma Rainey," from *Southern Road: Poems by Sterling A. Brown.* New York: Harcourt, Brace and Company, 1932. Used by permission of John L. Dennis.

Brown, William Wells, "The Big Bee" and "Hang Up the Shovel and the Hoe," from *Clotel, or, the President's Daughter.* London: Partridge & Oakey, 1853.

———, "Corn Shucking and Christmas Festivities," "Let My People Go," "Baptist Chitlins," "I Am Gwine to Glory," and "Voodoo in St. Louis," from *My Southern Home: Or, The South and Its People.* Boston: A. G. Brown, 1880.

———, "Song of the Coffle Gang" and "A Song for Freedom," from *The Anti-Slavery Harp: A Collection of Songs*, 3rd edition. Boston: Bela Marsh, 1851.

Cable, Mary, "Cinque," from *Black Odyssey: The Case of the Slave Ship Amistad*. New York: Viking Press, 1971.

Chase, Carolyn, "I Limit My Syllable Output." See Gwaltney, John Langston.

Clark-Lewis, Elizabeth, ed., "I was Leaving," from *Living In, Living Out: African American Domestics and the Great Migration*. Copyright © 1996 by Kodansha America, Inc. Reprinted with permission of the publisher.

Cox, Ida, "Wild Women Don't Have the Blues." Paramount, 1924. Reprinted with permission of MCA/Northern Music Company.

Cox, Jimmie, "Nobody Knows You When You're Down and Out." Reprinted with permission of MCA/Northern Music Company.

Crummell, Alex, "Eulogium on Henry Highland Garnet, D.D.," from *Africa and America: Addresses and Discourses by Alex Crummell*. Springfield, Mass.: Wiley & Company, 1891.

Dance, Daryl Cumber, "We Must, We Must, We Must," from *Honey Hush! An Anthology of African American Women's Humor*. New York: W. W. Norton & Company, 1998.

———, "Ruthville Post Office" and "Unrequited Love," from *The Lineage of Abraham*. Used by permission of the author.

———, "Why the Whites Have Everything," "In the Name of the Lord," "Bobtail Beat the Devil," "God Delivered 'Em," "I'll Go as Far as Memphis," "Let the Wheelers Roll," "Some Are Going and Some Are Coming," "Upon This Rock," "The Tar Baby," "Why the Black Man's Hair Is Nappy," "You May Fall in Yourself," "How?" and "Hot Biscuits Burn Yo' Ass," from *Shuckin' and Jivin': Folklore from Contemporary Black Americans*. Copyright © 1978 by the Indiana University Press. Used by permission of the publisher.

Davenport, Charles Cow Cow, "I Ain't No Ice Man." Reprinted with permission of MCA/Northern Music Company.

"Death and Burial," from *Southern Workman* 26 (January 1897): 18–19.

Delany, Sarah, and A. Elizabeth Delany, with Amy Hill Hearth, "Our Papa's People," from *Having Our Say: The Delany Sisters' First 100 Years*. New York: Kodansha International, 1993. Used by permission of Amy Hill Hearth.

De La Soul, "Ghetto Thang," from the album *3 Feet High and Rising*. Lyrics by Paul Huston, David Jolicoeur, Vincent Mason, and Kelvin Mercer. Published by Prinse Pawl Musick (BMI) and T-Girl Music L.L.C./Daisy Age Music (BMI) © 1989. Used by permission of publisher.

Diamond, Oswald, "Beef Ribs." Permission granted by Rozeal Diamond.

Diamond, Rozeal, "Rolls." Permission granted by Rozeal Diamond.

Dollard, John, "The Dozens: Dialectic of Insult." See Dundes, Alan.

Dorson, Richard M., "Mr. Rabbit and Mr. Frog Make Mr. Fox and Mr. Bear Their Riding Horses," "Why the Rabbit Has a Short Tale," "Straighten Up and Fly Right," "Polly Tells on the Slaves," "The Coon in the Box," "The Mojo," "How Hoodoo Lost His Hand," "John and the Twelve Jews," "The One-Legged Grave Robber," and "The Irishman at the Dance," from *American Negro Folktales*.

Bloomington: Indiana University Press, 1958. Reprinted by permission of Gloria Dorson.

Douglass, Frederick, "My Slave Experience in Maryland," from *National Anti-Slavery Standard* 5.51 (May 22, 1845): 202.

————, "O Canaan" and "We Raise de Wheat," from *Life and Times of Frederick Douglass, Written by Himself: His Early Life as a Slave, His Escape from Bondage, and His Complete History to the Present Time.* Hartford, Conn.: Park Publishing Co., 1881.

————, "Sandy's Roots," from *Narrative of the Life of Frederick Douglass, an American Slave,* 3rd English edition. Wortley, near Leeds: Printed by J. Barker, 1846.

————, "What to the Slave Is the Fourth of July?: An Address Delivered in Rochester, New York, on 5 July 1852." Lee, Mann & Company, 1852.

Du Bois, W. E. B., "Lay This Body Down," from *The Souls of Black Folk.* A. C. McClurg, 1903.

Dunbar, Paul Laurence, "The Colored Band," from *Lyrics of Love and Laughter.* New York: Dodd, Mead and Company, 1903.

————, "The Party" and "An Antebellum Sermon," from *Lyrics of Lowly Life.* New York: Dodd, Mead and Company, 1912.

Dundes, Alan, ed., "The Dozens," from *Mother Wit from the Laughing Barrel: Readings in the Interpretation of Afro-American Folklore.* Englewood Cliffs, N.J.: Prentice Hall, 1972.

Earle, Alice Morse, "Pinkster Day," from *The Outlook* 49 (April 28, 1894): 743–44.

Ellison, Ralph, "Rinehart, Poppa," from *Invisible Man.* 1952; New York: Vintage Books, 1972.

————, "Learning to Swing," from *Shadow and Act.* 1964; New York: Vintage Books, 1972.

Equiano, Olaudah, "The Slave Ship," from *Equiano's Travels: His Autobiography; The Interesting Narrative of the Life of Olaudah Equiano or Gustavus Vassa the African,* abridged and edited by Paul Edwards. Oxford: Heinemann, 1967. Permission granted by Heinemann International.

Fortier, Alcee, "The Elephant and the Whale," from *Louisiana Folk-Tales.* New York: G. E. Steckert, 1895.

Foster, Frances Smith, "Sloppy Salmon." Permission granted by Frances Smith Foster.

Franklin, The Reverend C. L., "The Eagle Stirreth Her Nest" and "What of the Night?" See Titon, Jeff Todd.

Frazier, Julia, "Charlie." See Writers' Program (Va.).

Freeman, Roland L., "Street Cries," from *The Arabbers of Baltimore.* Centreville, Md.: Tidewater Publishers, 1989. Used by permission of the author.

Frost, Adele, "My Life." See Hurmence, Belinda.

Fry, Gladys-Marie, "Night Doctors," from *Night Riders in Black Folk History.* Copyright © 1975 by Gladys-Marie Fry. Published by University of North Carolina Press. Used with permission of the publisher and the author.

Gabbin, Joanne V., "Pot Meals" and "Chicken Pot Pie." Permission granted by Joanne V. Gabbin.

Gage, Frances Dana, "Sojourner Truth," from *National Anti-Slavery Standard* 2 (May 2, 1863): 4.

Gilbert, Martha, "Corn Pudding." Permission granted by Martha Gilbert.

Giovanni, Nikki, "Yo' Mama," from *Gemini: An Extended Autobiographical Statement on My First Twenty-Five Years of Being a Black Poet*. Reprinted with the permission of Scribner, a Division of Simon & Schuster, from *Gemini* by Nikki Giovanni. Copyright © 1971 by Nikki Giovanni.

———, "I Always Think of Meatloaf." Permission granted by Nikki Giovanni.

Godfrey, Anne, "Interpret Dat." See Solomon, Jack and Olivia.

Gore, Bernice, "Bernice Gore." See Banks, Ann.

Govan, Sandra Y., "My Mama's Corn Pone." Used by permission of the author.

Grainger, Porter, and Everett Robbins, " 'Tain't Nobody's Business If I Do." 1922.

Greene, Melissa Fay, "Grandma" and "The Sheriff," from *Praying for Sheetrock*. Copyright © 1991 by Melissa Fay Greene. Reprinted by permission of Perseus Books Publishers, a member of Perseus Books, LLC.

Griffin, Fannie, "My Marster . . . Was a Good Man." See Hurmence, Belinda.

Gurley, Leo, "Sweet-the-Monkey." See Banks, Ann.

Gwaltney, John Langston, ed., "I Am a Hard Woman," "The Difference between Us and Them," "I Limit My Syllable Output," and "If You Ain't in the Know, You Are in Danger," from *Drylongso: A Self-Portrait of Black America*. New York: Random House, 1980. Used by permission of John Langston Gwaltney.

Handy, W. C., "Careless Love." 1926. By permission of Handy Brothers Music Co., Inc. New York, N.Y. Copyright renewed. International copyright secured.

———, "Beale Street." Memphis, Tenn.: Pace & Handy Music Company, 1918.

———, "The Hesitating Blues," Memphis, Tenn.: Pace & Handy Music Company, 1915.

———, "Joe Turner Blues." Memphis, Tenn.: Pace & Handy Music Company, 1915.

———, "The St. Louis Blues." Memphis, Tenn.: Pace & Handy Music Company, 1914.

Harris, Middleton, ed., "Caution" by Theodore H. Parker and "Black Blood," from *The Black Book*. Copyright © 1974 by Random House, Inc. Used by permission of the publisher.

Hatcher, William E., "No Other Preacher Could Walk like Him," "Light as a Feather," and "The Sun Do Move," from *John Jasper: The Unmatched Negro Philosopher and Preacher.* New York: Fleming H. Revell Company, 1908.

Hemenway, Robert, *Zora Neale Hurston: A Literary Biography*. Urbana: University of Illinois Press, 1977.

Hemings, Madison, "Life among the Lowly." *Pike County* [Ohio] *Republican* (March 13, 1873).

Higginson, Thomas Wentworth, "Prince Lambkin's Oration on the American Flag," "The Route Step," "Lay This Body Down," "My Army Cross Over,"

"One More Valiant Soldier," "Ride In, Kind Saviour," and "We'll Soon Be Free," from *Army Life in a Black Regiment*. Boston: Fields, Osgood & Company, 1870.

"Hold Him, Tabb." *Southern Workman* 26 (June 1897): 122–23.

Holmes, Sheila Louise, "Grandma, Grandma," from "Jump Rope Rhymes and Hand Games: Their Significance in the Educational Development of African-American Children." Thesis, Mount St. Mary's College, 1999. Used by permission of Sheila Louise Holmes.

Hughes, Langston, "Salvation" and "Rent Parties," titled "When the Negro Was in Vogue," from *The Big Sea*. Copyright © 1940 by Langston Hughes. Copyright renewed 1968 by Arna Bontemps and George Houston Bass. Reprinted by permission of Hill and Wang, a division of Farrar, Straus and Giroux, LLC.

Hughes, Langston, and Arna Bontemps, "Betty and Dupree," from *The Book of Negro Folklore*. New York: Dodd, Mead and Company, 1958.

Hungerford, James, "Juber," from *The Old Plantation, and What I Gathered There in an Autumn Month*. New York: Harper & Brothers, 1859.

Hunter, Rosa, "What Do You Want Here?" from *Southern Workman* 27 (March 1898): 57.

Hurmence, Belinda, ed., "My Marster . . . Was a Good Man" and "My Life," from *Before Freedom: 48 Oral Histories of Former North and South Carolina Slaves*. New York: Penguin Books, 1990.

Hurst, Fannie, "Zora Hurston: A Personality Sketch," from *Yale University Library Gazette* XXXV (July 1960).

Hurston, Zora Neale, "Zora Neale Hurston," from *Dust Tracks on a Road*. New York: Harper & Row, 1942.

———, Introduction, "Preparation for the Crown of Power," and "Behold de Rib," from *Mules and Men*. Copyright © 1935 by Zora Neale Hurston. Copyright renewed 1963 by John C. Hurston and Joel Hurston. Reprinted by permission of HarperCollins Publishers, Inc.

———, "Uncle Monday," *Go Gator and Muddy the Water*. New York: W. W. Norton & Company, 1999.

Jackson, Bruce, "Convict's Prayer" and "The Wanderer's Trail," from *"Get Your Ass in the Water and Swim Like Me": Narrative Poetry from Black Oral Tradition*. Cambridge, Mass.: Harvard University Press, 1974. Reprinted by permission of the author.

Jackson, Jesse, "Keep Hope Alive," from *Keep Hope Alive: Jesse Jackson's 1988 Presidential Campaign*. Frank Clemente with Frank Walkins, eds. Boston: South End Press, 1989. Used by permission of South End Press.

Jackson, Margaret Young, "Pompey," from "An Investigation of Biographies and Autobiographies of American Slaves Published Between 1840 and 1860: Based Upon the Cornell Special Slavery Collection." Dissertation, Cornell University, 1964.

James, Willis Laurence, "Raise Up," "I'm a Man," "John Henry," "Dam de Cap'm!"

and "Imagery and Nature of the Work Song," from *Stars in de Elements: A Study of Negro Folk Music*. First published in a special issue of *Black Sacred Music: A Journal of Theomusicology* 9, nos. 1 and 2 (1995), Jon Michael Spencer, ed.

Jasper, The Reverend John, "Light as a Feather" and "The Sun Do Move." See Hatcher, William E.

Johnson, Alonzo, and Paul Jersild, eds., "Testimony of Conversion," from *"Ain't Gonna Lay My 'Ligion Down": African American Religion in the South*. Columbia: University of South Carolina Press, 1996. Used by permission of the publisher.

Johnson, Clifton H., ed. "I Am Blessed but You Are Damned," "God Struck Me Dead," and "Pray a Little Harder," excerpts from *God Struck Me Dead: Voices of Ex-Slaves*, Clifton H Johnson, ed. Cleveland: The Pilgrim Press, 1993. Copyright © 1969 by United Church Press. Used by permission.

Johnson, Maggie Pogue, "What's Mo Temptin to de Palate?" from *Virginia Dreams/Lyrics for the Idle Hour: Tales of the Time Told in Rhyme*. Copyright 1910 by John M. Leonard.

Johnson, Ruth Rogers, "A Love Letter from de Lord." See Jones, Lealon N.

Johnson, Wendolyn Wallace, "Baked Shad," "Greens I," and "Greens II." Permission granted by Wendolyn Wallace Johnson.

Jones, Charles C., "De Eagle an Eh Chillun," "De Two Fren an de Bear," "Buh Lion an Buh Goat," "Buh Squirrel an Buh Fox," and "De Dyin Bull-Frog," from *Negro Myths from the Georgia Coast*. Boston: Houghton, Mifflin and Company, 1888.

Jones, Lealon N., ed., "A Love Letter from de Lord," from *Eve's Stepchildren*. Caldwell, Idaho: The Caxton Press, Ltd., 1942. Used by permission of the publisher.

Jones, Richard M., "Trouble in Mind." Reprinted with permission of MCA/Northern Music Company.

Jones, Richard O., "The Liberation of Aunt Jemima," from *When Mama's Gone*. Los Angeles: Milligan Books, 1998. Reprinted by permission of the author.

"Juba," from *Southern Workman* 24 (February 1895): 30.

Kein, Sybil, "Éh, La Bas," "Salé Dame," "Maw-Maw's Creole Lullaby," and "Zydeco Calinda," from *Creole Ballads & Zydeco*. Used with permission of Sybil Kein.

King, Martin Luther, Jr., "I Have a Dream," "Eulogy for the Martyred Children," and "Our God Is Marching On," from *Testament of Hope: The Essential Writings and Speeches of Martin Luther King, Jr.*, James Melvin Washington, ed. Reprinted by arrangement with The Heirs to the Estate of Martin Luther King, Jr., c/o Writers House, Inc., as agent for the proprietor. Copyright © 1968 by Martin Luther King, Jr., renewed 1996 by Coretta Scott King.

Latrobe, Benjamin Henry Boneval, "New Orleans Musical Instruments," from *The Journal of Latrobe*. New York: D. Appleton and Company, 1905.

Lincoln, Mabel, "I Am a Hard Woman." See Gwaltney, John Langston.

Lomax, Alan, "Didn't He Ramble," "Shooting the Agate," and "Voodoo Had Hold of Him, Too," from *Mister Jelly Roll: The Fortunes of Jelly Roll Morton, New Orleans*

Creole and "Inventor of Jazz." 1950; 2nd edition, Berkeley: University of California Press, 1973. Copyright © 1950, 1973 by Alan Lomax. Used by permission of the University of California Press.

McCray, Carrie Allen, "Freedom's Child," from *Freedom's Child: The Remarkable Life of a Confederate General's Black Daughter.* Chapel Hill, N.C.: Algonquin Books of Chapel Hill, 1998. Copyright © 1998 by the author. Reprinted by permission of Algonquin Books of Chapel Hill, a division of Workman Publishing.

Madden, T. O., Jr., and Ann L. Miller, "We Were Always Free," from *We Were Always Free: The Maddens of Culpepper County.* Copyright © 1994 by T. O. Madden Jr. and Ann L. Miller. Used by permission of W. W. Norton & Company, Inc.

Madison, May Anna, "The Difference between Us and Them." See Gwaltney, John Langston.

Malcolm X, "The Ballot or the Bullet" and "Message to the Grass Roots," from *Malcolm X Speaks: Selected Speeches and Statements,* George Breitman, ed. Copyright © 1965, 1989 by Betty Shabazz and Pathfinder Press. Reprinted by permission.

Malone, Jacqui, "Stepping: Regeneration through Dance in African American Fraternities and Sororities," from *Steppin' on the Blues: The Visible Rhythms of African American Dance.* Copyright © 1996 by the Board of Trustees of the University of Illinois. Used with permission of the University of Illinois Press.

Marshall, Paule, "Returning to Africa," from *Praisesong for the Widow.* New York: G. P. Putnam's Sons, 1983.

Melville, Herman, "The Handsome Soldier," from *Billy Budd.* Copyright © 1962 by University of Chicago Press. Used by permission of the publisher.

Montague, Dorothy, "Corn Pudding," "Fruit Cobbler," and "Sweet Potato Pudding." Permission granted by Dorothy Montague.

Moore, Quincy L., "Spicy Country Meat Loaf," "Jambalaya," and "Blackberry Bread Pudding." Permission granted by Quincy L. Moore.

Morris, Willie, "Going Negro," *North Toward Home.* Boston: Houghton Mifflin, 1967. Used by permission of Theron Raines.

The Negro in Virginia. See Writers' Program (Va.).

Nelson, Beulah, "I Was Leaving." See Clark-Lewis, Elizabeth.

"The New York Glide," from *Ethel Waters 1921–1923, The Jazz Chronological Classics,* vol. 796.

Northup, Solomon, "The Poetry of Motion," from *Twelve Years a Slave: Narrative of Solomon Northup, a Citizen of New-York, Kidnapped in Washington City in 1841, and Rescued in 1853, from a Cotton Plantation Near the Red River, in Louisiana.* New York: Miller, Orton & Co., 1853.

Odum, Howard W., "Marry Me," "Po' Boy Long Way from Home," "Look'd Down de Road," "Frisco Rag-Time," and "Railroad Bill," from "Folk-Song and Folk-Poetry as Found in the Secular Songs of the Southern Negroes," from *The Journal of American Folk-Lore* 24 (July–September 1911).

Oliver, John, "If You Ain't in the Know, You Are in Danger." See Gwaltney, John Langston.

Olmsted, Frederick Law, "Colored People of Richmond in 1852," from *The Cotton Kingdom: A Traveller's Observations on Cotton and Slavery in the American Slave States*, vol. 1. New York: Mason Brothers, 1861.

Parker, Theodore H., "Caution." See Harris, Middleton.

Parrish, Lydia, ed., "Anniebelle," from *Slave Songs of the Georgia Sea Islands*. 1942. Athens: University of Georgia Press, 1992. Used by permission of the University of Georgia Press.

Parsons, Elsie Clews, "Making Butter," "The False Message: Take My Place," "Mary Bell," "The Lazy Man," "The Clever Companions," and "Riddles," from *Folk-Lore of the Sea Islands, South Carolina*. Cambridge, Mass.: American Folk-Lore Society, 1923.

Patterson, Ruth Polk, "Hull Gull and Other Games," "Toys Fashioned in the Polk Family," and "The Seed of Sally Good'n," from *The Seed of Sally Good'n: A Black Family in Arkansas*. Copyright © 1985 by the University Press of Kentucky. Used by permission.

Perceley, James, Ivey Monteria, and Stephan Dweck, "More Insults," from *Snaps*. New York: William Morrow, 1994.

Pope-Hennessy, James, "Liable to Plot Rebellion," from *Sins of the Fathers: A Study of the Atlantic Slave Traders 1441–1907*. New York: Alfred A. Knopf, 1968.

Prahlad, Sw. Anand. "You Reap What You Sow" and "The Pot Calling the Kettle Black . . . ," from *African-American Proverbs in Context*. Jackson: University Press of Mississippi, 1996. Used by permission of the publisher.

Puckett, Newbell Niles, "Cures for Rheumatism," "Wedding Colors," and "Witches Who Ride," from *Folk Beliefs of the Southern Negro*. Copyright © 1926 by the University of North Carolina Press. Used by permission of the publisher.

Pyrnelle, Louise-Clarke, "The Goldstone," *Plantation Child-Life*. New York: Harper & Brothers, 1882.

Quarterman, Wallace, "Flying Africans." See Skinner, Elliott P.

Rainey, Ma, "Last Minute Blues." Paramount Recording. We have made every effort to find the copyright holder for this selection. If you have information regarding the copyright holder, please write to W. W. Norton, 500 Fifth Avenue, New York, NY 10110 (Attn: Amy Cherry).

Reese, Mayme, "Quilting Parties." See Banks, Ann.

Reisner, Robert, and Lorraine Wechsler, *Encyclopedia of Graffiti*. New York: Macmillan Publishing Company, Inc., 1974.

Rosenbaum, Art, "We Never Did Let It Go By," from *Shout Because You're Free: The African American Ring Shout Tradition in Coastal Georgia*. Athens, Ga.: University of Georgia Press, 1998. Used by permission of the publisher.

"Run, Nigger, Run, De Patteroler'll Ketch Yer," from *Southern Workman* 24 (February 1895): 31.

Russell, Maggie, "Testimony of Conversion." See Johnson, Alonzo, and Paul Jersild.

Saxon, Lyle, Edward Dreyer, and Robert Tallant, eds. "Photograph of King Zulu," "The Zulus," "The Black Indians," "Craps Rhymes," and "Craps Lines," from

Gumbo Ya-Ya: A Collection of Louisiana Folk Tales. Copyright © 1987 by Lyle Saxon, Edward Dreyer, and Robert Tallant. Used by permission of the licenser, Pelican Publishing Company, Inc.

Shelton, Jane de Forest, "The Election Day Festival," from "The New England Negro," from *Harper's New Monthly Magazine* 88 (March 1894): 533–38.

"Signs from the Hampton Folk-Lore Society," from *Southern Workman* 23 (January 1894): 15–16.

Skinner, Elliott P., ed., "Magic Power" and "Flying Africans," from *Drums and Shadows: Survival Studies Among the Georgia Coastal Negroes.* Garden City, N.Y.: Doubleday & Company, 1972.

Smith, Bessie, "Backwater Blues." Copyright © 1927 (Renewed), 1974 by Frank Music Corp. All rights reserved.

Smith, Bessie, and Clarence Williams, "Jail-House Blues." Words and music by Bessie Smith and Clarence Williams. Copyright © 1923 (Renewed) by Frank Music Corp. All rights reserved.

Smith, Chris, "Long Gone." Music by W. C. Handy. Memphis, Tenn.: Pace & Handy Music Company, 1920.

Smith, Ethel Morgan, "Aunt Honey's Rabbit Stew and Peach Wine." Permission granted by Ethel Morgan Smith.

———, "The Smell of Death," titled "Uncle Clem" in *From Whence Cometh My Help: The African American Community at Hollins College.* Columbia: University of Missouri Press, 2000.

Solomon, Jack and Olivia, comps, "Interpret Dat," "Lookin' for Three Fools," "The Laziest Man," "The Witch with a Gold Ring," and "Old Joe Can Keep His Two Bits," from *Ghosts and Goosebumps: Ghost Stories, Tall Tales, and Superstitions from Alabama.* Tuscaloosa: University of Alabama Press, 1981.

"Some Conjure Doctors We Have Heard Of," from *Southern Workman* 16 (February 1897): 37.

Spanier, Muggsy, "A Different Style." See Banks, Ann.

Sterling, Dorothy, ed., "Childhood" and "Looking Down on Her," from *We Are Your Sisters: Black Women in the Nineteenth Century.* New York: W. W. Norton and Company, Inc., 1984.

Stowe, Harriet Beecher, "Looking Down on Her." See Sterling, Dorothy.

Talley, Thomas W., "Love Is Just a Thing of Fancy," "Jump Jim Crow," "When I Go to Marry, "Old Man Know-All," "I'll Eat When I'm Hungry," "Slave Marriage Ceremony Supplement," "Antebellum Courtship Inquiry," "The War Is On," and "Jack and Dinah Want Freedom," from *Negro Folk Rhymes, Wise and Otherwise.* New York: Macmillan, 1922.

Theard, Sam, and Fleecie Moore, "Let the Good Times Roll." Words and music by Sam Theard and Fleecie Moore. Copyright © 1946 Cherio Corp. Copyright © renewed by RYTVOC, INC. All rights reserved.

Tindley, Charles Albert, "I'll Overcome Some Day," from *New Songs of Paradise: A Collection of Popular and Religious Songs for Sunday Schools, Prayer-Meetings, Epworth League Meetings and Social Gatherings.* Philadelphia: C. A. Tindley, 1923.

Titon, Jeff Todd, ed. "The Eagle Stirreth Her Nest" and "What of the Night?" by Rev. C. L. Franklin, from *Give Me This Mountain: Life History and Selected Sermons.* Copyright © 1989 by the Board of Trustees of the University of Illinois. Used with permission of the University of Illinois Press.

Toomer, Jean, "Barlo's Sermon," from *Cane.* New York: Boni & Liveright, Inc., 1923.

Truth, Sojourner, "Ain't I a Woman." See Gage, Frances Dana.

Tubman, Harriet. See Bradford, Sarah.

Turner, Nat, *The Confessions of Nat Turner, the Leader of the Late Insurrection in Southampton, VA, as Fully and Voluntarily Made to Thomas R. Gray, in the Prison Where He Was Confined, and Acknowledged by Him to Be Such When Read Before the Court of Southampton, etc.* Baltimore: T. R. Gray, 1831.

Turner, Patricia A., "AIDS" and "Attention," from *I Heard It Through the Grapevine: The Rhetoric of Rumor in Black Culture.* Copyright © 1993 Regents. Used with permission of the University of California Press.

Vassar, Esther, "Cornbread," "Applesauce Rum Cake," and "Aunt Maude's Sweet Potato Pie." Permission granted by Esther Vassar.

Walker, Margaret, "For My People" from *This Is My Century: New and Collected Poems.* Used by permission of the University of Georgia Press.

Warren, Edward, "John Koonering," from *A Doctor's Experiences in Three Continents.* Baltimore: Cushings & Bailey, Publishers, 1885.

Waters, Donald J., ed., "How Brer Wolf Caught Brer Rabbit," "The Irishman and the Moon," and "The Irishman and the Watermelon," from *Strange Ways and Sweet Dreams: Afro-American Folklore from the Hampton Institute.* Boston: G. K. Hall, 1983. Used by permission of Thorndike Press.

Watkins, Mel, "Missus in the Big House," from *On the Real Side: Laughing, Lying, and Signifying — The Underground Tradition of African American Humor That Transformed American Culture, from Slavery to Richard Pryor.* New York: Simon & Schuster, 1994.

White, Shane and Graham, "Fashion Plates," from *Stylin': African American Expressive Culture from Its Beginnings to the Zoot Suit.* Ithaca, N.Y.: Cornell University Press, 1998.

Wilson, Jack, "Magic Power." See Skinner, Elliot P.

Writers' Program (Va.). "Charlie," "Fire Sticks," and "We's Free," from *The Negro in Virginia,* compiled by workers of the Writers' Program of the Work Projects Administration in the State of Virginia. Copyright © 1940 by Hampton University. Courtesy of Hampton University Archives.

Index

mG 1/02